Robert Graves

ROBERT GRAVES

Sergeant Lamb of the Ninth

Proceed, Sergeant Lamb

Robert Graves Programme
General Editor: Patrick J.M. Quinn

Centenary Selected Poems
edited by Patrick J.M. Quinn

Collected Writings on Poetry
edited by Paul O'Prey

Complete Short Stories
edited by Lucia Graves

Complete Poems I
edited by Beryl Graves and Dunstan Ward

Complete Poems II
edited by Beryl Graves and Dunstan Ward

Complete Poems III
edited by Beryl Graves and Dunstan Ward

The White Goddess
edited by Grevel Lindop

I, Claudius and *Claudius the God*
edited by Richard Francis

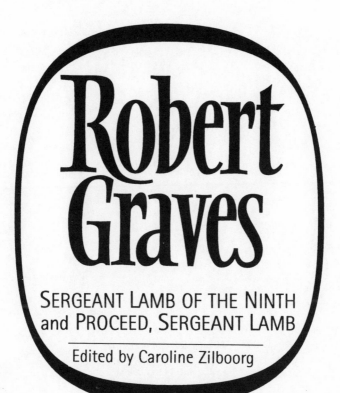

Robert Graves

SERGEANT LAMB OF THE NINTH
and PROCEED, SERGEANT LAMB

Edited by Caroline Zilboorg

CARCANET

First published in 1940, 1941.
Published in Great Britain in 1999 by
Carcanet Press Limited
4th Floor, Conavon Court
12–16 Blackfriars Street
Manchester M3 3BQ

A CIP catalogue record for this book
is available from the British Library.
ISBN 1 85754 281 9

The publisher acknowledges financial
assistance from the Arts Council of England

Set in Ehrhardt by XL Publishing Services, Tiverton
Printed and bound in England by SRP Ltd, Exeter

ROBERT GRAVES'S SERGEANT LAMB:
AN INTRODUCTION
Caroline Zilboorg

Private circumstances and public events brought Robert Graves in late 1939 to the idea of writing a historical novel on the subject of Sergeant Roger Lamb, a young Dubliner who had served with the Royal Welch Fusiliers (the 23rd Foot regiment) during the American War of Independence. The events of the three preceding years had made impossible a potentially quiet writing life in a secluded village in Mallorca. The conflict in Spain in 1936 had forced Graves to leave his home in Deyá for what at first seemed an indefinite stay in London; threat of a larger war soon made the United States seem an attractive alternative to an English exile for the duration. Laura Riding, Graves's intellectual and emotional partner since 1926, when he was still working at his first marriage to Nancy Nicholson, was eager for a change, but an interlude spent in Brittany on the eve of war did little to calm her excitable nature. Although world war was held at bay throughout 1938, a turmoil of inner passions defined the months Graves lived with an unstable community of friends in a large eighteenth-century château ten miles from Rennes. The group slowly dissolved during the summer and autumn as Riding, struggling with her own writing and with her grief in response to her father's recent death, grew increasingly distracted while Graves focused his attention on Beryl Pritchard Hodge, the young wife of Alan Hodge, Graves's friend and future collaborator.

By the time Graves and Riding left France for America in late April of 1939, Beryl and Alan Hodge were a significant part of their household. All four had been invited to stay indefinitely on a sprawling farm with new acquaintances, Schuyler and Kathleen Jackson, but Graves and Riding would first visit Tom and Julie Matthews in Princeton until cottage accommodation on the Jacksons' farm could be made ready for them. Central New Jersey and the farm in New Hope, Pennsylvania were not far apart; there were frequent trips back and forth, and Graves became aware of local history and the area's many Revolutionary War sites. In late May, the Hodges arrived in Princeton; in early June, the group moved into the Jacksons' farmhouse itself, still waiting for the cottage.

The visit proved an emotional disaster. Riding dominated the ménage, quickly taking over Kathleen's position not only at the dinner table but in her husband's bed. Manipulated and exploited, Kathleen broke down in late June and was, at Riding's instigation, taken away from her home and young children and confined in a mental hospital. Laura now freely committed herself to Schuyler, but Graves still struggled with his feelings for Beryl, to whom he was drawn both sexually and emotionally at the same time that he remained intellectually and creatively bonded to Laura. Beryl's marriage to Hodge had become merely an amicable alliance, and she obviously returned Graves' love, but was understandably wary.

Under these circumstances, Graves left America for England at the end of July. His intentions were mixed. He sensed the imminence of war and felt an obligation to participate in what looked rather like a reprise of the conflict of his youth in which he had served as an officer in the Royal Welch Fusiliers. In 1914, Graves had joined up immediately after the declaration of war and by 1915 was in France where he served until seriously wounded in July of the following year. Once physically recovered from the damage to one of his lungs, he returned briefly to the front in early 1917, but was soon ill with bronchitis and came back to England once more. He spent the remainder of the Great War in Britain, physically incapable of fighting at the front and his nerves shot. Miranda Seymour writes that in '1917 and 1918 he hovered on the brink of a nervous breakdown. Recovery took another ten years.'[1] As Martin Seymour-Smith notes, however, one seldom recovers from such experiences, and even towards the very end of his life, Graves, like so many other soldiers who survived that particularly disillusioning war, was to feel an inexpiable responsibility and guilt.[2] For such survivors, the Second World War was a reprise of the First; the intervening years, merely 'a long armistice'.[3] Such a frame of mind helps explain Graves's unqualified delight when his son David applied for a commission to the Royal Welch Fusiliers after completing his undergraduate degree at Cambridge in June of 1940. Graves's initial enthusiasm obscured the possibility which became a reality when David was killed in Burma in April of 1943, but certainly as

---

1. Miranda Seymour, *Robert Graves: Life on the Edge* (London: Doubleday, 1995), 60.
2. Martin Seymour-Smith, *Robert Graves: His Life and Work*, rev. edn, (London: Bloomsbury, 1995), xviii, 549.
3. Richard Aldington, *Life for Life's Sake: A Book of Reminiscences* (London: Cassell, 1968), 265. Aldington wrote this memoir in 1940 for the *Atlantic Monthly*, which began to serialise it in November; the second installment of Aldington's book appeared in the very issue that carried a brief review of *Sergeant Lamb of the Ninth*. Writing to Alan Hodge on 15 May 1940 about the title of the social history that would become *The Long Weekend*, Graves revealed his own view of World War II as a continuation of the Great War: 'Title still simmering. I think *Lull* ought to come into it. *Lull Between Wars* – A record of happenings in Great Britain between 1918 and 1939.' See *In Broken Images: Selected Letters of Robert Graves, 1914–1949*, ed. with commentary by Paul O'Prey (London: Hutchinson, 1982), 293.

a former soldier Graves was aware at some level in 1939 and 1940 of the moral and emotional complexity of serving a cause which, if one survived, would inevitably shape one through participation and suffering.

Both Graves's enthusiasm for a cause (England threatened) and his specific loyalty to his own regiment stimulated his interest in the material of the two historical novels he would write about Sergeant Lamb. Graves was also prompted by the pertinence of his subject (war) at the same time that he was attracted by its difference from the present in concerning another conflict (the American Revolution) in another place (the American Colonies).

On 25 September 1939, he wrote to Basil Liddell Hart that the War Office could only offer him the sort of desk job which seemed to Graves, now forty-four, particularly dull and useless. He was beginning, instead, the necessary research for a historical novel set in eighteenth-century America. Placing his remarks in the context of the previous war, he commemorated the date by adding under it, 'Good old Battle of Loos', then reported,

> I finally managed to get medically boarded for the Officers' Emergency Reserve, got passed Grade 2 which means that I can only be accepted for non-combatant and very dull corps – and decided that with so many people unemployed because of the war it was altogether unnecessary for me to do-my-bit in the Educational Corps or Army Pay Corps just in order to be in uniform – so I am calling it off...

Graves added that he felt free to do so 'because of my age and disability pension'.[4] Certainly the fact that he was beginning stimulating research on an extensive project must also have assuaged his poignant sense of obligation to participate directly in the war effort: Graves was not a teacher or an accountant; he was and knew himself to be first and last a writer.

Joined by Beryl in October, Graves struggled to build a new life in the relative calm of the house of friends, John and Lucie Aldridge, in Great Bardfield in rural Essex. He and Beryl would live here for the next seven months, and it was here that he would complete most of the research for and begin writing the large novel that, because of wartime paper shortages, would appear in two volumes, but which now appears in one, reflecting the single unified project which Graves's work on Lamb surely is.

Graves's letters during this period vividly convey his need for domestic safety as well as his growing excitement about the project which allowed him the strategic retreat both from the turmoil he had left behind in America and from the present war which defined his situation in

4. Robert Graves to Basil Liddell Hart, *In Broken Images*, 286.

England. In his late September letter to Liddell Hart, he reflected: 'Laura is short-handed over there and I have to work in order to support my family and various war-stranded semi-dependents.' Then he added, 'It occurs to me suddenly that the war which is very much "the Next War" rather than "The War" as it was last time is already over – I mean that we aren't fighting any Passchendaeles or Verduns this time' (286–7). In this context, and despite 'the publishing stagnation', Graves confessed his enthusiasm for his next project:

> I have been asked [by Methuen] to write an historical novel on the subject of the American War of Independence. I have a good centre character: Sergeant Lamb of the 9th and 23rd – and his journal which I have been reading is pretty good stuff. It will not be really fiction, but the real stuff enlarged by other contemporary evidences of the sort of thing that happened. I hate this sort of writing; but [it] can be justified as making readable what is not readable at all.

The project was appealing on several counts. Richard Perceval Graves comments that

> Robert was certainly very short of money at this time; and he felt under a great moral obligation not only to provide Nancy and their children with financial support, but also to look after the interests both of Karl Goldschmidt [Gay] and of Alan Hodge… Robert's solution to these financial difficulties was to begin work on what he hoped would be another *I, Claudius*, which not only would provide him with money, but would mean that he could offer secretarial and research work to his friends.[5]

As Graves settled into relative domestic tranquillity in Great Bardfield, he quickly moved ahead. On 13 November 1939, Graves wrote sympathetically to Liddell Hart, who was staying with friends in Devon, where the rural calm was helping him to recover from a nervous breakdown: 'Beryl and I have a disinclination even to go as far as London away from this place – which is now a home, with a cat and all.' Graves then described his rapid progress:

> I have read about 8000 pages of American War of Independency literature, word by word not skipping and feel I will soon know the scene well enough to begin my novel. Unfortunately I still am without one of my two key books: it is Sergeant Lamb's *Memoir of His Life*, Dublin, 1812 (298 pp) (*not* his *Journal of Occurrences in the Late American War*, 1809, which I have, the other key book). The memoir book is never quoted by the usual authorities and is exces-

---

5. Richard Perceval Graves, *Robert Graves: The Years with Laura, 1926–40* (London: Weidenfeld and Nicholson, 1990), 319.

sively rare and no copy in Fitzwilliam, Bodleian, British Museum
or the Trade. I am writing to searchers in Dublin and have advertised in America. It does exist, but only just, apparently. Then I am
sending someone to look up in (23rd) Regimental records for
Captain Julian's and Sir Thomas Saumarez's journals. When you
do get your books stacked and sorted I would indeed be grateful for
a list of your Americana. One of the very best written histories I
have come across is Winthrop Sergeant's *Life of Major André* (1865
or so), (Southern States) American and done in the purest English
detached style.[6]

Convinced in part of the value of Lamb's memoir because it appears to
him 'excessively rare', Graves reveals his own peculiar view of research as
an obscure and quantitative endeavour in which, like a schoolboy, one is
given credit for the amount one reads 'word by word not skipping'. It is
also clear from this letter that he has asked his son David to look for
Lamb's work in the Fitzwilliam, a Cambridge art museum, while in fact it
is logically and readily available in the Cambridge University Library,
whose catalogue has listed a copy, along with Lamb's *Journal*, since the
time of their publication. Graves's excitement and impulsiveness here
both sustain and shape his creative work, enabling him to carry on despite
financial and emotional pressures. Beryl later recalled that Graves identi-
fied so intensely with his subject that he would often lay an extra place for
the sergeant at meals during the winter of 1939–40.[7]

By the time Graves turned from reading to writing, he made progress
at an impressive rate. On 2 February 1940, he reported to Hodge, who had
now moved on to gathering material for a new book on which the two
would collaborate (*The Lost Weekend: A Social History of Great Britain,
1918–1939*, appeared later this same year), that he was writing two chapters a week.[8] His pace was not only a sign of mental health and renewed
creative energy, but to a degree of pressing necessity: in addition to
nagging debts, Laura was pushing him for funds and Beryl was pregnant.
A letter from Graves to Karl Gay on 26 January 1940 reveals the tension
Graves was experiencing. On the one hand, he was identifying himself
with Roger Lamb and thrilling to the dashing exploits of a Royal Welch
Fusilier; on the other, he was forced to regard his work as a commercial
enterprise. He told Gay that he had heard at length from Laura, who
wrote 'nicely' in one letter, then retracted her kindness in a second contradictory letter, indicating after all

that she doesn't want to see me in March and that there is no possi-

6. *In Broken Images*, 289.
7. Seymour, 284.
8. Seymour-Smith, 370.

bility of my helping in the *Dictionary*, which is being done in an entirely different way now, except by helping her financially from my *Sergeant Lamb* money; and that because of extraordinary expenses she cannot repay me the £540 paid to her in error last November [1939] from Random House, which Random House will now recover from my *Lamb* advance.[9]

Thus Graves's attitudes towards his work on the two Sergeant Lamb books are shaped by his decision to remain in England – a practical necessity at this point given war restrictions on travel – but also by a situation enforced by Laura's final rejection. Graves now struggled to cast his predicament in terms of volition and moral choice. Writing to Liddell Hart, he declared his patriotism:

It goes against the grain to leave one's country and friends in wartime, except for the very highest considerations – of aims transcending merely national or personal ones; and I cannot now see that to go to America in my present circumstances would be justified.[10]

These tensions between America and Britain, between Laura and Beryl, between the bizarre community of New Hope and the more traditional family Graves was establishing in the English countryside provide a biographical context which at one level helps to explain why Graves at this time should want to write about a historical struggle which was at once a war of independence, a revolutionary conflict, a secession, a break-up of a linked community, and the forging of an early commonwealth. But an understanding of Graves's life during this period, while providing a vivid sense of the creative process which fostered these novels, finally does little to help us read these two books, which are certainly in no way transparent or symbolic autobiography. Seymour notes that 'An argument can be made for seeing these books... as Graves's way of mythologizing the war between himself and Schuyler Jackson on a national scale, but even references to the River Schuykill fail to yield anything more suggestive than a name...'. She concludes: 'The decision to write a picaresque novel... can rather be interpreted as an outlet for Graves's frustration at finding himself in a second war and ineligible for active service.'[11] More importantly, the Sergeant Lamb novels offer fascinating evidence of a creative mind that invariably struggled with the nature of reality, with conventional parameters in art as in life, with the boundaries of genre and of truth, whether as fact or surreal experience. One can best approach the

9. *In Broken Images*, 290.
10. Undated letter, probably written in early February 1940, *In Broken Images*, 291.
11. Seymour, 284.

two novels by understanding Graves's own conception of them and by examining their relation to his sources.

Prose was not Graves's favourite form. Graves's novels are often very fine, although Graves routinely denigrated his fiction, indicating that they were written for money, as if that fact it itself undermined their merit. He confessed in 1952 in a letter to an unidentified recipient, 'Frankly, all I really care about is poetry – that is my life, not novel-writing.' Still, he continued, 'My next interest is history…'.[12] It is only natural, then, that Graves should have put a great deal of effort into his historical fiction, care which, despite the pace of their creation, the Sergeant Lamb books clearly convey. He had previously written five novels, and his prose now reveals his increasing conscientiousness and confidence in this genre. While Seymour-Smith thought that these two novels were 'solid and workman-like', he also found them 'his stodgiest work' since – a not necessarily logical conclusion – 'Their function was to bring solvency – and to guard their author against the kind of self-pitying introspection he hated.'[13]

In fact, the books' stodginess and the narrator's carefully crafted detachment are a direct result of Graves' unwavering and almost exclusive dependence on two sources, both written by Roger Lamb himself: *An original and authentic Journal of occurrences during the late American War from its commencement to the year 1783* (Dublin: Wilkinson and Courtney, 1809, 438 pp.) and *Memoir of his own life* (Dublin: J. Jones, 1811, 292 pp.). Graves doggedly follows Lamb chronologically through this ·material, placing the autobiographical record of Lamb's early life, contained in the first pages of the *Memoir*, at the beginning of *Sergeant Lamb of the Ninth*, while inserting other incidents from the *Memoir*, omitted by Lamb from the *Journal* as incidental or even unsuitably personal, at appropriate spots later in *Proceed, Sergeant Lamb*. In other words, Graves collapses the *Memoir* into the *Journal* so as to have one chronologically sequential account. It is no wonder that from the start he became concerned with the aesthetic and practical issue of length. Still thinking of the two novels as one volume, Graves wrote to Liddell Hart on 19 February 1940, 'My problem at the moment is how to keep the book within bounds. The libraries refuse to stock any book beyond 9 shillings and one can't publish a long book at that price now; and I have to give a very long, leisurely book to suit the date and characters.'[14] By spring, Graves realized that he would need to divide the whole into two books. Copying and paraphrasing more than he pruned, he was adding novelistic conversation and details to Lamb's accounts, while in large measure including Lamb's extensive quotation from other sources, often with the Sergeant's footnotes; the

12. Robert Graves quoted in Seymour-Smith, 369.
13. Seymour-Smith, 370.
14. *In Broken Images*, 292.

project was daily increasing in length. On 2 April 1940, he wrote to Karl Gay, 'As for *Lamb*: since I can't compress his story without making it read dry I have to follow it out at leisurely length feeling anything but leisurely myself and in the last eleven days I have written six and a half chapters.' He decided that, 'with a little doctoring at the join', it would break into two volumes of around 90,000 words each.[15]

Sergeant Lamb of the Ninth was published in September of 1940, while *Proceed, Sergeant Lamb* appeared in February of 1941. Widely reviewed and selling fairly well, the volumes brought in the money Graves needed. The distressed author of 1939 was beginning to feel more stable emotionally as well. In April of 1940, he had moved with Beryl from Essex to a house of his own at Galmpton in Devon, where their first child was born that summer and where Graves would spend the remainder of the war. He knew that his books about Lamb were uneven, and he felt understandably defensive about their merits. Aware that the novels did not wholly succeed as fiction, he defended their value as history. Graves boasted about what he called in January of 1941 'the only two books in existence to give an account of the whole war [of Independence] while also contriving to be readable.' He thought, in fact, that there was a good chance they would 'find their way into all school libraries especially in the U.S.A.'[16] At the end of the year Graves was readier to claim for at least the second volume the novelistic virtues of relevant theme and consistent character. Writing to his protégé, the young poet Alun Lewis, on 26 November 1941, Graves reflected: 'I think that when you have got the second *Lamb*, now called *Proceed, Sergeant Lamb*, you'll see that there is more than episodic interest to excuse the story – it is about the fates of war, with no dropped threads anywhere, Lamb being such a thorough fellow...'.[17]

Modern biographers, placing these novels within the context of Graves's life at the time, have struggled to emphasize occasional parallel elements. Robert Perceval Graves's perceptions are typical:

> He had certainly done his research well, and his re-creation of late eighteenth-century American life and manners and landscape is vivid and wholly believable: but although there are some excellent set pieces, the story is not merely 'discursive', as he had intended, but rambling to the point of tedium; while Sergeant Lamb himself, the main character and narrator, is extraordinarily shadowy. Just occasionally, the narrative is illuminated by flashes of pure horror... which remind us that Graves was writing this novel within a year of his appalling experiences in Pennsylvania; but for

---

15. This letter is quoted in Robert Perceval Graves, *Robert Graves and the White Goddess, 1940–1985* (London: Weidenfeld and Nicholson, 1995), 11.
16. Graves quoted in *Robert Graves and the White Goddess*, 17–18.
17. *In Broken Images*, 310.

most of the time he appears to be emotionally disengaged – like Sergeant Lamb, when he says: 'My mind is like a lake over which a storm has raged. It reflects only the blue sky and forgets the thunder and lightening.'[18]

Later scholars, who have given the Lamb novels only passing attention, tend to agree with Robert Perceval Graves and with contemporary reviewers that the strengths of these two books are the setting and the general impression created of the period. George Orwell, for example, praised *Sergeant Lamb of the Ninth* as 'a historical novel that rates our respect' (*New Statesman and Nation*, 1 September 1940, p. 291). An anonymous reviewer for the *Atlantic* wrote that he found the book on the whole 'disappointing. It has the factual verisimilitude... but it lacks vitality and... suspense' (December 1940, n.p.). J. D. Beresford in the *Manchester Guardian* decided that 'The book is documented with various contemporary evidence. It is a novel to be read for its detail rather than the development of its narrative' (13 September 1940, p. 6). Similarly, the anonymous reviewer in the *New Yorker* found it 'lively reading, with perhaps too much history and not enough novel' (2 November 1940, p. 85). While Stephen Vincent Benét thought Roger Lamb was 'a likeable and forthright fellow', he attributed what he found a confining eighteenth-century 'style and matter' to the fact that 'Mr. Graves has sometimes forgotten that he is writing a novel', creating a work that is finally 'painfully pedestrian' (*Saturday Review of Literature*, 2 November 1940, p. 5). The anonymous reviewer for the *Times Literary Supplement* liked the novel's 'period flavour' despite its 'Somewhat formless... storytelling' (14 September 1940, p. 469). H. A. Wooster encapsulated the generally mixed and finally uneasy response to *Sergeant Lamb of the Ninth*: 'The casual reader may object that he is getting his history too straight, but the thoughtful reader will appreciate the honest effort to recreate a period and succession of important events which have present day significance' (*Library Journal*, 1 October 1940, p. 808).

Proceed, Sergeant Lamb met with a similar reaction. Bonamy Dobrée in the *Spectator* was among the most positive reviewers: 'This volume is even better than the first; its romance is less fanciful, though equally exciting... Mr. Graves' own war-experience has served him as a historical novelist.' Dobrée concluded that 'the whole account is so coherent, so built up of verisimilitude... that Lamb lives with us by our side' (28 February 1941, p. 236). The anonymous reviewer for the *TLS* agreed: 'the narrative wears an extraordinary air of authenticity', making it appear to be 'uninhibited and almost artless personal testimony'. He concluded that 'Mr. Graves' art... has been to transcribe fragments from a crowd of eyewitnesses other

18. *Robert Graves and the White Goddess*, 18.

than Sergeant Lamb to match the Sergeant's devoted and sensible person-
ality' (22 February 1941, p. 89). Other readers found the tension between
fact and fiction more pronounced and problematic. J. D. Beresford found
the book 'vigorous and flavoursome' despite its 'ponderous eighteenth-
century style' (*Manchester Guardian*, 28 February 1941, p. 7), while H. A.
Wooster concluded with disappointment that 'The historical interest
outweighs the story interest and the appeal is to the reader already interested in the period' (*Library Journal*, 15 September 1941, p. 793).

Reviewers could not have been expected to take on the scholarly task of
examining Graves's sources, without which it is impossible to sort out just
what in these two books is fact and what fiction, or to discover just what it
is Graves has actually contributed to this account of Roger Lamb's experiences. Whatever Graves might have thought he was doing, whatever
impression he might duplicitously or naively convey, *Sergeant Lamb of the
Ninth* and *Proceed, Sergeant Lamb* are not novels. That is, Graves's texts
here are enriched by the advantages and suffer from the disadvantages of
his dependence on his sources. His idea of scholarship in these two books,
as earlier during his years as a student at Oxford, relies more on quantity
and inclusion than on quality and principles which would allow a more
judicious sifting and selection of information for fictional purposes. As the
responses of both contemporary reviewers and modern scholars attest,
such important novelistic elements as plot, character, point of view and
theme are ultimately sacrificed to facts and anecdotes about the political
and economic issues of the American War of Independence, for instance,
or details of specific troop movements and catalogues of equipment and
food supplies, or accounts of local terrain and customs in the American
Colonies from New England to the Carolinas – all material taken verbatim
or closely paraphrased from Lamb's own journal and memoir. Thus
Graves binds himself to the chronological structure, incidents and even
tempo of the two works. He omits moral treatises on such subjects as the
benefits of swimming and descriptive passages about such period interests
as national physiognomy, but he fleshes out individuals with names and
personalities only suggested by Lamb, specifically through conversational
sequences, and adds one particular character – Lamb's first love, Kate
Weldone Harlowe. The result is a very long, sometimes tedious and unfo-
cused work whose authenticity is evident throughout in Graves's usurpa-
tion of Lamb's own voice while the verbal exchanges of the characters,
Graves's own addition, make vivid and often amusing scenes from what is
present in Lamb's texts only in summary.

Still, the two books can best be understood aesthetically as one project
which at times succeeds as a travelogue in the spirit of such eighteenth-
and nineteenth-century works as Swift's *Gulliver's Travels* or Melville's
Typee. In this vein, Roger Lamb as narrator offers us a privileged glimpse
of the strange attitudes and behaviour of both the American colonists and

the native Indians as he moves from Boston to French Canada to the wilds of New York at Fort Ticonderoga and Lake George in the first volume, and in the second volume from New York City by ship to Georgia and then through the rural southern colonies and back to New York via the woods and rural communities of Maryland, Pennsylvania and New Jersey. While failing to convey the coherence of imaginatively informed historical fiction, the two Sergeant Lamb volumes sometimes succeed as poignant history as Graves' academic devotion to his sources leads him to quote long passages which detail such events as the British 'articles of capitulation', the terms of surrender drafted by General Burgoyne after valiant fighting at Lake Champlain and submitted to General Gates of the Colonial forces in October of 1777. Thus two pages of *Sergeant Lamb of the Ninth* comprise quotation from 'Minutes and proceedings of a Council of War, consisting of all the general officers, field officers, and captains commanding corps, on the Heights of Saratoga, October 13th, 1777.' The final effect is certainly moving, but does little to deepen our understanding of character or theme and only marginally advances the plot. That is, Sergeant Lamb's own wanderings – as a soldier in the ranks serving the will of his superior officers and as a prisoner of the Colonial Army who repeatedly effects an escape – seem determined ultimately by personal strengths (for example as a nurse and medical assistant) and weaknesses (for instance his passion for the attractive Kate) rather than by the larger events of history. Ironically, however, this individual life, with its charming if underdeveloped friendships with such eccentric characters as Mad Johnny Maguire, Terry Reeves and 'Smutchy' Steel, personalities Graves himself amplifies, is obscured by Graves's concern to tell the whole story, to get it all in, to recount all he has learned about the entire experience of the Revolutionary War on both a large and a small scale. Thus we are offered the story of General Benedict Arnold (with whom Lamb had only glancing contact, but whom he follows through the citation of contemporary sources) as well as details not in Lamb's own accounts – such as an amusing description of the eighteenth-century library at provincial 'Nassau College', later Princeton University, whose local history Graves would have discovered as a tourist during his visit with Tom and Julie Matthews in May 1939.

The resulting confusion of focus has a serious impact on the texts' point-of-view: Roger Lamb, the protagonist-narrator who tells us his tale from the perspective of a survivor settled again in Ireland in 1814, tends to disappear (this is particularly true in *Sergeant Lamb of the Ninth*, the weaker of the two books) as Graves, like Lamb, alternates between large- and small-scale events. The work is ironically at its best not when it is most historical but when Graves draws on and embellishes the personal narrative whose sources are the intimate details contained or sometimes only suggested in Lamb's own narratives. The structure of the volumes,

especially the first, however, depends on the very history which, for all its
interest, becomes something that prevents the attention to Lamb's life
which gives these books their particular dynamism and dramatic force.

In his 'Foreword', Graves claims that 'All that readers of an historical
novel can fairly ask from the author is an assurance that he has nowhere
wilfully falsified geography, chronology, or character, and that the information contained in it is accurate enough to add without discount to their
general stock of history.' One might rather assert that this is the least one
can expect of any historical account, but that from a novel, one necessarily
wants all this and more. Graves's claim, also in the Foreword, that his
work on Lamb 'suggested itself as a means of learning, as I wrote, why and
how the Americans had separated themselves from the British Crown',
also seems naïve: Graves here conflates author and reader, process and
product. His writing of the Sergeant Lamb volumes may well have helped
him to understand this war, but the reader comes to the 'novels' with
more than historical expectations. It is not even sufficient compensation
to read in the Foreword that Graves in 1940 'regarded the American
Revolution as the most important single event of modern times'. During
the Blitz, in full force by the time of the publication of *Sergeant Lamb of
the Ninth* in late 1940, the contemporary reader, who might well have been
drawn to Graves's work through a familiarity with the author's poetry and
prose shaped by his First World War experiences, could not be expected
easily to believe in the modern significance of the American War of
Independence, a conflict which occurred a hundred and fifty years earlier
and a continent away. Parallels – which Graves was apparently uninter-
ested in developing – between the American war and the two world wars
might have given his work a direct twentieth-century relevance; he might
have explored such common elements as the psychological significance of
fighting on foreign soil, the soldiers' longing for home and family, the
camaraderie among the British troops, their identification with the enemy
as young men like themselves, or even such shared issues as conscription
and rationing. Instead, he chose to emphasize historical accuracy in a
meandering account of another time and place, which except for its
central figure (a sergeant in the ranks) and its general subject (war), might
well be understood as an escape from the present, a distraction from the
private and public turmoil of Graves's and his readers' experiences during
this period.

In fact, what is most interesting in these two books about Sergeant
Lamb is just what Graves does not develop during this stressful time in
his own life and in the life of his nation and the world: personal relation-
ships, self-examination, the nature of love and loyalty, of physical, mental
and spiritual retreat – the last a personal struggle to establish a new life as
much as possible on one's own terms. One must never, of course, ask an
author to do what he has no intention of doing. That is, as a responsible

reader, one must evaluate the text the author has written and not the book one might have wished him to write. Yet this is just the point: despite Graves's disclaimer – that all we can ask of a historical novel is that it not contain untruths – both he and we know that by virtue of the genre, we expect more.

Ironically, the charm of the Sergeant Lamb books lies in the moments when just the issues Graves is careful to marginalize suddenly claim centre stage. Lamb's love for Kate, who keeps turning up at fortuitous moments; his jealousy of her husband, the knavish Richard Harlowe; Lamb's affection for his mates; his illnesses, pain, and tears as well moments of personal triumph and celebration are the strengths of these volumes, as Graves seems to know. His comments in the Foreword appear finally defensive, both of the books' obvious flaws and of his own reluctance to attempt the kind of examination which will make his 'novels' live.

Written at white heat, the works' weaknesses can perhaps be explained as simply the result of hasty effort, but they are to a greater extent, I feel, a product of Graves's desire to isolate and protect himself from the kind of emotional analysis the best fiction requires and communicates. He is too much the consummate artist to allow himself off so easily, and the Sergeant Lamb books ultimately reward the persistent reader with passages of just the sort of moving insight, consistent focus, dramatic plot and satisfying thematic clarity that one expects from good fiction and from Graves at his best. Thus the last hundred pages of *Proceed, Sergeant Lamb* realize elements often dormant or even absent in previous chapters. Lamb's adventurous escape and rescue by British troops still stationed in New York Harbour have sufficient drama to compensate for much of the pedantic historiography which precedes his satisfying reunion and self-affirmation – both of which seem all the more powerful and sincere for reflecting Graves' own physical and emotional as well as artistic and spiritual state in 1939–41. Lamb returns to Dublin to set himself up as a schoolmaster and, as the author tells us even before we begin the long work, to marry not the passion of his youth but the good woman of the regiment. In rural retreat with Beryl in Devon, Graves, too, was ready to reshape his career once more.

SERGEANT LAMB
OF THE NINTH

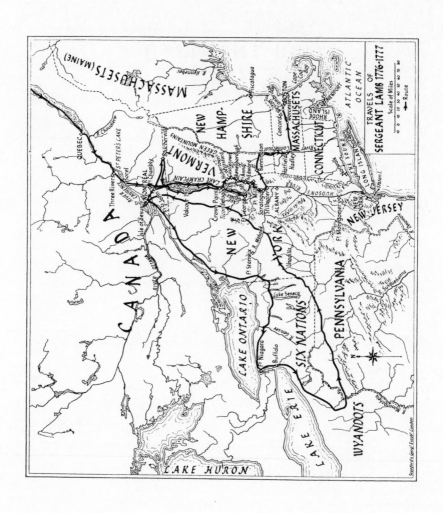

TRAVELS
OF
SERGEANT LAMB 1776-1777

Scale of Miles

Route

FOREWORD

I FIRST came across the name of Sergeant Roger Lamb in 1914, when I was a young officer instructing my platoon in regimental history. His experiences conveyed little to me at the time, because of my truly British ignorance of America and the Americans. However, I visited the United States twenty-five years later and stayed for some weeks with American friends at Princeton, New Jersey, where Washington's defeat of the Hessian Division of the British Army was a proud tradition of the town. It happened to be the time when King George and Queen Elizabeth were being magnificently welcomed by the President and people of the United States; and as an Englishman I came in for my share of the popular warmth. I naturally remembered Sergeant Lamb as a representative British soldier of the period and looked up his story. This novel then suggested itself as a means of learning, as I wrote, why and how the Americans had separated themselves from the British Crown. These were for me very serious questions – for I now regarded the American Revolution as the most important single event of modern times – and I had found them as equivocally treated in American as in English text-books of history.

Since *Sergeant Lamb of The Ninth* is not presented as straight history, I have avoided footnotes or other documentation. All that readers of an historical novel can fairly ask from the author is an assurance that he has nowhere wilfully falsified geography, chronology, or character, and that the information contained in it is accurate enough to add without discount to their general stock of history. I am prepared to give that assurance. I have invented no main characters, not even Chaplain John Martin, Sergeant Buchanan, Dipper Brooks, or the child born at the Quaker's house in the forest by Lake George. All the opinions on the war which are here put into the mouth of Lamb or quoted from his friends and enemies – however shockingly they may read now – are actual opinions recorded during the American War of Independence.

The letter reproduced as a frontispiece, by kind permission of the Lieutenant-Governor of the Royal Hospital, Chelsea, is the only one in Lamb's hand that appears to be extant. It is addressed to General Calvert, the Adjutant-General of the Army, and went as covering letter to his manuscript Memorial, applying for an out-pension at the Hospital. It refers to adventures subsequent to those contained in this book: when, escaping from his American prison-camp, he became Sergeant Lamb of The Twenty-third, or Royal Welch Fusiliers. These make a long story in themselves.

The date of Lamb's death is not known, the record having apparently perished when the Four Courts were blown up in 1922 by the Irish revolutionaries: but from information that Mr Dermot Coffey of the Irish Public Record Office has been good enough to supply, he appears to have lived until at least 1824. After his discharge from the Army in 1784 he became schoolmaster of the Free School at White Friars Lane, Dublin. He married Jane Crumer by banns in St Anne's Parish Church, Dublin, in January 1786.

R. G.
Galmpton-Brixham, Devon
1940

ROGER LAMB'S NOTE OF EXPLANATION

I CANNOT readily convey to paper the vexations and disappointments which attended the publication of the autobiographical book on which I had for so many years laboured, after school hours, and during the whole of my holidays, while master of the crowded Free School of White Friars Lane in this city of Dublin. I had written it as a faithful memoir of interesting events, not shrinking from any confession of error or boast of success, so long as I should keep to the truth.

In the year 1808, when it was concluded, I showed the manuscript to one or two of my old military comrades who resided in Dublin. They considered it pretty well as a story, and had little fault to find with its exactness as historical writing. But with the booksellers it was an altogether different matter. Few of these would deign so much as to look into the work, which they said was clearly of tedious and inordinate length as the life-story of so obscure an individual as I was; others read a page or two and then asked me, affecting to like it fairly, whether I would pay them a hundred guineas for the risk of publication. But I was a poor man, with a parcel of debts, indifferent health, and a numerous family to support; and had expected the tide of money rather to flow in the opposite direction.

The chief subject treated of was my campaigning experiences in the American War of 1775-83, which these booksellers professed to regard as 'a Lazarus' – their trade term for a subject that was not only dead but stinking. They refused to listen to me when I argued that the present hostilities with France would greatly favour the book, as calling attention to the thankless heroism once displayed in America by the same regiments then triumphantly engaged under Lord Wellington in the Spanish Peninsula.

This American war had, admittedly, been a war lost, and so was in general not a pleasant subject for the British people to dwell upon; and a shameful war, too, as fought against men of our own blood, the American colonists; and still more shameful in that these had been leagued after a time with our natural enemies the French, against whose agressions we had so recently defended them. Yet in spite of all this, we (if I may speak for the survivors of the British expeditionary forces in America) had nothing with which to reproach ourselves, nor could we hold ourselves the inferiors in either skill or courage to Lord Wellington's troops. Our common conviction was that it was not we who had lost the war – indeed there was hardly a skirmish or battle in which we had not been left in victorious possession of the field – but that it was lost by a supine and ignorant Ministry seconded by an unpatriotic and malignant Opposition. Nor could our view be readily disputed.

I put all this, perhaps almost too hotly, to Messrs. Wilkinson and Courtney, two enterprising booksellers of Wood Street to whom finally I brought the manuscript of my book. And I asked this question of old Mr Courtney: 'When is it, sir, that old campaigners speak most earnestly and warmly about the hazards, fatigues, triumphs, and frolics that they have lived through together?' 'It is' (I informed him in the same breath) 'when a new war is in progress and when the regiments whose badges and facings they once wore with pride are again hotly engaged, as now. Can such a subject as the American War be therefore called "a Lazarus", except in the sense that Lazarus was by a miracle raised from the dead and acclaimed by the crowds?'

Mr Courtney admitted the justice of my observations, and agreed that a great many retired officers could perhaps be found in Ireland and elsewhere to subscribe to a book which gave an account of campaigns in which they had themselves sometime fought.

Young Mr Wilkinson then undertook to read the book rough, which he did; and a few days later proposed to come to an agreement with me, as follows. Mr Wilkinson should have authority to solicit subscriptions in my name for a work entitled *A True and Authentic Journal of Occurrences in the Late American War*, in which he would include the more general and striking parts of my story and fat it up with extracts drawn from dependable works of travel and biography. He would excite the compassionate interest of the nobility, clergy, and gentry in me as a worn-out old soldier now surprisingly turned writer, and he would expunge from my work all judgments and incidents not consonant with that humble character. He fully expected an edition of fifteen hundred copies to be taken up; and undertook to pay me five pounds down and sixpence for each copy subscribed, which he represented to be very handsome payment indeed. If matters turned out as he hoped, he would publish the remainder of my writings, a more particular *Memoir of His Own Life: by R. Lamb*, as a separate work of a highly moral tone; he would not handle this himself but turn it over to a hackney writer, some hedge-parson or other, who could strike the note of contrition that the middling public would heed. For this work I should receive nothing but the glory of being the author of a second book, until after one thousand copies had been sold, when my reward should be at threepence a copy.

This was a wretched offer and at first I refused it with indignation. But presently I swallowed my pride and signified my acceptance, because of my great want of money and the wretched importunities of the tradesmen who were my creditors, small men almost as impoverished as myself.

Mr Wilkinson allowed me to assist him in the editing of my book. It was excessively painful for me to sit and watch him run his lead-pencil through its choicest passages with a reiterated groan of 'No, no, Mr Lamb, this will never do'. *This* was trifling, *that* was vulgar, *the other* would not only cause pain and offence but dry up subscriptions like a styptic. However, I now had somewhat less urgent need of money than before, since my recent application for an out-pension from the Chelsea Hospital had been immediately and unexpectedly granted – through the good offices of General H. Calvert (by whose side I had once fought) with His Royal Highness the Duke of York. I therefore wished to tear up the signed agreement made in an evil hour with these *cognoscenti* of literature, repay them the five pounds and have my book back. But they held me to my signature and I had no legal remedy against them.

Not once did Mr Wilkinson respect my plea to allow some particular or other to stand in his version. I therefore soon left him to finish his butcherly work alone; and I confess that I was sick at heart when the *True and Authentic Journal* was finally presented to me bound in calf, handsomely printed and with hardly a sentence left as I had penned it. That I received my twenty guineas was poor consolation, or that the list of subscribers to the work included such great names as Major-General W. H. Clinton, M.P., the Quartermaster-General of Ireland; Lieutenant-General Sir Charles Asgill, Bt., then commanding the Eastern District; and the Earl of Harrington himself, Commander-in-Chief of His Majesty's Forces in Ireland – it was no longer my book, no longer the truth as I had wished to tell it. The second volume was yet worse, a sad hotchpotch of religious sentiment and irrelevant anecdote; but it was at least gratifying for me to know that if I got nothing from it, the publishers got less than nothing (though they had shared their risks with a Welsh printer named J. Jones of South Great George's Street), for hardly a copy sold.

Much mortified, I prevailed upon an underling of Mr Wilkinson's (paying him a guinea) to find and restore to me the pencil-scarred manuscript; which Mr Wilkinson continually pretended, when I applied directly to him, that he could not lay his hand upon. Then I set myself, as a sort of penitential task, to rewrite the original story again, and in a manner that displayed even less regard than before for the susceptibilities of the nobility, clergy, and gentry; at the same time correcting numerous errors of detail that I ; had committed, or that had been fathered on me by the ingenious but unhistorical Mr Wilkinson. I trust that I have now done my duty by the jealous nymph Clio, whom the ancients figured in their legends as the Muse of authentic history.

R. LAMB
(December 1814)
The Free School,
White Friars Lane, Dublin.

CHAPTER I

THERE ARE more ways than one of telling a story. I could perhaps plunge as Homer does – whom I have read in translation – in *medias res* with my arrival at the city of Quebec in May 1776, when the American War had been already in progress for a year; and tell the story backward from that point until overtaking it again. But I consider it both more workman-like and more soldier-like a method to do as follows: first, to relate some particulars of my early life and peace-time service with the British Army in Ireland; next, before coming to my own experiences in the war, to venture upon a general account of its origins and commencement. Here I beg leave to point out a grave historical lack: namely, an impartial Detail of the more minute but no less important occurrences of the war which, as secret springs of a clock, actuated the visible pendulum and turned round publicly the hands of time. The only attempt at such a Detail of which I have knowledge is a work published in America, and written by a Member of Congress, but which I find to be exceedingly partial.

I first heard the name of America from my father, an industrious Dublin tradesman who dealt chiefly in seamen's necessaries, on the occasion of the news reaching our city of the British capture of Quebec in Canada from the French under M. de Montcalm. This was in November 1759, the year of victories, when I was not quite four years old. Great cheering and shouting was heard in our humble street, which lay contiguous to the Arran Bridge on the River Liffey, because it was a Protestant street and here was another victory to be celebrated over the Papists of our vicinity. My big brother Tom came bouncing in with the news, blackthorn in fist, huzza-ing and twirling in the air his frieze cap. But my father, upon learning that the gallant and affable general Sir James Wolfe, who had been Quartermaster-General of the Forces in Ireland but a year previously, had fallen in the hour of victory, sternly rebuked Tom's enthusiasm. He made him sit down quietly upon a stool and hearken to a geographical lesson upon the subject of North America which (my father said) was wholly ours now, for ever. This was, as I say, the first time that ever I heard tell of America, and the name was thereby endued for me with solemn associations of glory and grief. My father, I must observe, was a

man of much reading which strong native powers of intellect had led him
to digest and methodize; but he was by no means pious and gave me no
regular religious education, though he taught me at an early age to read,
cipher, and write a fair hand.

For many weeks after, a favourite play in our back garden was the
'Capture of Quebec', in which my brothers played the part of the British
forlorn-hope that swarmed up the Heights of Abraham (a withered apple-
tree) to the Upper City of Quebec (the roof of a wood-shed) where two of
my younger sisters and myself did duty for the French Army. Tom was
the eldest, and I the youngest of our family of eleven, of whom four were
boys. In the following year Tom sacrificed his life in defence of his
country, dying of a wound received on board a British frigate during a fight
in the English Channel. My father was gravely afflicted by the news, which
took the sweet taste of perpetual victory from his mouth and left only
bitterness. Hitherto he had used to take me every Sunday afternoon along
the North Wall and describe to me, in the most interesting and familiar
manner, the latest naval engagement of which news had reached him;
pausing now and then to illustrate the manœuvres of the ships with marks
scratched in the mud. He used the point of his stick, a curious twisted piece
of ivory, the spear of a sword-fish. But there was now no more of that, for
when one day I asked him: 'Father: tell me a battle!' he shook his head and
tears came into his eyes.

He replied: 'Ah, Gerry, dear child, I see your little breast has been fired
with the accounts I have given you. But I only related these things to form
your judgment: I would not have you become a fighting man, no, not on
any account. I have lost one fine boy already in fighting for his country.
Let us have no more talk of battles for a while.'

A year or two later, my two remaining brothers (as well as my favourite
sister) died of the confluent smallpox, so that I was left the only son of my
parents. I was nearly carried off myself, and being thus preserved unexpectedly was for some time so cosseted and indulged by my mother that I
became very wilful; and when my father began again to discipline me for
my faults I resented it greatly. I openly defied him, and allowed him no
alternative but a sterner discipline yet. My mother took my part, but
secretly, because she stood somewhat in dread of my father, who was of
powerful body and of temper difficult to govern.

I constantly visited the quays on the banks of the Liffey and soon
acquired the art of swarming up the masts of the vessels moored thereabouts. One day at the age of six I came near to destruction by imitating
the acts of some grown lads whom I had seen that same morning strip off
their clothes and jump from the steps of the old dock, in the place where
the new custom-house now stands. But whereas the boys had leaped into
the river at low tide, when the stream did not rise above their middles, I
inadvertently chose a time when the water was ten feet deep. I plunged to

the bottom like a stone and, my legs sinking in thick mud up to my knees, I was caught there fast. I would infallibly have drowned had not one of my father's customers, who was passing with a messmate, happened to see my plunge and happened also to be an expert swimmer. Observing, after a time, that I did not rise again to the surface, he immediately leaped in and took me up, almost dead. I was quite unconscious; but this excellent fellow laid me on the ground in the sun and stretched himself beside me. He blew with his mouth into mine, closing my nostrils with one hand, as with the other he expelled the air by pressing my chest closely. Then calling to his mate to continue the treatment, he also gave me a tobacco clyster, puffing up smoke of tobacco into my bowels with the broken stem of his pipe; and next rubbed my belly with his neckerchief. The last remedy of this series was a pinch of snuff in my nostrils. I sneezed, vomited, and so painfully recovered my senses.

This adventure, far from deterring me from the water, only made me eager to learn how to swim; and after some time I became such a proficient that, from off the bowsprits and round-tops of ships, I frequently leaped head-foremost into the river. I also delighted in the summer-time to float about in the sea at the river's mouth, lying quite stiff and straight, and suffering myself to sink till the water entered my ears; thus committing myself to the discretion of the tides. I could remain for several hours in the water in this manner, and would continue often until I grew drowsy and took little naps as I floated. I recommend swimming to the rising generation as a most healthy accomplishment, and immeasurably more useful than many which are at present taught at a very great expense.

My mind still ran upon naval battles and the seafaring life in general, and since my father no longer indulged me in my fancy I would prevail on seamen who came to the shop to tell me of their own experiences in the wars. My father was vexed at this curiosity of mine. He therefore took me by the hand one holiday morning and said: 'Come, Roger, my froward son, let us today walk farther than our usual custom. Let us visit the Four Jolly Rogers.'

I could not conceive what he meant by this play on my name, and hoped to meet with – I hardly know what, perhaps four big playmates. He took me along the South Wall and near the pigeon-house, in the direction of the lighthouse, talking to me of the hardships and dangers of the seafaring life, and enlarging on my own intractable disposition. At last he pointed to some large objects hanging above my head and said solemnly: 'There swing the Four Jolly Rogers, Roger, my froward son, and be careful that you don't one day make a fifth. For it is directly to those rusty chains that your present inclinations are leading you.'

The four hanged men, whose mouldering and tattered bodies were swaying in the breeze above me, on gibbets (as terrible examples to the people of Dublin in general and myself in particular) were Peter M'Kinley, boatswain; George Gidley, cook; Richard St Quintan and Andrew Zikermnan, mariners.

'These ruffians,' my father told me, 'conspired together and murdered the master, mate, and cabin-boy of a merchant ship, the *Earl of Sandwich* (out of Oratova, laden with wine, Spanish dollars, gold dust, and jewels), and also a Captain Giles, his wife, his young daughter, and a serving-boy. They then altered the course of the ship, which was bound for London, and landed some leagues from Waterford, where they loaded the ship's boat with treasure and left the *Earl of Sandwich* with her ballast-port open to sink, as she soon did, together with two cabin-boys whom they barbarously left on board. The four men subsequently came to Dublin and lived for a time in great luxury and excess.

'However, the ship was in some way buoyed up from the ocean-bed and a few days later came ashore near Waterford. That there was found no damage to her hull or masts caused much speculation; and upon M'Kinley disposing of about £300 worth of dollars to a Dublin goldsmith, the plot was suspected. Presently all four criminals were laid by the heels: who severally confessed to the commission of this horrid crime.'

He added many vivid circumstances to the narrative, with which I will not trouble my readers, though they still remain indelibly impressed upon my mind.

This was the first sight that I had ever had of corpses, and it caused such alarm and disgust in me, their flesh being rotted from the bones so that their anatomies showed plainly under their ragged clothing, that I said not a word but began to whimper and begged to be taken home at once. I could not sleep that night, and the day following I was found tossing in a violent fever of the brain. When this left me, I had no desire left for a seafaring life, since in the height of my delirium I imagined myself to be a cabin-boy sucked down with the ship; and this was a recurrent dream with me for many years following.

At the age of eleven I was taken under the charge of a youth of fifteen named Howard to stay for six weeks in a village of West Meath: at the house of his uncle Mr William Howard, a merchant of Jervis Street, and a close friend of my father. I had never before left my father's roof or lived in the country and the experience delighted me, though I was astounded at the pitiable condition in which these country people lived. Their only fare was potatoes and buttermilk, and their small, smoky cabins seemed to be pigsties in which humans were housed, rather than human habitations with occasional accommodation for pigs and poultry. On the first day that I was in this village I presented a little piece of sugar-candy to a ragged peasant boy of my own age: an act for which old Mr Howard reproved me, saying that the child had never tasted such a delicacy in his life. To give him a touch of it was cruel, as creating a new appetite and so making him dissatisfied with his lot. Mr Howard was a very religious gentleman, but,

I remember, stoutly opposed a project sponsored by the rector of the nearest parish, to set up Sunday school for the poor children: advancing the same reason, that it would lead to trouble as educating them above their station, and unsettling their minds. Perhaps he was right, for they seemed a happy, singing people in spite of all; and notwithstanding the drab hue of their faces, which could be ascribed to continual curing by peat-smoke, robust enough in frame. 'I envy them,' sighed Mr Howard, 'with all my heart I envy them. Not an old man among them has the gout, an affection that is slowly killing me.'

I was here accepted as the hanger-on and errand-boy of Mr Howard's son, who was a year older than his cousin, and had just obtained a commission in the Fourteenth Regiment, then stationed at Boston in America. They appeared very grand gentlemen to me, and I soon learned the newest oaths – 'Od's triggers', 'As God shall judge me', 'Prick my vitals', and the like – together with the fashionable London manner of speaking: to their great amusement. Mr Howard's son fancied himself as a swordsman, and so did the nephew, and together they taught me the rudiments of small-sword fencing. I became proud of this elegant accomplishment, which I took up seriously on my return to Dublin, though it was not altogether consonant with my station in society. I even entertained the idea of becoming a professional duellist – of the sort employed at that period by some great persons to fight their battles for them. The two Howard cousins amused themselves at the same time by putting me on a spirited horse, in order to see me tossed off; but somehow I managed to keep my seat, and before long, by perseverance, became a tolerable horseman and could even leap low walls and ditches.

Mr Howard's son was pleased with my usefulness to him and flattered by my devotion, which came very near to downright worship. At my instance, he wrote to my father, asking whether he might take me with him to America. My father was ready to comply with this unusual request, for I had been a great trouble to him at home; but it proved in the event that no situation in The Fourteenth could be procured for so young a boy as I then was. I was obliged to remain at home and the disappointment distressed me. I resolved at all events to depart for America as speedily as possible, and there attach myself to my hero. What ensued is a familiar sort of story, and I will therefore spare particulars of it: how an adventurous child goes to the captain of a vessel sailing for the Indies or America and asks to be engaged. The captain either laughs and tells the boy to run home, or else (which is more common) he engages him and then betrays him to his father, asking a sum of money for his release. Mine was the commoner case. My father paid the money, and took tribute from me with a stout stick.

At that period the administration of justice was greatly relaxed in the city of Dublin. It was almost impossible for persons to walk through some parts of the city (particularly on Sunday evenings) without encountering the most violent and sometimes dangerous assaults. Lower Abbey and Marlborough Streets on the north side of the city, and the Long Lane neat Kevin Street on the south, were the places of general rendezvous for 'Club Law', as it was vulgarly called. Here numbers of daring, desperate fellows used to assemble and form themselves in battle array according to their religious persuasions: then to batter one another with well-managed black-thorn sticks, showing neither mercy nor remorse.

In the case of death, which was frequent, the murderer was seldom discovered. On only one occasion that I remember was such a man appre-hended by the watch and tried for his life by the civil power. He did not deny that he had struck the fatal blow or profess any regret, pleading ancient usuage and that it was done in sport. Evidence was then advanced that the victim's skull was particularly thin, and the jury, upon retiring, instantly brought in a verdict of 'innocent', the foreman announcing very grandly on their behalf that 'a man with so un-Hibernian a cranial forma-tion had no right to stroll down Lower Abbey Street at five o'clock of a Sunday evening'.

I took no part in these encounters. As a small-swordsman I considered the blackthorn club beneath me, but would often condescendingly watch the battle from a distance, sword in hand lest I should become involved in a charge of the Papists. My only regret was that in my walk of life I did not encounter sufficient adversaries armed with my own weapon to keep my hand in practice; affairs of honour which called for recourse to the sword being a prerogative of the higher orders of society.

After the age of seventeen, when I had been for two years employed as clerk in the counting-house of a respectable tallow-chandler and soap-boiler, I grew weary of my lot. It was a continual regret to me that my father's means and interest were insufficient to secure me a commission in the Army, for which I considered myself by nature fitted. I read several treatises on strategy and military engineering, but this practice seemed to no purpose and I desisted. I thought then of persuading my father to let me change my employment and learn surgery in the hospitals, so that I might become an Army surgeon. But he would not grant me even this request. My disgust with tallow-chandling increased and I grasped at whatever distractions of a novel sort were offered to me by the city. The cockpit outside the barracks was my favourite place of call and I would wager there as much as half a guinea on a main, though my wages did not warrant my staking so much as a sixpence.

One memorable day, the 10th of August 1773, I was challenged to lay against that oddity, a hen-cock – that is to say, a cock with plumage resem-bling a hen's – which was to meet a famous shift-wing red, owned by a drummer of the garrison, that had won six good fights in a row. I offered to lay a shilling, which was all that I had of my own money in my pocket, but this was considered unhandsome by my challenger, an evil, black-browed, sallow fellow with a little grey cock tucked under his arm. So I dared to clap down on the board a whole guinea with which my father had that afternoon entrusted me – I was to take it to a tailor in discharge of a debt. The shift-wing, after a long quailing, was prevailed upon to set to the hen-cock, but with such evident alarm and dismay at what seemed to him a fowl of the opposite sex masquerading in spurs, that the hen-cock made short work of him: first tearing his throat and then, volleying over, striking him through the brain with the first heel-blow.

I had lately been forced to pledge my sword and a laced hat owing to similar mischances of play, and had no other resources left for concealing my peculation. I am sure that had I played the prodigal son and, going to my father, fallen on my knees with: 'Father, I have sinned against Heaven and before thee and am no more worthy to be called thy son', he would have rebuked but forgiven me once again. But pride would not permit this Christian course, nor a recollection of his good-humoured scorn at my parade of cock-fighting lore. Instead of returning home, I thought to myself: 'I am a man now and have no more fear of a father's curse than I have use for a father's blessing. To the devil with my father, the guinea, the tailor, the black-browed rogue, and that thief of a hen-cock! I still have a shilling to stake on the last fight.'

This fight was between the little grey cock and another of the same breed, but rather dark-winged. It ended in confusion, the company clamouring that the 'black fellow with the jaw on him' had played his cock foul. They fell on him in a body, but somehow he extricated himself unharmed from the hurry-burly and darted down the street, the little grey cock under his arm. I kept my shilling and the sport ended. Then I said to myself, 'Damn the whole lot of 'em! I still have a shilling for rye whisky: a man can get drunk as a tinker's wife for less than half that sum.'

I soon found myself in the public-house opposite the lower barrack gate, calling for rye whisky and puffing out my chest. Sergeant Jenkins, who kept the house, was a recruiting sergeant. He noticed that the top of my head overpassed the chalk line on the lintel that marked five foot six and a half inches, which was the height below which, at that time, no soldier could be accepted for enlistment. He therefore flattered me and gave me another drink, this time at the expense of the house. Then followed a close inquiry after my state of health: had I ever been troubled with fits, was I ruptured, had I the sight of both eyes? I satisfied him with these particulars without even considering his reasons for asking them, and he began to stroke my shoulders and croon over me: 'Aye, a fine, tall, brave dandy young fellow: the proper cut, the exact proper fit!' It so closely recalled an old farmer exulting over a pig to be carted off to market, that I laughed in his face. However, he joined heartily in the laugh, and soon he had me nobly drunk. Within half an hour he had trotted me before a Justice of the Peace and sworn me in; and lo, I was a recruit of His Majesty King George's Ninth Regiment of Foot, and committed to a martial career after all.

But Sergeant Jenkins was himself a trifle drunk and did not consider that I was enlisted in good form until, after the event, he had made me his customary recruiting speech in the following well-worn phrases:

'To all aspiring heroes bold – in which I include you, Mr Lamb – who have spirits above flattery and trade, and inclinations to become gentlemen by bearing arms in His Majesty's Ninth Regiment of Foot, commanded by the magnanimous General Lord Ligonier, let him repair to the drum's head (Tow-row-dow!) where each gentleman volunteer shall be kindly used and honourably entertained and enter into present pay and good quarters. Besides which, gentlemen – meaning yourself, Mr Lamb – for your further and better encouragement you shall receive one golden guinea advance, and a crown besides to drink His Majesty King George's health. And when you come to join your regiment you shall all have new hats, caps, arms, clothes, and accoutrements and everything that is necessary and fitting to complete a gentleman soldier. God Save their Majesties, and success to their Arms!'

'Huzza, huzza,' I replied fervently, gripping his hand.

When I came to my senses the next morning I was sick and sorry for what I had done; but another drink or two of whisky soon restored me, and I was able to go home to my father, accompanied by Sergeant Jenkins, and civilly informed him that I had joined the Service. I repaid him therewith the guinea out of my enlistment money and promised to settle another small debt from the sale of my present wardrobe so soon as a set of regimental clothes should be issued to me. He took the news pretty well, grasped my hand, and wished me good luck in my new life since I had failed so signally in the old. It is curious that his chief regret was that I had joined the Army in preference to the Navy: forgetting, I suppose, his former objections to my entering on a seafaring life. The Navy, for which my father had a predilection, having once served in a King's ship as boatswain, despised soldiers heartily. It was a preferential saying of seamen: 'A messmate before a shipmate, a shipmate before a stranger, a stranger before a dog, a dog before a soldier.'

The Army, it may be remarked, returned the odious compliment. 'Sailor' was a term of peculiar affront in the barrack-room, and in an officious hand-book issued about this time it was ordered that: 'You must enlist no strollers, vagabonds, tinkers, chimney-sweepers – or sailors.' And in another similar work it was remarked: 'Sailors and colliers seldom make good soldiers, being accustomed to a more debauched and drunken way of life than what a private soldier's pay can possibly admit of.' The severest and most disgraceful punishment that could be inflicted upon a soldier, beyond any quantity of lashes, or the Wooden Horse, or even the

Scavenger's Daughter was *Removal to The Navy*. *I* think it a great pity that such reciprocal abuses were and still are exchanged between the two Services: they breed jealousies and ill feeling that has often been fatal to our arms in a combined expedition on land and water. My father, I believe, regarded my choosing the Army in preference to the Navy as a slight both upon himself and upon my dead brother's memory; though, as I say, he took the news pretty well.

My mother was disconsolate and could not say a word of good-bye, but only wept.

CHAPTER II

I WAS lodged at the barracks for four days and employed there in a number of menial and disagreeable tasks for which I had not bargained, without even the satisfaction of being given a red coat to wear. I was also refused a pass through the gate lest I should be tempted to desert. On the 18th of August three other recruits and myself, under a Corporal Buchanan, were marched a distance of seventy-six miles by road to Waterford, where my regiment was then stationed. Of these three men, one was a 'dipper' or pickpocket recruited in Dublin Jail, and one a gin-shop keeper whose only means of escape from his creditors had been to join the Army. The third was a delicate young fellow named Richard Harlowe who was a man of some education and evidently owed his presence among us to some personal misfortune; though in all our long acquaintance he never let fall a single word as to his antecedents, and I was always too delicate to inquire into them. Harlowe and I struck up a sort of friendship on our march together, and I protected him from the insults of our two fellow recruits who sneered at him for a fine gentleman who found their company too low for him. I knew something of the art of boxing and made it clear that any malice that they showed towards him I would resent equally as if it had been directed against myself.

Our way lay through Timolin, Carlow, Kilkenny, and Royal Oak. It was for Harlowe and myself a matter of melancholy interest to contrast the magnificence of the country seats of the nobility and gentry, and the decency of the dwellings allotted to their retainers, with the sordid cots of the unprotected peasantry. Castle Belan, two miles beyond Timolin, was a case in point, the residence of the Earl of Aldborough. The house, which we turned aside to visit, stood near the junction of two streams, the Greece and the Arrow, with before it a wide lawn gradually sloping from a grove of high fir-trees to the gently flowing Greece, between two rows of elm and ash. The Earl was very busy at this time on the modernization of the house, which was built in the plain style in use under King George I; and this process when complete was to include a fruitery, hot-house, green-house, ice-house, a chapel, a theatre, a pheasantry, and two porters' lodges to each of the six approaches – twelve in all – and stone piers and sweep walls. Each

approach was an English mile in length from the house. There were artificial waters in the pleasure grounds besides the two streams aforesaid,
namely, ponds, canals, and a small lake replete with carp, tench, trout,
pike, cray-fish, etc., and with all sorts of domestic and foreign waterfowl.
His Lordship had, moreover, erected a spacious inn and planned to
construct forty slate farm-houses for the Protestant tenantry of his out-
domain. But a mile or two away from this island of opulence we came upon
a cluster of Papist cabins in the pitiful old style, of mud and turf. We
should have thought it impossible for human beings to exist in such abject
poverty, sloth, dirt, and misery: which was worse even than anything that
I had seen in County Meath as a boy – indeed seldom in all my subsequent
travels did I see such 'looped and windowed raggedness' or such pinched,
greenish animal faces as there.

A toothless old man to whom we spoke, told us among other particulars that there were not more than half a dozen ploughs in the whole parish;
that these were let out by their owners at a high rate, but that for the most
part the spade ruled hereabouts. The labourers were paid by their titular
employer, an absentee rector, not in money but in small potato-plots of an
acre apiece, for which they were charged six pounds a year; which they
worked out at the rate of fivepence a day. They ate no bread, but only potatoes, even on feast-days. Some of them were also, as a charity, allowed the
grazing of a cow. This serfdom was aggravated by their compulsion to pay
tithes (though illegally) on potatoes, turf, and furze, for the support of a
religion which oppressed and detested their own. At the time that we
passed through, there was almost famine in the village: as was customary
in the months of July and August when the old potatoes were exhausted
and the new not yet come to maturity. The cottiers were obliged to fall
back upon boiled cabbages and nettles with a little milk, so that many, as
usual, were dead of the flux. But once every week when their tyrants, the
tithe-proctor and the tithe-farmer, and the other Protestant gentry were
safely away at church together down the road – where a wretched out-at-
heels curate officiated – they would bleed the cattle fattening on the
summer grass to make themselves a holiday meal of black pudding. The
tithe-farmer bought the tithes from the tithe-proctor (who managed for
the rector) and each turned a profit by the transaction. The peasants were
the slaves of the tithe-farmer and were made to draw home his corn, hay,
and turf for nothing, and to give him their labour and that of their children
whenever called upon.

I presented the old man with a sixpence, which he gazed at with wild
joy and wonder. It was, he assured us with tears, the grandest coin that any
man in the village had seen since Christmas; and he would be careful about
taking it to some friends a great distance off to change it into half-pence,
lest the tithe-farmer should get wind of his riches. He wished me abundant
prosperity, health, glory, etc., etc., which grateful oratory I cut short by

remarking that a stout gentleman was coming towards us who had the very air and complexion of a tithe-farmer. The old man took to the hedge like a hare and I saw him no more.

In our journey we passed many places hardly less wretched than this.

Corporal Buchanan was of the blustering sort. He soon had cause for gratitude to Harlowe and myself, though he did not mitigate his severity towards us on that account; for just after dawn, in the barn where we were lodged, near the ruined Abbey of Craigenamanagh, I awoke to see Brooks the pickpocket rise secretly and rifle the pockets of the Corporal's coat. I raised the hue and cry and out he ran across the fields. I pursued him; but he had his shoes on, whereas I was unshod. He would have escaped, had not Harlowe pulled a stake from the hedge, caught and mounted a horse that was pasturing in a held, and ridden the fugitive down in the Abbey grounds. Brooks was conveyed for the rest of the journey with his hands firmly secured behind his back. There was, by the bye, a prophecy current in these parts that the fine ancient octagonal tower of the Abbey would fall down at last on the day when the Devil passed through Craigenamanagh. But it had a solid enough look.

On our arrival at Waterford, on August the 24th, we were put into the hands of an old drill-sergeant of the name of Fitzpatrick, who was a remarkably devout man – for a person of his profession. There were sixteen of us in his awkward squad, and on the first morning Sergeant Fitzpatrick addressed us as follows: 'My dear lads, now that you are set under my charge I will teach you to become good soldiers, if you will closely heed me. The Ninth Foot in which you have the honour of serving is the best regiment in the Army – barring always The Twenty-third, the Royal Welch Fusiliers, with whom I served throughout the Seven Years' War. For you know, my lads, that it is with a regiment as with a wife: you espouse her for life and are one flesh with her, you must never permit the least reproach to be spoken against her, as you love your own honour. I am, as it happens, a twice married man; The Ninth is my second wife and I honour her accordingly, but I cannot be untrue to the memory of my first. The Royal Welch Fusiliers were ever the boldest corps in the King's Army, and the truest on parade: and, what is more, we fought at Fontenoy, Dettingen, and Minden under the guiding eye of the Most High God and the inspiration of His saint, the Reverend Charles Wesley. But The Ninth is a very good regiment likewise.

'Understand, then (it is an order): The Ninth Foot is to be for you the *ne plus ultra* of martial perfection and you shall strive with all your might to keep it so.

'Next, my gallant lads, pay strict attention to what I say. These are my instructions with regard to you, viz: –

'The Recruit is to be taught the several duties of the soldier, by gradation and regular stages, as follows:

'First – his body is to be formed, the air of the clown to be banished, and a manly, soldier-like deportment to be acquired.

'Secondly – he is to learn to march with ease and gracefulness, and to be taught the Step.

'Thirdly – the handling of his arms and the Manual Exercise.

'Fourthly – firing, and the Platoon Exercise.

'Fifthly – firing with ball.

'Now, in the first stage, you must learn from me the true position of the soldier: fixing your eyes upon me and making me your fugleman. You must keep your body erect, without constraint. Observe, my heels are close and in a line, my toes a little ,turned out, my belly rather drawn in than otherwise, my breast projected, my shoulders are to the front and braced well back, my hands hanging down my sides with the palms close to the thighs. Observe especially my head: how it is turned somewhat to the right, so as to bring the left eye in a direct dine with the centre of the body, with my looks directed to an object to the right – the soldier's wife's chemise yonder hanging on the line.

'Come now, my brave boys, and we'll make a lucky start. Fall back against the wall of the privy in a line, the tallest soldier on the right, the shortest on the left.'

He had us back against the privy wall (our heels, calves, shoulders, the backs of our heads and palms of our hands all touching it) and kept us standing there, after correcting our position with stern judgments upon our boorishness, for fifteen or twenty minutes. The term 'Friday's children' was his most solemn abuse, by which he intended us to understand that we still formed part of the great animal kingdom, which included bears, asses, mules, puppies, and the round-shouldered ourang-outang. These the Almighty Lord created on the fifth day, Friday, before perfecting Man on the Saturday afternoon, and resting on the Sunday morning. Having then an immobile audience fixed before him, he would preach to us on the excellence of military discipline as moulding the man for duty and propriety in general, how it forms not merely good soldiers but good citizens and subjects to benefit the commonwealth. Sometimes in these addresses his eloquence carried him away, and we were like to faint in our upright posture; waiting for the sermon to finish, which, by the bye, it seldom did without the name of the Rev. Charles Wesley being somehow introduced into it.

It may be observed that the Rev. Charles Wesley and the Rev. George Whitefield, both Methodists, had been much persecuted in their early missionary journeys through Ireland and particularly by beneficed clergymen who happened also to be Justices of the Peace – the Cork Grand Jury made in 1749 a memorable presentment to the effect that 'We find and present Charles Wesley to be a person of ill fame, a vagabond, and a common disturber of His Majesty's peace; and we pray he may be transported.' However, the effect of their severe teaching upon the troops stationed in Ireland was approved by the commanding officers, as conducing to good behaviour and improved discipline; and the persecution died down. It has been said that the true victor of Minden was not Ferdinand of Brunswick but the same Charles Wesley whose inspiration made perfect Ironsides of our marching regiments.

Instead of beating us over the shoulders with a cane, as most drill-sergeants do, to correct the faults of recruits, Sergeant Fitzpatrick would chasten us in Biblical language. But, even this failing, would give the order, 'On your knees, down!' 'Now,' said he, 'you shall in unison humbly pray God to give you both the will and strength to become good soldiers of Christ and King George' – which order we were bound to obey, mumbling the words after him. When Smutchy Steel, the gin-shop keeper, stealing a sidelong glance to his left laughed aloud at the sight of his comrade, Brooks the Dipper, thus praying to order, Sergeant Fitzpatrick grew enraged. He seized Steel by the collar, swung him up in the air, though a heavy slouch, and hustled him off the parade-ground so powerfully that his heels seemed hardly to scrape the gravel; and threw, rather than gave, him in charge of the Main Guard. Smutchy Steel was instantly confined and spent the remainder of the day in the dark cell, with bread and water as his only subsistence. 'Well, then, my brave soldiers,' cried the Sergeant, returning very red in the face, 'you see the rapid fate that overtakes the man who dares interrupt your devotions. On the feet, up! Now that you are refreshed by prayer, it is an opportune time for you to attempt the Right Face, the Left Face, and the Right About Face. Therefore watch me, pray, with close attention. To the Right Face. First, place the hollow of the right foot briskly behind the left heel' (etc.).

This dark cell, or Black Hole, was a place approved of by general military regulations: it was ordered, however, by the Adjutant-General that though as dark and dismal as possible, the Black Hole should be free from damp and supplied with clean straw once a week.

It was our misfortune that we did not continue long under the instruction of good Sergeant Fitzpatrick: he was poisoned by a meal of shell-fish of which, in the excessive hot weather then prevailing, he should have had the sense to beware, and narrowly escaped with his life, his face and extremities swelling to an alarming degree. His charge was handed to a sergeant, nicknamed 'Mortal Harry' from his extravagant use of swearing, who completed with us the twenty-one days set aside for our first stage of training. 'O you truant offspring of a Drogheda pig and a Belfast chambermaid' he would shout at young Harlowe, for whom he reserved his choicest objurgations. 'Another false step and I'll pluck out your smoking liver with my own fingers, by the Holy Hyssop and Vinegar, so I will! I'll eat it raw with salt on – and relish it too, God damn me all hues and colours!' He taught us the Slow or Parade step, of seventy paces to a minute, timing us with a battered silver watch, and the Quick step of one hundred paces to a minute. The length of the pace was to be exactly two feet four inches, from heel to heel, and he hobbled our legs with straps so that we should not exceed this allowance. He would buckle on the straps himself and took delight in so tightening them that they constricted the flesh painfully. This cruelty roused our indignation but we were too wise to protest to an officer. At the end of that period, having at last, in the opinion of the Captain who came to inspect us, rectified the most prominent appearance of our awkwardness, we were each given his regimentals – coat, waistcoat, breeches, hat – a set of accoutrements and a Tower musket with its bayonet and ramrod. This musket, which weighed fifteen pounds, was a fine and trusty weapon, though most inaccurate at a longer range than fifty paces; and the yellow flint supplied with it was only good for fifteen rounds – the black flint used in gentlemen's fowling-pieces, with which the American armies were afterwards supplied from a rich vein at Ticonderoga, was good for sixty. For the loss of a musket we were fined one pound, ten shillings; for a bayonet, five shillings; and for a ramrod, two. Our complement of necessaries, valued at three pounds sterling, may be interesting to the reader to compare with that of the present trousered, booted, and short-haired days. They comprised: three shirts, two white stocks, one black hair stock with its brass clasps, three pair of white yarn stockings, three pair of oiled linen stockings to be worn on the march under half-spatterdashes, one pair of these same half-spatterdashes, two pair of black linen gaiters, one pair of long black woollen gaiters, one pair of linen drawers, one red cap, one cockade, one knapsack, one haversack, one pair of shoe-buckles and one of garter-buckles, one of black leather garters, two pair of shoes, and a machine to cut and cock hats. In addition we carried a cartouche case to contain four-and-twenty rounds of ball and powder, which were not to be used but in cases of necessity; for ordinary service we were expected to make our own cartridges and run our own bullets. We also carried two spare flints, a powder bag, a ream of whited-brown paper, a spool of pack-thread, three spare musket locks, a dozen of screw pins, three spare priming-pans, six iron ramrods, a bullet-mould, a cartridge-mould, an iron ladle to melt lead in, a worm for extracting cartridges that were fast in the breech, a turnkey, a hammercap, and a stopper. One pound of lead, half a pint of powder and a yard of paper made about fifteen cartridges.

We were next taught how to salute an officer of the Army or Navy, standing fast, giving him a full front, at the same time pulling off our hats with the left hand, and letting them fall in a graceful manner to the side. These hats were wide awkward affairs, not looped three-corner-wise, as in the time of the German wars, but only before and behind, so that they afforded neither shade to the eyes nor protection against sunstroke. The tall caps worn by the Grenadier companies were lighter and at the same time more noble in appearance.

Thus prepared we marched every morning from the barracks to the bowling-green near the water-front, to be instructed in the Manual Exercise. We learned how to stand with a firelock, how to shoulder, order, and present arms, how to fix and charge bayonets, and, finally, how to load and fire with ball. We were drilled for four hours every day.

The words of command and instructions which accompanied this exercise may be of interest, and I shall therefore as a specimen detail the loading instructions then in use. (The firelock, at the start, is dropped to the primary position, and at half-cock.)

Handle Cartridge! Draw the cartridge smartly from the pouch with the right hand. Bring it to the mouth, holding it between the forefinger and thumb. Bite off the top of it.

Prime! Shake a little powder into the priming-pan. Shut the pan with the three last fingers. Seize the small of the butt with the same three fingers.

Load! Face to the left on both heels, so that the right toe may point directly to the front, and the body be a very little faced to the left, bringing at the same time the firelock round to the left side without sinking it. It should in this momentary position be almost perpendicular (having the muzzle only a small degree brought forward) and, as soon as it is steady there, must instantly be forced down within two inches of the ground, the butt nearly opposite the left heel, and the firelock itself somewhat sloped, and directly to the front; the right hand at the same instant catches the muzzle, in order to steady it. Shake the remaining powder into the barrel from the cartridge, putting in after it the wadding and ball. Seize the top of the ramrod with forefinger and thumb.

Dram Ramrods! Force the ramrod half out, and seize it backhanded exactly in the middle. Draw it entirely out, and turning it with the whole hand and arm extended from you, put it one inch into the barrel.

Ram down Cartridge! Push the ramrod down, holding it, as before, exactly in the middle, until the hand touches the muzzle. Slip the forefinger and thumb to the upper end, without letting the ramrod fall farther into the barrel. Push the cartridge well down to the bottom. Strike it two very quick strokes with the ramrod.

Return Ramrods! Return the ramrod to its loops, strike the top of the muzzle smartly so as to fix the ramrod and bayonet in position.

The primary position varied between the ranks. For the front rank of the platoon, who dropped upon the right knee when it came to firing their volley, this position was fixed at the height of the breeches' waistband; for the centre rank, who stood fast, it was at the middle of the stomach; for the rear rank, who moved one pace to their right, it was close to the breast. The firelock was in each case kept horizontal. For discharging the firelock, the orders were *Make ready, present, give fire!* A trained platoon could fire two aimed volleys in the space of one minute, following these orders, and the motions became so mechanical that I have seen a man who had been knocked senseless in battle with a blow on his skull, yet continue loading and firing in exact perfection of discipline – though what mark his bullets were striking I could not well determine.

These instructions were simple by comparison with the old words of command, with their relevant explanation, that hung in a frame in our Sergeants' Mess, showing a date of ninety years before: when a musket was fired with a slow match, not flint and trigger, and supported on a rest.

The orders for firing, unloading, and reloading a musket were a sermon in themselves, viz.

March with your rest in your hand
March, and with your musket carry your rest
Unshoulder your musket
Poise your musket
Join your rest to your musket
Take forth your match
Blow off your coal
Cock your match
Try your match
Guard, blow, and open your priming-pan
Present
Give fire
Dismount your musket
Uncock your match
Return your match

Clear your pan
Prime your pan
Shut your pan
Cast off your loose powder
Blow off your loose powder
Cast about your musket
Trail your rest
Open your charge
Charge your musket
Draw forth your scouring stick
Shorten your scouring stick
Put in your bullet and ram home
Withdraw your scouring stick
Shorten your scouring stick
Return your scouring stick
Recover your musket

But at the present day a great improvement has been made even upon our expeditious orders; so that only ten words of command are given from start to finish in the same exercise.

CHAPTER III

MORTAL HARRY'S language outraged my sensibilities but broke no bones. Some of us recruits, namely Harlowe, Brooks, and myself, suffered far worse at the hands of Corporal Buchanan who had marched us down from Dublin and who was now in charge of the mess to which we were assigned. He drew our pay for us every Saturday, and on the specious pretence of guarding it safely for us, so that we should not run into temptations of women and drink, squandered the greater part of it himself. It paid the expenses of his weekly score at the public-house. According as it was thirsty weather or, not so thirsty, we received a greater or lesser proportion of our due; but, though provisions were very cheap in Waterford at the time, the allowance he made us was always below our needs. We complained continually in private among ourselves, but such was our inexperience that we did not dare state our grievance to the Captain commanding our company. Had the complaint been properly made, with the interference of a sergeant, we should most certainly have been redressed: but none of us came forward to bell the cat. Our apprehensions were increased by the fact of the Corporal's being a favourite with Lieutenant Sweetenham, our platoon officer. This Lieutenant was a well-intentioned but negligent gentleman, having been over-long in the service and without interest to secure his promotion: he suffered many abuses in his command to pass with impunity.

The first of us to contemplate desertion was Brooks the Dipper, but he did not confide in us, knowing of our objections to him. He was a dirty soldier and a liar, and would not relinquish his old trade when embracing that of arms; we were therefore not sorry one Sunday, when we were awakened by the morning gun, to find him gone. It added to our satisfaction to hear that, before absconding, he had stolen the whole of our pay from the pockets of our cruel Corporal: for we hoped now to reclaim it for ourselves. But the Corporal boldly told Lieutenant Sweetenham that the money was his own, all but a few shillings, since he had advanced us money earlier in the week for the purchase of pipe-clay, hair-powder, soap, and missing necessaries to lay out for the general inspection of our belongings that had been held. We were a pack of spendthrifts, so he had the impudence to tell the Lieutenant, in our presence too – and he eyed us malignantly as who would say: 'Dare to tell on me, my beauties, and you'll be confined in darky for ten days, every man Pat of you,' which was his common expression. Such was Corporal Buchanan's ascendancy over us that none of us durst nail his lie to the bench.

That evening Harlowe said to me: 'Lamb, a bargain is a bargain. I swore to serve the King as a soldier, for a certain payment. That payment is withheld from me and I am half-starved for want of it. The exercises are severe and I am punished for every trifling fault which my bodily weakness makes me fall into. I am resolved to desert the Service. If the Dipper can get off free, why not I? What I have suffered is enough to turn a man rank Jacobite. Aye, Waterford is a harbour of good omen: it was from here that King James II escaped from his enemies and sailed to freedom in France.'

I remonstrated with Harlowe, pointing out the manifest dangers of such a course; but he persisted in it. He said that the vessels in the Newfoundland trade that sailed from Waterford with cargoes of pork, butter, and potatoes were frequently short-handed, and he could no doubt stow himself aboard one of them and work his passage to America, which was his object. The harbour of Waterford extended about eight miles in length in nearly a straight line, all the way deep and clear, and having no rocks or sands that could obstruct the navigation; and that many small vessels were tied up in lonely parts would facilitate his escape. The name of America struck sympathetically in my ears, and, near desperate as I was myself, I began to think that his project was not so rash as I had judged. That evening, after a particularly warm day under Mortal Harry, I became fully determined to ally myself with Harlowe.

There was a manner of breaking out of barracks, known to two or three of us, which presented no difficulties to a pair of active men. The route began with the necessary-house. One man would there mount on the other's shoulders in order to climb a ten-foot wall, and pull up his comrade after him; a short stretch of this wall brought the venturers to a holly-tree, into the prickly branches of which they must leap, and so descend. A sentry had his walk along the outer wall of the barracks; but he could be eluded even on moonlit nights by making the passage in three stages. The first stage was to choose, for the leap into the tree, the moment when the sentry had turned the corner of the barrack wall, and to wait concealed in the foliage until he had reappeared and passed on again. The second stage was then to shin down the tree and lie concealed behind an elder-bush. The third was to wait for his second reappearance and subsequent disappearance, and thereupon to dash across a paddock and out of sight behind a hedge.

Corporal Buchanan was dead-drunk as usual on the night for which we planned our evasion, which was pay-day night of the ensuing week; and we therefore had no fear that our long absence at the necessary-house would be noticed by him. We stole out, about an hour after the evening gun, Harlowe carrying two wretched suits of slops which he had bartered at a marine-store against the fine silk handkerchief and decent hat in which he had enlisted. We undressed in the necessary-house and put on these patched and ragged duds, rolling up our regimental clothes and burying them in a sand-heap outside. It was a cloudy night and a little rain was falling.

We mounted the wall cautiously and silently and observed that the sentry was at that moment disappearing round the corner. We crawled along the top of the wall, which was irregular and difficult, and each in turn catching hold of a projecting bough of the holly swung ourselves into a crotch of the tree: where we crouched panting. Soon we heard the sentry's steps approaching and presently saw him ground his firelock in a very unsoldierlike fashion and begin to whistle and dance a jig to the tune of 'The Top of Cork Road'. We recognized him as 'Mad Johnny Maguire', a very humane and merry Northerner who had been among our comforters in these troubles. He had urged us repeatedly to bring our complaint to the company officer and brave the consequences, and undertook that all would be well if we did so. My heart pricked me that, should we succeed in deserting, poor Maguire must bear the blame and be confined for our fault: for our regimental clothes would be discovered and it would be known that we had passed through his walk. He might well be suspected as a confederate. However, it was too late now to turn back.

Hardly had Maguire shouldered his arm again and resumed his march, when we heard whispered curses and a rattle of stones, and two men came along the wall after us. For a moment we thought we were lost, and that this was a party sent to apprehend us. We lay perfectly still, not daring to move, and suddenly some one took a great leap off the wall into the tree, kicking Harlowe on the head as he went, and landing on my thighs. My assailant gave a muttered cry and seized me by the throat, but Harlowe instantly interposed, recognizing him. 'Hist, Moon-Curser,' he said. 'Leave off now, for God's sake. We are all friends. This is Gerry Lamb and I am Gentleman Harlowe. We are deserting too.'

Terry Reeves (nicknamed 'Moon-Curser' from his having been a linkboy before he enlisted) and his comrade Smutchy Steel were recruits of the same company as ourselves but of another mess; they had by a coincidence chosen the same moment for desertion. Terry was drunk and Smutchy a very oafish fellow; both were in their regimental clothes. It was a great embarrassment to both parties that we were simultaneously engaged on the same venture, for the risk of capture was thus more than doubled. But neither would 'give the wall' to the other, and Mad Johnny Maguire had come whistling back before the whispered argument in the crotch had finished. We were piled one upon the other, like fish in a creel, or like corpses along the covered way during a hot assault.

Then came a diversion: from the next sentry post on the right, a sudden hoarse challenge of 'Halt, who goes there?'

'Rounds,' was the reply. This surprised us, for the visiting sergeant of the watch was not due until midnight.

'What rounds?' the sentry called again.

'Surprise Grand Rounds.'

'Advance four paces, Grand Rounds, your Honours!' So quiet was the night that we could hear the smart slap of the sentry's hand at the swell of the stock, and the click of his heels as he presented his arm. For it was Major Bolton, the Commanding Officer of the Regiment, who accompanied by his adjutant officer, a drummer with a lantern, a sergeant, and a file of men, was making an unannounced inspection of the posts. Maguire's strolling step briskened up into a parade-ground stride, he ceased whistling, and retired around the corner again to await the officers' approach. While the Major was questioning the sentry in his duties and finding fault with him for being short of two buttons on his coat, we decided on a bold move. I slid to the ground and helped down Harlowe, who ran across to the elder-bush. Then I stayed to assist the two others for I reckoned that, since we must all sink or swim together it was to my interest to do so. How we managed to push heavy-footed Smutchy Steel under cover of the bush without Maguire hearing and challenging us, I do not know; but I imagine that his attention was so fixed upon the approach of the Grand Rounds that he discounted the nearer noises as unworthy of his attention. There were, as it happened, an ass and her foal pasturing near by, for the steps of which perhaps he mistook ours.

From behind the bush we heard Maguire challenge, in his turn, very fiercely, and after the same exchange as before, Major Bolton, the adjutant, and the drummer with his lantern came into view. Major Bolton warned Maguire to be on his guard that night, for there was a report that two soldiers contemplated desertion. 'And if you fail in your duty, my man, it will not be for lack of warning.' They passed on, and soon we were able to make the next stage to the hedge.

On the previous day we had marked out the vessel in which we proposed to stow ourselves away, moored at about a mile's distance from the barracks. She was a large, half-decked, cutter-rigged vessel, of the sort named 'droghers', and was evidently sailing soon, and for some distance, to judge from the water and live stock being carried aboard her as we watched. The cargo was birch-brooms and potatoes. Our two comrades had broken out in a blind despair rather than with any preconcerted plan, and they therefore attached themselves to us as guides to salvation; nor could anything that we might object make them quit our company. We passed along the road down which we were marched every morning to our drill, but took to the ditch every time that footsteps approached. After a few hundred paces we heard a regular tramp of feet in the distance and the sharp cry of a non-commissioned officer giving his men the step. We leaped into the ditch in no time, and soon a party of six men went by with fixed bayonets. Mortal Harry was in command and in their midst we descried the stumbling and miserable figure of Brooks the Dipper, his hands gyved behind him.

'Yes, my heathen jewel,' Mortal Harry was exulting, 'the drummers of The Ninth are Goliaths and Behemoths; they lay on like the red fiends of Hell itself. Won't they lift the skin off your eel's body, hey? Old Pontius Pilate's crew of Romans couldn't do better, by the Almighty God, no, they couldn't! By the time they have entirely done with you, you'll be howling for the raw hide of a cow to lap yourself within, my poor damned monkey, lest you bleed to death.'

An indescribable horror seized me at these words, spoken in such cold malevolent tones that they felt like the hand of death on my heart. To go forward, or return – either course now seemed equally perilous. Harlowe was for going forward at all events; therefore I went with him. We arrived without further hazard at the water-front, but I remember that it was rather with relief than anguish that I observed our potato-ship in the act of casting off and slipping down the tide.

'Now,' says I to Harlowe, 'you can do as you please. But I, for one, am returning. Be sure that it was the man at the shop from whom you bought these rags who betrayed us to Major Bolton; for we communicated our design to no one, and these two drunkards here acted on a sudden motion. We have no chance of escape; but we have a chance at least of making good our return, if we start at once.'

They all felt too miserable for disputation, and without a word turned homeward with me. After the passage of half an hour we were back again at the hedge and then ran across in pairs to the elder-bush. But Smutchy Steel, the awkward creature, put his foot in a rabbit-hole and turned his ankle, letting out a great screech. Mad Johnny Maguire was still on his watch, for it wanted a few minutes of midnight. He was standing at ease under the holly-tree. I had the presence of mind to anticipate his challenge, by crying out: 'Hist, Maguire, for the love of God raise no alarm! It's I, Gerry Lamb! Let me come forward and explain our case to you.'

He proved a good comrade to me once more; for, though risking a severe punishment for such a breach of discipline, he consented to let me approach unchallenged. I detailed what had occurred in a few words and pleaded earnestly with him to let us return to our duty, explaining that we had felt at the water-front the reviving energy of loyal motives, which had induced us to turn back in time. He revolved the matter for awhile in his head and then remarked quizzically, 'So it's deserting backwards you are, my fine cocks? By Heaven, it's a big thing you're asking me, Gerry boy. For if I were now to arrest the whole four of you, wouldn't it mean great glory to me, and perhaps a guinea from the company officer in recompense, beside?'

'Yes, John Maguire, we are indeed at your mercy. But pray hasten your decision, or the Visiting Rounds will be upon us.

He winked at me, shouldered his piece, and retired beyond the corner, as much as to say: 'Well, then, my name is Billy Hare, I know nothing.' So we returned safely, though it was a great business, hoisting Steel into the crotch and hauling him across to the wall; we could not prevail on him to stifle his groans. We were safely back at the sand-heap, and hurried changing back into our soldiers' clothes, before midnight tolled from the chapel bell, and the distant cries marked the progress of the Visiting sergeant.

As Harlowe and I re-entered the barrack-room, Corporal Buchanan awakened suddenly at the noise and turned up the lantern burning small beside him.

'From whence, in the Devil's name, do you soldiers come?' he inquired in the hoarse whisper of sleep.

'From the necessary-house,' we replied. 'We have, both of us, a touch of the colic.'

'How came that sand on your coats?'

'We tripped over a mound of sand in the darkness.'

'You drunken strollers, get you to bed at once,' he roared at us, and an instant later fell asleep.

Harlowe turned down the lantern wick, lest finding it still burning high in the morning he should be reminded of the incident; and then we crept back into bed. Never before in my life had I been so glad to be between blankets, as then. We had taken the precaution to thrust our ragged clothes, with a stick, deep into the night soil at the necessary-house, and there was now nothing more to fear.

A court martial sat upon Brooks the Dipper the next morning and he was found guilty of desertion, aggravated by the theft of his comrades' pay, and the additional crime of resisting arrest by the party sent to take him at the peasant's hut where he was found hiding. The sentence was three hundred lashes at the halberts. Major Bolton had accelerated these proceedings instead of letting Brooks lie a prisoner for a week or so, which would have been the more usual course. For he desired to make him an example to the two unknown men who, from the evidence of the slop-shop man, seemed also to be contemplating desertion. The sentence was promulgated at noon, and at three o'clock the regiment was formed up in a hollow square to witness its execution under the superintendence of the Drum-Major, who was answerable that the cat did not have more than nine tails, and with the surgeon standing by to decide at each stroke whether the continuance of the punishment endangered the man's life or his further usefulness as a soldier. I will say this for Major Bolton, and so will any man who ever had the honour of serving under his command, that he was an officer who combined strictness with magnanimity to a most remarkable degree. He avoided flogging as much as possible, and only resorted to it for such great crimes as required extraordinary coercion. For the common breaches of military laws and duties, he used to send the offenders to the drill field for a few hours, sometimes (to show his keener displeasure) making them wear their regimental coats turned inside out as examples of ill behaviour and disgrace. They were, moreover, prevented from going on any command or mounting the principal guards.

On this occasion, he did not shirk the horrid spectacle of Private Brooks's castigation, though it was well known that he had told the surgeon that his stomach churned within him on such occasions, and that he had great difficulty in restraining his vomit. I shall spare the reader the details of the proceedings, informing him merely that during the infliction of the punishment on my comrade's bare back, by the regimental drummers, the warm, youthful emotions operated in me to such an extent that I cried like a child. Harlowe, who stood next to me, fainted clean away, his firelock falling with a clatter at my feet.

The third drummer had just completed his tale of twenty-five lashes – each one of which was like a stroke against my own heart – and the victim's shrill screams had already turned to great sobs when Major Bolton, evidently much affected, strode forward to the halberts where he was bound, and in very moving, compassionate tones expostulated with Brooks on the greatness of his offences, and asked him, had he suffered enough?

When Brooks signified his repentance in grimacings, being unable to kind a voice, Major Bolton ordered him to be taken down and remitted the remainder of the punishment, on Brooks's promise of future good conduct. The parade was then dismissed.

As we came off parade, my feelings still very warm, I remarked to Terry Reeves, in the hearing of Corporal Buchanan: 'Twenty-five was for resisting arrest, Moon-Curser, twenty-five for desertion, but the remaining twenty-five, as the Major said, was for *that meanest of all crimes, stealing his comrades' pay.*'

The Corporal turned round sharply, but I was too wild to mind his glaring eye, and I believe that had he spoken a word of reproof, I should have called him thief to his face. However, he made no remark; and, fearing, I suppose, that his peculation might be made known to the Captain, he gave us that very night nearly two shillings apiece of our pay, holding back only the odd shilling of our due. However, the next week and the week following he still kept us on very unfair allowance, and I should yet have gone hungry had not Sergeant Fitzpatrick and his wife employed me to teach their young son writing and arithmetic. These people were very kind to me, frequently inviting me to their table, where they both plied me with the Rev. Charles Wesley's opinions and merits as well as with excellent porter. They paid me, besides, at the rate of one shilling and sixpence a week. I also managed to pick up an odd sixpence or so by making out reports for other sergeants and corporals; and was thus able to relieve my unfortunate messmates who still, however incredible this may seem, preferred starvation to complaint.

Harlowe, though a man of better education than myself, was unable to undertake such writing tasks as these, because he had never learned a clerkly hand, and had such a crabbed gentleman's fist that his writing was quite illegible.

CHAPTER IV

DURING OUR stay at Waterford I fell into many irregularities. The common girls of the town were lavish of their favours to the military, whose handsome facings and well-set-up appearance exercised a sort of fascination upon them; and since the Roman Church regarded such errors as venial, so long as the men they chose were not known to them to be married, I had much gratification at little expense. I also acquired a taste for the raw spirit distilled by the peasants from potatoes, which was as potent as it was easy to come by. However, my strongest prepossession was for gambling, and 'the Devil's picture book', as the Methodists term a pack of cards, was now my favourite study. Being inexperienced in barrack-room life, I was a regular loser in whatever games of chance I attempted. In Dublin I had acquired a sharp eye for those forms of cheating in which cards are secretly removed from the pack to the dealer's advantage, or the pack is arranged beforehand and only a pretence of cutting and shuffling made. But I had yet to learn the maxim, which it cost me a large sum of money to frame for myself: never to use an opponent's pack more often than my own. For though in The Ninth no one, I dare affirm, marked his cards with the faint thumb-nail scratches and notches used in the fashionable clubs of London, there was not a pack in use among us of which each card had not acquired a distinct character of its own by constant handling. A shepherd knows every ewe in his flock by some slight difference of appearance, which would certainly escape the eye of the stranger unless one happened to be blind, lame, or tailless: in this same way every owner of a pack knew his own cards at a glance, soon as dealt, even though there might be no broken corner or torn edge among them. This knowledge put him in the ascendancy over players who knew only half a dozen of them at most, even after playing several times with the pack.

Sergeant Fitzpatrick and his good wife used to counsel me strongly against my passion for gambling. He used to say: 'Private Lamb, the practice will involve you in severe difficulties. Even where money is not risked, the playing of cards administers to idleness and dissipation; and where money is risked, the winner proceeds with ideas of avarice, and the loser to recover his losses, until the precipice yawns equally for both.' And she would quote from a poem of which I do not recollect the title:

> Cards are superfluous, with all the tricks
> That idleness has ever yet contrived,
> To fill the void of an unfurnished brain
> To palliate dullness and give time a shove.

To supply the expenses of gaming, the privates sold their necessaries, besides squandering their pay: on such occasions they dreaded an officer's inspection of the barrack-room when they had to lay out their belongings for his scrutiny. But they almost invariably managed to elude punishment, by borrowing shirts, gaiters, stockings, and other articles of regimental appointment from comrades who happened to be sick or absent on guard duty. It was, among us, held a matter of honour to pay gambling debts within twenty-four hours of incurring them, and a man would rather commit crimes which even common and statute law punishes as capital offences than fail to meet such obligations.

In July 1774, our regiment received the route for the North of Ireland, and on our arrival there, by way of Dublin – where, to my satisfaction, I found my father more friendly disposed towards me – the companies were distributed among the various towns of Ulster. I happened to be ordered on command, in a detachment of twelve men under Lieutenant Sweetenham, to Saintfield, ten miles distant from Belfast. It was a small but neat town once extensively engaged in the linen manufacture; but then in decay. The neighbourhood of Belfast was very ill disposed to the British Government, because of the way in which its ministers had played fast and loose with Irish trade and industry. The greater cheapness of living and labour in Ireland has always rendered her a dangerous commercial rival to England. First of all we were forbidden to export cattle, so our landowners turned their land into sheep-walks, and a flourishing woollen industry was presently begun. This industry, which employed thirty thousand families in Dublin alone, was crushed in my grandfather's day by laws prohibiting the export of Irish wool or cloth, not only to England and the colonies, but to any country whatsoever. In compensation, a promise was made that our linen and hemp manufacture should be encouraged; but no sooner was the linen trade well established than innumerable restrictions were put upon it so that Irish should not compete with English and Scottish linen (which were subsidized by the Government) in any country in the world – nor even with Dutch linen, for fear the Dutch, in retaliation, ceased to buy English woollens.

As a result of this jealousy of the English manufacturers ten thousand or more weavers had since five years been obliged to emigrate to America, whence they wrote home letters full of rancour. The spirit of these weavers, who were all Presbyterians, was the Dissidence of Dissent, and was more obnoxious to our Protestant ruling classes even than Popery.

Many thousands of Presbyterians had previously emigrated to America, being driven from their homes at the beginning of the eighteenth century by the inquisitorial Test Act, though they had been among King William's staunchest supporters at the Protestant revolution. These had become backwoodsmen of the Western Border, and were to be among the fiercest and most redoubtable foes with whom we had to contend in the American War. From a great many inhabitants of Saintfield we therefore received black and sullen looks; none the less, the women here, as in the South, appeared very needy to court with our men, especially where there seemed a prospect of matrimony.

There was a very beautiful girl living at Newton Breda, two and a half miles distant from the inn where we were quartered, the daughter of a retired English merchant captain and a former lady's maid in the household of Lord Dungannon, whose seat of Belvoir lay adjacent. Father and daughter resided together in humble circumstances, the mother being lately deceased. I conceived a great passion for Miss Kate and would have made her my wife had she consented, since she was a Protestant like myself, and there was no obstacle to our union but my poverty. But she put me off with a tender firmness, and would not so much as allow me the smallest familiarity with her. I did not suspect that I had a rival, at least among the soldiery. The Saintfield horse-barrack lay empty at this time and I flattered myself that of all my comrades there was none to whom she could give the preference over me.

She continued to treat me with friendship and did not discourage my visits. Nor was her father at all averse to my visits at the house, though he made it clear enough that I must not deceive myself with any hopes in regard to his daughter until I held at least a corporal's rank. With my education, he said, and my natural talents, I might within a few years rise high in the Service.

To be brief: this Kate Weldone, who was dark-haired, well-featured, and of a gracefully rounded figure, and had, besides, remarkable wit and spirit, told me one day during her father's absence from the house that she was in great grief. She said that she would do almost anything in the world to recompense me if I would risk a crime for her sake.

I resented this question, and asked her whether she mistook me for a rapparee or bully.

But her misery was so remarkable that I softened towards her. Indeed, I presently assured her that I would commit almost any crime in the world, just for the satisfaction of pleasing her, so long as it were no vulgar crime, of theft or murder, and did not injure any of my comrades.

At this, she ran into my embrace and kissed me wildly. She swore that what she asked was in the interests of her own greatest happiness and would not hurt any one at all, least of all any comrade of mine.

'A strange sort of crime that hurts nobody, yet benefits you, my dearest

Kate,' said I. 'Very well. On condition that it is indeed exactly as you say, I hereby swear by my honour to do for you whatever lies in my power: and I shall leave the assessment of my reward to your generosity.'

Her father happened to approach the room at the moment, but we broke our embrace in time, warned by his difficult breathing. On his entry he did not observe the emotion under which both of us were labouring, and called for a dish of tea.

'I hear from the innkeeper, Private Lamb,' he said, after we had exchanged our usual civilities and his daughter had busied herself in blowing up the fire, 'that even were I willing to give you my daughter, which I am not, the marriage could not now be solemnized. Your Commanding Officer has today issued a general order to prevent private soldiers from marrying without written licence signed by the officer of their company or detachment. He has desired the ministers of the places concerned not to solemnize the marriages of soldiers without calling for such a paper from them.'

Miss Kate affected indifference to the news, and Captain Weldone then went on to repeat a rumour that orders were soon expected for us to be sent to Boston in New England, where the colonists were at this time in almost open rebellion. Major Bolton's action was read as a precaution against more soldiers' wives being taken upon the strength than could be received aboard the transports when we embarked for America. 'It's an ill wind, etc.,' he said. 'If you are sent, and a campaign develops, your promotion is likely to be accelerated, and on your return I shall, I trust, find no reason for refusing you my Kate, if she be still willing.'

This made me suppose that there was an understanding between the Captain and his daughter on the subject, that she had confessed to her liking for me, and that only my lowness of station and my poverty prevented the consummation of my hopes. I returned to our quarters in an elated frame of mind, and after buying drinks for the whole company called on my comrades for a game of cards. We played a while for very trifling stakes, since they were so far seduced in wealth that most of them had been forced to keg themselves: that is to say, they had taken a common form of oath not to borrow, lend, touch spirituous liquors or lose more than a penny a game at cards or dice, until they had saved enough of their pay to repurchase the necessaries which they had sold. The restriction seemed to irk my friend Harlowe, for he asked in a tone of challenge whether there was not a soul present who would dare to bet with him in visible coin. 'I have just bought a new pack of cards,' he said, 'and I'll break the seal for any one who will match me through the pack, card against card, the ace to take precedence over the king.'

He fetched the cards, broke the seal and shuffled them while I fetched drink for the two of us. He was my messmate and much obliged to me for a variety of services, and I therefore did not do him the discourtesy of watching him at the shuffle. He dealt out the cards alternately, so that we had half the pack each. They were smuggled Spanish cards, a sort which we favoured because they were both stout and cheap. They ran forty-eight to the pack, and Primero was our favourite game with them.

We matched card against card at threepence a sight, and when at the eighth card he was a shilling and threepence ahead of me, I called on him to double the stake: which he did.

At the twenty-fourth card I owed him eight shillings and ninepence and, desperate at the greatness of this sum, called on him to double the stakes again. He refused, saying that he would not run me into such a thicket as would tear the clothes off my back, thread and thrum; but I insisted, and my comrades called him a coward and told him in the language of the cock-pit to 'beak up and fight it out to the throttle'. So he consented, though with an appearance of comradely reluctance and concern; and when only eight cards were left to play I owed him sixteen shillings. I doubled the stakes again, and he consented 'to give me a chance to win the whole sum back'. But I continued to lose, at two shillings a card, twice out of every three times; and when the last card had been turned up, and I lost even that, my debt to Harlowe stood at the prodigious sum – for us – of twenty-nine shillings and ninepence.

There was dead silence for a while, and I sat stupidly fingering the cards with my left hand and drumming the Devil's tattoo on the table with the fingers of my right.

Nobody laughed, for it was well understood that I could not afford to quit my debt within the statutory time. I was well enough liked by the men, many of whom would have been willing to accommodate me with a loan, had they been able; but they were kegging themselves and could do nothing. For Harlowe they had no liking and avoided his company as much as they decently could, he being a bird of another feather than their own. Mad Johnny Maguire offered me one shilling and sixpence, which was all he had, and Terry Reeves two, which was more than he had in coin; but this sum, added to what I had in my pockets, still fell short of the debt by a guinea. All those present behaved like mourners at a decent funeral.

I burst out laughing and shouted: 'Oh, by the Holy, it's come to this, has it? Well, down goes the whisky, and that's the last drink I'll swallow for a long while, for now I'll be kegging myself to Harlowe.' As an alternative to paying a debt, if the sum exceeded one month's pay, a soldier might keg himself to the victor: that is, abstain from all drink and gaming and make over all his pay, except one shilling a week, to his creditor. Nevertheless, the creditor had the right to refuse to compound in this manner if he distrusted the debtor; and the debtor was then bound to obtain the money by some other means.

Harlowe looked narrowly into my eyes. 'And what if I refuse to let you keg yourself to me?' he inquired. 'Have you always treated me in so comradely a way that you should expect generosity or mercy now?'

I could not in the least understand what he meant by this, nor could any one else present. There were murmurs of astonishment and indignation. However, Maguire said: 'This is none of our business, lads. There's a she in the case, I'll be bound. Let us leave these bucks to settle it between them in private.'

'Comrades, I have nothing whatever on my conscience,' I declared, 'in regard to Private Harlowe. Indeed, since the time when we were recruits together, I have treated him with far greater delicacy, I think, than many persons of my acquaintance.'

There was a laugh at this, for only the night before I had dissuaded Smutchy Steel, whom enforced abstinence had made quarrelsome, from daubing the tap-room wall, as he threatened, with Harlowe's entrails.

'You must come outside,' pronounced Harlowe, 'if you wish to talk compound with me.'

We went out for a jaunt down the Newton Breda road.

'How have I offended you, Harlowe?' I inquired. 'For I know that you would not refuse me to keg myself to you, unless you considered yourself in some way injured.'

He did not answer me outright, but paced along by my side in a silence which greatly annoyed me.

I stopped in my stride, faced about, pulled him backwards by the shoulders and told him: 'Gentleman Harlowe, if you will have your pound of flesh, then by God, say so plainly like an honest Shylock. For then I'll go on the pad, cut the purse and throat of some innocent traveller and the money will be yours by morning, though I swing high for it.'

'No, Gerry,' he replied softly, 'it need not come to that. But I'll remit the whole debt and present you with my painted snuff-box, which you have so long coveted, into the bargain, if you will but give me the help, not of your side-arm but of your pen.'

I thought for the moment that he had gone out of his wits. I inquired, 'Am I to write out the whole of Pope's *Essay on Man* in a flowing hand, like a schoolboy punished for orchard-robbing?'

'No,' he said, 'two words would serve, almost.'

'Don't tantalize me further,' I cried. 'What joke are you driving?'

Thereupon he explained: 'I am bent on contracting marriage with a girl of this town. Not only is our scheme unknown to her father, who would object to it, but there is a general order posted this morning which prevents such marriages from being solemnized without the written permission of an officer. You know that Lieutenant Sweetenham has a strong antipathy to me, at any rate, and that he would reject my request, did I dare make it, with contempt. You write a good hand and are used by the Lieutenant as his amanuensis. You are therefore familiar both with his composition and his signature. Now, my proposal to you is that you shall counterfeit the

Lieutenant's signature to the licence and accompany me with it to the minister's house, to arrange for the solemnization of my marriage. If you will do all this, you are quit of your debt; and the snuff-box, too, is yours.'

I stared dumbly at him and many strange emotions stirred within my breast. How thankful I now am that I did not do what came uppermost to my mind, which was to take him by the throat and choke him in rage, scorn, and envy. For, like a flash, the explanation of the evening's events came upon me. The woman with whom he contemplated marriage could be none other than Kate Weldone. Her careful amity with me had been a mere pretence to conceal her infatuation for my comrade Gentleman Harlowe – against whom her father had conceived a strong prejudice on our first arrival at the town and whom he had told bluntly, he was an unwelcome visitor at the cottage. The petition that Kate had been on the point of disclosing to me and that I had undertaken in advance to grant, for love of her, was the very same that Harlowe had now converted into an obligation, by a downright cheat. For I was suddenly convinced that the cards had been rigged by him with this very object. I was sensible enough to reflect, however, that this fraud must have been unknown to Miss Kate, for otherwise she would not have troubled to plead with me in so melting a way; and that I could therefore not justly be incensed with her.

I therefore contented myself by saying shortly to my companion: 'I must think this over for a spell.' I turned on my heel and left him standing there.

It was a starry but moonless night and I had the luck to recognize old Captain Weldone as he passed me on the road, he not recognizing me. I could now count upon gaining admittance at the cottage and speaking to Kate, without recourse to any stratagem. She had already retired to rest, as I knew by the candle-light at her window; but I threw up a pebble and she presently put her head out and called, 'Is that you, my sweet Dick?'

Dick was Harlowe's name, so I knew that I had read the story aright. But nevertheless I carried on with my game.

'No,' said I, 'it's no sweet Dick, nor no common Tom or Harry, but it's myself, Private Roger Lamb. I have come to hear the service that I am to do for you, since it weighs so heavy on your mind.'

She descended after a while, with her hair loose upon her shoulders, and, upon my urging her, disclosed to me the very same plan of forgery that I had just heard from Gentleman Harlowe's lips, though she was more frank than he in naming him as her intended spouse. I simulated grief, surprise, and a great unwillingness, but she urged that I had given my word. I agreed at last, making one condition only, which she swore on her honour to keep: that she was not on any account to reveal to Harlowe her request of me, and that the very next words she spoke to him would be begging him to propose the plan to me himself as an act of friendship. 'If he does so, I will agree readily,' I assured her, 'and thus persuade him, against truth but in the interests of your own honour, that the object of my visits to this house has always been rather your father than yourself.'

She considered this more than handsome on my part, and with expressions of unmistakable affection, which I need not rehearse, promised never to forget the heavy debt that she was incurring. Presently I said good night and we parted.

On my way home to our quarters, I smiled sourly to myself at the comedy which would ensue: Harlowe would agree, at Miss Kate's instance, to urge me for friendship's sake to forge the document; and yet be greatly troubled in his mind lest I reveal to her, at my next visit to the cottage, in what manner that crime had already been forced upon me.

My spirits were totally restored by an incident upon the road. I passed by a poor thatched cabin from which issued the agreeable sound of a fiddle very masterly played; and the melody so plucked at me that I turned aside, pushed upon the door and entered. It was a scene of the most distressful poverty. That the inhabitants were Papists was shown by the wooden crucifix hanging on the rough earthen wall. I found them to consist of a sick man groaning on a straw pallet; an ailing young woman crouched before a low fire, over which potatoes were boiling unskinned in an old iron pot on legs; three half-naked dirty children tumbling in a corner; four starved fowls roosting on a beam; and an old grandfather with ragged white hair seated on a stool at the opposite side of the fire from the woman. It was he who was playing upon the fiddle, and his face was away from me as I entered.

He put down his instrument and spoke something to me in the Gaelic tongue without turning round. The woman translated for him. 'He says you are welcome, your Honour, and to be seated on this stool. He has not the English and he is blind; but he has the Sight. He told us this morning that a tall young soldier visits us this evening.'

I asked: 'What was that tune he was playing? It seemed to invite me to enter.'

She replied that the Gaelic words concerned a woman for whose sake a wise man would not trouble himself. She repeated them to me, and they may be Englished thus:

> O woman shapely as the swan
> Should I turn wan
> For love of thee?
> O turn those blue and rolling eyes
> On men unwise –
> They wound not me.

The old man spoke again. The woman informed me: 'My man's father says that he played the tune for your comfort '

'Thank him kindly,' I said, 'and pray give him this shilling if he will

consent to take a fee. But how in the world could he have known my need
of it?'

'I tell you, he has the Sight,' she returned.

The old man pocketed the shilling with satisfaction and seizing up his
fiddle again, resumed his playing to such an effect that my breast swelled
with the strangest alternations of enraged despair and amused equanimity;
and, having thus amused himself with me for a while, let the music drop
into a lullaby so compelling that I felt myself falling off into a deep sleep
where I sat on the stool.

I awoke with a startle, to find that the music had stopped and that the
old man was laughing at me.

'He has all the ancient gifts of music,' said the woman.

'It was a shilling well spent,' I rejoined, rubbing my eyes, and thereupon went over to shake my host by the hand. He retained my fingers in a
surprisingly powerful grasp, and I had the conviction that he was able to
read my inmost thoughts while so engaged.

He spoke at last and (as the woman gave me to understand) ran through
many exact particulars of my past life, including the story of my early
escape from drowning and my attempted desertion, promised me happy
issue to my present troubles, but a long and hazardous life to follow. He
also assured me of a future event so fantastical that I laughed outright to
hear of it: that when next I attempted desertion I should succeed in the
attempt and that I should be thanked for my pains by a general with a
shining star on his breast.

I returned to the tap-room in a sort of dream, but the familiar close
smell of the room restored me to my usual senses. I recollected the plan of
conduct that I had drawn up for myself before the distraction of that
fiddling lured me from the road.

As I pushed open the door, all eyes turned on me.

I said to Mad Johnny Maguire: 'Maguire, my good friend, I'll not
require your loan, nor yours neither, Terry Reeves, though I thank you
from the bottom of my heart.'

Terry Reeves asked: 'Have you compounded then with The
Gentleman?'

My staunch resolve was that in no possible respect would I be beholden
to my successful rival. I replied shortly: 'I am permitted to keg myself to
him after all.'

Harlowe started, but said nothing, for I continued: 'He has asked me
also, in return for this permission, to perform a certain small service for
him, and I have consented to that.'

Harlowe raised his eyebrows in an inquiring manner; I nodded good-
humouredly in his direction.

He fumbled in his pouch and drew out the snuff-box, which was a
pretty enough piece, with a painting on it of the Limerick coach with its

four matched horses at full gallop.

'I accept the token, Gentleman Harlowe,' I said softly. But, after helping myself to a pinch of snuff, I threw it to the back of the grate where the fire was crackling hotly under a kettle hung from a chain.

This seemed so droll and unaccountable an action that nobody had the wit to snatch the box from the fire for his own use: the company watched it slowly scorch and char, scrutinizing our countenances between whiles as if to read the riddle. Both Harlowe and I sat impassive, and they remained nonplussed.

Harlowe was the first to speak: 'Well, it was yours, Gerry Lamb. You have a right to burn or squander whatever is yours, I suppose.'

'I have kegged myself to you, Gentleman Harlowe,' I said, 'and I shall have arranged the other matter to your satisfaction before the coming pay-night.'

I was as good as my word, and Fortune assisted me smilingly. The next day was the 28th of July, which was kept in The Ninth as an anniversary of the Relief of Londonderry in the year 1689; at this exploit The Ninth had assisted, when the *Mountjoy*, with some of our musketeers aboard her, broke the boom across the river, and King James consequently raised the siege. Lieutenant Sweetenham called me in, an hour or two before his cele-bratory atoner, to copy for him in a fair hand some official papers to which he would then attach his signature. I considered whether to smuggle the marriage licence in among these papers, bringing them to him just before he sat down to dine with an ensign and another lieutenant, invited by him from neighbouring commands. But I rejected this project as too daring, though he was a man who, for negligence, seldom read through even the most important paper before he signed it.

Throughout the next day he was incapacitated from duty by a surfeit of roasted goose and of Madeira wine, four cases of which had been ordered up for this celebration; and on that afternoon, at four o'clock, Private Richard Harlowe was clandestinely married to Kate Weldone by a curate of Saintfield whom I had imposed upon. In Northern Ireland in those days it was not difficult, I confess, to find a minister to solemnize a marriage in a hurry and without proper ceremony: if he were visited in his front parlour at any time after noon, when it was ten chances in twelve that he would be perfectly inebriated.

I afterwards brazened it out with the Lieutenant. Upon his recovery, I reported to him, in a casual manner, that the marriage had passed without incident and that Private Harlowe had drunk his officer's health with grateful devotion.

'What marriage in the Devil's name is that?' the Lieutenant asked petu-lantly. 'I sanctioned none, so far as I am aware.'

'Oh, doesn't your Honour remember signing the permission after dinner last night, which I brought to you at your own urgent request?'

'I remember nothing at all of last night's events,' he complained. 'If you now told me that I stripped myself naked and waved my small-clothes in the air like a flag, shouting "Death to the Papist pigs", I would believe you, Private Lamb; not being able to swear to the contrary and knowing you for an honest man.'

'It is exactly what your Honour did,' I said, very truly, 'for we all witnessed it.'

Lieutenant Sweetenham did not push his inquiry into the marriage matter further, but buried his head remorsefully in his feather pillow; and that was the first and last that I heard of it from him. But I faithfully kept my kegging-contract with Harlowe, intending that every penny I paid him on a Saturday night would scorch his palm.

Old Captain Weldone took his daughter's marriage ill, and would not permit his son-in-law to lodge in the cottage during all the time that we were stationed there. However, he did not suspect my hand in it and I continued with my visits to the cottage, in order both to gratify the old man, who enjoyed my society, and to displease Harlowe. To Mrs Harlowe I was very civil and said nothing to wound her feelings. She would entrust messages to me for her husband, which it tickled my crooked humour to deliver to him with every outward show of good comradeship.

It was in this year that the octagonal tower of Craigenamanagh Cathedral fell down; and when we heard the news, we shook our heads. That the Devil was loose again in Ireland was ill news. It was said that he had not been sighted for certain in our country since his apparition to Saint Moling, near a thousand years before.

CHAPTER V

IN THE beginning of the year 1775 The Ninth was ordered to Dublin and Major-General Viscount Ligonier, the Colonel of the Regiment, arrived from England to inspect and take the command of it. His Lordship, who had fought at the battle of Minden, was generous, affable, and greatly beloved by the men. A regiment commanded by a peer can in general congratulate itself on this score, because as his coronet has elevated him above the society of his officers he can afford to unbend towards the rank and file to a degree that commoners would not dare – for fear of abating something of their dignity. Moreover, a peer can often win for his regiment privileges and advantages from the civil government that would be refused to a person of less consequence. It was said that, but for His Lordship's interest at the Castle, another regiment would have been given the Dublin duty, which was the most popular in Ireland.

Lord Ligonier's eye soon fastened upon Private Harlowe and myself as persons of superior education, fit for promotion as corporals; and the Sergeant-Major of the Regiment, under whose immediate command the non-commissioned officers came, and who was a complete sergeant, a good scholar, and a sensible, agreeable man, spoke up for us to his Lordship. There was increasing talk of our being sent across the Atlantic, and his Lordship held that a scattered sort of fighting would be likely to prevail in the woody and intricate districts in which America abounds. It was therefore to the common advantage that non-commissioned officers should be able to send intelligible messages in writing to their company officers. Harlowe and I were among the non-commissioned officers chosen to be instructed in the novel light infantry manoeuvres, lately introduced into the Army by General Sir William Howe and strongly approved by His Majesty the King. These manoeuvres were intended for use in broken country, the set hitherto employed having been designed rather for the open battlefields of Germany and the Low Countries. They were six in number and well designed to their purpose, and we of The Ninth were sent to the Thirty-third Regiment, then also quartered in Dublin, to learn them.

I am bound to record here that I felt a certain shamefastness, on visiting the barracks of The Thirty-third, who were commanded by the young Earl of Cornwallis, to compare their high state of appointment and the steadiness of their discipline with the slovenly and relaxed bearing of most of our own companies. One can always correctly judge a regiment's capacities by the behaviour of its sentries. I have already described how Maguire performed his sentry duty at Waterford, and might well have remarked then that his behaviour was not exceptional. I have seen men go on duty in The Ninth dead drunk and scarcely able to stand. But with The Thirty-third the sentry was always alert and alive in attention; when on duty he was all eye, all ear. Even in the sentry-box, which he never entered unless in a downpour of rain, he was forbidden to keep the palm of his hand carelessly on the muzzle of his loaded firelock; for this was considered as dangerous an attitude as it was awkward. During the two hours that he remained on his post the sentry continued in constant motion, and could not walk less than seven miles in that time. The Thirty-third thus set a standard of soldier-like duty which made me secretly dissatisfied with The Ninth, and which I have never seen equalled since but *by a single other regiment* which was brigaded with The Thirty-third under the same Lord Cornwallis, in the later campaigns of the American War. I resolved at least to bring the men who were under my immediate command into a state of discipline for which I should have no cause to blush.

On my return to the Regiment I was appointed to take charge of a squad of light infantry, thirty-three in number, for passing on to them the knowledge that I had acquired. I soon learned the accent of authority without which it is impossible to make men jump to their tasks, and Major Bolton was pleased to congratulate me upon the neat agility and grace with which my pupils performed the new manoeuvres. My employment did not preclude me from other duties such as guard-duties, and on more than one occasion I was appointed for the important Newgate Guard.

It was our ill luck, however, to be under the nominal charge of a captain, an Irish nobleman, who was noted more for punctilio and the flippancy of his tongue than for the acquisitions becoming his rank. He had not taken the pains to acquaint himself with the new exercises and when he appeared upon parade, usually far gone in liquor, to take over the direction of the squad from me, his orders were always confused and contradictory. I was then placed on the horns of a dilemma – whether to allow the men to be misled and mismanaged, or whether to interpret the Captain's wishes by supplying the correct words of command. In the first case I should be wanting in duty to the Regiment and the King, in the second I should be wanting in respect to my immediately superior officer, and in face of the men too. I chose the second evil and, when twice I had capped an impossible order with the correct one, he turned on me in a rage, threatening me with his cane if I would not pay him the proper respect. He added, with shocking imprecations, coupling the name of the Deity with expressions drawn from the common bawdy-house, that if I did not mind myself he would make a devil of me. I had the sense to reply with the becoming and respectful tone of a non-commissioned officer: 'Very good, your Lordship,' so that his anger abated somewhat. However, the squad, which resented this impious and unofficer-like manner of enforcing subordination, had the spirit to make a butt of the captain. Whenever thereafter he came upon the parade-ground they re-echoed in chorus and in a variety of ridiculous tones: 'I'll make a devil of you, you spawn of Satan.' The other officers, who came to hear of this irregularity and had already rated this young nobleman as more apt for caning his men than for storming half-moons, were not ill-pleased; and before long he found his situation so awkward that he sold his captaincy and left us.

My fellow-corporal, Gentleman Harlowe, always now avoided conversation with me. But in talk with others he used to sneer at me for the increased martiality of my bearing, and himself followed the usual fashion of The Ninth: which was to do well enough to scrape through his duties without disgracing himself or his company, but not well enough to excite admiration among civilian onlookers. 'We are a rough and ready regiment,' the saying was, 'and an old regiment, and we can fight as well as the best.' Upon his appointment to the rank of corporal, Harlowe had this great satisfaction, that his wife was permitted by her father to leave the cottage at Saintfield and enter upon effective rather than merely titular matrimony with him at Dublin.

The jail of Newgate was a small mean building, and in no degree suited to the respectability of a great city. It stood on the site of ground now known as the Corn Market, a short distance from High Street and contiguous to Thomas Street. It happened once in the range of my duty to have command of a guard there for twenty-four hours beginning on a Friday evening, at the time when a handsome young Papist, a dock labourer, was due for public execution. This was some time towards the end of February 1775. The sympathy of the city was much excited by his fate, for he had 'suffered the misfortune', as it was vulgarly expressed, to strangle his sweetheart. He had done this as a punishment to her for consorting with one of our drummers.

The guard-house was immediately outside the jail, with a sentry posted before it; and another sentry was posted inside in the entrance-hall. This second man was intended to assist a Mr Meaghan, who had an apartment there with his wife, and a tap-room next door, being employed in the triple capacity of turnkey, hangman, and ale-house keeper. The criminals were lodged upstairs and only allowed to descend if they could afford to pay for refreshment in Mr Meaghan's tap-room: and then no more than three at a time. It was a custom of prisoners, then as well as now, to beg from passers-by, by making loud appeals to their pity through the grated upper windows, from which they would let down a bag on a cord to receive alms.

I was passed word by my father, who had heard the noise from a neighbour, that a rescue was planned of the young culprit in my charge. I therefore resolved to omit no precautions against this taking place. As soon as I had relieved the sergeant of the old guard, I desired the turnkey to assist me in searching the prisoners' rooms for weapons or other instruments of escape. This was done, and two small stabbing knives found and confiscated. Next, I made it my personal care that no contraband should be insinuated into the alms-bag, which was most generously filled that night. On my first examining the bag I discovered a small fee, which I pocketed; and warned the crowd then that if they had any further donations to make they must use Mr Meaghan or myself as intermediaries. This announcement excited groans and howls from the dense crowd of Papists who thronged Towns Arch, the entry to Thomas Street; but I assured them with a resolute smile that if they did not remain orderly, I would disperse them with a ball or bayonet. And if this did not content them, I said, their friend the murderer would be refused by me even the money already collected, and thus disabled from 'wetting his throttle, the poor lamb', as the weeping women termed it. Since I meant precisely what I said, they credited me and subdued themselves.

I then permitted his relatives (whom Mr or Mrs Meaghan first searched, according to their sex) to attend his wake in the tap-room. They were eight in number, of whom two were his sisters; but my sentry with a loaded firelock standing at the door was sufficient to overawe them.

The prisoner was now allowed to descend and the stair-door was locked again after him. In short, rescue was impossible with such careful dispositions taken, and the family therefore settled down to merry-making. They had brought in a handsome brass-bound coffin which they placed upon the floor, and set six lighted candles upon it. This ominous furniture served as a board on which to spread a plentiful display of funeral bake-meats. There was punch, wine and spirits, besides beef-steaks, potatoes, cakes, green bacon, and a kettle of Hyson tea; and the murderer, whom they hugged and kissed perpetually, calling him their darling, their jewel, their poor, charming, handsome, disgraced Jimmy, was the heartiest man in the whole hearty assembly. After a time he charitably recollected that his comrades languished upstairs, and sent up two pints of spirits to them, with Mr Meaghan's permission, and a hamper of potato cakes and butter. This soon set the whole upper storey ringing with triumphant song, and the effect upon the crowds outside was a happy one. For it assuaged their anger against our men, whom, as comrades of the drummer, they had treated as the accomplices of poor Jimmy's ruin.

A priest, or one who professed to be such, presently came in to confess the murderer. He declared himself insulted when the sentry referred him to Mr Meaghan to be searched before he was permitted to enter; nevertheless, a horse-pistol was taken from under his frock. He exclaimed in confusion that he had quite forgotten that he carried such a thing, and, rather than aggravate matters, Mr Meaghan permitted him to enter 'now that his teeth were drawn'. I had seen this priest's sallow face before, but somehow I could not fit it with a priest's cap; and his name, which was given as Father Martin, awoke no memories.

His absolution of the murderer, after confession, was the signal for long faces, tears, and a sad keening of the sort which Shakespeare likens in one of his tragedies to a pack of Irish wolves howling to the moon. Soon every person in the room, barring the priest, was swaying about pitifully, clutching at his own windpipe in horrid anticipation of the choking in store for their relative when he reached his life's goal at Gallow's Green. Father Martin took his leave about midnight, and I closed this penultimate scene by ordering the removal of all the guests but two. For on the eloquent plea of the murderer's uncle, who quoted his own brother's case as a precedent, I suffered Jimmy to remain in the tap-room until dawn with his two nearest of kin, and there to play cards upon the coffin lid. There is a tale that the uncle cracked a joke out of season by trying to cheat him, and that Jimmy nearly became a double murderer; it may be true, but the same has been told of the last hours of many other culprits. At least, he was kept out of mischief by my indulgence, and although the crowd remained outside, chattering, cheering, and wailing all night, no rescue was attempted by them.

When I had returned to the guard-house from the taproom, after giving permission to Jimmy's relatives to remain with him, as above described, I found Terry Reeves in a state of the very greatest terror. On my asking what ailed him in Heaven's name, he withheld his reply for a little while, but then, drawing me aside, he inquired, 'Are you acquainted with that person?'

'What person?' I asked.

'The pretended priest,' he replied, shivering again.

'No,' said I, 'I do not know him from Adam.'

'He is a great deal older than Adam,' Terry assured me, 'and only one day younger than Almighty God Himself. That man is the Devil, the Father of Lies. Wouldn't I know that wet, black forelock of his anywhere in the whole world? I first met him when he was in the disguise of a student of physic at the Romish Seminary where I was employed in the coach-house. Ill luck follows him about, and a shivering cold wind.'

'I smelt no sulphur, dear Moon-Curser,' I said, joking to keep up his spirits, though my own spirits began to sink because I had noticed the same cold wind. 'A little diabolical sulphur would be welcome to fumigate this fetid place.' But now I felt my own skin creeping on my neck, for I had remembered where that face had appeared to me before – at the cockpit on the evening of my enlistment. Indeed he was the very man, the one with the little grey cock, whose challenge had ruined me. I took Terry with me

into the tap-room where we both fortified ourselves with drink. Terry
whispered to me: 'He must have come to claim poor Jimmy's soul.'

On the Saturday morning it was my unpleasant duty to see the prisoner
pinioned and mounted in the criminal cart or 'rumbler' for a procession
through the city; and almost I may say that no task I had subsequently to
perform in the whole course of my service – no, not in any of the six
pitched battles, four sieges, and other hazardous events in which I took
part – was ever so anxious as this. I knew that I could not count upon the
assistance of the city watchmen who were in general infirm and altogether
unfit for that dangerous duty which must occasionally devolve on the
peace officers and body of the police. To reach Gallow's Green we must
defy the threatening rabble who had now rushed up in extraordinary
numbers from all the Liberties and suburbs, to kill the whole course of the
High Street through which we must pass. Yet I think that what Terry had
told me comprised the greater part of my fear.

I was lucky enough to have won the respect of the crowd at Towns Arch
by my frank address to them on the previous night and by the praise given
me by the mourners at the wake for my politeness and easy bearing. I
disposed my little force with circumspection and spirit, first publicly
examining my men's arms and putting them through the loading drill in
the manner detailed in a previous chapter. I also was attentive to halt the
cart for a while in Thomas Street, where the High Sheriffs of the city were
awaiting us, while the murderer made an address of thanks to his sympa-
thizers and benefactors. Lest he should call for rescue or revenge in his
inebriated state, I sang out to him: 'Courage now, Jimmy, my fine cock!
Soon it will be all over, and you'll find yourself in Glory and in the
company of the Saints.'

This sentiment pleased the crowd as well as it did Jimmy himself; he
was good enough to wish me and the guard all good luck, and to confess
that he bore us no ill will. But the passage of High Street was most frightful
and at many points there was such a jostling and thrusting and such
screams of desperate rage from the populace that I thought I should at any
moment be obliged to order a volley. Moreover, I discerned among one
knot of men armed with cudgels, inciting them to attack, the wild face of
Father Martin: which turned me sick, though in effect the attack was not
made. We carried our firelocks at the port ready for instant action; Mr
Meaghan, at whom the curses of Dublin were chiefly directed, marching
between me and Terry Reeves.

All ended well. We arrived in safety at Gallow's Green, where the
victim uttered his last words in so low a tone that nobody could catch them,
and the halter being then fastened around his neck, the cart jerked off with
his feet and he was dead within ten minutes.

They made a ballad of it, which was hawked about the streets the next
day, to the effect that:

Poor, pretty, little Jimmy
Was hanged, not for stealing,
But for choking of his honey,
O that was his failing!

He drove out from Newgate,
He passed through the city,
His hands were tied behind him
And the ladies wept 'Pity'.

                                        etc.

It was set to an air combining the hilarious and the plaintive in equal
measure; while the chorus was nonsensical and comically designed to be
sung in a single breath:

Is there e'er a pretty lass, now,
From North Wall or South Wall,
Could entice poor pretty little Jimmy from
the sweet green gallow's tree, killa-ma-lee, killa-
ma-loo, whisky, piskey doodle-doo——
                                        Ranty doodle
di do, ring ding fol, lol, lol!

I give these particulars in some detail, not only for the purpose of
exciting surprise at the insecurity of the city in those times, and of waking,
by contrast, satisfaction with the present police establishment: but because
they are a help to an understanding of the notorious Cunningham affair,
in which Gentleman Harlowe was involved when he acted as sergeant of
the same guard a few weeks later. Cunningham, a famous highwayman,
was confined in Newgate Jail awaiting trial on a capital charge, and it
happened that it was I who handed over the guard to Corporal Harlowe. It
was my policy never to fail in civility to my former rival, and in this
instance I should have thought myself wanting in soldierly duty had I not
informed him of all matters affecting the conduct of the guard, which was
new to him. I warned him that Cunningham was a very bold fellow and
was suspected at this moment of conspiring with his fellow prisoners to
break out of jail; and described to him the precautions I had taken on the
previous night to forestall any such attempt. He did not answer me offen-
sively, since private soldiers were present and to do so would have occasioned a breach of discipline: however, he was very off-hand in his
acknowledgments of my report and plainly intended to pay no attention
whatever to it.

    That evening Cunningham and a companion obtained a file by means
of the alms-bag dangled from the window and contrived to saw the iron
bolts of their fetters nearly through. They called down the stairs through
the crack under the door for leave to descend, saying that they desired to

take punch in the tap-room before the door was finally closed for the night. The inner sentry passed word of this request to the outer sentry; which Corporal Harlowe granted without demur. Mr Meaghan had the fever in the room adjoining the tap-room, but Mrs Meaghan unlocked the door, and permitted the two men to descend, locking it again after them. When she had gone into the tap-room to draw the spirits ordered, Cunningham's companion delayed at the foot of the stairs, holding the sentry in talk. Cunningham let fall a coin which rolled behind the sentry, and stooped as if to search for it in the dim light. Instead, he broke off his fetter-bolts and knocked down the soldier, who was armed only with a bayonet, by swinging at him from behind with the fetters.

Mrs Meaghan, on hearing the noise, rushed out of the tap-room. She was seized by Cunningham and his associate, who tried to force the keys from her, but maintained a stout struggle for several minutes. She bit Cunningham's hand very savagely when he tried to stop her screams with it. In the end, however, they seized the key of the stair-door from her, in order to enlarge a third man, who was undergoing solitary confinement in the punishment cell. When he appeared, the three of them demanded from her the key of the outer door. She fastened it in her clothes, and refused to yield, though already well beaten and bruised. Mrs Meaghan made, indeed, the most astonishing resistance: the joints of two of her fingers were broken before they wrested the key from her.

By this time, the guard had been alarmed by the cries of the woman and were drawn up in front of the outer door. But notwithstanding the obstacle of an iron chain fastened diagonally across, the criminals unlocked the door, and, what was more amazing, contrived to escape in the face of the guard by darting out through Towns Arch, and without receiving the slightest wound. Cunningham, thus at liberty, was emboldened to resume his career of robbery. He eventually put himself in the way of being again apprehended and imprisoned, and made in the end a capital atonement for his many crimes. But that occurred some months later, and meanwhile the escaping of three prisoners proved disgraceful to Corporal Harlowe who, together with the guard, was confined for it, and became a private soldier again.

I debated with myself whether it would now be proper to offer Mrs Harlowe assistance, considering on what terms of less than friendship her husband and I had lived since her marriage. I decided in the end that I owed her no malice, seeing that she had not encouraged my suit more warmly than was needed to screen her real intentions from her father. Besides, since my fraud practised upon the minister and Lieutenant Sweetenham was also a fraud practised upon my friend and host, Captain Weldone, I felt it my duty to make provision for his daughter. I went to her lodgings and told her, with as much delicacy as I could muster, that I would be glad to afford her whatever assistance lay in my power until such time as her husband was released from confinement and could again provide for her.

It has always been a matter of perplexity to me, how far my attitude towards Kate Harlowe sprang from noble causes, and how far there was an admixture of irony because of my scorn for her husband. It would, I think, be just to say that the two motives, namely, that of pleasing and comforting her to the best of my ability, and that of showing her husband by contrastive generosity how shabbily I thought of him, were reconciled and intertwined. In any event, I never (let me swear) planned to coax away her affections from the man she had married, however obnoxious he might be to me, and from a comrade-in-arms too, however lacking in soldierly honour. Nevertheless, the effect of my visit was that her gratitude to me became confused in her heart with yet warmer feelings; and it was as much as I could do to play the virtuous Joseph and, with a cool word or two, disengage myself from her impetuous embrace.

The old passion now stirred again in me, and Kate was soon aware of it. Had not Gentleman Harlowe been released from confinement two days later I do not know to what follies my inclination might have led me. But the very fact of his now being put under my immediate command proved a sufficient check to my feelings; he was in my power, as any soldier is in the power of a corporal who cares to vent his spite, and I knew that the greatest punishment which I could inflict was to heap coals of fire upon his head, in requital of his former insults and injuries. This I did by treating him no worse than his fellow soldiers, and even a little better, as one who had received training as a non-commissioned officer.

All was not well with me, by any means. Kate Harlowe was seldom out of my thoughts, and whenever I met her in the streets, walking either alone or in her husband's company, the sight of her lovely face and figure was like a stab to me. Because of this preoccupation, I soon slipped back again into my former habits of drinking, gambling, and idleness. Indeed, I so far forfeited the confidence of my officers that I was warned by Major Bolton himself on one occasion that unless I soon sloughed off my negligence I would suffer the same degradation as Richard Harlowe.

In January 1776, when the American War had already been in progress for some months (at a cost so far to us of three million pounds sterling and two or three thousand casualities from wounds or sickness, whereas only one hundred and fifty of the enemy had fallen) I was seized with severe sickness at the Dublin Barracks. I was sent into the general military hospital in James Street (at present used as a barracks) and disabled to march with the Regiment on its receiving the route to the Cove of Cork, where it was to embark for North America. I was the only soldier of The Ninth obliged to stay behind for sickness, and the loneliness of my position, as well as regret for the intemperance which had caused my sickness, made me anxious for a rapid recovery. Early in March I thought myself enough recovered to leave the hospital. I immediately waited on Sir William Montgomery, our Army agent, in Mary Street. Here I was informed that The Ninth was supposed to be already on its voyage, and recommended to join the additional company belonging to us, employed in England on the recruiting service.

My parents and sisters were urgent with me to go with the recruiting parties, in order to detain me from the dangers of foreign service. I had indeed a great curiosity, on the one hand, to visit England, a single county of which seemed of more interest to me than the whole of North America; but on the other hand I considered that remaining aloof from the scene of warfare was not consistent with the manhood of a soldier. I resolved to repair to the Cove of Cork and sail, if possible, with the Regiment; or, if not, then in some later ship bound for the same destination, which was Quebec in Canada. Mrs Harlowe was among the wives who had elected to follow The Ninth to America, and it was perhaps the thought of standing well in her esteem that swung the balance of my judgment in making my choice.

So to Cork I went and found the Regiment still there, in spite of a delay I had undergone by the desertion of a recruit from Downpatrick, who had been entrusted to my charge and to whom I had advanced a fortnight's pay, knowing that I should be refunded whatever I thus gave him. Incensed and anxious that he should have no cause to plume himself upon 'running the old soldier' so much to my expense, I put up placards in the most public parts of the city, advertising the deserter in minute detail. I had the satisfaction to learn of his arrest, three days later, on the Drogheda Road. This man, by name Casey, was a Papist. Owing to the difficulty of finding recruits to bring our regiments up to full establishment, the rule against the enlistment of Papists had recently been waived. But few enough came forward: for that year and the next were among the most prosperous years for farming that Ireland has ever experienced, and the peasants had an inveterate dread of fire-arms, besides.

My valuable friend, Major Bolton, expressed himself pleased at my joining the Regiment, of which he then again had the command (for Lord Ligonier held too exalted a rank to lead us in person), and characterized me as a volunteer, since I might well have gone to England to beat up recruits. He therefore at once promoted me to the acting rank of sergeant in his own company, and used me occasionally in the capacity of confidential clerk.

On the 26th of April in the same year we embarked in a well-appointed expedition consisting of ourselves, the Twentieth, Twenty-fourth, Thirty-fourth, Fifty-third, and Sixty-second Regiments: with which bare statement I must close this account of my peace-time service in Ireland. Next, I will keep my promise and give some account of the origins of the American War then already in progress; and relate what had so far occurred in it. I will also make it plain why we were being embarked for Canada, which was not in revolt, rather than for the embattled American colonies.

It would not be amiss to mention here that the system of transports is a very bad one; the captains think only of their owners and of themselves, and take whatever liberties they dare with the troops and cargo entrusted to their bottoms. If the Government had sent reinforcements in royal vessels, which it did not, even where the need was most urgent, they would have arrived both more speedily and in better condition, and the course of the war would have changed materially. At least a thousand Highland volunteers sent over later in the war in slow-sailing, unarmed, unescorted transports never reached their destination, being ingloriously captured on the high seas by American privateers. Why did this system continue, to the great hurt of the nation? I fear that the reason preponderating was that certain influential men in the Government drew a commission of three per centum on the hire of these ships, and loved their wives and families too well to relinquish this perquisite.

CHAPTER VI

I WILL BEGIN my short historical survey of the origins of the American War with a single short sentiment that was freely and continually expressed by all classes and conditions of our people both civil and military, and on either side of the Atlantic Ocean, throughout the conflict: that it was 'a damned business, a very damned ugly business'. Yet I must in honesty add that, though the losses in lives and treasure that it entailed were in every way to be heartily regretted, yet the separation between the Crown and the Colonies must in the nature of things have come about at some time or other, and perhaps it was as well that it came when it did.

America, in her relation to Great Britain, was frequently presented at this time as a froward child who defied an indulgent parent. This figure was, however, in no sense apt: for America as a single consentient nation did not yet exist, and the diverse American provinces had each in turn finished with tutelage and put on the manly gown.

Now, there is nothing so absurd and so uncomfortable as when grown sons with families of their own are obliged from filial duty to stay under a father's roof, to keep fixed hours, conform to quaint usages, and draw pocket-money instead of wages for whatever labour they perform on his estate. It galls their pride and retards their ambition. The old patriarch may tell them: 'My sons, surely you are tolerably well off here? You can want for nothing in food, drink, clothing, or other comforts. I allow you each a wing of my mansion to yourself. I pay the tithes and the taxes on your behalf. There is sport enough in my coverts, and the labour that I require of you is light. The authority of my name is sufficient to protect you against all insult and danger. Where else in the world would you and your families find yourselves so well off as here, in this spacious and well-provided mansion? Are you so ungrateful then? Or what more can you want of me that I do not do? What restraint have I ever set upon you? I even – an unheard-of thing – have excused your attendance at family prayers. No, no! Be careful that you do not try my patience, my boys. And see, now it is past ten o'clock. Drink up your quart pots, kiss your mother, and off to bed you go with your wives, and pray let us have no more arguments.'

The sons have no answer to make, unless a low muttering that 'every grown man has the right to live where and how he pleases, in independence.' If they are men of spirit as their father is, sure as fate it will come to a quarrel in the end. This quarrel will blow out of some trifling domestic occurrence and the sons will perhaps have a poor enough case to present to the world. But they will push it to extremes, well knowing that the father must grow exasperated and stand on his authority when he finds that they are deaf to reason. For they fear that, unless they force the issue, they will become confirmed in their dull habit of dependence upon him, and forfeit all dignity of manhood. Their trouble is that a profound admiration for their father makes rebellion alike more difficult and more painful.

It is easy to be wise after the event. For my part I think that where quarrels are due they had best come soon. 'Bear and forbear' is an impossible counsel of domestic perfection. For a certain sort of son, complete independence is the only cure of his moods. Left to himself he will come, in time, to be a polished, respectable citizen of the world, and on civil terms with his father again.

So we come to the quarrel between the Crown and the American colonies. It may be objected that I cannot but be partial in judging the rights and wrongs of this case, seeing that seven of the middle years of my life were spent in America as a loyal soldier of King George after he had quarrelled with his revolted subjects. But I had cause to feel both respect and affection for the better people of America during those seven years, and would not therefore be willingly guilty of making any misrepresentation or suppression of fact that would aggravate an already bitter case. I may observe that I have in my time read a great number of American newspapers and pamphlets – printed in the war years on blue, yellow, brown, and black paper for lack of white – and listened to a large number of political conversations during the year and a half of captivity that I spent among them, and consulted numerous books since published in the United States. Especially I shall beware of sneers and airs of affected superiority as a Briton, in telling my tale. But where things were ill done on the American side I shall be no more ready to conceal them, from false delicacy, than if they had been done on ours.

To begin, then: the people of the colonies planted in North America enjoyed almost every privilege and liberty enjoyed by His Majesty's subjects at home, and were indeed by the various Royal Charters permitted to govern themselves by whatever laws, however odd, that it might please their provincial assemblies to frame – and many of them were mighty odd to our British way of thinking – so long as they did not conclude treaties with a foreign power. The allegiance that the colonists, or all but those of Massachusetts, gave the Crown for two centuries was spontaneous and unquestioning; and the whole American people, you may say roundly, thought it no more than justice that in return for the armed protection afforded their country by the British Army and Fleet, and for the monopoly of tobacco-manufacture, certain trade advantages should be required from them. The English, for example, prohibited the colonists, as they prohibited the Irish, to manufacture various goods in competition with themselves, or to purchase directly from foreign nations certain articles of commerce: England was to remain the sole provider and carrier as she had been at the first.

If any American thought that this bargain was unjust, he could find satisfaction in the thought that on his side it was being persistently evaded. England's claim to engross American trade had not been enforced for a century; there was smuggling done on a vast scale along the whole of the American sea-board. Nor could it be reckoned a hardship that the competition of American manufacturers with the English should be restricted. There were a few small manufactories in the villages of New England that kept hands busy in the long winter months and filled the pedlar's pack; but these were not provided against by the Acts of Trade. Nor were great manufactures for export in the English style ever seriously considered in America. In the first place, the success of such an enterprise must depend on there being a great number of poor people to do the work for small wages and long hours; but in those fortunate colonies there were (and still are) no industrious but unfortunate poor. Where land is cheap and rich, every man of energy who will work with his own hands can soon make an independency for himself as a farmer. Hired labourers or servants are therefore impossible to find but at very big wages; and the few there are know their value so well that the master must treat them most respectfully and indulgently, or down go their tools, on go their hats, and good-bye! As for slave labour, that could only be applied profitably to the raising and manufacture of tobacco in the Southern colonies. In the Northern ones, the severer climate made the clothing, housing, and feeding of negroes too great a charge on their masters, so that there were few black faces seen north of Maryland. These Acts of Trade had been in force for a century now, and acquiesced in as legally binding upon the colonies.

How was it, then, that the quarrel grew? The paradox that I have drawn above in the case of the restless sons and the patriarchal father holds here: that the quarrel proceeded from an increase rather than a diminution of admiration for Britain on the part of the colonies. One may not call it jealousy, for no American was ever guilty of so servile an emotion, but it was at least keen emulation – a desire to do deeds worthy of their blood, for which they would gain the credit in their own name, not merely as sons and allies of Great Britain.

The Americans were in general exceedingly proud of their British descent, and the name of an Englishman gave them an idea of all that was great and estimable in human nature: by comparison they regarded the rest of the world as little short of barbarian. By a succession of the most brilliant victories by sea and land – for which the bells rang and the people cheered as loudly in America as anywhere – Great Britain had recently subdued the united powers of France and Spain, the former nation outnumbering her in population by nearly four times, and the latter by three, and acquired possession of a vast extent of territory in both the Indies.

Since the contest with France had arisen on their account in 1757 and the Peace of 1763, by securing Canada to the British Crown, had freed the colonists from all fear of their ambitious French neighbours, they might well have been expected to add gratitude to respect. But gratitude is spontaneous and not forced, and the English were not always so considerate of the feelings of the freedom-loving American that this generous emotion was stirred.

It is certainly not true, as Dr Benjamin Franklin pretended, that 'Every man in England seemed to consider himself as a piece of a Sovereign over America, seemed to jostle himself into the Throne with the King, and talked of *Our Subjects in the Colonies*.' But certainly British soldiers would sometimes recall with too great satisfaction that, though a great number of Americans had fought alongside the English in these campaigns, it was only as skirmishers and auxiliaries: there being no American regiments of the line who could successfully oppose the trained forces of the French and Spanish in pitched battle or siege. Some even accused the Americans of cowardice; and there were stories current in the London clubs of a deprecatory and fantastic sort, of which the following will serve as an example. That at the siege of Louisburg, twenty years previously, the Americans placed in the van had run away without firing a shot; and that Sir Peter Warren, the British commander, had then posted them in the rear, assuring them that it was 'the custom of generals to preserve their best troops to the last; especially among the ancient Romans, the only nation that ever resembled the Americans in courage and patriotism'.

Now, the French being gone from Canada, the colonists felt less dependent upon the British than ever before. They believed that they could treat the former savage allies of the French – the Ottawa, Wyandot, and Algonquin Indians – with contempt; and that, because of the degeneracy of the Spanish nation, the Spanish posts in the Havana and New Orleans threatened little danger to themselves. Indeed, they counted themselves the unchallenged masters of the whole American continent and began to cherish large ideas of their coming greatness. My Uncle James, indeed, at the time when the peace terms were published in 1763 greatly lamented that Canada had now passed to the British Crown, for he said that with the removal of the French there would now be no check upon the ambitious and restless Americans; he would have favoured, instead, taking from the French the rich sugar island of Guadaloupe.

The American condition was, in truth, remarkably flourishing. Trade had prospered almost beyond belief in the midst of the distresses of a war in which they were so immediately concerned. They had paid themselves in two sorts of money: in English by supplying provisions to our troops, and in French by selling contraband to the enemy. Their population continued on the increase, despite the ravages and depredations of the French and Indians. They were a spirited, active, and inventive people, especially the residents of New England, and saw no limits to their future undertakings. As they entertained the highest opinion of their own value and importance and the immense benefit that the British derived from their connexion with America, they believed themselves entitled to every benefit and mark of respect that could be bestowed on them. And though, as I say, they were permitted to pass what laws they pleased for their own provincial government; though the Church of England exercised no authority over them; and though the existing arrangements of trade between themselves and Great Britain worked greatly to their advantage; they began to view the supremacy of the Crown with a suspicious eye.

So it was that the old game of befooling and thwarting the King's representatives – the regal Governors of the colonies – was taken up with increased zest by many of the Colonial Assemblies, especially in the North. This they were in a position to do, though the Governor had the power of absolute veto upon the laws that the Assemblies would pass, for they held the purse-strings. Unless he assented to their measures they would withhold his salary. There was always great mistrust between the Governor and the Legislature, even when a compromise seemed desirable. The Governors would not pass the laws that were wanted, without being sure of the money, nor the Assemblies give the money, without being sure that the laws would be allowed. The rather indecent bargain-and-sale proceedings that ensued were the rule rather than the exception.   .

These Governors were accused of being idle and haughty persons and of bringing in their trains a set of worthless rascals who paid their debts with the perquisites of office and gave the colonies nothing of value in return. That we in Great Britain cheerfully bore with the very same concomitants of monarchy did not concern the Americans. My jailers during my captivity were never weary of telling me that their fathers had left the Old World to escape from these monstrous inequalities of fortune and station there prevalent, which they would not allow to be foisted on them in the New. Certainly, America had served for several reigns as a wilderness into which to banish all the factious people who would not conform peaceably to established religious practice – Puritans, Baptists, Quakers, Presbyterians, and Papists – the liberality of the early provincial charters having been baits to these troublesome folk to emigrate. But that some at least of their parents had come over, not of their own free will, but by order of a magistrate and in chains, I was always too delicate or too cautious to observe. (True it is, that in the sixty years preceding the

Revolution no fewer than forty thousand felons had been transported to America from Great Britain, besides a number of persons kidnapped by the 'spirits' of the seaport towns and conveyed there against their wills to be sold on arrival as 'redemptioners'.)

A deal of loose talk was current in the Northern States about the New World's natural superiority in grandeur to the Old. Dimensions were compared, always favourably to America. Beside the wide Hudson's River, or the wider St Lawrence, the Severn was no more than a creek and the Thames a poor ditch; the biggest forest in England would seem no more than a coppice if set beside those of the northwestern parts of America; and how many times would the whole United Kingdom fit into the space of a single one of the greater colonies? 'A dwarf claiming sovereignty over a giant,' they said in Boston – Boston being the original seminary of all American malcontents and revolutionaries. Calculations were made as to how soon the population of the American colonies, which doubled itself every thirty years by natural increase, would overtake that of England: this time was expected to be reached about the year 1810. Then how foolish a case that would be, with a great and vigorous nation forced to bow to the superior wisdom of a smaller and weaker, that lived three thousand miles away!

So we come to the hullabaloo raised in America after the Peace of 1763. Then, since the national debt of Great Britain had been much increased by the expenses of the war and a multitude of extraordinary taxes were now being levied at home, as upon window-panes and wagon-wheels, it was thought equitable that Americans should contribute a trifle to the common stock, in the interests of their own security from invasion. Duties were therefore laid on all articles imported into the colonies from the French and other islands of the West Indies, the amounts to be paid in specie to the Exchequer of Great Britain. The colonists warmly remonstrated, asserting that they had hitherto furnished their contingent in men and money by the vote of their Colonial Assemblies; and that the British Parliament, in which they were not represented, had no right to tax them further. No attention was paid to these complaints, and they soon retaliated by forming associations to prevent the use of British manufactures until they should obtain redress.

This agitation was still in progress when the Red Indian, Pontiac, secretly knit up a confederacy of those Northern tribes who had formerly favoured the French, to which were added those of the West who wished for revenge, as having been dispossessed of their hunting-grounds by the sturdy and ruthless American backwoodsmen. Pontiac and his allies made a simultaneous attack upon our weak border posts in the neighbourhood of the Great Lakes and the Ohio River, and took scalps of nearly every one of the defenders. Lord Jeffery Amherst, who commanded our forces in America, found himself woefully short of troops: for after the Peace a quantity of British regiments had been disbanded and the few still stationed in America had fallen very low in strength. There had been costly expeditions sent to the Havana and Martinique, where the fever took off thousands of poor fellows. The Indians therefore were able to continue their ravages upon the borders of Virginia, Maryland, Pennsylvania, and New York, with increasing boldness and violence. Yet when Lord Amherst appealed to each of the colonies for local levies to assist him in his march against Pontiac's main forces, he met with a shabby enough response from almost every Assembly.

Partly it was that Lord Amherst, who soon resigned his command in disgust and sailed home, was held like the rest of our officers in America to have too haughty a way with the provincials. In the Canadian campaign he had seldom or never called the American colonels to a council of war, so that they knew no more of what was afoot than their own sergeants. Partly it was that a long-standing suspicion and jealousy existed between the colonies; so that if one colony held back from contributing to the common interest, the others felt no obligation to be any more active. But the chief reason why the provincials in general were so lukewarm was that they regarded soldiering as an unprofitable occupation in these roaring times and best left to the English, should they be martial-minded enough to undertake it. The provinces of Massachusetts and Connecticut made conditions which amounted to a refusal; Rhode Island did not deign to reply; New Hampshire excused herself; Pennsylvania would not send a single man; New York and New Jersey voted a mere thousand men between them – but two-thirds of these might not pass across their borders; Virginia had already sent men to her own frontier and could spare no more, so the Assembly pleaded.

It was two years before Pontiac's power was broken. By this time the colonies had grudgingly raised between them something better than two thousand men (of whom three hundred immediately deserted) to accompany the British punitive expedition. The most useful fighters were a few score of frontiersmen from Virginia; but the Virginian Assembly refused to pay their expenses and tried to fasten the cost personally upon the Colonel of the Sixtieth Regiment with whom they had marched. The King's men bore the chief brunt, and won, unsupported, the only pitched battle of this Indian war, that of Bushy Run. They felt more than a little resentment when they recalled that in the days of greatest peril to the colonies sixty invalids of Montgomery's Highlanders had to be dragged from hospital and conveyed in carts to the weakly-held frontier forts – because free-born Americans refused to make the war any concern of theirs.

Now for the famous Stamp Act. It seemed clear enough that, if left to their own resources, the colonies would be unable to agree upon secure measures of defence against depredations of Indians in their rear, or possible naval raids of French or Spanish upon their front and flanks. Fifteen thousand men was reckoned by the King's military advisers to be the lowest figure necessary for the protection of his possessions from Hudson's Bay to the West India Islands, and it seemed reasonable that the colonies should pay a part at least of the maintenance of these troops, having been such great gainers from the late war.

The new First Lord of the Treasury, therefore, Mr George Grenville, began considering ways and means. He consulted first with the London agents of the various Colonial Assemblies. He pointed out to them that the Acts of Trade and Navigation were being consistently evaded by the Americans. Even with the addition of the new duties, against which such indignant protests were being raised, the amount of revenue brought in did not pay one-third the cost of its collection! Would not the Colonial Assemblies, since these new duties displeased them, suggest an alternative method of raising money for American defence? But no answer came.

It may be noted that the famous Dr Benjamin Franklin, agent for Pennsylvania, then privately approved the quartering of British troops in the colonies as a reasonable measure, and as a security not only against foreign invasion but intestine disorder – for armed conflict between the various colonies, in disputes over land, was always threatening. The generality of Americans, however, held that, since no immediate danger seemed to hang over America, and since they had supplied several militia regiments in the late war, for the expulsion of the French from Canada, their obligations were now at an end. It was also held unjust that their militia officers, however extensive their experience of war might be, still ranked junior to the rawest officer from England who held a commission from His Majesty. But the main impediment to a favourable reply, when Mr Grenville raised this question, was that no two American Colonial Assemblies were ever known to agree, and therefore it would have been impossible, even had the principle of contribution been admitted, to fix the proportions of money that each colony should pay into the common fund for American defence.

The Government then, since the agents did not answer, saw no other alternative but to enforce the Trade and Navigation Acts by a tightening of the preventive system, to pass a Bill for the quartering of troops in America, and to pay the resultant expenses by new imposts in the form of stamp-duties. In the year 1765 the Quartering Act and its more famous companion, the Stamp Act, were passed.

The Stamp Act provided for the annual raising of £100,000, the whole of which was to be spent in America for defraying the costs of that country's defence. Since the population of America was something above two millions all told – exclusive of negroes and Indians – this amounted to a monthly charge of less than one penny a head. Yet what a howl went up! The loudest mouthed and most energetic dissentients in America were always to be found in Boston and the province of Massachusetts generally. The people of Massachusetts had once enjoyed a far more liberal charter than the present, but it had been withdrawn from them for their frequent defiance of the Crown, and their intolerant killing, whipping, and jailing of harmless Baptists and still more harmless Quakers. Massachusetts was a very litigious province as well, and the numerous irregular lawyers of Boston, who were demagogues to a man, chanced to be hurt in the pocket by this Act: for the new stamp-duties were (as had long been the case in England) applied not only to newspapers, pamphlets, playing cards, and dice but to all legal documents, nor might any but the regular lawyers now ratify documents with the stamps.

These lawyers roused the town mob to the most striking demonstrations of displeasure. On the limb of a large tree, as one came into Boston from the country, were hung two effigies, one designed for the Stamp Master and the other for a jack-boot, with a head and horns peeping out at the top. Great numbers of enthusiasts, both from town and country, flocked to see it. In the evening these poor, foolish effigies were cut down and carried in procession with shouts of, 'Liberty and Property for Ever. No Stamps!' But what became of them after, I do not know. The mob went next to the house of Mr Oliver, the Chief Justice of the colony, beheaded him in effigy, broke his windows and burned down a new building of his which lay adjacent. A few days later they also broke the windows of the Deputy Registrar of the Court of Admiralty, and entering into his house destroyed his official books and papers and much of his furniture. They served the Comptroller of Customs similarly, and drank his cellar dry in addition. As for the Governor himself, Mr Hutchinson, they wholly wrecked his mansion and not only carried off from it all his plate, furniture, and clothing, but scattered or destroyed the collection of historical documents that he had been thirty years at making. These mobs consisted, not of people of substance, but of a rabble who were as unqualified to vote in their provincial assemblies as the lawyers who stirred them up now were to discharge their assumed profession. They were, in fact, the forerunners and exemplars of the *Sans-culotterie* who, guided by a similar school of lawyers, were the smoke and flame of the subsequent Revolution in France.

The mobs of the other colonies did not lag far behind Boston in their excesses. At Newport in Rhode Island they burned the houses of two gentlemen who had in conversation supported the right of Parliament to tax the Americans. In Maryland the effigy of the Stamp Master, on one side of which was written 'Tyranny', on the other 'Oppression', and across the breast, 'Damn my Country, I'll get Money', was carried through the streets from the jail to the whipping-post and from thence to the pillory. After suffering many indignities, this effigy was first hanged and then burned. Similar outrages and frolics took place in New York and

Connecticut. On the day that the Act became law there were mock-funerals of Liberty in several towns, church bells tolled mournfully, minute-guns were fired and flags flew at half-mast.

Nor had the mob alone been the instrument of colonial discontent. The respectable General Assembly of Virginia had passed resolutions strongly protesting against the right of England to lay taxes on America. Of this Assembly, the famous George Washington was a member and a zealous speaker on the text: 'No taxation without representation.' But the boldness and novelty of these resolutions, when they were first presented to the Assembly, affected Mr Randolph, the Speaker, to such a degree that he struck upon the table with his gavel and cried out, 'Treason! Treason!'

It may be thought remarkable that the Virginians, who were the most aristocratic people of America, should have allied themselves with the libertarians of Boston in this protest against taxation. It would indeed have been remarkable, had the flourishing condition continued in which the province found herself when the war ended: for revolution is never made by affluent men. But peace commonly brings unemployment, as the energies that were devoted to destruction are relaxed and cannot at once be converted to constructive ends. Money is scarce, trade stagnates, merchants fail to meet their obligations and men tramp the country in search of employment that is nowhere to be had. All this took place after the Peace of 1763. The prosperity of Virginia was so closely linked to that of England that there were many bankruptcies among the planters; for the London market being glutted with tobacco, which few could afford to smoke or chew, the price of that commodity had fallen alarmingly. The employer of free labour has this advantage over a slave-owner, that he can at least turn his workmen adrift in difficult times: whereas the slave-owner must either house and feed his or sell them in a falling market.

Another cause of great discontent in Virginia and the South in general was that the planters did not receive a proper return for their crop even in the best of times: with British profits, charges for freight, commissions and taxes, the price of British goods sent to America in exchange for tobacco was, it was said, six times their real value. George Washington was just such a planter who had fallen into difficulties from these complicated causes: however, by a rich marriage he was protected against utter ruin. He was also one who, though a Colonel of Militia, and a soldier of experience in the Indian wars, had taken it ill that as an American he could not be granted a higher rank in the British Army than that of Captain, and had quitted the Service in a huff. To a man of his condition the Government's choice of such a time to tax America for the purposes of quartering an army on her soil was, of course, most offensive.

On the matter of taxation and representation the British Government took the following view: owing to the preservation without change of our ancient electoral system, certain decayed Cornish boroughs, for example, of a few houses apiece, still return forty-two members to Parliament between them – while great new cities, such as Birmingham and Manchester, have no members at all. Yet Birmingham and Manchester are virtually, it was held, represented by their manufacturers whose interest controls votes in other boroughs; and it was the same with the American merchants, who were indirectly a great power in the British Parliament. Why should Boston and Philadelphia be more tenderly treated than Birmingham and Manchester, cities of rather greater size than themselves?

To which the common American replied: that if the men of Birmingham and Manchester wished to live as slaves, that was their own affair: it did not suit the free populations of America.

To which the answer came again: 'If you would be free, then take concerted measures for your own defence, tax yourselves as you were first requested through your agents – do not burden Great Britain with the business. There can be no more proper a time than now for this mother-country to leave off feeding out of her own vitals the children whom she has nursed up. For, by your own showing, they are arrived at such maturity as to be well able to provide for themselves.'

But the Americans: 'The supposed danger does not exist, or is much exaggerated: if the French or Spanish invade our country we will turn them out easily enough, we reckon, and without your aid.' The hotter-mouthed among them cried, 'We want none of your lazy, foul-mouthed soldiery, hirelings of oppression, quartered upon us, nor of your arrogant, evil-living officers, instruments of a tyranny worse than death itself.'

Mr Pitt the Elder, who had ruled England in the glorious days of the French wars, was now out of office, suffering from a suppressed but deep-seated gout. This affection prevented him from making any great parliamentary exertions, and was even generally agreed to have impaired his powers of reason, though diminishing little from his fluency as an orator. At the third reading of the Stamp Bill he had warmly taken up the cudgels for the Americans, while tolerantly deprecating the turbulence of the Boston mob. His speech, spoken with great animation, paid witness rather to his continued warmth of heart than to his continued sagacity as a statesman. He declared that he rejoiced that America had resisted the despotic threat to her liberty which this Bill conveyed. Yet he did not suggest by what alternative means the necessary fund for America's defence was to be raised. Nor would he explain in what sense the old-established Acts of Trade, one or two of which he had himself sponsored, were any less despotic in intention than this Stamp Bill – unless it was that they were more easily evaded by the lawless American people than this might prove to be.

The irony of the situation lay in this: that the American boast, to be able to defeat the French and Spanish armies if they invaded the colonies, was taken seriously neither by the British nor by the Americans themselves.

Yet it now appears evident that it could have been made good, to judge by the fearful mauling that our armies encountered at their hands when we attempted the same thing.

The Stamp Act was soon repealed, in consequence of a petition to the King and to the Houses of Lords and Commons by a Continental Congress: to which novel institution all the American colonies sent representatives. That the petition was granted was, some will say, evident proof that *virtual* representation in our Parliament was more effective than the actual representation of any English city. Had Old York or Old Boston shown such ill temper over the stamp-duties as their namesakes across the Ocean had done, it would have been a matter for the constabulary and armed forces to settle without delay, nor would any Mr Pitt have pleaded for indulgence towards them.

The withdrawal of the Stamp Act was presented as a pure act of royal benevolence, and a Declaratory Act was at the same time passed, maintaining the authority of the British Parliament over the colonies, without any reserve.

Yet the mischief was now done, for where England had yielded once she might be expected to yield again. The problem of finding funds for the defence of America and of the West India Islands, on which the colonies were dependent for a great part of their trade, remained unsettled. Mr Pitt became the Earl of Chatham, accepted power for a while, grew worse of the gout and being unable to attend to colonial affairs, left his Chancellor of the Exchequer to act as he pleased in the matter. Now, the compromise tacitly agreed upon between England and America, at the close of the Stamp Act dispute, was that Parliament would refrain at least from imposing *internal* taxation, which was to be left to the Colonial Assemblies to manage, stamp-duties being counted as internalities. To the principle of *external* taxation, in the sense covered by the Trade Acts, the colonists gave a grudging consent; though to be sure, as an Irish Member of Parliament put it, there seemed but little difference in effect, whether money was to be taken from the coat-pocket or the waistcoat-pocket. This Chancellor of the Exchequer, Mr Townshend, therefore felt himself at liberty to crack on whatever external duties he pleased, and on various goods, among them tea, that had hitherto passed free of tax. Nor was the expected increase in revenue to be devoted to the quartering of troops in America, but to a fund for the regular payment of colonial governors and judges. Mr Townshend very properly explained to Parliament that in a country where lawlessness abounded and justice was often a matter of favour, the persons in chief legal authority must now be raised above the temptation to venality. But to the Americans it seemed that these fees were a bribe to the Governors and judges to settle all questions to the advantage of the King's friends. The associations formed to refuse English imported goods grew stronger than before, so that the value of such goods fell by a million pounds sterling in a single year. The mob grew still more turbulent, especially that of Boston and New England generally; and even the Loyalists began to think that America should now be treated with the former 'salutary neglect' that gave these low people no excuse for their outrages. To press for the payment of taxes which never could cover the cost of collection seemed like burning down a barn in order to roast an egg.

CHAPTER VII

IN THE summer of the year 1768, two regiments of Foot, The Fourteenth and The Twenty-ninth, and one company of Artillery, were sent to Boston to assist the magistrates and revenue-officers in enforcing the law. This measure was represented by the Boston politicians as if a great herd of lions had been let loose on the town to tear and mangle the inhabitants; but from what I have been told by men of The Fourteenth who later fought beside me in Canada and upper New York, the matter was altogether different – these soldiers felt themselves so many Daniels in the wild beasts' den. For the lawyers and the Congregational ministers, their allies, controlled the populace, the most sturdy and intemperate part of which lived in Fish Street and Battery Marsh. This mob, under the respectable dress of town-meetings, put terror upon all those who were accounted friends of England; by beatings, burnings, and that strange indignity of tar and feathers the use of which had been discontinued by our ancestors, so I have read, about the time of bad King John. No magistrate and no jury, whatever their real convictions might be, dared bring in a verdict obnoxious to the real rulers of Boston; it was endangering his own life and property for any officer of the law to call assistance of the military; and the individual British soldier accused, however falsely, of a crime, however trifling, was altogether at the mercy of these base-minded, factious, and enthusiastic people.

Constantly soldiers and even officers were arrested on frivolous charges, refused bail, and kept in jail until the case came up for trial; when, the prosecutors not coming forward, the case was dismissed and no explanation or satisfaction offered. On one occasion a soldier was arrested in barracks by a constable; since the warrant of arrest did not particularize the soldier by name, his officers appeared on his behalf in court to protest against this infringement of his rights as a citizen. They were thereupon indicted for riot and rescue and made to pay a heavy fine, while the magistrate thundered at them from the bench, threatening them with the vengeance of the town! Two soldiers of The Fourteenth, emerging one day from the hospital after a bout of fever and scarcely able to walk, were set upon by the mob and half-killed by sticks, fists, and boots. They appealed to Major-General Mackay, their commander, for redress and he condoled with them for their misfortunes. 'But,' said he, 'be advised and seek no revenge. For even if you can identify your assailants, as you say, there is no justice for soldiers in Boston. Here is half a guinea for each of you, my lads. Drink and forget.'

And it may not be credited, but it actually occurred to my knowledge: a soldier found guilty (I do not know how justly) of a petty theft was condemned to pay damages to the amount of some seventy pounds sterling, but not having so many pence was indented as a slave and sold for a term of years to the highest bidder! For the custom of selling white men into servitude was still oddly common in this land of liberty.

It may be asked, why did not General Mackay proclaim martial law and reduce the mob to reason by a warning shot or two? He was not permitted. Lord Chatham, the Prime Minister, had adjured the House in passionate tones: 'Let affection be the only bond of coercion: pass an amnesty over the errors of the colonists: by measures of lenity allure them to their duty.' The soldiers of the garrison had strict orders never to strike an inhabitant of Boston, whatever the provocation. This the Bostonians knew; and they took every advantage of their knowledge. Soldiers passing peacefully down the street would be saluted from their rear with cries of 'What cheer, lobster scoundrels?' or 'Hello, you red-herring rascals!' and pelted with stones or filth, the assailants then scuttling away. A sentry standing guard at the entrance to the Custom House or the Magazine would be mobbed by impudent youths, one plucking at his side-arm, another trying to knock off his tall cap with a stick, a third daubing with dirt his white buckskin accoutrements. And these young limbs of mischief would encourage one another: 'Don't be skeered, lads. He dursen't fire. He's a bloody-back coward like the rest.' This term of abuse, 'bloody-back', alluded, like the others, to the scarlet cloth of the infantry uniform; but glanced also at our military custom of flogging delinquents, by which the Americans professed at this time to be greatly shocked. Our men showed a great and disciplined forbearance at Boston.

It was indeed a strange place. The Saints, as the Bostonians were called in fun by the other colonists, were perfectly scandalized by the innocent military music of horns, clarinets, hautboys, and bassoons, especially when played after dark through the streets on the King's birthday, or the anniversary of the Gunpowder Plot, or St George's Day. Their wives and daughters would shudder and draw their skirts aside if they passed a soldier in the streets. In certain peculiar moral observances, such as the limitation of Sabbath Day travelling, or the abstention from black-puddings, they were near as strict as Jews. Yet for scheming, evading, overreaching, hoodwinking, and, in a favourite phrase of their own, being 'smart men', the people of Massachusetts in general and of Boston in particular were a byword in the remaining colonies. As for Boston

Common – to see the women who sneaked out there at night for clandestine pleasure with the soldiery, you might well (said my informants, with an oath) have believed yourself on Wimbledon Common or Blackheath!

Next came the so-called 'Boston Massacre' of March 1770. A private of the Twenty-ninth Regiment, passing early one Saturday morning along a public rope-walk, was hailed by some ropers there, and asked, 'Would you like to do a job of work?' He replied innocently enough that he would gladly undertake work to supplement his meagre pay. 'Then come and clean out our coffee-house' (as they termed a privy) 'you damned rascal bloody-back,' they cried. Says he: 'Boys, I have a prophecy to make. Before much more hemp has been twisted on these walks, your backs will be bloody too.' A fisticuff fight began, three of his comrades running up to defend him, but all these men dutifully refrained from using their side-arms. An officer approaching, the fight was broke off before a decision was reached, but not before the prophetic soldier had engaged the ropemakers in a friendly enough spirit, for he was an Irishman, to fight it out on the Monday morning following – but teeth, nails, and kicking barred. On Sunday the Congregational ministers – the same who used to rant in the pulpits about the Demon Bishops of Britain and how, among other perquisites of episcopacy, every tenth-born child was ravished from its mother's side, along with the tithe-calf and the tithe-pig, for his monstrous appetite – these having got wind of the coming appointment, preached that a massacre of the honest ropers was secretly intended by the British, and that this diabolical plot must be forthwith frustrated. So our four champions, accompanied by a few comrades, all equally unarmed, were astonished on arriving at the agreed place of encounter to find a great number of men drawn up with clubs and sticks to oppose them, the ministers darting among the crowd with cries of exhortation and defiance.

They stood and laughed. At this the mob began to hurl stones, and the bells of a neighbouring church started pealing, setting off all the other peals in Boston. 'Town-born, turn out!' was a cry taken up in all parts of the town.

The mob then moved away from the rope-walk under the influence of a tall, large man, wearing a red cloak and a white wig, and approached Murray's Barracks where they dared the soldiers at the gate to come out and fight like men; at the same time pelting them with snowballs in which stones were wrapped. The soldiers' only answer was a silent contempt; and a passing officer ordered them into barracks. The same ringleader then withdrew them from the barracks and harangued them earnestly. They uttered huzzas and cried: 'On to the Main Guard!' and breaking up into distinct divisions converged on the Custom House in King Street by different routes. Captain Preston, the officer on duty, called out a sergeant and twelve men of the guard with bayonets fixed on their muskets. This order was to protect the sentry, who was now being pelted with snowballs by the rabble. On the appearance of this party, frantic shouts arose of: 'Cowardly bloody-backs! You dursen't fire agin us. Fire, I say, you bloody-back slaves!' The most furious group, composed of sailors who had lost their livelihood by the British interruption of the smuggling trade (the mainstay of this city of Saints) advanced to the very points of the bayonets with most unsaintly oaths and execrations.

Captain Preston pushed his way through the ranks and begged the fellows to go quietly home and play at snowballs among themselves, if they would avoid bloodshed. But the sailors now tried to strike the muskets down with their clubs, and a blow was aimed by one of them at the Captain himself, which he avoided. Among the guard were comrades of the soldier who had been sold into slavery by the miserable action of the magistrates; and one man (the same who gave me this account) had lately been offered by a lawyer the sum of fifty pounds to swear a false affidavit against his own lieutenant, a most humane and excellent officer. Their lungers itched at the triggers.

A sailor struck a soldier on the arm with a club at the moment that the red-cloaked ringleader was shouting back at the Captain. 'Do your worst, damn you! We ain't afeared!' The man's musket went off, but without effect. One of the rabble then happening to shout, 'Fire, my men, fire!' in mimicry of an English officer's tones, this was mistaken for Captain Preston's own order. Several men discharged their pieces. Four sailors fell dead and seven more wounded, two mortally.

To convert an indifferent cause into one that seems to have over-whelming justice on its side, there is nothing so convenient as a martyr: and here was a whole maniple of martyrs. The town broke immediately into full commotion; but, upon the Governor promising to commit Captain Preston and his men to jail and to withdraw the whole of the garrison behind the walls of Castle William, which was a barracks on an island in the harbour, there was no recourse to open fighting. Yet the whole of the colony of Massachusetts threatened to avenge the 'dastardly crime', as it was described. Fantastically distorted accounts of the occurrences were sent back to England by the penmen of Boston, which the Opposition newspapers published *in extenso* as a means of discrediting the Ministry. Two revolutionary leaders, of whom one was the well-known Mr John Adams, a self-taught lawyer, then came forward, politically enough, to offer themselves as counsel for the prisoners at their trial. Captain Preston, the sergeant, the sentry, and ten men of the guard were by aid of his eloquence honourably acquitted of the charge of murder. The two remaining men, who were said to have initiated the volley, were found guilty of manslaughter but punished only lightly. Any other verdict would have been plainly scandalous and a damage to the revolutionary cause; yet that these honest soldiers escaped with their lives was advanced as a signal proof of the impartiality of American justice. And at the same time the mob-leaders and ministers did not hesitate to speak of 'the Boston Massacre', as if there had been a grave miscarriage of justice, the British having secretly overawed the jury by threats.

I have by me an old copy of the Boston *Gazette* of March 1771, referring to the Boston Massacre, in which is mentioned that rancorous Whig, Mr Paul Revere, whose exploits at the beginning of the Revolution have been very dramatically recounted, but without great relation to the truth:

> In the Evening there was a very striking Exhibition at the Dwelling-House of Mr Paul Revere, fronting the Old North Square. At one of the Chamber-Windows was the appearance of the Ghost of the unfortunate young Seider, with one of his Fingers in the Wound, endeavoring to stop the Blood issuing therefrom; near him his Friends were weeping: And at a small distance, a monumental Obelisk, with his Bust in Front: – On the Front of the Pedestal, were the Names of those killed on the Fifth of March: Underneath the following Lines,
>
> > 'Seider's pale Ghost fresh bleeding stands,
> > And Vengeance for his Death demands.'
>
> In the next Window were represented the Soldiers drawn up, firing at the People assembled before them – the Dead on the Ground – and the Wounded falling, with the Blood running in Streams from their Wounds; Over which was wrote FOUL PLAY. In the third Window was the Figure of a Woman, representing AMERICA, sitting on the Stump of a Tree, with a Staff in her Hand, and the Cap of Liberty on the Top thereof, – one Foot on the Head of a Grenadier lying prostrate grasping a Serpent – Her Finger pointing to the Tragedy.
>
> The whole was so well executed, that the Spectators which amounted to many Thousands, were struck with solemn Silence, and their Countenances covered with a melancholy Gloom. At nine o'clock the Bells tolled a doleful Peal, until Ten; when the Exhibition was withdrawn, and the People retired to their respective Habitations.

King George, who was at that time in the full vigour of his powers, the sad lunatic strain not having yet revealed itself, chafed at the confusion into which national affairs had fallen. No fewer than three Prime Ministers had resigned office within a space of seven years. He decided that his Kingdom must for a while at least be managed by a Ministry which would pursue a continuous policy and be proof against faction. He therefore instituted a system of personal government – that is, government under his own direction – the parliamentary leadership being given to Lord North, a well-intentioned but slack-minded Tory. Lord North was bound to the King by a stronger tie than mere loyalty, being his near cousin: his mother had been the daughter of one of George II's German mistresses. At the King's gracious desire Lord North removed the vexatious 'Townshend duties' that had occasioned such a falling-off in the American trade, reserving only a single one, namely, the tax on tea, as a token that the King did not waive his sovereign rights. Thus a great landowner, who freely allows the people of a neighbouring village to walk through his park land, nevertheless for one day in the year keeps the great gates shut from sunrise to sundown and admits nobody: lest a 'right of way' be created which might somehow be inconvenient to him or his heirs. The duty on tea was chosen to be retained as one which, after reckoning in the cost of its collection, yielded practically no revenue to the Crown and could therefore not constitute a legitimate grievance. This measure had a good effect upon trade, which soon recovered its former volume, especially since the American associations formed against the importation of English-manufactured goods had now achieved the hidden object for which they had been intended The shelves of the American merchants were at last cleared, and without loss, of the huge stocks which they had laid in at the close of the French war, before trade had become depressed by the confusions of peace. Yet the two great questions outstanding, that of providing for the external defence of America and that of protecting loyal persons from the molestation of the 'Liberty Boys' (as the revolutionaries now styled themselves) remained unsettled. Matters improved still more in the following year, 1771, there being an alarm of war with Spain. The colonists showed themselves agreeable now to red-coats being quartered among them, and even gave assistance to royal recruiting-parties: our regiments being considerably under strength owing to desertions.

However, in the next year the alarm passed and the agitation against the British continued steadily in New England. It was given substance by an act of the famous and venerable Dr Benjamin Franklin, already mentioned, the inventor of the lightning-conductor for houses, who was then Deputy Postmaster-General of America and resident agent in London of the colony of Massachusetts. Dr Franklin had by some unknown means possessed himself of certain confidential letters written by Mr Hutchinson, the Governor of Massachusetts, whose house and collection of historical documents had been destroyed in the Stamp Act riots, and of Mr Oliver, Lieutenant-Governor, whose house also had been burned on the same occasion: both men very respectable in their private character. In these letters, written to influential friends in England, they had expressed themselves very freely and with pardonable warmth upon the situation of affairs in America, recommending that the Government should adopt more vigorous methods in support of its authority. Let Parliament clap a padlock on the mouths of the over-eloquent orators of Boston, whose one aim was to preserve the remembrance of every disagreeable occurrence that had ever passed between the soldiers and the townsfolk, who ranted ceaselessly on the 'blessings of liberty', the 'horrors of slavery', the 'dangers of a standing army', but only with a view to keeping the popular mind continuously inflamed, and with a fixed aversion to the truth.

These private letters were conveyed by Dr Franklin to his friends of the Massachusetts Assembly where they were read aloud to one hundred and five members by Mr Samuel (not John) Adams. This other Adams was an enthusiast by whom the well-known Committees of Correspondence had been founded, which guided particular towns, not only within his colony but scattered throughout all the others, to concerted action against the Crown. These private letters, then, which Dr Franklin with patriotic and lofty excuses thus mischievously published (some say because of a private pique against the Governor, whose Sabbatarian principles he had offended, and against the Lieutenant-Governor, perhaps in revenge for the rifling of his own private correspondence by secret agents in the British Post Office), threw the Assembly into a violent flame.

By a majority of over twenty to one they voted that the tendency and design of these letters was to subject the Constitution and introduce arbitrary power into the province. They humbly petitioned His Majesty to remove these two men for ever from the government of Massachusetts: asserting that they, teeing 'no strangers or foreigners but bone of our bone, flesh of our flesh, born and educated among us . . . have alienated from us the affections of our Sovereign, have destroyed the harmony and goodwill which existed between Great Britain and Massachusetts and, having already caused bloodshed in our streets will, if unchecked, plunge our country into all the horrors of civil war.' Dr Franklin himself conveyed this petition, the sincerity of which may well be questioned, to the King, before whom it was laid in Council. But it became known that the letters on which the petition was grounded had been purloined by this same Dr Franklin, and the Committee of Lords therefore considered it a somewhat indecent affair. Dr Franklin, called in evidence, would not reply to interrogation, the petition was thrown out, and Dr Franklin was dismissed from his Deputy Postmastership. This was thought to be to his satisfaction; for it would prove to the Bostonians that he was ready to suffer from his attachment to their cause – being still somewhat suspect to them as having been a warm supporter of the Quartering Act and the Stamp Act. In the event, he was rewarded by his fellow-countrymen, a year or two later, with the Postmaster-Generalship of the United States.

Every one on this side of the Atlantic, as on the other, has heard of the 'Boston Tea-Party' which was the immediate occasion of the American War; but how it came about is not, I find, so generally known.

The East India Company stood on the brink of bankruptcy, one reason being that it had lost many hundreds of thousands of customers in

America. Until the new duty had been placed upon it, tea had been, after hard liquor, the favourite beverage not only of the white Americans (especially of the women, who were perfect addicts to it) but of the Indian savages, who boiled it regularly twice a day in the kettles suspended over their wigwam fires. Four million pounds' worth of tea had now accumulated in the London warehouses, and the Cabinet thought to help the East India merchants out of their difficulties by allowing them to sell some of this surplus treasure direct to America at a reduced rate. That is to say, the Company was allowed a drawback of the whole tea duty then payable in England, while the Exchequer continued to claim the duty of threepence on the pound payable by America. This arrangement greatly vexed the Bostonians. It was not only that this slight but aggravating threepence had become a symbol to them of liberties denied – for the watchword, 'No taxation without representation', was by now made to cover external as well as internal imports; but that it damaged the private interests of their leaders and put many of themselves out of employment. Colonel 'King' Hancock, of the Sons of Liberty, had made a large fortune by smuggling East India tea from Holland, where it was sold at one shilling a pound; having in combination with a few associates handled no fewer than five thousand chests in two years, and engaged a great number of seamen and others in the trade. The new tea being offered for sale far cheaper, even with the duty added, than what Hancock sold (and indeed cheaper than in England, since the English duty was higher than the American) would undercut the profit, amounting to near two hundred per centum, that he was drawing from his venture. It was Colonel Hancock's friend, Mr Samuel Adams, who personally directed the 'daring action', as it has been called, of the fifty Boston mobsmen who, on December 16th 1773, disguised as Mohawk Indians, boarded the British tea-ships on their arrival at Boston harbour, and threw the whole of their cargo, three hundred and forty-two chests, overboard. In the immediate and particular sense it was not daring: Mr Adams knew well that the troops would not be called out from Castle William to save the tea, since their orders were to intervene in civil disturbances only if blood were shed; nor would the magistrates take any action against him subsequently, for fear of a coat of tar and feathers, even if they were not of his own opinions. But it was a daring action in the sense that it challenged reprisals against the town of Boston as a whole.

This was not the only consignment of tea that was sent to America at that time; and Mr Adams's Committees of Correspondence in the principal towns of the continent had made preparations for concerted action against its acceptance. The Pennsylvanians greeted a tea-ship on its arrival at Philadelphia, the capital city, with such execrations and threats that the captain turned about and sailed down the Delaware River again and straight home. At Charleston in South Carolina the tea was taken ashore indeed but heaped into a damp cellar, where it was soon utterly spoiled by the mildew.

On being informed of the destruction of the tea, King George considered himself personally affronted, but was considerate that the other cities of America should not suffer for the fault of Boston, where, as he knew, all the present troubles had been fomented. No action was therefore taken against them in the matter of their refusing the tea, but Boston must be sharply punished as a general warning.

In March of the year 1774 'The Boston Port Act' was passed: to 'discontinue the landing and discharging, lading and shipping, of goods, wares, and merchandize at the town of Boston or within the harbour' until such time as the East India Company had been compensated by the city for the loss of the tea, which was valued at £15,000. The business of the Custom House and the seat of Government transferred at the same time to the port of Salem, seventeen miles distant. The unfortunate Mr Hutchinson was not considered equal to the task of governing Massachusetts in these aggravated conditions: he was instructed to hand over his office to General Gage, a gallant and capable soldier, who had been wounded by Col. Washington's side in the late war, had married an American lady, and was greatly esteemed by the better people of America. It was remembered that on the repeal of the Stamp Act in 1769 his house at New York had been brilliantly illuminated. General Gage had also been appointed Commander-in-Chief of the Forces in America.

Let nobody think that the name of Boston figures too importantly in this account. But for Boston, it is difficult to see by what means the necessary separation between England and her colonies would eventually have come about. In Boston alone existed the active resolution to rebel. At the close of the war, a Boston statesman whose name it is not hard to guess wrote of his own part in initiating the general movement (against the inclinations of so many of his countrymen) as follows:

Here in my retreat, like another Catiline, the collar around my neck, in danger of the severest punishment, I laid down the plan of revolt: I endeavoured to persuade my timid accomplices that a most glorious revolution might be the result of our efforts, but I scarcely dared to hope it; and what I have seen realized appears to me like a dream. You know by what obscure intrigues, by what unfaithfulness to the mother-country a powerful party was formed; how the minds of the people were irritated before we could provoke the insurrection.

Can this justification of end by means be admitted as proved, if the end was so little appreciated by the greater part of those for whom it was conceived, even when the war had been for some time in progress? That the end was not generally appreciated does not, of course, argue against its rightness; for in my opinion the American quarrel was inevitable, and in the long run salutary, though a very ugly, damned business while it lasted.

Let me speak more explicitly. I had been told, before I sailed for America, that this was a civil war, a rebellion of recreant Englishmen against their rightful Sovereign. Yet I came to realize before I had been many weeks on the scene of action that it was no civil war. Americans are not merely another sort of English, but are in effect Americans, a nation in their own right. Transplant English roots, herbs, or pulse to America, even to that part of the continent which most nearly resembles England in climate, and in three years what will have occurred? The difference of soil and air will have brought about notable alterations in your plants: in some cases for the better, in others for the worse, but at least a pronounced change. It may be that a crop which was feeble in England and required much care will have grown as rank as a weed over there. Or it may be that after three years there is such a degeneration of seed (as with the cabbage and the turnip) that you will be obliged to send home for fresh. It is the same with fruit, poultry, and cattle. Some varieties thrive enormously, some come to no good at all, all alter. Is it therefore surprising that the English race should also alter on transplantation to this continent? Three, nay, two, generations are sufficient for your Englishman to be transformed (or transmogrified) into a different being. He becomes a native American, who walks, works, plays, speaks, looks, feels, and thinks in a way peculiar to the country; and who, once he becomes aware of these changes in himself, can no longer be ruled by gentlemen, though as learned, eminent, or gracious as you please, sent over from England with royal letters patent.

The town of Boston, however Jesuitical its leaders may appear to our British judgment, however graceless its mob, was right in its main contention; aye, and bold and even, one may say, heroical in maintaining it. Three thousand five hundred able-bodied citizens were not many to challenge so great and powerful an Empire as the British.

The heraldic flag of the American Republic consists of *bars* and *mullets* (vulgarly 'stripes' and 'stars') which commemorate in number the colonies of the Union. It was first hoisted on New Year's Day, 1776. The simple family coat of General Washington, America's saviour and first President, are recalled in this flag: for it consists of the very same bars and mullets, though not so numerous. I consider it remarkable that the young Republic instead of coining the new motto *E pluribus unum* (which is to say, 'One composed of many'), should not have boldly taken over Washington's own, as well as his heraldic charges: for it was EXITUS ACTA PROBAT – 'the end justifies the means'.

CHAPTER VIII

TIDINGS OF the Port Act were received by the Bostonians with most extravagant tokens of resentment. The text of the Act was printed on mourning paper with a black border and cried about the streets as a 'Barbarous Murder'. The terms 'Whigs' and 'Tories', for want of better, now being introduced into America (the former covering those who favoured the action of the Bostonians, and the latter those who condemned it as turbulent and unwarrantable), a regular persecution of the Tories throughout New England now began. These Tories were for the most part people of property and education, descendants of the first settlers; but their barns were burned, their cattle driven, their families insulted, their houses broke into, and they themselves forced either to quit or starve. 'A Tory', the Whigs held, 'is one whose head is in England, whose body is in America, and whose neck should be *stretched.*' If any one of them was caught alone and unarmed he was seized and led for mockery and detestation from township to township – 'as by law is provided in the case of strolling idiots, lunatics, and the like'. Soon many hundreds of them had screened themselves in Boston, in the neighbourhood of the barracks. Servants of the Government were most brutally handled, and even ministers of religion whose Toryism was held offensive by their congregations found their cloth no protection to them. One had bullets fired through his windows, another merely had his pulpit nailed up, but a third was put into the village pound, as if he had been a strayed pig; where red herrings were thrown over for him to eat, in mockery of his affection for the red-coats. Only in the case of physicians was a touch of Toryism condoned by the Liberty Boys: from consideration of the ladies whose exigencies could not be denied for a mere political reason.

But a striking discrepancy was discovered by a number of thoughtful Americans between the professions and acts of the Boston agitators. One judicious writer who 'eschewed politics as if they were edged tools' complained about this time that there was something excessively absurd in some men's eternally declaiming on freedom of thought – while not permitting an opponent to open his mouth on the subjects in dispute, without danger of being presented with a coat of tar and feathers, or being

obliged to run like a criminal dog into the nearest woods with the hue and
cry behind him.

At the instance of the revolutionary party at New York a Congress of
Delegates was now called from all the colonies to deliberate on the critical
state of their affairs. This Congress, at which Georgia alone of the colonies
was unrepresented, met at Philadelphia in the autumn of 1774. The fifty-
one delegates declared themselves outright Whigs: urging the Bostonians
to persevere in their opposition to the Government until their chartered
liberties should be restored to them, engaging to support them in this aim
to the best of their powers, and passing various resolutions of American
unanimity – in which they even artfully tried to include the French Papists
of Canada. They avowed, however, their allegiance to King George and
drew up a petition in which they entreated him to grant them peace,
liberty, and safety. This civility to the King was added as a sop to the representatives of Pennsylvania and New York, who opposed many of the resolutions and absented themselves from the proceedings for several days. A
common front was only marshalled by the energies (to quote an American
gentleman who was on the spot) of 'Adams with his crew, and the haughty
Sultans of the South, who juggled the whole conclave of delegates'.

The Bostonians had framed an agreement, which they called 'A Solemn
League and Covenant', by which the subscribers engaged in the most
sacred manner to 'discontinue commercial intercourse with Great Britain
till the late obnoxious Acts are repealed'. This was also taken up by large
numbers of people from the other provinces. When General Gage
attempted to damp the effect of this covenant by a proclamation against
mutiny, they retorted that the law allowed His Majesty's loyal subjects to
associate peaceably in defence of their rights; and he could not deny this.
Nor could he do anything by legal methods for the proper protection of
the Tories, since a Whiggish unanimity had now been forced on all instruments and accessories of the law – magistrates, jurors, and witnesses alike;
or even by military means, since the force at his disposal consisted of four
weak battalions, which were wholly insufficient to the task of policing so
great a province. The men of Massachusetts had now begun secretly to
arm themselves and openly to drill; and a rival government to General
Gage's, a provincial congress, had resolved to raise the number of these
avowed rebels to twelve thousand men and invited the other New England
provinces of Connecticut, Rhode Island, and New Hampshire to assist
them with eight thousand more.

To relieve the distress of the people of Boston, liberal gifts were sent in
money and kind from other towns of the province, and from so far away as
South Carolina. The merchants of Salem and Marblehead, which lay adjacent, placed their wharves at the disposal of their colleagues of Boston; but
these towns soon lost the use of their port, from destroying a cargo of tea
which arrived in it.

Desertions from the Royal Army became frequent and were due to a variety of causes. In the first place, the daily sixpence which was the pay of a common soldier, was insufficient for his subsistence (because of the heavy stoppages made from it for clothing and other matters, under the title of 'Off-reckonings') even in England. In America, where prices were one-third higher for all European articles, a soldier was never out of debt, unless he happened to be a model of sobriety and thrift. Troops garrisoned in America were always being tempted with offers of employment at high wages by prosperous farmers of the back districts; and with such offers now went an undertaking from the Committee of Correspondence of the township concerned that no sergeant's party of his regiment would be suffered to arrest him as a deserter. If intending deserters could bring their muskets and side-arms with them, so much the better: the sum of twenty dollars apiece was offered by the rebels for Tower muskets in good repair.

Now a new and disgraceful employment was offered to the necessitous soldier: he could count upon fifty pounds sterling in gold money if he consented to become a drillmaster and teach the American volunteers their platoon-exercise for use against his King and his comrades. Many soldiers consented, especially those with particular grievances against some officer or sergeant; smothering their sense of guilt under a professed concern for the cause of Liberty. Others remarked that they had volunteered as soldiers to fight for King George, and that, though surrounded and insulted by hordes of his enemies, they were not permitted to use the arms that had been entrusted to them for this very purpose. If the pride of England had thus decayed, they declared, there was no temptation to remain loyal soldiers, to sweat, shiver, pull off the hat, run into debt, grow decrepit in a thankless service, and every now and then (for some slight dereliction of duty) be tied up to the halberts and helped to two score of lashes laid on by a lusty drummer. They might just as well pass over to the Americans, who for all their uncouthness were men who stood up for their rights, who contrived to eat and drink heartily, to go well clothed and well shod, and were hospitable to new-comers.

The troops were encamped on Boston Common, just outside the town, and, the desertions growing more frequent, in spite of the death penalty being ordained for the crime, General Gage was one day heard to remark to his staff: 'We are bleeding to death by damned driblets, gentlemen, and I am resolved to stop the flow with a tight bandage.' Whereupon he gave orders for the fortification of Boston Neck, which separated the town from the country behind, and placed his most trustworthy men on guard there to see that no one went out or came in who had no right to do so. But the revolutionary leaders represented this protective bandage rather as a noose tied around the neck of Boston to throttle her. The country people and Bostonians were exceedingly impudent to our sentries as they passed and repassed the lines with their carts. One carter was stopped going out of town with some nineteen thousand ball cartridges, which were taken from him. He had the effrontery to approach Headquarters with a demand for their redelivery, saying that they were for his own use in hunting! The request was of course refused, but, says he: 'Foh, then, it don't matter, I reckon. That was only the last parcel of a very great quantity I have carried out in this cart at different times; and all for my own use in hunting.'

Next, the inhabitants of Newport, in Rhode Island, dismounted forty cannon, which were provided for the protection of the harbour, and carried them off for the use of the revolutionary forces; and the New Hampshire men seized a great quantity of Government stores in the fort of Piscataqua, albeit without bloodshed. Evidently war had grown imminent, and was indeed confidently announced in September 1774, many months before it actually broke out. Then Colonel Israel Putnam of Connecticut, that old hunter of bears and Indians, wrote by express to New York, during the first session of the Continental Congress, that the King's troops and ships had that instant begun an indiscriminate massacre of the wretched people of Boston. He called for aid from every direction. The report caused despair and rage in Philadelphia, to which city it was instantly transmitted, and remained uncontradicted for three days. Colonel Putnam, who was an honest man, was, it is thought, imposed upon by some agent of the political Mr Samuel Adams, who wished by this false news to force the Congress, by no means unanimous, to declare itself as resolutely as in the event it did. Here I may observe that the most dislikeable man in America, to the English, was this same Sam Adams, with his agued hands and twitching face, his tongue (as was said) alternately dripping honey and venom, his unkempt person, his restless eyes, and ever-empty pockets. He had not long before avoided prison, when charged with defalcation as tax collector, by the interposition of his partisans in office.

General Gage wrote to the Government about this time: 'If force is to be used at length, it must be a considerable one. To begin with small numbers will only encourage resistance and not terrify.' Since it was estimated that the Americans could raise a force of one hundred and fifty thousand men with knowledge of firelocks, he asked for fifteen thousand men to be stationed at Boston, ten thousand at New York, and seven thousand more to protect Canada against invasion by the Americans.

He had taken what precautions he could against a rising; removing the powder and arms from magazines in the vicinity and storing them all in Castle William. He had also, by the bye, deprived that arch-smuggler, Colonel 'King' Hancock (afterwards President of the Congress) of his commission as Commander of the Massachusetts Company of Cadets. These cadets were gentlemen who used to attend the Governor, but since many of them now feared what the mob might do to themselves and their property should they continue in this service, the company was disbanded. They returned to the General the Standard that he had presented to them on succeeding Mr Hutchinson as Governor. Mr Oliver the Lieutenant-Governor and almost all of the new councillors appointed by a royal *mandamus* had by now been obliged to resign by threats against their lives.

There were some disturbances of a lesser sort in the town. Mr Samuel Adams, in the presence of a number of British officers, during a town-meeting on March 5th in the Old South Meeting House, moved that the thanks of the town should be presented to Dr Warren, who had just spoken, for his elegant and spirited oration, and that another should be delivered on March 5th next to commemorate the *Bloody Massacre* of five years previous. Several officers began to hiss, others cried, 'O fie, fie!' and an officer dressed in gold lace regimentals with blue facings, whose name or regiment I cannot learn, advanced to Mr Adams and Colonel Hancock, who was also present, and addressed them in severe terms. He told them that the Army resented the phrase *Bloody Massacre*, Captain Preston having been fairly tried and honourably acquitted by a Boston court of the charge of murder. The Americans making some reply, the renewed cries of 'Fie! Fie!' were misheard as an alarm of 'Fire, Fire!' and the whole place was thrown into a bustle. Women shrieked, men swore, and many persons leaped headlong out into the street from the lower windows. The drums of the Forty-third Regiment, which happened to be passing, increased the confusion: Mr Adams, Colonel Hancock, and others present evidently feared that they were about to be apprehended by an officer with a warrant. The meeting was nearly cleared in two minutes, but no lives lost or violence used.

Two days later a man was caught who had attempted to buy from a soldier of The Forty-seventh the lock of his musket. Men of this regiment stripped, tarred and feathered the American and, seating him on a truck, in that manner paraded him through the town for the best part of the after-noon. The officers of The Forty-seventh lent no hand to this excess (which the Americans imputed to them) but turned a blind eye. The affair was much disapproved of by General Gage.

While I was in Dublin, about April of the year 1775, my father showed me the following two letters, copies of which he had been permitted to take by his friend and patron Dean Evelyn of Trim in Meath, whose son, the author, was serving in Boston as a captain in The Fourth, or King's Own Regiment. It expressed so clearly the resentful sentiments of the British forces in America at that time that I take leave to reproduce them here *in extenso*, but omitting personal particulars interesting only to the family.

To the Rev. Doctor Evelyn [his father], *Trim, Ireland*

BOSTON CAMP, *October* 31*st* 1774

MY DEAR SIR,

It happens so seldom that we have the opportunity of a King's ship going from hence, that we are glad to lay hold of every one that

offers to let our friends hear from us; they must be a good deal
alarmed for us indeed, if ever they see the bold and desperate
resolves of every village in New England, and must conclude that
two or three thousand poor fellows of us must have long since been
devoured by men of their mighty stomachs; but here we still are in
our peaceful camp, and in the same situation as when I last wrote to
you; nothing of any consequence has happened, but great preparations for hostilities making on both sides. We, on our part, have fortified the only entrance to the town by land, and thrown up a very
extensive work in front of it. We have got General Haldimand, with
the 47th Regiment and part of the 18th, from New York, with more
artillery and military stores; two other Regiments, the 10th and
52nd, are coming in from Quebec, part of them already in the
harbour; and we have a man-of-war, and two companies of the 65th
from Newfoundland.

The good people of these provinces are getting ready as fast as
they can; they are all provided with arms and ammunition, and every
man who is able to use them is obliged to repair at stated times to the
place of exercise in order to train; in short, the frenzy with which the
people are seized is now got to such a pitch, that it can go but little
farther, and they must either soon, very soon break out into civil war
or take that turn which the people of England did at the time of the
Restoration, and wreak their vengeance on those who have seduced
and misled them. I believe never was so much mercy extended to any
nation on the face of the earth: they are now in an absolute, open,
avowed state of rebellion, and have committed every act of treason
which can be devised, but that of openly attacking the troops, which
they publicly declare their resolution of doing as soon as they are
prepared, and the season will allow them, and they feel bold.

The people of England, in the time of Charles the First, behaved
with decency and moderation compared with these. The 'North
Briton', 'Whisperer', 'Parliamentary Spy', 'Junius', etc., are dutiful
and respectful addresses compared to the publications here; never
before did I see treason and rebellion naked and undisguised; it is the
only occasion upon which they lay aside hypocrisy. We expected to
have been in barracks by this time, but the sons of liberty have done
every thing in their power to prevent our accommodation. As it was
found difficult to furnish quarters for so many men, it was resolved
(to avoid extremities) to build barracks on the Common, where we
are encamped; for some regiments timber was provided, and the
frames pretty well advanced, when they thought proper to issue their
orders to the carpenters to desist from working for the troops, upon
pain of their displeasure. And one man who paid no attention to their
order, was waylaid, seized by the mob, and carried off, and narrowly

escaped hanging. However, the Government have procured distilleries and vacant warehouses sufficient to hold all the regiments, and our own artificers, with those of the men-of-war, and about 150 from New York and Halifax, are now at work upon them, and we hope to get into them in ten days or a fortnight. They have also forbid all merchants from furnishing their enemies with blankets, tools, or materials of any kind, and have endeavoured to hinder our getting bricks to build chimneys in our barracks, and threatened to prohibit all provisions being brought to market; but the force of English gold no Yankey can withstand, were it offered to purchase his salvation. I can give you no description of the 'holy men of Massachusetts', by which you can form a just idea of what they are. There are no instances in history to compare them by; the Jews at the time of the siege of Jerusalem seem to come near them, but are injured and disgraced by the comparison.

I beg my best love to all my friends; I should be glad to hear something of them when you have a spare half-hour.

I am, dear Sir,

Your ever affectionate,

W. G. EVELYN

To the Reverend Doctor Evelyn [his father], *Trim, Ireland*
BOSTON, *February* 18*th* 1775

MY DEAR SIR,

About the 10th of this month, I received your letter (the only one I have got from you) dated the 2nd of November, though it was not opened, as mine to you had been, yet it did not fall short of it in expense, as every letter we receive by the New York Packet costs us threepence for every pennyweight; for which reason I wish our friends would endeavour to write to us by vessels bound to Salem or Marble Head, or try to have their letters sent in General Gage's bag, as Mr Butler sends his to his son, and saves him by that means fifteen or twenty shillings a-month. If you would be kind enough to enclose any letter for me to him, I am sure he would be so obliging as to send it to the Secretary of State's office in England, and I should receive it with the General's despatches.

That lies innumerable should be circulated in your papers with regard to what is passing here is no way strange, when in this very town, where we are upon the spot, the most false, impudent, and incredible relations are every day published concerning us; but the fact is, the authors know them to be false, and that not a person in this town (of about twenty thousand inhabitants) believes a word of them; but they are calculated for the poor deluded wretches in the country, who are all politicians, and swallow everything they see in those seditious papers (and none other are they allowed to read) with a credulity not equalled even in old England; and by this means is the spirit of faction kept alive, and the schemes of a few enterprising, ambitious demagogues made to pass upon the people for their own act and deed. I said *of a few;* a great many doubtless appear to be concerned in carrying on the business; but would you believe it, that this immense continent from New England to Georgia is moved and directed by one man![1] a man of ordinary birth and desperate fortune, who by his abilities and talent for factious intrigue, has made himself of some consequence, whose political existence depends upon the continuance of the present dispute, and who must sink into insignificancy and beggary the moment it ceases.

People in general are inclined to attribute the ferment that at present subsists in this country to a settled plan and system formed and prosecuted for some years past by a few ambitious, enterprising spirits; but in my opinion the true causes of it are to be found in the nature of mankind; and I think that it proceeds from a new nation, feeling itself wealthy, populous, and strong; and that they being impatient of restraint, are struggling to throw off that dependency which is so irksome to them. The other seems to me to be only the consequence; such a time being most apt for men of abilities, but desperate fortunes, to et themselves forward to practise upon the passions of the people, foment that spirit of opposition to all law and government, and to urge them on to sedition, treason, and rebellion, in hopes of profiting by the general distraction.

This is the case of our great patriot and leader, Sam Adams. Hancock, and those others whose names you hear, are but his mere tools; though many of them are men of no mean abilities. Hancock is a poor contemptible fool, led about by Adams, and has spent a fortune of thirty thousand pounds upon that infamous crew; has sacrificed all he was worth in the world to the vanity of being admitted among them, and is now nearly reduced to a state of beggary. The steps by which the *sons of liberty* have proceeded, and the strides with which they are now hasting to rebellion and civil war, are set forth in a very masterly manner by a writer (on our side), under the signature of Massachusettensis; which papers, as far as they have been hitherto published, I have enclosed to Mr Butler at the Castle, directed for you; they will give you a better idea of the nature of this important contest than any on the other side, which are composed of sedition, treason, misrepresentation, and falsehood, framed by villains of the first water, and greedily swallowed with the credulity of ignorance, and the malignant zeal of inveterate fanatics.

---

1 *Scilicet:* Samuel Adams.

It is but very lately that a Tory writer dare appear, or that a Printer could be prevailed on to publish any thing on the side of Government; and nothing now protects them, but the presence of the troops in Boston. Those who have remained in the country, whose circumstances and situation would not admit of their leaving their families, are hourly in danger. Some are prisoners in their own houses; a mob constantly mounting guard about them, lest they should escape; and others have been treated with the utmost barbarity. Words cannot give you an idea of the nature of the lower class of people in this province: they are utterly devoid of every sentiment of truth or common honesty: they are proscribed throughout the whole Continent, and possess no other human qualities but such as are the shame and reproach of humanity.

As the event of this very important question depends upon the determination of the people of Great Britain, and as they have such unhappy divisions, and so many dangerous enemies to their country among themselves, it is impossible to form any conjecture about it. We who know our own powers, and the helpless situation of the people, consider it as the most fortunate opportunity for Great Britain to establish her superiority over this country; even to reduce it to that state of subjection, which the right of conquest may now give her the fairest title to; at least, to keep it in that state of dependency which they are now avowedly attempting to free themselves from, and which, had they waited for another century, they would probably achieve. Though the point at present in view is, to be independent of Great Britain, and to set up for themselves, yet I do not believe the most sanguine of them have any expectation of accomplishing it at this time; but they hope to make some approaches, and to gain something towards it. In this struggle their great dependence is upon the tenderness and clemency of the English, who they imagine will consider them under infatuation, and will give up some points to them out of humanity, rather than push matters to extremity; and indeed, they may with reason think so, for under no other Government on the face of the earth would they have been suffered to perpetrate so many horrid villainies, as they have done, without being declared in a state of rebellion, and having fire and sword let loose among them. From the accounts given by the faction, people would imagine that the colonies were unanimous to a man in their opposition to Government, but the contrary is the fact; there is a very large party in our favour, and thousands inclined to our side, who dare not openly declare themselves, from an apprehension that Government may leave them in the lurch; this you may depend upon as a certain truth, that those gentlemen who have declared on our side are men of the best property in this country, and those who before these troubles were in the highest esteem, and most respected among the common people.

The hour is now very nigh in which this affair will be brought to a crisis. The resolutions we expect are by his time upon the water, which are to determine the fate of Great Britain and America. We have great confidence in the spirit and pride of our countrymen, that they will not tamely suffer such insolence and disobedience from a set of upstart vagabonds, the dregs and scorn of the human species; and that we shall shortly receive such orders as will authorize us to scourge the rebellion with rods of iron. Under this hope have we been hitherto restrained, and with an unparalleled degree of patience and discipline have we submitted to insults and indignities, from villains who are hired to provoke us to something that may be termed an outrage, and turned to our disadvantage; but these are all treasured up in our memories against that hour in which we shall 'cry havock, and let slip the dogs of war'. Excuse my indignation, I cannot speak with patience of this generation of vipers. If any troops should be ordered from Ireland with officers of distinction, I should beg your interest to procure me some recommendations.

You must not believe implicitly the reports that are spread of the deaths and desertions among the troops; there have been some, and some regiments have been more unlucky than others; but it is very trifling, when you consider that no pains or expenses have been spared to seduce our men. Our regiment, nevertheless, has not lost more than we usually have done in the same length of time in Great Britain. The weather is delightful beyond description, and we are in perfect good health and spirits.

Wishing the same to all friends at home,

I am, dear Sir,

Your ever affectionate,

W. G. E.

Dean Evelyn died in his Dublin residence a few days before I sailed for America and Captain Evelyn did not long survive his parent. On August 27th of the same year he led the British advance in the battle of Long Island, being with the Brigade of Light Infantry, and took five American officers prisoners who were sent in advance to observe the motions of our army in the direction of Jamaica Pass. The overwhelming victory of that day was in great measure due to this capture. He was mortally wounded at the skirmish at Throg's Neck two months later.

CHAPTER IX

THE AMOUNT of troops for which General Gage called staggered the Ministry. They had already voted him a reinforcement of ten thousand men, which had been thought more than handsome: and the troops now actually stationed in Boston amounted to about four thousand. The Earl of Sandwich, the First Lord of the Admiralty, refused to believe that the threat was so serious as was made out. He pronounced the Americans cowards (though unknown to him personally) and regretted that there was no probability of our troops encountering without delay two hundred thousand of such a rabble, armed with old rusty firelocks, pistols, staves, clubs, and broomsticks; and of exterminating them at one blow Colonel Grant, in the Commons, agreed with the noble Lord: 'the colonists possess not a single military trait and would never stand to meet the English bayonet'. He had been in America, he said, and disliked their manner of speaking equally with their way of life, and held them to be 'entirely out of humanity's reach'. Colonel Grant was taken up by Mr Cruger, an American-born member, and reminded that his own services in the Alleghany mountains had been of no very triumphant character. (The speaker called Mr Cruger to order before he could say more.) However, Lord North considered these views too sanguine; and since it was impossible to send the troops that General Gage demanded, without stripping the whole Empire, he made a new attempt at conciliating the Americans. He undertook to exempt from taxation any province which would of its own free will make a reasonable contribution to the common defence of America and provision for the support of the civil government.

The Whig Opposition had encouraged their friends in America to believe that England could not or would not make war on them, the country in general being so averse to this, or at least would not venture more than a short campaign. It was true that England stood to lose by the conflict immensely more than she could gain; for the prosperity of the manufacturing towns in the North of England depended largely on the continuance of close relations with the colonies, and the London merchants alone were owed close on a million pounds by their American customers. The chief Opposition speaker, Mr Fox, now assured the House that the Americans must and would reject Lord North's offer with contempt. To accept exemption from a tax, as an indulgence, and on condition of performing an act equivalent to paying it, would be to admit a principle of liability which every American would oppose with his life's blood. In the Lords, the Earl of Chatham, the gout still heavy on him, spoke of the disdain with which the whole world and Heaven itself regarded the forces entrenched behind Boston Neck: 'An impotent general and a dishonoured army, trusting solely to the pick-axe and the spade for security against the just indignation of an injured and insulted people.'

But Lord North's offer of exemption from taxation came too late in any case; for the first skirmish of the war had already been fought, with the loss of many lives, and from either side complaints of barbarities done contrary to English usage. This was the Lexington affair and it gave an interesting foretaste of the style of fighting that our armies might expect when the campaign began in earnest.

General Gage, having been informed that an important quantity of military stores had been collected by the revolutionaries at Concord, about twenty miles from Boston, decided to seize these by the sudden secret descent of a large body of troops. At ten o'clock on the night of April 18th 1775 a contingent of some seven hundred picked men, namely, the flank companies (the Grenadier and Light Infantry companies) of the twelve or thirteen battalions of the garrison were rowed over in boats with muffled oars from the town, and up Charles River for a mile or two. They were there disembarked and began a silent march on Concord. Though they proceeded with the greatest caution, securing every person whom they met, in order to prevent the alarm being spread, they soon found by the continual firing of guns and ringing of bells that they were discovered. By five o'clock in the morning they had reached Lexington, after a march of fifteen miles: where militia and minute-men (troops so-called from their readiness to rise to arms at a minute's notice, though continuing mean-while at their ordinary trades) were drawn up on the green to oppose them.

Major Pitcairne, who commanded the advance guard, rode forward and called on them in the King's name to disperse. But they would not. At this moment some shots were fired from a house facing the green, wounding one man and striking the Major's horse in two places. The Americans, however, declare that the Major fired first, with a pistol, and that the English in consequence were to blame for the sequel. Our people at once returned the fire, killing and wounding eighteen of the militiamen, who broke and fled. The march to Concord was then resumed, where the advance guard found no muskets or ammunition, but spoilt some barrels of flour, knocked the trunnions off three old field-pieces, and cut down a Liberty pole – a sort of May pole which was used by the Sons of Liberty as a standard and rallying point of rebellion. There then ensued a sharp skirmish for the possession of a bridge over a river beyond the town. Many

Americans and British were killed. It was declared by our people, and furiously denied by the other side, that some of the dead and wounded were scalped by Americans who had adopted this savage and singular custom from the Red Indians. If this was indeed so, it was not remarkable. The Government of Pennsylvania, of which the respectable Governor Penn and Dr Benjamin Franklin were members, had, but a few years before, offered a bounty for Indian scalps, male and female. Also there was precedent for the taking of white scalps: many had been lifted from Frenchmen in the late war by the Rangers of Connecticut, an act which they glorified.

Here I may interpolate a few remarks upon scalp-taking. The Indians set so much store upon the taking of scalps that it was regarded as of less honour to kill three men in battle and leave them undespoiled than to take the scalp of one, even if he had fallen to another's tomahawk. It was not, as is supposed, the general practice of the scalper to remove the whole fleece of hair, but only the central lock. This, twisted and grasped in the left hand, gave the needed purchase for scaring and scooping from around it, with a knife, a little piece of the skin, about the size of a priest's tonsure. Should the victim be bald, however, or short-haired, the Indians would rip off more, often using their teeth to loosen the skin from the bone. If the scalp were taken in revenge for some injury, as was almost always the case, that of a woman or child was prized more highly than that of a man. A wounded person who has been scalped very often recovers, though the hair never grows again on the crown of the head. I observed one or two scalped men in the back parts of Virginia when I was in captivity there, and lodged with a settler who proudly showed me a pair of scalps that he had himself ripped from Cherokee Indians that he had shot. He had dressed them in Indian fashion by sewing them upon a hoop with deer sinews, and painting them red for the sake of show.

On their retirement from Concord, after two hours' halt, the British troops were shot at, the whole length of the march, by Americans concealed behind stone walls, of which there were many in the cleared land, or behind trees in the uncleared parts, and taking every advantage that the face of the country afforded them. They never showed themselves in bodies of more than a few men at a time, and immediately retired when any movement was made against them, yet persisted about the column like a swarm of mosquitoes. The column being confined to the road and unable to extend to protect their flanks, because of the continual obstacles of stone walls, dense woods, and morasses to be encountered, suffered very heavily. A minute-man, supported perhaps by a single neighbour or kinsman, would conceal himself behind a bush at fifty paces from the road, and as the tail of the column was passing would discharge his single shot, his companion holding his fire in case there were retaliation. Then they would lie still until the danger had passed.

These countrymen were bred to the musket or rifle-gun from boyhood, and their experience of fighting against the Indians, or of stalking bears, deer, and other game, had taught them a mode of fighting which to our people seemed mean and skulking; but it certainly caused us much damage and themselves very little and transgressed no rule of civilized warfare. In Europe, to be sure, armies advance towards each other in solid mass, the lines perfectly dressed, with standards flying, drums beating; and tear away at each other with disciplined and simultaneous volleys. But that manner is only a custom of warfare, not a rule; and the Americans saw no reason why they should adopt it to their own disadvantage. Whenever during the war their Continental Line, who were trained in European style, dared to engage our people in a pitched battle they were almost invariably routed; for the British Army was second to none in the formal manner of fighting.

It was surprising that our men escaped as they did. They had already marched twenty-five miles, with smart fighting thrown in, and on empty stomachs, too, for their provision carts were captured. When they reached Lexington again, where a force of eight hundred men, including the main body of the Royal Welch Fusiliers, came hurrying up to their relief, they had expended all their ammunition; and their tongues were hanging out, like dogs', for thirst and weariness. There were two six-pounder field-pieces with the newly arrived troops, which were used with deterrent effect against the Americans; who were by now treading close on the heels of the exhausted column, groaning in derision, 'Britons Strike Home!' and uttering their war-cry of 'King Hancock for Ever!' Despite these guns, the Americans continued with irregular shooting from flanks, front, and rear. Our men threw away their fire very inconsiderately and without being certain of its effect; for many of them were young soldiers, who had been taught that quick firing struck terror into the enemy. But, on the contrary, doing so little execution, it emboldened the Americans to come closer. The noise of battle now brought up fresh reinforcements of Mohairs (as these soldiers without uniforms were contemptuously called in the English ranks) from all the surrounding countryside; and the fatigued column must run the gauntlet of successive companies of cool marksmen, who were often commanded by the Congregational minister of their township, dressed in his preaching clothes. It is said that for want of material these warlike men of God had suffered their religious books to be converted into wadding for their cartridges, especially the hymnals of Dr Isaac Watts. Then: 'Put a little Watts into 'em, Brethren' was a catchword of the day.

The firing was now heavy from the houses on the roadside, and the British were so enraged at suffering from an unseen enemy that they forced open many of these buildings and put to death all the defenders; in some cases, seven or eight men. Often they found these houses apparently deserted; but soon as the march was resumed, the defenders climbed out of their hiding-places and the popping shots began again from the rear.

Before the day was out the enemy numbered some four thousand men, yet no more than fifty were ever seen together at a time, out of respect for the six-pounder guns. No women and children were, I believe, encountered during the day, all such having doubtless been removed from the neighbourhood at the first warning of battle; certainly none were deliberately killed in the houses, as the American leaders alleged against us to incite the vengeance of their followers. It is true that, notwithstanding the efforts of the officers, a few soldiers carried off small articles of plunder from the houses thus broken into; but the day was too hot and the men too weary for the practice to become general.

At length the straggling column reached Charlestown Neck, near Boston, where the guns of the men-of-war anchored close by protected them, and the rebel fire ceased. The Grenadiers and Light Infantry had marched forty miles and eaten nothing for a day and a night; and it was past midnight of the 19th before they reached barracks and bed. Our casualties were near three hundred men killed and wounded, including a number of officers; the Americans lost only a third of that number. Many providential escapes from death were reported. The Earl of Percy, who commanded the relieving force, lost a button shot off his waistcoat; a man of my acquaintance had his cap blown three times off his head and two bullets through his coat, one of these carrying away his bayonet. Lieutenant Hawkshaw of the Fifth Fusiliers received a bullet through both cheeks, which also removed several teeth; but did not by any means regard this as a providential escape. He had been accounted the greatest beauty in the Army and was now bitterly mortified in the sad alteration to his appearance.

The affair at Lexington animated the courage of the Americans to the highest degree, insomuch that in a few days their army amounted to twenty thousand men and was continually increasing. Congress appointed George Washington to be Commander-in-Chief of the American armies. His fighting service had ended sixteen years previously, nor had he ever commanded above twelve hundred men. He was chosen chiefly as being a wealthy aristocrat from Virginia, in order to flatter the South into common action with the revolutionary North. John Adams proposed his name. He first enumerated the high qualities that a commander-in-chief should possess, and then remarked that, fortunately, such qualities resided in a member of their own body. At this 'King' Hancock was all satisfaction and smiles, believing that the speaker could only be pointing at him, and Mr Adams afterwards wrote that never in his life had he seen so sudden a change on any man's face as on John Hancock's when George Washington's name was mentioned in place of his own. Samuel Adams seconded the nomination, which was passed unanimously. General Washington, in accepting, declined to take any payment for his services: which gave him much popularity.

Boston was now completely invested and those critics were confounded who held that a regiment or two could force their way through any part of the continent, and that the very sight of a grenadier's cap would be sufficient to put an American army to flight. The news was especially gratifying to Colonel Hancock, who was to have been charged on the day of the battle with defrauding the customs by smuggling to the tune of half a million dollars. The lawyer he had briefed for his defence was Samuel Adams.

There was worse to come: the battle miscalled that of Bunker's Hill. About the end of May 1775 reinforcements of British troops arrived in Boston under the command of Generals Howe, Clinton, and Burgoyne, whose services in the preceding war had gained them great reputation: bringing up the number of troops in the town to some seven thousand men. A few days later General Gage issued a proclamation to the Americans who 'with a preposterous parade of military arrangement affect to hold the Royal Army besieged': in which he offered pardon to all who would lay down their arms, and thus stand separate and distinct from the parricides of the Constitution The only persons excepted from this pardon were Colonel Hancock and Mr Samuel Adams. No revolutionaries offered their submission in reply.

Opposite the city of Boston and separated from it by the Charles River, which was about the breadth of the Thames at London Bridge, another peninsula of much the same size as Boston's jutted towards it, and was similarly joined to the main land by a narrow neck. Charlestown lay at one corner of the flat head of this other peninsula, which was formed mainly of a steep ridge, Charlestown Heights, whose two humps were known as Bunker's Hill and Breed's Pasture; of which Bunker's Hill was both the loftier and the farther from Boston. General Gage, observing that Charlestown Heights commanded the whole of Boston, decided on the precaution of occupying Bunker's Hill. He was, however, forestalled by the revolutionaries, who had spies everywhere. Learning of his intention, they decided to seize the hill and fortify it themselves: to show their power and provoke the British to a battle in conditions favouring defence rather than attack.

On the night of June 16th 1775, then, a detachment of some twelve hundred Massachusetts militia crossed Charlestown Neck with entrenching tools and set hastily to work under the orders of an engineer. Because of some mistake it was the lesser hill, Breed's Pasture, close to Charlestown, that they pitched upon; which was a less defensible position and did not offer so ready an escape over the Neck. Here they worked with such diligence and silence that before dawn they had nearly completed a strong redoubt, mounting ten cannon, and a six-foot high entrenchment which extended one hundred paces to their left, facing Boston.

When discovered by the British troops at about five o'clock the redoubt was plied with an incessant cannonade from the line-of-battle ships and floating batteries in the river, besides the cannon that could carry across from Boston, three-quarters of a mile distant. Most of the Americans soon ran, including all the gunners, who took four guns off with them, crying that this was murder and that they had been betrayed. However, about five hundred of them coolly continued their work, which they completed about noon; for because of the steep elevation the damage done by our cannonade was not so severe as was predicted.

Meanwhile General Gage as Commander-in-Chief called his major-generals together for a council of war. General Sir Henry Clinton, supported by Generals Sir William Howe and John Burgoyne, proposed (very correctly) sending round a picked force of Grenadiers, supported by artillery, to make a landing on the neck of the Charlestown peninsula, which was not two hundred paces wide, and so cut off the retreat of the Americans. This might well have been done without loss. We held command of the water, which was navigable to shallow craft on either side of the Neck, and the Americans encamped on the Neck were in no posture to stand an attack with bayonets. Those on the peninsula must then have chosen between starvation or surrender.

But General Gage opposed this plan. He resolved instead to land a considerable force at Moulton's Point (the right-hand corner of the peninsula, as you look across from Boston) and drive the rebels off the heights by force of arms. He could not resist giving the troops the chance for which they had been so long clamouring: which was to come to grips with the enemy and give them a good drubbing. Boston had lately been a cramped and miserable station, a by-word for high prices and low fever. All longed for a sortie. 'Once let us get into the back country,' cried General Burgoyne, 'and we'll soon find elbow-room!'

Two thousand five hundred troops were therefore landed at Moulton's Point under the command of Major-General Sir William Howe. At three o'clock in the afternoon the advance began, one division deploying against the enemy's left, intending to turn it and seize Bunker's Hill in the rear; another making a frontal attack against the Redoubt on Breed's Pasture.

The day was exceedingly hot, the grass stood knee-high. Yet the men, dressed in their heavy greatcoats, were burdened, besides their rifles and ammunition, with blankets, heavy full packs and three days' provisions a man – the whole weighing above 100 pounds; Mr Commissary Stedman, the historian, rates it at 125 pounds. They advanced very slowly, the ground being broken by a succession of high fences; and the ridge, though at its highest point it rose no more than one hundred and ten feet above the river, seemed to them like Snowdon or the Pyrenees.

The Americans had now been greatly reinforced and, before the close of the battle, numbered more than three thousand men. Of these a thousand from New Hampshire and Connecticut, good men, went to line a long fence, of stone below and rails above, which protected their left. This

barricade lay 'refused' – that is, somewhat behind the line of the entrenchment – and along lower ground. They had stuffed the interstices with
grass, and the front was protected by another rail fence of the zigzag or
Virginian sort. The advance was not supported by artillery as strongly as
it should have been; for at least four reasons. In the first place, the guns
that fired grape, that most horrific shot, were mired in a soft patch. In the
second, the shot in the side boxes of our six-pounders were, by an error,
twelve-pound balls. In the third, the Chief of Artillery, Colonel
Cleaveland, was not with the batteries, being absent at a Latin lesson,
which is to say that he was spending his morning in company with pretty
Miss Lovell, daughter of the master of the Latin School. In the fourth,
General Gage had failed to arrange with Admiral Samuel Graves, with
whom he was not on the most cordial terms, to cover his advance on the
right. Gun-boats of light draught or the *Symmetry* transport, which
mounted several eighteen-pounder guns, might have raked the enemy
position from end to end.

The battle was joined near simultaneously along the whole half-mile of
the position, but our men were allowed to fire their volley too soon – the
Americans not yet even showing their hats above the entrenchments,
except for a few look-out men and officers. General Putnam, who was
mounted and seemed to be in effective command of the American forces –
though there was no hierarchy of rank as yet in this disorderly army –
galloped from point to point and swore to shoot any man who fired before
the enemy came within point-blank range. The Americans feared and
obeyed this violent man, who, by the bye, claimed to have killed and
scalped a number of Frenchmen in the previous war. Guided by him, the
Massachusetts officers ran very boldly along the parapet, kicking up their
men's muskets.

When at length the American volley was permitted, the execution done
was terrible. Not only was the general fire well aimed – 'Aim at the waist-
belt' was their cry – but they had marksmen armed with rifle-guns whose
sole charge it was to pick off the royal officers, conspicuous in the bright
sun by the glittering gorgets at their throats. The attack was broken all
along the line, the front ranks withering away; the remainder, finding
themselves leaderless, retired out of range, re-formed and again advanced
against the enemy, the companies being now generally commanded by
sergeants. The oldest officers and soldiers engaged, among them some who
had fought at Minden and other great battles of the Seven Years' War,
declared it was the hottest service they had ever seen. The enemy were
employing slugs and buckshot in their firelocks, and the wounds that
ensued were the despair of our surgeons.

The second attack failed, as the first had done, though personally led
by General Howe. It was he who had taken the forlorn-hope up the
Heights of Abraham on the glorious day that General Wolfe captured

Quebec from the French and made Canada ours. He soon found himself standing alone, before the rail-fence, the whole of his staff of twelve officers having been either killed or wounded, though he was unhurt. He was a tall, large, swarthy man, somewhat of a voluptuary; and very German in appearance, being descended, like Lord North, from George I and a German mistress, though she was a different one from Lord North's grand-dam. His coolness and officer-like behaviour on this occasion cannot be too much applauded. He went over to the troops who had been flung back from the Redoubt and ordered them to unbuckle their packs and remove their greatcoats, together with all other impediments to action. 'The third try is lucky, my brave boys,' he is reported to have said, 'and this time we'll take the bayonet to 'em only.' If he said this, it was a long speech for him: for he was almost as silent a man as his brother Admiral Sir Richard Howe, whom the sailors called 'Black Dick'. He kept his self-possession so wonderfully that when a certain general officer, meeting him later upon the field of battle, made a teasing remark about the costliness of 'this new sort of light infantry tactics' he only grinned in reply.

The British batteries in Boston, and the ships' guns, now punished Charlestown with red-hot balls and carcasses (or incendiary shells), for enemy musket-fire from the houses and the meeting-house steeple had been galling our left. Soon five hundred wooden houses were in one great blaze. The smoke and cinders blew into our soldiers' eyes, already sore with the sweat pouring from their brows, and made them swear loudly; yet they answered General Howe's summons with a cheer and, for the third time, advanced intrepidly against the Redoubt. This time the Americans, who were pretty short of ammunition and lacked bayonets, would not face the assault, though outnumbering our people by two to one. With their trousers rolled high above their naked feet and ankles, they scrambled out of the trenches. The majority of them got safe back across the Neck, which was now swept by the ships' fire, but many were caught. The Grenadier company of the Royal Welch Fusiliers, with which in after years I had the honour to serve, had the post of honour on this occasion, and lost every man but five of its three-and-thirty: nevertheless these five managed to make good an oath of vengeance sworn after the first attack against a certain sharp-shooter. He stood upon a cask placed on the *banquette* of the Redoubt, three feet above his fellows, and was known to have wounded their company officer, Captain Blakeny, and accounted for three subaltern officers besides. He was perfect at a hundred paces and was kept constantly nourished with loaded rifles by his comrades. This champion maintained his fire to the last; but the Grenadiers, when they came up with him, and he fought with his rifle-butt, drove their bayonets through his vitals again and again. It was said that three of our officers were in the first assault shot in the back by men behind. This was not deliberately done, the men's loyalty being beyond question: it was, I believe, due to crowding and over-lapping at the corner of the Redoubt.

So exhausted were the troops, and their losses so calamitous, that General Howe did not pursue the enemy over Charlestown Neck and on to their headquarters to Cambridge. He contented himself with occupying Bunker's Hill and fortifying it. The Americans thereupon fortified Prospect Hill, at a little distance beyond the Neck (a place with which I was two years later to form a long and miserable acquaintance), and gave our people to understand that they were prepared to sell this eminence at the same price as the last. Our casualties were nearly one thousand men, and ninety-two officers, among these Major Pitcairne, who fell with four balls in his body, the last one fired by a negro soldier. The Americans lost some-thing more than four hundred killed and wounded, and five guns out of the six that remained.

The general comment among the men was that we had taken the bull by the horns, but would have been better advised to sneak round behind, as mastiffs do in bull-baiting, and fasten upon a softer part. It was also commonly agreed that it had been a mere libel on common sense to take post at Boston of all places in the whole continent, unless in overwhelming strength; for the city was commanded all round – a mere target or Man of the Almanack, with the points of the swords directed at every feature. It was not many weeks before the rebels also seized and fortified Dorchester Heights to the southward, and so served us notice to quit.

There were innumerable other complaints of blunders committed by our generals: for example, that General Gage had permitted all his cabinet papers, Ministers' letters, etc., and private correspondence with Loyalists to be stolen out of a large closet, or wardrobe up one pair of stairs on the landing at Government House; and that his wife was a prime treasoner, in secret communication with the enemy, to whom she disclosed all his mili-tary plans and dispositions. It was also urged that we should have lost no time in purchasing the American generals. I have heard Captain Montrésor, an American Loyalist and at this time Chief Engineer in America, declare that even General Israel Putnam could to his certain knowledge have been bought for one dollar a day, or eight shillings New York currency. He added that the following generals could have been obtained at a still more modest expense, viz. Lasher, the New York shoe-maker; Heard, the Woodbridge tavern-keeper; Pribble, also a tavern-keeper from Canterbury in England; Seth Pomeroy, the gunsmith, and the other Putnam, namely Rufus, a carpenter of Connecticut. This Captain Montrésor was a bitter man, with a burden of grievances against fate and the British Government: he was six times wounded and six times lost his baggage in twenty-four American campaigns, yet was refused the rank corresponding with his important and extensive command; a restless ball was roaming in his body, resisting excision; he suffered from a hydrocele, a fistula, and a nervous spasm; the revolutionaries had burned to the ground his house and his out-houses, barns, and offices on Montrésor's Island, afterwards Talbot Island, eight miles from New York, for which he could obtain no restitution – and all these troubles were not one-half of his tale of woe. I expect that a modest allowance for exaggeration must therefore be made in his assessment of the venality of these Americans. He hated them so prodigiously for being tradesmen, rebels, and generals all together. I think that he had a grudge against Israel Putnam who had served with him at Niagara in 1764 in the Indian War. Yet he was one of the best-informed men and clearest speakers upon the situation in America to whom I ever had the privilege to listen. I later served under his son, a courageous officer of the Royal Welch Fusiliers, and heard many praises in many quarters of the old Captain and his wife: they kept open table in New York throughout the Revolution, when provisions were excessively dear, and converted their large mansion into a hospital for wounded Officers. The whole family was ruined by the war.

CHAPTER X

I CONCLUDED a previous chapter with an account of how I terminated my peace-time service in Ireland at the Cove of Cork, early in April 1776: by embarking for Quebec with the Ninth Regiment in which I was then a non-commissioned officer. The reason why ourselves and five other regiments of the Line, of which we were the eldest, were being sent to Canada was that news had reached England of a dangerous attempt on the part of the Americans to seize Canada, which was only lightly held by us. The enemy were under the command of Benedict Arnold, of Connecticut, an enter-prising militia colonel, and Brigadier-General Montgomery, an Irishman who had formerly held the King's commission. It was commonly feared that our expedition of relief might not reach Quebec in time to prevent an insurrection of the French inhabitants, who numbered about five thou-sand, or the surrender of the small garrison for some other reason. How strange a war it already appeared! General Montgomery had, twenty years before, played the hero beside Sir William Howe and Sir James Wolfe during the famous capture of Quebec from the French.

It is important to distinguish the motives which prompted this inva-sion. The Americans' ostensible motive, which was to free the Canadians from British tyranny, must be taken at a heavy discount. A few dozen malcontents in Montreal and elsewhere may have been stirred by the appeal to revolt made by the American Congress of 1776; but in general the Canadians, who were all French, found themselves pretty well off under British rule. They rightly suspected the American offers of help in 'knocking off their chains' as too effusive to be disinterested. The fact was that the Americans wished to secure Canada mainly for reasons of strategy. They feared a British attack by land upon New England, and they wished to deny us naval bases in the St Lawrence River. There were, besides, powerful Red Indian tribes resident in Canada, which then extended through the central part of what is now New York State, and behind the western boundaries of the other colonies, as far south as the great Mississippi River. These the British might persuade to light the flame of war along the whole inland frontier from New England to Virginia. If the Americans could strike suddenly and victoriously at the Canadian posts and prove that the British were not invincible, they might perhaps swing the Indians across to their own side. However, the more immediate object of their invasion was the capture of military stores from our arsenals at Montreal, St John's, Quebec, and other places, of which they stood in great need.

In England, no news had been received from Quebec for some months, owing to the freezing of the St Lawrence River, which cut our communications by sea. The last dispatches that had come were sent in the *Adamant* frigate, together with a few prisoners, on November 12th of the previous year. These told how Colonel Arnold's men had burst into Canada by the back door, that is to say by way of the Kennebec and Chaudière rivers, and, after a march of incredible hardship and exertions over unmapped country were now within a mile of Quebec. Moreover, General Montgomery's column was knocking at the front door, having moved up by the more familiar route of the Lakes George and Champlain; and the important posts of St John's and Chambly, with their garrisons, had already fallen to him. Montreal, a city of twelve thousand inhabitants, the largest on the whole American continent, was to be abandoned to this second column for want of troops to defend it; so that in all Canada no place of importance but only Quebec remained in our hands.

It seemed evident that, soon as we disembarked upon the farther shore of the ocean, we would find ourselves hotly engaged with the American colonists, whose fighting abilities the news of Lexington and Bunker's Hill had warned us not to underrate. It was therefore with indescribable emotions that early in the morning of April 8th I stood on the deck of the *Friendship* transport and eyed my native country, as we prepared to leave the harbour. It was bitterly cold for that time of year, though the sun was shining brightly, for a strong north-easterly wind blew. The exit to the cove was by means of a somewhat narrow strait. On the right hand stood the fortifications and the solidly built barracks which we had just quitted; the green hills beyond, spotted with white flocks of sheep, looked delightful as a background to the intervening blue waters. I leaned over the rail, gazing at them, and wondered when, if ever, I should look on them again. There was a certain luxuriousness in my melancholy, which almost drew tears from me, as it did from many of my messmates who were exceedingly drunk. In the *Swallow* transport, which lay a cable's length from us, the military band of The Ninth was playing a lively air, and similar strains proceeded from several other ships of the three hundred which composed our convoy. Two fine frigates were to escort us: we could make out their top-sails at the head of the line.

Soon we heard the boom of signal guns, every mast-head broke out with bunting; one by one the ships' crews heaved up their anchors and away slid the ships. The wind was favourable, the tide ran fast, and soon we were racing out through the strait with huzzas and nautical melodies, and the barrack buildings dwindled in the distance. I took a deep tug at my spirit flask, and after one more lingering view of Ireland, went below.

Mr Lindsay, the Scottish surgeon of The Ninth, who had been pleased to take a kindly interest in me, had given me much useful advice; for he was sailing in another and larger transport. I had inquired of him how best to keep myself and the men under my immediate supervision in good health during our passage. He observed, first, that during the first two weeks of sailing there was generally little sickness, except the usual nausea which persons unused to the sea feel and which have no ill effect. Against this sickness, abstinence from fluids was proper, and he recommended magnesia and walking on deck. After this first fortnight, however, a different diet became necessary. The men were given spirits and water instead of small beer, and were obliged to eat salted meat. This diet was not unwholesome, unless the water were putrid, which, however, was common both on the transports and the ships-of-war. Mr Lindsay recommended sweetening the water for the men of my mess by hoisting the butts out of the hold and pumping the contents with a hand-pump from one butt to another; and continuing this method every day, for three days, before the water was put into the scuttle-butt.

'Above all,' said Mr Lindsay, 'if any of your men be sick, avoid if possible letting them be sent to the sick-bay, which has the worst circulation of air and which breeds disease in those who are confined there for some other cause – such as a broken limb – from the stench of their fellow-patients' evacuations and putrid sweats. This bay is in general dark and its cleanliness but little inspected into. To save life, good air is indispensable.'

On the surgeon's advice, I commenced a regimen of diet and living which was intended to season me for the severities and fatigues in store. I ate and drank sparingly, chose for my berth a place under the main hatchway, and slept on the boards.

Mr Lindsay had spoken very passionately in my hearing about the negligence which condemned good men to die of disease on ship-board. 'More men by far are lost through injudicious management than by the violence of the most malignant diseases, especially in hot quarters of the globe. Putrid fevers are caught from the smell of the bilge-water lying at the ship's bottom: this becomes dangerously fetid from the soft loam and muddy matter of the ballast, along with the filth thrown down by the crew. This noxious air acts so powerfully that articles of silver taken into the hold are quickly turned to a black colour; and that the men who pump this water from the bilge are often overcome with giddiness, headaches, and fatal fevers. Great heavens, surely in an empire established, as ours is, in the ocean, the inquiry of the Medical Faculty and the constant care of naval officers should be particularly devoted to maintaining cleanliness on board and making arrangements, both in shipbuilding and general nautical economy, to keep vessels well ventilated! Ill health among troops stowed together in cramped quarters on ship-board promotes riots, quarrels, and ill behaviour: terrible accidents may derive from causes which at first seem insignificant. If only the whole of the Regiment could be transported in one vast ship, so that I might be able to exercise some guiding control over the health of men and officers! But I cannot be everywhere at once in a flotilla of forty craft, and naval surgeons are not provided except on warships; nor will the generality of officers heed me when I impress upon them the graveness of their responsibility for the men's health.'

We experienced rough weather almost as soon as we drew out of sight of land: we split one of our top-sails in a very high wind and broke some of our rigging, in which many sea-fowl became entangled, blown there by the force of the gale. The *Friendship*, in which the celebrated American privateer Paul Jones happened to have served his apprenticeship, was an old, crazy ship and rolled horribly, the gunwales being frequently under green water and the decks awash; so that the Captain was obliged to shut all the hatches. Hardly a soldier or soldier's wife but was overcome by the most dreadful nausea, and since we were all landsmen on board, we fully expected the ship to founder: but most of us were past caring. This ill weather continued for four days, though the hatches were not battened down for more than twenty-four hours, and at the end of that time the greater part of the men were still prostrated. It was not until much later that we recollected an Irishism of one of our recruits sufficiently to laugh as it deserved; he had come down from a visit to the deck in an ecstasy of terror, bawling out: 'O honeys, listen to me! We are all sure to be drowned, for the ship is sinking! Yet we shall be avenged, by my soul, for if she goes to the bottom that rogue of a captain will be accountable for our lives when we reach Quebec!'

At the height of the gale a soldier's wife was brought to bed; on which occasion, as the only person aboard with the least pretence to surgical knowledge and the least affected of any of the troops by sea-sickness, I was called upon to act as man-midwife. Another soldier's wife, who could not rise from her cot for weakness, offered me meanwhile not always coherent advice. I delivered the child creditably within three hours, and it survived the voyage. It will be wondered at, that I had the resolution to attempt this operation, when I tell my readers in what a place it was performed. The poor woman was stowed with two others and their husbands, all prostrated, besides three children (one of whom had a quinsy, from which it subsequently died) in a cabin which was a cube of seven feet – that is, seven feet long, seven feet broad, and seven feet high. Among these others was Mortal Harry and his wife, whom, when I first set eyes upon her and heard her tongue, I judged at once to be God's requital on him for his own wicked character. For one thing only I could feel grateful: that Harlowe and Mrs Harlowe were not of this number. She was being employed as lady's maid, on another ship, by the wife of the adjutant.

After a week the weather improved, though the sun seldom pierced the clouds, and I was able to spend a deal of my time on deck. Lieutenant Sweetenham, who commanded the troops on the *Friendship*, was desired by the Captain to keep the private soldiers between decks as much as possible, since they interfered with the management of the ship. He consented, though I had already acquainted him with Surgeon Lindsay's views about the healthfulness of fresh air. I now urged that to spend a mere two hours a day on deck, which was all that they were now allowed, and which was occupied by arms drill, was a prejudice to their health; but the Lieutenant continued to defer to the Captain, at whose table he ate, and nothing was done in the matter. Lieutenant Sweetenham was a veteran officer, worn out by the service, to whom a disagreeable voyage was no novelty and who also considered that the men should not be pampered on any account. However, I went to the Mate, who happened to be acquainted with my father and was a good-natured man, and asked permission for the men directly under my charge to be allowed to come up on deck during his daylight watch to perform fatigue duties under his supervision. To this he was pleased to agree, since it saved his own men labour. I would allow no man to plead nausea as an excuse from this duty and was often obliged to tie a rope about some of the lazy ones, and have them hauled out into the fresh air by their more vigorous messmates. As a further precaution against contagious disorders, I made every man wash and comb himself every morning; and every day, unless it rained, had the beds brought up on deck to be aired, and the berths sprinkled with vinegar. In consequence, I had far fewer men on the sick list in my mess of twenty-five than in the other, which was Mortal Harry's, or than in messes of other transports.

Brooks the Dipper, on the thirteenth day of the voyage, so far forgot the promise of good conduct that he had made to Major Bolton that he stole a linen shirt from Smutchy Steel's knapsack. Smutchy reported the loss to me and I knew at once where to seek for the missing garment, there being no dram-shop keepers aboard to act as receivers of purloined goods: I found Brooks wearing it under his own.

When Lieutenant Sweetenham was informed of the crime he decided to flog Brooks on the coming Sunday after divine service: 'for,' he said, smiling, 'who knows but that if I defer the penalty until we reach America, we may all be drowned beforehand and justice cheated? The King made a pretty hard bargain, Private Brooks, when he engaged you.'

Brooks decided, on the contrary, that he would rather drown than suffer another lashing. The next afternoon, soon as I brought my mess upon deck for our daily fatigue duty, Brooks broke from the party and running forward to the forecastle, leaped headlong into the sea. The vessel in a moment made her way over him, and he arose at the stern. We were travelling at a rate which seemed about that of a man walking fast. I instantly ran to the cabin where the Captain and the Lieutenant were dining and crying 'Man overboard!' burst in without a knock: for which lack of manners I was called a 'damned insolent rascal' by the Captain, who continued with his meal unperturbed. He presently complained, in a surly way, after eating a mouthful or two, that this pother came of permitting troops to go on deck at irregular hours. Nevertheless, at Lieutenant Sweetenham's insistence, he ordered the ship to be put about, and the boat to be hoisted out and manned.

I then returned anxiously to the deck and was relieved to make out the form of Brooks, at a little distance ahead of us, swimming strongly. He hoped, I dare say, to be picked up by some other ship of the convoy, at least a dozen sail of which lay astern within half a mile of us. He was soon over-hauled and it was with some difficulty that the sailors could force him into the boat. When he was brought back to the ship he was ordered between decks and a sentinel placed over him until the Sunday morning. However, that night he was found to be in a high fever and continued very bad until almost the last day of the voyage, when Lieutenant Sweetenham mitigated the award to forty strokes of the rope's end, which was as much as he was judged capable of enduring. These were duly inflicted.

On the last day of April, at about nine o'clock, a little girl, the elder of the two grown children from the married cabin, came running up to me and, 'O, Mr Lamb, dear Mr Lamb,' she cried, 'I believe that mother will murder father. For pity's sake, Mr Lamb, come at once and unbuckle them.'

I could not, in humanity, assure the child (who was, perhaps, seven years old) that, for all I cared, both her parents, who were Mortal Harry and his wife, Terrible Annie, might tear each other to little shreds and goblets and be heartily welcome. I therefore hurried to the cabin, where I found the place in indescribable confusion, for breakfast had been in progress when the battle began. On the floor, in the narrow space between the bunks, the two drunken creatures were rolling among the wreckage of their meal, grappled together with the fearful, deadly fury of snake and vulture.

I had once been warned by my father never on any account to intervene in any quarrel or altercation between man and wife. 'Each,' he said, 'will equally resent it and make common cause against you.' But here was an exception to an excellent rule, for, being both beside themselves, neither seemed to notice my presence, not even when with a great effort I disen-gaged the woman's clutching hands from Mortal Harry's throat, so that he was narrowly preserved from throttling.

They rose – he to a crouching, and she to a kneeling posture – and glared at each other, without a word. His face was mottled with blood, and one ear torn. At last he said in an odd, pitiful, complaining tone, to curdle the blood – and using no oaths, neither, which was remarkable: 'So you are too fine a lady to eat salted pork, are you, Annie, you touchy, passionate, ill-natured, contradictory woman? You would rather see me drowned first, you say? My dear, is that the truth now? You would rather see your Harry drown?'

'It would make my heart sing psalms, you great Limerick ape,' she replied, 'to know that you were fifty fathoms under the keel.'

Without another word Mortal Harry rushed out of the cabin and up the companion-ladder. The woman went slowly prowling after him, hissing between her teeth. I remained behind, to pacify the children and restore some sort of order to the cabin; for the sake of the poor mother of the child that I had delivered, who lay screaming in an hysterical manner, with a blanket thrown over her face. Suddenly the alarm of 'Man overboard!' was raised, and we felt the jar of the vessel being turned hard about. We were making six knots at the time, and there was a heavy swell. I hurried on deck to find Terrible Annie leaning against the fore-mast, laughing at her loudest. This occasioned great scandal among the seamen who heard her, for Mortal Harry had sunk to the bottom like a plummet and was seen no more. They threatened to throw her after him if she did not cease her cackle; but nothing would make her desist, so I called a drummer and a file of men who forced her below.

Let me here interpose as a remarkable fact that this poor widow had no difficulty at all in funding another mate; but so just were the workings of Providence, or whatever supernatural power regulates these matters, that the man she hit upon was Buchanan, the very same drunken corporal from whose depredations we had suffered so severely as recruits. The conclusion of that story I will not here anticipate.

Accidents are generally found to run in sequences of three, and this was no exception to the rule. Casey, the recruit whom I had been at such trouble to apprehend when he tried to desert in Dublin, was on deck four days later, during the drill hour; I was in charge of the parade. He had been provoked throughout the voyage by his comrades, who taunted him with the name of Jail-hound and with a legend of his having hanged his old mother in order to gain a small legacy by her decease. This he took very ill, and his obvious discomfiture encouraged his messmates to tease him further. It is true that he had been recruited in Downpatrick Jail, where he was confined on suspicion of some crime of violence, but murder was never imputed to him. When I gave the parade an order to stand easy, after the completion of an exercise, they proceeded as usual to chaff Casey. I did not prevent them, because that was outside my range of duty and, besides, the man had treated me very badly in deserting after I had advanced him money from my own pocket. Smutchy Steel now made some blockish remark, which was like a spark in the priming-pan. Casey stood and harangued them all in a high screaming voice, uttering dreadful curses upon them, and wishing that they might all soon become miserable and comfortless captives in the farthest parts of America, and suffer at their enemies' hands all and more than he had lately suffered from his supposed comrades. Then, in his full accoutrements, he ran and leapt off the fore-castle from exactly the same spot that Brooks and Mortal Harry had chosen before him. The great deep swallowed him up in a moment.

These deaths greatly sobered the remainder of us, especially Smutchy Steel, who came to me the following day and asked as a favour whether I would instruct him in reading and writing! I readily consented and he learned very quick. There were no further casualties among the troops, in spite of salt-tack, weevil-ridden biscuit, and an increasing foulness of the water with which we mixed our grog. Even of this water there proved to be an insufficiency, the Captain having as a speculation filled a number of our water-butts with porter for sale to the Quebec garrison on his arrival. He prevented me also from sweetening the water for my mess in the manner recommended by Surgeon Lindsay, by withholding the hand-pumps necessary for the task lest we should damage them. I fell back upon the alternative method, of scalding the water with irons made red-hot in the galley-furnace. The butts were old wine-butts, improperly cleaned, and in consequence many of us suffered much from dysentery, a miserable complaint for which the only specific we had was to swallow in brandy the rust scraped off an anchor-stock. The captains of transports were in general a set of men who had their own interest far closer at heart than the welfare of their country.

Towards the middle of May we approached the Banks of New-foundland, which are a surprising range of sunken mountains, extending in a direct line not less than three hundred and thirty miles in length, and about seventy-five in breadth. The top of the ridge, which at its highest reaches within five fathoms of the water's surface, is frequented by vast multitudes of lesser fish on which the excellent cod feeds, fattens, and multiplies in inconceivable quantities. Though hundreds of vessels have been laden for centuries past from thence, no scarcity or decrease of cod happens.

During the greater part of our passage across the Banks we never saw the sun, owing to the thick, hazy atmosphere which prevails in that part of the ocean. For two days together a total darkness like midnight covered the sky, so that a continuous firing of guns and beating of drums was needed to enable the ships of the convoy to keep due distance and avoid fouling one another. There was also the danger of running down fishing-vessels, from whose unseen decks hoarse shouts of warning against collision frequently arose. In spite of such risks it was customary for convoys to travel along a depression in the middle of the Banks, which was named the Ditch. The water here was as calm as in a bay, though the winds on either side were extremely impetuous.

At last came a stiff wind and with it a break in the fog. We saw the disc of the sun, dim and red, but gradually blazing with what seemed to us more than its usual splendour. In the welcome light we observed how numerous a congregation of fishing-vessels, large and small, lay about us. In times of peace, we were told, more than three thousand sail were annually to be counted there. A vast flock of seafowl was in attendance on the vessels, wheeling above them and ever and again swooping down to the decks to snatch up a cod's head or some other fishy prize. Besides the familiar gulls and many larger birds of the same feather, we observed a flightless, swimming, knowing sort, called penguins. They were sporting in pairs here and there, and ducking deep down in the water in chase of fish. Here the sea was no longer of the usual azure blue, but of a sandy white colour. We were now permitted to supplement our diet of salt meat and maggoty biscuit with fresh-caught cod. We baited a hook first with the entrails of a fowl and soon pulled up a fish. The hook was then baited with the entrails of this fish, which was gutted in its turn, and presently we were hauling in cod as fast as one can imagine. The water magnified the size of them so that it seemed almost impossible to get them aboard, and their struggles were very obdurate.

The right of fishing on these Banks, though by the law of nature it should have been common to all nations, had been appropriated by the French and British, who at this time had frigates constantly cruising there to prevent encroachment by ships of other nations. And, by an Act of the previous year, the revolted colonists of New England had been excluded from the Banks, though it was on the cod-fishery that their wealth had been founded and was still largely maintained. The New Englanders took this very hard, and the fishermen of Marblehead and Salem who lost their employment because of the Act were, as privateers, to do us more mischief in the war almost than any other class of Americans.

We passed close by several of these fishing-vessels, which had galleries erected on the outside of the rigging from the main-mast to the stern, and sometimes the whole length of the ship. On the galleries were ranged barrels with the tops struck out, into which the fishermen would get to shelter themselves from the weather. The stay of these vessels on the Banks was but short, for the method of curing was as quick as the catching. As soon as the cod was hauled up, the fisherman cut out its tongue, then passed it to a mate who struck off its head, plucked out liver and entrails, and tossed it to a third hand, who drew out the bone as far as the navel; then down the carcass went into the hold. In the hold stood men who salted and ranged the cod-fish in exact piles, taking care that just sufficient salt was laid between each row of fish to prevent them from touching.

It was on this sunny day, May 14th, that we first saw icebergs; but these were small bergs floated down from the St Lawrence River. Four days later we had a view of the mountains of Newfoundland, covered with snow. We had been forty days at sea without landfall and this dreary island was therefore very pleasant to our eyes. On the following day we entered the noble Bay of St Lawrence our fleet being all in sight. We doubled Cape Rosier and found ourselves in the St Lawrence River itself, which at this place is no less than ninety miles in breadth, with very boisterous water. Soon we were boarded by our first visitor from the New World, at whom we all gazed with the greatest interest, as if to divine from his appearance what sort of fate we were destined to encounter

He was a French-Canadian pilot, a low-statured, yellow-faced, merry man dressed in seal-skin jacket, well-tarred trousers and stout sea-boots. He affected also a prodigiously long pig-tail, bound with eel-skins, a heavy gilt crucifix about his neck and a round cap of white fox fur.

It was from this person that we heard the first particulars of the recent fighting, which had favoured our arms. The frigate had the day before signalled the fleet the good news that, though Montreal had been in American hands for some months now, the British standard still flew at Quebec. The pilot assured us, it was not to be expected that the Americans would stand their ground much longer, hearing of our approach. It was therefore with relieved minds and no immediate expectation of battle that we continued our voyage up the river.

We passed by Bored Island, so called from an opening in its middle through which a small schooner might pass with her sails up; and Miscou Island with its excellent harbour, in the offing of which a fresh spring spouted up to a considerable height from the salt water; and the Island of Birds, shaped like a sugar-loaf, which gave off a most insufferable stench from the droppings of the innumerable sea-fowl that nested upon it – we sent our boat to it, which returned laden with eggs; and the large Island of Anticosti which, upon my inquiry, the pilot represented as absolutely good for nothing.

In the third week of May, we saw, for the first time since we left Ireland, houses and cultivated land: a number of pleasant-looking French plantations upon Mounts Notre Dame and St Louis. Our navigation grew slow; for, after the river narrowed to about nine miles across at Red Island, shoals, sunken rocks, and whirlpools became frequent. It was here that I caught my first sight of the Indian aboriginals: three of them (of whom one appeared to be a chief by his feathered head-dress) passed within musket-shot of us in a birch-bark canoe, which they paddled downstream with inconceivable celerity. Their faces were painted with green stripes and they paid no attention at all to us when we hailed them.

Before the week was out we had passed by several more islands, but these for the most part well inhabited and cultivated. Stone churches, wayside crucifixes, and neat, whitewashed buildings with boarded roofs were now to be seen almost everywhere; and well-kept woods of red pine-trees, valuable for their profuse yield of turpentine, which we thought very graceful besides. The river-water was sweet to the taste at last, having been brackish for the first three hundred and thirty miles up from the ocean.

In the fourth week we entered a part of the river where the stream was no more than a mile across, and came to our destination – the noble port of Quebec, remarkable for being able to accommodate one hundred ships of the line at four hundred and twenty miles distance from the ocean. The newly arrived troops were not permitted to go ashore, except for a short fatigue-duty across the river at Point Levy, since there was fighting promised for them farther up the ever; but disappointment was assuaged by the fresh meat, poultry, and vegetables brought aboard. I was fortunate enough to be an exception to this rule against the allowance of shore-leave; for I was sent to the Upper Town with a detachment of The Ninth, which as the eldest regiment was chosen to provide guards for the day. I had a great curiosity to visit Quebec, if only for the sake of childish memories of the Heights of Abraham (represented by our wood-shed) and the death of that hero, Major-General Sir James Wolfe.

CHAPTER XI

WHEN THE Americans had entered Canada that autumn, the Governor, Sir Guy Carleton, escaped down the St Lawrence River from Montreal in a dug-out canoe, by night, and with difficulty reached Quebec. Our pilot described him as 'a man of ten thousand eyes, very courageous'. He was evidently prudent besides, for he had immediately expelled from Quebec, together with their families, all persons of military age who refused to take up arms for the King. On December 1st General Montgomery joined Colonel Benedict Arnold before the city and mounted his cannon for a siege. By a perfect novelty in military science he placed them on platforms of snow and water congealed into solid ice. The shot, however, was too light to make any great impression on the defence; whereupon, after consulting with his officers, General Montgomery determined on a general assault to be delivered simultaneously in two quarters, for the night of December 23rd. He boasted that he would eat his Christmas dinner in Quebec or Hell. Yet he was forced to go back on this undertaking because of the clearness of the weather: since, for a successful assault, he needed the cloak of a snowstorm. Difficult as the situation of the defenders was, with great scarcity of fuel, short rations, a wide circuit of walls to defend and a restless alien citizenry to keep in check, that of the besiegers was far worse. No unanimity existed among these troops, composed of contingents from several colonies, of whom only the Virginian riflemen, being better shod than the rest, did not now have their enthusiasm frozen to death. The temperature had fallen so low that it was found impossible to touch metal with the naked hand lest it should strip off the skin. Even in the city it was sufficient employment for the soldiers to keep their noses from the frost-bite, and several sentries lost the sight of their eyes from the extreme cold.

How any at all of the Americans managed to survive, I do not know. The Virginians wore white linen smocks, which were so obviously unfitted for use in winter that a legend arose among the French peasantry that they were impervious to cold. In the accounts that spread of their exploits the word *toile*, which means 'linen' in the French language, became changed to *tôle*, which is 'sheet-iron', and a legend will doubtless go down to posterity of ogres clad in white, frost-proof, iron armour, who sought to invade the country. To add to their discomforts, a severe epidemic of smallpox raged in the enemy camp. Desertions from the New England companies were frequent, and many men avoided duty by feigning sick; for which crime they had halters put around their necks and were paraded in derision before their comrades, and then lashed. What made matters yet worse was that sufficient pay in hard money for these troops was wanting. The injunction of the American Congress against alienating the Canadians' affections was so strict, that necessary supplies of food and clothing might not be seized from the country people, nor could they be compelled by any means to accept the new American paper money, termed 'Continental currency'.

General Montgomery had no alternative but either to attack or to retire, for he failed in all attempts to seduce the French population of Quebec to revolt. Messages to that purpose had been shot over the walls tied to arrows, and one emissary, a woman, had somehow contrived to gain admittance: she was seized, tried, jailed, and then drummed out with ignominy.

The distinguishing badge adopted by the Americans, who had no common uniform, was hemlock worn in the hat; but General Montgomery, now deciding on an assault for New Year's Eve, replaced these withered sprigs with a paper badge on which was inscribed, in each soldier's own handwriting: 'Liberty or Death!'

In the words of our French pilot, who appeared greatly tickled by the circumstance – 'By Gar, ze General he oblige to try zat day – last day possible.'

'How the last day possible?' we had asked.

'Ze New England militia, zey finish, at finish of year; zey go home goddam quick, finish of year, by Gar.'

The assault was delivered at about five o'clock in the morning of the New Year of 1776 with the aid of a blinding blizzard. The garrison, though warned beforehand that an attack was expected, were distracted by two feints at an escalade made at distant points of the defences, which were no less than three miles in circumference. Many of our men were also incapacitated by having drunk too deeply the health of the New Year. With little opposition the Virginian riflemen, under their gigantic commander Colonel Dan Morgan, forced their way into the Lower Town, which was a large suburb of wooden houses contiguous to the River, and there penetrated to the foot of Mountain Street, which zigzagged upwards to the Upper Town. Here they found the sally port of the lower barrier open, by mistake; and the French levies soon came running down past our well-placed batteries there in whole platoons, to give themselves up as prisoners. This barrier was captured at the first rush. But, instead of pressing on, the Virginians loyally waited: this was their agreed rendezvous with General Montgomery's column, whose attack was being made at some little distance away. They waited in vain, for he was dead, shot through both thighs and the head by a sudden discharge of grape in the moment of assault.

Colonel Benedict Arnold, under whom the Virginians were serving, was adjudged to be the boldest and most skilful soldier in the whole American Army. If he had not had the misfortune, a few minutes before, that his leg was shattered by a musket ball, he would never have permitted the delay and Quebec would doubtless have fallen, for the upper barrier of Mountain Street was only weakly held. But, by the time that the Virginians came to know that they could only count upon their own exertions, the British had rallied and were strongly placed behind the upper barrier. The chance had slipped. The American plan had been to fire the Lower Town, in order to provide a screen of smoke for the storming of the Mountain Street barriers, but this was not effected, and, when morning came, such of the Americans as had not already retreated were surrounded and captured. The enemy lost between six and seven hundred men and officers, more than half their force, in killed, wounded, and prisoners: the British losses were less than twenty. Yet Colonel Arnold had the temerity to encamp within three miles of the city, where smallpox and misery continued to diminish the numbers of his men. Even so, General Carleton was not to be tempted to attack: he lay close in the Upper Town. In April the Americans were reinforced, so that they numbered about two thousand men: but these were insufficient for a renewed assault. On May 3rd three British warships forced their way through the floating ice, to the great encouragement of the garrison. The Americans then broke camp and retired hastily up the River St Lawrence.

Let me conjure up a picture of Quebec as I saw it from mid-stream of the river, on the morning of May 28th 1776. At the water's edge was a cluster of warehouses and dwellings, the Lower Town, and behind them rose a cliff consisting of slate and marble, upon which, behind batteries and palisades, stands the Upper Town. In the middle of the cliff ran a serpentine road, Mountain Street, and a zigzag footpath with a hand-rail led up past the great grey palace of the Roman Catholic bishop; and, on the left, a little above it, stood Castle St Louis, the residence of the Governor, a long, irregularly constructed, yellow building of two storeys. The Castle was thought to be out of range of guns, because of its elevation, but this proved an error: for one evening of the siege a shot passed through a room next to that where General Carleton sat at cards with his family. Beyond were seen the slate-covered spire of the Cathedral surrounded by the spires of other religious buildings, namely, those of the Jesuits, the Franciscan Recollects, the Ursulines, and the Hotel Dieu, and by many tall and beautiful trees. To the left of Castle St Louis was a rounded pinnacle of dark slate, known as Cape Diamond where was a square fort, the Citadel of

Quebec; and on the highest point of the pinnacle a look-out box, an iron cage formerly used to house the bodies of felons. Cape Diamond stood upwards of one thousand feet above the level of the water.

Such a sight was beautiful in the extreme and improved by the numerous ships anchored in the intervening waters; but from a close view, when I went ashore for the Guard, many imperfections appeared. The fortifications, though extensive, wanted much in regularity and solidity, and, the parapet being broken down in many places, the ways of communication between the works proved rugged in the extreme. A number of houses, moreover, had been destroyed for fuel by the besieged inhabitants; shot and shells had continually defaced and burned the remainder; and the pavement of Mountain Street had been purposely torn up – in order that the shells might bury themselves in the ground before they burst and so spread less of death – and not yet replaced. Besides this, the streets were very narrow and dirty, and the buildings in general were small, ugly, and inconvenient. But I was delighted with the Canadian women whom I saw as I passed through the town; they were not beautiful but had something to set off this defect, a charm of behaviour and a lively neatness which is more difficult to forget than to describe. I was amused, too, by a curiosity, namely a great number of broad-shouldered, short-legged dogs yoked in little carts bringing country produce to the market.

The Guard of which I was the Sergeant, under a good-humoured young lieutenant named Kemmis, was a double one: over the St John's Gate, at the south-east of the city looking across the Charles River, and over the American captives in the solidly built jail near by. General Arnold's attack, which was made at this point, must have been the maddest possible, for the gate and the walls adjoining were stupendous and not to be attempted without heavy artillery.

I was shocked at the appearance of the captives: they had suffered terribly during the siege, though General Carleton had showed them as much humanity and consideration as he could afford. Their living had been salt pork and salt fish, biscuit, rice, and a little butter, but there was no means of providing them with remedies against the scurvy, which many of them, already weakened by the smallpox, took very badly, so that their teeth had loosened and dropped out and their flesh seemed to be rotting on their bones. Their clothing was ragged and verminous, and all their laughter had long forsaken them, giving place to a fixed melancholy. An attempt had been made by them to escape on April 1st, with which was connected a plan for seizing St John's Gate and admitting Colonel Arnold's forces into the city; but it miscarried. The cause of this failure was that common to almost all American war-like enterprises' the refusal of inexperienced participants to subordinate themselves to the experienced. Towards the completion of their plan only one obstacle still remained to be surmounted: which was the removal of a block of ice that prevented their prison door from opening outwards. Two good men were chosen to creep out and whittle this obstruction silently away with the long knives of which they were possessed; but a pair of meddling know-alls anticipated them by chipping at it with axes – which noise the guards overheard. All was discovered, and the conspirators were thereupon manacled and put in foot-irons. This hindrance to their taking exercise in the prison parade depressed their health further and aided the scurvy, of which many scores of them perished. Governor Carleton, however, had allowed them fresh beef about the middle of April and relieved them of their fetters, soon as the city was relieved. He had also distributed clothing to the naked. Thus I did not see them at their worst, though what I saw was shocking enough.

When I called out one of them, by name James Melville, or perhaps it was Mellon – I disremember – to discourse with me, what he disclosed rang so piercingly in my ears that I could never afterwards forget it. He said: 'If ever I am released from this jail and get home to our people, and fight again – before God I swear that I will never again suffer myself to be taken prisoner in my versal life. I have lost the half of my soul here, seared away by those cold irons. Look at me – you English soldier – I was as hale and stout a man as you in September last when I marched with the rest from Cambridge in Captain Dearborn's company. Nor was it the Kennebec River that did this for me, despite the hideous woods and mountains, and the tarnal hunger and heavy loads; nor the Height of Land where I wore the flesh from my shoulders at the Terrible Carry. Nor was it the Chaudière River, where we waded knee-deep for miles in the icy alder swamps, the abode only of herons and adders, and fed upon raw dog-meat and the bark of trees, and I roasted my leather shot-pouch and ate it; and also had the flux, nation bad upon me. Nor was it the complicated distresses of the campaign before this city, in the coldest winter but one that the oldest man can recall, and in rags of uniform. It was these solid prison walls, and the foot-irons.'

He added that, while he could complain of no unkindness on the part of the British, the Canadian militia had taunted these Americans often and threatened torture and death, though in effect doing nothing. 'But our worst enemy proved he who should have been our friend, a villain named Dewey, chosen from among us to be our quartermaster sergeant. He defrauded us of a great part of our provision, so that we had not above three ounces of pork and not half a pint of rice and two biscuits a day. Yet the Lord of Hosts delivered us out of his hands. The villain took the smallpox, which soon swept him off the face of the earth.'

I asked this soldier, the first native-born American with whom I ever conversed, a variety of questions. He told me that he had used his musket at Lexington in April 1775, marching with his neighbours from Hubbardston in Massachusetts, and that his enthusiasm for the cause of

Liberty had first been fired by a Methodist preacher, lately arrived from Ireland, a most persuasive speaker. This preacher had taken his text from Nehemiah iv. 14: *Be not ye afraid of them: remember the Lord who is great and terrible, and fight for your brethren, your sons and your daughters, your wives and your houses.* 'He had a face the colour of a biscuit and a black, wet lock hanging over his eyes. His words were like swords,' this man Melville said.

I asked him, what quarrel he could possibly have with King George. He replied that this preacher, along with the rest, had assured him that the King, not content with forcing him to drink that noxious weed tea, plotted to establish Popery in New England.

'But the King at his Coronation abjured Popery in the most solemn fashion,' said I, smiling. 'He is no more a Papist than you are.'

'Ah,' said he earnestly, 'so you may believe. But I dare swear that he is not the first great person to forswear himself when it was to his convenience. What of the Quebec Act of two years ago? Was that the Act of a Protestant Monarch? It established Popery in Canada as the State Religion, tithes and all. Now missionaries will breed here under the royal protection and spread like flies over our border and seduce all our young people.'

'Well,' said I, 'I see no great harm in granting the French-Canadians permission to continue worshipping God as freely in their ancestral manner as do your allies, the Papists of Maryland; indeed, I consider it a necessary and humane measure. It pleases me to know that on a Sunday, after the Romish service is over, General Carleton with his officers and soldiers resort to the Cathedral for their own worship; and neither party demands the reconsecration of the edifice between whiles.' I would gladly have said much more on this issue, remembering with shame my wretched fellow-countrymen at Timolin, and all along the road from Dublin to Waterford, wishing for humanity's sake that a Quebec Act could be passed by the Irish Parliament, so that the tithes sweated from these poor wretches could at least be paid to priests of their own faith, for the spiritual comfort that would accrue. But I did not wish to make a gratuitous parade or confession before this American of the ills from which Ireland suffered; and kept strictly to the matter in hand.

I am of an inquiring turn of mind and had already been at pains to find out as much as possible about the conditions obtaining in Canada. I was therefore able to tell him: 'As for the other main provision of the Act, against which your Congress has protested as fastening fetters upon the Habitants of Canada – namely, that of re-establishing the French Civil Law except in criminal cases – I am informed that the English-speaking settlers, who are outnumbered as two hundred to one by the French-speaking, have been the only persons to complain. Indeed, I hear that we have forced on the French of this province a greater measure of liberty than they can well digest: they are said to abominate trial by jury, deeming their Seigneurial judges as more likely to give them justice than a parcel of tradesmen crowded together in the jury box.'

At that very moment, as we talked together in the main doorway, a tinkle of a bell was heard up the street; and we saw how the people prostrated themselves before the Host conveyed by a robed priest to a dying man in a house near by. Acolytes carried lighted candles before the sacred wafer, which was enclosed in a gilt box laid upon a purple embroidered cushion, and handsome young nuns of the Ursulines walked behind, with their eyes fixed upon the ground. A number of soldiers were in the street, including Highlanders of the Royal Emigrant Regiment and German mercenaries from Brunswick who had sailed in the convoy that had arrived just ahead of us. But one and all obeyed the Governor's orders and doffed feather bonnet, cocked hat, or grenadier's cap as the procession passed; and, as required, the sentry at the gate presented arms.

'Faugh,' exclaimed this Melville, when they had passed, 'if that is not the dissemination of Scarlet Popery, what tarnal other name would you give it?'

'Good manners,' said I, 'which I am always pleased to witness. I wish we had more of them back in my own country.'

'I watched that same crew perform over a Frenchman in the hospital a month or two ago,' he remarked in a hollow voice. 'The nuns came and read over him, and then the priest entered and they fetched in a table covered with a white cloth, and lighted two wax candles about three feet long and set them on the table. The priest had on his white robe, and the nuns kneeled down, and he stood and read a sentence, and then the nuns a sentence, and so they went on for some time. Then the priest prayed by himself, then the nuns by themselves, and then the priest again. Then all together they read a spell, and finally the priest alone. Then the priest stroked the man's face; then they took away their candles and table. But the man died for all that, I should nation well reckon.'

He described Colonel Benedict Arnold as the most terrible man in America, and said that it was a pity that he was so much of a gentleman.

I pretended not to pay much attention to this, so that his tongue might run on unchecked. 'There was Colonel Easton of Connecticut who disputed the command with Colonel Arnold at Crown Point last year; Colonel Arnold made it a matter of honour and called on him to draw. Colonel Easton pacifically refused, though he had a hanger and a case of pistols on him; so Colonel Arnold kicked his posterior tarnal heartily, which Colonel Easton could not forgive him.'

'You don't like gentlemen, then, in New England?'

'Law for me, no! They are Tories and enemies of Liberty. But a few are well disposed to us and have military talents, so we employ them. General Montgomery was one such, and a good man in his way. General Philip

Schuyler is another, but he gives himself aristocratic airs and was once mighty surly to an honest blacksmith who came uninvited to visit him in his mansion at Stillwater. But General George Washington is a nation worse than all, and if he had his will would put only gentlemen in command of us; we hold him in great suspicion. He is tarnal friendly with Colonel Arnold.'

'I am informed that Colonel Arnold is a druggist and bookseller. How comes he then to rank as a gentleman?'

'Why, he married the High Sheriff's daughter in his town, commanded two companies of the Governor's Guards, and is a pretty considerable merchant. He boasts of his descent from a former Governor of Rhode Island, and he dresses tarnal proud. Well, he took a pet against Colonel Easton, as I have said; and he quarrelled with Colonel Enos, whose three companies later hooked it off from us at the Kennebec River; and with Major Brown, whom he named a damned thief for taking more than his share of the plunder captured at Sorel; and with Colonel Campbell, whom he accused of cowardice; and with Captain Handchett, whom he threatened to arrest for the same thing. Now, I hear he has retired to Montreal because General Wooster, who came up with the reinforcements in April, would not consult his advice.'

'Tell me,' said I. 'Who appoints your officers? Is it General Washington?'

He spat upon the ground. 'Law for me – no, no! We would accept none of his appointment. We want safe men, not men of quality, nary one of 'em.'

I could not resist interjecting sarcastically that quality was sometimes no bad thing, especially when compared with mere quantity. But he did not heed me and continued: 'The Continental Congress appoints generals and colonels and such, and we appoint the rest, from captains down.'

'Whom do you intend by "we"?' I asked in some bewilderment.

'The soldiers who are to serve under him. Our captains and lieutenants are voted for by a show of hands. They are pretty respectable tradesmen – such as hatters, butchers, tanners, shoemakers – and many of them worth several thousand dollars. But, let me tell you, that for all they are very warm men, they resemble our ministers in this – if they do not please us we do not obey, but we bid them hook it off in nation quick time.'

This raised such a ludicrous picture in my mind that I heartily laughed, which offended him. He told me: 'Scoffers will also have their portion in the hell that is prepared for the unrighteous.'

'Who told you that?' I asked, still laughing a little.

'The same preacher of whom I spoke – the Reverend John Martin was his name.'

'The Devil!' I exclaimed involuntarily, at the coincidence of two Irish priests of the name of John Martin, both with sallow faces and a black forelock, the one a Papist and the other a shouting Methodist. With that I dismissed the American; but before the Guard was relieved and we returned to the *Friendship* I gave him an old shirt and a pair of stockings, for which he wrung my hand gratefully.

General Carleton came to inspect us that same afternoon and complimented Lieutenant Kemmis upon our appearance and bearing, which gave us no little satisfaction. Let me describe this famous man who saved Canada for the Crown – not only by his activity and gallantry in this war but by his considerate framing of the Quebec Act mentioned above, which consolidated the loyalty of the French. He was tall, raw-faced, with a very large nose and a great diffidence in conversation; the best military instructor of his day and the most generous man alive. General Carleton had a quaint humour: when, two months before Quebec was relieved, the Americans had sent him a message warning him that the townspeople would revolt unless he surrendered, he gave no reply, but ordered a great wooden horse to be placed upon the walls, close to this Gate of St John. This was to signify that the treachery of the wooden horse of Troy would not be repeated by American emissaries in Quebec. When his staff reproached him for 'shooting too high for the Americans', who were not well read in classical legends and would be nonplussed by the horse, 'O, by God,' he said, 'I'll soon remedy that. Put a bundle of hay before the beast and write in bold letters on the wall, using tar: "When this horse has ate his hay, we surrender."'

After the relief of the city his good nature was such that he issued the following proclamation:

> Whereas I am informed that many of His Majesty's deluded subjects, of the neighbouring provinces, labouring under wounds and divers disorders, are dispersed in the adjacent woods and parishes and in great danger of perishing for want of proper assistance, all captains and other officers of militia are hereby commanded to make diligent search for all such distressed persons, and afford them all necessary relief, and convey them to the general hospital, where proper care shall be taken of them: all reasonable expenses which may be incurred in complying with this order shall be paid by the Receiver-General.
>
> And lest a consciousness of past offences should deter such miserable wretches from receiving that assistance which their distressed situation may require: I hereby make known to them that as soon as their health is restored they shall have free liberty to return to their respective provinces.

General Carleton also fed and clothed the sick whom the Americans, when they broke the siege, had abandoned in their hospitals. I heard from one of our men who happened to remain in Quebec during the week following our departure, that General Carleton visited the prison and spoke to the captives there in a very affable and familiar tone.

He asked: 'My lads, why did you come to disturb an honest man in his government, that never did any harm to you in his life? I never invaded your property, nor sent a single soldier to distress you. Come, my boys, you are in a very distressing situation, I see, and not able to go home with any comfort. I must provide you with shoes, stockings, and good warm waistcoats. I must give you some good victuals to carry you home. Take care, my lads, that you do not come here again, lest I should not treat you so kindly.'

He was as good as his word, though owing to the war, and one thing and another, James Melville and his comrades did not sail home until August; they had all voluntarily signed papers promising on their honour never to take up arms again against His Majesty. They sailed in five transports, and the General presented to the officers of each transport a cask of wine and five sheep as ship's stores. Mgr Briand, the Bishop of Quebec shamed them with a gift of two casks of wine, eight sugar-loaves and a number of pounds of green tea. The tea offended their political consciences and they respectfully refused it; then the good Bishop, to prove that he had not acted with malice, gave them an equal amount of the best coffee in exchange. This set animosity against tea was most violent in the early years of the war. The same James Melville, or Mellon, informed me that his comrade Sergeant Dixon, who lost a leg below the knee with a thirty-six-pounder ball before Quebec, was advised by a surgeon, who had amputated the limb, to drink some tea in default of brandy: for this would stimulate the desired reaction. The lady of the house where he had been brought made a dish of the beverage, which Dixon put away from him with detestation exclaiming: 'No, madam: it is the ruin of my country.' Nor could he be prevailed upon to forgo his resolution and touch this 'nauseous draught of slavery'; but, lock-jaw ensuing, he died.

The Reverend Samuel Seabury, who was to become the first bishop of the Protestant Episcopal Church in America, had recently written a humorous refutation of Congress's commercial policy: they recommended, in retaliation of the tea duty, an agreement against exporting all goods to Great Britain and Ireland. He was a farmer of his own glebe land in Westchester County, near New York, and did not wish to lose his Northern Irish market for flax-seed, of which he had in the previous year threshed and cleaned eleven bushels. He put it thus:

> The common price now is at least ten shillings. My seed, then, will fetch me five pounds ten shillings. But I will throw in the ten shillings for expenses. There remain five pounds. In five pounds are four hundred three-pences. Four hundred three-pences, currency, will pay the duty upon two hundred pounds of tea – even reckoning

the exchange with London at two hundred per centum. I use in my family about six pounds of tea. Few farmers in my neighbourhood use so much; but I hate to stint my wife and daughters, or my friendly neighbours when they come to see me. Besides, I like a dish of tea too, especially after a little more than ordinary fatigue in hot weather. Now, two hundred pounds of tea, at six pounds a year, will just last thirty-three years and four months; so that, in order to pay this monstrous duty on tea, which has raised all this confounded combustion in the country, I have only to sell the produce of a bushel of flax-seed once in thirty-three years.

But the Reverend Samuel Seabury, as a minister of religion, should have known better than to play the rationalist, confusing substance with symbol. As the elements of the Lord's Supper are held to suffer a divine transformation in the hands of the priest: so Pekoe and Hyson were believed by the Americans to suffer a diabolical transformation when handled by the excise-man.

CHAPTER XII

WE SAILED up the St Lawrence on the first day of June, our destination being Three Rivers, a village which lay about half-way between Quebec and Montreal and some ninety miles from each; it was so named from the three rivers which joined their current close above it and then fell as one into the St Lawrence. Here we expected that the enemy would make a stand.

In our passage we were entertained by many beautiful landscapes, the banks being in many places very bold and steep and shaded with lofty trees, now in young leaf. What particularly struck our attention was the beautiful disposition of the towns and villages we passed. Nearly all the settlements in Canada were situated upon the banks of rivers; which was by no means the case in other parts of America, as I afterwards found. The churches appeared frequently and seemed kept in the neatest repair, most of them showing bright spires of tin. It puzzled me why these spires did not rust; but I later discovered that it was from the dryness of the air and from a method they have of nailing on the squares of tin diagonally, the corners folded over the heads of the nails, so as to keep moisture from intruding. The houses were of logs, but much more compact and better built than those which I was to see in the rest of America: the logs were more closely joined and, instead of being left rough and uneven on the outside, were trimmed with the adze, and whitewashed. It was pleasing beyond description to double a tree-covered headland in the evening and perceive one of these villages opening to view, its houses close upon the river, rosy with the setting sun, and the spire of its church twinkling bright through the leafy trees.

The air became so mild and temperate that we imagined ourselves transported into another climate; yet I noticed that hardly a house on the whole river had its windows thrown open; for the French-Canadians loved a close, stifling heat as dearly as they loved the tobacco-pipes which gurgled constantly in their mouths – I once saw a boy of three years puffing away at one.

The tide still ebbed and flowed in the river as far as Three Rivers, but not many miles beyond. We disembarked about twenty miles below this place, where the left-hand bank was flat, and much corn and fruit was grown. This was June 5th, and we marched along the river-road all day, with the regimental music ahead of us, funding great enjoyment in the use of our legs. We remarked upon the extraordinary speed with which the crops sprouted and the trees leafed, soon as winter had departed, as also upon the very slovenly manner of farming here in use. It appeared that manure was seldom put upon the fields, considered already rich enough by nature, but was instead thrown into the river. The sandy earth was merely turned up lightly with a plough and the grain scattered in furrows which were far from regular. More than half the fields also had been left without any fences, exposed to the teeth and hooves of cattle. However, the Habitants were beginning to be more industrious and better farmers; because, since the English came, the greed and rapacity of their feudal landlords, the *Seigneurs*, had been somewhat curbed. Beforehand, it was not worth their while to accumulate any surplus of corn or maple-sugar or fuel, because it would all be taken from them under one pretext or another; but now they counted on the protection of the Governor and were assured of a steady market for their produce, owing to the energy of the English merchants of Montreal and Quebec, who sent boats to collect it on fixed days. Yet for their *Seigneurs* they still had a habit of reverence, and were bound to them by certain ties of vassalage, such as being obliged to take their corn to be ground only at the *Seigneur*'s mill, under payment of a heavy fine, however inconvenient the journey.

The *Seigneurs* lived in a simple style and were often poorer than their vassals, for they were forbidden by pride to engage in the tilling of the soil or any mechanical task; but at the sight of a beaver hat, however shabby, every red night-cap was doffed. This disgust of mechanical employment was shared by the vassal, who was usually related by marriage with a Seigneurial family, and, though he condescended to till the soil, would hold it beneath him to set up as a blacksmith or boot-maker. In consequence, the Canadians had great scorn for the invaders from New England when they were aware that even their officers were tradesmen and artisans.

The women of the Seigneurial class affected long cloaks of scarlet silk, in contrast with those of a similar colour, made of cloth, worn by the plebeians, and a kind of worsted cap with great coloured loops of ribbon. If any woman without a right to these distinctions were to be seen attired in them, they would be torn from her, even in a crowded gathering.

The peasant girls were very pretty, but only the young ones; for their beauty closed prematurely. They wore charming sleeveless bodices in blue or scarlet, petticoats of a different colour and wide-brimmed straw hats. Some sat spinning in the open air outside their house doors. They did most of the farm labour, the men being in general indolent, except when on some adventurous expedition in search of furs. The farms were not in general large, grazing thirty or forty sheep, and about a dozen cows, along with five or six oxen for the plough. The cows were small, but very good for the farmers' use. The people seemed not only immeasurably better circumstanced than the peasants of Ireland, but (a comparison I was able to make in later years) a great deal better than most of the English themselves. Every dwelling-house had a small orchard attached and at evening the return of the herds and flocks from the woods was a very pleasant sight. The swine were also allowed to roam wild in the woods; these were very fierce, and the hardy manner of their life greatly improved the flavour of the flesh and the quality of the bristles for brush-making.

We halted in a small village about an hour after disembarking, and Lieutenant Kemmis, who knew a little French, asked a French farmer, who had come out of his house to watch the troops go by, how far it was to Three Rivers. 'Oh,' replied he, 'about twenty pipes, sir.' This strange method of computation, which was the common one on the river, represented time rather than distance: the time that it would take to smoke a pipe, according to the element which one used, land or water, and in the latter case according to whether the journey was upstream or down. For men walking along, in the leisurely stroll used by these Frenchmen, 'a pipe' was about three-quarters of a mile.

The same farmer, who, in spite of the warmth of the weather, wore a coarse blanket coat tied about his body with a worsted sash, and the habitual red woollen night-cap, invited the Lieutenant and myself into his house for a drink. It was of a single storey, with three or four compartments and a large garret a-top, where in winter he stored his frozen provisions.

I looked about me with interest. The interior of the living-room was neatly boarded and the furniture plain and solid. There was a close iron stove with a long line over it for the drying of dish-clouts and clothing. Strips of stout paper were still tightly pasted about the window to keep out the blasts and snow of winter. A crowd of about thirteen people, seated at a long table on stools, were eating their dinner with wooden spoons from wooden bowls (hollowed out from the knots of the curly maple-tree) and drinking cider from tankards of unglazed earthenware. Their bread was sour and black, and the dinner was a great pot of potatoes, cabbage, and beef boiled to shreds. The smell in the room was a curious admixture of sweat, stew, garlic, tobacco, and sulphur. We had not been there above five minutes when we felt our heads beginning to swim, for the stove was roaring hot and giving off noxious fumes.

'Good God, my friend,' exclaimed the Lieutenant, 'do you never open the window even in the hottest day of summer?'

Our host ruminated a while and then shook his head.

'And why not, pray? Would it not benefit your health?' For the Lieutenant was aware that the French were much subject to the consumption, which these stoves invited.

He puffed at his pipe. 'It is not a custom of the Habitants,' he told us at last; and I was to learn that this same reason was habitually given by his countrymen for many other eccentric refusals to behave in a common-sense manner. So we drank off our cider, which was very rough in the mouth, thanked him, and staggered out again into the road – a very good one too, because the Corvée of France was still in operation hereabouts, which provided forced labour for the maintenance of public works. This road was ditched on both sides and curved in the centre for dryness, and the ruts constantly filled up with stones. A pleasant breeze blew off the river, which was about two miles broad, so that vessels of considerable size sailing in midstream appeared like wherries.

We had the luck to observe two sea-wolves sporting in the river, within musket-shot. To have disturbed them by a volley would have been a wanton act, for had we wounded or killed them we should not have been able to recover their bodies; nor did we need fresh meat, being abundantly supplied with very good beef. The sea-wolf, so-called from his howling, is an amphibian creature. His head resembles that of a dog. He has four very short legs, of which the fore ones have nails, but the hind ones terminate in fins. The largest animals weigh upwards of two thousand pounds and are of different colours. Their flesh is good eating, but the profit of it lies in its oil, which is proper for burning and for currying leather. Their skins do excellently for travellers' trunks, and when well-tanned make shoes and boots that do not admit water, and lasting covers for seats. I never saw a sea-cow, though this animal was also found in the river: larger than the sea-wolf but resembling him in figure. The sea-cow is as white as snow and has two teeth, of the thickness and length of a man's arm, that look like horns and are of the finest ivory. These beasts were seldom taken at sea, and on shore only by a stratagem. The people of Nova Scotia used to tie a bull to a stake fixed on the shore to the depth of about two feet of water; they then covertly tormented him by twisting his tail until he roared. As soon as the sea-cows heard this they would take it as a signal from one of their own kind and swim towards the shore; when they reached shallow water they would crawl to the bull on their short, awkward legs and be taken without difficulty.

I later saw several schools of porpoises playing about in the river: each was said to yield a hogshead of oil, and of their skins were made warm musket-proof waistcoats. They were mostly white and when they rose to the surface had the appearance of hogs. At night, if I may use an Irishism (being Irish born), they often caused beautiful fireworks in the water, especially when two schools crossed each other, a continuous stream of light gliding with each member and curving in and out.

It must not be thought that we were so distracted by the interesting sights of our march that we forgot the purpose for which it was made; namely, to throw back the American invaders out of Canada. We felt indeed an unquestioning assurance that the Americans, fighting not in defence of their homes but as invaders of a foreign country with which they had nothing in common, would have no chance against us. They would lack the opportunity to shoot from behind stone walls at a column in line of march as at Lexington, or to defend a prepared position against frontal attack as at Bunker's Hill; nor could they count upon the assistance or even the neutrality of the Habitants. They were accustomed to fight as individuals not as an army; and in battles in open country, as this was, victory must always attend the side which shows the most perfect discipline and the closest subordination to the instructions of its commander – so long as he be not a perfect fool, as very few of our generals happened to be.

The Americans who opposed us consisted of three several expeditions. First, the two thousand besiegers of Quebec, who upon General Carleton's sortie early in May – 'to see', as he said, 'what these mighty boasters are about' – had fled almost without resistance, abandoning the whole of their artillery and stores. To these were added two thousand new troops under General Tomson, who had been sent up from Boston to assist at the capture of Quebec; they could be spared for the service because General Howe had in March been forced to evacuate Boston, bag and baggage. That they arrived too late was due to mismanagement and dissension. Besides these, three and a half thousand men had arrived under General Sullivan, and Colonel Benedict Arnold from Montreal with his three hundred veterans. This was a respectable force in numbers, but we had thirteen thousand men to set against their eight thousand, and were far better served with artillery. The Americans were reported to be concentrated at Sorel, some forty miles up the river from us and on the other bank. Between them and us lay the broad Lake of St Peter with its thousand islands, which would be the next stage of our journey up to Montreal.

We arrived at Three Rivers, after being ferried over the intervening stream on *batteaux*, a sort of barge peculiar to Canada, flat-bottomed and with both ends built very sharp and exactly alike. The sides were about four feet high and there were benches and rowlocks for oarsmen; the *batteau* also carried sail, though it was very awkward either to sail or row. Its advantage was that it drew very little water and could be propelled by poles, where there was no wind and where oars would not serve. The poles were about eight feet in length, extremely light and shod with iron. The current in the centre of the St Lawrence River was so strong that to stem it a crew must keep close to the shore and use their poles in unison. The *batteau* was steered by a man with a pole in the hinder part, who shifted it from side to side to keep the course even.

We found Three Rivers a place of disappointing size, though the third town, in point of importance, in Canada. It contained but two hundred and fifty houses, most of them built of wood and indifferent in appearance, two extinct monasteries, an active convent of Ursuline nuns, and a barrack with capacity for five hundred troops. The town used to be much frequented by Indians, who brought furs thither down the rivers after which it is named; but by this time the trade had been diverted to Montreal as being a more accessible market to the Indian trapping-grounds, and Three Rivers was no more than a port of call between Montreal and Quebec.

My company were lodged for the night in a barn belonging to the Ursulines and were shown great kindness by the Chaplain of the sister-hood. He invited Lieutenant Kemmis and myself to enter a part of the convent which could be visited without leave of the Bishop – as the part where the nuns dwelt could not. We were conducted to a handsome parlour with a charming view of the convent gardens, and presently in came gliding the Mother Superior and a bevy of lay-sisters, who were not bound by the same strict vows as the other women. I could only nod and smile, but Lieutenant Kemmis offered a number of gallantries in halting French, which greatly pleased the old woman. The dress of the Order, a poor one, consisted of a black stuff gown, a handkerchief of white linen with rounded corners looped about the throat, a head-piece of the same material which allowed only the centre part of the face to show, a black gauze veil which screened half even of that and overflowed the shoulders, and a heavy silver cross suspended from the breast.

We were shown specimens of the handicrafts of the Sisterhood, by selling which they helped to support themselves; and were expected to purchase some specimens, which we did. It is unusual for soldiers on the eve of a battle to fill their pockets and knapsacks with a heap of keepsakes in fancy-work to send to their friends – but we could not disappoint these poor women. We bought from them two pocket-books, a work-basket, a dressing-box, all of which were made of birch-bark embroidered in elk hair, dyed in various brilliant colours; also some models of Indian toma-hawks, scalping-knives, calumets, and those birch-bark canoes for the manufacture of which Three Rivers was famous. They packed them up for us very neatly in little boxes kept for the purpose, of the same bark.

The next day we spent in drill, both by platoons and companies, and Major Bolton impressed upon us that what we had perhaps regarded hith-erto as idle ceremony had a practical and deadly purpose. He declared that we must show the same steadiness and unanimity upon the field as upon the parade. In the afternoon I went from curiosity to watch a number of Indians at their canoe-making, a work performed with the utmost neat-ness. They began with a framework of thick, tough rods of the hickory nut-tree, bound together with remarkably stout strips of elm-bark. Over this they sewed, with deer sinews, large strips of birch-bark, which resembles that of the cork-tree but is of much closer grain and far more pliable. A thick coat of pitch was laid over the seams between the different pieces. The inside was lined with two layers of thin pieces of pine, laid in a contrary direction to each other. A canoe of this sort was so light that two men without fatigue could carry one on their shoulders, with accommodation for six persons. It was wonderful to see with what velocity these canoes might be paddled: in a few minutes a keel-boat rowed by an equal number of men with oars would be left behind, a mere speck on the river. But they were very easily overturned by the least improper movement; and the Habitants preferred more solid canoes hollowed out from a single log of red cedar.

The work was entirely performed by women, who undertook all the labour of the tribe: such as procuring and transporting fuel, planting corn and vegetables, cooking, dressing skins, doctoring, making household instruments and utensils. The men supplied the food and defended the camp, but considered it beneath them to undertake any other labour.

I observed a number of men lounging about on the bank, smoking their calumets, a combination of pipe and axe. One of them, sitting cross-legged in his blanket-coat with a black face and untrimmed locks, which I was told signified mourning and unsatisfied revenge, offered me a handsome otter-skin pouch. I opened it and found inside a lump of tobacco in one compartment and dried leaves in the other. Upon my looking puzzled, he took the pouch from me, extracted the tobacco lump, cut it into shreds in the palm of his hand with his scalping-knife, rubbed it together with the dry leaves, which were of the sumach-tree, and finally, drawing my pipe from my waist-belt, where I had put it, stuffed the bowl with the mixture. He struck fire into a bit of touchwood with his flint and steel, kindled the pipe and put it between my lips. These were simple and familiar actions but performed with indescribable harmony and grace. Except in their war-dances or when they were intoxicated, I never saw an Indian make any movement or gesture that was not beautiful to the eye. I sat for some minutes watching this man, who appeared to be a very sincere and honest smoker. He never removed or replaced his pipe in his mouth without due solemnity, and the act of inhaling the smoke seemed to be closely akin to some religious ceremony. He remained all the time in the profoundest melancholy. A squaw who could speak a little English, of the simple ungrammatical sort used by the Montreal traders, told me his story. He had lost three children from the smallpox, and his brother had been scalped during a fur-getting voyage in the far north. He wished to go to war himself in order to change his luck, but his Sachem had restrained him. His name was Strong Soup, and he wore tied on his legs the furs of polecats, which were the insignia of acknowledged valour. The polecat furs he had won for a deed of desperate daring against the Algonquins, undertaken to erase the stigma of a previous misfortune: when he had fled from the same Algonquins weaponless and leaving his breech-clout in their hands. His revenge was to kill three Algonquin warriors, two squaws, and the only infant child of their chief; lifting four scalps in the act. The popular jeer against him in the matter of the lost breech-clout was there-upon forbidden by his war-chief by means of the public crier.

One other incident of interest occurred while I was here. The woman who told me Strong Soup's story had two children with her, an infant and a girl of perhaps seven years old. The infant was swaddled in a blanket and bound tightly to a piece of board somewhat longer than itself. Bent pieces of wood protected the child's face, lest the board should fall, and it was suspended upon the branch of a birch-tree within reach of the mother's hand: she kept it swinging from side to side like a pendulum while still engaged in her canoe-making. The little girl was covered with a loose cotton garment and was very forward. She came behind me and fingered my accoutrements in a way that the mother regarded as unmannerly. The punishment was not a string of curses or a slap, as it would have been in Ireland, but a stern look and a handful of water scooped from the river and flung in her face, which abashed the child so much that she crept away and hid beneath a canoe. To comfort her, I presented her with a sewing-box that I had bought from the nuns; which she gazed at with evident exulta-tion, and said an eloquent speech of thanks.

'What does she say?' I asked the woman.

'She wish you kill plenty bears, plenty deer, take many scalps. Say your hand like a sieve, give very good gifts.'

The woman and the child had most delicate, harmonious voices, which was the rule rather than the exception, I found; whereas every Indian, almost, with whom I ever conversed spoke as if he had a hot potato in his mouth or a heavy weight upon his chest, pronouncing his words labori-ously from the lower part of his throat and moving the lips only very slightly.

The women were dressed in moccasins, leggings, and a loose short shirt like the men, but fastened with silver brooches at the neck. They also wore pieces of blue or green cloth folded closely around their middles and reaching to the knees; and silver bangles on their wrists. I shall have more to say later on the subject of these interesting people; but I cannot post-pone a record of my astonishment when the squaw with whom I had been conversing took down the cradle from the tree and, unswaddling the young child, hugged it for a while to her tawny bosom – for I perceived that its body was as fair as that of an English child. I was to observe later than even negro children were not perfectly black when born, but acquired their jetty hue gradually; just as in the vegetable world the first tender blade of spring, on peeping through the soil, turns from white to pale green, and to emerald only when May is come.

We were asleep on straw in the barn of the Ursuline Convent when the drums suddenly began to beat and in came Lieutenant Kemmis, calling for his groom. He appeared to be in great animation.

'Well, my gallant lads,' he cried, 'we are to have a smack at 'em this morning, it seems. See that you fall in quick and without confusion. Sergeant Lamb, pray inspect the men's arms and ammunition. Pay especial attention to the flints. If any appear worn, serve out new from the box – you have the key?'

'Very well, your Honour.... Fall in, men, and tumble to it! Your Honour, are they upon us?'

'They crossed over a brigade of fifty *batteaux* last night from Sorel and landed at Point du Lac, about ten miles upstream from here. We are ordered to join the vanguard with the flank companies of the other regiments.'

Soon we were marching out into the darkness along the river-road, in column of route. Our company, being the eldest light infantry company present, had the right to lead the column of route. It was daylight before we came upon their vanguard. They were marching along the river-road in a careless manner, like a congregation coming out of church, as if not expecting to meet with any opposition. They were slender, loose-limbed men dressed in dark green hunting shirts, long mud-coloured breeches, with tan gaiters, They wore tan ruffles around their necks, at the bottom of their coats, on their shoulders, elbows, and about their wrists. Their hats were round and dark with a broad brim folded up in three places, and in one fold was stuck a sprig of green. This colouring, being in perfect imitation of the hues of a forest, made them very inconspicuous in woody country, whereas a red coat showed up like a poppy in a stubble-held. Here, however, in the open land between blue water and the brilliant fresh-green of young corn they were not indifferent targets. We quickly executed one of the new manœuvres that we had learned from The Thirty-third in Dublin, shaking out across a cornfield. There we fired two very disciplined volleys, to the great scandal and grief of the farmer, who tried to head us off with shouts and curses, caring nothing for the bullets which were already whizzing about him. '*Sacré Nom du Grand Archange Saint Michel et de tons ses anges inférieurs – éloignez-vous bien vite de mes putats, assassins, on je vais le dire au Général Carleton.*' Which, it seems, was to say: 'Sacred Name of the Good Archangel St Michael and all his inferior angels, get you gone quick from my potatoes, you hired robbers, or I shall go and complain to General Carleton!'

A bullet happened to strike the pipe out of the honest fellow's mouth, and a clay splinter gashed his cheek. Suddenly realizing the hazards of his position between two tares, he leaped like a hare for the ditch, and lay there cursing and shouting. The burden of his song was that he would on the very next day get aboard his boat and descend to Quebec to complain of the outrage to General Carleton, who never failed to give redress.

The Americans did not stay within range, but ran to hold a slight ridge where they began to scoop shallow trenches in the light soil. Reinforcements came up on either side. Our orders were to hold fast and conserve our fire: if they attacked, we were to charge bayonets and meet them as they came.

This being the first skirmish I ever was engaged in, it really appeared to me to be a very serious matter, especially when the bullets came whistling by our ears. There were a few veterans among us who had been well used to this kind of work, among them old Sergeant Fitzpatrick, who went about with a hymn of the Rev. Charles Wesley's upon his lips and a devout anger in his eyes. But Mad Johnny Maguire took it very easy. 'Oh, by the powers, my honeys, take it easy!' he said. 'This is but only the froth of battle. I was with the dear Ninth in Sixty-two when we stormed the Moro Fort at Havannah. That was the real brew, full and deep, by Jesus Christ!'

He had told us all, during my inspection of their arms and pouches that morning: 'Now there's no need to be alarmed if you hear the sound of a bullet fired against you, for that means it isn't there. It's the bullet you don't hear that's the bother, for often you notice afterwards that it has killed you.'

'Did that often happen to you, Johnny Maguire?' we asked him.

'Not to the best of my recollection,' he answered very seriously, 'but I had a devil of a big fright once or twice.'

Soon the cannon from the vessels in the river began to roar, and the held-pieces which accompanied the van shot over our heads. The fire from the river was particularly severe, for the ships stood in close and blazed from the flank at point-blank. In a battle all sense of the passage of time is absent, as in childhood or during play at cards when the stakes are high. It may have been five minutes or half an hour before we observed that the Americans were going away in two's and three's and that their fire was slackening. We charged bayonets and sprang forward at them with a shout. They made no attempt to stand, which would indeed have been folly in their situation. They had suddenly learned that a brigade of British troops had been landed from transports some distance in their rear, and their one thought now was to regain their *batteaux*, lying a matter of three miles away, before they were cut off. A few valiant or obstinate men stayed behind, firing to the last, but singularly little execution was done: in the whole course of the day our army lost no more than a dozen men killed or disabled. The retreating colonists had not far to run before they were in woodland: we pushed so rapidly ahead, to prevent their making a stand on the road, that their laggards took to the trees.

The Americans won the race to the boats, of which only two were taken, and were soon safe away among the islands and shallows of St Peter's Lake, where our ships could not pursue them. Two generals, several inferior officers, and two hundred men surrendered in the woods. I had no personal adventures to boast of afterwards; the only American whom I shot at, as he ran from me in the forest, I missed. So ended the brief, glorious, and unremarkable battle of Three Rivers: of which the Americans later spoke as if it had been a great victory, declaring that as many of our people had fallen as at Bunker's Hill, while their own losses were insignificant.

On the day following, we left Three Rivers and were put aboard our transports with all expedition; the wind springing up fair, the fleet sailed towards Sorel. The greatest breadth of St Peter's Lake, through which we were now sailing, was about fourteen miles, and its length about eighteen. The number of islands here was so extraordinary that it was impossible not to feel astonishment that such large vessels as visited Montreal could pass between them; and indeed the channel was very intricate. Lieutenant Kemmis found the prospect highly romantic, especially since many islands were peopled with camps of Indians dressed in their festival clothes to salute the convoy as it passed, and birch-bark canoes were continually speeding in and out of the vessels, the Indians shouting lengthy exhortations and greetings. The only intelligible part of these was an insistent demand for Christians' fire-water, as spirits were called; for, until the English landed on the American continent, no intoxicating liquors were known to these happy people.

The *Friendship* grounded on a sand-bank in the very middle of the lake. Some men were sent out in a boat with an anchor, which they dropped in deep water; this gave us purchase to heave the vessel clear, so that we were only stuck fast for two hours. However, it was found impossible to recover the anchor, which loss caused such grief and vexation to the Captain as I should not have expected him to express for that of the whole ship's burden and company. With captains of hired transports, it was evident that the crew, the cargo, and the welfare of their country were but secondary objects. One of them about this time gave the frigate guarding a convoy the slip, and got safe into Boston with a cargo of fifteen hundred barrels of gunpowder, which he sold to the Americans for a sum which made him rich for life.

Our journey from Three Rivers to Sorel at the head of the lake took five days, which was one too many, for upon our disembarking we found the fires of the American encampment still burning, but the men gone. It was here that we saw the last of the *Friendship*. We disembarked with all our baggage and, leaving the St Lawrence (which runs eight miles an hour at this point), marched south up the Sorel River towards Lake Champlain. A second column pursued another part of the American forces towards Montreal. We began our march in three columns under the command of Lieutenant-General John Burgoyne, M.P., an officer of the greatest experience and universally esteemed by his men, yet somewhat of a grumbler and too easily carried away by his natural eloquence into an exaggeration of injuries received from, and faults committed by, those in authority over him. It was an excellent army, and a great many men served in it who had fought against the French and Spanish. The mistakes that we committed were therefore totally different from those of the Americans: accustomed only to warfare in Indian fashion, they erred in too little regularity of organization and discipline, we often in too great rigidity. Our arrangements for the march, for bivouacking, for reconnaissance of ground, for the placing of outposts, and for the supply of ammunition, victuals, and forage, were admirable; as they were throughout the war, consistent with circumstances. But we were always a few hours' march behind the retreating enemy, who, notwithstanding their haste, took care to destroy by fire all *batteaux*, ships and military stores that they could not take with them, and many houses besides.

Their distresses were very great: a British army of superior strength hanging close on their rear, their men obliged to haul loaded *batteaux* up the rapids by main strength, often to their middles in water. They were likewise very short of lead for running their bullets, of paper and thread for cartridge-making, and of every sort of medicament. This last was the most serious lack of all, since great numbers of them were labouring under that terrible disease, the smallpox, which always struck so fatally in America. We had orders not to handle any belongings left behind by them in their flight, nor to occupy any dwellings where they had lodged. Their dead and dying being left behind in considerable numbers, we provided regular burial squads, consisting of men who had already had suffered from the disease.

The sickly season of the year had come, and the Americans felt such terror of death by smallpox that they suffered themselves to be inoculated against it by their surgeons – that is, the fetid matter from one suffering from the disease was pushed under the fingernails of a healthy man. The intention was that he should take the disease, but not badly, and thereafter be immune against the natural infection. In America, ever since the great epidemic of 1764, it had been the custom to have inoculation frolics: to make up a cheerful party of persons of both sexes, in a spacious house with an enclosed garden, for all to be infected together. They could count on two or three days in bed, and six weeks of quarantine spent in pleasant lounging, drinking, amatory and political discourse, cards, prayers, and horse-play. In these conditions, a few were seriously sick, some died, but very many lives were saved. However, the present was no time for such a frolic; the poor creatures being already worn out with the hardships of war and unable to endure the poison. Moreover, no quarantine was possible and those who were inoculated passed on the disease to their comrades. The surgeons were ordered to discontinue the practice, but this did not hinder the men from inoculating one another and performing the operation in a very dirty manner. Though the fatigues of our march were great, we could, I am sure, have overtaken the Americans had instinct not kept our men from increased exertions: we slackened our pace sufficiently to avoid infection from our sick adversaries.

The Canadians showed violent resentment against the invaders for bringing so much ill luck and so little real money into the country. Many of them had been influenced by hopes of gain or by prophecies of a British defeat to take a decided part in the Americans' favour; and this against the warnings of their priests, who refused to confess any rebel. Nor could the clergy have well been expected to adopt any other course of action, Congress having been so highly indiscreet, not to say double-faced; for while pretending great attachment to the Habitants in their struggle against British oppression, they had at the same time published an address to the people of England, which totally contradicted this. The address warmly indicted Parliament for the countenance it had given to Popery in Canada, which they declared to be the dissemination of impiety, persecution, and murder in every part of the globe. Now, though Congress had assured these Canadian rebels, but a few months before, that 'we will never abandon our Canadian friends to the fury of our common enemies', they were left exposed to the heavy penalties annexed to the crime of aiding or comforting His Majesty's foes. The retreating army could only recommend the rebel Habitants to throw themselves on the mercy of the Government; and this, though ironically intended, proved to be good advice. To the best of my knowledge (I was in Canada for twelve months after this) none of them was either imprisoned or otherwise punished by General Carleton.

On June 17th we came to the hills of Chambly, some forty miles beyond Sorel and there took possession of the old French castle. We found that all the wooden buildings of the place, and all the boats too large to be dragged up the rapids, had been reduced to ashes. The French people hereabouts were greatly relieved that in this new war they were not to be called up for forced labour, as in the old days. We were told that General Montcalm had once visited the castle in the last war to assure himself that it was in a correct posture of defence; the peasants came dropping on their knees about him to implore him to abate the oppression and tyranny of their militia captains. Among others, the owner of the saw-mill complained that, loyal subject of King Louis though he was, he had been reduced to extremities by the Corvée – his harvest was lost, his family starving, and his two remaining horses had perished of overwork that very day. Monsieur Montcalm looked sternly at him and then, thoughtfully twirling his Cross of St Louis, remarked: 'But you have the hides still, have you not? That's a deal, a great deal!'

It was at Chambly that our General Prescott had been captured by General Montgomery in the preceding year, together with eleven ships and several companies of men of the Seventh and Twenty-sixth Regiments. He was soon exchanged with the Americans for General Sullivan, who was now opposing us, and put in command of Newport, Rhode Island; but there he was again captured by a party of raiders as he slept, and carried off without his breeches. He was a very peevish, foolish man and suffered tortures from the gout. Our people then bought him back in exchange for another American general, Charles Lee; not so much because they needed poor General Prescott as because the return of General Lee to an enemy command would embarrass General Washington, to whom he was openly hostile. General Prescott won the jocular title of 'Continental Currency'.

On the next day we occupied the redoubts at St John's; where the enemy in their precipitation had left behind twenty-two pieces of cannon, unspiked and with their ammunition unexploded. The country that we had marched through until we came to Chambly was flat and without interest except for the unusual birds, flowers, trees, and animals. We saw grey squirrels, and deer; and Smutchy Steel had the misfortune to catch a creature resembling a bushy-tailed grey cat streaked with white, which was pursued towards us by a pair of our dogs. This animal, which the Canadians called Devil's Child, discharges its urine when attacked, which infects the air with an intolerable stench. Smutchy had his black linen gaiters soiled and was fain to strip them off and abandon them. There were sweet wild raspberries in plenty beside our route.

A bear crossed a clearing and I had a snapping shot at him, but missed. This animal was rather shy than fierce; he would seldom attack a man, and fled in terror from a yapping dog. Only in July was he dangerous, for this was his mating season and he was abominably jealous. Then he grew very lean for passion and rage, and abstained from eating. His flesh acquired so disagreeable a relish that the Indians would not eat him; but, this season over, he became fat again and ate his kill of honey, and of wild grapes and other autumnal fruit.

Of trees there were an infinite and delightful variety, many of them excessively tall, and very few exactly corresponding in foliage or bark to British trees. For example, there were three different sorts of walnut-tree – the hard, the tender, and the bitter. Of the tender, the wood of which was almost incorruptible in water or the ground, the Canadians made their coffins; the nut of the bitter yielded a very good sort of lamp-oil; the nut of the hard was the best to eat, but caused costiveness. There were beech and elm in great abundance, and the sugar-bearing maple, and cedars, and wild plum, and cherry.

But every local advantage is set off by disadvantages. When we camped at evening we were obliged to clear off the underwood and cut away the small trees from about us: on such occasions we were constantly assailed by enormous swarms of mosquitoes. They could not be kept from attacking us even by the smoke or flame of large fires, which we were always obliged to kindle. The fine perfumes and blooming abundance of such luxuriant regions as these are thus lost from enjoyment by man. For the loss of peace and comfort caused by angry and odious vermin nothing can compensate; and an Englishman's blood being richer or less hardened against mosquito bites than the American's, he suffers almost to madness.

We pressed on for a week past the swamp of St John's and Nut Island, until we reached the northern reaches of Lake Champlain, which was narrow and long, running south for a hundred miles to Crown Point, where it was linked with the smaller waters of Lake George. For want of boats we could not pursue the enemy farther, and they had several armed vessels on the lake besides. But we had seen them safe out of Canada, and between the smallpox and the fighting they had in a month lost five thousand men. The smallpox accounted for by far the greater number of these. We heard that at one time two of their regiments had not a single man in health, another only six, a fourth only forty – two more were nearly in the same condition. If the rest of the war were to take the same course, we would soon be home again. However, we were obliged to pause now in order to transport a fleet up to Lake Champlain sufficiently strong to outgun the enemy's schooners which patrolled it and prevented our further advance.

CHAPTER XIII

THIS HIGHLY important task of shipbuilding was commenced on July 4th, the very day that the United Provinces signed the famous Declaration of Independence, formally breaking their ancient connexion with the Crown and people of Great Britain. This declaration anticipated by a few days the arrival of Admiral Howe at Staten Island, close to New York (where his brother, the General, was in command of an expeditionary force that had landed there) with orders from King George for the pair of them to act as Commissioners for restoring peace, though at the eleventh hour. Colonel Paterson, the Adjutant-General of the Forces, was sent with a letter to General Washington as the Commander-in-Chief of the American armies, stating that the Commissioners were invested with powers of reconciliation, and that they wished their visit to be considered as the first advance towards that desirable object.

After the usual compliments, in which, as well as through the whole conversation, he addressed General Washington by the title of 'Excellency', Colonel Paterson entered upon the business by saying that General Howe much regretted the difficulties which had arisen, respecting the address of the letters to General Washington. For, a few days before this interview, General Howe had sent a letter directed 'To George Washington, Esquire', which the latter refused to receive, as not being addressed to him in his official capacity. Colonel Paterson explained that the address was deemed consistent with propriety, and founded upon precedents of the like nature, by ambassadors and plenipotentiaries, where disputes of difficulties of rank had arisen. He added that General Washington might recollect he had himself last summer addressed a letter to General Howe, 'To the Honourable William Howe, Esquire'. Lord Howe and General Howe, he said, did not mean to derogate from the respect or rank of General Washington, for they held his person and character in the highest esteem; and the direction, with the addition of '&c., &c., &c.,' implied everything that ought to follow. The Colonel then produced a letter, which he did not directly offer to General Washington, but observed that it was the same letter which had been sent, and laid it on the table with the superscription 'To George Washington, &c., &c., &c.'

The General declined the letter. He said that a letter directed to a person in a public character should have some description or indication of it, otherwise it would appear a mere private letter. It was true that '&c., &c., &c.' implied everything, but they also implied anything. The letter to General Howe, now alluded to, was an answer to one received, under a like address from him, which the officer on duty having taken, he did not think proper to return, but answered it in the same mode of address. He should absolutely decline any letter directed to him as a private person, when it related to his public station.

Colonel Paterson then said that General Howe would not urge his delicacy any further, and repeated his assertions that no failure of respect was intended.

After an exchange of views on the subject of the treatment of prisoners on both sides, Colonel Paterson proceeded to say that the goodness and benevolence of the King had induced him to appoint Admiral Lord Howe and General Howe, his Commissioners, to accommodate this unhappy dispute; that they had wide powers and would derive the greatest pleasure from affecting an accommodation, and that he (Colonel Paterson) wished to have this visit considered as marking the first advances to this desirable object.

General Washington replied that he was not invested with any powers on this subject by those from whom he derived his authority. But, he said, from what had appeared or transpired on this head, Lord Howe and General Howe were sent only to grant pardons. Those who had committed no fault, wanted no pardon. The Americans were only defending what they deemed their indisputable right.

Colonel Paterson said, 'That, your Excellency, would open a very wide held for argument.' He confessed his apprehensions that an adherence to forms was likely to obstruct business of the greatest moment and concern.

Colonel Paterson was treated with the greatest attention and politeness during the whole business, and expressed acknowledgments that the usual ceremony of blinding his eyes had been dispensed with. At the breaking up of the conference, General Washington strongly invited him to partake of a small collation provided for him, which he politely declined, alleging his late breakfast, and an impatience to return to General Howe, though he had not executed his commission amply as he wished.

While these two royal Commissioners, the Admiral and the General, were endeavouring in their civil capacity to effect a reunion between Great Britain and the Colonies, in order to avert the calamities of war, Congress seemed more determined in opposition. They ridiculed the power with which the Commissioners were invested 'of granting general and particular pardons to all those who, though they had deviated from their allegiance, were willing to return to their duty'. Their general answer to this was that 'they who have committed no fault want no pardon'; and immediately entered into a resolution to the effect that 'the good people of the United States might be informed of the plan of the Commissioners, and what the terms were with which the insidious Court of Great Britain had endeavoured to amuse and disarm them, and that the few Americans who still remained suspended by a hope, founded either in the justice or moderation of their late King, might now at length be convinced that the valour alone of the country was to save its liberties.'

This was immediately followed by another resolution, in order to detach the Germans who had entered into the service of Britain. It was penned in these words:

'Resolved, that these States will receive all such foreigners who shall leave the armies of His Britannic Majesty in America, and shall choose to become members of any of these States, and they shall be protected in the free exercise of their respective religions, and be invested with the rights, privileges, and immunities of natives, as established by the laws of these States; and, moreover, that this Congress will provide for every such person, fifty acres of unappropriated lands, in some of these States, to be held by him and his heirs as absolute property.'

So there was clearly no other course to be followed but to prosecute the war with energy: and the campaign began with an attack upon Long Island and the capture of New York. Yet the same aggrieved Captain Montrésor, whose remarks upon the supposed blunders of the British I have already quoted, was very hot against this attempted reconciliation. He stigmatized as a greater blunder than any: 'The sending of the two Howes out as Commanders-in-Chief and Commissioners for restoring peace, with the sword in one hand and the olive-branch in the other; and these two at the same time avowedly in the Opposition and friends to the Americans!' It is true that General Howe did not prosecute the war with remarkable energy, and that the memory of his elder brother who had died in America in the previous campaign, greatly beloved by the colonists, made him more tender than he otherwise might have been towards them. He rejected the view common to most of his subordinates that 'we must be permitted to restore to the King his dominion of the country by laying it waste and almost extirpating the present rebellious race, and upon no other terms will he ever possess it in peace.' Yet Captain Montrésor's hint of General Howe's disloyalty to the royal cause cannot be readily accepted; nor the story that was current in the barrack-rooms that the King had warned both General Howe and General Clinton, when they evinced reluctance to serve in America, that they must either do so or starve. It was, I believe, more sloth than disloyalty that kept General Howe from pressing his advantage at the close of this year, when General Washington was almost beat and the war only kept alive by this eminent soldier's peculiar courage and by the steadfastness of a handful of his adherents, to whom Congress showed itself a worse enemy than any officer of the Crown.

Mention has been made of German mercenaries serving with our forces. To their participation in the war and to that of our Indian allies, the strongest objection was raised both by the Americans themselves and by the Whig Opposition in Great Britain; though hardly with reason, granted the propriety of fighting a war at all. Was there any novelty in the hiring of German mercenaries either by ourselves or by any other nation? There was not. In the Seven Years' War we had employed great numbers of them upon the battlefields of Europe, where the war was won that freed America from the power of the French. Protestant Germans had been called into Great Britain itself to help in the suppression of the Jacobite rebellions of 1715 and 1745: as was natural, seeing that we had set a German Protestant dynasty upon the throne of England, while the defeated Papist dynasty had been Scottish. The Sixtieth Regiment, or Royal Americans, consisting of four battalions who were foreigners almost to a man, had not only protected the colonies from the incursions of the Indians under Pontiac but had been used as a police force against the turbulent border people of Virginia and Pennsylvania, to the great gratification of the provincial Assemblies of those colonies. Or was the consideration that these merce-naries were Germans, rather than Swiss or members of some other nation, a source of irritation to the Americans? Again, no. Great numbers of Germans were already residing in America and had been welcomed as the most peaceable, industrious, and valuable immigrants of all; and I have already quoted the resolution of Congress offering citizenship and land to every German soldier who cared to desert. (The ingenious Dr Franklin made sure that this offer came to the notice of those for whom it was intended, by printing it in German and wrapping it around a large number of packages of tobacco, which he allowed to be captured by Hessian foragers; it had a magnetic effect upon intending deserters.) When the question was later raised of a common language, other than English, to unite all the States under a Federal Government, the German was very favourably considered and, but for the opposition of those who favoured the Hebrew, would, I believe, have been adopted.

Or was the vexation that the Americans felt caused by a sense that the Germans should never have been employed in a civil war of British against British? Then the Americans should certainly have refrained from an appeal to the Canadian-French to rise against us, and should never have sent an army to annex Canada; since this was a war of aggression and not to be represented as one fought in defence of their own liberties.

The fact was, the Americans were aware of the very low point to which the war establishment of Great Britain and the Empire had been reduced, and believed that the regiments that could be spared for the purpose of suppressing the Revolution would be totally insufficient for the purpose. A number of Highland clansmen forced to leave their homes because of elevated rents and the poverty of the soil were glad to enlist in our Army; but few other recruits could be beaten up, even among Irish Papists, notwithstanding the increased value of the bounty paid on enlistment and a dangerous leniency in assessing the requisites of height, age, and health in a serving soldier. Nor was the militia of Great Britain in a fit state to be called out for the defence of their country, to take the place of troops sent abroad. The Americans did not reckon on our raising mercenaries at the tremendous expense that was clearly necessary. They believed we would consider that the wisest course was to cut our losses at once: for the cost of the war had already enormously outweighed the possible financial gains to be won by victory. But Great Britain never reckons profit and loss in a monetary sense when she considers her national honour at stake. There was talk of supplementing our forces in America by the hire of twenty thousand barbarous and hardy Russians from the Empress Catherine, and almost they were sent; but the Empress was in the end persuaded to refuse by her friend King Frederick of Prussia. She wrote to King George in her own hand, somewhat impertinently, to the effect that she had not only her own dignity to consider, but his also. To lend him troops in such numbers would be to imply that he was one of those monarchs who could not suppress with his own armies a rebellion in his own domains. Besides, she would not risk the loss of her brave subjects in another hemisphere of the globe, and so far removed from all contact with herself. This was a great disappointment to our people in America, who considered that the employment of the Russians would be in the highest degree politic; not only were they good soldiers and accustomed to extremes of cold and heat but, not having any connexion with America, nor understanding the language, were 'less likely to be seduced by the artifice and intrigue of those holy hypocrites in Congress'.

However, there are always soldiers to be bought somewhere on the Continent, if the price offered be high enough: for in Germany especially soldiers are like cattle, and, in loyalty to the rulers whose property they are, and, in hope of plunder, will go wherever they are led or driven. They are trained, like spaniels, by the stick. The Duke of Brunswick had a few soldiers to sell. He was a relative by marriage of King George and undertook to provide four thousand infantry and three hundred dragoons in return for fifteen thousand pounds a year paid into his Treasury during their absence abroad, and thirty thousand a year during the two years following their return to Germany. They themselves were to receive the English pay corresponding with their ranks. As a Prince who professed to study the interests of his country, the Duke only detached from his regular forces two battalions of infantry and the dragoons, nor did he supply any horses with the latter. The remainder of the contingent were makeweights of an extreme wretchedness, young boys and worn-out old men unprovided with any material of war or the simplest soldier's necessaries: they must be clothed and armed on their arrival at Portsmouth. The officers were veterans, living on half-pay which the Duke now threatened to withhold from them if they would not march at his orders.

The Landgrave of Hesse drove a harder bargain with King George, for he had better troops to offer and was well informed of our exigencies. The Hessians were tall, vigorous, well-trained men and so docile that it has always been a proverb in Germany that Hessians and cats are alike born with their eyes closed. He had twelve thousand of them disposable, and thirty-two pieces of artillery. The pay was to be English pay, but a bounty of £110,000 a year was also to be given the Landgrave so long as the troops remained out of his Principality, and for a twelve-month afterwards. For every soldier killed in action a compensation of thirty dollars was also agreed upon. Moreover, England was to pay for clothing and equipping these troops, and the manufacturers of Hesse were to enjoy the profitable contracts. The Landgrave followed the grocer's fashion of his cousin of Brunswick in, as it were, sanding his sugar and adultering his tea: he mixed in with his Hessian subjects the off-scouring and scum of every barrack-room in Europe. By these means he raised his country from squalor to affluence, built roads, libraries, museums, seminaries, an opera house, and I do not know what else for the comfort and delight of his remaining subjects.

As for the troops sold to King George by the Margrave of Anspach, they were a bad case; they were forced aboard the transports that were to take them overseas by the use of heavy whips and volleys of musketry. Yet this was not a numerous contingent, and for the most part the Germans were as ready to do what was required of them as our own sailors forced to serve by the press-gang – which, by the bye, was exceedingly active at this time. We served beside the Brunswickers on several occasions during the campaign in the North but seldom with any sense of pleasure or security in their companionship. Except for 'Old Red Hazel', as our soldiers named General Riedesel, their commander, his two well-trained regular battalions, and the dragoons, they were like a stone round our necks. There seemed no intermediate age among them between grandparents and grandchildren, with the grandparents in the majority; they marched ill, worked slowly, complained much, were ridden with terror of death and were, in brief, wholly unfitted for an active and stern campaign in the frightful woods and deserts that we were to pass through. The famous Prince de Ligne has remarked that a soldier is not at his best when the sap has ceased to mount; most of these poor fellows were already withered – leaf, branch, and root.

A great outcry was also made when it was learned that we were employing Indian warriors against the colonists. It is true that the Indians were cunning, savage, and relentless, but if one side thought fit to employ them as scouts and skirmishers, the other would have been mad to forgo the same military advantages – for they were unequalled in this sort of warfare. It must be noted that the Americans were the first to invite the savages' assistance in their war against us; for in 1775, while we hesitated, Congress had determined to purchase and distribute among them a suitable assortment of goods to the amount of forty thousand pounds sterling to gain their favour. They also sent a speech to them, couched in the simple language always used on such occasions:

Brothers, Sachems and Warriors! We, the delegates from the twelve United Provinces, now sitting in general congress at Philadelphia, send their talk to you, our brothers.

Brothers and Friends, now attend! When our fathers crossed the great water, and çame over to this land, the King of England gave them a talk, assuring them that they and their children should be his children; and that if they would leave their native country, and make settlements and live here, and buy and sell and trade with their brethren beyond the water, they should still keep hold of the same covenant chain, and enjoy peace; and it was covenanted that the fields, houses, goods, and possessions, which our fathers should acquire, should remain to them, as their own, and be their children's for ever and at their sole disposal.

Brothers and Friends, open a kind ear! We will now tell you of the quarrel between the counsellors of King George and the inhabitants of the colonies of America.

Many of his counsellors have persuaded him to break the covenant chain, and not to send us any more good talks. They have prevailed upon him to enter into a covenant against us; and have torn asunder, and cast behind their back, the good old covenant, which their ancestors and ours entered into and took strong hold of. They now tell us they will put their hands into our pockets without asking, as though it were their own; and at their pleasure they will take from us our charters, or written civil constitution, which we love as our lives; also our plantations, our houses and goods, whenever they please, without asking our leave. They will tell us that our vessels may go to that or this island in the sea, but to this or that particular island we shall not trade any more; and in case of our non-compliance with these new orders they shut up our harbours.

Brothers, we live on the same ground with you; the same land is our common birthplace; we desire to sit down under the same tree of peace with you; let us water its roots, and cherish its growth, till the large leaves and branches shall extend to the setting sun and reach the skies. If anything disagreeable should ever fall out between us, the twelve United Colonies, and you, the Six Nations, to wound our peace, let us immediately seek measures for healing the breach. From the present situation of our affairs, we judge it expedient to kindle up a small fire at Albany, where we may hear each other's voice, and disclose our minds fully to one another.

Subsequently they besought the Mohawk nation to whet their hatchets against us, on the curious ground – among others – of the probable increase of Popery in Canada! They also persuaded Jehoiakin Mothskin of the Stockbridge Indians to take up the hatchet, who warned 'King' Hancock, as the President of Congress, that they must expect him to fight not in the English, but in Indian fashion. All that he desired was to be informed where his enemy lay. He was regularly enrolled in the Army of Massachusetts. Sir Guy Carleton had attempted in that same year to win over the Six Nations from the seductions of Congress; and had accordingly invited their chiefs, in a language they understood, to 'feast on a Bostonian and drink his blood'. This meant no more than to partake of a roasted ox, of the sort brought up from New England by the drovers, and to wash the meat down with a pipe of wine. The American patriots, however, affected to understand this speech in a literal sense. It furnished a convenient instrument for operating upon the passions of the people, the more so as it was well known that the Mohawks were not by any means averse to eating the flesh of their foes. This they did (as also the Ottawa, Tonkawa, Kickapoo, and Twighee tribes), not from bestial gluttony but from a belief that the estimable qualities of the man they had slain, which centred chiefly in the heart, could be absorbed by the victor who partook of that organ roasted. Most Indians, however, looked upon cannibalism with the same horror that we Europeans do.

How to look upon our Indian allies was a question which greatly puzzled us. It was said that at one period the Indian had not been so ready to pick quarrels and perform wanton barbarities as then; and that Penn the Quaker, who founded the Commonwealth of Pennsylvania, proved that his policy of fair, generous, and pacific dealings with the Indian chiefs was never disappointed by any act of spite or ingratitude on their part. He went unarmed in their midst, ate of roast acorns and stirabout with them, and even on occasion shook a leg at their dances. When the first English settlers arrived in New England they were at pains to cultivate the friendship of the Indians of those parts, who often succoured them in their worst need, when nearly dead of cold and starvation. It was only a hundred years later that wars arose. The cupidity or cruelty of individual colonists had excited the communal vengeance of the Indians. Similarly, the Quakers did not forfeit the affectionate respect of the tribes until overreaching them in the purchase of lands: they had covenanted to buy from them as much land as could be walked around in a day, but ran rather than walked, and quite omitted the usual custom of sitting down now and then, for good manners, for a smoke and a meal.

Gradually a very evil view came to be adopted by the colonists as a means of stilling the prick of conscience: namely, that the Indians, being heathen, had no claim upon the Christians for fair treatment. In the frontier districts of America, such was the readiness with which offence was taken against an Indian, that should a warrior so much as slap a white man for committing a criminal offence, the act would be eagerly seized upon and exaggerated, the whole white population would rush to war and the tawny men be hunted from their homes like wild beasts. Nor did even the adoption of Christianity serve to protect Indians from the animosity of the Americans: as witness the massacre in 1763 of the twenty peaceful, psalm-singing Conestogas at Lancaster in Pennsylvania by a mob known as the Paxtang Boys – they first burned the Indian houses early one morning and killed six, and later broke into the workhouse where the magistrates had put the fourteen survivors for safe keeping and killed them all – man, woman, and child. They scalped them too, in order to collect the bounty offered by the Government of Pennsylvania for Indian scalps of either sex. The Paxtang rascals were not grudged this blood-money or in any way punished for their wicked action.

There was no peace possible on the frontier, since agriculture, by which the settlers lived, and hunting, by which the Indians lived, are trades that cannot be practised compatibly in the same district; the plough and axe are always the victors. The Indians naturally resented being driven from their ancestral hunting-grounds, without compensation, and from the tombs of their ancestors, and were at their wits' end how to act, for the American pioneers were terrible men and avenged their own losses, ten lives for one. These pioneers, being of a restless and dissatisfied turn of mind, not untainted with greed, instead of keeping within provincial territories where millions of acres remained unoccupied (but all had to be paid for), crossed the boundary lines into Indian territory with no by-your-leave and began to behave in a most proprietary manner. The Indians' only hope now was to recover some of their losses at least by profiting from the disagreements of the white men. They sold their military services to the French, the English, the Americans in turn at the highest price obtainable.

They became, in effect, banditti and made war not for glory or for any generous motive but only in order to obtain money, rum, guns and powder – necessities of which they had once never even known the name. Many of them were now regular camp-followers, and periodical beggars at the gates of forts and trading-houses; and the alms or stipends given them to avert their hostility were sufficient, wretched as they were, to destroy their self-dependence. Supplied with munitions of war, their propensity for mischief was quickened by the increased means of gratifying it; and they knew their power to enforce tribute by intimidation.

Thus the Indian, who in his natural state was generous and hospitable and expected generosity and hospitality, had been to such a degree spoilt by his dealings with the white races that to expect him either to forget his wrongs suffered at their hands, or to relinquish new appetites that he had acquired and return to his simple state, was manifestly foolish. Even Dr Franklin, who had disapproved of the Paxtang Boys and who had joined in the 'good talk' quoted above between Congress and the Six Nations, believed firmly that the only solution to the problem of how to deal with the Indian was a gradual extermination of all the tribes.

Revenge is the emotion that burns most hotly in a savage's breast, nor is he careful to distinguish between a particular wrongdoer and the wrong-doer's associates. Let me take an example from the abuses of the fur trade, which were almost incredibly enormous. The Indians assembled at Montreal, Three Rivers, or some other trading-place in the autumn, to exchange the skins taken in the past season for arms, ammunition, blankets, and other articles needed for their support. For two or three hundred pounds' worth of peltry, the product of a whole year's hunting with all its concurrent fatigues and dangers, the hunter was plied with brandy and then given a kettle, a handsome firelock, a few pounds of powder, a knife, a duffel-blanket, some paltry ornaments of tin for his arms and nose, together with paints, a looking-glass, and a little scarlet cloth and cheap calico to make a dress for his squaw. The whole was not worth one twentieth part of the furs which the Indian had brought in. If then the firelock which he had been given proved as unserviceable a weapon as it too often was, despite its showy appearance, and burst at the first discharge, wounding him, he would be like to seek revenge, not on the fraudulent trader who supplied the weapon, but indiscriminately on the first party of white men whom he encountered.

CHAPTER XIV

IN THE journal of occurrences that I kept posted throughout this Northern campaign, a gap occurs between June 26th 1776 and the last day of September in the same year. These three months were among the busiest and happiest in my life. In company with all the rest of the Army under the command of General Sir Guy Carleton I was busy shipbuilding. As has already been remarked on an earlier page, vessels were needed on Lake Champlain to oppose the American fleet now cruising up and down upon its waters and hindering our advance, for on either side of the lake the virgin forests presented an impenetrable barrier to invasion. Sir Guy had sent in haste to England for a number of gunboats, in sections. These could be reconstructed in the dockyard at St John's which lay, as I have said, well above the rapids of Chambly that hindered direct navigation between Lake Champlain and the St Lawrence River. There was a vessel of one hundred and eighty tons, the *Inflexible*, in building at Quebec; Sir Guy ordered her to be taken to pieces and shipped up the river in *batteaux* together with the carpenters who had been engaged upon her construction – she was likewise to be completed in the dockyard at St John's. The *Inflexible* carried eighteen twelve-pounders and was ship-rigged. Two schooners lay at Montreal, the *Maria* armed with fourteen six-pounders, and the *Carleton* with twelve. These were sailed at once to Chambly and, rather than lose the time of taking them to pieces, it was proposed by the naval lieutenant who commanded the *Inflexible*, to convey them upon a cradle overland to St John's; and that the troops should be called upon to build a road for them. General Carleton acquiesced and we set to.

This was a very slow and tedious business, for it meant felling thousands of trees and levelling off the stumps, and hauling the vessels forward by means of cables fixed to windlasses at every twenty yards. Our men lost a great deal of weight by sweating, and much skin from their hands; but this hard work was on the whole beneficial to their health, as was also the copious ration of spruce beer now served out to us as a preventive of scurvy, for we were again living mainly on salt meat and biscuit. At the end of a week, in spite of all we could do, we had advanced the *Maria* no more than half a mile. The General, perceiving that this mode of conveyance would engross more time than the other, ordered the two schooners to be taken to pieces and reconstructed at St John's in the same manner as the *Inflexible* and the gunboats. Some of us were then employed in the hauling of two hundred laden *batteaux* up the Chambly rapids, which demanded almost incredible exertions; others at the ropewalk at St John's in making rigging; others in assisting the Royal Marines to improvise stocks and slip-ways, to reconstruct the schooners and the gunboats (which carried one brass field-piece apiece, varying from nine-pounders to twenty-pounders), and to build, besides the *Inflexible*, a flat-bottomed *radeau* or raft, to mount twelve guns and a number of howitzers, also a gondola with seven nine-pounders, numerous long-boats and a whole fleet of *batteaux*.

My company happened to be employed at first in outpost duty, three miles into the forest from St John's, where we occupied a block-house protected by a screen of Indian scouts. It was very pleasant thereabouts. As well as the other Canadian trees before mentioned, the paper birch grew plentifully around us, and that rich shrub, the aralia, with numerous flowers and a high pink fragrance, also a wild gooseberry, the honeysuckle of the garden and strawberries in abundance. We were next set to building barracks for the troops and artificers. American block-houses never varied in plan. They were constructed of roughly trimmed logs, placed one on the other and overlapping at the corners. Each length of timber in roof and walls was so jointed as to be independent of the length next to it; so that if a piece of artillery were played upon the house only that timber which was struck would be displaced; indeed if one half of the construction were completely shot away, the remainder would stand firm. There were two storeys, a shingle-roofed loft, and a chimney constructed of brick or dressed stone; the upper storey, reached by a ladder, projected two or three feet beyond the walls of the lower one. Each of these storeys was supplied with a couple of pieces of cannon and four port-holes, so that the cannon could be trained in any direction to resist attack. There were also loop-holes for musket-fire in all the walls, and holes in the floor of the upper storey – both at the projected sides, to fire down upon the enemy if he attempted to storm the lower part, and in the centre should he succeed in gaining an entrance. Each block-house served to lodge a hundred men, and there was an apartment in the upper storey for the officers. The building was made weatherproof by clay daubed in the interstices of the timber, and proved snug enough in winter if the two fireplaces were well supplied with dry fuel. A block-house was a very strong defence, unless the enemy succeed in firing it by incendiary shells, especially when placed on a little knoll in a clearing, as ours was. The barracks that we built were only rough affairs, of untrimmed logs, but sufficient to the purpose; it was not to be expected that they would be needed for more than short use. Some of our men became handy with the axe, though it would have needed years more at the task to make them equal in expertness with the Canadians or with our American foes.

On one of the rare days when I was free to leave my duty for an hour or so and visit the dockyard I found that the two schooners, *Maria* and *Carleton*, had been reconstructed in a mere ten days; but even this prodigy of expedition was surpassed by the building of the frigate *Inflexible*. Her parts only arrived at St John's on September 4th, her keel was laid on September 7th, and she was all rigged, armed, and ready to sail by the end of that month. Only sixteen shipwrights built her, and one of these was so badly wounded by an adze on the third day as to be of little service.

One evening at the block-house, where I happened to be in command, since the two company commanders were absent at a general conference of officers, and the other officers were out hunting with their dogs, I visited my chain of sentries. I heard a challenge at some distance away and a deal of argument. Presently Mad Johnny Maguire and another soldier brought along for my examination two persons who wished to pass through the posts.

'Who are they, Maguire?' I asked. There was only a feeble light and they had halted at a few paces from me.

'That I do not know, Sergeant,' he grumbled. 'I have had many and various customers pass through my post since first I stood sentry, but here's a pair of queer fish that beat and bewilder me entirely. There's one who says he's a warrior, though, by Jesus, he's a squaw unless my two eyes are liars; and the other calls himself Captain Brant and speaks better English than I do, yet he's a rogue of an Indian for all that. Who knows that they an't a couple of Yankee spies, such fancy fellows as they are, upon my soul!'

I brought them into the officers' apartment at the blockhouse, where I could question them at greater convenience and without the inquisitive stares of the men. Maguire had not deceived me as to their appearance. The person describing himself as Captain Brant was clearly an Indian of blood, tall, slender, and of commanding appearance. He wore elegant deer-skin leggings trimmed with gold lace, moccasins with diamond buckles, a blue military topcoat with tarnished silver buttons, good lace at his cuffs and throat, a pair of excellent duelling pistols in a holster at his side, and several strings of wampum about his neck. His head was bare and shaved clean, but for his scalp-lock which was dyed vermilion. His face was streaked with war-paint.

The other, introduced as Sweet Yellow Head, wore a red velvet dress with a silver girdle, bangles, and long Spanish ear-rings, a necklace of garnets and small white beads, a wrapper of white fox fur, and a fusil slung on his shoulder. His face was delicately powdered and rouged, and his long, braided hair, with its vermilion-streaked parting, was dyed bright yellow. He walked in an exaggerated mincing manner, rolled his eyes coyly about, constantly tossed his hair, and in a word behaved exactly as a gay young ensign would do at a regimental theatrical performance when called upon to play the heroine in a farce.

Captain Brant spoke severely to this creature in the Mohawk language, which I did not understand, and evidently bade him conduct himself in a more seemly fashion. Then he asked me in a deep voice: 'Sergeant, where are your officers?'

I told him that I was in command at the block-house and asked him his business. He replied: 'I am a great man of your allies, the Six Iroquois Nations. I am Thayendanegea, the Mohican war-chief. My English name is Captain Brant. In the month of May last I fought in the company of Captain Forster at the engagement of The Cedars, thirty miles from Montreal. We took near five hundred Yankees as prisoners; it was great glory. Yet for the love of Jesus Christ, who died for us all, I restrained my warriors from taking scalps and from burning alive a Yankee captain whom they had secured.'

'That was a noble action on your part,' I remarked dryly, 'and I applaud you for it.'

'I thank you, Sergeant,' said he. 'I persuaded my people to do no more than nick a few of their ears, as we do with cattle, to claim possession.'

'That must have angered them excessively,' said I, and he nodded.

'But,' said he, 'they were revenged upon our people for this indignity, for when some of our warriors stripped them of their military finery to wear themselves, the smallpox infected them, and many died.'

He told me that the American Congress had not only refused to ratify a cartel for an exchange of prisoners made between Captain Forster and Colonel Arnold, on the ground of Captain Forster's inhumanity in the matter of the nicked ears, but had demanded him to be delivered up to them by General Carleton to answer for his conduct in this 'atrocious massacre'. Congress, Thayendanegea conjectured, took this unheard-of course to spite Colonel Arnold – though why they did not rather fulfil the agreement than leave their hostages in the hands of so merciless an enemy, only Mr Samuel Adams perhaps could explain.

Said I: 'No doubt Mr Adams and his kind regard their troops only when Heaven makes them victorious.' I continued: 'Yet I find it a little singular that you speak English so well, and that the name of the Saviour is on your lips. How does that come about?'

'Easily answered,' replied Thayendanegea (which means, in the Indian tongue, 'holder-of-the-stakes-made-by-the-parties-in-a-wager', or 'mediator'). 'As a youth I attended the missionary school of the Reverend Doctor Wheelock at Lebanon in the colony of Connecticut, and embraced the Christian religion. I am a well-read man. I assisted Doctor Barclay in revising the Prayer Book as translated into the Mohawk tongue, and Doctor Stewart in translating the Acts of the Apostles. I have myself made a translation of the Gospel of Saint Matthew and have converted numbers of my people. I am acquainted with many English men of letters, including your famous Doctor Samuel Johnson, the lexicographer and author of that pertinent pamphlet, *Taxation no Tyranny;* to whom his *fidus Achates*, Mr James Boswell, introduced me.'

'From whence do you come now? I had no notification of your approach.'

'From General Herkimer of the New York Militia at Unadilla, in New York Colony, one hundred and fifty miles to the south-west of this place. He called me to a conference.'

'You have been treating with the enemy!' I exclaimed. 'Do you dare tell me so?'

'He had been my friend and neighbour on the Mohawk River and I could not refuse to parley with him. It might be that he wished me to take a letter to Sir Guy Carleton, offering his submission to the King. I agreed to a rendezvous at Unadilla, where a large hut was to be erected in an open space between his encampment and ours, a mile apart from each. We covenanted to leave our arms behind us, and to meet with only ten men in the suite of each. This was done.

'We shook hands and exchanged general talk, he seeking to know my mind, I to know his. The old man spoke much about peace and how greatly to the advantage of the Mohawk nation it would be if we embraced the sacred cause of Liberty, or at least remained neuter. I spoke to him like a brother, warning him that the cause of rebellion was one accursed of God. He grew impatient. He asked me how much money Sir Guy Carleton had paid me for my services in the cause of tyranny, and undertook to double this sum and to give every member of my suite a rifle-gun and other gifts if we would join his forces. I was offended. I asked, did he take us for dogs? I sent my warriors running back for their rifle-guns to show him that we were not beggars. They discharged a volley in the air and uttered a war-whoop, to his great consternation. He said: "You have broken the covenant," and he was right. For in my impetuosity I had forgotten that no weapons were to be brought to the hut. Then he said: "Tomorrow let us meet again, tomorrow in the morning, and talk quietly without anger on these matters." We agreed that only four of us were to be present at the meeting.

'That evening a squaw, who was living as the wife of an American named Waggoner, came secretly to me; she made me swear to spare her husband if she disclosed a plot to take my life. I swore. She was a good woman and to be trusted. "Father," she said, "tomorrow the General and his three men, my husband among them, will have pistols concealed in their shifts. When he proffers you his snuff-box and you go forward to take a pinch, it will be the signal to them to murder you with a volley."

'The next day I went to the hut with my three men, all unarmed. The General spoke to me very mildly, like a dove, and asked me whether it would be the act of a Christian to permit savages to fall upon my co-religionists, to burn, kill, and destroy them. I replied: "When I was at Lebanon, learning at the feet of the Rev. Dr Wheelock, he told me that war was evil. But, Neighbour Herkimer, were not your people the first to take up arms in this war?" "Never mind about that," said he hotly. "God damn it, my friend, we were but defending our liberties." I said: "The Rev. Dr Wheelock, that excellent man, taught me and my friends that the first duty of a Christian was to fear God, and the second to honour the King. Now you both blaspheme God and try to win me, by bribery, to take up arms against your King." He turned pale with rage and said to me: "Let us not bandy arguments, Captain Brant, but know each other for open foes, since you will not listen to the voice of conscience. Let me offer you a pinch…"

'I interrupted him: "No, General Herkimer, I will have none of your SNUFF." At that word, which was a signal, five hundred of my warriors sprang from the long grass where they had lain concealed, dressed in their war-paint and brandishing their arms. "Now," says I, "you see, Neighbour Herkimer, how unwise it would have been for me to accept your snuff. I would have sneezed you into your graves. You are in my power, but since we have been friends and neighbours, I will not take advantage of you. We have both been at fault, I to forget yesterday that rifles were not to be brought near to the hut; you to come here today with a pistol concealed in the bosom of your shirt. But let me assure you of this, that if ever we meet again before the hatchet is buried, I know well which scalp, of our two, will adorn the other's wigwam." So we came away through the woods, and here I am.'

'Can such treachery be possible?' I asked. 'I have heard that General Herkimer is much regarded among the Americans as a gentleman of honour.'

'That may be,' he replied. 'But with American gentlemen there is this reservation to their code of honour: as none would ever believe the oath either of a whore or an Indian, so one would not hold oneself bound by any oath sworn to a whore or an Indian. They seldom cloak their sentiments, neither. I would rather a thousand times deal with a poor French farmer or a raw British subaltern officer than with General Washington himself, who is the most honourable man in their whole army, barring only Philip Schuyler.'

It came into my mind to ask him what his opinion was upon negro slavery, which I regarded as a detestable practice and incompatible with the Americans' claim in their Declaration of Independence that all men have an inalienable right to be free. Says he: 'That is a matter for their consciences. The Congress of Massachusetts raised the subject two years ago, but upon their considering the ill effect that a motion condemning slavery would have upon their friends in the South, the matter was allowed to subside. I am told that General Washington is an attentive and just master to his slaves, and there are many like him in this respect. Should I settle down to farm an estate when this war is over, I should assuredly employ negro slaves. No Indian is apt to the labour of farming, and no white man would care to work for an Indian. Besides, the blessed Bible countenances slavery, saying, "Ham shall serve his brethren."'

I objected to this conclusion, declaring that there was a world of difference between service and slavery. Then he told me a fable current among the Indians, which I consider not unworthy of repetition here.

The Great Spirit, God, made the world. It was solitary and very lovely to look upon. The forests were rich in game and fruit, the prairies abounded in deer, elk, and buffalo, the rivers were well stocked with fish. There were also countless bears, beavers, and other fat animals, but no sentient being was present to enjoy these good things. God then spoke: 'Let us make man.' And man was made; but when he came up before his Maker he was of a pale, whiteish colour. God was sorry, He had pity on the poor pale creature and did not resolve him into his original elements, but permitted him to live. God tried once more, determined to improve upon his handsel task, but inadvertently ran to the other extreme, making his second man of a black colour. He liked this black man even less than the white, but at the third trial he was fortunate enough to accomplish his design: he made a red man, and was content.

These three men were very poor at the first. They had no lodges, no houses, no tools, no traps – nothing. All of a sudden down came three large chests from the sky on ropes; and the three men, the red, the white, and the black, watched their gradual descent. They landed in a meadow. God said: 'My poor white eldest-begotten, you shall have the privilege of first choice from these boxes. Open them, examine them, choose your portion.' The white man opened, looked, chose. The chest was filled with pens, ink, paper, sand-castors, spectacles, nightcaps, chairs and tables. He put spectacles on his nose, a nightcap on his head, took a pen in hand, sat down on a chair at a table, and began writing out his accounts; nor did he pay any further attention to the proceedings. God thrust the black man aside and said, 'I do not like you, the red man has the next choice.' The red man chose a box filled with tomahawks, war-clubs, traps, knives, calumets, and a variety of other useful objects. He thanked his Maker and went off proudly into the wilderness. God laughed with pleasure. The black man had what was left. It was a chest full of hoes, sickles, water-buckets, ox-whips and shackles; and this slavish lot has been the lot of the negro ever since, and so will ever be.

I should add to this that the Indian would slay a negro with as much unconcern as a dog or a cat. I heard of an Indian woman of rank who had a negro slave captured in a raid from an estate in Virginia; application was made to her for the return of this negro, who was a remarkably tall, handsome fellow. She listened quietly to the American officers who came after their property, but was determined not to gratify them. Instead, she stepped inside her lodge, fetched a large knife and walking up to her slave, without any sign of emotion plunged it into his belly. 'Now,' she said to the Virginians, 'you can have him if you wish.' The negro lay writhing on the ground in agony until one of the warriors compassionately put him out of his pain with a blow of a tomahawk.

While I was thus agreeably conversing with Captain Brant, his companion had sidled out of the room and begun conversing with the men in the lower apartment. Hearing angry oaths, loud laughter, and shrill falsetto cries, I hastily drew out the wedge, or stopper, from a musket-hole in the floor and gazed down. Sweet Yellow Head had taken a fancy to Sergeant Buchanan, who had just entered the room, and now pursued him with disgusting advances, which the troops found very ludicrous but which enraged the Sergeant beyond measure. He flung the Indian from him, seized a musket and would have shot him had I not loudly bawled out: 'No, no!' from above him. This prompted Corporal Terry Reeves, who stood by, to knock up the musket and disarm him; and I then hurriedly descended the ladder by way of the trap-door.

Thayendanegea came after me, and thanked Terry and myself for our good services. Said he: 'If this sergeant had killed my poor cousin, I should have been obliged in honour to avenge the death, as his nearest relation. I am deeply grateful that no blood has been shed. My poor cousin is a *bardash*, born neither one thing nor the other; God knows the reason but not I. He is a brave man and the fleetest on his feet of our whole nation. He has married three men and been faithless to all. I should not have let him out of my sight.'

He called his cousin to him, and publicly chastised him, to the great amusement of the barrack-room. Thereupon, bidding me good-day and assuring me that I could always call upon his services were I ever in need of them, he went off under the escort of Terry Reeves and another soldier in the direction of the camp, taking Sweet Yellow Head with him. On the following day another Indian arrived at the block-house with a fine buck upon his shoulders and a great basket of cranberries in his hand, as a present from Thayendanegea for myself. I recognized the Indian as Strong Soup, his locks still untrimmed, his face still black in mourning. He told me that his squaw having died, his Sachem had at length permitted him to join the war-party; soon his luck would change. I would have given him a present; but he refused, saying that Theyendanegea had forbidden him either to ask for or accept anything, unless it were a fill for his pipe. The fresh meat was so seasonable that I filled his pouch with tobacco, and he appeared gratified. He skinned the buck for me very dexterously and cut it into steaks. The cranberries we boiled in maple sugar.

CHAPTER XV

TO JUDGE from reports that reached us, the American armies were a most haphazard and disorderly assemblage of men. They could be roused to desperate and courageous action in defence of their homes, but were altogether impatient of discipline. The regimental officers were often the servants, not the masters, of the men; and known for their obsequiousness and easy humour rather than for military qualities; they were also constantly engaged in struggles among themselves as to who should be the highest in office. We all heartily laughed at a report which our informant, an American volunteer in the transport service, swore was true, of a Connecticut captain shaving one of his men, for a fee, on the parade-ground; and how another was cashiered for stealing and selling his men's blankets, which he did as a revenge for their having insisted that he throw his pay into the common stock! However, one of our people who had served in 1762 upon the Spanish Peninsula told me that this very sort of thing was known in Europe also: at Lisbon a Portuguese officer would supplement his meagre pay with journeyman tailoring and cobbling, and his lady would take in washing – nor was he above asking alms of passers-by as he mounted the guard at the gates of the Royal Palace at Lisbon. Yet at least, our man said, the Portuguese service had never suffered from the spirit of insubordination that reigned in the American. There it was so strong that, as we now know, General Philip Schuyler resigned his command rather than be forced to 'coax, to wheedle and even to lie to carry on the service'; and that General Montgomery had on more than one occasion informed his officers that unless they would obey his orders he would quit the service and leave them to cut one another's throats at their pleasure. General Washington himself declared that, had he seen what was before him, no earthly consideration should have wooed him to accept the chief command; for discipline was impossible while men considered themselves the equals of their officers and regarded them no more than a broomstick. These three were all generals in the aristocratic way, and were greatly hindered in their efforts to improve the fighting efficacy of the forces: by two or three humbly born colleagues who had won general's rank, not because of proved military experience or talent but because of their known inveterate rancour against the British and a talent for ingratiating themselves with members of Congress. General Washington made many enemies in Congress by his too ingenuous plea that gentlemen and men of character should be given the preference in the allotment of commissions.

The length of service fixed by the various provincial Assemblies for their militia varied greatly, but more than a year was never required of them. Volunteers might engage themselves to serve for six months or a year, for six weeks or four weeks, or for as long as it pleased them. A militiamen might buy a substitute and many did so, from the dregs of the population; the American Army contained numbers of ruffians so hired, transported felons and such, to whom the Mosaic allowance of thirty-nine lashes was a contemptible punishment – they would offer, after receiving it, to suffer as much again for the fee of a pint of rum. These regiments were continually fluctuating between camp and farm. A soldier would announce unceremoniously to his captain: 'See here, Neighbour Hezekiah, my old woman writes to tell me that she has but one nigger and my boy left on the farm, since the hired man was called. She has all the ploughing to do yet for the winter grain, and ten loads of hay to get in. Within ten days she'll be lying in, and my elder daughter is tarnal sick with fever. I believe now, I must make my way home to Waterbury tomorrow, battle or no battle.' When he went, he took his firelock and the powder and shot served out to him, and seldom returned. The Connecticut men were the worst offenders in this respect; but the staunch Virginians accused the New Englanders in general of having an 'ardent desire to be chimney-corner heroes'.

When we British enlist, we know what to expect from a soldier's life; but with the Americans the motive of Liberty, which spurred a peaceful man to take up arms on an impulse, was often insufficient to nourish him as a soldier. Washington is reported to have written to Congress at this very time that: 'Men just dragged from the tender scenes of domestic life, unaccustomed to the din of arms, and totally unacquainted with every kind of military drill are timid and ready to fly from their own shadows. The sudden change in their manner of living, particularly in their lodging, brings on sickness in many, impatience in all, and such an unconquerable desire of returning to their respective homes that it not only produces shameful deserters among themselves, but infuses the like spirit into others.'

There was a great shortage among them of arms and ammunition, the commissariat service was irregular and often the men went hungry; for Congress had little force of authority and could only request, not compel, the States of the new Union to provide rations for the troops stationed on their soil. Much meat and flour was lost by careless transport; for example, wagoners with a load of pickled pork would broach the casks and let the liquid escape in order to lighten their load, so that the meat would be rotten before it could be issued.

There was great quarrelling and jealousy among regiments sent from different parts of America. The 'Buckskins' of the South railed against the 'scurvy damned Yankees' of the North, the Yankees against 'the haughty coxcombical Buckskins'; but these enemies were united in their dislike of the people of the middle provinces, who seemed to them undisguised Tories and rank Britainers. How they fought the war out together to a successful issue is a standing mystery to us all; despite the gross errors and treacheries of our fellow-countrymen in England, and the aid that the French, Dutch and Spanish afterwards provided.

While we were completing our fleet, the Americans at the foot of the lake were attempting to strengthen theirs; though in addition to all the other disagreeables enumerated above, the continuance of the smallpox among them, the increasing sickliness of the season and an utter destitution of all necessaries and comforts made it almost impossible for them to hold their ground. An average of thirty new graves a day were dug daily at Crown Point. Had it not been for the reckless and indomitable spirit of Brigadier-General Benedict Arnold, their commander, they were already vanquished. General Arnold, who had considerable maritime experience from his trading voyages to the West Indies, asked Congress for three hundred shipwrights to be sent at once to help his men construct thirty gondolas and row-galleys, to reinforce the three schooners and the sloop already under his command. The gondolas were a large sort of *batteau* manned by a crew of forty-five; the row-galleys were keeled and carried a sail, their complement being eighty men, and were both faster and handier than gondolas in open water. He also desired a frigate of thirty-six guns to be constructed, but the carpenters did not appear in the numbers expected. By the end of September, when we were ready with our fleet, the newly constructed American boats numbered only four galleys and eight gondolas. These were, however, not vessels to be despised, being very well-gunned. Their fleet could at any single time bring thirty-two of their eighty-four pieces to bear on any quarter; ours disposed of only forty-two guns in all, if I leave out of computation the radeau *Thunderer* and our single gondola, both of which proved unmanageable. Our advantage lay in the frigate *Inflexible*, which was better than any vessel they could boast, and in our crews. For not only had a number of regular naval officers offered themselves for lake service, from the royal squadron that lay at Quebec, but two hundred prime seamen from the transports had come forward too. Arnold's fleet was manned by landsmen, the three hundred mariners from Marblehead that he expected not arriving until after the engagement.

On October 4th, our little squadron sailed out under the command of Captain Pringle, with General Carleton aboard the schooner *Maria*, our flagship. That same day my company, with the rest of the light infantry, had orders to draw a week's rations and move along the western shore of the lake, a screen of Indian scouts protecting us. This we did, and strove to keep abreast of the fleet. The woods were very dense and because of quays and other difficulties we could make no more than a few miles a day before bivouacking at night. General Carleton had expected to find the enemy on the eastern side of the lake, and in consequence we had no hope of witnessing a sea-battle. However, we were lucky enough to come within sight of Valcour Island, some forty miles on our way, at the moment when General Arnold's fleet, which was sheltering in a small bay within full view of the shore, no more than half a mile from us, was engaged by our ships. Valcour Island was two miles in length and had high cliffs. There were many Indians friendly to us encamped upon it at the time. The Americans lay in a half-moon formation, close together. They were so disposed, we observed, that few vessels could attack them at the same time, and these would be exposed to the fire of the whole fleet. Our ships, driving with a strong north-easterly wind, had overshot the island, before discovering the enemy, and were under the disadvantage of attacking from the leeward.

We were spectators of the whole battle, taking post on the shore, each company digging itself an entrenchment, from behind which it could prevent the Americans from landing, if they were forced ashore by the cannonade of our ships. It was an awful and glorious sight. A little before noon, Arnold's flagship, the *Royal Savage* schooner, and four galleys got under way. They ran down with the wind against the *Inflexible* frigate as she drew slowly under the lee of the island. But the *Royal Savage* was mishandled and dropped to leeward, coming unsupported under the fire of the *Inflexible*, which headed our line. Three heavy shot struck her and she ran ashore on the southern point of the island, where a great number of our gunboats came up and silenced her from short range. One of them was sunk. As an Irishman, I was proud to know, watching this fine fight, that the matrosses who served in the gunboats were drafts from the Irish Artillery in Chapelizod. General Arnold abandoned the ship and trans-ferred himself and his flag to the *Congress* galley; where for want of trained artillery-men he was obliged to point and discharge every gun himself, stepping rapidly from one to the other, like a person touching off fireworks on the King's birthday.

The *Inflexible* could not make any headway, because the wind was blowing from the north, but the schooner *Carleton*, which followed, caught a flaw from the cliffs which fetched her nearly into the middle of the American fleet. There her commander intrepidly anchored with a spring on her cable; which is to say, a rope attached from one side of the stern to the anchor, by hauling on which a broadside could be fired at the foe alter-nately from starboard and larboard. There she did much execution among the Americans, sinking a gondola, but suffered severely herself. Half of her crew were killed or wounded, her commander was knocked senseless, another officer lost his arm and only Mr Edward Pellew, a lad of nineteen, remained fit for duty. (He was to become Admiral Sir Edward Pellew, now Commander-in-Chief of our Forces in the Mediterranean, and the most famous of all our frigate-captains in the French Wars.) The spring being shot away, the *Carleton* swung bows on to the enemy and her fire was silenced. Captain Pringle in the *Maria* signalled to her to retire, but she could not, and two gunboats came to tow her off; her hull had been pierced in many places and she had two foot of water in her hold. Meanwhile the commander of our radeau *Thunderer*, not being able to come into action, went with a boat's crew aboard the *Royal Savage* and turned her guns on the two larger enemy galleys, *Congress* and *Washington*, who returned the fire.

The noise of the cannonade was tremendous and was tossed back and forth in echoes across the water between cliffs and woods. Our men held their fire, for the enemy were out of range; but the Indians, who had rushed up on hearing the noise and were dancing about and yelling in their excitement, fired a great number of useless shots across the strait. We also distinguished musket-fire from the cliffs of Valcour where a large number of Indians were congregated. Two enemy boats were now seen making for the *Royal Savage* in an endeavour to retake her; but in good time our people set her on fire, and before the boarding-party could arrive she was blazing hotly and soon blew up with an awful roar.

There was a lull in the fighting, of which we took advantage to eat our biscuit and dressed meat, and some of us even slept a while. As the afternoon wore on, the breeze changed direction, and to our great satisfaction we saw the *Inflexible* slowly tacking up the strait, followed by the *Maria*. By evening she had worked to within point-blank range of the American squadron and with five heavy broadsides silenced the whole line.

It was growing too dark to distinguish friend from foe, and to avoid being rammed or boarded, the *Inflexible* fell back; the whole squadron thereupon anchored in a line across the strait. The Americans had suffered severely. Two gondolas and the *Congress* galley had been badly holed, most of the officers had been killed or wounded, and they had blown away nearly all their ammunition. We had orders to keep a strict watch all night lest the Americans attempted to land on our coast; for that seemed their only hope of escape from this predicament. The breeze fell and a thick mist overspread the lake. We were very cold that night and crowded near our campfires.

When at about eight o'clock in the morning a southerly wind sprang up and the view cleared, we were surprised to find the Americans gone. General Arnold had contrived to bring the whole fleet away safely under cover of the mist and the extreme obscurity of the night. They had stolen out 'in Indian file', as it were, through a gap in the British line, with a dark-lantern on the counter of each vessel to guide the one following. The *Congress* brought up the rear of the column, for Arnold was always a laggard in any retirement. Three months before he had been the very last man to quit Canada in the retreat, riding back for a view of our vanguard and with difficulty escaping capture by our light infantry. For his beaked face, angry eye, and towering ambition the Indians named him 'Dark Eagle'.

General Carleton was enraged to kind that his prey had escaped, and was in such a haste to take up the pursuit that he sailed off without leaving us orders; so we kept our posts for another day but sent out scouts, north and south. That evening he returned again, believing that the Americans had gone up the lake, after all; but we brought him word from the Indians that the vessels had been seen hiding behind Schuyler's Island, eight miles down; they were weaker by two gondolas, which could not be patched into sea-worthiness, or lake-worthiness rather, and had been scuttled.

The wind had now turned round and was blowing up the lake. It hindered both the Americans' retreat to Crown Point and our pursuit. Their remaining six gondolas were slow and delayed the rest of the fleet, so that though they had a start of fifteen miles, from the moment when General Carleton once more turned about, he had a hope of catching them. Our orders were to continue down the lake so soon as daybreak came. We could not move rapidly enough to be present at the coming battle. It took place at noon that day, October 13th, in the lower narrows of the lake, at a place called Split Rock, about twelve miles above Crown Point and thirty from Valcour Island. The wind was now north-east. Here the *Maria* schooner, with the *Inflexible* and *Carleton* close astern, having greatly outdistanced our gunboats and the rest of the fleet, came up with the Americans. Split Rock was a strait between two rocks, just wide enough for our large ships to pass through, and with a very rapid current. The action lasted two hours; we could hear the noise of the cannonade brought down the wind, and mended our pace; though we knew that this was to no purpose.

Our ships were victorious; but General Arnold by fighting a delayed battle contrived to save part of his fleet, which got safely away, viz. two schooners, the sloop, two galleys, and one gondola. But the *Washington* galley struck early in the action and was taken with a general aboard, General Arnold's second-in-command; and, as for the *Congress* galley and the four remaining gondolas, they were lost. By General Arnold's orders they were pulled to windward where our men could not pursue, except in small boats, then steered into a creek about ten miles from Crown Point, but on the other side of the lake from us, run ashore and set on fire.

As usual, General Arnold was the last man to leave the post of danger. He stayed aboard the *Congress* until the flames had fairly caught her, whereupon he clambered along the bowsprit and leaped down to the beach. He and his men came safe back through the woods opposite Crown Point, after a skirmish with the Indians; then he saw a great smoke across the water, and learned that the Americans, on hearing the noise of gunfire from up the lake, had at once sent off their sick and baggage from Crown Point, set all the buildings there a-fire, and were now falling back on the fortress of Ticonderoga. So General Arnold went there likewise. Ticonderoga was fifteen miles below Crown Point, and its newly built fortifications were reputedly of great strength: they had been laid out for the Americans by a Polish military engineer who has since become famous on other fields of action – the patriot Thaddeus Kosciusko.

It was three days before we rejoined General Carleton, who had landed at Crown Point, and four more before the main body of our army appeared, transported on a fleet of *bateaux*. Meanwhile we encamped in a place called Button-Mould Bay, after the abundance of pebbles, thrown up on the shores, of the exact form of a button mould. Where those of wood or horn could not be procured, they would make excellent substitutes. When the Army came ashore we continued towards Ticonderoga, with our light infantry companies to the front as usual, in two columns, one on either side of the lake. Some of our vessels approached within cannon-shot of the enemy works, but the attack was not pressed. General Carleton judged it too late in the year to continue the campaign, even if we could quickly reduce Ticonderoga, which appeared doubtful. The intention had been to push on into the heart of New York State and to take the town of Albany on Hudson's River, where there was an important arms manufactory. General Carleton foresaw that communications with our base in Canada would be long and difficult, and now that the Americans had their harvest in, great forces of frontiersmen and militiamen from every part of New England would be free to beset us on all sides. It was no light task to march an army, of inferior strength to the enemy, through one hundred miles of tangled forest in the American winter. Old General Phillips, of the Artillery, was for taking a crack at the defences of Ticonderoga, which he swore were easily taken, and wintering there. General Phillips had gained great glory at; the battle of Minden, by galloping his guns ahead to harass the broken French; General Riedesel, who had also been present at this battle, in the service of Prince Ferdinand of Brunswick, agreed with him now that the enemy redoubts were more pretentious than strong. But General Carleton would not heed. 'Let us leave the Americans alone,' he said, 'and they will destroy themselves more effectively than could we: if the events of the past year have been any indication of their quality as soldiers.'

On the last day of October we were withdrawn up the lake, on *batteaux*, much to the relief of the Americans.

The colonies were now in the way to lose the war, largely from their common tendency to set the desire of personal irresponsibility before the ideal of national independence. Boston had been abandoned by us, but New York city and the seaward ports of New Jersey occupied by very large forces. General Howe had beaten General Washington's army in several engagements; and, before the year was out, forced him across the Delaware River into Pennsylvania. Moreover, we had occupied Rhode Island, one hundred and fifty miles farther up the coast towards Boston, and in the coming year a converging attack was to be made simultaneously on the revolutionaries by three armies – ours from the northward, by way of the lakes; the New York army from the southward, up the valley of Hudson's River; and another army from the eastward, with Newport, Rhode Island, as its base, marching through Massachusetts. The King very sensibly decided that the tinder and dry fuel of rebellion lay in the Northern provinces. If the conflagration could be stamped out there, it would die out elsewhere for want of nourishment. The South was green wood, slow to catch, and the Middle provinces were damp straw. It was unfortunate, however, and shameful too, that this plan of campaign, which was a Ministerial secret, should have been disclosed to members of the Opposition and published by them in the newspapers, copies of which reached America. The enemy were thus forewarned, many months in advance.

Our return up the lake to Canada was without adventures, and the beauties of Nature that unfolded themselves before us seemed the more fascinating now that for some months at least the hideous spirit of war need not hover between. The autumnal hues of the woods surpassed language, for their variety, and afforded infinitely more satisfaction than when all had been uniformly green. Sunsets and rainbows appeared tumbled among the forests. The gaudy reds and yellows intermingling with the dark green of the pines and the shadows of the rocks, as we threaded our way between the islands, were reflected in the placid blue waters of the lake. At some points the mountains were in a blaze of glory, and yet as Sergeant Fitzpatrick remarked, 'like the Burning Bush that astonished Moses, they are not consumed'.

I had brought a fishing-line on the campaign and amused myself by baiting a hook with a shred of ration beef and seeing what I could pull up. One morning I had a bite; I struck, and pulled up a singular dark brown fish with horns like a snail and a cat's visage. As it lay struggling in the bottom of the boat, I observed that it could lift or retract these horns at pleasure. I had the curiosity to touch one of them, to see whether it would draw them completely into its head, but I was punished by a severe numbing sensation, passing right up my arm, which stung so painfully all that day that I was incapacitated for duty. It was explained to me by Lieutenant Sweetenham, who was in our boat, that the horns of this creature, which was called a cat-fish, were naturally charged with the electric fire or principle which the celebrated Dr Franklin first drew down from heaven by a kite-string. Its flesh proved fat and luscious, very much like that of the common eel; the fins were bony and strong.

On November 2nd we disembarked at St John's again and were marched for two days through the woods till we came to Montreal, the first inland city of the American continent. It was built upon an island thirty miles in length and about twelve in breadth, formed by a divarication of the River St Lawrence, and containing two large mountains. The Ninth were to be quartered upon the Isle of Jesus, which was an island within this island, being about three miles in length and a little less in breadth and contained by two inlets of the river. The Isle of Jesus was cleared of woods and had a church and a number of farmhouses, as well as the barracks put up for our accommodation, and provided us with a very agreeable place of repose after our labours of the summer. The troops were rarely given leave of absence to visit Montreal, but we were one day marched by Lieutenant Kemmis to the top of the higher mountain of the Montreal island in order to enjoy what he described as the most sublime view in all North America.

This was a most fatiguing journey, for there was no regular path to be discovered, and we were in full marching order for the exercise; but even the greatest grumblers of the company confessed, when we gained the summit and had well eaten and drunk of what we brought with us, that the prospect was an ample compensation. A vast coloured sea of woods stretched out before us, through which whirled the huge stream of the St Lawrence. Far below us in the near distance we could descry the city of Montreal in the sunlight. It made a narrow oblong square, on a low ridge parallel with the river, sloping down evenly to the water-front and divided by regular well-formed streets. All the houses, almost, were whitewashed. A high plastered stone wall surrounded the city, consisting of curtains and bastions; and beyond, except on the waterside, were a dry ditch and a sort of glacis surmounted by a parapet loopholed for musketry. These defences were not strong and had been raised by the French long ago as a protection against Indians armed with bows and arrows, rather than a European enemy. The city was so situated, as we could see, that no works could be raised to enable it to stand a regular siege: for it was commanded by many eminences near by. There were numerous elegant houses in the suburbs, but these did not catch the sun so handsomely as those inside the city, which were covered with tin-plates, instead of shingles, for fear of fire. Fires, due to the inhabitants' attachment to red-hot stoves kept burning all night, had so often destroyed the city that it was now built wholly of stone with sheet-iron shutters to the doors and windows; which gave it, as one walked down the street after dark, the appearance of an assemblage of prisons. We lifted our eyes from the city and looked south-east across the river to the distant hills of Chambly; and beyond them to the Green

Mountains of Vermont, about sixty miles away, capped with snow – the residence of our enemies.

Our English-speaking guide bade us beware of serpents, which abounded in these woods, but he confessed that they were frightened off by the regular tramp of marching boots and would not bite unless surprised by the stealthy approach of a single person in moccasins. Only the copperhead snake, he said, was so torpid and sulky that he would not move out of the path though an elephant approached, but would infallibly strike at him as he passed. I may add, however, that no elephant had as yet visited the American continent; nor was one brought there for a show until some years after the Revolution.

This guide discoursed much upon snakes – the rattlesnake, whose skin, when the animal is enraged, exhibits a variety of beautiful tints, and who gains a new rattle to his tail for every year of his noxious life. Later, I saw two or three of them scuttling from me in the woods. This creature is greenish-yellow in colour, as thick as a man's wrist and about four feet in length. The Indians esteem his flesh as whiter and more delicate than the best fish. His sloughed skin, charred, pulverized, and swallowed with brandy is the best-known specific against rheumatism.

The guide told us a very deplorable story of an American farmer of the Minisink who one day went to mowing with his negroes, but wore boots as a precaution against being stung. Inadvertently he trod on a snake, which immediately attacked his legs, but, as it drew back in order to renew its blow, one of his negroes cut it in two with his scythe. They prosecuted their work all day, and returned home when the sun set. After dinner, the farmer pulled off his boots and went to bed. He was soon after seized with a strange sickness at his stomach. He swelled up and died before a physician could be procured. A few days after his decease his son put on the same boots, and likewise went to the meadow to work. At night he pulled them off, went to bed, and experienced similar sufferings of sickness as took off his father. A little before he expired a doctor came, but, not being able to assign the cause of so singular a disorder, he pronounced both men to have died by witchcraft. Some weeks after, the widow sold all the movables for the benefit of the younger children, and the farm was leased. One of the neighbours who bought the boots, presently put them on, and fell sick, as had happened in the case of the other two. But this man's wife, being alarmed by what befell the former family, dispatched one of her negroes for an eminent physician who, fortunately having heard of the dreadful affair, divined the cause, and applied medicines which recovered the man. The boots which had been so fatal were then carefully examined, and he found that the two fangs of the snake had been left in the leather, after being wrenched out of their sockets by the strength with which the snake had drawn back its head. The bladders which contained the poison, and several of the small nerves, were still fresh and adhered to the boot.

The unfortunate father and son had both been poisoned by wearing these boots, in which action they imperceptibly scratched their legs with the points of the fangs – through the hollow of which some of the astonishing venom was conveyed.

The best specific against rattlesnake bite is the juice of a sort of plantain-leaf: it was accidentally discovered by a Virginian negro who desperately rubbed it upon his leg to soothe the agonies of a bite, as he lay by the wayside. The negro not only recovered from the poison, but was emancipated by his master as a reward for this service to humanity.

The same guide told us also of a small, speckled, hissing snake with spots which glow with a variety of colours when he is enraged; at the same time he blows from his mouth a subtile and nauseous wind that if drawn into the mouth of an unwary traveller will infallibly bring on a mortal decline; for there is no remedy against it. He tried our credulity further with an account of the whip-snake which, he said, pursues cattle through wood and meadow, lashing them with his tail, until overcome with the fatigue of the chase they drop exhausted to the ground, where the whip-snake preys upon their flesh. This was perhaps true, but we could not accept his account of the hoop-snake which thrusts the extremity of his tail into a cavity of his mouth, where it catches fast with an arrangement like a pawl and ratchet, and then rolls forward like a boy's hoop with such extreme velocity that neither man nor beast can hope to escape from his devouring jaws.

There was a silence of a few moments after this tale, which Mad Johnny Maguire took the privilege of breaking, as he was the oldest soldier among us. 'Oh, what a darling monster that must be, from which nobody has ever escaped alive to give so sensible an account of his habits! But he's nothing at all compared with the serpents of Killaloo that Saint Patrick drove out of my country when he first came. They banged all: they could wrap their necks about a rifle-gun and squint along the barrel, and both load and fire it with their tails! But the Saint prayed at them, and waved his staff at them, and told them to quit before the Sunday following, and off they went, howling. The proof that I'm not codding you is that not a single specimen of the breed is still to be found on the shores of Ireland. Let us hope, by Jesus God, that they did not take ship to Canada.'

CHAPTER XVI

MAJOR BOLTON was taken from us to command the Eighth Regiment; they were stationed partly at Magara, by the world-renowned waterfalls which lie between the Great Lakes of Ontario and Erie, and partly at Detroit on the waterway joining Lakes Erie and Huron. We were sorry to lose so considerate an officer, but my private feelings were the more affected by the news of his removal when I learned that Private Harlowe, who was now his orderly, was going along with him. I did not care twopence whether or not I ever beheld Harlowe himself again in the whole future course of 'my versal life', but his wife would naturally accompany him; and let me here confess that for months past I had been tormented by longing thoughts of her. Struggle as I might against the spell that she had cast upon me, her face invaded my dreams and constantly stood before my imagination at all hours of the day, especially when I was in a relaxed condition of body after some heavy duty. I had not set eyes on her since we sailed from Ireland, for the women and children had remained behind with the baggage-guard during our advance to St John's and had been removed to Montreal when we proceeded up the lake. Now, at the first consideration, I was deeply grieved that I should not see her about the camp in the Isle of Jesus, as I had imagined that I would; but, at the second, there came a feeling of relief. For the sick temptation to run on evil courses, as well as the innocent pleasure of looking upon a face that I heartily loved, would be removed by her residence at Niagara. I busied myself in my military duties and began to look forward with keen expectation to the winter, which was the social season in Canada and always passed with great good cheer and merriment – especially in the neighbourhood of Montreal, where there were numerous sports performed in the ice and snow every day, and dances near every night in the better sort of houses. But first came the time called the Indian Summer, marked by a reddish, hazy, quiet atmosphere; the woods were close and warm with the exhalations of fallen and rotting leaves, which bred melancholy thoughts.

However, I was to be absent for some time from my comrades. We had not been in our new quarters above three weeks, during the last few days of which it snowed almost incessantly, so that the ground was covered to a depth of about four feet, when Captain Sweetenham, as he now was, sent for me. 'Sergeant Lamb,' he said, 'Colonel Guy Johnson is inquiring after you, and Corporal Reeves and yourself are to wait upon him this afternoon at his residence near the Place des Armes in Montreal.'

'I do not know the gentleman, your Honour,' said I.

'He is an Irishman, the Superintendent of the Indian Department of our Government and a person of great consequence among the tribes. Colonel Johnson has asked for three months' leave of absence to be given you for a special mission, in case you wish to accept it.'

'I shall be glad to go on any mission,' I answered, 'and the more adventurous the better it will please me. In Corporal Reeves's company I would dare go anywhere.'

'You will hand over your duties to Sergeant Buchanan,' the Captain said. 'Inform him so.'

I touched my tall cap and departed, with a pleasurable sense that my friend Thayendanegea was at the bottom of this business; and, upon my arrival at Montreal with Terry Reeves, I found that it was so. Terry and I made the journey in a hired cariole, a sort of carriage upon runners which the horses of the country could draw with ease, through ice or snow, at the rate of fifteen miles an hour. The people of Montreal were very curious in the way that they fashioned their carioles in every possible variety of design, such as the representation of some beast or fowl, a Venetian gondola, a Quaker shoe, a whale, or a monster goldfish. This one simulated a black swan, and was well provided with blankets. The cold was so severe that the St Lawrence itself was now nearly all frozen over, though there is a ten-knot current at Montreal; but Terry and I were surprised that we felt so little inconvenience from it. The reason was the superior dryness of the air. Perhaps this dryness excused a habit of the Canadian which seemed barbarous to us, namely of allowing his horses, sweating after a journey of perhaps twenty or thirty miles, to stand for hours on end, without any covering at all, outside the door where he had gone visiting.

The journey into Montreal was doubled in length by our driver constantly stopping, whenever he came to a wayside shrine or crucifix, to climb down and say a prayer. He was not to be deterred from this practice even by Terry's threats to cut off his treasured queue with a jack-knife, did he not shorten his orisons. It then occurred to me that the word of command, '*Marche-donc*', spoken to the horse in tones simulating those of his master, would likely enough set our chariot in motion. The plan succeeded, and the driver, hearing our loud farewells, leapt up, cursing, from his knees and rushed after us. It was fortunate that the horses recognized his voice and presently pulled up, for neither Terry nor I knew the word for 'Whoa!', and might well have been arrested for the theft of a cariole. The fur-clad driver was quite breathless from his long run when he climbed up into his seat, which enabled me to anticipate the French sentence which I knew was choking in his throat. *'Je vais le dire au Général Carleton,'* said I, very severely.

Then I offered him a drink of spirits and presently we were good friends again. He only descended for a short prayer at one more shrine, where was represented the sponge, vinegar-bottle, spear, and various other instruments mentioned in the Gospel chapters concerning the crucifixion of Jesus Christ; the whole assemblage surmounted by St Peter's cock.

Montreal presented a very animated appearance, for this was the season when the Indian fur-trappers assembled with their peltry to sell to the resident merchants. The city then took on the appearance of a great fair, with booths adorned with fir-branches set up in all public places for the sale of every conceivable object of utility or luxury. We saw numerous painted, pipe-smoking Indians, with capes over their head and shoulders wadded with feathers, and the squaws dressed in their finest clothes with jewellery, ribbons, and dyed plumes; British officers on horseback in full regimentals of flashing gold, silver, blue and scarlet; merchants whose Parisian extravagance of dress was intended to impress the Indians with an idea of their consequence; priests, friars, lay-sisters; armed parties of British soldiers in travel-worn greatcoats, marching to fife and drum; groups of animated French Habitants of both sexes' the women in long scarlet cloaks, the men in their sleekest furs, and swarms of warmly muffled, exuberant children; fantastic carioles jingling and whirling up and down the narrow streets; and, in the squares, frequent statues of men, monsters, beasts, and birds fashioned of heaped snow and glazed to perfection by pails of coloured water dashed over them.

At the Place des Armes, a sort of square which was used before the Conquest as a parade-ground for French soldiers, we were directed to the house of Colonel Guy Johnson, who had succeeded his recently deceased father-in-law, Sir William Johnson, in his Superintendency. We were given rum in an ante-room, where stood glass cases full of curiosities of Indian domestic manufacture – such as embroidered wampum-belts, pouches and tobacco-pipes of intricate manufacture, weapons of various sorts, and ceremonious head-dresses. The corporal on duty gave us an account of them, and told us among other surprising things that the 'wampum' or shell-beads, strung on leather, which are of universal currency as money among the Indian tribes, are coined in Old England: wampum was formerly made by the Indians themselves in the form of crude beads of baked white clay, but then of sea-shell, which we could cut by machinery much more expeditiously and regularly then they by hand, to the shape and size of the glass bugles worn on ladies' dresses. The shell used was that of the clam, a large sort of scallop found on the coasts of New England and Virginia, and the purple sort was more esteemed by the Indians than the white: they would pay an equal weight in silver for it.

This corporal was one of the armourers employed by the Indian

Department for mending the firelocks of friendly Indians; but he had the week before been wounded in the hand by a drunken Indian and withdrawn from his employment until it healed.

Colonel Johnson presently sent for us, and was most affable. He said, 'My friend Thayendanegea has an invitation to offer you.'

Thayendanegea was at table with him, in a company of several other war-chiefs of the Six Nations – Senecas, Oneidas, Onondagoes, Cayugas, Tuskaroras, and Mohawks – among them the Chief Sachem of the Mohawks himself, by name Little Abraham. This venerable person, it seems, secretly favoured an alliance of the Confederacy with the revolted colonists, and was now doing what he could to incline his inferior chiefs to that course. But Thayendanegea and his very active wife Miss Molly, with whom he lived in monogamous union on account of his Christian faith, were leaders of the opposition to Little Abraham; and their influence seemed to be preponderant at the table. The cloth was spread with beef-steaks, salted bear's-legs, dressed capons, and a number of fricassees and complicated confections in the French style which the Indians universally preferred to our English style of cooking. They were all to some degree intoxicated and had, as was their wont before sitting down to drink, given their weapons into the safe keeping of one of their number, who was pledged for the occasion to keg himself. However, on so ceremonious an occasion it was not to be expected that they would risk their dignity by any recourse to violence. For Indians of rank deemed it highly becoming to accommodate their manners to those of a distinguished stranger, especially a host, and they were wonderfully observant; so that you would seldom find a well-born Indian behaving other than with ease and gentility in the most select company, if a hint were but supplied him, before his entry, of the forms expected. Yet the Colonel was visibly restraining his impatience with the unusual and unexpected ill manners which one or two of his guests were showing. I was told later that the offenders on this occasion had recently been the guests of a Brunswick officers' mess at Three Rivers, and the greater licence for horse-play and raillery there permitted to the intoxicated had given them an incorrect notion of what would be fashionable in Montreal at the residence of a British officer of rank.

Just as we entered, Thayendanegea was addressing in English a Seneca chief named Gyantwaia, or 'Cornplanter', who was gravely balancing a bottle of Madeira upon his nose (distinguished for a gold nose-ring with a little gold bell-pendant dropping to his upper lip). Thayendanegea said very civilly to him: 'My courageous ally and brother, it impresses me vastly to observe your feats of *leger de nez;* but perhaps the hilarity of the occasion has blinded your eye to the fact that *a lady is present!*' – indicating Miss Molly, who modestly turned away. Then improving upon the occasion, for Cornplanter (whose father, by the way, was a Dutch settler from Albany in New York) seemed somewhat abashed, Thayendanegea added: 'And if our generous host will permit it, we will now cease our potations of his very fine liquors, which have somewhat disequilibriated our judgment. Instead, we will keep my wife, Miss Molly, company in a dish of tea, which as the rebellious colonists regard as noxious to all disloyal persons, so we may well drink with pride and gratification in honour of our ally and father, King George.'

Little Abraham was put in a cleft stick by this artful orator. He could not refuse to drink tea without discourtesy to Miss Molly, who was sitting there in the quality of a Christian matron, not an Indian squaw; yet he feared that to partake of the beverage would constitute a declaration in favour of the British side in the conflict, and that the Americans would have news of it, and cease to give him presents.

He said, in halting English, that the Madeira wine had so confused his wits that he did not know with which part of his face to drink, and that therefore he would abstain.

Thayendanegea pressed his advantage – and it was remarkable that, from courtesy to his overlord, he never failed to rise from his chair whenever he spoke so much as a word in his presence: 'My father, were you to embrace the Christian faith and read our Scriptures, you would learn into what shameful dangers the sin of intemperance is apt to lead such venerable old men as the patriarch Noah and yourself; nor would you drink anything but tea, avoiding the fermented juice of the grape. I will send you a present, tomorrow, of fifty pounds' weight of superior tea, to refresh your whole household.'

Cornplanter, who was of Little Abraham's way of thinking, spoke up in his behalf; he had not Thayendanegea's command of English, but was not without eloquence. He said, in substance: 'My brother and ally, I thank you. Your words are very pretty. But we would not wish the Colonel to think that his wines are either so worthless or so injurious to us that we reject them and call for tea; which is no more than boiling water poured upon a dried herb. To call upon him for tea at such a social time would be to violate the custom of the white officers, with which I am well acquainted.'

Thayendanegea smiled pleasantly: 'My dear friend, do as you think fit, and no doubt my revered father, Little Abraham, will do likewise. But avoid provoking the Colonel to laughter. You talk of your knowledge of the white officers' customs, yet know no better than to *eat that peach unpeeled!*'

Leaving his two opponents, both now thoroughly disconcerted, to please themselves whether they drank tea or no, Thayendanegea dismissed the matter as settled. He waved a greeting to Corporal Reeves and myself with his pipe and asked us directly, without preamble, whether we would care to accompany a hunting expedition of his tribe towards the southwest. He said that General Carleton had wished aloud, in his presence, that our light infantry could be acclimatized to American forest life, especially in winter-time, so that they could contend on equal terms with the revolutionaries. Thereupon, said Thayendanegea, he had offered the General to act as schoolmaster to one or two of them at least, who could pass the lesson on to the rest – as in the monitor system now in use in the popular schools of Great Britain. Remembering our names and his debt to us in the matter of Sweet Yellow Head, he had then asked the General whether Colonel Johnson might apply for our temporary release from The Ninth for the purpose of accompanying him; and the General had consented.

Few invitations could have given me keener pleasure, but I had observed that it was regarded as a virtue among the Indians to appear indifferent to good news or bad; that no man would be esteemed a good warrior or a dignified character who openly betrayed any extravagant emotions of surprise, joy, sorrow, or fear on any occasion whatsoever. I replied calmly that if the General approved the plan, it would please me well; and that I and my comrade would be ready to set forth at whatever time was most convenient to him on the following day. Thayendanegea named a rendezvous on the road half-way between Montreal and our barracks, and after the exchange of a few civilities we took our leave.

Colonel Johnson went with us into the ante-room and advised us, if we would have an interesting and prosperous journey, to live as nearly as possible in the Indian style: in which we would find, if we were philosophers, more matter for admiration than for disgust. He said: 'They are, contrary to what is usually said of them, a sensitive, generous, and poetical people. Their apathy is only assumed, and proceeds from no real want of feeling. No people on earth are more alive to the calls of friendship or more ready to sacrifice everything they possess to help an ally in distress. If they appear greedy, that is no more than the reverse side of their generosity. Do you dress Indian fashion, observe their ways, cultivate their goodwill and forget nothing you learn. The hunting expedition on which you are going is, in reality, a missionary tour undertaken by Thayendanegea to excite the whole confederacy of the Six Nations to take up the hatchet for us in the coming campaign.'

The Colonel was then obliging enough to put us in the hands of his clerk, who undertook to provide us with Indian clothes and necessaries, which we signed for, and to claim the amount thus expended from the paymaster of the Regiment. We both chose to wear round beaver caps with flaps for our ears; deerskin leggings, dark blue cloth breech-clouts, red riding-frocks, and fur-lined half-boots; also whiteish capes of buffalo-skin, reduced to silky softness by a laborious process of dressing them with the brains of the dead beast. Terry fixed in his cap a little silver badge of Britannia seated, which was the device verbally conferred on The Ninth by Queen Anne. This later won him an Indian name which I have forgotten, the significance of which was, at all events, 'husband-of-the-woman-with-a-fork'. I may here mention that I was complimented for my willingness to indulge in any adventure or prank that was on foot, with the name *Otetiani*, or 'always ready'. But often we were called 'Teri' and 'Geri'. Both of us had rifle-guns, that we had picked up during the American retreat from Three Rivers, and which were weapons of precision. With a little practice I could hit a board the size of a man's head at two hundred and fifty paces.

'Remember,' said Colonel Johnson to us in parting, 'this invitation is a great honour to you, and I would have you remember that your behaviour and bearing will everywhere be remarked, and that if you win the esteem of your hosts this will reflect well upon the British Army as a whole. I may say that I have satisfied myself by inquiries from your commanding officer that you are worthy of the choice.'

The party, who were at the rendezvous the next day, consisted of Thayendanegea, Strong Soup, and four young warriors of rank, with their squaws. Were I to recount our adventures and wanderings of the next three months it would make a volume in itself. I will be brief then, and confine my account to a few particulars. Thayendanegea took us for a tour of the whole territory of the Six Nations, which lies between Lake Ontario and the headwaters of the Susquehanna and Delaware Rivers. We proceeded first along the shores of Lake Ontario until we came to the Falls of Niagara, and then striking south-west, below Lake Erie, for a short excursion into Wyandot territory, made a circuit through the northern borders of Pennsylvania and so back by the Susquehanna River, the Mohawk valley, and the hills to the westward of Lake Champlain. I was surprised at the high degree of civilization in the several Indian settlements that we visited in the fertile region of the Susquehanna, which must have been very beautiful in the summer. We were everywhere welcomed and feasted and Thayendanegea succeeded by his oratory in persuading many hundreds of warriors to join our standard.

The winter was not expected to be an intensely cold one, nor did it prove so. The approach of intense cold was always known in advance to the Indians by the behaviour of the birds and beasts that migrated in great flocks and droves in the autumn before: bears and pigeons coming down from the northern regions of Canada and swimming or flying over the St Lawrence River into the province of New York, black squirrels, on the contrary, crossing over into Canada at a narrow piece of water just above the Falls of Magara. Nevertheless, it froze very hard already; and on the first night when we encamped in the snowy woods far from any human habitation, Terry Reeves and I stared at each other in fearful surmise, wondering how we should live through the night. The Indians, however, soon cleared away the snow from a place under the shelter of an overhanging rock and piled it up high to form the walls of a hut. The squaws cut and plaited together brushwood hurdles which made the foundation of a roof, over which more snow was heaped, but a small orifice was left to allow the smoke of our camp-fire to escape. The interior of this dwelling soon became extremely warm, and after dining well upon the fresh pork we had brought with us from the city, seethed with potatoes in an iron kettle suspended above the blaze, we wrapped ourselves in our buffalo capes with our feet to the fire and slept in great comfort until dawn; the squaws taking turns to watch and mend the fire.

Thayendanegea amused us with tales of his first experience of life among the white men at Lebanon; how he was frightened by the way that the family gazed at him as if they wished to kill him, and disconcerted by the fire being built at one end of the house and not in the middle, and scandalized by the wife of the Rev. Dr Wheelock when she ordered her husband to go outside and feed the chickens for her, for she was busy. He blacked his face as a sign of affliction and sat apart from them in the barn for two days; but to please his father, who had sent him to this place, he did not run away, and soon he became reconciled to the white man's ways. He told us an anecdote of another young Indian, a chief's son, who had come with him to Lebanon, and was directed by Dr Wheelock's son to saddle his horse. The Indian refused to do so on the ground that this was a menial office, unbefitting a gentleman's son. 'Pray, do you know what a gentleman is?' young Wheelock had asked. He replied, 'I do. A gentleman keeps racehorses and drinks Madeira wine. You do neither, nor does your father. Saddle the horse yourself.'

It was fortunate for us that Thayendanegea could speak English perfectly and could teach us a little of the Mohawk tongue. We learned more for ourselves by a study of the Book of Common Prayer, a copy of which he presented to me, printed at New York seven years previously: which we could compare in memory with the English liturgy. It is not generally understood that there is no language common to all the Indians and that often neighbouring tribes speak in a manner as little intelligible one to the other as the English and French. Nor is it always possible to learn by the use of gestures the name of common things, because of misunderstandings. If a savage wishes to teach a traveller the word for 'head', and puts his hand upon his crown, it is possible to mistake him: he may be wishing to indicate 'top', or 'hair', or 'thought' as resident in the head. When I offered one of my companions, who enjoyed the peculiar appellation of 'Kiss Me', some tobacco from my pouch, and he put out his hand for more, uttering a word which I took to mean 'give me more', it proved later that the significance was 'only a little, please'.

It is said that the very word 'Canada' derived from a misunderstanding. It was the reply given by an Indian to the original European discoverer of the mainland, who haughtily asked, 'What is the name of this desolate country?' When the first settlers came to study the language, the word proved not to be the name of the country at all, but an injurious expletive.

It was a habit of our hosts upon a march to keep perfectly silent and follow one behind the other, constantly glancing from side to side. To this habit we naturally conformed, and soon I came to understand it as not merely due to caution, the constant fear of being surprised by an enemy, but to a concentration of attention upon the natural features of the landscape; so that Indians never lose themselves in a country through which they have once passed. To a European eye, one wild stretch of forest is much the same as another; to the Indian, a rock, or a withered branch, or a knotted bole, is noted for its unique shape, and its relation to neighbouring objects, and becomes an unforgettable landmark.

This was the season when bear, squirrel, wild-cat, and many other beasts of the forest take to their long winter rest in hollow trees or caves, and remain there asleep until the snows melt and the warmth of the sun awakens them. The Indians took pleasure in awakening the beasts before their time, and startling them from their hiding-places to kill them for their fur and flesh. Into such a method of hunting we were soon initiated. One of the party came upon the trail of a bear, which they all agreed was not above three days old; and we followed it for perhaps fifteen miles, though in places it was obliterated by new snow and we had to cast about until we hit it once more. We had three bear-dogs with us, a breed between the bloodhound and mastiff, and when we reached the hollow whiteoak where our quarry was concealed they set up a dismal barking and howling.

We formed a circle around the tree, where the bear's clawmarks were clearly distinguishable on the bark, and waited for the emergence of our quarry. To rouse him out, the Indians had applied a blazing torch to the hole, at the height of a man's head, by which he had entered. Soon thick clouds of smoke could be seen, issuing from a small hole a good deal higher up; the fire having caught the pine-branches that the bear had drawn together to stop the lower hole as a protection from the cold. We heard a choking, a coughing, and a grumbling noise. The bear emerged, a large, reddish brute, half-stifled by the smoke, and scrambled out from the upper hole. The Indians all fired at once, but they are as wretched marksmen with a gun as they are wonderful with the blow-pipe or the bow, and the bear was not even wounded. He descended at his ease, and while his enemies darted away behind trees, he stood blinking stupidly. Then Terry, who was posted on the other side of the tree from him, came around and shot him in the shoulder. This roused the bear to fury, and he made a rush for the warrior Kiss Me, whose head he espied behind a bush, but Kiss Me avoided him by springing nimbly aside. The dogs now set upon Bruin. He killed one with a blow of his paw and hugged another to his breast, but was struck down with a dexterously hurled tomahawk from Thayendanegea's hand, that caught him on the side of the head. I stepped up swiftly and put him out of action with a bullet through his head. The ball that the Canadians used for bear is a very heavy one, of the size of thirty to a pound; but the frontiersmen of New York and Pennsylvania preferred one of half that weight.

The killing of the bear caused much satisfaction, and he was soon flayed with skinning knives, and cut up with tomahawks. The choicest parts were taken off with us, but the rest left where it lay. I noticed that the paws, which are held in great estimation as a delicacy, were gashed with a knife, and were hung in the smoke-hole of our hut that night to dry. Later, we ate them stewed with young puppies, which is a traditional dish on all festive occasions; and not to be despised by Europeans.

It is said that the bear, who never lays in any store of provisions and yet is as fat when the thaw comes in May as when he began his sleep in the previous November, is a good deal subsisted by licking his own greasy paws; but this is an unlikely tale. Natural philosophers believe that the bear, by discontinuing the process of sweating when in this lethargic state, is saved from those losses of the constitution which other animals, not similarly gifted, repair by regular eating and drinking.

When we came into Seneca territory I was greatly astonished with the precision with which the young men of this nation would kill little red squirrels or big black squirrels, such as were not yet a-bed for the winter, with their long blow-pipes, of cane reed. The arrows were not much thicker than the lower string of a violin, headed with tin, and feathered with thistledown. They were propelled through the tube by a sharp puff of the breath, and at fifteen yards these marksmen never missed, but drove them through and through the squirrels' heads. The effect of these weapons was at first like magic: the tube was placed to the mouth, and the next instant the skipping squirrel on the bough fell lifeless to the ground. North America is remarkable for its variety of squirrels, among which are many that burrow and some that fly.

On one occasion, when we were in need of fresh meat, a number of squirrels were seen at the top of a hollow tree; the trunk was hewn at with tomahawks and the squirrels presently slain as they jumped clear of the toppling tree. We were told that such a practice was permitted by the Great Spirit, but not the felling of a tree for the sake of wild honey, which was unlucky and would result in death.

We hunted a great variety of animals – the stag, the caribou, the elk – and came one day to a colony of beavers, where the Indians, with no thought of compassion for these harmless and social creatures, broke down their dam and so drained the water from the artificial lake that they had made in a stream, and left their cabins high and dry. The beavers, hearing a barking from the lake-side, tried to escape from the back doors of the cabins, which led to the woods; where the Indians shot them. The cabins were built upon piles and divided into apartments spread with fir-boughs, each large enough to contain a male and a female. There were also store-houses in each hut proportionate to the number of the company that built it; it is said that each member knows his own store and would scorn to steal from his neighbour. The apartments were very fresh and clean. Beavers are big creatures, weighing from forty to sixty pounds, with a flat, oval tail, rat-like head, and webbed hind-feet. How they sink the piles for the cabins is as absurd a tale as any, but true, nevertheless. Four or five of them gnaw a stake through with their teeth, sharpening one end; with their nailed fore-feet they dig a hole in the bottom of the stream; with their teeth they rest the stake against the bank; with their feet again they raise it and sink it in the hole; and with their tails they whisk clay about it to make it secure. They also interweave branches between the piles to secure them.

The Indians have never considered, as British sportsmen do, the propriety of sparing an occasional pair of any kind of animal for breeding purposes; but have killed all indiscriminately, so that many of the rarer fur-bearing animals are in danger of one day becoming extinct. The most beautiful animal that I saw was the ermine; a squirrel-like creature with fine white fur and a jetty spot at the end of his long, bushy tail. In the summer his tail-tip only would remain unaltered in hue, the rest of his fur turning as yellow as gold. I was shown the track of a marten, which appeared the footstep of a larger animal; but this was occasioned by his jumping along in his pursuit of small birds and giving the marks of both feet at once.

The Indians concentrated their minds so closely upon the chase as hardly to have time for any other topic of interest, though I was occasionally questioned upon life in Europe. I took pains, in answering through the mouth of Thayendanegea, to present my own former condition, and that of my fellow-countrymen in Ireland, as far more splendid and prosperous than it was. My father, I told them (may God forgive me!), was a merchant who owned a number of vessels and a great warehouse full of scarlet cloth, looking-glasses, guns, beads, kettles, compasses, and all useful things. He daily took out a great map of the world and told his captains where to send his goods for trading purposes.

The Indians did not dispute the first part of the story, but disbelieved in the map, when Thayendanegea informed them that the design of the whole world could be reduced to little upon a single sheet of paper. However, they are never so indelicate as to give a person the lie: they said, 'We dare say, brother, that you yourself believe this to be true, but it appears so improbable to us that to assent to it would confuse our minds in respect to other related subjects.' I had with me, in an oiled silk bag, a map of the River St Lawrence and the Great Lakes. They understood the principle of a map: for in giving directions to a traveller, they would often trace on the ground with a stick the course of a river and indicate the natural features of the surrounding country. I showed them Buffalo Creek, down which we were travelling at the time, and 'There are the Falls of Niagara,' I said, 'and there is Lake Erie, and, if you cross the water at this point, in a matter of ten days or so in a canoe you will reach Detroit, and so upwards to Lake Huron.' They were fascinated, and exclaimed 'Wa-wa!' in astonishment.

'Then,' said I, 'if you shrink this map to a tenth the size, the directions and shapes remain the same, and there is room on the paper for my home in Ireland, and for the hot lands in the south, and for all the rest of the world.'

They confessed that they had been at fault and begged my pardon; so that the lie about my father, which I told in order to enhance my consequentiality among them – for they have a great scorn of indigent and ill-born persons – passed as Gospel truth.

Terry and I were in perfect health. He had a flux on the third day, but this was soon cured by a medicine that they gave him, decocted from a sort of fungus that grows on the pine. The squaws are the physicians of the tribe and carry medicine bags containing herbal remedies for wounds, snake-bite, and the commoner ailments. So healthy is the blood of these Indians (and I may say that they have the best teeth and sweetest breath of any people I know – by the bye, the cigar-smoking New York Dutch have the worst) that they recover rapidly from the effects of wounds that would be fatal in a European. I inquired closely into the appearance and properties of these herbs, many of which I was able to recognize in their green state when the summer came again, and add to my military *pharmacopoeia*.

Near Lake Seneca there was a solemn conference of chiefs in a fine grove of butter-nut trees upon a hill, where it was resolved to support the British cause to the utmost. As we approach the Senecan village of Buffalo. Terry was accidentally shot in the leg by a *feu de joie* of welcome to us. He remained there in Cornplanter's lodge to recover of his wound, much to my regret. Terry took an Indian girl to wife, which was an inconsiderate action on his part, for these women are remarkably faithful, and he could not hope to keep her with him on his return to the Regiment; the life of a soldier's wife in a crowded barrack would be death to a girl trained in the freedom of the woods and lakes. However, who am I to judge of Terry? For, on my resuming the journey, I fell into what will be judged by my readers to be still graver error.

CHAPTER XVII

WE WERE passing through the territory of the Wyandots, who are in general hostile to the Six Nations, being allied with their principal foes, the Algonquins and Ottawas; but in the words of one of our warriors, by name Bear-Whose-Screams-Disturb-Sleep, the war-hatchet was 'now buried under a few leaves and sticks, and though restless was not showing its edge to the light of the sun'. In other words, we could count upon passing safely through the territory unless we happened to encounter some Indian who had a private blood-feud against a member of our party. One afternoon, as we were gliding through a forest fifty miles to the south of Lake Erie, close to French Creek, Kiss Me told us: 'I smell a camp-fire. Fish is frying. Let us go to it.' So marvellously keen was his smell that we followed up the wind for a distance of five miles before we came to the encampment; which we approached, weapons in hand, with extreme caution in order to assure ourselves that the strangers were friendly.

We came upon a scene of great animation; two warriors were strutting about in the circle of the fire. They were making speeches and counter-speeches in a resentful tone, with a great amount of descriptive gesture of a very vivid and graceful variety. Though they were clearly incensed, one with another, the common forms of politeness were not outraged: each waited patiently without interruption, though with a mocking smile upon his lips, for the other to finish his say. They continually referred to a woman, the evident subject of their quarrel, who was seated before the fire, with her back turned to me, at a point equidistant from the two disputants. She was dressed in a soldier's red jacket and her hair was tied with a coloured handkerchief. She appeared from her posture to be weeping.

I did not understand a word of their language, yet my heart swelled and shrank to the rhythm of their eloquence, and I had a strange sense that it was my fate, not the squaw's, that was being debated. Suddenly one of the orator's, who, to judge from the murmurs of the onlookers, appeared to be having the worst of the encounter, rolled his eyes, uttered an exclamation of defiance, and rushed at the woman with upraised tomahawk. It was as if to say in the plainest language: 'Sir, if I do not win this prize from you, why, you shall not enjoy her, neither.' The unfortunate creature would infallibly have perished, had not some one at my side uttered the ceremonious word in the Mohawk tongue which signifies 'I am revenged', and fired at point-blank range with his firelock. The Indian dropped with a bullet in his breast, his tomahawk flying high into the air and lodging in the branch of a tree; instantly, Strong Soup, who was the murderer, sprang into the circle, struck the dying man with his club (as symbolically claiming the victory) and began scalping him before the eyes of all. The assembly sat dumbfounded, but doubtless a fierce battle would have ensued a moment later had not Thayendanegea, with a shout to our party to hold their hand, darted forward, pipe in hand, and stood smiling in the friendliest manner imaginable at the company.

The pipe to the Indian is as the white flag to civilized people, and universally respected among them. They did not stir from their pacific postures, but listened to him attentively. It seems that these were a delegation of Ottawas passing through Wyandot territory on a visit to our American adversaries at Ticonderoga. The dead man was the very person who had killed Strong Soup's brother in the previous year and initiated his run of ill luck: his name was Mad Dog, and the murder had been committed in wantonness and in a time of supposed peace. Thayendanegea assured the Ottawas that his own intentions to them were perfectly peaceful; let the nearest of kin to the murdered man charge himself with the continuance of the private feud, but let no new public war be set on foot.

The Indians, who were aware that they were surrounded and at our mercy, were glad to agree to Thayendanegea's proposal. It so happened that no kinsman of Mad Dog was present in the delegation, and though any person might, if he cared, assume the burden of a feud by a public declaration to that effect, nobody loved the dead man well enough to risk avenging him. We all now came from behind our trees, pipe in hand, to join the gathering as guests. I had the curiosity, as I was passing, to glance at the face of the squaw who had so nearly played the Helen to a savage war of Trojans and Greeks – but started back with so profound a shock of astonishment that I was hardly sensible what I did or said in the succeeding moments. The woman was none other than Kate Harlowe. I caught her up in my arms and pressed her to my bosom with a thousand expressions of love, joy, anxiety, and amazement; nor did she resist these endearments, but clung close to me and muttered in a broken voice that she was happy at last.

Kate Harlowe had run from her husband at Fort Chippeway, which lay three miles above the Falls of Niagara, in a fit of vexation. If her account was true, as I have no reason to doubt, she had reproached him for infidelity with a half-breed Indian woman, and he had retaliated by calling her a name which, once spoken by a husband to a wife, is never either forgotten or forgiven. He had then named me as her paramour and she, while denying this, declared that she wished, nevertheless, that it had been so: that she had learned from Johnny Maguire the full story of what had happened at Saintfield. He had thought to cheat me into forging the marriage licence for them, she said, but I had already undertaken to do so in pure chivalry of spirit, etc., etc., and she now heartily regretted her infatuation for a cruel, treacherous, good-for-nothing, prating, Papistical, *hedge-gentleman*. 'Ah, now!' she said, 'between the hedge-gentleman and the gentleman, what a great gulf is fixed – over that no horse can leap or bridge be thrown! Gerry Lamb is a true gentleman and the shame is on you. So good-bye, Hedge-gentleman Harlowe, and be damned to you, body and soul!'

He replied briefly and scornfully that it was a good riddance for him, since Marie Jeanne (the Canadian woman) was worth fifty of her sort of woman; and that the faster she went, the better he would be pleased.

It was her intention to take her life by throwing herself into the river above the Falls aforementioned. We had lately passed by this prodigious cascade and I now shuddered to think of the death to which she had so nearly consigned herself. The pitch which the stupendous volume of water acquired was horrific beyond any previous idea that could be entertained of it. A stupefaction seized me when I beheld an entire furious river, half a mile wide, precipitating itself into so dreadful a chasm. The huge hollow roar of descending waters could be heard at a distance of twenty miles on all sides, and more than forty miles in the current of a favouring wind. From the shock occasioned by it a tremulous motion was communicated to the earth for several rods around, and a constant mist beclouded the horizon, in which rainbows appeared from the shining of the sun. The foliage of the neighbouring pines was besprinkled with the spray, which depended upon the branches in thousands of little icicles. Below this terrible cataract were always to be found the bruised and lacerated bodies of fishes and land animals which had been arrested by the suction of the voracious waves, as also shattered beams and timbers. Yet so strange is the mind of woman that (as Kate assured me), the reason that she did not plunge in and allow herself to be drawn down to death in the Falls was that the water, in which large masses of ice were whirling, appeared to her too cold by far!

As she was hesitating on the bank she was approached by a womanish person who, from Kate's description, can have been none other than the *bardash* Sweet Yellow Head – though what his business in those parts could have been, I have no guess – and spoke very sympathetically with her, evidently divining the circumstances in which she was placed. He told her in broken English, mixed with French, that he was often unfortunate too, that unrequited passion and the cruelty of men made him long for suicide; but that he always refrained, in the confidence that his luck would change if he preserved his equanimity. Kate laughed to be sister in distress to so extraordinary a person, who undertook to help her, if she wished. He would use his influence with a friend among the Ottawas, who was crossing the river that day, to take her with him into the State of New York, where she would no doubt find a new lover among the white settlers of the border, where women were scarce, and there initiate a new and happy life. Sweet Yellow Head assured Kate that her virtue would not be assailed against her will. The Indians were never a lecherous people, as are the negroes, and there is no record of a white woman being violated by one of them, though many have lost their lives and scalps.

The man-woman was as good as his word. Kate returned to Fort Chippeway, where she provided herself with money and clothing suitable for a long journey through the wintry forest, and was soon under the protection of this Ottawa delegation, consisting of twenty persons. Two young chiefs of the party fell in love with her, for white women exercise a certain fascination for tawny men, and each had in turn pressed his suit. She had no liking for either of them and was obliged to adopt the character of a coquette, for fear of offending both. At last it was decreed by the leader of the party that since she had not said plainly, as she should have done, that she would have neither, to avoid dissension in the camp she must plainly declare for one, and be his. So began the dispute which ended in the death of the unsuccessful suitor.

It thus remained to settle with the other chief, to whom Kate now by decree belonged; but that was an easy matter. The Indian, being guilefully informed by Thayendanegea that I was her husband and that perfect love existed between herself and me, was content to relinquish his claim. He was highly gratified when I gave him, in quittance of my obligation to him, the map which had excited so much interest among my companions. The spot where we were now standing I marked upon the map with an allegorical scene in lead pencil: Feathered Turtle (for that was his name) shaking hands with, or rather presenting a flipper to, myself. I was represented as a lamb holding a firelock in the Make Ready position. He shook hands very warmly with me, and wished me long life and many sons.

We spent the evening very pleasantly in the company of these Ottawas, and Kate and I slept together that night, with her blanket beneath and my buffalo-skin above, in the character of man and wife. The ecclesiastical forms of marriage seemed so remote from us here in the wilderness that the invidious word 'adultery' never sounded in the conscience of either. Harlowe had repudiated her, and she him; she and I were now living Indian-fashion, and in Indian-fashion I had won her by purchase. Our reciprocal desires smothered all consideration of the future, for both of us, having been in the company of savages for so many weeks and obliged to conform exactly to their ways, dwelt like them carelessly in the present. But in order to justify myself formally, I permitted myself to be enrolled as a member of the Mohican nation.

Thayendanegea performed the ceremony in the presence of my fellow warriors. He bade me strip myself naked, and with the bone of a wolf, the knuckle-end of which was cut to tooth-like points, he scratched me from the palm of one hand along the upper part of the fore-arm, across the breast and across the other arm to the palm again. In like manner he scratched me from my heels upward to the shoulders, and from the shoulders again to the feet over the breast, and again up the reverse part of my arms and across the back. The lines drew blood from me along their entire extent, but I knew better than to flinch or cry out. He told me then, 'I have made you dreadful,' and desired me roll in the snow; which I did. Then he washed my wounds with a decoction of medicinal herbs and bade me keep apart from my wife for the space of seven days. He also set before me a spruce-partridge roasted in bear's grease. This food was symbolical of the qualities of a warrior; for the spruce-partridge makes a thunderous noise with its wings when in flight, and when hiding from a foe is remarkably difficult to discover. Thus I was to be endued with fury for the onset of battle; with patient cunning for the ambush; and with the strength and courage of a bear at bay. In conclusion, Thayendanegea presented me with a small stick whittled in the shape of a war-club, as a talisman.

Other white men have been adopted into the tribe as a mark of honour, notably Lord Percy and the American General, Charles Lee; but none, I believe, with the full native ceremony which made me a Mohawk in fact, not merely in name. Thayendanegea then took me in his arms and embraced me tenderly. While my wounds still smarted I allowed myself to suffer another operation, for which I have ever since had every reason to be thankful. Hair on the face is considered very unsightly by the Indians, and they remove it, roots and all, with the help of a small pliable worm made of flattened brass wire. Though I would not, merely to please them, allow them to remove my eyebrows and lashes, I suffered them to pluck out my beard. The instrument was closely applied in its flat state to my chin, where the hair was already growing luxuriantly, and compressed between finger and thumb; a number of hairs caught in the spirals were then drawn out with a sudden twitch. The operation, though exquisitely painful, was not a lengthy one; and when I consider how much fatigue and pain is caused in a lifetime by the daily operation of shaving, I wonder that more people, soldiers especially, do not summon up resolution and submit patiently to depilation in this manner.

Of the feasts that we attended in our journey the greatest was given to us by the Cayugas, who were the most violent in their desire for a war against the Americans. The festivities were attended by hundreds of persons. In this religious ceremony – it was this rather than a social occasion – each warrior appeared dressed and painted in simulation of the animal sacred to his family: for the tribes are divided into families named the Bears, Buffaloes, Stags, Pigeons, Eagles, Frogs, and so forth. Some therefore were covered with a buffalo's or a stag's hide, having the horns extended; others wore dresses of feathers in a variety of grotesque devices; the Frogs' bodies were entirely naked, but painted with green and yellow. I had been adopted by Thayendanegea into his family, the Wolves, and dressed accordingly with a wolf's mask and his bushy tail. All our faces were daubed with vermilion and black, since this was a war-dance, laid upon a coating of bear's grease. In his preparations for the masquerade each warrior was most sedulous to make the ferocity of his face the most ghastly and glaring possible; for this he used a small looking-glass, which enabled him to apply the colours with great nicety, but, frequently growing impatient with the result, he would wipe off the whole picture with a cloth and recommence from his natural skin.

When all was ready, we sat down on our hams in a circle around a great fire, near which a large stake was fixed. After a while the war-chief of the Cayugas arose, as the person of greatest respectability present and, placing himself in the centre, by the stake, began rehearsing all the gallant exploits of his life. He dwelt upon the number of enemies he had killed, describing with gestures how he stalked them, struck them down, scalped them – how he stole horses, ripped open enemies' lodges as an insult, did this and that atrocious deed. His recital, which was spoken with great fluency and dramatic earnestness, cannot have lasted less than three hours. He was greeted with great acclamation and cries of *Etow! Etow!* He continually knocked against the stake with his war-club, making it the witness to the truth of his boasts. I could follow the whole tale by his pantomime gestures. Especially I enjoyed his stealing of the horses of the Wyandots: how after much waiting and watching he had crept up to the horses, stooped down to cut their hopples, mounted the finest, seized another by the forelock and galloped off with both. He rode his tomahawk during this account, as children do broomsticks, making use of an imaginary whip to indicate the necessity of rapid movement, and glancing continuously over his shoulder at the pursuing foe. When he had done, we all arose and joined in a hopping dance, leaping about and brandishing our weapons; I should have preferred a fiddle to the monotonous beating of the drums, but the exercise after so long waiting in the cold was grateful. The Indian war-drum was a piece of hollow tree over which a skin was stretched, with kettles formed of dried gourds filled with peas. We passed around the fire in a circle with our bodies bent uncouthly forward, and uttered the same low dismal sounds, without variation, being the words '*blood, blood*', '*kill, kill*;' and ever and again raised the famous Indian war-whoop. This ferocious cry consisted in the sound *whoo-oo-oop!* which was continued so long as the breath lasted, and then broken off with a sudden lifting of the voice. A few modulated the cry with howling notes, placing the hand before the mouth to effect this. In either case, the whoop carried for an immense distance.

Thayendanegea was next, and he went through the same performance, though in a somewhat different manner. He told of his martial exploits, but also of his travels across the Great Water and threw a rich humour into his tale with imitations of the strutting lords, fashionable ladies, snuff-taking bishops and other London notables he had encountered, to the infinite delight of the gathering. He concluded with a passionate invective against the rebellious Yankees who had taken up arms against their long-suffering father, King George. He finished, and we all danced again. Two fat bucks had been put to roast at the great fire and whenever a man felt so disposed he would glide to the nearest carcass and cut off a great slice of meat for his own use. So the performance continued, Mohicans and Cayugans taking the floor alternately, until I thought it would never end. There was a person appointed to stand outside the circle and rouse any member of the audience who showed the least signs of sleep.

The celebration went on for no less than four whole days and nights. The speeches and dances persisted with unabated energy, fresh meat was continually put upon the spit, and the fire ever and again replenished. On the second day I was called upon to recount my own deeds of valour. I had not much to relate; but not wishing to lower myself in the estimation of my hosts and comrades I told resounding tales in English of the exploits of my regiment at the Battle of the Boyne and the assault of Athlone, and its service in many important fights in Spain during the War of the Spanish Succession, concluding with a dramatic recitation from Shakespeare's *Hamlet*, which I had by heart, in the course of which, in the character of the mad Prince, I was able to exhibit my skull at lunging and parrying with a small-sword, in contest with an imaginary foe. My performance was greeted with prolonged applause and Thayendanegea was good enough not to betray the cheat to the company.

It was February before we approached Montreal once more, and at each step I took my heart grew heavier. I had been living with Kate in a fantastic fairyland in which I would willingly have continued for the remainder of my life, so much did forest-life please me; but that the small insistent voice of Duty began to speak in my ear and to remind me of my service to my Sovereign. The parting from my new but well-tried friends would not have been so painful had it not meant equally a separation from my squaw (as I had affectionately named her); and my squaw, to judge from certain infallible signs, would before the summer was out seal her union with me by the birth of a child. We were at a loss what course to take. Kate could not return in my company to The Ninth, where she was well known, nor go to The Eighth without me, bringing her husband the gift of a bastard. We both felt with bitterness the irony of fate in condemning our separation, who loved each other so tenderly. And why must this be? Because I was but a sergeant, and she a soldier's wife. That General Howe and General Burgoyne each openly consorted with the wife of one of his commissaries, was condoned as a fashionable peccadillo, but the same fault in us would be regarded as heinous and vulgar. We shed tears when we perceived to what a strait our thoughtlessness had brought us. Indian women have certain simples, such as the sumach flower, which they use to procure abortion, but Kate would have none of them, saying that she wished to abide by what she had done, nor add the crime of murder to what had but been loving folly.

Thayendanegea, seeing me sitting very pensively apart one day, asked me gently what trouble was eating at me, and I told him the whole story. He continued thoughtful for a while and then begged me not to despair: he would arrange the matter for us both without scandal. And so in the event he did.

I will never forget our last discourse together. Kate was not fretful or passionate, but spoke reasonably with me. I had the chance, she said, to remain with her and with the fruit of our love, either wandering through the forests in the company of these good friends of ours – whose ways, though savage, were gentlemanly and considerate – or settling in a cote which we might build for ourselves in the wilderness under their protection. Surely that was in every way better than to return alone to my military life? Did I choose the former case, she promised me as faithful duty in the capacity of wife as if the ceremony performed at Newton Breda had been between herself and me, and not between herself and Richard Harlowe. In the latter case, she would harbour no ill feelings against me; but I must clearly understand that, saying good-bye to her now, I would say a perpetual good-bye. If ever afterwards we happened to meet she would feign not to know me, and would not address a single affectionate word to me; and, as for the child, I must renounce my paternity of it – what became of it need not interest me. She would take full responsibility for its birth and upbringing.

What can I say? What could I say then to her? As we spoke together in the snow, under the shadow of a tall white-pine behind which the sunset shed a glorious dying glow over the wide St Lawrence valley, I heard the music of the bugles from the British camp and the boom of the evening gun, and I knew that I could never choose as she wished me to choose. My skin was white, not tawny; my weapon of assault the bayonet, not the tomahawk; my birth British, not Mohican. As I kissed Kate adieu, my heart was heavy as a stone and I told her that I could not ask her forgiveness, since I did not deserve it. But I begged her to accept, as a token to tie around the neck of the child, a pierced silver groat of King Charles II that my father had given me in my boyhood and that had ever since hung about my neck on a string. She accepted it; then, taking me solemnly by the hand, she made me swear, by the name of God, never so long as she lived to divulge to a soul what had passed between us. She went back to the camp-fire of the Indians without another word.

CHAPTER XVIII

ON MY return to barracks at the Isle of Jesus, I found it difficult to accommodate myself immediately to civilized customs, and was glad to be told that in ten days' time I would be sent out in an officer's party to train twenty non-commissioned officers in the arts that I had learned from the Indians. Meanwhile I detested the disorder and quarrelsomeness of barrack life. Since Major Bolton went, there was little care shown for the well-being of the men: they were not regularly and usefully employed, and preferred idleness and drinking to that healthful indulgence in sport which kept the Canadians merry. A whimsical notion occurred to me: how salutary it would be if a Colonel, with a perfect indifference to precedent, were to put the men under his command to school during such periods of enforced idleness! It would be vain, of course, to hope for signs of genius in the pupils, but at least all could be taught to read and write a fair hand, and to state a plain matter intelligibly upon paper, which so few were able to do, even among the sergeants. Nor would it be ill for such an innovator also to instruct his young officers in the military science, in which on the whole they were dangerously deficient, especially in that of military engineering.

The quarrelsomeness of which I complained was not confined to the ranks, for officers frequently called one another out to avenge imagined affronts. One ludicrous case occurred. A Captain Montgomery of The Ninth, who had a very prominent nose, happened to leave his lodging to go to the Mess, not four doors away, when he met with Lieutenant Murray emerging from thence. 'God bless me!' cries the Lieutenant, 'your nose is frost-bit.'

The Captain was very tender on the subject of his nose and because it was not half a minute since he had stepped into the street, believed that he was being bantered. 'God damn you, sir, for your impertinence!' he cried.

Lieutenant Murray could not let this pass, and says he: 'Sir, let me repeat in all civility that you have a large nose that is frost-bit. Go, rub it in snow to make the blood circulate and keep away from a fire, else you will have but a short nose.'

Captain Montgomery very fiercely: 'Mr Murray, my second will wait upon you tomorrow morning to arrange a rendezvous.'

Lieutenant Murray: 'Sir, frostbite occasions no sort of pain, and you are therefore unaware that what I say is true. Rub your nose at once with snow, or mortification will ensue. Or, perhaps, get your second to perform the service for you.'

The Captain went blustering into the mess, and 'God bless me!' every one cried, 'Your nose is frost-bit! Keep away from the fire in heaven's name! Outside at once, and rub it well with snow, else you will lose it for sure.'

So out he went, to rub his nose with snow, and though a greedy man and sharp set with hunger missed a very good meal; exactly as Lieutenant Murray, that waggish Irishman, had intended when he had rehearsed the scene beforehand with his brother-officers. And the Captain that same evening made the Lieutenant a handsome apology.

It was remarkable to me that none of the men attempted to learn how to glide along the frozen river on skates. Perhaps they thought that to do so would be presumptuous, for several of the officers had provided themselves with skates and had instituted a skating club. I had myself learned the sport from the Indians, who could cover immense distances by this means of progression; it may not be credited but, for a wager, three Indians not long before had skated in a single day, between dawn and dusk, all the way from Montreal to Quebec – a distance of one hundred and eighty miles! However, this glory was purchased with death, for two instantly expired on reaching their goal and the third did not survive above a week. Contiguous to the frozen river's sides, the ice supplied a flat and level ground to go on, but in the mid-current the passage was rugged and hilly. This was occasioned by the powerful force and rapidity of the water underneath, throwing up fragments of broken ice. Standing upon a rising ground of ice thus formed, you might perceive the most grotesque appearances and figures, sometimes of human beings, beasts and birds and of almost every object which the earth offers the eye.

My journey with the non-commissioned officers proved uneventful and pleasant; Lieutenant Kemmis conducted us. He was a gentleman who never affected, as many young coxcombs do, that the epaulettes upon his shoulders had given him the power of knowing better than his subordinates in rank upon every conceivable subject. While avoiding to appear publicly in the character of my pupil, he inquired beforehand from me how marching, cooking, sleeping, and other matters were regulated among the Indians, and gave his orders accordingly; whenever an occasion arose where he was at a loss, he had no false shame in asking my advice.

Our tour was to Three Rivers, through the woods on the northern side of the river and back through the woods on the opposing side. We stopped for a night at Three Rivers and drank with the Brunswick Grenadiers at

the barrack. The Germans I found a very strange people, combining fortitude with superstitious panic, kindliness with brutality, mechanical skill
with sheer stupidity, erudition with a plentiful lack of wit. Those with
whom we spoke seemed to have no notion of the cause they were engaged
in, or of the probable course of the campaign, nor had they any curiosity
to inform themselves. Their thoughts ran on pay, plunder, their families
in Germany, and God. They were for ever singing psalms and hymns, and
had less idea of diverting themselves with sport even than our men. Their
attention to religion had, in a manner of speaking, been their downfall, for
the Duke of Brunswick's press-gang had caught most of them as they
emerged from their parish churches one fine Sunday morning.

I have heard it said that if one is acquainted with five Britons, one is
acquainted merely with five several Britons; whereas to be acquainted with
a similar number of Germans, from whatever principality or walk of life
they might be taken, is to know all Germans. Their humours and character
are said to vary but little between whole multitudes, and Lieutenant
Kemmis informed us that a Roman historian who lived about the time of
the Emperor Nero had remarked, even at that early date, that the German
tribes known to him exhibited a remarkable sameness of behaviour. Thus
it is that they are more subject to sympathetic infection by joy, fear, or any
other emotion than any nation in the world: let ten men go weeping
through a street in a German town and soon the entire countryside will be
in tears; or let them dance, and a long procession will follow them of
passionate dancers. At Three Rivers the emotion was melancholy and the
words: '*Werd ich meine armen Kinder nimmer wieder sehen?*', 'Am I ne'er to
see my poor children again?' From this they proceeded to a conviction
that, no, they would never live to revisit their homes. Parties of twenty or
thirty men would relate to one another a conviction that death was soon
coming to them; whereupon they moped and pined, obsessed with the
notion, and nothing could cure them of it.

I endeavoured to argue a couple of them, who drank with me, out of
this settled presentiment. It was to no purpose: the Rider upon the White
Horse was close upon them, they said, and they could not escape the stroke
of his scythe. Already scores of them were dead from no visible ailment,
but merely from superstition. A sergeant took me miserably by the hand
and led me into a long, unheated room appropriated as a *morgue*, the place
where dead bodies were kept until the thawing of the frozen ground
permitted them to be decently buried. '*Alles meine guten Kameraden,*' he
said wistfully, pointing about him.

It was a very strange and laughable sight that met my gaze, for the
superintendent of the *morgue*, an apothecary, was evidently a very fanciful
fellow. He had taken the bodies of these poor, pig-tailed, leather-breeched
Germans, while still warm, and placed them fully clothed in various lifelike postures where death and the weather preserved them stiffly. Some

were kneeling with hymn-books in their hands, their jaws open as if singing; others seated in chairs with cold pipes in their mouths; many leaning against the wall with hands in pockets or one leg carelessly crossed over the other; one man standing balanced on his head and hands.

At first I could not imagine them dead, despite their ghastly countenances, but dead they were. Two big tears trickled down my Grenadier's cheeks and wetted his great moustachios. '*Ach,*' he sighed, '*bald komm ich auch*', 'Soon I too shall come hither.' And he raised a hand at various heights from the ground to indicate the respective sizes of unfortunate children who soon would be left fatherless, by his decease, at Wolfenbuttel in Germany.

He told me the characters and professions of the dead men, as if he were a guide in a museum of wax-works. Most of them were 'good comrades' from Wolfenbuttel; but there were many strangers too. This was a fringe-maker from Hanover, a surly fellow; that, a whimsical creature, a discharged secretary from the post office at Gotha; that, a renegade monk from Wurzburg, but a good comrade; that, an upper steward from Meningen, a very pleasant man who could play the organ, but a thief; that, a cashiered Hessian major, very proud and evil; that, an unsuccessful playwright from Leipzig; that, a poor, bankrupt Bavarian pastry-cook; the one in the corner a retired Prussian sergeant of Hussars, who spoke no more in life than now in death.

As I came away I pondered a metaphysical question: whether in the same way as these Germans draw death upon themselves by the power of superstition, so a man might repel death by a contrary superstition of invulnerability – such as I myself had lately come to feel. 'Aye,' said I, 'but only so long as this presentiment of life is vouchsafed. It will vanish suddenly one day when that bullet is run into the mould which is destined for my skull alone.'

I communicated to Lieutenant Kemmis a plan I had for rousing the spirits of our company when we returned to Montreal, namely of instructing them in the Indian ball-game, called by the French *la crosse*, which was a prime divertisement among the Mohicans. The ball was similar in materials and construction to that used by our Irish schoolboys in their ancient game of hurry, but was propelled with two sticks, or *crosses*, one in each hand, resembling large battledores. The field of play measured three hundred feet in length, with goal-posts at either end through which the contending parties sought to drive the ball with their sticks. The party that effected this twelve times in all was accounted victorious. The parties might trip, strike, grapple, wrestle, knock away each other's sticks, or employ any stratagem whatsoever, provided that the ball were propelled only with the stick and that no man lost his temper and shed blood. These matches among the Indians, of which I witnessed several while in Buffalo settlement, were played with intense excitement. The greatest chiefs and most distinguished warriors took part in them, and important sums were staked upon the result by the spectators. The players, who were naked and slippery with bear's grease, played with a furious hilarity that was perfectly indescribable and grew most desperate as the game advanced until but one more point remained to be notched by the winning side. The most remarkable circumstance was that no player was ever slain.

Lieutenant Kemmis readily agreed to my proposal for forthwith playing the game on the ice, with ten men a side, and himself for umpire. We improvised the *crosses* and the ball, and were soon sufficiently adept at the game to look forward with pleasure to imparting it to our men at the Isle of Jesus and playing matches in rivalry between the several companies. However, Lieutenant Kemmis, fearful of accidents, barred fisticuffs and kicking, and bade us play in our waistcoats rather than stark naked.

After our first game, which left us with limbs very stiff, but in the highest spirits, I wished that I were in General Riedesel's confidence and could recommend the sport to him as a medicine for his dispirited heroes.

We were aware that, with the end of winter, our period of inactivity would come to an end, and our campaign be resumed. To me, Canada had proved a very kind foster-mother. Indeed, it occurred to me that, were I ever obliged to remove from my native country and inhabit another, this would be my choice, though situate within winter's peculiar meridians. The climate of Montreal was especially salubrious and did I but take pains to master the French tongue – for the Canadian French are very loath to learn the English – I might with industry and a small principal settle myself here very comfortably indeed. This feeling of gratefulness, still warm in my breast, will excuse that I have dwelt at such length upon the beauties and natural curiosities of the province.

I had the good fortune to visit Montreal on Holy Thursday, which they called *La Fête Dieu*, and which generally coincided with the departure of winter. On that day, at eleven o'clock in the forenoon, a great procession of the clergy in general, and the friars of all the monasteries, attended with a band of music, moved out from the great church and passed down the streets, occupying nearly half a mile of ground. They bore lighted candles in their hands.

The townspeople had prepared for this ceremonial by procuring large pines and firs from the woods, with which they lined the streets on both sides, making the boughs connect at the top, so that the religious spectacle proceeded under an umbrageous shelter, as if through a grove of living trees. The centre of the procession was occupied by the Host laid upon an open copy of the Scriptures in Latin, with a white cloth spread over, and above it a crimson canopy borne by six venerable priests. Boys in white vestments scattered flowers while others swung silver thuribles which they constantly wafted towards the Host, so that the smell of incense made the streets fragrant; and all the people sang joyful anthems. Protestant or no Protestant, I was pleased to pull off my cap, as had been ordered by General Phillips, the City Commandant, out of respect for the innocent emotions of these gay, good people – who fell with one accord upon their knees as the Host passed – and for the superb solemnities of the Romish Church.

On Holy Thursday the yellow wax candles that had been used in the ceremonial were cut into small pieces and distributed to the faithful, for a small pecuniary consideration, to be used as charms against tempests. If such a stump were lighted when the wind rose, its fury would – they thought - soon abate. A woman who kept a grog-shop near the barracks, with whom I was a favourite, presented me with one of these relics; informing me of its powers, and solemnly warning me against using it except for the purpose I have mentioned. I put it in my knapsack, after thanking her gravely, and thought no more about it.

Before the end of March the thaw had begun, Montreal having three weeks' advantage of Quebec in the matter of the spring's arrival, and it was no longer safe to play *la crosse* or perform our military exercises upon the frozen river. The river had been the parade-ground for some time past, for the snow lay deep upon the ground, but upon the ice it thawed daily in the sun and froze to small ice overnight – moreover, a steady footing was provided for the troops by the sweepings of the stables and byres which were thrown out upon the ice to be carried off when it should break up. One day, as we were at our platoon exercise, a sharp crack sounded under our feet like a discharge of grape and the ice split across from bank to bank. We broke ranks in alarm and one man was injured by a bayonet in the general *sauve qui peut*, but the crack was of no immediate significance. However, the warm weather continued and soon the ice along the bank gaped with great chasms. Frequent roars of breaking ice were heard from the centre of the river, where the fantastic ice-mountains had formed. As the waters became swollen by the melting of the snow, these mountains fell into the stream and were hurried down towards Quebec with tremendous impetuosity: until becoming wedged in narrow places between islands and heaping up there again in the form of new mountains. The greatest roar of all was heard at midnight of the last day of April when some obstruction, half a mile downstream from us, gave way. When we awoke in the morning, there was the river flowing clear and blue under the cloudless sky, and we were true islanders again; instead of carriages and sleighs driving across from the barracks to the mainland, canoes and *batteaux* came dancing down.

However, so long as there remained fragments of ice in the river, no navigation was possible to ships of burden, for these bergs, when frozen to the bottom, were no less dangerous than a rock – or than a charging sperm-maceti whale, when afloat.

We were distressed to learn that among the many victims of the thaw was Major Bolton, who was drowned in the Lakes on his way to Montreal, by the *batteau* he was in striking a submerged lump of ice with great force and sinking forthwith. Richard Harlowe brought us the melancholy intelligence; and in consequence of his employer's death he was obliged to quit The Eighth and be restored to the strength of The Ninth. When he was asked what had become of his wife, he replied that he feared her drowned in the Falls of Niagara, pursuant upon a threat that she had made him in a fit of rage. He affected to be disconsolate, and, whether or not he had banished from his mind all memory of his half-breed mistress, he at least refrained from boasting to us of that conquest. Towards me, he continued sullen and reserved.

During a fortnight the roads had been impassable, but now were quite dry and even dusty. Spring came with a rush, and we had hardly congratulated ourselves upon its delightful appearance when it passed on and gave place to summer. In a very few days the bare trees were in full leaf and the barren, frozen ground was green with grass and decorated with innumerable flowers.

Our annual supply of clothing, the new suit for every man for which stoppages were made from our pay, had not yet arrived, and we were told that we must commence the campaign in our old clothes, most of which were in a very ragged condition. But, to make them more presentable, all with long coats were told to reduce them to jackets, and their hats into caps; the cloth remaining over to be used as patches for rents and burns. The caps were now to be furnished with cockades of hair, but no hair being provided we were expected to go foraging for it – as the Israelites of old were expected by their task-masters to furnish themselves with straw for their bricks.

Terry Reeves, who had lately returned to us, his wound healed, and very sorrowful to be parted from his Indian squaw, led a foray of about twenty men of our company into a paddock where a herd of cows was grazing; intending to cut the hair from the ends of their tails. The plan miscarried. The farmer and a number of relatives who happened to be present in the farm-house, because of a funeral feast in progress there, rushed out with sticks and began laying about them with great fury. Two soldiers had their heads broken and their bodies severely bruised before they could be rescued; they were foolish enough the next day to complain to Major Forbes, their officer, of this 'premeditated assault'. Major Forbes told them downrightly that they had got no more than their deserts. In the first place, it was an inhumane act to cut from the tails of cows those hirsute appendages provided by Nature for switching away the flies that so greatly plagued them in the hot season; in the second, they had evidently gone without their side-arms, which should always be worn, being the same to a soldier as a sword is to an officer; in the third, horsehair was far superior to cow's hair for the making of cockades. Terry therefore led a new expedition, under cover of darkness, to the artillery barrack at Montreal, where sufficient hair was secured for the whole company from the tails of the gun horses and officers' chargers found unguarded there in the stables.

CHAPTER XIX

OUR LIGHT infantry and grenadier companies were transported across the St Lawrence River and marched to Boucherville, where we found the flank companies of the other regiments assembled, and took part with them in combined manœuvres under the approving eye of General Burgoyne.

General Burgoyne had spent the winter in England, together with several other officers of the army in Canada who were, like him, members of Parliament, and had there endeavoured to persuade the Ministry that he was far fitter to command the expedition against Ticonderoga than General Carleton. He alleged that General Carleton had been slow to press his advantage in the previous campaign, when he might have taken Ticonderoga almost without loss, and thus struck a resounding blow against the rebels; and that General Carleton was by no means beloved of the troops.

Now, the Secretary for War was Lord George Germaine. The greater part of the Army was unaware who this person might be, and gave no attention to the matter. But one day in this same summer I was greatly astonished to learn some particulars of his previous history. It happened in this manner. I had come upon old Sergeant Fitzpatrick and two sergeants of the Twentieth Regiment who, the day being July 31st, were drinking together in our bivouac. All wore roses in their caps to commemorate the glorious victory of Minden of which this was the anniversary, for before the battle the troops had lain in a rose garden and thus gaily decked themselves in contempt of the French. Now up rode stout old General Phillips. He stopped to shake the hands of his comrades-in-arms, but, says he, very sharply to Sergeant Fitzpatrick: 'How come you by this rose? I never heard that The Ninth fought at Minden.'

'No, General Phillips,' rejoined the sergeant, 'but The Twenty-third did so fight, with whom I then had the honour of serving, and in the leading line too. I remember your Honour on that occasion, how you split no less than fifteen canes on the rumps and sides of your sweating horses in bringing the guns up. And if I may make bold enough to say it, sir, I am right glad that today we have no Lord George Sackville in command of our cavalry.'

This Lord George Sackville had been in command of the British cavalry on that famous occasion and behaved very ill. An order had been given to the infantry to advance when they heard the beat of a signal drum. An aide-de-camp in a hurry conveyed the message that six British battalions and two of Germans were to advance at the beat of the drum; but this became mistakenly changed into an order to advance 'at beat of drum'. This they did forthwith, very courageously, despite a cruel cross-fire of artillery, before the French were marshalled in position; and by their unassisted efforts drove off the held a great mass of enemy infantry and – an unheard-of feat – a force of French cavalry of double their number. Lord George Sackville was hastily desired by Prince Ferdinand, the allied Commander, to pursue the routed French with his cavalry, but he stood fast, either from cowardice or because of personal pique against the Prince, pretending that he did not understand how the movement was to be carried out. Our noble Colonel, then plain Captain Ligonier, came galloping up to ask Lord George why he delayed. A Colonel Sloper, of the cavalry, cried out to Captain Ligonier, pointing in exasperation at his Lordship: 'For God's sake, repeat your orders to *that man*, that he may not pretend to misunderstand them, for it is near half an hour ago that he received orders to advance and yet we are still here. You see the condition he is in!' But the moment had passed, and Prince Ferdinand was robbed of the fruits of what was, even so, the most resounding victory of the whole century. Lord George Sackville, being in due course court-martialled, was found guilty and very rightly adjudged unfit ever again to command British soldiers in the field.

General Phillips now looked at Sergeant Fitzpatrick in a very peculiar manner. 'No,' said he shortly, 'Lord George Sackville does not command the cavalry of this Northern army, but Lord George Germaine sits in his chair at Downing Street; and there directs and co-ordinates the military operations of the Northern, the Southern, and the Eastern armies.'

One of the sergeants of The Twentieth then remarked: 'Aye, your Honour, I am sorry to hear that – for though I know little about this lord I have read that he is a sad Whig, having even been approached by that rascal Charles Fox to lead the Opposition. They say that he refused only because – as he frankly owned – to lead an Opposition was an ill paid and thankless task, and he had debts of honour which must be paid at all events. I cannot think that he will manage his task well. But better a thousand times to have such a Whig in the Secretary's chair than a traitor of the quality of Lord George Sackville.'

General Phillips very gravely: 'They are one and the same person. "*That man*", when he inherited the Germaine estates, changed his name accordingly.'

Well, this Lord George Sackville, or Germaine, nursed a long-standing hatred against a number of generals and other officers: all such as had avoided his company since the notorious court martial fixed so sable a blot upon his name. Among these was General Carleton who had, besides, refused to job for him politically; and his Lordship therefore lent a ready ear to General Burgoyne's insinuations, and even recommended to the King that General Carleton should be recalled from the Government of Canada. King George scented rancour and prejudice. He consented that General Burgoyne, as an energetic officer, should be put in command of our expedition; yet he retained General Carleton in his government. General Carleton was much mortified and sent in his resignation: for General Burgoyne, as an independent commander, would now be taking orders directly from Lord George Germaine, General Carleton's professed enemy, and at the same time making requisitions upon the resources of Canada which must be supplied willy-nilly and with all dispatch. When this resignation was refused, however, General Carleton very loyally and generously did everything in his power to assist the arms of his supplanter.

It will be recalled that the British plan of attack was a simultaneous converging upon Albany, on Hudson's River, of three armies: General Howe's northward from New York, General Prescott's westward from Rhode Island, ours southward from Canada. To co-ordinate the movements of three separate armies requires a watchful and controlling central power, great nicety in calculating times and distances, and perfect secrecy. The task would be formidable enough in a country so enormous as America, and with so difficult communications by land and river, even when the three armies were directed along interior lines of defence, namely lines drawn from the centre of the country outward to the frontiers; but was quite desperate when these armies must simultaneously attack inwards from positions on the frontier separated from one another by hundreds of miles of wilderness, and with no possibility of communication between them. For if then the central armies were well handled in opposition, they would mass in superior force against each of the three converging columns in turn, and destroy them piecemeal. It was plain madness to allow such a plan to be directed by any person at all, however gifted, from a distance of three thousand miles away – let alone one who had never set foot in America, or had any notion of conditions there, who relied for his information on prejudiced and inaccurate sources, who could not keep regular office hours or a secret, and who bore an inveterate grudge against the whole British Army. Yet such was the indulgence given by King George, long before he had shown any other signs of the lunacy that afterwards deprived him of his sovereignty, to Lord George Germaine!

I may here append that King George was as unfortunate in his choice of a minister to control his ships upon the sea, as in his choice of a minister to control his armies upon land: for the First Lord of the Admiralty was the ill-living, revengeful, and incompetent Earl of Sandwich, known to all as 'Jemmy Twitcher', after the libertine of that name in Mr Gay's comedy of *The Beggar's Opera*. It was he who, twenty years before, had been High Priest of that blasphemous and orgiastic fraternity, the Hellfire Club, *alias* the Society of the Monks of Medmenham Abbey; nor had he changed his nature since that day. He was as cordially hated by his admirals as Lord George Germaine by his generals, for he added hypocrisy to ill-living, and wilful mismanagement of the Navy to hypocrisy. When the Court and Cabinet were set upon revenge against the notorious John Wilkes, the libertarian, whose unseating and reseating as a member of Parliament was the chief political topic of the years before the war, his Lordship was called upon to discredit him in the House of Lords. He did so by reading aloud to the scandalized house a ribald poem composed by this Wilkes, and asked the Lords to brand it as an impious and obscene document; as if their Lordships were unaware that the same John Wilkes, who had also been a Medmenham monk, had printed this composition some years before, for private circulation in the club. Shortly after this, at a performance of *The Beggar's Opera*, that odious character, Mr Peachum, whose practice was virtuously to peach on his scoundrelly associates when they were of no further assistance to him, set the whole house in a roar by remarking how surprised he was that Jemmy Twitcher should peach. As for this Jemmy Twitcher's mismanagement of his office: he starved the dockyards, sold contracts through his mistress, Miss Ray, who presided at the Admiralty as if a coroneted countess and was an unconscionable bargainer, allowed our strength in line-of-battle ships to fall far below the modicum needed for the safety of our coasts, yet lyingly informed the Lords to the contrary, pretending that three times as many frigates were in commission as was actually the case. He also oppressed and cheated those deserving old sea-dogs, the Greenwich Pensioners, who were under his sole charge; and conspired to ruin by calumny and subterfuge a number of eminent and courageous captains and admirals of the Navy – among them 'Black Dick', General Howe's brother, and 'Little Keppel'. But in spite of all these wicked actions the noble Earl remained in power, as did Lord George Germaine, until the war was irretrievably lost: namely, five years after the period of which I am now writing.

However, we could then know nothing of what lay in pickle for us, and had perfect confidence in General Burgoyne, in our own arms, and in the righteousness of our cause.

Our fleet had been strengthened by a new frigate, the *Royal George;* and a radeau, big as a castle, which was sunk at St John's by the Americans in the previous year, had been raised from the river-bed. Our army consisted of some four thousand British troops and three thousand German. Two thousand Canadian levies had been expected to swell our numbers but the service proved unpopular. No more than one hundred and fifty appeared in arms with us; they hung back even from transport work. Besides these, there were the Indians, many hundreds of whom had promised to take up the hatchet.

At the beginning of June 1777 we marched out of Canada by way of St John's and encamped on the western side of Lake Champlain; where we waited for *batteaux* to transport us, under convoy of the fleet, to the southern extremity of the lake, close to Crown Point.

In our passage down the lake we frequently encamped upon the islands, the brigades regularly following one another, and making about seventeen to twenty miles a day. The order of progress was so regulated that each brigade occupied at night the encampment vacated in the morning by the brigade preceding. It would have been a very pleasant time had it not been for the mosquitoes, which were more venomous here than anywhere else on the American continent, but only at Skenesborough, a little farther to the south, where (as General Washington himself averred) they would not scruple to bite through boot and stocking. At this time great clouds of turtle-doves were migrating from New York State past us into Canada; they were decorated with beautiful plumage of shifting hues and were much wearied by their long flight. It was with difficulty that they gained the trees near our bivouac to roost upon, and some even dropped into the water and drowned. Our people struck them down from the branches with sticks and wrung their necks as they fell. Turtle-doves furnished subsistence for six weeks of the year to the Canadian farmer, who erected ladders from the ground to the tops of the pines where the flocks were accustomed to resort. The turtle-doves perched upon the ladders, several to each rung. Coming softly to the trees by night with a musket full of small shot, the Canadian would fire upwards along each ladder and seldom fail to kill or wound forty or fifty birds, which he would subsequently eat in a delicious fricassee with garlic and sour cream.

An event remarkable, even if it can be dismissed as coincidence, occurred as we were approaching Crown Point. Picture to yourself the scene: a fine June day with the wide lake undisturbed by a breeze, and the whole army in array, forming a perfect regatta, a great number of Indians paddling ahead in their birchen canoes, twenty or thirty to a canoe, followed by the advanced corps, our Light Infantry and Grenadiers, the Canadians and a few American Loyalist volunteers, upon the gunboats; next, the two frigates, *Royal George* and *Inflexible*, towing large booms, the schooners, sloops, and other ships a little astern, including the newly raised radeau which transported the heavy artillery; after them the first brigade, with scarlet uniforms and flashing arms, in a regular line of *batteaux* and with the three generals in their smart pinnaces following next, the second brigade, an equally brave sight, with the German brigades supporting; and far in the rear, the sutlers and camp-followers pushing along in a variety of craft.

The crystal surface of the lake became an indefinitely extended mirror reflecting the calm heavens, the tall trees of the islands past which we sailed, the great flock of laden boats and ships. It was like some stupendous fairy-scene of a dream, which the waking fancy can hardly conceive.

In our gunboat it happened that nobody was supplied with a tinder-box, though several of us felt the need of a pipe of tobacco. However, I rummaged in my knapsack and found there a dry piece of the fungus which I kept as a specific against the flux, together with a burning-glass and a candle-end of yellow wax. I concentrated the rays of the sun in a focus upon the fungus, which soon broke into flame when I blew upon it; where-upon I lighted the candle from this tinder and it was passed from hand to hand among the smokers on the benches.

All at once the sun was darkened by a cloud and a most violent and unex-pected tempest blew up from the Green Mountains to the north-east, so that the whole vast sheet of water was agitated in a terrible manner. A small sloop carrying but little sail, not fifty yards from us, was laid flat on her side by the first gusts and the crew were obliged to chop away the masts in order to right her. I thought that the greater part of the army must of necessity be swallowed up, for the *batteaux* were most unmanageable vessels in rough weather and now heaved about frightfully. Suddenly a superstitious thought crossed my mind: I had inadvertently lighted the Holy Thursday candle in a flat calm and had therefore been instrumental in loosing the very danger that these two inches of bees-wax had been intended to allay! I noticed that one of my comrades still held the lighted relic under the shelter of his greatcoat, where he was endeavouring to kindle his pipe from it. I snatched it from him, when it was instantly extinguished, and, lo, the storm began sensibly to abate. The whole brigade of *batteau* weathered the storm safely except for two, carrying men of The Ninth, both of which swamped just as they got close in shore, but our comrades were within their depth and lost neither their lives nor their arms.

At the mouth of the River Bouquet, where we finally disembarked, a great body of Indians joined us, and General Burgoyne held a Congress with their chiefs and principal warriors. Not only had the Six Nations appeared in full strength, but their sworn enemies the Algonquins and Wyandots also. General Burgoyne addressed them through an interpreter in his oratund manner, as follows:

CHIEFS AND WARRIORS,
The Great King, our common Father, and the patron of all who seek and deserve his protection, has considered with satisfaction the general conduct of the Indian tribes, from the beginning of the trou-bles in America. Too sagacious and too faithful to be deluded or corrupted, they have observed the violated rights of the parental power they love, and burned to vindicate them. A few individuals alone, the refuse of a small tribe, at the first were led astray: and the

misrepresentations, the specious allurements, the insidious promises, the diversified plots in which the rebels are exercised, and all of which they employed for that effect, have served only in the end to enhance the honour of the tribes in general, by demonstrating to the world how few and how contemptible are the apostates! It is a truth known to you all, these pitiful examples excepted (and they have probably, before this day, hid their faces in shame) that the collective voices and hands of the Indian tribes, over this vast continent, are on the side of justice, of law, and of the King.

The restraint you have put upon your resentment in waiting the King your Father's call to arms, the hardest proof, I am persuaded, to which your affection could have been put, is another manifest and affecting mark of your adherence to that principle of connection to which you were always fond to allude, and which is the mutual joy and the duty of the parent to cherish.

The clemency of your Father has been abused, the offers of his mercy have been despised, and his further patience would, in his eyes, become culpable, in as much as it would withhold redress from the most grievous oppressions in the provinces that ever disgraced the history of mankind. It therefore remains for me, the General of one of His Majesty's armies, and in this Council his representative, to release you from those bonds which your obedience imposed – Warriors, you are free – go forth in might and valour of your cause – strike at the common enemies of Great Britain and America – disturbers of public order, peace, and happiness, destroyers of commerce, parricides of state.

The General, then pointing to the officers, both German and British, who attended this meeting, proceded:

The circle round you, the Chiefs of His Majesty's European forces, and of the Princes his allies, esteem you as brothers in the war; emulous in glory and in friendship, we will endeavour reciprocally to give and to receive examples; we know how to value, and we will strive to imitate your perseverance in enterprise, and your constancy to resist hunger, weariness, and pain. Be it our task, from the dictates of our religion, the laws of our warfare, and the principles and interest of our policy, to regulate your passions when they overbear, to point out where it is nobler to spare than to revenge, to discriminate degrees of guilt, to suspend the uplifted stroke, to chastise and not destroy.

This war to you, my friends, is new; upon all former occasions, in taking the field, you held yourselves authorized to destroy wherever you came, because everywhere you found an enemy. The case is now very different.

The King has many faithful subjects dispersed in the provinces, consequently you have many brothers there, and these people are more to be pitied, that they are persecuted or imprisoned wherever they are discovered or suspected; and to dissemble, to a generous mind, is a yet more grievous punishment.

Persuaded that your magnanimity of character, joined to your principles of affection to the King, will give me fuller control over your minds than the military rank with which I am invested, I enjoin your most serious attention to the rules which I hereby proclaim for your invariable observation during the campaign.

I positively forbid bloodshed, when you are not opposed in arms. Aged men, women, children, and prisoners must be held sacred from the knife or hatchet, even in the time of actual conflict. You shall receive compensation for the prisoners you take, but you shall be called to account for scalps.

In conformity and indulgence of your customs, which have affixed an idea of honour to such badges of victory, you shall be allowed to take the scalps of the dead, when killed by your fire, and in fair opposition; but on no account, or pretence, or subtility or prevarication, are they to be taken from the wounded, or even dying; and still less pardonable, if possible, will it be held to kill men in that condition, on purpose, and upon a supposition that this protection to the wounded would be thereby evaded.

Base, lurking assassins, incendiaries, ravagers, and plunderers of the country, to whatever army they may belong, shall be treated with less reserve; but the latitude must be given you by order, and I must be the judge on the occasion.

Should the enemy, on their parts, dare to countenance acts of barbarity towards those who may fall into their hands, it shall be yours also to retaliate: but till this severity be thus compelled, bear immovable in your hearts this solid maxim (it cannot be too deeply impressed), that the great essential reward, the worthy service of your alliance, the sincerity of your zeal to the King, your Father and never-failing protector, will be examined and judged upon the test only of your steady and uniform adherence to the orders and counsels of those to whom His Majesty has entrusted the direction and honour of his arms.

After the General had finished his speech, they all of them cried out, '*Etow! Etow! Etow!*' and after remaining some little time in consultation, Little Abraham, as the most respectable and aged Chief among the Six Nations rose up, and made the following answer:

I stand up, in the name of all the nations present, to assure our Father that we have attentively listened to his discourse – we receive you as the Father, because when you speak we hear the voice of our Great Father beyond the Great Lake.

We rejoice in the approbation you have expressed of our behaviour.

We have been tried and tempted by the Bostonians; but we have loved our Father, and our hatchets have been sharpened upon our affections.

In proof of the sincerity of our professions, our whole villages able to go to war are come forth. The old and infirm, our infants and wives, alone remain at home.

With one common assent, we promise a constant obedience to all you have ordered, and all you shall order, and may the Father of Days give you many, and success.

They all cried, '*Etow, Etow*', again, and the Congress then dispersed. A war-dance followed that same evening.

I sought out Thayendanegea meanwhile in his wigwam, who greeted me with every mark of friendship. He was in full war-paint and grasped in his hand a war-banner, consisting of a spear dressed with coloured silks, feathers of the spruce-partridge and skins of polecats. I inquired privately of him the whereabouts and condition of Kate. He told me that she was under the protection of Miss Molly in his abode by the Genisee River, and already big with child; but counselled me to forget her. She had informed him of her decision never again to be my squaw, in any event, once I had quitted her for the sake of my Duty; she would return to Harlowe, soon as her child was born, for the sake of her duty as a wife. As my friend, Thayendanegea remarked, he deeply regretted her resolution, for (clenching his hands tightly together) he knew our hearts were and would always remain thus united in love, though in body separated. He added, however, that as a Christian he felt obliged to applaud Mrs Harlowe's resolution, reminding me that whom God had joined, no man should put asunder, etc., etc.; a text which I heard with a certain feeling of remorse, being now again in British dress and company. My life in the woods during the previous winter seemed but a beautiful and idle dream.

I asked, what would become of the child? He replied: that was provided for already.

CHAPTER XX

IF GENERAL BURGOYNE had in a manner made injudicious use of political power to supplant General Carleton in the command of our army, no scandal was caused by it; and General Carleton, as I have told, was very loyal in doing all within his power to ensure the success of our invasion of the United States. He even prevailed upon a few Canadian Habitants, during the very period when crops were sown, to hire him their teams for drawing our transport wagons and engage themselves as boatmen upon the lakes; others he set to improving the defences of St John's, Chambly, and Sorel. This decent amity was not shown in a corresponding situation upon the American side, where the Commander of their Northern army, Major-General Philip Schuyler, was assailed in Congress by the intriguing New England representatives, headed by Samuel and John Adams: on the ground that he was a secret Loyalist. They pointed out, truly enough, that he valued the aristocratic spirit, which inspires officers to command and soldiers to obey, before the spirit of Liberty, which makes all men believe themselves the equal of, or superior to, those who are their betters by birth or education. They found an ally and instrument in Major-General Horatio Gates, who had been Adjutant-General of the Americans during the siege of Boston and was now second in command to General Schuyler.

This General Gates was no gentleman in behaviour and sensibilities, whatever his quality by birth, nor was he endowed with any officer-like gifts, though he had once held a commission in our Army, which was well rid of him. He was an urbane, sneaking, and ambitious person of good presence, with a talent for ingratiating himself into the confidence of mediocre men by traducing persons of character and merit: General Washington was later to feel and suffer from his spite. Although set by General Schuyler in command of the American advanced forces at Ticonderoga, General Gates murderously (as they themselves complained) left his people there to their fate. They were now suffering more pitiably than ever from bad food, disease, and lack of medical supplies. All were living in poor, thin tents and without greatcoats or suffi-cient blankets; and a third part of them were even obliged to go shoeless in a temperature that stood fixed below zero on Fahrenheit's thermometer.

It is said that New Englanders had never sworn or taken God's name in vain until this experience of the camp at Ticonderoga forced them to it; where 'that most foolish and unaccountable of vices' took such root among them that every second word was now either the name of God or some base part of speech smacking of grogshop or nanny-house.

In November General Gates went down to Baltimore in Maryland, where Congress was assembled, and up again in February to Philadelphia, in which city their next session took place: insidiously pressing upon the Congress-men in lobbies, lodgings, and the street his superior fitness to command in General Schuyler's place.

Congress at last yielded to his persistent voice and passed a resolution giving him the independent command of the troops based upon Albany, just as General Burgoyne had been given an independent command of the troops based upon St John's. However, General Schuyler did not assent so amiably to his supersession as had General Carleton. He suggested to his powerful friends in New York that this was an act of spite against him for the part that he had once taken in a land-dispute between New York and Massachusetts, over the possession of what is now known as the State of Vermont; and New York thereupon elected him as their representative to Congress, where he rose to demand an official inquiry into his conduct. This put the two Adamses into an awkward position; and in the end his merits were publicly acknowledged and he was sent north to resume his authority from General Gates. He arrived back at Albany early in June, the same time as we began our expedition down the lake; and immediately appointed Brigadier-General St Clair to the defence of Ticonderoga, as a less offensive choice to the Massachusetts men than Brigadier-General Benedict Arnold, who was otherwise more fitted to undertake it. The next scene in this farce was that General Gates, who had not yet visited his army at Ticonderoga, grew reckless with rage and ran once more to Philadelphia to call Congress to account for their double-dealing!

General Burgoyne issued an Order of the Day to us on June 30th, to the effect that tomorrow we embarked for our assault upon Ticonderoga (which was fifteen miles distant from Crown Point, where we were assembled) and thence would drive forward into the interior of the enemy's country. The services required, he declared, were critical and conspicuous; but at all events 'this army must not retreat.' The British regiments of the Line, besides The Ninth, that embarked upon this hazardous campaign were very reliable ones, viz. The Twentieth, Twenty-first, Twenty-fourth, Twenty-ninth, Thirty-fourth, Forty-seventh, Fifty-third and Sixty-second.

No one can deny that we did very well at Ticonderoga, which was a double fortress consisting of the old French works, greatly improved, lying on the western side of the water, and a heavily fortified hill named Mount Independence, on the eastern. These two positions were linked by a bridge more than three hundred yards long, of colossal construction and protected by a massive boom. It should be explained that a short distance below Ticonderoga, to the west, occurred the crooked northern passage to Lake George; the broad continuation of Lake Champlain to the southward was called the South River.

My company had been formed with the light infantry companies of the other regiments into a battalion commanded by Colonel Lord Balcarres, an experienced and courageous nobleman. We expected very severe fighting, for the defences of Ticonderoga showed an even more formidable aspect than they had done when we stopped short before them in the previous October. Yet the exertions we called upon to make were in the pioneering, rather than the military, way. The fact was that the Americans, reduced by the negligence of their generals to but three thousand men, were hardly sufficient in numbers to man the existing works. They had therefore neglected to fortify Sugar Hill, a rocky eminence, rather less than a mile in their rear, which rose six hundred feet from the water at the point where the South River and the Lake George inlet divide. They fondly imagined that, because they could not spare troops to construct and man a redoubt on Sugar Hill, it was not only inaccessible to British artillery, but out of range; though, as we later learned from prisoners, General St Clair had a few months before satisfied himself by experiment that a twelve-pounder shell carried from the fortress to the summit, and could therefore carry in the contrary sense too.

General Phillips saw at a glance that Sugar Hill easily commanded the fortress; and remarked that 'where a man can go, a mule can go; and where a mule can go, a gun can go.' He called in the Lieutenant who was Engineer-in-Command of the Army, and asked whether he and his sappers could in a reasonably short time construct a road to the summit, up which gun-teams could haul howitzers of eight-inch calibre, light twenty-four pounders, and medium twelves. The Engineer visited this place – for we had by now environed the position for near three-fourths of its circuit, advancing through the woods with great caution on either side of the inlet, while the naval force kept in the centre – and was at first staggered by the broken rocks, the matted creepers, the huge fallen timber that encumbered its steep sides. Yet he undertook, if provided with sufficient fatigue-men, to make within twenty-four hours something that was worse than a turnpike road, but better than no road at all. So it was arranged, and my company was among those called upon to act as labourers upon this road. This was July 4th, the day which the Americans celebrated as Independence Day, and we could hear cheers for the United States of America coming down the wind to us. In the evening a dozen rockets were set off by them, and then one more, in honour of the thirteen States.

Under the Lieutenant's direction we heaved, pushed, fetched, carried, and sweated. A spur to our exertions lay in the consideration that if we could not thus force the enemy to evacuate their works by a threat of being shelled into Glory, General Burgoyne would call upon us to make a frontal attack upon them. We did not fancy a second Bunker's Hill victory; to advance across open country under fire of well-posted batteries, until we came to the tangle of forest-trees felled with their branches towards us, and finally, as we emerged in disorder from thence, to be picked off, one by one, by their excellent riflemen. A few lucky ones of us might make a lodgment and go at the enemy with the bayonet – who, as we knew, were ill-provided with this handy arm – but at a cost of perhaps half our force.

By dawn of July 5th a sort of road had been completed up Sugar Hill and the guns hauled up it on pulleys, by the combined powers of men, mules, horses, and oxen. As daylight grew, we were rewarded for our exertions by being permitted to peep through telescopes at the enemy works, where it was possible to count the defenders of each redoubt, and the guns in each battery, and to observe the enemies' vessels riding behind their gigantic bridge. Said General Phillips to us: 'Thank you, my brave lads, for what you have done tonight. Let us rechristen this hill "Mount Defiance".' Then the guns were laid, and shells and grape were sent plunging down into Mount Independence, and into the old French fort.

It was an unpleasant awakening for General St Clair: he must choose either to hold his ground and lose his army, or quit his ground and lose his character. For the Americans had set great store by Ticonderoga ever since it had been captured from us, two years previously, by the fanatical Colonel Ethan Allen 'in the name,' as he said, 'of the Great Jehovah and the Continental Congress'. To yield the place without a struggle would strengthen the factious power of the New England Congress-men against General Schuyler and himself. He called a Council of War of his colonels, and there urged that to take the less glorious course of retiring, while they still could, would be ultimately of more benefit to their country. They assented, and he made the most of the short time that remained for getting away what he could of his men, stores, and artillery. Nothing could be done by them until nightfall, on account of our observers on Mount Defiance; but the sun no sooner set than two hundred *batteaux* were laden with baggage and sent off under escort of the five galleys that still survived from General Arnold's fleet; while the troops followed on foot. They did not take the usual route down the Lake George inlet, for the brigade in which we served commanded that water from a hill named Mount Hope, which we had seized without opposition and hastily fortified; we had two brigades of artillery there with us, besides. Instead, they took the only remaining route, which was down the South River, the troops in the old French fort marching over the great bridge and down the farther bank. A building was fired by one of their lesser generals, in spiteful disobedience to General St Clair's orders, which lit up the scene and discovered great activity. However, it was doubtful whether they planned a sortie or a retirement, and we therefore stood to arms the greater part of the night. At daybreak an Indian scout, who had crept into the French fort under cover of darkness, reported that the enemy were gone. Immediately, we who were on piques duty were ordered to enter the works; where General Fraser himself planted the British flag upon the rampart. After a short examination of the place, to make sure that the enemy nowhere lay in ambush for us, we hurried to the great bridge in order to search the works on Mount Independence.

This bridge was supported by twenty-two sunken piers of timber, the interstices being filled with separate floats, fifty feet long and thirty wide, strongly fastened together with iron chains. It was likewise defended, on the Lake Champlain side, by a boom composed of very large pieces of timber, fastened together by riveted bolts and double chains. Through this bridge the British seamen from our fleet were busily cutting a passage to allow the frigates to sail in pursuit of the enemy galleys and *batteaux*. Some were demolishing the boom; others had already removed a part of the bridge itself, between two of the piers; a third party were unshackling one of the great floats, to tow it away. They reckoned, by nine o'clock in the morning, to have cleared away an obstruction upon which the Americans had bestowed incredible labour over a period of ten months. We were obliged to halt a few minutes while we built a slight gangway for our passage over the breach.

Upon reaching the farther side we possessed ourselves of the heavy battery that defended the bridge. There we came upon four Americans lying dead drunk upon the ground beside a cask of Madeira. We counted ourselves very fortunate in this, for we observed that the matches were lighted and they had evidently been left behind to fire the guns off at our approach and blow us to pieces; but the wine had allured them to forget their instructions and drown their cares. The heads of some powder-casks were also knocked off and powder strewed in a train to them, with the object of injuring our men as they gained the works. A number of Wyandot Indians had attached themselves to our party, from a hope of scalps and plunder, and were curious in examining everything that lay in their path. One of them caught up a match that lay upon the ground with some fire still alive in it and began waving it about, the sparks flying in all directions. 'Down on your faces!' I shouted in alarm to my comrades, and not an instant too soon, for a spark dropped upon the priming of one of the guns. It discharged with a great roar, but in any case would have done no injury, for by some error the muzzle was elevated above the level of our heads.

Here, though I fear to impair the verisimilitude of my story with anything so preposterous, I cannot forbear to mention an incident which had occurred on the previous day. There were, as it happens, many reliable witnesses of it, and Lieutenant Anburey of The Fourteenth has recorded it in his well-known *Travels Through the Interior Parts of America*.

A little after dawn, Smutchy Steel, being a sentinel of our piquet guard, observed a man in the woods reading a leather-bound book. He challenged him, with 'Who goes there?', but the man was so closely intent upon his studies that he did not reply 'Friend' nor make any other response. Smutchy abstained from use of the bayonet, but ran up and seized him by the collar of his coat. Awaking from his reverie, the intruder said very calmly that he was Chaplain to the Forty-seventh Regiment, but could otherwise give no account of his presence there. Smutchy bade him stay where he was until the relief came; whereupon he was taken before Captain Montgomery, the nearest officer, who sent him under escort to General Fraser. General Fraser suspected him to be a spy, for The Forty-seventh were stationed two or three miles in the rear, and he thought himself acquainted with the face and name of every clergyman attached to the forces. He began to ask him several questions about the Americans, remarking that if he consented to answer them fairly he would escape hanging. The stranger pretended to be perplexed and persisted in his first story.

'Come, come,' said General Fraser, 'a person in your dishabille cannot pretend to be a man of God going about on his lawful occasions. Own to the cheat, pray, or it will go hard with you.'

'Sir,' said the prisoner, 'you have only to send to the Colonel of The Forty-seventh, and he will inform you who I am. I reported for duty at his headquarters yesterday evening with a letter of credit from the Governor-General of Canada.'

'And your name?'

He gave his name.

He was sent for examination to General Burgoyne, where his story was confirmed. I had no share in these proceedings, but Terry Reeves came running up to me at about seven o'clock with pale cheeks, and 'Oh,' he cried, stuttering, 'I have seen him.'

'Seen whom, Moon-Curser?' asked I. 'It was a ghost or banshee, by the look on your face.'

'Worse,' said he. 'It was the Devil. Him whom we last saw in the Newgate tap-room, the day that little Jimmy was tucked up.'

I shuddered involuntarily. 'You are dreaming, dear Terry,' says I. 'Or is it the apple-brandy?'

'Gerry Lamb,' he replied very solemnly. 'Would I ever mistake the sallow face, and the loose, wet lock, and the ugly chin to him, this side the grave? Or would you yourself, Gerry?'

I have already confessed to my superstitious weakness in the matter of the Holy Thursday candle. It will not therefore seem surprising to my readers to learn that this appearance, or apparition, of the Reverend John Martin worked strongly upon my imagination. It seemed a presage of the utmost calamity to our forces, though our great successes of the following

week seemingly belied it. What is more curious still, this Popish priest, or
Methodist minister, or Chaplain of the Established Church, this Reverend
John Martin, once more disappeared so soon as he rejoined The Forty-
seventh; but reappeared as suddenly, a fortnight later at Skenesborough,
for a single day, and was thereafter lost to us. It has ever teased me to know
whether or not the letter of credit from General Carleton was a forgery, or
whether he had actually imposed himself upon that excellent personage.

We now explored Mount Independence; it was clear of Americans; and
the rest of the brigade coming up, we set off again in pursuit of the enemy.
The day was sultry, with the sun boiling behind a thin screen of clouds.
We marched without a halt from dawn until one o'clock over a number of
steep and woody hills, by a very rough track. A party of Indians went
ahead, who being unencumbered by packs and heavy clothing could
advance far more smartly than we; they brought back a score of stragglers
to us, and we learned from these that the American rear-guard was
composed of chosen marksmen under the command of a Colonel Francis,
one of their best officers. General Riedesel's Brunswickers were in our
support, but they could not keep up with us on the march on account of
heavy accoutrements and old age.

We were taking the Hibberton road, a roundabout route to
Skenesborough, which was the American base near the extremity of the
South River. We had halted about two hours and partaken of our dinners
when General Riedesel rode up. He appeared in considerable excitement,
and, 'Why, Red Hazel, my old friend,' General Fraser bantered, 'what
means this flashing eye, this surly visage?'

He answered in tolerably good English that his Goddamned old pigs
were straggling and he could not prevail upon them to mend their pace.

Said General Fraser: 'Do not blame them, General. I remember no
march so fatiguing as this in the whole course of the Seven Years' War in
Germany. Here, accept a present of gingerbread. It was taken from the
Americans at Ticonderoga out of a parcel left over from their celebrations
of Independence.'

General Riedesel scrutinized the gingerbread, which was gilt and baked
in the form of a mermaid. He gave her an amorous leer, then, with a sudden
snap he bit her head clean off, and burst into an enormous peal of laughter
– which so infected those who stood by that all immediately were
convulsed with mirth. The mermaid's head then becoming lodged in the
General's windpipe, he had like to be choked, but that Captain
Montgomery, who rode up, smote him in the back with his fist. The
gobbet shot out across the road, and he subsided, gasping and wheezing.

We marched on towards the enemy, who had gained Hibberton. When
our scouts reported that they had halted three miles from us, about two
thousand in number, we chose a defensible situation and lay that night on
our arms. We slept until three o'clock in the morning, much tormented by

the insects, and then renewed our march in the half-light. Two hours later we came up with the Americans and found them busily employed in cooking their provisions, though with piquets posted.

Then began a skirmish which, since the Americans were compelled to fight, became a pitched battle. When the piquets were driven in, our Grenadier battalion was sent round to cut them off from the Skenesborough Road, which ran through Castleton; so they turned instead towards Pittsford which was thirty miles to the east, along a steep, rocky road. The Grenadiers, to intercept them, climbed a hill so sheer as to seem inaccessible; they could only gain the summit by laying hold of the branches of trees and hauling one another up the rocks by main force. Being thus headed off, the Americans showed fight and, while some attacked the Grenadiers, others turned about and fired at our light infantry companies as we hurried after them. Those Americans who had axes hurriedly felled trees, to serve as a breastwork behind which to receive us.

The brushwood was exceedingly thick and tangled, and their marksmen took careful aim at us as we stumbled up against the breastwork. I was proud to find how steadily our men behaved, though we could preserve no sort of order or dressing, nor use the manual exercise for platoon firing in which we had been perfected during our training. We made an improvement *ex tempore* upon it, however, by abstaining from any use of our ramrods: after loading and priming we merely struck the breech of the firelock to the ground, which sent the cartridge down, brought it to the present, and fired. We maintained a certain unity of action by singing in unison *Hot Stuff*, a rousing song that now enjoyed the same popularity among us as the famous *Liliburlero* (that chased King James out of three kingdoms) had enjoyed among our predecessors of The Ninth at the relief of Londonderry, the capture of Athlone, the victory of Boyne Water. With dry throats and swelling hearts we sang:

> From rascals as these may we fear a rebuff?
> Advance, Grenadiers, and let fly your hot stuff!

Each side in this engagement, which lasted near two hours, afterwards claimed to have been greatly inferior in numbers to the other. My belief is that the sides were about equal, though the tenseness of the woods and the excitement of the occasion ruled out any counting of polls. It ended when General Riedesel, who had been impatiently waiting for his lagging troops to appear on the field and have their share in the glory, hauled forward fifty men of his vanguard and brought them into action. He bade them beat drum, blow fife and bugle, shout, sing battle-hymns and fire their muskets into the air to suggest to the enemy that they were the whole Brunswick Brigade; and this they did. The hullabaloo turned the scale: the Americans, who had lost their brave Colonel Francis, slackened their fire, and we charged with the bayonet. They did not receive us, but all ran off

– except those who surrendered, and one or two lurking fanatics who remained behind, concealed in bushes, waiting for the chance to shoot at the 'tyrannical British officers'. One of these succeeded in killing a well-beloved captain of ours, as he was examining some official papers taken from Colonel Francis's pocket-book, and escaped unavenged. As I ran in the direction of the shot, I came upon Sergeant Fitzpatrick kneeling alone and bareheaded in a little hollow. He was giving thanks to God that his life had once more been spared, in the solemn words of the Psalmist: 'O God the Lord, the Strength of my Salvation: Thou hast covered my head in the day of battle.' His calm and tranquil aspect checked me in my bloody course; I returned to my comrades.

Smutchy was cleaning his rifle when he discovered, to his surprise, that in the excitement and confusion of battle he had put no fewer than four cartridges into his piece. His mouth being so busy with *Hot staff*, he had not thought to bite off the ends: he had snapped his piece in vain, because he had also omitted to prime the pan. If these cartridges had exploded together the overcharge would have burst the gun and perhaps injured him fatally. 'However,' Smutchy said, 'there was no confusion as to my baggonet'; and, glancing at it, I observed blood upon the blade. There was a sudden sick revulsion in my belly at the sight of a fellow-creature's blood smeared on steel, and I went apart into the bushes and vomited.

This having been a hand-to-hand engagement, unlike my first skirmish at Three Rivers, I must describe the course of my feelings during and after it. Before the fight opened, I was seized with apprehensions, in the knowledge that my life hung upon awful accident. This natural instinct, the anxiety for self-preservation, caused a quick pulsation and agitated my breast; so that during the hot climb up the hill-side my lungs came nigh to bursting. But, at the moment when the first bullet whizzed by me, all emotion vanished, my breast calmed, and my limbs drew upon an unsuspected source of energy. I was entirely lost in the ardour of the battle, wherein it was my duty not only to fight but to direct others in fighting. Reflection upon the brutal nature of war or the sanctity of human life suffered temporary suspense; I acted like one in a trance; and trees, bushes, my comrades, the enemy, were as one sees pictures dancing in the flames of an open fire. It was not until we came to burying the dead that a thousand severe and painful feelings recalled the thoughtful mind and all the affections. The sight, especially, of dear comrades agonized with mortal wounds harrowed the recesses of my heart – some writhing and groaning in misery, some with brains oozing from shattered skulls, others sitting up or leaning on their elbows, pale with loss of blood, observing with a dull horror the extent of their injuries. I suffered sorrowful pangs, too, for the ragged enemy dead, whose cause their stubborn courage had in a manner ennobled. Worse than this, we found among the bushes two unfortunate Americans, wounded in the legs, who had lost their scalps to the

Wyandots, but were pronounced recoverable by the surgeon. It was shocking to see a live man so ferociously disfigured; and I wondered that I had ever allowed myself to be enrolled in an Indian tribe.

I found occasion for reflection, too, upon the hairbreadth escapes with which many had been blessed in battle, while others were terribly taken off in the first onset. Lord Balcarres, our tall, gallant commander, whose glittering uniform made him the target of every rifleman in the American rearguard, had his coat and trousers pierced with about thirty balls, yet escaped with a slight flesh wound in the hip; while Lieutenant Haggard of The Marines was shot dead between the eyes in the opening attack, and Major Grant of The Twenty-fourth through the heart, before ever the battle was joined – having been twice wounded in previous wars at this very placer

Not only solemn emotions possessed my unwrought mind. I recall with what an excess of laughter I greeted the story of Captain Harris's wound and his humorous sally. He was commanding the Grenadiers of The Thirty-fourth when he was struck, and scrambled on hands and knees to the shelter of a tree. Lieutenant Anburey of The Fourteenth, passing by, asked him: 'Are you badly hurt?' Though in great agony from a broken hip-bone, he clapped his hand to the part adjoining, which had also been pierced, and with an arch look, replied: 'You can ask my a—e, Anburey, you can ask my a—e!'

Now, a disagreeable happening to be related will show that the agreed rules of civilized warfare were either despised as tyrannical or not well understood by the New England soldiery. Stratagems and ruses are one thing, but to trade cunningly upon the mercy and humanity of the foe, quite another. General Schuyler, for example, made use of a legitimate and witty ruse about this time. He arranged for a letter written by himself, as from a Tory partisan behind the American lines, and enclosed in the false bottom of a canteen, to fall into General Burgoyne's hands, which perplexed him for days.

But an altogether different case was presented at this battle of Hibberton (or Huberton or Hubbardtown as it was indifferently named). Two companies of Grenadiers stationed in the skirts of the wood, close to a clearing, observed a force of about sixty Americans coming across this clearing with their arms 'clubbed' or reversed, the recognized sign of soldiers who wish to surrender. The Grenadiers held their fire and stood in a relaxed posture, ready to disarm such voluntary prisoners; but when these had come within ten yards they turned their muskets round in a single concerted motion, and, firing a destructive volley upon the Grenadiers, ran as fast as they could into the contiguous forest.

This seeming treachery greatly exasperated the surviving Grenadiers, who gave no quarter for the remainder of the campaign; but I would name it ignorance rather than treachery – a mistaken application to warfare of a principle allowed as legitimate in trade throughout New England. The principle was that of *caveat emptor*, 'let the purchaser beware of being over-reached', and the good people of Massachusetts and Connecticut would tell you droll tales for your entertainment of how they had tricked and defrauded, not only strangers but friends and neighbours, in a manner that in Great Britain or Ireland would bar them from the society of respectable men. I was a long time accustoming myself, during my residence in America, to this moral obliquity, which I will say, however, very positively, did not belie their natural good fellowship and hospitality. Rather it was a sort of sport with them, as among the knavish, jovial horse-swappers of Yorkshire, or the tinkers of my own country. Yet it must have caused a householder a deal of inconvenience never to be sure that the sack of corn that he had accepted as 'country pay' – for where coin is scarce one must pay in kind – might not in reality be one-third corn and two-thirds chaff mixed with earth; or that in a consignment of hams that he had bought for his winter use from a travelling merchant, one-half might not be made of bass-wood, carved and painted to a lifelike similitude of the sample he had approved. If he were duped, he was expected to laugh heartily and to remark: 'I guess it was a regular pedlar's trick and serves me well right for being so green and sleepy-eyed.' Nor was scriptural authority wanting for this smartness. The son of Sirach in the *Book of Wisdom* had declared: 'A merchant shall hardly keep himself from doing wrong, and a huckster shall not be declared free from sin.'

The enemy had fled in great disorder, leaving two hundred dead on the field, and many more disabled by wounds: besides, the remains of a whole regiment, two hundred men, gave themselves up. But we did not press the pursuit for fear of out-running our supplies, of which we were so deficient that our breakfast that morning was bullock's flesh broiled in the wood-ashes and eaten without bread or salt; these animals were found running in the wood. We were not to know that General St Clair's failure to reinforce his rear-guard had been due to the contumacious refusal of two militia regiments to march; and that, had we pressed the pursuit, we might have captured prisoners by the thousand, and supported ourselves upon the food and ammunition that they strewed behind them in their rout.

General Fraser had immediately dispatched a messenger to General Burgoyne, should he be at Ticonderoga, acquainting him with his success. He now desired to send the same message to him at Skenesborough, should he have succeeded in destroying the enemy's forces at the bottom of the South River, and reached that place, whither he himself now intended to march. He therefore called for a volunteer to carry the message ahead of his advance; and when I informed his aide-de-camp that I had lived for three months among the Mohawk Indians, and was ready to go, the mission was confided to me. The General allowed me to choose a companion; Mad Johnny Maguire at once recommended himself. We set off together a few minutes later, being ordered to travel as expeditiously as possible. We took the road through Castleton, a wretched hamlet of twenty houses, which lay a few miles away. This place we avoided by a circuit, for fear of meeting the enemy, but stumbled on a great stone jar of cider in a field near by, covered with grasses against the sun, and refreshed ourselves from it.

It was not until the middle of the morning that we observed armed Americans: a large party of militia marching up the road towards us.

CHAPTER XXI

OUR FLEET, having forced the bridge at Ticonderoga, had pursued the
enemy vessels down the South River and overtaken them in the afternoon
previous to our Hibberton battle. There was no escape for the Americans,
who were at anchor in South Bay, a naval station close to Skenesborough.
Two of the five galleys struck their flags, the remaining three were burned
by their own crews: of more than two hundred *batteaux* the most were
captured and the remainder sunk. The Americans, as they retreated, set
fire to their stockaded fort, their storehouses, saw-mills, forges, repair-
sheds, slips. The flame caught the hanging forest above the station, and up
it all went in the greatest conflagration imaginable. Not one earthly thing
was saved for the Americans, of whom about thirty were intercepted and
captured by men of The Ninth, who had been disembarked before the
attack began and ascended the hill from the flank. Others fled towards
Castleton; and these were the men whom Maguire and I now observed
coming towards us down the Castleton road.

Since we had no wish to engage in any fighting, we concealed ourselves
in the bushes and let them go by; our vanguard would snap them up, we
judged, in an hour or two. I had suggested the precaution of turning our
jackets inside out, so that the fustian lining should show, instead of the
scarlet, and render us less conspicuous – but Maguire said that this fashion
reminded him too sadly of punishment drill at Waterford Barracks; he
begged me not to make it an order. Since the scarlet of both our jackets was
faded almost to a brick colour from long exposure to the torrid sun, I
consented.

A party of about twenty Americans went by, arguing loudly among
themselves on politics, their muskets slung. Behind them came two more
men, a little dandiacal officer and a huge hairy-bosomed private soldier
who limped. The private, as he passed our lodge, cried to the other: 'Hold
hard, Andy, there's a tarnationed stone in my shoe. I must halt to shake it
out.'

'I am thankful of a respite, Neighbour Benaiah,' replied the officer
smoothly, sitting down plump a few paces from us. 'But, hark ye, I can't
rightly agree with you that the Britainers intend to push on beyond

Skenesborough. I calculate that 'tis but a feint to deceive us, and that's the reason of the plan of attack being openly published and advertised these months afore. No, my dear Benaiah, Johnny Burgine an't a-going to march down south on Albany with but eight thousand men agin the full thirty thousand we can oppose to him – for who's to guard his communications, eh? Be sure old nasty Carleton won't, seeing that he is Johnny's mortal foe and eaten with jealousy. No, no, dear Benaiah, and Billy Howe an't a-going to move up North to meet him, neither, and I'll tell you for why. I calculate old Billy Howe's a-going to transport his army by sea and land to the neighbourhood of Boston – for Boston, as we all know, is the centre and hearth of Independency; and Johnny Burgine, he'll return all his men, but a few, back up the Lakes and down the St Lawrence River and join forces with him within the month. The Britainers an't such fools as they pretend, not by nation much, that they an't. I'm bound back home to Boston to repel the landing with God's help, and I'm a-taking the company with me.'

'No, neighbour Andy,' said Benaiah, 'that you are not. You shall stay here to captain us, you tarnal skunk, or we'll shoot you for sure. No hooking it off and giving us the slip, mind, you jockey! The bloody-backed rascals are here, and here we'll fight 'em, so soon as ever we have refilled our pouches and sacks.'

The officer attempted to reply, but Benaiah with a growl told him to hold his rattle. Just then we heard shots, as of a brisk skirmish at some distance away in the direction whither we had been proceeding; whereupon the two Americans arose, the man Benaiah coolly and resolutely, his officer showing great apprehension, and passed on.

Maguire and I, who had both experienced a great desire to burst into laughter during this confabulation, now went cautiously in the direction of the shots. They ceased as we approached, and soon we came in sight of a detachment of our own regiment, under Captain Montgomery, who had secured a number of prisoners and were about to return to Skenesborough with them. We directed Captain Montgomery in the pursuit of Captain Andy's company; and in return he told us where to find General Burgoyne, to whom our message was addressed. We delivered it to him that evening, having come a matter of thirty miles, and arrived three hours in advance of the brigade. General Burgoyne was most affable to us and greatly encouraged by the news. Our reward was a bumper of Madeira wine apiece.

On his informing us that The Ninth had been detached that morning in pursuit of the enemy, who were retreating by Wood Creek towards Fort Anna, and that hard fighting was there expected, we begged leave to be allowed to join them; our excuse was that we bore a report to Lieutenant-Colonel John Hill, who now commanded The Ninth, of the losses we had suffered at Hibberton. These included the captain of our Grenadier Company, dead of his wounds, and a lieutenant seriously injured. The

General consented to our petition, and we joined Captain Montgomery, who was proceeding in the same direction. The next morning we were rowed up Wood Creek, which was shaded by enormous trees, in cedar-wood canoes: a gracious voyage. At the point where we were obliged to disembark because of obstructions in the stream made by the retreating enemy, we found ourselves in a camp of about five hundred Algonquin and Wyandot Indians, under the charge of the Deputy-Quartermaster-General of our army, Captain J. Money of The Ninth; they directed us to the Regiment. Several of these savages wore bloody scalps attached to their belts, and I observed with horror and disgust that one of these was that of a fair-haired woman. The warrior who wore it seemed fatigued after a long journey, and was rolling in the grass to refresh himself, as if he were a horse.

After marching along difficult roads and wading through rivulets, where the bridges had been destroyed by the enemy, we overtook our comrades about dusk. They had captured a number of American boats in Wood Creek laden with luggage, women and invalids, and were now encamped within a quarter of a mile of Fort Anna, which appeared to be strongly held. The fort consisted of a wide square formed by palisades with loop-holes between; inside was a large block-house and a store-shed. The whole stood on a slight eminence above the creek, with a sawmill adjacent, the mill-race of which gushed from a steep wooded hill.

I handed the message to Colonel Hill, who complimented me upon the speed with which I had delivered it. Knowing that I had some slight knowledge of surgery, he bade me report to Surgeon Shelly (who had exchanged with Surgeon Lindsay from another regiment) as his mate; for a hot engagement was expected. Maguire he ordered to remain with Captain Montgomery's company. We lay upon our arms all night, and I confess that I slept well, undisturbed by fears of the morrow, for I now accounted myself a veteran soldier. Lest the enemy should slip away from us, we had posted piquets on the skirts of the wood around the Fort, in front of which there was a cleared held of about a hundred paces broad. The enemy did not hold the sawmill, which lay outside the palisade.

The weather was sultry and a storm approached, to judge by the distant rumblings of thunder to the northward; but when dawn showed, the sky was still clear, though sudden gusts of wind blew hither and thither.

A man then came running out from the Fort, pursued with musketry-fire, which, however, did not injure him. He declared breathlessly that he was a loyal subject of King George and willing to serve in our ranks. Being questioned, he said that the thousand men in the Fort were in great consternation, as expecting to be attacked and stormed by us immediately. By the detachment of our flank-companies to General Fraser's division, The Ninth were reduced in strength to less than two hundred men, including the officers. Colonel Hill therefore instantly sent off a message to General Burgoyne, asking for support; for the rest of our brigade lay eight or ten miles away. The pretended deserter then slipped away, and it proved that he had been sent to spy out our weakness: for within half an hour the Americans came pouring out of the Fort with great fury and shouting.

The sentinels of the piquets immediately discharged their pieces, and their comrades hastened up from the woods to support them. A number of Americans fell. The remainder ran back to the palisade, re-formed, and came on again with redoubled violence. From where I stood with Surgeon Shelly, carrying his salve-box and bandages in my hand, I could see nothing, for the woods were very thick; but Captain Montgomery came marching by us with his company and we fell in behind. The noise of musketry in a close wood is very terrible, the discharges echoing from tree to tree and the bullets smacking among the leaves. Our whole line held firm and we shot down a number of men; but the rest ran across our right flank and we could hear their officers bawling to them to 'Follow up, follow up.' Colonel Hill then put us to a severe test of drill by bidding us change front and retire up the hill to our left. At this moment a party of Americans in blue and buff came at us, firing as they advanced; Captain Montgomery fell, wounded in the thigh, from which the blood rose in a little fountain. Surgeon Shelly had just finished dressing the wound of another man with my assistance. He ran to the Captain's side and says he to me: 'Sergeant Lamb, while I press upon the artery, wind the tourniquet tightly, close above.'

I complied with his order. We were glad of Mad Johnny Maguire's protection, for he ran forward with charged bayonet and sent the foremost Americans back; then returned to us, observing in a matter-of-fact voice, to the wounded Captain: 'They don't take the bayonet home, your Honour, so naturally as they should.'

I had nearly fixed the tourniquet ligature to Surgeon Shelley's satisfaction, when they came on again. 'Run, Sergeant; run, Maguire, my good man,' cried the Captain between his groans. 'Leave me, for I can't follow.' Off ran Maguire, but I remained for another few seconds until the bandage was secured and the Surgeon could remove his thumbs from the artery; then I, too, dodged among the trees, the bullets crashing about me and the enemy pouring up like a mighty torrent. I was thus the last man to ascend the hill; but heartily blamed myself as I ran that I had lacked the wit to snatch up the salve-box and the roll of bandages. These were now captured, together with Surgeon Shelly and the Captain. However, it was too late to return for them.

This manœuvre of Colonel Hill's was brilliantly executed: for indeed the Regiment, though rough in camp and on parade, was ready enough on the held, and we all made the summit of the hill except a few men. Here the ground was more open, and our companies drew up in Indian file, facing the enemy, each leading soldier discharging his piece in turn and then running to the rear of the file to reload; so that we maintained a well-directed fire for nearly three hours. I took my turn in the line of Lieutenant Westrop's company, who was shot through the heart as he stood by my side. A few minutes after, a man a short distance upon my left received a ball in his forehead, which carried off the roof of his skull. He reeled round, turned up his eyes, muttered some nonsensical words as if he dreamed, and fell dead at my feet.

Soon our fire slackened, for our ammunition was well-nigh expended; and the enemy, perceiving this, boldly ran across our front to cut off our retreat, nor could we prevent them.

Just at this critical moment, when all was still, came a cry that made my heart leap with joy and threw the Americans into the utmost consternation: 'Whoo-oo-oooop' resounded through the woods. Grounding my firelock, I clapped my hand to my mouth and, 'Whoo-oooo-oop', I replied, wildly modulating the note as I had learned, in welcome to the approaching Wyandots and Algonquins. The Americans scattered incontinently and, the fight being over, The Ninth formed upon the hill. Colonel Hill then led them down to the seizure of the Fort; but I remained behind to play the surgeon.

It was a grievous sight to see the wounded men bleeding on the ground. What made it more so, was that the rain, of which only a few great drops had hitherto fallen, came pouring down in a deluge upon us; and, still to add to the misery of the sufferers, there was nothing to dress their wounds, now that the salve-box was gone. I took off my shirt, tore it up and with the help of a soldier's young wife, Jane Crumer (the only woman who was with us, and who kept close by her husband's side during the engagement), made some bandages from these strips and from the hem of her petticoat, and bound up each man's wound in turn. I had held Jane in affectionate regard for some years. She was a slight-figured girl, not beautiful in a picturesque sense, but with an excellent speaking voice and fine eyes – a niece of Sergeant Fitzpatrick, with whom she had lived before her marriage. Little Jane had attended the arithmetic lessons at Waterford that I gave to his boy, and proved my aptest pupil.

Soon Maguire came in search of me, and, 'By the Holy, Gerry, my jewel,' says he in great excitement, 'I can hardly see you for the rain that's in my eyes. Now here's a packet of news for ye. Those bloody savages who saved us were no Indians at all, but only Captain Money's codding. For he brought them up when he heard the battle noise, but they wouldn't come; so he sent them away and came running up alone, and it was he who uttered that whoop, not they, the heathen beggars – they were four miles hence. What's more, the rebels burned down the block-house and the saw-mill, but the rain has put the flames out and hardly a stick is charred, Glory be to Jesus, and amn't I lucky to be alive?'

I stopped the flow of his talk by making him help Mrs Crumer and myself in conveying those of the wounded who could not walk, to a woodman's hut some hundreds of yards away, the nearest place of shelter. This hut had been the scene of a skirmish towards the end of the battle, for one of our companies had seized it for use as a fort when the enemy tried to outflank us. The work was excessively fatiguing, since we must carry the poor fellows in blankets slung upon poles, and the rain made the ground very slippery.

We had come back from the hut for our third load, and there still remained nine men incapable of movement, when up rode General Burgoyne himself, with his jolly face and jutting chin, together with his 'family', or staff, in order to view the battlefield. Recognizing me, 'So you arrived in good time to share the glory, my brave Sergeant,' he cried in a booming tone. 'Tell me, now, how did the battle go?'

I pointed out the positions, which he noted carefully – in order, I suppose, to remark upon them in his dispatches; and I then made bold to ask him for men to be sent to help me with carrying the wounded, which he obligingly consented to arrange.

Then he said: 'Should any of the Americans surprise you while you are performing this meritorious and humane duty, you must have a letter to give to their commanding officer, which should ensure the preservation of your life – if, indeed, the leaders of this rabble in arms have bowels of compassion like ordinary men.' He desired his aide-decamp to lend him his back as an escritoire; and then and there, using a pen, a strip of paper and a pocket ink-horn, indited a very eloquent plea for my life and signed it with a tremendous flourish.

I thanked him and he galloped off. Jane Crumer looked after him, and then back at me, and laughed softly. 'There now,' she said, 'I confess I am quite disappointed. I expected him to pull out tinder, flint, taper, wafer, tape, and all, and seal the letter in headquarterly style. Why, he never even used a sand-castor!'

However, the General did not forget us. He sent up a dozen men of the Twentieth Regiment to act as a carrying party. I dispatched Maguire and Mrs Crumer to Colonel Hill, to acquaint him with my situation; and the Colonel sent back Maguire, together with three other men and a quantity of provisions. The Colonel informed me that he was ordered to return to Skenesborough and that he left the wounded in my charge. Among these was Lieutenant Murray, with a flesh wound in his calf, who made merry with two fellow-Irishmen who were boasting of the blood they had shed in the service of their King and country, and the gravity of their wounds. In his blunt manner he exclaimed: 'By heavens, my good lads, you need not think so much of being wounded – for, by Jesus God, there's a bullet in the beam yonder by the door, and devil a compliment or pension will that poor timber earn!'

The losses of The Ninth on that day were thirteen killed and twenty-three wounded of all ranks; the gains were thirty prisoners, some stores and baggage and the Colours of the Second Hampshire Regiment of the Massachusetts army. We were commended in Orders.

As for myself, I remained for seven days as surgeon in charge of the hut, whither a supply of salves and bandages was sent up from Skenesborough, and a load of other necessaries. I encountered but one American, by name Gershom Hewit, of Weston, Massachusetts, a poor fellow whose right hand had been broken by a ball, and his leg injured. When I espied him, he was lurking in a thicket near our hut, in the hope of picking up scraps of food that we threw away. I had him covered with a musket when I told him to advance and be recognized. He expected me to shoot him out of hand, and was infinitely grateful when, seeing that he would never be able to soldier again, I dressed his wounds, provided him with victuals and drink, and sent him hobbling back to his own folk. He promised most faithfully not to reveal our whereabouts to his compatriots; which promise he kept.

We expected every moment to be attacked, and fortified the hut as best we could, cutting loopholes so that the wounded men also could fire on the enemy; but we were never molested, though every night during our stay we heard the noise of axes, as the enemy felled trees to hinder the advance of our army. We were proceeding against Fort Edward, on the upper reaches of Hudson's River, their new rallying-point. At the end of that time we returned to Skenesborough. All the wounded men, except three who died, were then nearly fit for duty; for, in preference to the drugs sent me, I had used a vulnerary recommended to me by the Indians, a sort of hartshorn which I found growing near the hut.

Now, Skenesborough was owned by a Scottish gentleman named Skene, a major on half-pay, who had served hereabouts in the previous war, and had been so taken by the beauty of the place that he obtained by Royal Patent a grant of 25,000 acres at the foot of the South River; and began to establish a great domain. It was he who owned the block-house and saw-mill at Fort Anna, and every other building for miles around. He was a Loyalist, and entertained General Burgoyne in a very magnificent way at his house in Skenesborough. Some say that all our subsequent misfortunes were due to this person. For though we were distant by land not more than twenty miles from Fort Edward, the effort of transporting our artillery and stores by this route would be gigantic because of the frightful nature of the country intervening: but all difficulties were denied or minimized by Major Skene, who calculated that a great military road cut from his quay to Ford Edward would render his estate more valuable by many thousand pounds. The alternative was to take us back by water to Ticonderoga, and thence to sail down Lake George, where the enemy could offer us no opposition. This would take four days with favourable

weather; and from Fort George, at the lake's end, a good wagon-road ran
to Fort Edward – the defences of both places being in a ruinous condition.
These stormed, another week should have brought us in triumph to
Albany; had we left our heaviest guns behind.

However, General Burgoyne took the advice of his host. After two days
but two miles of road had been built, notwithstanding the incredible exertions of men and teams; and General Burgoyne should then have acknowledged the error and called the task off – as did General Carleton when we
sweated over-much to drag the two schooners entire from Chambly to St
John's. But Major Skene pretended that more favourable ground lay
ahead, and reminded the General of his Order of the Day at Crown Point,
'This army must not retreat', which piqued his honour. General Burgoyne
had, moreover, sent his fleet of *batteaux*, his own and those captured, up
the South River for supplies, and was ashamed to send a fast ship to recall
them. He determined to continue the work at all events, the more so as
many hundred of provincial Loyalists had arrived in the camp, some with
arms, some without, and their expert services could be applied in the
pioneering way.

General Philip Schuyler lay at Fort Edward with the beaten American
army, amounting to little more than four thousand men; and had left in our
hands above a hundred pieces of artillery and large supplies of flour and
beef. Two regiments of New England militia he found so disorderly, and
so addicted to plundering, that he dismissed them from his army; and what
was left could not be depended upon as a fighting force. Yet he was
resolved to spare nothing, not even his own good name, not even his life,
to promote the cause of Independence which lay so near his heart. At Fort
Edward there were cannon lying about on the grass, but no gun-carriages,
and scarcely any entrenching tools; insufficient camp-kettles and not five
rounds of powder and ball for his muskets. He could not hope to hold the
place, but only to delay us until reinforcements were sent him. He had
already angered Congress by a letter to them protesting against their
dismissal of one of his surgeons without his leave; and now John Adams
was saying that the 'patriot armies will never successfully defend a post till
they have shot a general' – meaning Generals Schuyler or St Clair – 'who
has yielded a fortress, uncontested, to the enemy.' However, for the vict-
ualling of the army that remained to him after the desertions and his
dismissals, and for the delaying of our advance, General Schuyler could
draw upon his private fortune. He was the proprietor of an ancestral Dutch
domain at Saratoga on Hudson's River, some miles downstream from Fort
Edward, which was regarded as the best managed estate in all America, and
where hundreds of skilled labourers were engaged in his service. Soon
their axes, too, were added to those which we heard ringing in the forest,
and marvellous obstruction they caused.

The woods here were composed chiefly of oaks of different variety, and the tough hickory, the hemlock, the beech, intermixed with great numbers of the smooth-barked Weymouth pines. They grew to a great height, though none appeared to be more than two feet in diameter; indeed, the girth of the woodland trees of North America was very small in proportion to their height and trifling in comparison of that of the forest trees at home – they sprang up so close together here, and in such rivalry of the sun, that their force was spent in gaining height rather than thickness. These trees, General Schuyler's soldiers and lumberers sent crashing to the ground, at intervals of a few paces, across every path and trail, creek and rivulet, between ourselves and Fort Edward; and ditchers with spades laboured, also, to dam and divert these waters to our hindrance. While he was thus adding hugely to our labours, General Schuyler was also subtracting from our subsistence by driving off all flocks and herds, and carting away or burning all standing crops which lay within the utmost range of our foragers.

It was while I was in the hut at Fort Anna that the Reverend John Martin reappeared at Skenesborough and preached a sermon to the troops on a Sunday morning. This was said to be a very dove-like, unwarlike address and more fitting for a parish church at a harvest festival than for the present occasion, which was a thanksgiving service for the success of our arms. The text was 'Be ye not like unto the ox and the ass, that have no understanding.' After the sermon a *feu de joie* was fired by the whole army, with artillery and small arms. We heard the noise in the distance and could make nothing of it, though we guessed it to be the explosion of a magazine.

I have spoken of the mosquitoes of Skenesborough, that bred there in the stagnant waters under the protecting shade of great trees, as the most malignant of all in America. The inhabitants were proof against their venom, but on us they raised great watering pustules precisely like those of the smallpox. The only sure relief was to be looked for in volatile alkali, of which we possessed scarcely any; but immediate bathing in cold water was better than nothing at all. To scratch was most dangerous, and many men were deprived of the use of their limbs for days from swellings due to this imprudence; two were obliged to undergo amputation. These insects added to the hardships of our men, whom on July 17th I rejoined, returning to my own company in the Light Infantry battalion. The road had then attained but one-third of the length projected, and the obstacles were growing more and more numerous. Exclusive of the labour of hauling away the fallen timber, we found it necessary, before we had done, to construct no less than forty bridges and a causeway, two miles in extent and consisting of large timber laid transversely, over a quaking morass. Nor were the bridges mean feats of engineering: many measured as much as forty feet in height and two or three times that in length, straddling over deep and muddy rivers. Occasionally small parties of the enemy attacked our piquets, but were easily repulsed.

The common soldier's labour now began to become severe in an extra-ordinary measure. Though working through a difficult country in the hot, sickly season, he was obliged to bear a burden which none except the old Roman veteran ever bore. He carried a knapsack, a blanket, a hatchet, a haversack containing four days' provisions, a canteen for water, and a proportion of his tent furniture. This, superadded to his accoutrements, arms and sixty rounds of ammunition made a great load and large luggage indeed. Yet the German grenadiers, with their enormous swords, long-skirted clothing, heavy brass-fronted caps and big canteens holding about a gallon, were even worse circumstanced. The carrying of the rations was the greatest grievance to our men, who all held to the opinion that we should rather have been taken round by water at our ease than forced to these cruel labours. Many succumbed to the temptation to pitch the whole contents of their haversacks into the mire, exclaiming: 'Damn the provisions, we shall get more at the next encampment! The General won't let us starve.'

It was the last day but one of July before we reached Fort Edward, having taken twenty days to cover as many miles. This place consisted of a large redoubt with a simple parapet and a wretched palisade, and barracks for two hundred men; and stood in a little valley near Hudson's River upon the only spot not covered with forest. The Americans had withdrawn at their leisure thirty miles to the southward; General Schuyler, very properly, as I have indicated, risking to be court-martialled as a traitor and coward for the sake of luring us deeper into American territory. The farther we advanced, he was aware, the greater the numbers of militia and frontiersmen who would come out in defence of their homes, and the longer and less defensible our lines of communication. General Schuyler was even single-minded enough so to yield ground as to make a battlefield of his own domain and expose it to ravage and destruction by both armies. This conduct had its expected reward. The 'proud Bashaw of Saratoga' (as his back-biters named General Schuyler) was once more superseded in active command by General Gates; though, much to the chagrin of the Adamses, the courts-martial upon him and General St Clair failed to commit either to the firing-squad.

Unluckily for us, General Washington, who took the part of both these excellent officers in their disgrace, now insisted to Congress that, at least, General Benedict Arnold should be employed by General Gates in a subordinate command; and they consented. It was, however, with some difficulty that he persuaded General Arnold to go to General Gates's assistance, for he was labouring under a resentment. When in the February of that year five American Brigadiers had been raised in rank to Major-General, General Arnold was not among their number, though his services enormously outweighed theirs, and all were junior to him. Washington gave Congress his opinion of this unpardonable slight put upon the most capable officer in their army, and wrote to General Arnold himself, very delicately expressing his sympathy and begging him to take no hasty action, for he would 'do all in his power to correct an act of such flagrant injustice'. General Arnold was touched by General Washington's warmth and replied that 'every personal injury shall be buried in my zeal for the safety and happiness of my country, in whose cause I have repeatedly fought and bled and am ready at all times to risk my life.'

Had the matter not been thus arranged, and had General Washington, moreover, not reinforced this Northern army by stripping his own of some of its best troops – and sending up, besides, camp-kettles, shovels, pick-axes, field-guns and small-arms ammunition from his own arsenals, the campaign would have no doubt ended in a very different manner. Such disinterested conduct as his was by no means universal among the leaders of the American Revolution and deserving, in this instance, of his coun-trymen's highest praise; for General Washington was not certain but that our Southern army under General Howe might not suddenly attack and overwhelm him.

The jest of it was that General Gates, when he returned to his command, found himself far from welcome. Indeed, a strong brigade which had arrived from Vermont was for turning back in disgust, unwilling to serve under him, and other regiments expressed the same disinclination. But the magnanimous General Schuyler urged them not to make his supposed quarrel their own: for he had no quarrel.

CHAPTER XXII

THREE DAYS before our arrival at Fort Edward, there had occurred a sad murder by a party of Wyandot Indians, led by a powerful chief named The Panther, of a Miss Jane M'Crea who lived with a relative of General Fraser's in the neighbourhood of Lake George. The occasion was the abandonment of Fort George, at the southern end of the lake, by the American garrison; and the flight, either to the American or the British camp, of almost all the settlers of the district, for fear of marauding parties. Since the news of Miss M'Crea's fate made a great noise in Great Britain and America at this time, I shall take the liberty of relating it in the words of that great American partisan, Dr Ramsay:

> This, though true, was no premeditated barbarity. The circumstances were as follows: Mr Jones, Miss M'Crea's lover, from an anxiety for her safety, engaged some Indians to remove her from among the Americans, and promised to reward the person who should bring her safe to him, with a barrel of rum. Two of the Indians who had conveyed her some distance on the way to her intended husband, disputed which of them should present her to Mr Jones. Both were anxious for the reward. One of them killed her with his tomahawk, to prevent the other from receiving it. General Burgoyne obliged the Indians to deliver up the murderer, and threatened to put him to death. His life was only spared, upon the Indians agreeing to terms, which the General thought would be more efficacious than an execution, to prevent similar mischiefs.

The above account has been challenged by some, who deny that Mr Jones, an officer in a newly raised corps of Loyalist sharpshooters attached to our army, ever made any bargain with the Indians; and say that Miss M'Crea was found wandering in the woods. Others explain that the dispute arose between The Panther and a chief of the Ottawas who met the party as it was escorting Miss M'Crea to our camp in all civility and decency. Be this as it may, The Panther, also named 'The Wolf' by some authors, arrived in camp with Miss M'Crea's scalp in his belt, which had hair of a yard and a quarter long. Some of the many poets who later versified upon her fate described these tresses as being 'black as raven's wing'; others made them 'yellow as ripe Indian corn.' I cannot satisfy my female readers upon this question. The Panther was, it seems, unaware of the heinousness of his act, which was that expected of an Indian man of honour: it was held decent to avoid unnecessary bloodshed between fellow-warriors by sacrificing the subject of dispute, whether horse, dog, or woman, so that neither party should triumph. He consented at last, when he was acquainted with the sorrow and grief of Mr Jones, to sell him the scalp for a trifling consideration, though Indians in general are most chary of parting with these relics even at a very high price. (Mr Jones, by the way, never subsequently married but, surviving the war, retired to Canada, a morose and taciturn man.)

Had the threatened execution of The Panther taken place, his brothers-in-arms would have been bound by custom to revenge themselves upon our sentinels and advanced posts, for he was held in great esteem by them. General Burgoyne did very well not to press the matter, against the remonstrances of General Fraser. The chiefs of the confederacy of Wyandots, Algonquins, and Ottawas, then called a council under the presidency of a Frenchman, Monsieur St Luc le Corne, who had once led them in their wars against the English. At this meeting they informed General Burgoyne that their warriors were most discontented by the restraint in which they were kept, as never before when they had served as allies of the French. M. St Luc remarked: 'General, we must brutalize affairs, you know.' General Burgoyne replied warmly: 'I would rather lose every Indian in my army, Monsieur St Luc, than connive at such enormities as you would condone.' The next day, therefore, these tribes deserted by the hundred, loaded with such plunder as they had collected; only Indians of the Six Nations being left with us, and not many of these.

It cannot be a matter of much surprise that the murder of Miss M'Crea and General Burgoyne's pardon of The Panther were painted in the darkest and most disagreeable colours by the Americans, and that reports of similar outrages were fabricated by them and printed at large in their newspapers to discredit us. Dr Benjamin Franklin, who should have known better, circulated a document of his own composition, purporting to be an extract from a letter written by a certain Captain Gerrish of the New England Militia. This piece, which appeared in the *Boston Independent Chronicle*, described in minute circumstance the taking of booty from the Seneca nation, among which were eight packages of scalps lifted from American soldiers, farmers, women, boys, girls, and infants. A forged invoice and explanation from one James Cranford, trader, to Sir Guy Carleton in Canada was appended, and his supposed request 'that this peltry be sent to the King of England'.

But it astonished me later to learn that such cheap lies obtained circulation and credit even at home. *Saunders' News-Letter* of August 14th 1777 gravely asserted: 'Seven hundred men, women, and children were scalped on the sides of Lake Champlain. The Light Infantry and Indians scoured each bank, women, children, etc., flying in turn before them.' Now the fact is, that between St John's and Crown Point there were not more than ten human dwellings, the whole country being upwards of eighty miles of woods and wilderness. Could inhabitants who never existed be either scalped or made to fly before their enemies? Yet, necessary as it would seem for such public scandal-mongers to acquaint themselves with the topography of the places in which they fix their scenes of horrid action, their readers are usually as ignorant and willing to believe evil as themselves were to concoct it, so that the lie travels far. As a former light infantry man I hold this libel against my Corps in particular detestation.

At Fort Edward our expedition was faced with a further stubborn task, namely to clear our communications with Fort George, twenty miles from us, which was to be our base of supplies. General Schuyler, who was not superseded until a fortnight later, had sent a thousand axe-men up each of the roads and tracks connecting these places. Moreover, the road, once cleared, must be solidly laid to bear heavy transport. For between us and Albany, our destination, lay two broad and swift rivers over which our artillery must somehow be conveyed: thus, in addition to the artillery itself and our supply wagons we must also bring along large numbers of *batteaux* and a quantity of planking to form two solid pontoon bridges. One-third of the team-horses expected from Canada had not arrived to haul for us, nor could our foragers, scour the neighbourhood as they might, discover more than a mere fifty ox-teams. Thus a deal of the hauling was by man-power.

Great ill feeling was caused among us that the Brunswick foraging-parties failed to add to the common stock the cattle and sheep they took, yet drew from this stock their share of what we put in. We seldom now tasted fresh meat, but were reduced to our British salt beef, salt pork, and biscuit once more; and while our officers were content each to take all his worldly goods upon his shoulders in a knapsack, the German officers positively refused to be separated from their superfluities, but maintained a great train of vehicles to carry them. Our officers felt that this was unjust, and regretted having left at Ticonderoga, in the Light Infantry storehouse, many comforts which had become necessaries in a climate of this sort, and which could be conveyed upon a single tumbril. Colonel Lord Balcarres wrote asking General Burgoyne's permission to send a small party back to 'fetch a little baggage'. This permission was refused, on the ground that no party of men, however small, could be spared; and it was desired that no officer, either, should be given leave of absence for this purpose.

Lord Balcarres thereupon went in person to General Burgoyne and said frankly that he stood greatly in need of certain articles, such as shirts and stockings, left at Ticonderoga, and must fetch them at all events. Though he had been forbidden to send out any party of men, however small, nor any officer, he warned the General that he would obey this order only in the letter – he would send out a single sergeant, as being neither an officer nor a party of men. General Burgoyne took this in good part, but enlarged upon the danger to such a lonely emissary, for the woods were filled with prowling rebels. Lord Balcarres thereupon declared that he had a man in mind for the task who could be counted upon successfully to accomplish it; and was then good enough to name Corporal, acting as Sergeant, Roger Lamb of The Ninth.

General Burgoyne recollected me as both the messenger sent on from Hibbertown and the surgeon with whom he had spoken at Fort Anna. He not only consented but ordered that, if I accepted the mission, I should hasten the delivery to him of a quantity of other stores newly arrived at Ticonderoga, taking command of the recruits and convalescents there and bringing them back with me as escort. The cause of General Burgoyne's anxiety for the stores was that his advance was held up for lack of them. His foolish counsellor, Major Skene, had advised him to supply himself at the expense of the enemy, who had a richly stocked magazine and supply-base at Bennington, thirty miles to the south-eastward. Major Skene declared that the supplies at Bennington were but weakly guarded, that the district was populated with none by Loyalists, and that the Brunswick Dragoons, who still lacked horses, might have their choice of several hundred that were collected there. General Burgoyne thereupon sent off a force of Germans, with an advance guard of Indians, who, coming up against a strong force of New Hampshire militia and farmers from Vermont – under General Stark, a former British officer who had been overslaughed for promotion and now took handsome revenge – were utterly routed, losing five hundred men and all their artillery, ammunition and wagons. Thus his need of fresh supplies was worse than before.

Lord Balcarres now sent for me and explained what he wished done, without disguising the dangers of the journey. 'But,' said he graciously, 'my opinion of you is already so high that I feel perfectly sure that you will successfully undertake for us this very necessary service. See, here is General Burgoyne's pass, made out in your name.'

I undertook the commission with alacrity, not a little proud to be chosen as the depository of his Lordship's confidence and that of our Commander-in-Chief.

We were stationed at Fort Miller at this time, which lay fifteen miles beyond Fort Edward. The month was early September, although I cannot now recall the day, since my journal remained unposted for two months from July 8th, the day of the fight at Fort Anna. I set out from Fort Miller at noon, taking with me no blanket, but only some provisions, a rifle and twenty rounds of ball-cartridge. That it was a hazardous journey I knew well, for several of our men had been attacked when bringing up supplies or running messages. However, I kept off the beaten track, like an Indian, and by four o'clock came safe to Fort Edward – where a sergeant of the regiment stationed there gave me a drink of rum – then off again towards Lake George, after ten minutes' halt.

In this lonely journey through almost continuous pine forest, broken with tangled clearings, I met with no single soul, and stopped but once or twice by the way to refresh myself with the wild raspberries of excellent flavour that there abounded. I recalled, with little satisfaction, that this was the very way that had been taken by the wretched survivors of the Massacre of Lake George two years before my birth. The victims of this massacre were some scores of British soldiers – the number is not exactly known – together with their women and children. They were the garrison of Fort William Henry at the lake head, who had capitulated from hunger to the French general, Monsieur de Montcalm. He had allowed them all the honours of war and a safe convoy under guard to Fort Edward, but his callous and inhuman subordinates permitted these unfortunate people, whose ammunition had been taken from them, to be plundered and murdered by the Indians in the French service, led by M. St Luc le Corne.

One of the survivors, Captain Carver, wrote very pathetically of his escape. Being first robbed of his coat, waistcoat, hat, buckles, and the money from his breeches pocket, he ran to the nearest French sentinel and claimed his protection, who only called him an English dog and thrust him back with violence among the Indians. He was next struck at with clubs and spears, most of which he dexterously dodged, though a spear grazed his side, and some other weapon caught his ankle. When he took refuge among a party of his countrymen, the collar and waistband were all that remained of his shirt. The war-whoop then sounded and a general murder began, with the scalping of these defenceless men, women and children; yet French officers were observed walking about unconcernedly at some distance, shrugging and smiling. The circle of the British becoming greatly thinned, Captain Carver burst out from it, but was caught at by two stout chiefs, who hurried him to a retired spot where they could dispatch him at their leisure. He had almost resigned himself to his fate, when an English gentleman of some distinction, as Captain Carver could discover by the fine scarlet velvet breeches he wore, his only remaining covering, happened to rush by; and one of the Indians relinquished his hold, intent on this new prize. The velvet breeches showed fight, and Captain Carver broke away in the bustle; glancing around, he saw the unfortunate gentleman dispatched with a tomahawk – which added both to his speed and desperation. To be brief, after many similar hazards, the Captain escaped to the briary forest and, after three days in the cold dews and burning sun without sustenance, and with the loss of a shoe, reached Fort Edward at last more dead than alive.

Heaven evidently avenged the massacre by striking down Monsieur de Montcalm at Quebec and finally driving the French from Canada. As for the Indians, they perished of smallpox, which they took from the French, almost to a man; for while their blood was in a state of fermentation and Nature was striving to throw out the peccant matter, they checked her operations by plunging into cold water, which proved fatal to them. The reason that the French were held in such esteem by the Indians was that they interfered little with tribal customs, not even acknowledging the unwritten law of Christendom that all innocent and defenceless persons of whatever nationality, and especially women and children, must never in any circumstances be deliberately resigned to the barbarity of savages. They even winked at the practice of cannibalism, for about this same time Monsieur de Carbière's Ottawan Indians drank British blood from skull-goblets, and ate British flesh broiled, as Father Roubaud, a Jesuit priest, has testified in his history.

In avoiding the road, I made a circuit through the woods which brought me past a broad sixty-foot waterfall to the very pond near which the massacre took place. It was now called Bloody Pond. Dark had fallen and the dews were chill. The shallow waters of the pond were covered with beautiful white lilies. I was greatly fatigued by this time, and withdrawing from the pond to a deep part of the wood, lay down to sleep under a tree. The night dews awakened me shivering with cold about two hours later, and I resumed my march. I was no Indian, and had from drowsiness lost my sense of direction. By three o'clock in the morning I had no notion where I might be. Happening to see a light on my left, I cautiously approached it and perceived that it came from the open door of a log-house, against which was outlined the figure of a man wearing a large round flopped hat.

As I stood there, wondering what he might be, whether rebel or loyal, I heard a sudden shivering cry and a few unintelligible words, as if some woman or child were being put to the torture. Confused thoughts of Bloody Pond still crowding my head, I strode forward with my piece primed and cocked, resolving to take instant vengeance on the villains, come what might.

I called to the man: 'Hold up your hands, I have you covered' – with which summons he complied. Coming close, I found him to be a man of sturdy frame with unpowdered dark hair cut short and hanging around a white hat; his face was of a wild, melancholy cast. He smiled at me and asked in a smooth, wheedling, yet not unpleasant voice: 'What dost thou here with that weapon of murder, Friend?'

I pushed him aside and burst into the room – and there saw at once that I had absurdly mistaken the cry: the agony was not that of death, but of birth. A woman lay on a wooden bed in the corner of a plain, neat room, her face covered with her hands, her knees drawn up; and another woman, wearing a little black bonnet, was ministering to her in the capacity of midwife. I checked my impetuous career, and turned back in shame to the

man in the doorway. 'Forgive my foolishness, sir,' I said. 'I was confused.
I had thought it was the Indians at work.'

'Have no fear of the Indians. They are an honest and well-conducted
folk, unless they are abused, or partake of ardent spirits and so become
tired.' ('Tired' I found to be his term for 'intoxicated'.) 'They have shown
me and my family much kindness, for the sake of William Penn, who was
their friend.'

I then observed that he was a member of the Society of Friends, or
Quakers, and not a wet Quaker, neither – the sort who affect silver buckles
on their shoes, lace ruffles at neck and wrist, and powder on their hair –
but of the dry sort who wear drab, threadbare cloth coat and breeches,
cotton stockings, and plain, square-toed shoes.

'I was going out to the patch to commune with the Lord, praying Him
to mitigate the suffering of this poor soldier's wife,' he said simply. 'Wilt
thou accompany me, friend, and join thy prayers to mine? For it is written
that "When two or three are gathered together in Thy name" – here he
lifted his eyes reverently to Heaven – "Thou wilt grant their request." My
inner voice assures me that thy steps were directed to my door for this very
purpose.'

I answered nothing, but went with him; and presently we kneeled down
together in the dews at the edge of a held of tall hemp which he had
planted. There he began to pray with exceeding slowness, trembling in all
his body as he wrestled with the words. They came out one by one, often
in repetition, as if wrung from a strict compression of his heart: 'Grant –
O Lord – to this – my – poor – poor – sister – my – sister – now – O Lord
– labouring – labouring – labouring – with child – cheerful – courage –
now – oh – humble – courage – to endure – endure – O – Lord – to endure
– the punishment – of her mother – her mother – who sinned – her mother
– our mother – Eve – who – sinned – in Eden.'

'Amen,' said I greatly affected; and as we rose from our knees, the
woman's pangs lessened, for we heard the other comforting her and calling
her 'poor soul' and 'dear honey'. But the child was not yet born.

'Who is the woman?' I asked, in a low tone outside the door.

'Friend, I do not know her name. She was brought to my house by a
Mohican Indian, a follower of the Christian Thayendanegea, or Captain
Brant, a chief of that nation. She affirms herself to be the wife of a soldier
in the Ninth Regiment and relates that she was braving the perils of these
woods alone and on foot, from Montreal, in order to come up with him.
She was seized, she says, with the sickness of labour in the forest, where
she must have perished had the Indian not found her and brought her to
me. Yet I wonder that she is dressed in Mohican fashion, not in English
dress.'

The Quaker woman then emerging, I asked her trembling: 'Will she
live? Does all go well?'

She replied shortly, 'With God's help. There is nothing amiss.'

The pangs began again at that moment, and the woman returned to the house. I was so torn with emotion that I caught at the Quaker's sleeve and, cried I, 'Come back, sir, to the hemp patch, and let us wrestle this out together.'

He was nothing loath, and turned back with me.

I do not know what I prayed in my agony of heart, but the honest man knelt by me and cried, 'Amen, Amen!' to my wild outpourings, until the cries from the cabin ceased; and presently the woman in the bonnet came out with a little creature wrapped in a cloth and, says she, 'Josiah, O Josiah, kiss 'un, the sweet little girl.'

Josiah took and kissed the child fervently, and so did I, with indescribable emotions. 'The mother is sleeping now,' the woman said.

I told the good Quaker, who begged me to enter his house and partake of a dish of tea: 'No, I thank you, Friend Josiah – for a true friend you have been to me – I cannot accept. I must go forward to Fort George, according to my orders. Direct me, I beg, for I am lost.'

He said piously, 'No man is lost who loves God and his neighbour.'

Now that dawn was at hand, he showed me the path plainly, and I thanked him.

I said, 'Friend Josiah, tell the woman, whoever she may be, that Sergeant Roger Lamb of The Ninth will be passing this way again in about four days' time, with a party of men, and will be happy to convey her to the army in one of the wagons. And tell her this, that I wish her and the child well, from the bottom of my heart.'

I made him repeat these words exactly after me, shook hands with him in affectionate farewell, and directed my steps towards Fort George.

I reached this place as the sun rose; and upon my presenting to the officer in charge of the garrison my letter from General Burgoyne, he provided me with a captured American *batteau* to take me up Lake George to Ticonderoga. The Canadians called this lake by the elder name of Lake Sacrament, from the purity of its water, which they were in former times at the pains to procure for sacramental use in their churches. The bed was of fine white sand, giving a pellucid clearness to the lake, which was four-and-thirty miles long and nowhere more than four miles wide. Lake George embosomed above two hundred islands, which were for the most part but barren heath-covered rocks garnished with a few cedar and spruce trees. There was abundance of fish here, such as the black bass and a beautiful large speckled trout, remarkable for the carnation of its flesh. I drowsed rather than slept in my passage through this romantic waterway, which was performed in the finest weather.

We went ashore at Diamond Island with a message for the Captain in charge of the stores-depot there. The island was so called from the transparent crystals that abounded in the rocks upon it. A soldier of The Forty-

Seventh presented me with one which he had found lying loose in the sand, consisting of a six-sided prism, terminated at both ends by six-sided pyramids. When placed on a window-sill in the sun it threw little rainbows on the walls and ceilings, he said. Diamond Island was once overrun with rattlesnakes, whose sloughed skins lay about on all sides, and was in consequence avoided by every one. However, one evening a *batteau* conveying a herd of hogs was caught in a storm while sailing near by and overset. The Canadians and the hogs swam together to the shore, where the former spent the night in the trees and the latter ran off earnestly grunting. The next day the Canadians hailed a passing vessel and were taken off: but some time later, returning to the island, they found the hogs immensely fat, and hardly a single rattlesnake remaining. When they slaughtered one of these hogs they found by what means the island had been rid of its noxious tenantry; for its stomach was full of the undigested remains of rattlesnakes.

Near Halfway Island I witnessed a curious sight, namely a migration of grey squirrels and black: of whom hundreds were attempting to swim across the lake, which was then as smooth as glass, from the western to the eastern shore. We passed a number of their drowned corpses; and others which we overtook, nearly exhausted, ran up into the *batteau*, upon our putting down an oar before them. The boatman secured a dozen of them and said that he would put little chains around them and tame them for pets. Their bushy tails had acted as a sort of float to support them in the water; but the legend that they will raise their tails to act as mast and sail in a breeze I judge ridiculous.

A great curiosity hereabouts was the double echo, which our boatman showed us by calling out in a shrill voice the name of his wife, Louise Marie, which was repeated in melancholy fashion by the curved sides of a mountain, from two distinct quartets at once. I confess that my heart cried, 'Kate, Kate' no less loud and longingly, though my tongue was silent.

For the rest of the journey I slept. A brisk southerly breeze, springing up, carried the boat swiftly forward under sail. Disembarking above the Falls, I made the rest of my journey on foot to Ticonderoga, by way of Mount Hope, passing by a camp of American prisoners of war and several storehouses, and arrived late that same night. I was a day completing my business at the Fort, and two days more in retracing my way down the lake. I now conducted a brigades of *batteaux* containing a great deal of baggage and stores, and recruits and convalescents to the number of sixty. In addition, a crowd of Canadian French came with me, supplied by General Carleton at General Burgoyne's request, to work the *batteaux* on Hudson's River. I urged upon my command the necessity of speed, and kept every man who could work an oar, busy in urging the craft forward.

While I was at Ticonderoga I noticed the remains of a bonfire that some of our young officers had made, of an enormous stack of paper-money issued by order of the American Congress. Several tightly bound quires of bills, of high denomination, had remained unburned and hardly scorched. It occurred to me that it was as foolish an act to destroy these printed promises to pay in specie, as it would be to tear up a private note of hand. I therefore placed the bulk of them to store and took a commission for myself of five thousand dollars. The bills that I chose for myself were of twenty-dollar denomination, as being less bulky for my haversack, and had upon them a rude cut of a zephyr in a cloud disturbing the ocean waves, and the motto *Vi Concitate*, or 'Disturb with force!' I thought the device appropriate, though to *raise the wind* by the issue of such paper unbacked by specie was a doubtful procedure, and when the fraud was discovered by the common people was likely to cause great dissension. The four-dollar notes, which I rejected, showed a wild-boar running on a lance, with the printed sentiment, 'Either death or a decent life'; it was not clear whether the Revolutionary cause was represented by the resolute lance or by the courageous boar.

Returning without adventure to Fort George, I hastened to call upon the Quaker Josiah, during the time that the wagons were being loaded from my brigade of *batteaux*.

I knocked at the door, my heart beating loudly against my ribs, and waited with the utmost impatience to be admitted. Receiving no reply to my summons, I pushed open the door. There was nobody at home, but a weak cry from an adjoining room sent me hurrying to where the child was lying in a cradle of maple-wood, its tiny body covered with gauze against the mosquitoes, and naked because of the great heat of the day. Around its neck was tied my Charles groat on a slight blue ribbon.

I could not wait, for my military business was urgent; but I had the good fortune to meet with Josiah half a mile from the hut. He informed me that the negress who attended his wife, an emancipated slave, had two days previously lost her infant, of a cough. Kate Harlowe had thereupon resigned the child to the care of this woman, and the guardianship of the good Quaker and his wife, saying that she herself had no milk to give it, nor was the battlefield any place for a mother and her new-born child. But her place as a wife was beside her husband. The very day after I left her there, Josiah said, she had bidden the family farewell and set out to meet her husband, though against their wishes and continued entreaties.

The Quaker turned and walked a little of the way with me back to the Fort. He spoke very honestly of the shortcomings of numbers of his co-religionists. Not only were there Wet Quakers, who loved the world too well, but (it seemed) there were even Free Quakers who bore arms in the war. Yet, he said, such plain murder – if I would forgive the term, being a soldier – was perhaps less heinous in the eyes of God than the hypocritical action of some of his former companions at Philadelphia. In refusing to serve in the wars, or to pay the tax imposed upon them for their refusal, they acted in conformity with their faith; but he detested that they had voted the sum of twenty thousand pounds for 'wheat, barley, and other grains', letting it be known that among 'other grains' might be counted those of gunpowder – and thus becoming accessories of murder. In disgust of which unrighteous folly he had left them, and come to live in the wilderness.

I asked him: 'Friend Josiah, if you think me a murderer, why do you walk at my side in so social a fashion, and talk with me so pleasantly?'

He replied: 'Our Lord, Jesus Christ Himself, did not hold himself apart from the Roman soldiers, nor even from a Centurion, their officer. And John the Baptist bade soldiers be content with their pay.'

'If Saint John said that indeed, surely he was condoning murder? For the payment was for their being soldiers, namely for the practice of killing.'

He made no reply, but paced on with compressed lips.

I asked him again, thinking that perhaps he had not heard me: 'Expound, Friend Josiah: why did he who was counted worthy to baptize the Saviour of Mankind thus address soldiers, bidding them be content with their pay?'

He answered, 'Had even the Saviour Himself told them, "Thou shalt not kill", they would have mocked at Him (though such was the command of the Father), for they had taken the soldiers' oath to Caesar and could not unsay it. They were already murderers, as thou sayest. To them could be given no higher notion of virtue than they were capable to follow. And to thee, friend Roger, as my inner voice assures me, the Lord would not say, "Thou shalt not commit adultery," for thou knowest this commandment well, yet hast disobeyed it in a manner that cannot be undone. Instead, He would say, "Keep thy evil imaginings away from this woman, since she is the wife of another, and pray God that thou fallest not again into the same snare."'

With that he grasped my hand, the tears wetting his cheeks, and left me. His last words were: 'The child will be taught to worship God in this Wilderness.'

I returned very pensively to Fort George, where I made inquiries after Kate Harlowe, whose path would have led her past the outer sentinels; but she had not passed that way. I concluded that the sound of my name had refreshed her affections, and that she had returned to the company of the Mohican Indians rather than link herself again with her husband Harlowe, and thus bring equal pain upon herself and me.

The next evening I had the gratification of conveying the stores and baggage in safety to the army, and of being thanked by my officers for the manner in which I had executed the orders confided to me.

CHAPTER XXIII

BY MY conveyance of these stores, the army was the richer by a month's supply; and the bridge of boats being thrown across Hudson's River two miles above the village of Saratoga, on the 13th and 14th of September 1777 we crossed and encamped on Saratoga plain. Here the country was exceedingly beautiful but utterly deserted by its inhabitants. We of the Light Infantry formed the vanguard and, following down the opposing bank, soon came upon a delightful stream, the Fishkill Creek, peopled with exotic wildfowl, broken into artificial cascades, and trained around several tiny islands planted with unusual flowering shrubs. Beyond, a broad green lawn sloped easily down to the water's edge, and at its head stood General Philip Schuyler's spacious mansion, with a row of noble pillars extending its entire length from ground to roof. The mansion at Skenesborough had been very well, for so remote a place, but it was by comparison with this but a large and well-appointed block-house. This had both elegance and maturity and we saw clearly that the spirit of subordination, rather than that of 'Liberty, Liberty, Liberty' animated the General's artisans and tenantry, whose cottages could be seen in the distance clustered around a good-looking church.

The transition from the hideous and unkempt country about Fort Edward to this European paradise was striking. We found ourselves treading with humility and soberness, as we flanked the lawn in order to search the house, avoiding to violate the well-tended flower-beds and the neat borders of the gravelled paths, and stopping delicately between the rows of cabbages. It might almost have been Castle Belan, near Timolin, which I had visited as a recruit on my march to Waterford; but that here painted wood was generally employed instead of bricks and stucco. The house was embellished within, as we had expected, with solid and beautiful furniture, rich hangings and carpets, china and silver in glass-fronted cupboards, of which but little appeared to have been moved. In the dining-room we observed two or three lifelike portraits of General Schuyler's ancestors who were notable Dutchmen, and a fine equestrian portrait of His Majesty King George. Out of respect for the decency of these surroundings we abstained from plundering the least thing, but searched the attics, cellars, and outhouses, discovered nothing and passed on; but left a guard against the depredations of our Indian allies. The solid grist-mill, saw-mill, barns, and other buildings were also found clear of the enemy.

There was but one road in the neighbourhood, following the course of Hudson's River down to Albany, thirty miles away: it was flanked by forests, commanded in many places by rocky heights and often separated from the broad flood of the river only by a precipice. This was the road we must take, and many tributary creeks and thick forests lay between us and our destination; and, as a half-way obstacle, the deep and rapid Mohawk River. The enemy was encamped ten miles from us, at Stillwater, in a strongly entrenched position known as Bemis Heights. Our communica-tions with Canada were long and exposed; we had with us but a month's provisions; most of our Indian allies had left us; and what with the losses at Bennington and elsewhere, we were reduced to less than six thousand troops, including Germans and American Loyalists, against perhaps four-teen thousand of the enemy. The odds against us were increased by the greater discount that must be made in our case for men necessarily employed on other services than that of fighting: such as baggage and ammunition guards, and attendants upon the sick and wounded. Not three thousand of our men, of whom something better than two thousand were British, could be put into action at any given time; whereas the American fighting strength fell short of their total forces by far less. We did not, however, allow ourselves to consider the possibility of a check. Being ordered to attain Albany, there to join hands with our Southern army under General Howe, which was to advance up Hudson's River, we were resolved at all hazards to reach this rendezvous before our supplies failed: where we would be once more provided with all necessaries.

A very disagreeable circumstance was that a diversion of ours, to the westward, had signally failed. This was made by Colonel St Leger, who had gone by way of Lake Ontario and taken with him a battalion of American Loyalists, a few regulars and a thousand Indians of the Six Nations, led by Thayendanegea, under the guidance of Colonel Guy Johnson's brother, Sir John Johnson, Bt. Colonel St Leger routed and killed General Herkimer in a stubborn battle – though Thayendanegea was disappointed of his neighbour's scalp – and besieged an American force at Fort Stanwix, which seemed upon the point of surrender; he hoped soon to possess himself of the whole valley of the Mohawk River, a place well known for the number of settlers who remained loyal to King George. But General Benedict Arnold upset all his plans by a cunning stratagem. He prevailed upon a half-witted Dutchman, Hon Yost Schuyler, whom the Indians, because of his peculiar ways, held in a sort of religious awe, to go among the Indians and announce with excitement the approach of an enor-mous army of Americans under General Arnold. This he did. The Indians were alarmed and inclined to believe this tale, for Hon Yost – who performed this cheat in order to save from the gallows his Tory brother, whom General Arnold held – displayed a coat riddled with what he said were British bullet-holes. Sir John and Thayendanegea pooh-poohed the tale, but it was confirmed by an Indian in Arnold's pay who came up shortly afterwards; he, when asked, 'Are the Americans few or numerous?' pointed above his head at the leaves of the forest. After him came another Indian, whose lie was that General Burgoyne's army was cut in pieces and General Arnold hurrying to Fort Stanwix by forced marches. Indians, though not cowards, have always sedulously avoided pitched battles, preferring to harry the flank and rear of an advancing foe. These tribesmen now, persuaded by The Cornplanter of the Senecas, immediately decamped, in spite of all the persuasive eloquence and rum that Sir John offered them; the Loyalists followed, and Colonel St Leger, left with only his few regulars, had no alternative but to break off the siege and retire too. Most of the Loyalists had flung away their arms in terror; so that the Indians, balked of other scalps, took a few of theirs in disgust of such cowardice. Among Indians, to lose even an arrow was considered unwarrior-like, and for the like misdoing or mischance a man was flogged on the bare back by his women folk. Sir John and the Colonel each blamed the other for the common misfortune and drew their swords upon each other. Murder would have been done had Thayendanegea not interposed and recalled them to their duty as Christians.

From the Schuyler mansion we followed the road for three miles between forest land and continuous fields of fine wheat and Indian corn, half a mile broad. Of these, some had been harvested; some burned by Vrouw Schuyler, the General's wife, as she quitted her home at our approach; but a great deal left standing. The harvest was very welcome to our Commissaries, and men were instantly set to work to garner, thresh, and grind the wheat, at the mill, into flour. The maize was cut as forage for our beasts. Still we encounted no enemy, and the whole army moved forward on the following day, September 15th, encamping that night at a place called Devaco – or Dovegat, or Dovacote, or as you please – which lay on a crooked inlet of the river, where the cornfields ended. Beyond this place innumerable obstacles were encountered, such as felled trees, broken bridges over the numerous streams and rivulets which fed the river, and the road itself was cut away wherever it ran at the edge of a height. The army halted for two days while engineers and pioneers repaired this damage, and our Indians went forward as scouts to note the enemy's disposition. We then advanced to within three miles of the enemy's position, halted, and sent forward the repair-parties once more. On September 18th our engineers were obstructed by the enemy in their task of rebuilding a bridge, and we guessed that on the next day we would come to grips.

All this time it had rained heavily, which made our advance the slower, but our people's greatest wish was that the bad weather would continue, for rain spoilt musket-fire, by wetting the priming-pan, as effectively as it had hindered archers in the ancient days by slackening their bowstrings. If it came to push of bayonet, we believed ourselves the victors. We had, moreover, confidence in our own steadiness under fire, in the experience of our officers, and in the comradely unity that bound us all together, barring only some regiments of the Germans.

The American fortifications on Bemis Heights, a hill contiguous to the river, had been laid out by the same engineer, the Polish patriot Kosciusko, who had planned those at Ticonderoga; and were executed in the same swift and solid way by American labourers. But, as at Ticonderoga, the Americans had omitted to hold or fortify a hill, lying a short distance away, which overlooked their stronghold. General Burgoyne was aware that General Gates, in the lobbies of Congress, had presented the yielding of Ticonderoga as a very heinous offence. He therefore hoped that this other fortress would be held by General Gates with the stubbornness wanting in General St Clair; and that, even when it was raked by our guns from the commanding hill on the left, the whole American force would be kept cooped up in it. If this happened, great slaughter would be done. We could encircle the Heights by working round through the woods, and cut the road behind, whereupon any man who attempted to escape must either face our volleys from the woods that surrounded the fortress, or swim the river.

On the next day, September 19th, battle was joined. General Phillips, with the Germans and the heavy artillery, pushed up the road which ran close along the river. General Burgoyne with four battalions, of which The Ninth formed the reserve, and four light guns, took the centre; while General Fraser, with the Grenadiers and ourselves (the Light Infantry battalion), a battalion of American Loyalists, one regular battalion, the rest of the artillery and a few score Indians, was sent to make a wide circuit through the woods on the right. Our task was to seize the hill afore-mentioned which was the key to victory, while the other columns provided a diversion. A combined assault through broken and thickly wooded country is always difficult to achieve in unison, unless signals be given by bonfire, mirror-flash, or signal-gun. It was therefore well that a signal had been arranged, for the centre and left could not have foreseen how long a time would be spent by us in arriving at our agreed position, which was abreast of them at two miles' distance from Bemis Heights. The ground we had to traverse was a frightful tangle of rocks, thickets, ravines, bog-holes, briar-patches, standing trees, and trees overset by a hurricane of some years before. An occasional relief to this wilderness was found in what the country people termed 'clever meadows', namely unexpected grass-grown clearings; the flocks and cattle that came by devious paths to graze on them belonged to the farmstead of one Freeman, built on a hill near by, which formed our centre.

It was late in the morning before we were able to fire our signal-gun, in default of a mirror-flash, the sun being obscured, to which General Burgoyne and General Phillips replied with other guns; and then forward we went. It appears that General Gates had no notion but to do just as General Burgoyne had hoped – to stay snug in his trenches and tamely permit himself to be surprised and raked from the hill. But, unfortunately for ourselves, General Arnold was in a position to challenge and dispute this inept method of waging war. He had recently, after all, been raised by Congress to major-general's rank; as a reward for opposing a British landing on the Connecticut coast, where he happened to be on a short visit to his sister, and, though our people succeeded in destroying the important magazine of Danbury, taking tithes of their forces as they retired. His conduct on this occasion, where again he was foremost in attack and hindmost in retreat and but narrowly escaped death, had commended him so highly to the army that General Gates came to hate him very deeply.

Now General Arnold demanded, with eyes that seemed to shoot out fire, permission to lead out at least a part of his own Division in the direction from which the first signal-gun had been heard, in order to prevent our outflanking the Heights. General Gates refused this request, with a demand to General Arnold to mind his own business; but to one angry man was joined another, the same Colonel Dan Morgan of the Virginian Riflemen who had come so near to storming Quebec two years previously. Colonel Morgan, having been exchanged against a British colonel captured by the Americans, had re-formed and trained his regiment until it was the most formidable in their whole army. The marksmen it contained were now for the most part not Virginian backwoodsmen but Presbyterian Ulstermen settled in Pennsylvania, and some Pennsylvanian Germans. They could march forty miles in a day, subsist on jerked beef and maize-porridge, and for mere sport would often shoot apples off one another's heads, taking turns, at sixty paces. Both Arnold and Morgan had been drinking hard liquor all that morning, in a manner to make them reckless of what they said or did, yet not so as to destroy their judgment of what needed saying or doing. They railed at their Commander in so contumacious a manner that he was terrified for his own safety: for General Arnold kept clapping a hand to his pistol and swearing terribly. Finally General Arnold declared that if he could not go with permission he would go without, and at the head of his entire command; whereupon General Gates yielded sulkily, saying that he might take Colonel Morgan's riflemen and half a brigade of New England militia, but no more.

These forces came out against us about noon, on a front of two miles, and drove in our screen of Indians. The Loyalists and Canadians could not hold their ground either, but ran through our ranks. There ensued a very confusing skirmish, in which the Americans advanced with too great impetuosity, running in two's and three's against our leading platoons. We caught them with well-directed volleys, killed a number and took twenty prisoners. But they were far swifter of foot than we, and avoided the bayonet. The one failing of the rifle-gun, as against the musket, which it enormously outranged, was the difficulty of reloading. Towards the end of the war, little use was made of these weapons of precision, since it was found that delay between shots more than counterbalanced the advantages of their exactness.

It happened that our company under Captain Sweetenham was heavily engaged in this onset; he and I, with ten others, found ourselves separated and surrounded by a large number of riflemen who were dressed in Indian fashion, with no covering at all but leggins and breechclout. The Captain was soon wounded in the shoulder and the foot, four other men fell and the remainder of us had no choice but to retire, plunging into a ravine choked with tall reeds and escaping through a cedar thicket. It fell to me to cover the retreat, for the others went off in a hurry, forgetting that the Captain was able to proceed but slowly. A bullet carried off my cap, another grazed my side, a third broke the lock of my fusil, which I was forced to abandon. A company of The Fourteenth coming up in support, the fire grew very hot, but the Americans broke off the fight when the cry of a wild turkey, many times repeated, sounded through the woods: it was Colonel Morgan's rallying-cry, which they instantly obeyed.

After attending to Captain Sweetenham's wound, I sent him off under Mad Johnny Maguire's escort to the general hospital in the rear; and felt content that I had in a manner made amends for the trick that I had once played on him in forging his signature. Then I returned to the scene of the combat, intending to rearm myself with a musket of one of our dead or an American rifle-gun and the necessary ammunition. I was proceeding cautiously back through the cedar thicket when I heard the voices of two men passing my front, and crouched behind a bush. It was a large, heavy rifleman driving a disarmed British non-commissioned officer before him with the muzzle and butt of his piece; the prisoner pleading for mercy.

'Now, my wee lad,' cried the rifleman in a thick Ulster brogue, which I will not attempt to reproduce in writing, 'Sit you down, for we must have a clack together.'

Richard Harlowe – he it was – had lately been raised to corporal's rank and detached to our company to take the place of another who had fallen sick. He sat down, as bidden, on a tree-stump within view of my lurking-place, and the rifleman stood over him in a threatening posture.

'Don't think I do not know your bonny face, Ralph Pearce, or exult in having you here in my power at last; though be sure I should be glad enough to have Colonel Pearce, your father, sitting next to you, who drove me from my house and trade in Lurgan town, and forced me to sail here across the black ocean. Come now, Ralph Pearce, you who married my little sister Molly against your father's wish and mine; and who threw her off when he threatened to disinherit you; and who afterwards cheated at the cards and was dismissed from your regiment; and trafficked with the Pretender; and went back to poor Molly, to rob her of the jewels you had given her, and broke her heart: tell me now, Ralph Pearce, for I am curious to know – will you die with an easy heart?'

Richard Harlowe, or Ralph Pearce, made a sobbing noise in his throat, begging for his life to be spared. 'No, Alexander Bridie,' he said, 'no, I am not fit to die. Spare me, in Christ's name, for I am not fit to die.'

'I have lived a rough life,' continued Alexander Bridie, 'I have taken life in revenge for one-twentieth less of injury than I have suffered at the hand of the Pearces; and when we have taken life, we folk at the head of the Susquehannah River, we take the scalp too. With you, my charming Ralph, I shall reverse the procedure: first your scalp, and afterwards your life.' He drew out a long Albany knife and whetted it across his palm.

I was struck with confusion by this recital. Should I hazard my own life for the sake of this scoundrel Harlowe, rushing unarmed to his rescue, when by his death I should so greatly profit? Yet if I left him to his fate, would not my conscience ever afterwards reproach me for having not only seduced the wife of a comrade-in-arms, but stood idly by while he was mutilated and murdered?

My better feelings prevailed. I ran forward, halloing, with a rotten stick grasped in my hand as my only weapon; which seeing, Harlowe somer-setted backwards over the stump, dodged among the bushes and was free.

Alexander Bridie brought his piece to his shoulder, aiming at me, and I gave myself up for dead. But suddenly he himself staggered and fell down dead, as a flying tomahawk fetched the back of his head and cleft his skull almost in two.

As I stood staring, a lithe figure came mincing from behind the cedars and with giggles and squeaks, squatting upon his hams, took up the rifleman's fallen knife and with it excoriated the accustomed trophy. It was the Mohican *bardash*, Sweet Yellow Head, and after him appeared the majestic form of my friend Thayendanegea, with three new scalps swinging at his girdle.

Thayendanegea clasped me to him, embracing me fondly and calling me 'my son Otetiani'.

He took me apart into the thicket and said: 'I have news for you, dear Otetiani. This expedition has failed, as did the other expedition we made two months ago against Fort Stanwix; when Arnold, the Dark Eagle, tricked us. I am now about to fetch the Red Men home. I have explained to General Burgoyne my decision and urged him to retire while there is yet hope. But he will not listen. He is infatuated.'

I asked, 'Thayendanegea, what has occurred?'

He replied, 'Nothing has occurred. That is the devil of it.'

'How do you mean?'

'The Southern army was a hundred miles distant from Albany when the campaign began. Now it is not half this distance away – no, it is twice that distance. For General Howe has transported twelve thousand troops to the mouth of the Delaware River and is advancing against Philadelphia, as though he had no interest in us and were waging a private war of his own. General Washington opposes him. The few thousand men that remain in New York, under General Clinton, are insufficient to come to our help up Hudson's River.'

'But the Eastern Army that was also to converge upon Albany from Rhode Island?'

'It has not started. It will not start. General Burgoyne has been sent out on a fool's errand. Now also, my allies report that a strong division of Americans under General Lincoln is advancing against Ticonderoga to cut off your communications with Canada; already, I think, they will have done so. I told General Burgoyne: "I must now take my nation home. If we stay, your people and mine, yours will be captured as being white men, but ours will be massacred as being red. Why do you stay?" He replied, "I cannot believe that General Howe, or Lord George Germaine, would so deceive me. It is a fiction, is it not, confess, brave Thayendanegea, to excuse your departure?"'

'And did he credit you in the end, my Father?'

'He did, and, to his honour, bade me depart in peace and take all my nation with me. You are enrolled in my nation, dear Otetiani. Come with me, since I have permission for you to come. Come, and reside with us again. We love you dearly, my son. According to the Christian law, Mistress Kate is the wife of another; nevertheless, you will be accounted as married to her according to Mohican law, if you acknowledge her child as yours. She is now at our town of Genisee, her heart consumed with love for you.'

'She has positively assured me, Father, that she will never again speak to me.'

'She tells me this: she gives you now another chance to rejoin her. We will take off the little one from the Quaker's hut and find a wet-nurse for her from among our own nation. It is ill that a white child should drink the milk of a black woman. You will be happy with your wife and daughter. You will fight in our battles, and be revenged upon the American rebels, and assist in winning back America for King George.'

Almost he tempted me, but since I had clung to my way of duty before, I resolved not to swerve from it now, our cause being in such straits. I showed him my deep gratitude for his concern in my behalf, but declared that I could not so stretch my good conscience as to decamp from my post in the hour of danger. I would rather perish nobly in good company than live with Kate and bear the disgraceful name of deserter.

He told me, after a long silence: 'Dear son, you have chosen right.' He embraced me, and departed.

Meanwhile, the aspect of the battle had changed. General Arnold with three thousand men had counter-marched from the flank to the centre, where he attacked General Burgoyne, who was holding the house and the paddock of Freeman's Farm with eight hundred regular British troops. Here the action was very heavy, with shot for shot and bayonet against clubbed rifle, for nearly four hours. The American marksmen climbed into the tops of high trees and there took popping shots at our officers, for twenty of whom they accounted. General Burgoyne himself was nearly taken off, a rifleman wounding his aide-de-camp (who rode in fine furniture) in mistake for him. Three subalterns of The Twentieth, none of whom had exceeded the age of seventeen, fell, and were buried that night in a common grave. Our battery of four brass guns was several times taken and retaken, but the Americans could make no use of them, for so often as they were lost, our gunners, of whom but a quarter remained unwounded, carried away the linstocks – to fetch them back once more when the guns were recovered. Had General Gates reinforced Arnold, as he was constantly urged to do, the line would have given way, for The Twentieth were near breaking. But he did nothing, and we were saved by General Phillips who, towards evening, brought up some field-guns at a trot and treated the enemy to a great shower of grape. Behind him came General Riedesel's Brunswickers to take the enemy in flank. General Phillips himself rallied The Twentieth, who had lost half their number in killed and wounded, the Minden veterans acclaiming him with a hoarse shout. The Americans fell back. Though General Arnold, on foot now and pistol in hand, urged them to a crowning effort, they were exhausted and could do no more. In the gathering darkness he led them round in safety behind the impenetrable thicket which covered the American centre. So the battle ended, but for slight encounters as a few Americans, lost in the forest, tried to regain their lines through our posts. By midnight all was silent.

We lay upon our arms that night and at daybreak moved forward to within cannon-shot of the enemy, where we strengthened our camp by cutting down large trees, which served for breastworks. We threw our dead together into wide, shallow pits, and scarcely covered them with clay; the only tribute of respect allowed to fallen officers was to bury them apart from their men. Among the Massachusetts dead were found one or two young women, who, from the fact of one of them having a cartridge clasped in her hand, had no doubt accompanied their husbands or brothers on service in order to load spare firelocks for them in the line of battle. General Fraser shook his head when this circumstance was brought to his notice. 'When women are brought into this damned business,' he said, 'it argues a resolution that will take some beating down.'

Taking all the results of this battle, our advantages from it were few indeed. We kept the field, but the possession of it was all that we could boast, for we were so much weakened that we could not at present press the attack. The Loyalists had nearly all gone off with the Indians. Their disappearance left us at a loss, from their having evinced a wide knowledge of this district and served us in the capacity of guides. Such levies are always precarious assistants to regular troops; they shrink from blows and scanty subsistence and their untrained condition gives them a temper easily dispirited by reverse. It needs the training of years and the tradition of former battles before a regiment can gain that cool presence of mind which will carry it forward unguardedly, to destroy itself if necessary in the cause to which it is devoted.

Two days later a letter reached General Burgoyne from Sir Henry Clinton at New York, confirming Thayendanegea's ill news. This was the first messenger from the South that had arrived since the campaign began in earnest, nor had a single one of General Burgoyne's own ten messengers succeeded in passing safe through hostile territory. The letter, written in cipher, ran merely: 'You know my poverty; but if with 2,000 men, which is all that I can spare from this important post, I can do anything to facilitate your operations, I will make an attack upon Fort Montgomery: if you will let me know your wishes.' Fort Montgomery, on Hudson's River, lay eighty miles to the south of Albany.

This placed General Burgoyne in a predicament. Now, if he decided to extricate our army from the difficult position in which it was caught and, disobeying orders, retired to Canada, he would be behaving very shabbily towards General Clinton, who counted on him to advance. Yet the longer he waited, the more insecure his position. He had that very day been informed that the American General, Lincoln, had successfully attacked our posts and depots about Ticonderoga and the northern end of Lake George; and that he had captured nearly three hundred of our men, several gunboats and the whole of our remaining *batteaux*, with their crews, rescued a thousand prisoners and possessed himself of Mount Defiance, Mount Hope, and other outworks of the fortress. We were thus cut off from Canada.

General Burgoyne sent the same messenger instantly back to General Clinton, with a reply written small on thin paper, and screwed inside a silver bullet. The messenger reached Fort Montgomery, which, by General Burgoyne's account, he expected to kind in British hands, and there inquired of two soldiers, whom he took to be Loyalists, for General Clinton. Such incredibly ill luck attended this expedition that the person before whom he was taken was not Sir Henry Clinton, but a distant relative of Sir Henry's in the American service, who was then Governor of the State of New York. No sooner had the messenger discovered his error than he turned aside and swallowed the silver bullet: which was, however, recovered by means of an emetic. Upon its being unscrewed, the message was found and General Burgoyne's intentions discovered: which were to hold General Gates in play while Sir Henry made a diversion below Albany to draw away his troops. But General Burgoyne revealed that our supplies would not last beyond October 12th.

The messenger was immediately hanged as a spy. 'Out of thine own mouth shalt thou be condemned', was the jest that hurried him into eternity.

We kept within our fortifications for the next few days, not having sufficient strength to attack the Americans, but being most averse from retreat. We hoped also that our continued presence at Saratoga would serve the obscure and perplexing strategy that had fixed us in our present situation, at least by preventing General Gates from marching with his fourteen thousand men to the aid of General Washington. General Burgoyne could not have guessed that he was the victim of a monstrous blunder; but it was so. The story is as follows. Lord George Germaine had in May drafted a dispatch to General Howe, ordering him to march up Hudson's River. This dispatch was in reply to one from General Howe, who did not agree to the plan for co-operating with General Burgoyne in this manner, but favoured instead an attack upon Philadelphia, as the enemy's capital city. However, upon calling at the War Office one morning, on his way to Sussex for a holiday, and funding the draft not yet copied fairly out, Lord George Germaine could not wait to sign it, but continued on his journey. The dispatch was therefore not signed, and therefore not sent, and his Lordship either clean forgot about it or assumed that it would take care of itself. Unfortunately, in another dispatch Lord George had, it seems, approved of the attack upon Philadelphia as a subsidiary enterprise; and General Howe was therefore unaware that he was still expected to assist in the attack upon Albany, or that our army had already set forth single-handed upon this project.

The American General, Charles Lee, who often hit the right nail upon the head, remarked of General Howe, not altogether unkindly: 'He shut his eyes, fought his battles, drank his bottle, had his little whore, received his orders from North and Germaine (one more absurd than the other), shut his eyes, and fought again.'

Though we did not yet know it, the battle had brought out much bad blood in the American camp. General Gates, 'that man-midwife', as General Burgoyne privately named him for his sneaking and unctuous ways, made no mention whatever, in his report to Congress, of General Arnold's presence upon the held of battle; and the chief colonel of his staff spread the absurd story that General Arnold had avoided the fight and spent the whole day in camp, drinking. By this means the single person who prevented us from storming the Heights and breaking through to Albany, and who had therefore saved General Gates's reputation, if not his life, was teased and provoked into mutinous rage. He resigned his command. Every Northern general but one, General Lincoln, then signed a memorial entreating General Arnold to remain with them for one more fight at least; but General Gates withdrew his command from him, and allowed him to remain in the camp only in the capacity of a private person.

The war-like feeling of New England was intense at this time, largely because of the indignation and alarm that had been inculcated in the various provinces by reports of Indian savagery. The militia mustered in enormous numbers and for once paid attention to their officers; deserters were whipped and returned to duty by the Selectmen of their townships – one father even sent back his two recreant sons in chains to the General commanding a Provincial division with the Roman request, 'Deal with them as they deserve.'

CHAPTER XXIV

ON OCTOBER 6th our rations were diminished by one-third, because of a great shortage of provisions, but without exciting any murmur or complaint in the camp. We were already reduced to salt pork and flour, with a little spirits; not even the officers being able to procure tea, coffee, or fresh meat. Our regimental clothes were in a sad state, not having been renewed that year: they had become rotten from the great variety of weather in which we had worn them and ragged from the briars and rough country through which we had fought our way. Our horses also went hungry; for the river-side pastures were soon exhausted, and covering-parties to protect our foragers could not be spared. Most of all we felt the want of sleep, for the forests around us were alive with the enemy, who kept us continually upon the alert and compelled us to lie upon our arms for a great part of each night. The Americans even had the assurance to bring down a small field-piece to fire as their morning-gun, and so close to our quarter-guard that the wadding from its discharge flew against our works.

We had heard a great concerted howling two nights before from the right of our position, which disturbed our sleep; and the same noise arose again on the night following. General Fraser believed that it proceeded from dogs belonging to our officers, who had gone off by night to hunt; he ordered them to be confined, under pain of any stray dog being hanged by the Provost of the Division. However, upon the noise continuing and scouts going out to investigate, it was found that great packs of wolves had assembled and were howling as they scratched at the shallow graves of our poor comrades; nor would they be balked of their banquets, but continued their horrid cries until they had dug up the flesh and consumed it.

On this same night General Burgoyne called his chief officers to a Council of War. He told them, that our army had evidently been intended from the first to be *hazarded* and that it might now require to be *devoted*. He asked their advice. Generals Fraser and Riedesel were for retiring at once to Canada, General Phillips gave no opinion, General Burgoyne himself was for making one last attempt to force a passage to Albany. There being no objection raised to his view, about noon of the next day,

October 7th, he took out fifteen hundred of us with ten guns, against the enemy's left, in an attempt to turn them off Bemis Heights. The Generals above named commanded the three divisions. What was left of our army stayed in the camp, except the batmen who went out for forage under cover of this advance. Before we set out we were given our last issue of rum, to hearten us.

We advanced in good order to within a short distance of the enemy's works, where we halted in a large field of uncut wheat and shook out along a zigzag fence, posting our cannon in rear. We were inviting an enemy attack, hoping to cause them heavy losses and then to press victoriously upon a rout with the bayonet. We of the Light Infantry held the right of the line, and my company, being the eldest there, held the extreme point. At four o'clock the battle began with an attack upon our left by many thousands of the enemy. There our Grenadiers sustained the attack with great firmness; but the Americans broke the Brunswick regiment to the Grenadiers' right, and General Riedesel and his staff used their swords among the fugitives to rally them behind the guns. We were then quickly recalled from our position, where we were already hotly attacked by Colonel Morgan's force, to save the Grenadiers from destruction. They were fighting hand to hand now against odds of ten to one, and some of our field-pieces had been taken and retaken five times.

To break off an action against superior numbers without loss is a matter of great difficulty; General Fraser accomplished it for us by ordering a charge-bayonet which sent the riflemen running. But, alas, to twelve marksmen had been consigned the task of aiming at the person of General Fraser and none other. Dressed in the full uniform of a general, with laced furniture upon his iron-grey charger, he presented a most conspicuous target. One bullet grazed the horse's crupper, another passed through the mane, but a third pierced the General's body, passing in close under the breastbone and out near the spine. He was carried away, mortally wounded, and the command of the right wing devolved upon Lord Balcarres.

This was the first occasion that I saw General Benedict Arnold in action. He had been forbidden by General Gates to leave camp, but had struck with his sword at an officer sent to restrain him, wounding him; and then galloped into the fray with oaths of fury. He was in an ecstasy of enthusiasm, to which resentment of General Gates, natural courage, and a great deal of hard liquor contributed perhaps in equal measure. He rode in undress, and bare-headed, directly across our front, waved a sword about his head, shouted in a cracked voice and grimaced in high excitement. The New England militia troops were inspired by him to unusual valour wherever he led. He carried three whole regiments of Massachusetts infantry with him in a dense body against the centre, where the remainder of the Germans broke before him at the second charge. A comic aspect of this heroism was provided by an aide-de-camp of Gates, who had orders to arrest General Arnold and bring him back to camp. The unfortunate man was made to play follow-my-leader throughout the day and led into some mighty hot spots, but never came near enough to lay his hand upon the angry man's collar.

General Gates himself was not seen by his troops during this action: he spent the greater part of the day in discourse with a wounded prisoner, Sir Francis Clark, whom he was trying to persuade, by political argument, of the righteousness of the American cause. Sir Francis, who was dying, did not budge from his convictions, and, says General Gates to one of his aides, 'Did you ever hear such an impudent son of a bitch?'

It was a stiff rear-guard action that we fought, some companies retiring while the others faced about and fired volleys with precision and effect. We were now covering the retreat of the centre and the left, but were sufficient to the task and came safe back at last into the camp, where we hurriedly refilled pouches and cartouche-cases. All the guns had been lost, by the shooting down of the teams: without these it was impossible to haul them back. Twenty-five officers had been killed and wounded in the space of less than an hour, and several experienced sergeants, including my friend and benefactor Sergeant Fitzpatrick, who died very easily, shot in the lungs. 'Well, Gerry,' he said panting, as I bent over him, 'I believe I have got my furlough – to the Promised Land. The Rev. Charles Wesley always bade us build our hopes of what God might do for us hereafter on what He has done for us here. I trust to that. My loving duty to poor Mrs Fitzpatrick, my affectionate wishes to my niece Jane, my compliments to the Captain, and God bless you!' Soon after, he expired.

General Burgoyne had escaped unwounded, though shots had pierced his hat and his waistcoat. The batmen had been surprised in the act of cutting fodder and came back empty-handed.

This was not the end of the day. General Arnold next rode against our camp with a brigade of Continental troops. He unwisely chose the position held by the Light Infantry and supported by heavy pieces of artillery. We gave his Americans' musket-fire and grape as they tried to rush the open space in front of Freeman's Farm; and repulsed them with great loss. Even this did not daunt General Arnold: in the fading daylight he effected a combined assault on the horseshoe redoubt which covered the right of our position. Here the German reserve was stationed, and his attack this time did not miscarry, for he broke through the weak Canadian companies that lay between the Germans and ourselves and took the position in rear. The Brunswick colonel was killed; his men fired a last volley and then surrendered. General Arnold was entering the sally-port, sword in hand, when his horse rolled over, stone dead. As he was pitched from the saddle, a wounded German fired at him point-blank and shattered the thighbone of the same leg that had been broken below the knee at Quebec. General

Arnold prevented an American soldier from bayoneting his adversary, swearing that the German was a fine fellow and in the way of his duty. The pursuing aide-de-camp here finally caught up with General Arnold. 'General Gates's compliments,' he gasped. 'You are to do nothing rash, but return at once to the camp.'

General Arnold called a surgeon, who shook his head on examining the wound and recommended amputation. 'Goddam it, sir,' cried this remarkable man, 'if that is all that you can do with me, I shall see the battle out on another horse.'

As for our people, they were greatly fatigued, and even the sentinels found it hard to keep their eyes open. I was busied with the wounded, until late that night, when an order came to us to abandon our post and take up a new position half a mile in the rear, on the height above our general hospital. This natural fortress lay close to the road and the river and was protected by a deep ravine. The order was obeyed with the greatest regularity and silence. We could hear the Americans bringing up their artillery for an attack at dawn, and thus the wisdom of the withdrawal became apparent, for our camp was not cannon-proof and the enemy had outflanked us by the capture of the horseshoe redoubt from the Germans.

Early in the morning General Fraser, who had dictated and signed a last Will, breathed his last: his request was to be buried by us without any parade within the great redoubt. All that day we offered battle, and several brigades of the enemy formed against us in the plain with the evident intention of assault. However, a howitzer shell from our batteries, bursting in the middle of a column, caused such carnage that they all ran off into the woods and showed no further inclination to attack. An assault across a level meadow against so strongly entrenched a force as ours was too much to expect of irregular troops; and it was a mistake on our part to discourage them by howitzer fire before the attack was well launched. To have met them in the open would have been a most agreeable change from the continual wood-fighting and skirmishing in which the advantages of our discipline had been lost. In a dense thicket every man is his own general, and subordination to orders where combined movements are impossible of execution becomes a vice rather than a virtue, for the most obedient soldier is at the greatest loss.

At sunset, since the enemy did not attack, we buried General Fraser, carrying the corpse in procession up the hill in full sight of both armies. Generals Burgoyne, Phillips, and Riedesel joined the cortege. The Americans, regarding the prosecution of the war and the killing of our officers as of more importance than scruples of reverence to the dead, cannonaded the procession; and their shots threw up the earth around us as we stood bare-headed at his grave, attentive to the service. I have since heard it said that on perceiving their error the Americans fired a minute-gun only, as a mark of respect; but if so, they used shot in mistake for wadding.

The chaplain of the Artillery, Mr Brudenell, continued his steady reading of the office without alarm or hesitation throughout the cannonade.

At nine o'clock we were obliged to move back again, for the Americans were marching in great force to turn our right flank; we abandoned our general hospital, with five hundred sick and wounded, to the enemy. Terry Reeves was among the wounded, and I said farewell to him with a heavy heart, for he had fought very gallantly and proved a true comrade to me. Our company was with the rearguard, General Phillips commanding us. It was two hours before the order came to march, and we had for some time expected a night-assault by the enemy, who re-formed in the same place as they had left that morning. We could see the twinkling lanterns which the officers carried, and their movements up and down the lines. Yet, we came off safely, and the enemy did not pursue us until late on the following day, which was October 9th. For lightness of travel we had left behind our tents and other furniture.

This was a miserable journey, the rain pouring down without ceasing, and the road exceedingly bad and muddy. The Americans had again broken down the bridges over the creeks, which must be repaired to allow our wagons and guns to pass and then broken down once more to hinder the enemy's advance. Our *batteaux* in the river which had kept abreast of our advance now returned with us, the crews poling them with difficulty up the shallows. The train of wagons, as the rain grew worse, became bogged and not to be extricated by any means, the horses being weak for lack of fodder and our own strength quite worn out. These wagons had been hastily constructed of green wood in Canada and the warping of the timber made them very stiff to drive, even in the best of weathers. We held no conversation among ourselves on this march, so heavy our hearts were, nor cracked a joke, nor sang a song. We halted for some hours, at Dovegat, where we formed in expectation of an assault. None came, and on we went.

I found myself in ill company, that day, trudging beside Richard Harlowe. The knowledge that he was indebted to me for his life seemed to embitter him yet further against me; but on the contrary (by a strange infirmity of human nature) warmed my heart towards him. This infirmity the great Shakespeare noted in his tragedy of *Julius Caesar*, where the memory of how he had once saved Caesar's life from drowning weighed more with Cassius – when invited to join in murdering him – than any memory of kind treatment at Caesar's hands. I even offered to carry Harlowe's musket for him, since he limped from an inflamed heel and seemed unable to support the weight; but he sullenly refused and I did not repeat my offer.

So we continued in a silence disturbed only by the horrid imprecations of Corporal Buchanan, who had been sent to take Sergeant Fitzpatrick's place in our company. At nightfall our vanguard reached the village of Saratoga, and found that a large body of the enemy had seized the rising ground on the near side of the Creek, where the Schuyler mansion stood, and were fortifying it. However, the rain prevented the enemy from using their rifle-guns and they were pushed across the ford by threat of bayonet; where they joined another large body that was fortifying the opposing bank in order to cut off our retreat. So fatigued were most of our people on arrival at Saratoga – we had spent near twenty-four hours in accomplishing a march of eight miles – that they were indisposed to cut wood for fires, to dry their drenched clothes, but lay down as they were upon the sodden ground. I remembered, however, the situation of a hen-house near General Schuyler's range of barns and storehouses, and, with the permission of an officer, led my company to it out of the rain.

About the middle of the night I was overcome by a terrible nightmare. In this dream I fancied that I was caught in a raiding party of Wyandot Indians, my arms were pinioned and I was led away to be burned. I struggled against my captors with all my strength, but unavailingly, and was lashed with strips of elm-bark to a stake. There a fire was kindled about my feet. The Indians mocked and jeered me, seizing brands of hickory wood from the fire and scorching my flesh with it in every part of my body, without pity. Foremost among my persecutors was Richard Harlowe, who at last seized a bucket of red-hot embers and emptied it on my head, crying: 'Coals of fire! Coals of fire! There's nothing burns the head like coals of fire!' Then the Reverend John Martin appeared in the guise of a Wyandot sachem. He grinned at me and, said he, 'Here I am again. Ye'll never be rid of me. I am here, there, and everywhere, like the Royal Artillery.'

The heat was unbearable, the flames roared high, I was choking with the smoke; and then some one seized me by the middle and threw me across his back. He staggered with me out through the flames, and laid me upon the grass. I awoke then, to know that the fire at least had not been a dream, and that Smutchy Steel had rescued me from the blazing hen-house, when I was near smothered. The fire had been providentially noticed by Lieutenant Kemmis as he went to his lodging at the mansion; he ran up and shouted a warning. My comrades awoke, but could not escape, for the door proved to have been secured from the outside with a stout snib. Had the Lieutenant not been at hand to enlarge us, by turning this snib, we should infallibly have burned to death.

Some flaming straw from the hen-house, being carried upwards by the heat, now lodged in the roof of a barn near by and the whole range of buildings caught fire. We were hard put to it to rescue from the flames the sick and wounded who had been housed there. My two hours of sleep before the conflagration were the first that I had enjoyed since the third night before; and I slept no more that night, neither, Our company discussed together who could have been the incendiary, but came to no conclusion. It was remarked that, of those who had taken shelter in the hut, only Richard Harlowe was absent when the alarm was given. But, there being no other circumstance to incriminate him, he was not charged with arson, and the matter subsided.

On the next day, October 10th, the *batteaux*, with what little provisions remained in them, were constantly fired upon from the other bank of the river, which was distant but thirty yards. Many fell into the hands of the enemy, and several of the boatmen were killed or wounded. We now recrossed the Fishkill Creek, and General Burgoyne sent a force of artificers up the river, under a sufficient escort, to occupy and repair the pontoon-bridge built for us four weeks previously. They found it still afloat and the task would have been completed by the following daybreak had not their escort been urgently recalled by General Burgoyne, who wished every available soldier to be present with him for a battle which he hoped might be decisive for our arms. A company of Loyalists, left behind as a guard, fled upon the approach of a small body of the enemy, and the artificers were forced to do likewise. But General Burgoyne at least succeeded in sending his military chest safe back into Canada, under slight escort, assisted by the Indians.

We were entrenched on the low ridge of hills overlooking Fishkill Creek and its artificial islands, and a broad space was now cleared of everything that could afford cover to the enemy. By an unkind necessity of war, the Schuyler mansion on the opposite side of the creek was, at General Burgoyne's order, burned to the ground, for it afforded an admirable shelter behind which General Gates's army might mass for the assault. My heart was sore to see this noble house and the mills beside it go up in flames; and my high estimation of General Schuyler's character was confirmed when later I learned that he bore us no ill will for this destruction, declaring that, had he been in General Burgoyne's shoes, he would have done the same. He had, indeed, in the first year of this war, ruined the beautiful estate of his neighbour Sir William Johnson, Bt. (father of Colonel Guy and Sir John Johnson), which was situated in the Mohawk valley: carrying off his Scottish tenantry as prisoners and killing his famous herd of peacocks, the feathers of which his militiamen stuck in their caps as trophies.

It was raining still, and indeed rain fell continuously for a whole week from the time of our retreat. 'So much the better for us,' we thought, fingering our bayonets with expectant ardour. In the middle of the morning the American attack was launched under cover of a thick fog. Their vanguard, consisting of above a thousand of their regular troops, covertly passed over the Creek and advanced towards us up the slope. At that moment the fog lifted and their whole line was disclosed. We gave them grape-shot and platoon-fire and waited for their nearer approach in order to charge with the bayonet; but they broke and ran in remarkable disorder. We expected them to re-form and return to the assault, but in vain. Instead, their centre halted and took post, facing us, on the other side of the Creek, while Colonel Morgan led his large command two miles upstream and there crossed; wheeling round, he then halted on the fringe of the forest which bordered our right flank. Three thousand more Americans pushed along the farther bank of Hudson's River, now denuded of our forces, capturing a number of our *batteaux* with their crews. Opposite us they posted batteries of guns which could rake our position from end to end. They also placed guards on all the fords and ferries as far upstream as Fort Edward, and built a redoubt commanding our pontoon-bridge.

General Riedesel now proposed to General Burgoyne to abandon our baggage and guns and retreat during the night, forcing a passage over a ford four miles below Fort Edward, and striking across the forest to Fort George before the enemy beyond the river could be reinforced. General Burgoyne refused, still hoping that the Americans would dash their army against us in a wild onslaught.

On the following morning, October 11th, some of us were given the dangerous and difficult duty of transporting the sacks of provisions from the *batteaux* upon our shoulders into the camp, and rolling up the barrels. Musketry and shell-fire from across the river killed many of our number.

Very great indeed were the distresses which we were called upon to suffer, yet they were borne with fortitude; and we were still ready to face any danger when led on by officers whom we loved and respected. Numerous parties of the militia now joined the American forces, so that General Gates was soon at the head of twenty thousand men. They swarmed around us like birds of prey. By our losses we had been reduced from the seven thousand men with whom we set out from Canada to half that number, not two thousand of whom were British.

Our camp was a mile and a half long, and half a mile broad. We were exposed to continual round-shot from the enemy batteries, which made it inadvisable to light fires: for the smoke or flame provided a target at which aim was immediately taken. Thus we were obliged to subsist upon raw victuals – salt pork and a paste made with flour and water. Moreover, the whole army was provided with but one spring of water, which was muddy, and we were feign to drink puddle-water or rain caught in our caps. To fetch water from the Creek by day was to be shot dead; and three armed parties who went down under cover of darkness did not return. We were greatly galled by popping shots from the riflemen in the tree-tops; and, in the small redoubt where we were huddled, would amuse ourselves by hoisting a cap upon a stick above the parapet. Instantly shots would be fired at it, and it would be perforated by two or three balls. We were forbidden to reply, in order to save our ammunition for the general assault that was still expected, and took this very hard. Soon we were beyond caring for the cannonades. We lighted fires, regardless of the danger, baking our flour paste into the usual cakes upon stones laid in the embers.

Our store of spruce-beer was expended and any one who possessed a reserve of rum could kind a ready market for it at one guinea the pint.

At another Council of War on the next day, October 12th, General Riedesel prevailed upon General Burgoyne to attempt the retirement that he had refused to make two days before. Five days' rations – all that remained – were therefore issued to us by the Commissaries, and we awaited orders to issue from the works when dark came. However, our scouts reported that the enemy had sent out so many detached parties that it would now be impossible to execute this retreat without setting the whole American army in motion against us. General Burgoyne therefore changed his mind once more, for though he trusted General Riedesel, he did not trust the Germans under his command. It was notorious that they were suffering too greatly to be dependable marching companions; and had concerted to fire one volley only, if attacked, and then to club their arms in token of surrender.

I was now assisting the surgeons in a building which was a principal target of the American artillery – a log-house of two storeys well advertised to them as constituting our general hospital. It was suspected by these over-ingenious people that our generals would be smart enough to make the hospital serve a double purpose, by sheltering themselves and their families under a roof that invited a humane respect. Some slight colour for their belief was provided by Madame Riedesel's ornamental calash which stood near the door; this pretty blue-eyed lady and her three young children having taken refuge in the cellar of the building. Therefore the round shot came bounding in and out of the upper chambers where we were at work. A surgeon, Mr Jones, had his leg so crushed by flying masonry that we were obliged to amputate it. In the middle of this operation, which he endured with great fortitude, another ball came roaring from across the river, and when the dust had cleared we found that Surgeon Jones had been dashed from the table on which he was laid and was lying groaning in a corner: his other leg had been taken clean off! This was only one of many horrible happenings, of which a full Detail would turn the stomach.

The wounded were crying out for water, and we had none to give them. A batman volunteered to run down to the Creek and bring up water in a pail, but he was struck down before he had gone many steps. Then the same Jane Crumer, who had assisted me at Fort Anna, and whose husband was among the gravely wounded, cried out that the Americans were not such beasts that they would fire at a woman. She went leisurely out from the hospital, paused by the dead man to unclasp his fingers from the pail that they still clutched; then, waving amiably to the enemy across the river, she continued to the water-side, drew water, curtsied her gratitude and returned. Not a shot was fired at her. She went to and fro with her pail until she had fetched sufficient for all.

On October 13th, General Burgoyne summoned yet another Council, to which all officers from the rank of Captain upwards were invited. It is said, that to Major Skene, who was present, General Burgoyne remarked with a pardonable show of irritation: 'Sir, you have been the occasion of getting me into this quagmire. Now be good enough to show me the way out.' To which Major Skene made the absurd reply: 'Scatter your baggage and stores in every part of the camp, and while the rebel militia are scrambling for the plunder, you will have time to get away in safety.' This remark, however, was not recorded in the minutes of this proceeding, which may best speak for themselves.

Minutes and proceedings of a Council of War, consisting of all the general officers, field officers, and captains commanding corps, on the Heights of Saratoga, October 13th, 1777:

The Lieutenant-General having explained the situation of affairs as in the preceding Council, with the additional intelligence that the enemy was intrenched at the fords of Fort Edward, and likewise occupied the strong position on the pine plains between Fort George and Fort Edward, expressed his readiness to undertake, at their head, any enterprise of difficulty or hazard that should appear to them within the compass of their strength and spirit. He added that he had reason to believe a capitulation had been in the contemplation of some, perhaps of all, who knew the real situation of things; that, upon a circumstance of such consequence to national and personal honour, he thought it a duty to his country, and to himself, to extend his council beyond the usual limits; that the assembly present might justly be esteemed a full representation of the army; and that he should think himself unjustifiable in taking any step in so serious a matter, without such a concurrence of sentiments as should make a treaty the act of the Army as well as that of the General. The first question he desired them to decide was:

Whether an army of three thousand, five hundred, fighting men, and well provided with artillery, were justifiable, upon the principles of national dignity and military honour, in capitulating in any possible situation?

Resolved, *nem. con.* in the affirmative.

Question 2: Is the present situation of that nature?

Resolved, *nem. con.* that the present situation justifies a capitulation upon honourable terms.

General Burgoyne then drew up the following letter directed to General Gates, relative to the negotiation, and laid it before the Council. It was unanimously approved, and upon that foundation the treaty opened:

After having fought you twice, Lieutenant-General Burgoyne has waited some days in his present position, determined to try a third conflict against any force you could bring to attack him.

He is apprized of the superiority of your numbers, and the disposition of your troops to impede his supplies and render his retreat a scene of carnage on both sides. In this situation he is compelled by humanity, and thinks himself justified by established principles, and precedents of State and of War, to spare the lives of brave men upon honourable terms.

Should Major-General Gates be inclined to treat upon that idea, General Burgoyne would propose a cessation of arms, during the time necessary to communicate the preliminary terms by which in any extremity he, and his army, mean to abide.

General Gates then transmitted the following proposals to General Burgoyne; whose answers are appended:

(1) General Burgoyne's army being exceedingly reduced by repeated defeats, by desertion, sickness, etc., their provisions exhausted, their military horses, tents, and baggage taken or destroyed, their retreat cut off, and their camp invested, they can only be allowed to surrender prisoners of war.

Answer: Lieutenant-General Burgoyne's army, however reduced, will never admit that their retreat is cut off while they have arms in their hands.

(2) The troops under His Excellency General Burgoyne's command, may be drawn up in their encampments, where they will be ordered to ground their arms, and may thereupon be marched to the river side to be passed over in their way towards Bennington.

Answer: This article inadmissible in any extremity; sooner than this army will consent to ground their arms in their encampment, they will rush on the enemy determined to take no quarter. If General Gates does not mean to recede from this article the treaty ends at once. The army will to a man proceed to any act of desperation rather than submit to this article.

General Gates did recede from this article, and the following was substituted in its stead:

The troops to march out of their camp with the honours of war, and the artillery of the entrenchments, to the verge of the river, where their arms and artillery must be left. The arms to be piled by word of command from their own officers. A free passage to be granted to the army under Lieutenant-General Burgoyne to Great Britain, upon condition of not serving again in North America during the present contest; and the port of Boston to be assigned for the entry of transports to receive the troops whenever General Howe shall so order.

It becoming generally known to both armies that the articles of capitulation were being discussed, the enemy's fire slackened; and, though the rain continued, our condition was sensibly bettered. Our remaining oxen and other cattle were slaughtered and some fresh meat distributed to us. Our people began to greet and discourse with the Americans on the opposite bank of Hudson's River; and a few riflemen even emerged from the forest on our right and exchanged rations and keepsakes with the Light Infantry and Grenadiers. On the morning of October 18th Mad Johnny Maguire came down to the river with me and several others. My comrades began shouting across the water friendly challenges to wrestling and boxing matches, and a big fellow with a gun seven foot long cried out, evidently to me: 'You now, the tall sergeant with the moon face, will you kindly oblige me with a sweet turn at the blackthorn stick?'

These were the accents of the city of Dublin, and I burst into loud laughter. 'No, my Kevin Street bully,' I replied. 'The small sword is my weapon.'

The American grew very wrath and 'Don't you dare to laugh at Cornelius Maguire, you rascal lobster,' he said, 'or I'll swim over this stream and scuttle you with one blow, so I will.'

At this, something appeared to strike Mad Johnny Maguire's mind very forcibly. He darted from our midst and plunged into the river. 'Och, Corny, Corny,' he cried, 'I hardly knew ye.'

Cornelius Maguire, seized by a similar impulse, plunged in to meet him. They found their feet on a shallow place near the middle, where they hung on each other's necks and wept. Their 'Och, Johnny, my darling brother', and 'Och, Corny, my jewel', soon cleared up the mystery for us. Cornelius Maguire had emigrated to America twenty years previously, at about the same time that Mad Johnny Maguire had entered the British Army. Each had been totally ignorant that he was engaged in hostile combat against the other's life.

Our minds were set at rest on October 18th, when we learned that General Gates had yielded to General Burgoyne's threat of a desperate assault, should his demand for honourable terms be rejected, and that the articles were now signed. It was consoling that we had preserved the dignity of the British character and extorted from a successful foe, vastly outnumbering us and straining every nerve to tarnish our honour, so plain an admission of the awe in which they held our enfeebled arms. We were aware, however, that General Gates was prompted to rapid compliance not only by our resolute front but by news of Sir Henry Clinton's capture of Forts Montgomery and Clinton with a charge-bayonet five days before. The Seventh, Twenty-sixth, Sixty-third, Fifty-second, and Fifty-seventh were the regiments employed on this honourable service. The great iron chain-boom, weighing fifty tons, there stretched by the enemy at prodigious expense across the river, had been speedily removed, and our ships freed to sail up the river as far as Albany. General Gates feared for his arsenal in that town and resolved to finish off one business before becoming involved in another. It consoled us for the surrender of our thirty-five pieces of brass ordnance and our five thousand muskets, to learn that General Clinton had captured more than that amount of cannon, together with great stores of powder and provisions, in Fort Montgomery.

Our minds were filled with delightful thoughts of a safe and prompt return to our own land, where we might hold up our heads as men who had fought stoutly, and where we would also find great arrears of pay awaiting us to console us for our present indigence and hardships.

Mad Johnny Maguire and his brother fell into a severe dispute, since they were resolved never again to part, as to whether Johnny should now discharge himself from the British Army and settle down with Corny on his farm at Norwalk in Connecticut, or Corny should quit the American Army and the two together go west into the new territory of Kentucke. The moral issue was debated with great warmth and, their fraternal love being as strong as their respective loyalties, it was with difficulty that we could restrain them from reciprocal injury.

CHAPTER XXV

OBEYING OUR officers' orders, we piled up our arms in a meadow, near the confluence of Fishkill Creek and Hudson's River, and emptied out our cartouche-cases. It was found that not fifteen rounds a man remained to us. A great stench arose in this meadow from the decaying bodies of horses that lay about it. They had been allured there, from the deep ravine where we kept them within the camp, by the scent of rich grass – the enemy shot the poor beasts down as soon as they began grazing. There were soldiers who now wept at being parted from the muskets that they had carried so long and cared for so well, and that seemed almost a part of themselves; and I own that for days I missed the familiar weight of my piece upon my shoulder, and felt in a manner naked without it. No American troops were present at this melancholy scene, General Gates having confined all to camp except a few companies of riflemen who lined the fringes of the forest as a precaution against any treachery on our part. Lieutenant-Colonel Hill preserved the colours of The Ninth by taking them off the staves and sewing them in the lining of a mattress. He eventually was able to present them to His Majesty at St James's Palace, who rewarded his faithful services with the appointment of aide-de-camp to himself and the full rank of colonel.

That same day, October 17th, we were marched off in the direction of Boston. We passed through the long ranks of our enemies, who had spent the whole morning scrubbing and cleaning their persons and firelocks in order to make the best appearance possible. There were fourteen thousand of them in the parade and some thousands more posted in reserve. The men were in general taller, thinner, and more sinewy than ours. Our veterans remarked that they would have liked these rebels better had they shown that command of mind which should dignify an army when victorious in the field; for it seemed to them that the features and tones even of the American regular troops betrayed an improper exultation. Lieutenant Anburey of The Fourteenth, in his published account of these transactions, has written: 'As we passed the American enemy, throughout the whole of them I did not observe the least disrespect, or even a taunting look, but all was mute astonishment and pity.' Neither I, nor such of my surviving comrades as I have consulted, can account for the discrepancy between what we saw and what the Lieutenant saw, unless by the suggestion that we were of a more jaundiced and irritable temper than he: for pity there was none, but either sour looks or good-humoured sallies at our expense, to which we did not care to reply. The truth is, we had been so scribbled against, by their newspaper writers and pamphleteers, as base mercenaries and British scum, and so preached against by their ministers, who represented us in Biblical imagery as mere monsters – with swords for tongues, claws for hands, hoofs for feet, and our mouths dripping with the blood of children and virgins – that few Americans could cast out this strong prejudice from their minds. Add to this, that we could hardly expect from peasants, fighting in defence of their homes, the same courtesies as passed, for instance, between our armies and the French, when professionally opposed in battle upon the neutral soil of Germany or the Low Countries.

The American regular or 'Continental' troops wore buff and blue uniform with stout knapsacks, and carried muskets, twenty thousand of which had been secretly bought from our enemies the French by an American emissary in Paris; the riflemen were conformedly dressed in linen hunting shirts and legging; the militia were clad, according to their own parochial fancy, in coats of military cut but of many different stuffs, colours, and facings – their firelocks also showing much diversity of quality and pattern. Besides these troops there also were numerous companies of well-whiskered rustics in workaday dress, many of whom carried immensely long guns of the sort used for duck-shooting, but some only pitchforks or knives bound to poles to serve as pikes. It was the monstrous many-coloured, fleecy wigs affected by the elder men that caused us most amazement and recalled the times of Good Queen Anne, when men wore haystacks upon their heads.

The Americans certainly had proved very smart in repairing their deficiencies of warlike material. We had at first thought that they would have to yield for want of gunpowder: for the quantities that they won by capture, or by sale from the Spanish, French, and Dutch were wholly insufficient to their needs. But a simple countryman had approached the Massachusetts Assembly with a specimen of his own manufacture of gunpowder, from the salt-petre contained in rotten stable-refuse, and undertook to show them how more could be made in eight months than the province had money to pay for. His process was adopted. Flour-mills, which were very numerous in New England, were thereupon converted into mills for gunpowder, and of this product there was soon a superfluity. The Americans also were very short of lead for bullets and ran into their moulds clock-weights, waterspouts, cisterns, leaden ornaments from house-fronts, statuary, and printers' founts of type, and were reduced at times to pewter spoons and dishes. Paper for cartridges, neither too thin nor too thick, was hard to come by, and the Continentals were supplied on one occasion with a whole edition of a German Bible printed in Philadelphia. The leaves of vestry-books were also much used in New England for this purpose. In one respect, we learned, the smartness of the Yankees recoiled upon them. For the French muskets supplied being insufficient to the needs of the whole American army, the militia were sometimes served out with trade-muskets, showy and defective, that had been manufactured for sale to the simple fur-getting Indian, or to the African chiefs of the Guinea Coast who took them in exchange for slaves. They frequently burst at the first discharge and proved fatal to the soldiers who bore them. Most of the muskets used against us were manufactured by country blacksmiths in imitation of the Tower musket, but not to a single standard, so that if a part were damaged the piece would be useless until a new part could be forged to match.

When the head of our column arrived opposite the enemy's general headquarters, General Burgoyne in plumed hat and a rich new uniform delivered up his sword with a flourish to General Gates, wearing a plain blue frock, cocked hat, and spectacles, who received it courteously and returned it to him. The other officers were likewise permitted to retain their swords and fusils. Major Skene, by the bye, wrote himself down humbly as 'a poor follower of the British Army'. During these proceedings their musicians played the tune of 'Yankee Doodle', which had now become their national paean, a favourite of favourites, and used alike among them as the lover's spell, the nurse's lullaby, and the soldier's marching song. The word 'Yankee' signifies 'coward' in the Cherokee Indian tongue, but from being used as a term of reproach it had become a word of glory to all New Englanders. The verses of the tune were exceedingly frivolous.

During the delay of some minutes caused by the compliments exchanged between the Generals, I found myself halted opposite some Massachusetts troops: I believe they were a Captain Morean's company. Among these I recognized James Melville, or Mellon, who had been prisoner at Quebec. I asked him: 'Fighting again? Did you not give your parole?'

He grinned and replied: 'They gave me a paper to sign. But I owe King George nothing. A forced promise, I'll swear, is no promise.' He then asked his officer for permission to break ranks and give me a drink from his flask: which was refused, as the orders were very strict against this. Yet he tossed the flask to me, I drank rum from it and was about to toss it back when he cried to me that I might keep it in return for my former benefits to himself; which I did, gladly.

We now retraced our steps once more along the road to Stillwater, which was a gloomy enough stage on our two hundred mile journey; encamping on the hill over the ravine where we had abandoned our tents and our wounded. The tents were gone, but the hospital was still crowded with our sick, who were receiving considerate treatment. To my joy I found Terry Reeves sitting at the door on an upturned keg, nearly recovered from a bullet wound in the foot; he did not wish to be parted from us again and hobbled forward with the company the next day. We were shocked to discover on a visit to General Fraser's grave that some rough Americans had added to their former disrespect of his obsequies by exhuming the corpse. Their excuse was that they thought that we had concealed guns in the grave, and muskets in the coffin. It was certainly their custom to credit us with a 'smartness' altogether foreign to our British nature; but more likely the hope of these frontiersmen was to find, in the pockets of the General's uniform, a watch, or money, or some article of value that had been overlooked by the mourners in the anxiety and solemnity of that evening's work.

We crossed Hudson's River by General Gates's bridge of boats at Stillwater; the township was very well named from the sudden calming of the turbulent stream opposite it. The American army passed us, marching down to Albany against General Clinton's small army – which, however, soon retired upon hearing news of our disaster.

That morning a thanksgiving sermon had been preached before the American army. The Chaplain fully set forth to his hearers that the Almighty had done more for them than they had done for themselves. He preached from Joel ii. 26: 'But I will remove far off from you the Northern army, and will drive him into a land barren and desolate, with his face towards the East Sea, and his hinder part towards the Utmost Sea; and his stink shall come up, and his ill-savour shall come up, because he has done great things.' Great things our Northern army had indeed accomplished in the way of battle, and none could deny it; that General Howe had not come to our assistance with his twenty thousand men, or that General Clinton's force had marched too late, was no fault of ours. Now we were, in the words of the text, being driven into a land barren and desolate, with our face towards the East Sea; and as for our stink and ill-savour, the inhabitants of the country soon made it plain to us how grossly their nostrils were offended.

Saratoga was distant from Boston some two hundred miles. From the outset of our march we experienced much hardship, sleeping in barns and being given but scanty provisions. The way before and about us presented an uncheering appearance, mountainous and uncultivated, with no pleasing scenery to amuse the eye. I was now able to congratulate myself on my prescience in burdening myself with the Congress bills, which passed current in these parts. I still retained one thousand dollars of them. The remaining four thousand I had given to the surgeon of the hospital to purchase comforts for the poor fellows under his charge; which gift, I believe, saved many of their lives. Of what was left I kept one hundred dollars for my own use and divided up the remainder among the men of my company: I regarded it as plunder and to be put into the common stock. We therefore fared better than most of the army so long as this money lasted. New England rum, which we purchased at Bennington, the first place of pleasant appearance that we arrived at, kept us alive through the very cold nights of our passage over the Green Mountains. Many soldiers paid for their drams by selling their cartouche-cases, which seemed unnecessary luggage now that our muskets were taken from us. The mountain roads were almost impassable to our wagons, and when we were half over, a heavy fall of snow occurred, which caused several men to die of cold. A soldier's wife bore a child under the lee of a baggage cart that cruel night, and both survived.

The Americans were very glad to sell our people Continental paper in exchange for 'hard money', as they termed gold and silver. At Bennington, in Vermont State, they offered nine paper dollars for each golden guinea, thus halving the professed value of the paper, and when we had crossed the Green Mountains and arrived at Hatfield and Hadley in Massachusetts, on the Connecticut River, we could get eighteen. The price of guineas grew still better, the nearer we came to Boston, and by the time we had passed through the back country of Massachusetts and approached the sea-board, we came to realize how low was the confidence of the more sagacious Americans in the ability of Congress to redeem these paper promises. For at Worcester, two or three days' march from our destination, we could get as much as thirty-five dollars for a guinea. As the war continued, the value of a paper dollar declined to less than one penny, and at last the entire issue, having served its purpose of raising the wind, was silently repudiated. But what appeared strange to us was that though the Americans depreciated Congress money in this way, by offering to sell it to us at so great a discount, yet always, whenever they sold any article at a price in paper dollars and we paid in hard money, they made no allowance for the difference in exchange; but for the honour of their country reckoned a paper dollar the equal of a silver one. We were the Egyptians, as it were, whom these Children of Israel – who, by the bye, bore Biblical names almost to a man – spoiled of our silver and gold.

In this march we were able to make many comparisons between the appearance and manner of life of the inhabitants and what we recalled of the Canadians and our own people at home. First, let me say, that though the wants of the country owing to the war were already very great, from its reliance upon England for stuffs and manufactured goods of quality, the inhabitants appeared well-fed and cheerful, and immeasurably better provided with the conveniences of life than the country people of Ireland. The women were dressed in bright and well-fitting clothing and had a remarkably independent air. Every place through which we passed was now raising two or three companies of troops to join General Washington's army, so that on the industry of these women depended the life of the countryside, and well they knew it.

I must observe here that no town that we came to had a settled or finished look, nor can it have been solely a fault of the war that life was here universally lived as if it were a doubtful campaign against the forces of Nature; with no opportunity to enjoy the fruits of victory, but a constant impulse to engage in new battles. Accidents that in our own country would serve to drive a man half mad seemed here to produce little alarm or agitation. Nothing was either splendid or beggarly, and when a man was knocked down, he speedily picked himself up again in a manner impossible on our Continent. The labourer was everywhere content with a house of rough logs, unwhitewashed, unpainted, and not always boarded even on the inside. All around this habitation was, in general, as barren as the sea-beach, without flower-beds, paths, or lawns, but only heaps of cast rubbish and refuse; and if there was a cultivated plot called a garden, they used the plough to it, not the spade. Especially there were never any forest trees left standing for shade or adornment in the neighbourhood of a dwelling: Americans detested trees as much as our farmers detest weeds or stones. From the face of the country being everywhere overspread with forest the eyes of the people became weary of it: so that I have read of Americans landing on barren parts of the north-west coast of Ireland and expressing the greatest surprise at the 'improved state' of the country, so clear of trees! I never but once during all my seven years in America saw a well-laid out and completed estate, and that was General Schuyler's at Saratoga that we had been obliged to devastate. What contributed to the untidy and hasty effect of North American negligence was the stumps of trees left standing where virgin forest had given way to the plough. They were not grubbed up but allowed to rot slowly, while the plough avoided them with crooked furrows. They stood up two or three feet at the natural height of an axe-stroke; since a man could cut many more trees in a day in this style than if he levelled the stumps with the ground. Hedges were lacking, being held to rob the soil; and instead everywhere ran rough fences of various construction, which were more convenient than charming.

This want of attention to the amenities of life had been hereditary from the first settlers. Land and timber were cheap, labour dear, and a man would be held a fool who spent his time beautifying his home and its environs, when he might be planting an orchard of fruit-trees or clearing a few acres of forest to make into a maize-field. It may be recorded here that the only American who was ever known to grub up the stumps of his trees at once was their General Stirling, who called himself Lord Stirling. He had come to England, before the war, to pray for the revival in his favour of the extinct Stirling peerage, but the House of Lords disallowed his claim and forbade him under pain of public disgrace to assume the title. When the

Americans popularly conceded it to him, he showed his gratitude by a sincere and steady devotion to their cause. He was most adhesive to the dignity of his rank, and the removal of the tree stumps was in keeping with these punctilious traits of his character.

The cattle hereabouts were numerous and extraordinarily large; and so were the hogs, which they fattened upon maize. Maize, or Indian corn, was the only grain to which the climate was favourable; for wheat was inclined to the blight, barley grew dry in the ear before maturity – so that ale was a rare delicacy in America – and oats yielded more straw than grain. But Maize throve exceedingly and was the staple for both man and beast.

These Americans were so little gregarious that a rural township never consisted, as in Canada or anywhere in Europe, of a social collection of houses, inns, and places of religion surrounded by the fields and orchards of the inhabitants: we seldom saw more than a dozen houses together and the rest were here, there, and everywhere. It was as if each family wished to assert its independence of neighbours and form a village consisting of its own house and barns. When a son married, he would seldom be content, I was told, if he could not remove with his wife to a distance of two hundred miles away or more, and clear new land with his own axe.

I must say that America was certainly no Lubberland, or Land of Cockaigne, where the streets are paved with half-peck loaves, the houses roofed with pancakes, and where the fowls fly about ready roasted, with knife and fork plunged in their backs, crying, 'Sweet, sweet, come eat me!' It was the land of hard work and steady habits.

The women were brisk and handsome and kept their youthful looks some years longer than ours at home, though their hair turned grey sooner. For some reason, the climate did not appear to encourage wrinkles, and old men and women had a ruddy, smooth look which would contrast very cheerfully with the crumpled parchment faces of our own parents and grandparents. Their teeth, however, were very bad and their breaths sour, which some attributed to their hasty manner of eating and to immoderate fondness for molasses – which they consumed at every meal, even with greasy pork. Another cause may have been the great severity of the winter which kept them short, for months together, of green vegetables and salads and also encouraged them to profuse tippling of spirits. New England speech seemed to proceed rather through the nose than the mouth, yet was not unpleasing in effect, if the person discoursing was one of sensibility; and was so clearly articulated that, where a number of people were talking together in a crowd, an American voice, though not raised, could be distinctly heard cutting through the confused babble of the rest, with hardly a syllable lost.

New Englanders were, then as now, generally esteemed the most inquisitive people in the world. They greatly lacked for entertainment in the country and made up for this with gossip and with minding the business of other people. No stranger who arrived, however greatly fatigued, at an inn but was pestered by the company and by each newcomer who dropped in, to reveal his name, destination, origin, family condition, trade, intentions, and political colour. This provided good sport, for the stranger was always suspected of misleading his interrogators, who would try to trick him into contradictions. If he proved sulky, hospitability would dry up, and if he asked questions in return he would get more grins than answers. It can be conceived, then, what interest the passage of our army excited, especially when it was learned that among our officers were no fewer than six members of Parliament and a number of peers. Lieutenant M'Neil of our regiment was annoyed at the giggles and ironical curtsies of a row of very handsome young women who came out to see us at Worcester; and when a small queer great-grandmother in a tall hat, standing a little beyond them, raised her hands to Heaven and stared at us with astonishment, he turned to her tartly: 'So, Mother Goose,' he said, 'must you too come wandering out to see the lions?' She replied archly: 'Lions, lions! I declare now I had mistook you for lambs.'

We were sorry for young Lieutenant Lord Napier. He was much troubled by the curiosity of the women at the house where he was lodged, who imagined that a Lord must be something more than man and kept peeping in at doors and windows, in the hope of seeing a creature with angel's wings or a devil's hoof and tail, or I know not what else. At last four of them, pushing boldly into the room inquired: 'We hear you have got a Lord among you. Pray now, which may he be?' Then they looked sternly at Lieutenant Kemmis, as if to say: 'Dare to deceive us and it will be the worse for you.'

Unfortunately for Lord Napier, he was fresh from a tumble in the mud, and had not yet got his clothes sufficiently dried to allow the dirt to be brushed off; one side of his face was bemired, too. But Lieutenant Kemmis, knowing that there would be no peace until these women were satisfied, pointed to his Lordship and cried out in the resonant tones of a herald-at-arms: 'Ladies, there you behold the form and person of the Right Honourable Francis Napier, of His Majesty's Thirty-first Regiment of Foot, Baron of Merchiston in the Kingdom of Scotland, Baronet of Nova Scotia, Hereditary Lord Almoner to the Akhoond of Swat, Grand Squire of Gotham, Lord of a hundred inferior lordships in the Land of Cockaigne, Knight Grand Cross of the Order of Liliburlero, and much besides which I have forgot. Gaze on him, ladies, for you will never look upon his like again.' They gazed very attentively at his Lordship, who blushed beneath his mud. At length one of them exclaimed: 'Well, if *that* be a Lord, I never desire to see any other Lord than the Lord Jehovah.' Nevertheless, a number of other women came in to see the show, for which privilege they had paid entrance-money to the landlord.

The last stage of our march was from Weston to Prospect Hill, near

Cambridge, which lies six miles from Boston. Exceedingly heavy rain fell, but our people bore up very well and sang choruses as we approached the end of our travels, to proclaim that our spirit was undaunted. The most sanguine among us did not imagine that we would have less than two or three weeks of waiting before the transports appeared which would take us home to Britain; but it was argued that the cost of keeping so many men in fuel and provisions would prompt the people of Massachusetts, whose Court had passed resolutions for procuring suitable accommodation for our army, to be rid of us as speedily as possible – or so soon at least as we were no longer able to pay for our subsistence in coin.

Meanwhile we determined to make the best of our lot, which was, to be short, deplorable. We were put that evening, drenched to the skin, into the temporary barracks that had been erected for the shelter of the revolutionary troops during the siege of Boston. These had since been dismantled and allowed to fall into utter decay. In a number of cases thirty or forty persons, men, women, and children, were indiscriminately crowded together in one small, miserable open hut. Our provisions and fuel were on short allowance, our bedding was a scanty amount of straw, and we had no furniture of any sort but our own camp-kettles, and these General Burgoyne had with difficulty saved for us from the enemy, who wished to seize them as legitimate plunder.

How mercifully is the future hidden from the eyes of man! Had it been revealed to us by an Angel that our army, by Congress's profligate repudiation of the Convention, was to remain in captivity for five miserable years, I believe the great mass of us would have run mad, falling upon our guards with our bare hands in a desperate attempt to wrest back our freedom.

In what manner I myself, after having been closely confined for a twelve-month, succeeded in escaping to the British Army in New York, and there took up arms once more against the Americans; and travelled, before the war was over, through another eight states of the American Union, Northern, Southern, and Middle, is a separate story from this. For I then changed my title from 'Sergeant Lamb of the Ninth' to 'Sergeant Lamb of The Twenty-third, or Royal Welch Fusiliers'. Yet into that account Kate Harlowe must again enter (whom now I thought altogether lost to me) and several comrades of The Ninth, who also escaped, and Mrs Jane Crumer, and even that unaccountable personage, the mock-priest John Martin. But, for the present, I have told enough. I have, it will be observed, endeavoured to demark the right line of duty and behaviour which the soldier in the ranks ought invariably to pursue. I may have lost my aim, but even in its failure I trust that my motive will be thought laudable.

PROCEED, SERGEANT LAMB

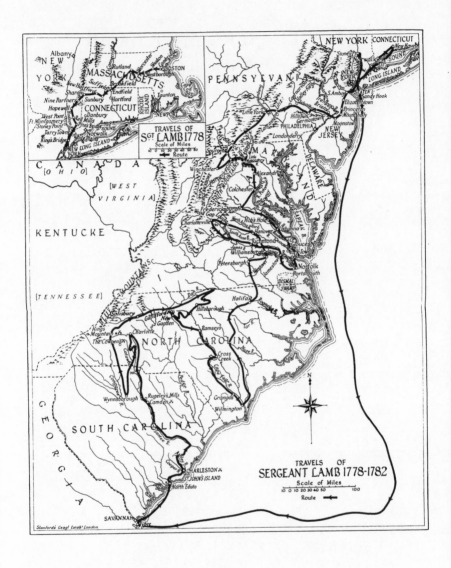

TRAVELS OF
Sᴳᵀ LAMB 1778
Scale of Miles
0 0 10 20 30 40 50 60
Route

TRAVELS OF
SERGEANT LAMB 1778-1782
Scale of Miles
10 0 10 20 30 40 50   100
Route

FOREWORD

Proceed, Sergeant Lamb is the sequel and conclusion to my *Sergeant Lamb of The Ninth.* Lamb's own rather disjointed *Journal* and *Memoir*, published in Dublin in 1809 and 1811, provide the bones of the story: the body has been built up from a mass of contemporary records, British, American, French and German. No incident of any historical importance has been invented or distorted. There has been too much, rather than too little, material to draw upon: for a start, no less than three officers of Lamb's regiment, The Twenty-Third, or Royal Welch Fusiliers, kept journals of the American War – Captains Julian and de Saumarez, and Colonel Mackenzie.

The frontispiece, reproduced by kind permission of the Lieutenant-Governor of the Royal Hospital, Chelsea, is in Lamb's own handwriting – the first sheet of a Memorial sent in 1809 to the Duke of York, applying for a veteran's pension. It concludes:

'That Memorialist, being now far advanced in life, humbly solicits your Royal Highness to recommend him for a military pension, which would smooth his declining years and be most gratefully received as a remuneration for the many times he has risked his life and limbs in His Majesty's service.

That for the truth of these facts, he most humbly refers to General H. Calvert and Colonel Mackenzie.'

Colonel Mackenzie (the one who kept the journal) had been adjutant of The Twenty-Third at Boston and Deputy-Adjutant-General at New York. Lamb had reported to him in New York when in 1782 he escaped there from captivity for the second time. General Sir Harry Calvert, as a newly-joined second-lieutenant, had been helped through his first guard-mounting at New York in 1779 by Lamb, an experienced sergeant. He was now Adjutant-General of the Army and saw to it at once that Lamb was awarded an out-pension of one shilling a day – a generous amount at that time – and excused the formality of coming to Chelsea to establish his identity. The official reason for the award in the Hospital ledger is 'worn out'.

There is no record at the Hospital of Lamb's death. However, a reference to him by the Reverend W.B. Lumley in a mid-Victorian memorial volume of the Methodist Church in Ireland shows that 'worn out' referred only to Lamb's capacity for further soldiering. He was still alive and working hard fifteen years later, at the age of seventy. 'The best known of the teachers of Whitefriar Street Day School was Mr Roger Lamb, who for nearly forty years superintended it with great fidelity and great advantage to the boys under his care. The grandson of this good man is now the eloquent and learned Dr Chadwick, Dean of Armagh.'

A descendant, Miss E. Chadwick of Armagh, has kindly searched among family papers for a portrait or other record of Roger Lamb, but without success.

Lamb's story has come close to me in several ways. My paternal great-grandfather and grandfather, possibly even my father – if Lamb survived for a few years after his retirement were Dubliners of Lamb's day. Admirals Samuel and Thomas Graves, who successively commanded the British fleet in American waters, were cousins of my great-grandfather, who was Chief of Police at Dublin and subscribed to Lamb's *Journal* before publication. (The well-known Massachusetts family of Graves, stemming from Thomas Graves of Hatfield, the town on the Connecticut River through which Lamb passed as a prisoner, have a common ancestry with the Irish branch to which in the War of Independence they were 'fratricidally opposed'.)

But the chief link that I have with Lamb is that I had the honour of serving, like him, in the Royal Welch Fusiliers during a long and bloody war; and found their character as a regiment, and their St David's Day customs, happily unaltered since his day.

R.G.
Galmpton–Brixham, Devon
1940

CHAPTER I

In the first volume of this authentic relation of my career as a soldier, I told of my birth at Dublin in the year 1753, my enlistment in the Ninth Regiment of Foot at the age of seventeen, my peace-time service in various barracks of Ireland, and my campaigning in Canada and the State of New York in the years 1776 and 1777. For the benefit of those who have not been able to peruse the first book, I will now give a short Detail of other matters that will give them a running start into this second and concluding volume of my adventures.

I was fellow-recruit with four men, who afterwards fought by my side. These were: my good friend Terence Reeves, who had been a link-boy in the city of Belfast before his enlistment and was therefore nick-named 'Moon-Curser'; Alexander, called 'Smutchy', Steel who had once kept a Limerick gin-shop, and when I first served with him was but a clumsy slouch; Brooks the Dipper, a bad and dirty soldier, who had been recruited in a jail; and lastly Richard Pearce, the felonious son of an Ulster nobleman, who had taken refuge in the ranks of The Ninth, under the assumed name of Harlowe, from the just vengeance of the Law.

This Pearce, or Harlowe, married Kate Weldone, the woman whom I loved, and took her with him to Canada on campaign; but when he proved faithless, she ran off into the woods from Fort Niagara where he was stationed. Kate then for a while lived with me as my 'squaw', while I was by my officer's permission absent from my regiment and learning the Indian arts of battle from certain Mohican warriors, led by their gifted war-chief, Thayendanegea, or Captain Brant. A girl child was later born to Kate at the house of a Dry Quaker in the wilderness by the foot of Lake George. The wild untrammelled life of the Indians had not only fired my fancy but also satisfied my judgment as offering the philosophic mind far more for admiration than for disgust. However, the call of military duty restrained me from following my passionate inclination, which was to continue with Kate (and the sweet fruit of our illicit love) as a member of the Mohican nation into which I had been duly initiated by the aforesaid Thayendanegea. I continued a loyal soldier of King George III. Kate and the child, when last I had news of them, were the guests of Thayendanegea's wife, Miss Molly, at Genesee village in the territory of the Six Nations – far beyond the confines of New York State.

Another fellow-soldier of mine was a veteran, Mad Johnny Maguire, who had fought in America with The Ninth when Savannah Town was taken from the Spaniards. His elder brother, Cornelius, was a farmer of Norwalk in Connecticut; the two met by chance, at the close of my narrative, after a battle in which, each unknown to the other, they were fratricidally opposed. It was Mad Johnny who had done a good service to Steel, Harlowe, Reeves and myself, when, being all recruits together, we repented in time of a desperate plan to desert the Army, which we had almost put into execution. Johnny let us return through his sentry post before we were apprehended, the reason for our rash decision to desert having been the ill-usage we suffered from the corporal of our mess, a petty tyrant by name Buchanan.

The above particulars I reckon sufficient to afford my readers a knowledge of the names and characters of such of my fellow-soldiers as have principally figured in the history hitherto. Now two other persons of civilian status, must be presented to them: the first, a young, slightly formed woman, Jane Crumer, the wife of a private soldier of The Ninth. Mrs Crumer attended very devotedly to our wounded after we captured Fort Anna, below Lake Champlain, and later risked her life at Saratoga to fetch water from a creek under the rifle-gun fire of American marksmen posted on the opposing bank. The remaining character is difficult of description: he was a lean, lantern-jawed Irishman, with a black wet forelock and a cajoling tongue. His name was the Reverend John Martin. He appeared to me first on the day of my enlistment in the year 1770 at a cock-fight, where I lost money that was not mine to lose; he wore no clerical garb on that occasion but carried a dark-winged cock under his arm. Later he appeared in the guise of a Romish chaplain at Newgate Jail in Dublin, the day that one Pretty Murphy, a murderer, was hanged, and myself acted Sergeant of the Guard. Finally this Reverend John Martin was seen by Terry Reeves in the year 1777, on the day before we took the fortress of Ticonderoga; he was then garbed as a Chaplain of the Forty-Seventh Regiment, and was reading a leather-bound book close to the enemy's works. Terry Reeves believed this fantastical personage to be the Father of Lies himself; nor would I myself now swear that he was indeed human flesh, rather than a conjoint fancy of our disordered brains.

Now for the circumstances in which I found myself in November 1777, the month in which this new volume opens. I had attained the rank of corporal, and was performing the duties of a sergeant, in the Light Infantry company of The Ninth. The Ninth formed part of Lieutenant-General Sir John Burgoyne M.P.'s army. This army, consisting of British regular troops and some German mercenaries, had in the summer of 1777 invaded New York State by way of the Canadian Lakes and Hudson's River. In October of that year, we were cut off and forced to capitulate, at Saratoga on Hudson's River, by an American army outnumbering us by four to one, commanded by General Horatio Gates, a renegade Briton. However, so evident was our resolve to fight on to the death rather than surrender ignominiously, that General Burgoyne succeeded in wresting from General Gates far better terms than we had a right to hope; namely, a pledge to send us home safely to Great Britain in return merely for our laying down our arms and undertaking not to serve again in the American continent while the war was still in progress. We duly yielded up our muskets and ammunition and what remained of our artillery; thereupon marching through wild country, under the escort of our enemies, to Boston, the so-called 'City of Saints', which lay some two hundred miles away to the east. Here, according to the Convention signed between the two opposing generals, transports were to be sent from New York, which was in British hands, for our repatriation. Pending the arrival of these ships, we British were crowded into miserable derelict huts on Prospect Hill, a few miles from Boston; yet, in the confident hope of speedy relief, we did not allow our present hardships to daunt us. We numbered about two thousand whole men, and some hundreds of sick and wounded. The German prisoners had been sent by the Americans to better quarters, in the hope that they would desert our cause.

THE WEATHER was very bad, the rain pelting in at the open windows; we were saucy and improvident enough on the first night to tear down some of the rafters to keep the fire alive in the grate – an act for which our guards greatly abused us. But this was still November, before we settled into the full misery of winter. When December came, those of us who could lie down at night, and the many who sat up from the cold, were obliged frequently to rise and shake the snow from our clothes, which the wind drifted in at the openings. Our officers were removed from us and quartered in the University town of Cambridge, become an arsenal for military stores, where but few students remained at their Latin studies – for war is the enemy of the Humanities – and those were little boys. Our officers' accommodation was scarcely better than ours, though many fine houses, the property of American loyalists, lay empty there as the common prey of plunderers.

Officers, quartermaster-sergeants and soldiers' wives were given passes, renewed each month, to go from their quarters for a distance of a few miles; but none was allowed any nearer the city of Boston, that emporium of rebellion, than Bunker's Hill and Breed's Hill (where the battle was fought) on the hither bank of the Charles River. That the common soldiers were not allowed out of the barracks was considered a great hardship, the more so since Colonel David Henley, the American commandant of the camp, forced us to buy all our provisions at two store-houses which he set up there for his own profit. By him we were charged greatly above the market price for every sort of commodity.

Our upkeep and support was paid in paper by Congress, who demanded to be reimbursed by General Burgoyne in gold and silver at the nominal value of the notes! When General Burgoyne protested at this fraud, the answer came: 'General Burgoyne supposes his solid coin to be worth three times as much as our currency. But what an opinion must he have of the authority of these States, to suppose that his money could be received at any higher rate than our own in public payment! Such payment would be at once depreciating our currency with a witness.'

What was worse, we soldiers had huge stoppages made from our pay on account of pretended damage done by us during our passage through the State of Massachusetts; it was alleged that we had burned fences, destroyed hay, grain and flax, and plundered houses of furniture. There was no redress against this plain lie and grievous injustice, for we were prisoners; and the claimants, who eagerly caught at the chance of recovering, by a recital of invented losses, real losses caused them by the war, would not be denied. General Gates was heartily cursed by the rank and file for his condonation of this smart dealing.

I was appointed by Lieut.-Colonel Hill to be temporary Surgeon to the Regiment, for Surgeon Shelly, captured in the fighting at Fort Anna, had not been returned to us; and thus I became in a manner an officer. Yet I was not asked for my parole as the officers were, and remained with my comrades on Prospect Hill. I frequently needed to visit the townships of Watertown, Mystic and Cambridge to purchase drugs and comforts for our sick. The better sort of Americans whom I met on these occasions treated me with hospitality, but I was often insulted by those whose business had been ruined by the war, or who had lost relatives in the fighting. What seemed to puzzle them was that I could be an Irishman and yet loyal to King George who, I was persistently told, governed my country with monstrous oppression.

I was often urged to desert and to take up the profession which in New England, and indeed in most colonies of America, was practically engrossed by my fellow-countrymen – namely, that of travelling school-master. It was said, I could pick up a good living by going from one out-of-the-way township to another and teaching the boys and girls to read, write and cipher. My pay would be 'country pay' that is, payment in kind: my board would be found, my clothes and boots kept in repair and in addition I would, each schooling season, receive a barrel or two of flour, some lengths of yarn, a few fleeces, a keg of molasses and so many cords of wood. There was great store set here upon education and much reading done, though religious and political argument in tract and newspaper comprised the greater part of this. Thrifty parents who could not afford to pay the Irish schoolmaster would often smuggle their children into the back rows of his class and bid them learn all they could before the cheat was discovered. I was smilingly warned that I must be a pretty slick man to avoid being overreached by my prospective pupils and their parents.

In order to avoid offence, I would tell those who urged me on this course that if ever I took to the profession it would be at home in Ireland, where ignorance was far more prevalent than in their enlightened country, and the need for Irish school-masters correspondingly greater.

I came upon many sights that interested me greatly. In the streets of Cambridge, for instance, I saw an entire house being rolled on logs, fitted with wheels, to another situation. The house had been raised on four screws placed at the corners and the logs thrust underneath. I had the courage to ask the owner the reason for his removal, and, says he very frankly: 'My wife's mother is a scold, yet I can get no satisfaction against her from the deacons, who fear her tongue as much as I do. I am a peaceable man and am therefore removing to a distance beyond the tether of her infirmities.'

Many young women rode by me, unescorted, eyeing me with remarkable boldness. They were mounted upon the horses peculiar to New England – a fine-headed, long-maned, goose-rumped, cat-hammed breed, with switch tails. When the snow lay thick on the ground I passed on the road many large sleighs, to seat a dozen persons, drawn by two or four horses and jingling with bells, but not decorated in the pleasant manner of the Canadian cariole. In these sleighs, large parties of young men and women were accustomed on moonlight nights to go out for a drive of two or three hours to a distant rendezvous with a similar party from another town: they drank, danced and caroused all night and returned to their common avocations the next morning without taking any sleep. In Ireland such a custom would be judged very imprudent, but here they thought nothing of it.

The most disagreeable part of my outings was when I must pass the American sentinels at the camp gates. They were militiamen, of an age either too advanced or too immature for more active service. The granddads, as we generically named the bushy-wigged elder sort, were in the main cold-blooded, querulous and slow; whereas the grandchildren, as we named the fifteen-and sixteen-year-olds, were hot-blooded, self-important and impatient to be doing great deeds on the held of battle. The granddads usually kept us waiting on some excuse or other, pretending that our passes were forged or that we were not the persons named in them; and if we showed impatience they protracted the delay yet further. The grandchildren threatened and insulted us, but were not so slow about their business.

One sentry, a Select-man (or church-elder) of Cambridge, held me up for three days in succession. On the third day I said to him: 'Surely, my friend, we need not run through that long rigmarole yet again?'

'I thot I told you to halt!' he drawled, presenting his piece at my breast. 'I swear now, if you attempt to pass, I'll blow you to pieces with my blazing-iron. I do not know you from Adam, you rascal.'

Now supervened a laughable yet somewhat disgusting incident which has been recounted by Lieutenant Anburey in phrases which I could not better for delicacy. A soldier's wife of the tough breed, who had followed the drum for thirty years, and could carry burdens like an ox, cook like a witch, forage like a Hessian, and outswear Mortal Harry himself at his prime, came bustling out from the camp, a short clay pipe in her mouth, and a dirty pass in her hand. Long Winifried was her name and some years before she had borne without flinching a sentence of one hundred lashes laid on her bare back: for the crime of stealing the Town Bull of Boston, slaughtering him and hacking him into beefsteaks. Long Winifried waved the paper in the old Select-man's face and was for passing on. He flew into a passion and called on her to halt, or he would fire. She turned back and gave him Billingsgate oratory in a scorching flood, to the effect that she was hastening to buy a little milk for her sick grandchild and he would cut his pranks at his own peril – she would not be halted. As the Lieutenant writes: 'When the old man was so irritated as to present his firelock, the woman immediately ran up, snatched it from him, knocked him down and, striding over the prostrate hero in the exultation of triumph, profusely besprinkled him not with Olympian dew but, 'faith, with something more natural. Nor did she quit her post till a file of sturdy ragamuffins marched valiantly to his relief, dispossessed the Amazon and enabled the knight of the grisly caxon to look fierce and reshoulder his musket.' But, for myself, I did not wait for this concluding scene, hurriedly snatching up my fallen pass and running away down the path, lest I be cited as an accessory after the fact.

On the morning of December 13th, I went out from the camp to Cambridge, which lay two miles off, in order to attend upon. Lieut.-Colonel Hill. He was sick and had desired me to come and bleed him. The sentinel that day was a young sickly boy who gave me no difficulty at the gate, and I therefore looked forward to a pleasant excursion, it being a clear Sunday morning, with the church bells pealing and the sun shining brilliantly across the thin snow.

I had crossed Willis Creek and nearly reached the Colonel's house at the outskirts of Cambridge, when I was stopped by my enemy, 'the knight of the grisly caxon', but in his quality not of sentinel but of Select-man. He informed me that I was contravening three of the oldest and most venerated laws in the province at one and the same time: the first, by carrying a bundle upon the Sabbath Day – for I had in my hand a little canvas case containing cupping instruments; the second, by being seen in the streets during the hour of Divine Service; and the third, by proceeding along a road for more than the Sabbath Day's journey allowed to the Jews by the prophet Moses.

I pleaded that I was going upon an errand of mercy and obeying the orders of my superior officer; but he was very fierce and would not listen to me. He confined me instantly to a dungeon in the town jail, which was dark, empty and very cold, and kept me there upon bread and water until the next day; drily remarking, as the key was turned upon me, that I was but a young bear with all my troubles before me. Two small doors with double locks and bolts shut me from the exercise yard; two small windows, strong grated with iron, introduced a gloomy light to the apartment and were without a single pane of glass. I slept upon a little damp straw. In this place I was kept for two days and nights, without even being able to go outside for the necessities of nature; but must add my sum to the noisome litter deposited in the corner by previous malefactors. Nor was I permitted to send a message to my commanding officer, explaining why I had not waited upon him; no, they marched me back to the Camp, where they cast me into the prison-hut, next the guard-room, where our people were confined for slight or imagined faults by the American guards, without prior reference to our own officers. This prison-hut was a worse place than the Cambridge jail, being very damp and verminous, but at least I had company. The first to greet me there was Terry Reeves, who had been arrested in my absence. He asked me with surprise what brought me into confinement; and indeed it was the first time in my whole service that I had found myself in that disgrace. 'The Book of Deuteronomy, I believe,' I said. 'And what brought you here?'

'Tobacco-juice,' he answered with equal brevity, and told me his story. He had been suffering greatly of a toothache and the only relief he could find was in rum, of which he drank above a pint upon an empty stomach. As he was walking from his hut to the guard-room, where he was about to put in a report on men fallen sick, he saw a person approach him dressed in a rough frieze overcoat with a woollen cap upon his head. This person, who was chewing tobacco, squirted the juice from the corner of his mouth across Terry's path, wetting his boot. Terry cried in vexation: 'Hold hard and keep your yellow spittle off my feet, damn you!' The man replied: 'I squirt where I please, you scoundrel. I am a major in the Massachusetts service.'

To which Terry made answer: 'If that be so, which I doubt, you are no credit to the Provincial service. To spit on a soldier's boot is a beastly habit in an officer.' Whereupon the officer arrested Terry.

Corporal Buchanan was also confined. His charge was: 'being found in possession of a spade, knowing it to be stolen from the guard.'

The Commandant of the Camp, this Colonel David Henley, was a very drunken, passionate person, and the author of most of our troubles, by inflaming his subordinates to cruel treatment of us. On the day after I was confined in this prison-hut, a number of quartermaster-sergeants attended the Deputy-Adjutant-General's office for the monthly renewal of their passes. He railed at them all for the disorderly noise which, so the guards informed him had arisen on the previous night from the huts. Sergeant Fleming of The Forty-Seventh stating, as an excuse, that none of us had been able to sleep because of the cold – which was very true – Colonel Henley clenched his fist and shook it at the Sergeant crying: 'You rascals,

I'll make damnation fly out of ye. For I will myself one of these nights go the rounds and if I hear the least word or noise in your barracks, I'll pour shot amongst ye and make flames of Hell leap out of ye and turn your barracks inside out. Moreover, my merry men, the sentinels inform me that when they stop ye for your passes, you look sulky at 'em. Were I a sentinel, and you did so to me, I would blow your brains out, aye, were you Whaley, Goffe or the Devil himself.'[1]

Three days later this Colonel Henley came on horseback with some other militia officers to release several of us who were prisoners, in order to make room for others, the prison-hut being overcrowded. He called us out in order of rank, myself first, then the two corporals. Having read out our crimes he made many very scurrilous remarks to the three of us, which I heard with indifference, Corporal Buchanan with feigned awe, but Terry Reeves with indignation. Finally he told us that the Ninth Regiment gave more trouble than any other corps. Terry Reeves, who could never hold his tongue, then remarked archly: 'I believe, Sir, that General Schuyler and General Gates were both of your opinion during the last campaign.'

Colonel Henley, feeling his dignity challenged, grew very angry, and began to thunder at Terry.

Says he: 'You hired cut-throat, how dare you insult a Provincial officer, as you insulted Major McKissock yesterday? Do you venture to tell your British majors that they are a discredit to their service?'

'No, sir,' replied Terry unabashed, 'for I tell no lies.'

This was as much of the conversation as I heard, for Colonel Henley catching a smile as it stole across my face, ordered me back to close confinement.

I am informed that, after I had gone, Terry continued: 'However, Sir, I am sorry if I insulted the Major; but I could not have known him to be of held rank because of his civilian dress and his unofficerlike habit of chewing and spitting. I own that I was in liquor, owing to a toothache, and therefore I am ready to beg his pardon if I seemed disrespectful in manner.'

Colonel Henley in a rage: 'By God, Sir, had it been me you served so, I would have run you through the body. You're a great rascal, I guess.'

Terry Reeves remained undaunted. He replied: 'Sir, I am no rascal, but a good soldier, and my officers know it.'

'Silence, you coward Englishman!' cried Colonel Henley. Another

---

1 This expression, often heard in New England, refers to the two famous Swordsmen and Regicides from whom the general pardon was withheld at the Restoration. They had fled to New England, where they lived under assumed names in the town of Hadley. Goffe once routed a swaggering fencing-master who came to give a display at Boston, himself armed with only a wet mop and a cheese, tied in a napkin, which he used as a shield. The fencing-master, whose sword was at each lunge received in the cheese and his face dabbed with the mop cried out: 'Who are you in the name of God? You must be either Whale, Goffe or the Devil himself.' R. L.

officer, Major Sweasey, called Terry a rascal and raised a whip to strike him.

But Terry Reeves would not be silenced. 'I am no coward, Colonel Henley, and I will not be so abused by you. If I had arms and ammunition I should soon be with General Howe, fighting for my King and Country.'

'Damn your King and Country! When you had arms, you were willing enough to lay them down,' was Colonel Henley's strange rejoinder.

Terry Reeves cried: 'Sir, I tell you, I will not hear my King abused.'

Colonel Henley again called him to silence, and then Corporal Buchanan must put in his oar with: 'Hold your tongue, Corporal Reeves, when the officer bids you.'

Terry in disgust turned on Corporal Buchanan: 'Damn you, you fawning fellow, why don't you stick up for your King and Country?'

'Be silent, Terry, or you'll be getting us all into trouble,' muttered Buchanan.

Terry would not be silent. 'God damn them all,' he cried in a loud voice. 'I'll stand by my King till I die.'

Colonel Henley in great scorn; 'This is a free country, rascal. We acknowledge no Kings here.'

'No, I believe not,' said Terry, 'or none but King Hancock.'

This excited a laugh among the grandchildren on guard, which so infuriated the Colonel that he cried to them: 'Silence, boys, and let one of you run him through for a scoundrel!'

None of them stirred, for in America there is a tribute of respect always paid to a ready tongue, and they reckoned that Terry Reeves should not be murdered for his.

Colonel Henley then leaping off his horse, seized a fire-lock with a fixed bayonet from one of the lads, and ran at Terry. Terry leapt back a pace, so that the steel did no more than prick him in the left breast.

Colonel Henley white with passion: 'Another word, and I'll drive it through your body.'

'I don't care,' cried brave Terry. 'For I'll stand by King and Country till I die.'

The Colonel made another push at Terry's heart with the bayonet; but Smutchy Steel, who was one of the new prisoners waiting for accommodation in the hut, leaped forward to the rescue, calling to Buchanan to do the same. The two of them knocked up the firelock, and the bayonet passed harmlessly over Terry's shoulder.

Thereupon an ancient corporal of the guard drawlingly interposed, saying to the Colonel: 'No, I swear, Neighbour Henley, you shan't kill this man, for he was committed to my charge by Major McKissock whom he insulted. You may do as you like with the other rogues, but this Corporal Reeves is my prisoner and I'm answerable for him to Major McKissock, who's my own company officer.'

Major Sweasey then dismounted and besought Colonel Henley to return Terry to the prison-hut; in which plea he was seconded by another officer present. Colonel Henley at last consented.

Terry was brought back into the hut, bleeding profusely from an upward stab three inches long. He exclaimed still in unquenched indignation: 'Damn them all, I'll never allow my King to be abused while I live!' I was fast by the legs, but he came to me and I could dress his wound with the bandages which I carried in my canvas case.

CHAPTER II

THE CRUEL excesses of an individual such as Colonel Henley, and their effect upon several of his subordinates, cannot be enlarged into an indictment of the whole American nation, and I may here note that in time of war the greatest magnanimity towards the enemy seems always to be shown by the troops most directly engaged in the fighting, whereas the meanest and most inhumane feelings prevail in the bases and camps far remote from the hostile scene. Nor would I disguise from my readers that at New York, where the prisoners taken from the Americans were confined in hulks in the harbour, the treatment that they received, it is said, greatly exceeded in malignity what we were now experiencing. It should be observed that the Commissary of Prisoners was an American Tory, as were most of the prison-guards, and these revenged themselves for past injuries upon their unfortunate fellow-countrymen. Nevertheless, the negligence of the high British officers responsible for the well-being of these prisoners cannot escape censure; and the Provost-Marshal, Major Cunningham, a beast in human form, was (I regret to record) an Irishman. When charity supplied a vessel of broth to his starving captives, he would divert himself by kicking it over, and watching the poor creatures lap the liquor from the foul floor with their tongues. The rulers of Massachusetts when they learned of the barbarities which had been done on the hulks, and at Major Cunningham's jail in Walnut Street, New York, naturally retaliated upon us.

I will not therefore enlarge at inordinate length upon our sufferings at Colonel Henley's hands, merely relating an incident that occurred early in the new year of 1778, while a number of our people, myself among them, were watching a parade of the American militia. Their unhandiness with arms was the subject of a silent merriment among such veteran spectators as ourselves, though we contrived to keep straight faces. Colonel Henley, who commanded the parade, became aware of our close interest and shouted: 'Off, you rascals, and clear the parade; or it will be the worse for you.'

We immediately turned about and began to pick our way carefully through (he mud, those of us who were behind waiting for the rest of the

crowd to get clear before following them. 'Damn you,' cried Colonel
Henley, 'I'll make you mend your pace!'

At that moment, Corporal Buchanan, looking over his shoulder, saw
the militia soldier who was performing the manual exercise as fugleman to
the rest, by a maladroit movement drop his musket to the ground.
Buchanan could not restrain his mirth, but gave way to a roaring laugh.
Colonel Henley, setting spurs to his horse, ran at him with his sword.
Buchanan avoided the thrust and made good his escape, but the sword
wounded in the left side a corporal of another regiment. Colonel Henley
then rode back to his men. He 'was straightening, as he went, the sword
which, being of inferior make, had bent nearly double against the
corporal's ribs. He then ordered his men to load and come back with him
to hunt Buchanan down and blaze at him when found. Though unarmed
ourselves, we all felt ourselves in honour bound to protect our comrade
from death, and shouted to the Colonel that he would only catch his man
by a general massacre of us all.

Colonel Henley had already given the first order for a volley in our
midst; but Major Sweasey, who then fortunately appeared, implored him
to desist. The Major proposed instead that the British officer in command
of our huts be asked to arrest Buchanan and confine him for trial. Colonel
Henley unwillingly consented, and we dispersed. In the end Buchanan was
given up as a prisoner and sentenced to a few days' imprisonment for disrespect.

When, however, two more of our soldiers were wounded by the instigation of Colonel Henley, separately, on a single day, General Burgoyne
demanded a special court-martial of this infamous person. The plea was
granted and he himself acted as prosecutor, speaking very eloquently and
sharply and calling the Americans to a reminder of that due sense of the
rights of mankind that they had expressed so ably in their Declaration of
Independence. Yet it will readily be imagined that Colonel Henley was
acquitted of the four crimes charged against him, the court being
composed of his associates, and the evidence of the militiamen (who had
been well rehearsed beforehand) being preferred to that of British eyewitnesses. It was alleged in his defence that we had daily and hourly offered
insult and insolence to our guards, and to the Colonel himself by our resolution to protect Buchanan; and that the Colonel was a warm-blooded but
benevolent officer animated only by a desire to protect his country from
affront. The perjury was unashamed. Terry Reeves' rejoinder on the
subject of King Hancock was distorted into the absurd statement: 'King
Hancock is come to Town. Don't you think him a saucy fellow for coming
so near to General Burgoyne?'

General Burgoyne's prosecution of this American colonel was much
spoken of, and that the verdict was an acquittal was used against him by
Americans and by his enemies at home as putting him in the light of a

mischief-maker. Yet we soldiers loved him for his warm championship of our cause, and his action was on the whole successful: for though Colonel Henley 'for public honour' was formally reinstated in his command after the trial, he was removed a week later, and a more humane colonel named Lee replaced him. Colonel Lee did away with one great evil: he granted our people passes for the purchase of provisions, so that the extravagant price of commodities at the two stores on the hill dropped down to the market rate.

On January 10th, two days after this incident upon the parade ground, I walked over to Charlestown Neck to make a few small purchases from the farmers in the neighbourhood of the burned village of Charlestown. Terry Reeves, who had recovered of his stabbing wound, had been chosen to act quartermaster-sergeant of The Ninth and provided with a pass to accompany me.

I said to him: 'Let us now pass over Bunker's Hill and Breed's Hill and see how the battle went.' This we did, and we were resting in the ruined redoubt which had been the scene of the fiercest fighting in this battle when we heard footsteps approach. Looking over the parapet, we found ourselves confronted with a person whose disagreeable aspect will by this time be so familiar to readers of my former volume that I will spare them a fresh account of it, as being unchanged. It was, let me ask them to believe, once more the Reverend John Martin, but this time dressed as an American Congregational minister.

I silently gripped Terry's shoulder to impress upon him that I would face the thing out boldly and that I expected him to stand by me; but I could feel, by the shudder that took him, that he was almost dead with fear.

'Good day to you, holy man,' I cried. 'And who pray, may you be? For this is the third time that you and I have met, yet we are still unacquainted.'

'I disremember any such meeting,' said he in an off-hand way. 'Yet to be sure, you have an Irish accent.'

'So had my father,' I replied sternly. 'But that is neither here nor there. I asked you your name. Then give it!'

'I am the Reverend John Martin,' he said, suddenly very humble, 'a chaplain of the Rhode Island militia. I see that you belong to the captured, or Convention, Army. Many of your British comrades were killed hereabouts three years ago. Do you happen to be acquainted with a charming play, *The Downfall of British Tyranny*? I am not the author, but I mended a few lines, you know.'

'A wretched, patched production, they tell me,' I said, though I had never heard of it before.

'No, no,' the false priest persisted. 'An altogether delightful one. It hits them all off. Admiral Tombstone (meaning Admiral Graves, ha, ha!) relates in tarry-trousered style: "Many powdered *beaux*, *petite maîtres*, fops, fribbles, skip-jackets, macaronies, jack-puddings, noble-men's bastards and whores' sons fell that day." '

'No more of that,' said I, 'or with my fists I shall resent the insult to the Army.'

'No offence was intended,' he said hurriedly, 'A play is but a play, a harmless thing. But, good Sergeant, I myself took part in the battle. Indeed, it was I who, the night before, in the absence of Colonel Gridley, the patriot Engineer, oversaw the construction of this very redoubt. I lied above a thousand men at work.'

'Tell me more,' said I, staring into his eyes, 'and I'll believe less.'

But he would not meet my gaze, and tried instead to fascinate Terry, who was now quaking like a man in a fit.

'Oh,' said he, when I repeated my injunction in a louder voice. 'Just as you wish. Well, then, on the next morning I went down into Charlestown yonder with a spy-glass, for a look at the foe. A cannon-ball came hurtling through the house where I was taking refreshment, the property of a Mr Cary. It fetched off my hat, without touching me, and I returned to the Hill. There I sent a message back to General Ward at Cambridge for rein-forcements, judging the force in the redoubt to be weak; and, in answer a little after noon, up comes Colonel Putnam with the Connecticut men.'

'So,' said I, 'you took quite a prominent part, you say, in directing the battle?' I sneered at him, for I could see that every word was a fabrication, and shook off all my fanciful terrors.

'That was nothing to what followed,' he continued, in hurried tones, his voice gradually rising. 'I returned in person to headquarters at Cambridge, in order to press General Ward there to send forward wagons for the safe conveyance of the wounded. On my return the fighting was very warm. I stood down by that fence,' [pointing to the left, as we faced Boston] 'where the Connecticut men, intermixed with some Irish compa-nies, were engaged with the Welch Fusiliers. The Irish inadvertently fired upon our line, but I ran forward and called on them in the Old Irish tongue to desist. The Connecticut men, not understanding this language, suspected treachery; but the Irish listened to me, and all was well.'

'So you too are an Irishman,' I said, very severe, as if I had learned this for the first time. 'Now we can discourse on common ground. Continue!'

He went on, his eyes flickering about like a candle-flame in a draught, 'I had girded on an Irish long sword that day, and it was well that I came so armed. The British pushed around the end of the fence by the water, and damned me for a clerical dog, saying that they would have my life. A Welchman fired point-blank at me and rushed upon me with his bayonet. I let out his bowels with my sword. Then I engaged, cut and thrust, with an officer who drew his hanger; I slew him too with a stroke on the neck. I lost but a button sliced off my coat.'

Then I said to this parson: 'Did I believe that you were either an honest man, or a clerk in Holy Orders, which I do not, I would spare you punishment. But you have sailed under too many false colours and proved a bird of ill omen to my comrade and myself on too many occasions. Now I am about to "change my luck" in Indian fashion by making your feathers fly.'

I turned to Terry. 'Terry,' said I, 'for the honour of our Army, and of Ireland, I am resolved to give this liar a thrashing – "be he Whaley, Goffe or the Devil himself". Lend me the loan of that little hickory club you were carrying.'

Terry cried: 'No, no, Gerry. Let be! He will do us some mischief.' But I snatched up the club notwithstanding, from where it lay in the trench, and swung at the false priest's head.

He dodged, and leaped nimbly over the parapet – I tripped, felt curiously numbed, as if I had touched a catfish, and was slow in following. When I had surmounted the parapet and gazed about me, he had disappeared as cleanly as if he had never been!

Terry stared at me in a dazed way. 'Oh, Gerry,' he faltered, 'it's a brave boy you are, surely. When I meet that Devil I feel always like a frog before a black snake, and there's no hiding it. I am sure now that when we return to Camp there'll be black news waiting for us.'

I reproved him with: 'Terry, you must not allow these sick thoughts to weigh with you. Take a stick to the Devil and he leaps off and vanishes; for there is no power or force in lies. That you are a gallant man we know, from your defiance of Colonel Henley. I think that his Reverence will not show himself again to us in a hurry.'

'If he were mortal flesh,' said Terry, still in a whimpering voice, 'I should not care. But he is as old as the wickedness of the world.'

On our return to the Camp we found that Terry's gloomy prediction was justified, and confirmation given to the headless rumours that had for long been flying through the Camp. The Convention of Saratoga, solemnly entered into by General Gates, was not to be ratified by Congress, and we were therefore to be kept prisoners for an indefinite time!

Here, as always, when treating of the American Congress, a distinction must be made between the real motives guiding their policy, and their professed motives. Their excuse for not ratifying the Convention was that General Burgoyne had called American public faith in question by unjustly charging a militia colonel with attempted murder and by complaining further that the wretched accommodation given his officers at Cambridge and to ourselves at Prospect Hill did not agree with what had been stipulated; and that therefore if he could express himself so warmly, he might well be himself meditating a breach of the Convention! Furthermore, we had retained our empty cartouche boxes and our cross-belts when delivering up our arms at Saratoga, and this (though it had not

been insisted upon by General Gates that we should do so) was a failure to
conform with the spirit of the agreement. Nor, they complained, had our
officers supplied them with a personal description of all our non-commissioned officers and men – for which no express demand had, either, been
made. Finally, when because of the danger and difficulties of bringing
transports into Boston during the winter months, it had been demanded
of Congress that we should be permitted to march to Providence in Rhode
Island, where the harbourage was more convenient, and be fetched off
from there, they pretended to regard this as an attempted evasion of the
Convention, and the preparation for an offensive movement.

The fact of the matter was that Americans in general, and New
Englanders in particular, hate to be overreached in a bargain, and when it
became known to Congress that General Gates, with our army surrounded
and outnumbered by five to one, had yet yielded to General Burgoyne's
menace of a desperate attack and let us go freely, they felt cheated and
looked for a legal loophole by which to escape. General Lafayette, a young
French officer of fortune who, with the rank of major-general, was now
one of General Washington's military family, told Congress that it would
be a very foolish action to ratify the Convention. He pointed out that even
if we were not sent back to America we could still serve as garrison troops
elsewhere in the Empire, and release other regiments to take our places.
Further, we might thereupon be actively employed against the French,
whom the news of our surrender would surely now encourage into an open
alliance with the Americans against us. General Lafayette urged these
military considerations more readily because the proposed breach of faith
affected only the American Republic, not his own country. It is said that
General Washington and other men of honour were not of his way of
thinking. They remonstrated indignantly at the weak and futile pretexts
used by Congress to avoid their obligations. Nevertheless, General
Lafayette succeeded in overriding all scruples by advancing as precedent
an alleged breach, by our Government, many years before, of the
Convention of Kloster Seben, where the French were the losers.

The Convention being not yet directly repudiated, we still had hope at
least of being exchanged against American prisoners. Meanwhile, there
were rumours running among our guards of an attempt on the part of
Admiral Howe to enter Boston with his fleet and rescue us; and great
excitement was caused one night by the lighting of a chain of beacons from
hill to hill, which brought the militia up from a great distance to repel an
attack. However, it was but a false alarm designed by the Americans to
stimulate popular distrust in the public faith of Britain.

Our captivity had begun to grow very wearisome, from the lack of
employment and hope deferred, but we comforted ourselves with an
assurance that the Spring would soon be upon us, and that the new
campaign would be decisive for British arms. It was notorious that General

Washington, who alone of American generals kept an army in the field during this winter, had been reduced to great straits by his enemies in Congress, who starved him of supplies, and by the desertion of his militia, who were impatient of the discipline that he imposed upon them. Less than three thousand men remained under arms with him in the camp at Valley Forge by the Schuylkill River, and General Howe, snug in Philadelphia, refrained from attack only because he believed that the force of the Revolution was already broken by the jealousies and rivalries of its leaders.

Our watchword was 'Patience'.

However, before the year was much older, news came that the Colonists had done what we never believed them capable of doing – they had signed an armed alliance with our mortal enemies the French and thus renounced for ever the name and tradition of Englishmen! France from the beginning of the contest had secretly encouraged the Americans in their opposition and supplied them with munitions of war, while at the same time amusing Great Britain with declarations of the most pacific intentions. What made matters worse was that the traitors of our Opposition were in constant treaty with the American agents in France and openly rejoiced when news reached them of General Burgoyne's capitulation at Saratoga.

I am sorry to relate that the American agents who visited our camp, and constantly pestered us with threats and cajolements in an attempt to make us desert, had considerable success with some regiments even thus early in our captivity; though but little with The Ninth. We were promised our freedom, citizenship and liberty to pursue our trade in any State in which we chose to settle; and, if we cared to enter their army, the rank and pay of an officer for every man of three years' service and upwards! Even the newest recruit of ours could turn a large fee by becoming a deserter; for the well-to-do farmers or manufacturers called out as militiamen now found it next to impossible to engage substitutes and were willing to offer almost any price for such. Remarkable it is how few men took this bait, and how many of those who did were but pretended deserters, and crossed over into New York at the earliest opportunity. However, the whole band of The Sixty-Second was seduced except the Master, and went to dispense *Yankee Doodle* and other patriotic airs to a Boston regiment; and once we recognized a soldier of The Forty-Seventh, who had deserted three years previously, riding up to the camp in major's uniform at the head of a supply column. Our officers had the mortification of taking orders from him.

On April 15th, when the Spring had suddenly appeared, and we saw green grass again for the first time since our captivity' our brigade (which consisted of the Artillery, the Advanced Troops and The Ninth) was paraded one morning and told to prepare for a march to Rutland in the

interior of the province; because the Council of Boston had decided that
we should fare better there. It happened very fortunately for us that a
vessel under a flag of truce had arrived at Boston from New York two days
previously with some necessaries for us, including blankets, linen and
medicaments; else we should have been in a wretched state. We were
marched along the same Worcester road which we had taken on our
journey to Boston and halted about midday at a place called Weston, our
destination that night being Westborough which lay at twenty-five miles'
distance from the camp. I was resting by the roadside, avoiding as far as
possible any converse with the inhabitants of the place, who were exer-
cising their wit at our expense, when I heard my name called and an
American militia sergeant came forward from the crowd and gripped my
hand.

I did not at first recognize him but he swore that, being indebted to me
for his life, he must at least insist on my taking refreshment with him at a
tavern near by. He was one Gershom Hewit, whose wounds I had dressed
after the fight at Fort Anna. I declined at first to go with him, lest I might
be apprehended for quitting the column, but he undertook to write me out
a pass, and his offer of a glass of mimbo – that is to say, hot rum and water
sweetened with molasses – was very inviting; so I went with him up the hill
to the tavern.

Hewit took me into a private apartment where the mimbo was set
before us. When the landlord had departed, he clapped me on the back in
a very cordial manner, and told me that we had met again in a fortunate
hour, since it now lay in his power to do me a very considerable service; in
quittance of his debt to me.

When I asked him what that could be, he told me in evident expectation of my acceptance, that if I would desert the King's service and a cause
which was, I must admit, both an evil and a lost one, he had it in his power
to make me the surgeon of his regiment, at very good pay – for he had been
commissioned that very day to find a man to fill the vacancy!

Said I: 'Sergeant Gershom Hewit, you have formed a mistaken opinion
of my character. I thank you for your offer of this surgeon's commission
and for your present hospitality, but I must decline to talk treason with
you, even in a private apartment.' I took up my smoking glass and toasted
the health of King George, adding, 'If you will not drink with me, I must
drink alone.'

I drank alone, for he arose and left me without another word. I stayed
a minute or two more in the room, reading a well-thumbed copy of *Poor
Richard's Almanack*, for the year 1744, published at Philadelphia by Dr
Benjamin Franklin, that lay upon the chimney-shelf.

There was a rhyme in it that struck my eye, and I memorized it for the
edification of my comrades. It referred to the New England custom of
'bundling', namely the supposedly chaste lying in bed together of young,

affectionate, unmarried persons of opposite sexes for the sake of company
and the saving of fuel; this was still universally practised among the
common people hereabouts, who held that the man and woman (being
already sanctified by Grace) could not yield to temptation. The mother of
the girl concerned would usually tuck the pair in bed herself and blow out
the light. It may be remarked here that love-children were frequent in
America; but the man almost invariably married the woman whom he had
seduced, and the advantage of a large population in so extensive and rich
a country excused the fault even if it were not repaired by subsequent
wedlock; so long as it was not incestuous or too often repeated by the same
woman. Bundling was the subject of much raillery, and I found that if ever,
while in American company, I looked grave at jests on this head, I was
adjudged a person of evil imagination who doubted the innocence of my
hosts. The rhyme ran:

> Biblis does solitude admire,
> A wondrous Lover of the Dark:
> Each night puts out her Chamber Fire
> And just *keeps in a single Spark*;
> 'Till four she keeps herself alive,
> Warmed by her piety, no doubt;
> Then, tired with kneeling, just at five
> She sighs – and lets that Spark *go out*.

I thought: 'These are a people whom I will never come to understand.
If the practice be indeed blameless, how come the country people to take
such delight in salacious jokes on the subject? Or, if it be vicious, how do
the ministers, who hold such a sway over the people, tolerate and even
encourage it as innocent?'

At this point of my reflexion there came a noise of angry shouting from
the common tap-room of the inn, crashes as if a battle were in progress,
and screams of grief and indignation from the women of the house. I
learned later that a company of our artillerymen had followed me to the
tavern for a drink of mimbo, and that Sergeant Hewit, after leaving my
presence, had attached himself to their company and attempted to wean
them from the Service. They had made scornful replies, which the
Americans present had resented, and a battle was joined with stools and
fists. Three drinking-glasses were broken, but no injuries done to the
contestants beyond a few bruises. The artillerymen had made good their
retreat and rejoined their column just as it marched off.

The landlord, fearing that he would get no satisfaction, cried out in my
hearing, just as I was quietly taking my departure: 'I have a hostage, wife,
never fear. I'll squeeze payment out of him, I swear.' He ran up to me,
catching at the collar of my jacket and, says he: 'You rogue of a Britonian,
you will pay me for these broken glasses, or I'll have the Law on you.'

I replied: 'Landlord, you know as well as myself that I was not in this room while the stools were flying, but in the parlour.'

'O what a wicked falsehood!' cried his dutiful wife and daughters; 'You were the ringleader of the party, O fie! O fie! We saw you with our own eyes.'

'This will cost you sixty dollars, young man,' said the landlord very severely. 'You see, there are witnesses.'

I turned to the landlord's wife and asked in a smooth voice: 'Can you tell me, Madam, for I have been long parted from my Bible by the accidents of war, which is the number of the Commandment – is it the Tenth or the Ninth? – which prohibits the bearing of false witness?'

Yet she was not abashed. 'The Commandment prohibits only the bearing of false witness against a neighbour, and the Gospel makes it nation plain (in the chapter concerning the good Samaritan) that only he is a neighbour who does a man a friendly service. You have done us no such friendly service. You have come into our land to lay it waste and destroy our young men, as the Assyrians came into the Land of Israel; and I have neither love for you nor pity.'

'Summon Sergeant Gershom Hewit, then, Madam,' said I, 'for he can call me neighbour, and he will testify that I am not culpable of these breakages.'

'No, no,' exclaimed the landlord, 'you can't escape us that a way. Neighbour Hewit, though he brot you here, is greatly obliged to me and would not injure my trade. The Commandment forbids the giving of false witness against a neighbour, but it does not insist that one should volunteer to give true witness even when called upon. Come, come, don't be het up, but pay me my sixty dollars. Nay, I'll be content with fifty, for the sake of peace.'

I could not by any means prevail on them to summon Sergeant Hewit, who had returned to his own house with a bruised head; for all were aware of the obligation under which Sergeant Hewit stood to me.

Now, I had four guineas in gold concealed in my shoes, each one of which was now worth at least fifty Continental paper dollars. Rather than be committed to jail and separated from my comrades, I would willingly have drawn on this hoard to pay the fine. Though the injustice was monstrous, the landlord had me in his power. Unfortunately, however, this way out was barred: once I discovered my hoard, the landlord would take it all away, and even make a virtue of his great benevolence in compounding with me for twenty odd dollars instead of fifty

Fifty dollars in paper was not so stiff a price as appears at first sight, perhaps only double the value of the broken glasses. For the Americans had been dependent on Britain and Ireland for almost the whole of their glass-ware and crockery; therefore three years of war, and (before the war) the strong associations of colonists to avoid the use of English manufactured goods, and finally the rapid depreciation of the paper-currency, had sent up the value of the simplest household utensils from halfpence to dollars. Breakages were almost impossible to renew, and I may mention here that when General Gates, after the capitulation of Saratoga, had entertained General Burgoyne and his staff at a banquet; no more than four plates and two drinking-glasses could be found for this purpose in the whole American camp.

In short, I refused to pay, but told them that they were at liberty to take me to a magistrate where they might prove the crime against me if they could. There was a deal of whispering together among the men who had been engaged in the brawl with the artillerymen, and presently one of them came forward and asked me: 'Say, you rascal lobster, kin you clip?'

I told him I was no barber, but he angrily bade me not to be witty at his expense. He then explained that he wished to know whether or no I was fleet of foot.

'Is this a challenge?' I asked.

'No,' he said very slowly, 'not exactly a challenge, but a tarnal provocation.'

The mob guffawed at this rejoinder and it was now borne upon me that they had concerted to make me 'run the gauntlet' to the nearest magistrate's house. Running the gauntlet, or gantlope, between the ranks of a regiment, of which each man was armed with a switch or strap, was a punishment lately borrowed from the British Army by General Washington for introduction into his own; together with the more formal punishments of flogging and riding the wooden horse. The last-named very painful punishment (which consisted of setting the offender a-straddle upon the edge of a board six feet above the ground, with muskets tied to his feet) was only awarded for serious offences, such as horse-stealing and desertion. General Washington discarded it, in the end, because of the permanent injuries it often occasioned; but by permission of Congress, the legitimate allowance of stripes in flogging was at the same time raised from the Mosaic limit of thirty-nine to that of five hundred – though, I believe, seldom more than two hundred were awarded. Running the gauntlet, which combined entertainment with castigation, was the sentence usually inflicted throughout the American forces upon soldiers who failed in their duty. The whole regiment being made the executioner, the drummers were relieved of the peculiar odium which their disagreeable duty as floggers brings upon them in every army; and there was also this advantage, that the criminal was left to the mercy of his comrades, who laid on lightly or heavily according to their estimation of the gravity of the crime and his character as a soldier.

I was kindly excused the precaution usually taken to ensure that the victim did not escape lightly, viz. a sergeant with a bayonet placed at the runner's breast walking slowly backwards to check his pace. They took me to the tavern door, and pointing out the magistrate's house at a hundred yards' distance down the hill, which was conspicuous for an American flag flying from a staff, 'There, damn you,' one cried, 'Look at the Stripes of Liberty!' Presently their leader gave me the word 'Go!' I instantly darted off. I was young and active and the slope accelerated my pace, so that I received but few blows, though a score of people, armed with hickory sticks, aimed to strike me as I passed.

The magistrate himself, a red-faced man wearing a monstrous corn-yellow wig, was on the stoep, or raised platform, which surrounded his house; he appeared to be enjoying the fun very heartily. As I leaped into the sanctuary of his parlour, he pretended surprise at my unceremonious haste, and asked me gruffly, where were my manners? The landlord soon arrived, carrying the broken glasses on a tray for a testimony against me, and claimed the fifty dollars from my pocket. But he said: 'Come now, I swear I'm a merciful man. I'll accept forty, and that's dog-cheap.'

The magistrate called me a rogue and a common brawler and, without hearing my defence, threatened me with the hulks at Boston, where I should be fed on bread and water, did I not instantly pay. I persisted in declaring that I had no part in the outrage and challenged any person to come forward and prove it against me, demanding fair play. I observed that I had evidently raised a scruple in the conscience of the landlord's wife and daughters: for they did not venture to swear against me. Yet, the landlord himself being very insistent, the magistrate rejected my plea and repeated that to the hulks I must go, unless I laid down the mulct upon the table.

Then I said: 'As for the money, Sir, you cannot either by squeezing or threats get blood from a flint, or coin from a pauper. You are at liberty to search my pockets, and take what you find, but more cannot be effected. I have always understood the folk of Massachusetts to be a reasonable people.' Then I produced two dollars in Continental paper and an English sixpence, all of which I laid upon the table. 'As for sending me to Boston, that will only cause you trouble; nor will it pay for the drinking-glasses, which (I repeat) I did not break; and so Sergeant Gershom Hewit, who owns himself under an obligation to me for the saving of his life, would be glad to testify, were he summoned.'

The magistrate, I judged, was chary of offending Gershom Hewit. After some consultation among themselves, the matter was arranged to the general satisfaction. The price of the glasses was to be made up by a voluntary contribution of the whole company, who demanded in return the pleasure of striking at me once more, having succeeded so ill on the former occasion.

I was therefore brought to the door and held by the magistrate and his sons until my enemies were each man posted between the house and the Westborough road, all prepared to strike me. The magistrate asked for the word 'ready'; and when they gave it I was let go. Once more I darted along the line, though the ground did not favour me as before; and despite that the number of my assailants was greatly increased by the news of my arrest, which had spread through the town, I did not receive in all more than a dozen blows. Their confusion and eagerness to deal strokes upon my unprotected head spoilt their aim, and I dodged, checked and ducked with an agility that surprised even myself. They did not pursue me after I had gained the road and by rapid marching I was enabled to join my companions. However, I felt my body and head sore for many days afterwards.

CHAPTER III

ON OUR arrival at Rutland, ten miles beyond the township of Worcester, we found no preparation made for us. In a region of forest remote from any houses, we were given axes with which to fell a great number of trees, and to cut pickets from them of the length of five and twenty feet, sharpened at either end. These pickets we were then ordered to drive firmly into the earth, very close together, so that a pen was made enclosing a space of two or three acres. Only when this was accomplished were we allowed to build log huts for our shelter and accommodation; to procure boards for which we must fell more timber and convey it to a saw-mill some miles away. We were, however, allowed a few nails for our carpentry. For chairs we were content to use tree stumps or round blocks; two blocks with a plank laid over made a table; pegs served instead of cupboards.

At one angle of the pen a gate was erected and outside the gate stood the guard-house. Two American sentinels were constantly posted here and no one could go out unless he had a pass from the officer of the guard; but this was a privilege in which few were indulged, except for the felling and transport of timber. Other sentinels stood at convenient distances around the pen, armed with loaded weapons. Our provisions were rice and salt pork, delivered with a scanty hand, nor could we obtain any drink but water, unless we paid a high price to the guards. The favourite liquor in these parts was cider.

American agents were very active in attempting to procure our desertion; but little attention was paid to them except by the worst soldiers. It will not be found surprising when I relate that Brooks the Dipper was seduced from his duty. He was tempted to sell himself as substitute for a hatter of Danbury, but soon deserted the Connecticut militia regiment to which he was posted and escaped back into the State of Massachusetts, where he was safe from apprehension, and there went to live as servant with a private family. Corporal Buchanan also left us, never to return. He had been appointed sergeant to kill a vacancy that had occurred and given money by his officer to provide shoes for the company; for he had been a cobbler before his enlistment. His pass took him as far as Worcester, where leather was to be bought, and there he bundled with a young woman at an inn, and was tempted to carnal intercourse with her. She agreed not to cry out 'rape!' only when he undertook to give her all the shoe-money. Apprehensive of punishment if he returned empty-handed, he went away to the town of Taunton, which lies about forty miles to the south of Boston; where he obtained employment at a shoemaker's and was set to do bespoke work, the customers bringing leather to the shop to be made into shoes. From his wages, and from the sale of children's shoes and whangs from the leather left over from the bespoke tasks, he contrived in six months to save a considerable sum of money. Thereupon he sent a letter to a man of the same trade as himself in the Fourteenth Regiment, urging him to desert and proposing that they should set up together in business on their own. But though Sergeant Buchanan painted the pleasures of freedom and employment in very lively colours, the man remained faithful.

In this pen we continued without employment or sufficient food, the Americans evidently intending to encourage our desertion by this means; but it was constantly impressed upon us by our officers that Congress would in the end be obliged, for the public honour of the nascent American Republic, to fulfil its obligations by our release. We therefore continued patient. Our sufferings were aggravated by a decision of General Sir Henry Clinton, who had superseded General Sir William Howe in the command of the Forces in America, no longer to send us our pay in specie. His view was that so much coin as was due to us should not be put in circulation among the Americans, who would use it for purchasing arms from France; and that this would be an inducement to them to detain us longer. Many persons from the Southern states, where Congress money was less regarded even than here, had journeyed up to our camp at Prospect Hill for the purpose of exchanging paper for coin. They had to act cautiously, for the transaction ranked as treason. Two German officers, about this time, very unkindly informed against a Virginia merchant who would not give them for their guineas as much paper as they demanded; and had him packed off to prison! Thus we suffered for the public good, and the paper money issued to us was so unwelcome to the Americans, because of its daily depreciation, that though they did not dare to refuse it, they informed us either that they had nothing to sell of what we needed, or that our money was counterfeit. It must here be observed that an immense quantity of well-counterfeited Congress notes had been printed in New York by American loyalists, and widely scattered in Revolutionary terri-tory to undermine public faith in the genuine issue, already tottering. The paper that we tendered was therefore naturally suspect as being supplied to us by the Paymaster in New York.

We amused ourselves with boxing matches, leap-frog, races, and with card-playing so long as our worn packs held together; and also undertook theatrical performances of Shakespeare, for which I was frequently selected, as gifted with a good memory, to take principal parts. My greatest hit was as Edgar in the *Tragedy of King Lear* and I remember the hearty laugh that went up when it fell to me to complain of hunger in that character, being in one scene disguised as a ragged Tom o' Bedlam: how 'rats and mice and such small deer, Have been Tom's food for seven long year.' This touched a responsive chord, for we eked out our provisions with all manner of small birds and animals which we snared. And it was notorious that I had been badly bitten in my left hand, which festered, by a flying squirrel which I had tried to catch for the pot. And also: 'Hopdance cries in Tom's belly for two white herring. Croak not, black angel: I have no food for thee.' What would we not have given for a well-cured Dublin herring!

Jane Crumer was a popular actress and once played Desdemona to my Othello. She was, besides, the object of universal admiration and pity for the constancy which she showed to her husband. This poor fellow had indeed recovered bodily health after the head-wound he received in the fighting at Freeman's Farm, but though still a fine-looking man and a Hercules in strength was by that blow left for the remainder of his life a poor puzzle-witted innocent, unfit for any but the simplest field labour. Mrs Jane was better off for money than most of us. To reward her services at Saratoga in fetching water from the river, the wounded officers who had benefited from her gallantry had thrown money into her lap to the amount of no less than twenty guineas.

In the course of this summer we became very familiar with the beautiful birds of the country, which we encouraged to visit us by scattering crumbs: the cardinal bird, the feathers of which were as scarlet as a new uniform coat; the blue bird, a sort of small jay, which united in its plumage all the various shades of blue from the pale-blue of early dawn to mazarine and the Royal blue of silken facings; the fire-bird which was of pure flame colour; and the hanging bird whose plumage of orange was variegated with black. Jane Crumer was given by a sentinel a nest of the hanging-bird, which resembled a hornet's nest and was suspended by hemp stalks from the extremity of a bough. The young ones proved very tractable and she taught them a variety of tricks. They would take crumbs from her lip, chirp in unison, cease at a signal, and even 'die for their country'. There was also a bird which the Americans called a robin on account of his rufous breast, but which was three times the true robin's size, and songless. These birds were greatly inferior in song to those of Ireland: we heard no twittering exultant lark, no plaintive nightingale, no melodious thrush. As for the bird which they called a blackbird and which was of the size of our blackbird, but with a collar about his neck of iridescent blueish feathers, I took a great dislike to the species. These birds had no sweet fluting song but made a harsh disagreeable noise which caused them in some parts of the country to be named 'grackles'; they were great thieves, and tyrants to lesser birds, besides being disgracefully lecherous.

A pair of grackles had a nest in a tree on the other side of the pen when we first came, and a sentinel one day shot the cock-bird for sport. This we at first thought wanton, but the widowed hen, by some means which we could not determine, called a new cock-bird to her but a few hours later, who entered into all the duties and privileges of the conjugal state. The sentinel thereupon shot this cock too, and lo, the next morning the undis-consolate widow had found a third mate. Seven cock-birds this same sentinel shot and each time the hen-bird mysteriously summoned a new one from the skies. 'Last of all the woman died also,' remarked this waggish New Englander, quoting from the Gospels, and this time discharged his small shot at the hen herself. He killed her, but the body hung suspended upside down by the claws to the bough where she was sitting. Even in death she did not lose her attraction for the opposite sex; but two days later, when her body was already decaying, a new cock appeared and began to puff out his feathers and strut and go 'grackle-grackle' at her, in the manner which we had observed in the previous courtships of this very promiscuous bird.

Being distant from any township, we saw no fruit trees in blossom, which was the great beauty of Massachusetts in the Spring, but hard by the gate there grew a beautiful dogwood tree, a sort of white rose-bush, having at first more flowers than leaves, and highly ornamental. The wood of this bush or tree was very hard and fibrous; we used it for tooth-brushes. Branches of dogwood were tied about the necks of cattle in the summer, for a virtue it possessed of reviving them if they were exhausted by the heat of the sun. The flowers lacked the odour that might be expected of their beauty. Indeed, as the birds were in general without song, so the flowers were in general without smell. Once the orchard blossoms had gone, there was no more to expect in the flowery way. Summer in New England had no shepherd's rose or honeysuckle, just as Spring came and went without primroses, cowslips, bluebells, daffodils or daisies.

However, in the woods about us there were chestnut, walnut, cedar, beech, oak, pine, and the graceful tulip-tree with its curious leaves and tulip-shaped green flowers which it bore for a fortnight together; the sassafras, the flowers of which were employed by the Americans as an agreeable substitute for that bane of their country, tea, and also as a fast yellow dye for woollens; and the red-tasselled sumach, the leaves of which the Indians smoked, and likewise used as a vulnerary, as I have related in my former volume.

The nights were very noisy in this camp on account of a colony of frogs in a marsh near by, which made a noise like a crowd at an Irish cattle fair, with numerous different tones and voices intermixed. There were also whooping owls and a night-hawk named 'whip-poor-will', from this phrase which his repeated cry suggested; he was also called The Pope from the word 'pope' which he ejaculated when he alighted upon a bough or fence-rail.

Summer passed languidly, and still we remained shut in the pen. Our officers were allowed to lodge in the farmhouses of the neighbourhood and come in amongst us for the purpose of roll-call and other matters of regularity. But they complained of frequent ill-treatment from the inhabitants, and Mr Bowen, who was now appointed the regular surgeon to The Ninth (so that I was returned to my ordinary duty) was one day set upon with a whip by a Select-man who accused him of trespassing on his estate. When he resented the insult with a blow, Mr Bowen and two officers who accompanied him, but had taken no part in the scuffle, were haled away to the common guard-room of the camp. Here they were kept for some days and obliged at night to sleep upon the floor, where the guards squirted tobacco-juice upon them for amusement and jested profanely at their expense. It seemed that Mr Bowen would be a long while away from us, being later confined by the civil power to the town jail of Worcester. I was therefore again appointed temporary surgeon and allowed a pass, as at Prospect Hill: much to my pleasure (though I sighed on Mr Bowen's account), since the confinement of the pen was heavily oppressing my spirit. However, Mr Bowen and his companions succeeded after a few weeks in enlarging themselves. They briefed a lawyer of Worcester who undertook (for a considerable fee) to prove a flaw in the charge against them. He did, in effect, convince the Assize Court that the charge was unproved: for it specified a crime against the United States, when it was evident that the breach of peace (which he did not deny on his clients' behalf) could only affect the single state of Massachusetts!

In August I was given the full rank of sergeant, to supply the vacancy caused by Buchanan's desertion. Hitherto I had done the duties of a sergeant and borne the title without drawing the pay of the rank or enjoying its privileges. It was rare for a man without interest to be advanced to sergeant's rank in so little as eight years' soldiering, and I was not a little proud of myself.

In September we heard that Sir Henry Clinton had once again applied to Congress in behalf of our army. In a letter addressed to the President of Congress, and dated New York, September 19th 1778, he had acquainted Congress that His Majesty had given him positive injunctions to repeat his demand, namely that the stipulations of the Convention of Saratoga be fulfilled, and to require permission for our embarkation at the port of Boston in transports which would be sent thither.

Congress sent the following answer, which the Earl of Carlisle (one of the Commissioners for Peace then at New York) described very justly as 'uncouth and profligate':

SIR,
    Your letter of the 19th was laid before Congress and I am directed to inform you that the Congress make no answer to insolent letters.
                              Signed, CHARLES THOMPSON, *Sec.*

This news caused a despair among our people, and many who had seemed most loyal made no secret of their intention to desert, now that there was no honour or advantage to be gained by remaining steadfast. Even Mad Johnny Maguire took the decision to abscond. He came and shook me by the hand and, said he, 'Gerry boy, I'm off now. Now don't you look vexed at me. For while I am here kept prisoner by the Americans I am no longer in the King's Service – now, isn't that so? And if you tell me that it is any sort of desertion to leave a service that I am no longer in, then by the Holy, you're a liar! Since I may not serve my King with arms in my hand, then I scorn to eat idle bread at his expense, however poorly. So, my darling Gerry, I'm off. I shall labour on my brother Corny's farm, as he has asked me, until times change. For I'm losing my robustness and my love of living, and that's a great sorrow to me.'

I could not find it in my heart to be vexed with Mad Johnny Maguire. I pressed his hand, avowing the sincere hope that we should meet again when the war was over. But in saying this, I was well aware that the war might yet be prolonged for months and perhaps years, now that the fainting American cause had been revived by French aid. I feared too that the Spanish and Dutch would also lend a hand, when they perceived how hard set upon we were; and these fears were not long afterwards proved to be well founded.

In October I was provided with a pass to visit the town of Brookfield, a long day's march to the southward. It was a melancholy duty with which I was charged by my officers, namely to visit Sergeant Buchanan and Private Brooks in their last hours, they being both deservedly sentenced by the Assize judge to death by hanging for the crime of murder. The first news that we received of this sentence was contained in a letter to Lieutenant-Colonel Hill from Sergeant Buchanan, which ran in terms something like these:

To Lieutenant-Colonel John Hill, Cmdg The Ninth Regiment in the Convention Army at Rutland

HONOURED SIR,

It is with great grief and true contrition that I lay before you my present case. You will be aware that in the month of May last I was commissioned by my company officer to provide boots for the company, and that I was supplied with the sum of one hundred and fifty dollars in Continental paper to purchase leather, thread, lapstone, awls &c for the making of them. This money was stole from me at an inn and getting no satisfaction for the loss, but being ashamed to return without, I repaired to the town of Taunton, where I worked at my trade in order to make good my account: Having saved so much, I bent my way back to Rutland in July, hoping for forgiveness from your Honour; when I fell in with Private

Thompson, who had run off from the Grenadier Company and who informed me that I hail been posted as a deserter and Sergeant Roger Lamb appointed in my place. I thereupon resolved to escape to Montreal, where I had left behind me my wife and infant child, in the hope of obtaining pardon by means of General Sir Guy Carleton, to whom I would report for duty.

On my route to Canada, I passed through this town of Brookfield where I was noticed by a Mrs Spooner, daughter to the well-known General Ruggles, who was remarkable for her attachment to the Royal Cause and offered to assist me with every means in her power to run safe through to Canada. Unfortunately for her, Mr Spooner her husband was very hot in the Rebel cause, and this occasioned domestic disagreement and a murderous odium in her heart against him. The common bond of attachment to His Majesty's cause drew Mrs Spooner and myself together, so that I became greatly enamoured of her, though unaware that the reciprocal warmth which she professed for me was only a sham. For her object (I am now aware), was to make me her Cat's Paw, and to be rid of her husband in order to marry her hired man. On Mr Spooner's going for a journey to Boston, she disclosed to me a plot she had arranged for removing him by poison as he dined at a wayside inn; overcoming my scruples by observing that he was an officer in the Rebel Army and therefore to slay him in time of war was 'killing no murder'.

This plot miscarrying, on account (she said) of his drinking so heartily at the inn that he vomited up the poison, he returned unexpectedly to his residence and discovered me sitting in the parlour, at which he expressed much displeasure and, using many profanities, which I will not Detail here, ordered me to begone. Mrs Spooner found me another lodging, and secretly communicated with me there, by means of the hired man, her paramour. She assured me that if I assisted her to rid the world of this Monster, she would confer considerable property upon me in goods and land and accompany me in the quality of my wife wherever I wished. I replied that I shrank from perpetrating any deed of violence and that I owed a duty to my wife and infant child; to which she replied that I was a soldier and would be failing in my duty if I hesitated to do away with so violent an enemy of my Sovereign. If I consented, she would safeguard me as far as the Canadian border (where her husband possessed property which would be hers at his death), describing me as her man-servant if I would not consent to be called husband; and there let me run across to freedom.

At this juncture, Private Brooks of my Company happened to pass through Brookfield while 'whipping the cat', which is a cant term in use hereabouts for obtaining casual employment at farm-

houses during a vagabond life. In a foolish hour I took Brooks into a
partnership of the intended violent transaction, promising him half
the hard money that Mrs Spooner had undertaken to give me. Mr
Spooner having ridden some distance from home in the day, we
determined to dispatch him on his return at night. Brooks was
chosen to be the executioner, for I shrank from embruing my hands
in the blood of an unarmed man; and of Brooks' former desperate
character your Honour will not be ignorant.

That evening Brooks, armed with a heavy log of walnut wood,
waited in a convenient corner near the door of the Spooner mansion
and fractured the skull of this ill-fated gentleman as he made his
entrance. We threw the body down a deep draw-well and Mrs
Spooner then provided us with a quantity of money and advised us
to keep out of the way until Mr Spooner's disappearance should be
accounted for by her in some credible manner. She could not,
however, prevail upon the hired man to remain with her. He went
off in our company, saying that a woman who could exult as she did
over the battered body of her husband was no wife for him. His
defection caused Mrs Spooner much distress and she was rash
enough to inform her neighbours that a party of British deserters had
robbed her house and, after murdering her husband, had carried off
his body. The hue and cry was therefore raised and we were apprehended at the town of Linn, where I was working in a shoe manufactory. Thus our common guilt was discovered, and the body drawn
out from the well.

It was not until the hand of the Law was laid upon my shoulder
that I became fully aware of the horrid nature of the crime to which
I had been accessory, and when sentenced to death by the Assize
Judge I became in a manner resigned to my fate. For I was advised
by the Congregational minister who visited me in prison that, were
I to be truly penitent and make complete confession of my scarlet
wickedness, he would inform me how to enter into eternity with a
calm mind, trusting in the extraordinary mercy of God vouchsafed
to sinners. My heart was touched and immediately I knelt down to
pray with him. After wrestling in prayer for some hours, I saw the
light and knew in my heart that I was pardoned by God! My comrade
in wickedness, Private Brooks, has also undergone a total change of
heart since we were confined, and awaits with impatience the stroke
of death which will set his soul free from its erring body and admit
it into everlasting mansions.

May it please your Honour to forgive both of us in your heart for
the disgrace that we have brought upon the Regiment, and of your
well-known generosity of mind to send one of our former comrades
to us here to be present at the hour of our execution, so that we may

not die wholly encompassed by strangers upon this alien soil. We would esteem it a great favour were Sergeant R. Lamb to be selected for this service, as being a suitable repository for our last wishes and farewells, and a person whose forgiveness for past offences we both hope to hear from his own lips.

    I am, Sir,

your greatly obliged and truly penitent Servant, the Sinner

J. BUCHANAN

(formerly Sergeant)

BROOKFIELD TOWN JAIL
    Oct. 15th 1778

During my expedition to Brookfield, which I accomplished in a single day, I refreshed myself at a wayside inn and was there given by the land-lord, a judicious person, an account of the recent progress of the war, which disproved or clarified many wild rumours that had been current in our camp. He informed me that peace proposals had been made to Congress by the British Parliament, and Commissioners sent to imple-ment these, soon after the news of the French alliance had been published. These proposals included an abnegation of the right to tax America, as of every other sovereign claim which might stand in the way of the free devel-opment of the American people, and an amnesty for all rebels – if only the link which joined the two countries, a common fealty to the Crown, might not be dissolved. But so much hatred against Great Britain had now been stirred up, and the people of America hoped for so great an extension of their trade by the French alliance, that Congress shortly rebuffed the Commissioners. This decision grieved a great many Americans who still considered themselves English; but they were powerless against the clam-orous voices of the Patriots, who considered England a nation doomed to well-merited destruction.

Our main army under General Clinton had at the end of June quitted the city of Philadelphia (where General Benedict Arnold was now appointed military governor), and, falling back across New Jersey, had checked General Washington's Army in the stubborn rear-guard action of Monmouth, and come safe back to New York. General Washington had moved to Hudson's River, which he crossed; he then encamped at White Plains, on the Highlands, threatening New York and making his principal stronghold on the river the fortress of West Point, about half-way upstream to Albany. Our forces at New York had then carried out one or two very energetic and successful forays on either side of Hudson's River, and against towns and islands of the New England coast. Great booty was taken and much shipping of a privateering sort destroyed.

As for the French, they had hitherto disappointed the American hopes, though a fleet of theirs greatly outnumbering our own squadron had arrived in American ; waters and attempted, in conjunction with General Sullivan and a large force of New England militia, to cut off and capture the British garrison of Newport, Rhode Island. ; A common disgust soon arising between these precarious allies, the French had taken offence and sailed away. Moreover, a party of amorous French sailors in Boston so offended against the morals of this saintly place that a French officer was killed in the streets by the citizens. The alliance would have been ended there and then, had not the Massachusetts Council, fearful of the consequences of this act of popular folly, hastily voted a monument to the murdered Frenchman. The crime was politically charged against captured British sailors and ourselves, the wretched Convention Army! Many of General Sullivan's men had meanwhile deserted to our forces and, his siege of Newport becoming dangerous, it was raised. In fine, the war was not going so disadvantageously for our cause, after all; though against our successes must be set the capture by American privateers of near a thousand British merchantmen of a gross value of £2,000,000.

The same landlord also gave me news of a very bloody raid by American Loyalists and Indians of the Six Nations on a frontier district of Pennsylvania: one whole valley, that of the Wyoming river, was completely devastated, and many prisoners burned at the stake. I said, I sincerely hoped that this account of Indian savagery was no less exaggerated than previous ones.

He showed no animosity to me as a soldier in the British service, but only a sort of pity, which I resented as strongly. He told me that he had visited Dublin some years previously, and asked in a very sincere way, how I could reconcile my duty with my good sense? Though I evidently did not regard myself as a slave, and had a pride in my loyal subordination, did I not consider the free soil of America as in every way preferable to that of Ireland? He said that, for his part, he had seen so many unpleasant sights amidst the grandeur and pageantry of the rich in Dublin City that the total impression was one of pain and horror. Such hosts of street beggars, such troops of poverty-stricken children, such a mass of degraded poor people! How the labourers of Ireland, and of England herself, he said, contrived to live with such low wages and such high prices for the staple commodities, was above his comprehension. Yet with all this poverty and woe, taxation was laid upon the public with merciless severity, to fatten the minions *of* royalty and provide pensions and sinecures for the idle gentry. He showed me a newspaper where the present miserable condition of Ireland was set forth, and where it was reported (without much exaggeration, as my readers will be aware) that my country was then nearly ruined. The rupture with the colonies had closed the chief market of the linen trade, the provision trade was annihilated by a Royal proclamation, the price of black cattle and wool had sunk, thousands of manufacturers were forced to lock up their works. In Dublin bread had risen to famine prices and hungry crowds paraded the Liberties, carrying a black fleece in token of their distress; while in the country 'the wretches that remained had scarcely the appearance of human creatures'.

I felt it difficult to restrain my tears, as I perused this journal, for thinking of the want to which my own parents and sisters would necessarily be reduced and of my present impotence in affording them any help; yet the landlord's questions did not have the effect upon me that he intended. I informed him that, though he might consider it a depravity in me, I would in all events remain loyal to the King to whom I had sworn allegiance; and that the present distresses of Ireland and England were largely caused by the Americans' repudiation of this same allegiance, which had caused enormous suffering and expense in all three countries.

He remarked: 'You are an unusual sort of Irishman, I guess. Is it not true, pray, that the native character and political propensities of your people have ever been toward rebellion – that the Irish have ever been uniformly intolerant of the rule of the English Kings?'

'That, Sir,' I replied, 'is a calumny which has become hereditary to historians, The reverse is the case: during a matter of twenty reigns that have succeeded the first submission of the Irish princes, the fidelity of Ireland to the Kings of England has been very seldom interrupted. Irish soldiers have often been brought over to England to protect their sovereigns against the insurrections of British rebels. During the same period above thirty civil wars, greater or less, raged within the larger island – four British monarchs were dethroned, three murdered.'

He changed his tack: 'Well, if you are right and I have been misinformed, then on the contrary I am astonished that the unrelenting cruelties and misrule of the British governors have not goaded you into disaffection: for my part, I would never live upon any but free American soil.'

I replied, as to this, that I suspected the political well-being of a country that cast out its Tories, equally with that of a country that hanged its Whigs. But I contented him by saying that there were many customs and inclinations in America that pleased me, and that might with profit be transplanted into Ireland: for example, the hospitality and mutual assistance afforded to one another by the back-country people, and the high value set upon education. Yet I swore I would never turn my back upon the land of my birth, and would labour on my return to do all in my power to better its condition in the light of my novel experiences – as a loyal subject of the King.

It was not until some months later that I received news that my father had deceased in Dublin almost on the very day of this conversation, in poverty and debt, and in great grief at a report that had reached him of my death in the fighting at Saratoga. He died, however, at a time when Irish affairs were beginning at last to right themselves. It will be remembered how, at the close of this same year, King George was graciously pleased to consider the demands of my fellow-countrymen, to which on the 4th of November (Dutch William's birthday) they called his attention with loyal if extraordinary manifestations. On that day forty thousand Irish Volunteers, who had been enrolled to repel the raids on our coasts threatened by the American privateer captain, Paul Jones, paraded before King William's statue on College Green in Dublin City; firing volleys into the air, waving flags and trailing cannon to which were tied placards inscribed, 'Free Trade or This!' The display had immediate effect. In December, Resolutions were adopted in the Parliament at Westminster, granting to us Irish the free export of our products and manufactures, and privileges in trading with British colonies equal to those enjoyed by the merchants of England and Scotland.

At Brookfield I procured admission to the jail with little difficulty, by telling the turnkey that the Methodist minister who was Chaplain to the prisoners would know that I was expected to arrive. The Chaplain was fetched and brought me to the cell, where I was greeted by Buchanan and Brooks in such sanctified phrases that I was perfectly astonished. Both implored my pardon, which I readily gave, for the frauds, deceits and cruelties that they had practised upon me – some of which I had no knowledge of, while others I had forgotten and attempted forthwith to convert me to their own religious ecstasy. Brooks before his confinement had not only been notoriously profane but almost illiterate; yet since his confinement he had attended so much to a devout perusal of the Holy Scriptures that he could now read them with facility, explain them to his unhappy cell-mates in an edifying manner and even select the chapters most appropriate to their sad condition.

The day of execution, which was that following my arrival, was a severe trial for me. I wished to humour the poor fellows by letting them suppose that they had affected my conversion; but honesty forbade. It was not that I was a disbeliever, or that I was addicted to evil courses. for I now lived, of necessity almost, a regular and decent life – but that to profess a change of heart would mean abandoning all hope of resuming my connexion with Kate Harlowe and our child. For this still remained with me the sweetest dream of all and altogether ineradicable from my fancy.

Mrs Spooner, the murderess, was to die on the same day, but indulged loud hopes of escaping condign punishment. She pleaded pregnancy as an argument for being respited, and seemed impenitent a good deal. Her Tory opinions, however, fastened the noose tightly about her throat, and sealed the fate of her unborn child. The gallows were fixed at a distance of two miles from the jail and a holiday crowd of sightseers attended; who were punished for their idle curiosity by a great storm of thunder, followed with copious rain, that all of a sudden broke upon them from a fine and serene sky and drenched them to the bone. Mrs Spooner met her end with hysterical screaming and fierce vituperations; but Buchanan and Brooks remained true to their new-found convictions and died with the name of Jesus upon their lips.

I must add one last note to my account of this ignominious catastrophe. Buchanan's widow, known as 'Terrible Annie', who had been Mortal Harry's widow before, and that of a drummer in the Thirty-Third even before that, was not sorry when the news of his death reached her at Montreal. She was a woman with the same mysterious power as the American hen-blackbird, or grackle, of attracting new mates to console her in her frequent widowhood. Her fourth husband was a quartermaster-sergeant of the Forty-Seventh Regiment, and passed for the greatest rogue in the whole Service.

CHAPTER IV

EARLY IN November 1778, when we had already, by considerable labour and thought, improved our slight huts so as to make them snug enough to shelter us through another severe New English winter, we were given our route for the back country of Virginia. Our destination was said to be Charlotteville, which lay near eight hundred miles away. The object was that the Southern States should bear their share of the expense of maintaining us, especially now that we were without pay from our own authorities; also, that we should be moved beyond reach of rescue. We were in great distress for want of money to undertake this march, and our commanding officers met to consult upon a means of procuring some. General Burgoyne had returned to England on parole, and General Phillips, who now commanded, spoke very warmly on the subject of our want of cash, protesting his inability to effect anything: 'Good God, my lords and gentlemen, what would you have me do? I cannot make money. I wish to Heaven you could slit me into paper dollars – I would cheerfully submit for the good of the troops.' However, the Paymaster somehow succeeded in obtaining enough currency to enable us to march, something less than two hundred pounds sterling in value but an enormous mass of paper; and this was distributed to the regiments. Our chief remaining distress was the raggedness of our jackets and breeches. Unfortunately, a ship that arrived at Boston under a flag of truce, with the uniform clothing long overdue to us, came just too late for its distribution to us. The march could not be postponed. However, we obtained some shoes, linen and blankets and on November 10th said good-bye to the pen. We resented having been tricked into clearing so many acres of forest-land and building enough good huts to accommodate several American families; for this would add greatly to the wealth of the proprietor without any benefit accruing to ourselves. However, we did not in revenge burn down our barracks, lest the route be countermanded.

From Rutland we marched south-east at about twenty-five miles every day, under guard of a regiment of Pennsylvanian Germans, and passed the Connecticut River at Endfield. This stage of the journey had little novelty for us, since we had made our way across the same part of Massachusetts, though a little to the north, a year before during our journey into captivity. Yet it was interesting to me to note the different degrees of civilization and prosperity attained in this region or that through which we passed. These were announced by the several sorts of fences that enclosed, first, the cleared land, where all was level; next, the half-cleared, where tree-stumps remained among the corn-stubble; and lastly, the uncleared, where the oaks and other hard timber were as yet only girdled and left to the wind for felling. The rudest sort of fence was a tangle of the light branches of trees; the next rudest was the Virginian fence, made by trunks of trees laid one upon the other at an obtuse angle, in a zigzag manner – a drunken man hereabouts was said to 'make Virginian fences' when he tacked to and fro along a road; then came the post and rail fence; and when a farmer had achieved so settled a dominion that he could go to the trouble of clearing his land of stones, he piled them up to form a wall with a ramp of earth, into which he drove palings of split timber – but this was very rare to see.

We were on the whole extremely fortunate in the weather, which was temperate and clear, though the frosts were severe during the nights when we bivouacked in the dismal fir woods, seeking shelter in the crevices of the rocks; and the rutted roads crackled with ice every morning. 'I swear God has turned Tory,' a surly old dame cried, looking angrily up at the blue skies as we marched past her door. General Washington had been considerate enough to supply wagons for our women and children, of whom there were about two hundred with us.

Our route now lay through the northern borders of Connecticut, but most of the so-called townships (as Endfield, Suffield and Sunbury, which we passed in this order) were not regular towns: each consisted of one or two hundred scattered farms belonging to a single corporation that sent a member to the State Assembly. A meeting-house or church, with perhaps an inn and one or two houses, marked the centre of this township, but often the church stood singly. We observed that the interior of many houses that we passed was only half finished. The man who cleared the land and constructed the house from the felled trees had usually completed only one half of it and left the other a mere shell (though with roof and glazed windows complete) to be boarded and furnished within by his son when he took a wife. We were pleased by the swarms of healthy children who rushed out of every house on our route, and by the handsomeness of the women who passed us on the road, often riding alone on horseback or driving their own carriages. The weather continuing fine, they were dressed in white aprons, calico gowns and elegant hats. We learned that though every man was a farmer, most men also plied some mechanical trade, as tanner, sawyer, whitesmith, blacksmith, physician or tooth-drawer. Besides, every woman was mistress of so many domestic arts, including spinning, weaving of woollens and linsey-woollens, broom and basket-making – in which labours she was assisted by her children – that the country was in a manner independent of the industry of cities.

We marched through a fertile river-valley at New Hartford, where were abundance of geese and turkey-birds, and hogs of a prodigious size wearing around their necks triangular wooden collars which prevented them from breaking the fences of the cultivated fields. Horses and cattle wore a similar contrivance. There was a scent of cider-making in the air, or perhaps they were distilling cider into apple-jack spirits.

At the small town of Sharon some of us were allowed by a woman to inspect an exceedingly ingenious mill invented by one Joel Harvey, for which he was awarded twenty pounds by the American Society of Arts and Sciences. One water-wheel set a whole complicated machinery in motion for threshing, winnowing, grinding and bolting wheat; and for simultaneously beating and dressing hemp and flax. But the two branches could be disconnected if necessary, and only one operation maintained.

Now we had reached the confines of the State of Connecticut and were approaching Hudson's River in the State of New York. The time had therefore arrived for putting into effect a daring resolution that I had formed so soon as news reached us of our proposed transplantation to Virginia: I would quit the column of march and make an escapade to General Clinton's army in New York! In this venture the river itself would be my guide to safety, nor would I need to follow it more than seventy miles downstream from the point where our army was intended to cross over. I concluded that it would be much more agreeable, and indeed less dangerous, to have companions in my flight and therefore considered which of them I should approach.

I naturally first sounded Terry Reeves, as the most courageous and resourceful man in the Regiment, but he would not hear of the attempt. He asked, was I unaware that our officers (fearful of the regiments' being, at our eventual return to Europe, reduced to mere skeletons) had issued orders that any soldier absent from his corps for more than four-and-twenty hours should be returned as a deserter, and if brought back again by the American civil or military power, should be flogged without mercy? I replied that I was not unaware of this, but that the hope of striking another blow for my King and Country weighed more with me than any such orders. I could not convince Terry, and went away sadly. Smutchy Steel, however, now an excellent soldier, showed himself eager to accompany me. He said that, much as he loved Terry, he could not be sorry that he was not to be one of us: for Terry brought bad luck on himself and his companions in any venture, and never seemed to escape some injury – which was true enough. He recommended as our third companion Richard Harlowe, who had that very morning expressed a wish to 'make a run for it'. Smutchy reminded me that Harlowe was acquainted with the French and German languages, which would perhaps be of great service to us – especially the German, when it came to outwitting our guards. There were few companions whom I would have selected with less eagerness than Harlowe, but what Smutchy had observed about the usefulness to us of foreign languages struck me as very true; nor was anyone else of our acquaintance so gifted. 'Very well,' I said to Smutchy, 'let it be Harlowe, for beggars cannot be choosers. But do you speak to him yourself on my behalf. I have no wish to approach him directly.'

Smutchy presently reported that Richard Harlowe was ready to join our company. We were then at a place named Nine Partners, about forty miles to the north-west of the place where we now learned we were to cross. Smutchy obtained from Jane Crumer, who borrowed it from one of the soldiers' wives, an almanack for the current year 'being the second after Leap Year and second of American Independence, calculated for the meridian of Boston by Daniel George.' He handed me the book, saying with satisfaction 'There is good news for us here.'

I opened at random and, to cod him, began to read a passage upon how to rear turkeys successfully: 'Plunge the chick into a vessel of water, the very hour if possible, at least the very day it is hatched, forcing it to swallow one whole peppercorn, after which return it to the mother, &c.'

'No, not that,' he protested.

I read again: 'The Foreign Vintage rival'd by the Gardens of America: Or, a Receipt to make WINE as good as most that is imported, and much cheaper. To a Gallon of Water, add a Gallon of Currants — '

'No, no,' he protested again rather testily.

I read further: 'The highest price is given at the Printing Office in Newbury Port, for all sorts of Linen and Cotton RAGS – the smallest pieces are (in proportion to their bigness) as serviceable as large. Good WRITING-PAPER will be given in exchange, at a very low price, if wanted' – 'why, Smutchy, have you a mind to sell your old shirt for. a sheet of foolscap?'

He tore the book from my hands. 'Now, don't be so provoking, Sergeant Gerry,' he said. 'Read here where the page is turned down. There's a new moon in two days' time, November 18th, at ten o'clock at night; and there the coming weather is forecasted also.'

Indeed, for all my jesting, it was a matter of awful concern to us both what aspect the Heavens would wear for our flight. So at last I consented to read the prophecy for the next five days: *flying clouds and strong south winds which bear down all before them, and perhaps some rain or snow*. MORE FOUL WEATHER. 'Now, I wonder,' says I, laughing, 'is that the truth or just another smart Yankee trick to overreach us?'

'Neighbour Daniel George wouldn't dare deceive his public with regard to the moon,' was Smutchy's surmise, 'and I expect he knows the usual run of the weather in these parts. Well, then, the moon will not trouble us, being too young; As for the rain or snow, let it be rain and the more rain the better, for the sake of the powder in the rebels' priming-pans, and of the darkness. Faith, let it be as dark as the inside of a poacher's dog, I don't care. As for the strong south wind, that same will blow in our faces and bring us news of danger the sooner. God save Great Daniel George, I say.'

The country between Nine Partners and the river was well cultivated, and the inhabitants were for the most part Dutch. All this country had formerly belonged to the Dutch Republic which, I believe, exchanged it with the King of England for the spice-lands of Surinam. A few of our officers were well bitten by the Dutch landlord where they lodged at Opel, or Hopewell, our next stage. He and his family behaved very civilly and attentively to them and would scarcely permit them to pay for what they had consumed. The officers, thereby concluding that the household were Loyalists, opened their hearts and observed that it was a great shame that British officers should be put to such expense, which ought to fall upon Congress. The landlord then ran from the room and made out an enormous bill, which he insisted upon being paid. The officers, declaring it to be exorbitant in every particular and three times what had been agreed, this Dutchman said: 'Yes, gentlemen, but I had thought that Congress were to defray all your expenses, and did not wish to be severe upon them. Now that I know that it will fall upon you, I can't take a farthing less than this bill.' They were compelled to discharge it.

It was on November 17th, from our bivouacs in a wood a few miles beyond Hopewell (a name of good omen) that we made our attempt to regain our freedom, at breakfast-time on the morning of our departure. The Army was to cross Hudson's River that afternoon; and General Washington himself would be present to see it go by. Richard Harlowe had cultivated the acquaintance of a German corporal of the guard and now obtained permission from him to go to a house a hundred yards beyond the line of sentries, in order, he said, to buy a few eggs. He promised two eggs to the Corporal. After being gone for about three minutes, he came back (as I had suggested to him) as if to reassure the German that he contemplated no desertion. His account was that the farmer was sawing wood and would not give his wife the key of the hen-house, which he kept locked against the depredations of the soldiery, until he had finished his daily stent. This task would take him a good hour, which was longer than we could afford to wait; but it could be shortened if two or three British soldiers could be found to help him with it. The Corporal believed this story, because the sound of a saw could be heard proceeding from the farm; and Harlowe, with his consent, then called upon us to bear a hand. We agreed with feigned unwillingness.

We walked slowly through the trees to the farm, in order to allay the Corporal's suspicions; but immediately we were fairly out of sight began running away through the woods, avoiding any beaten track, and within a few minutes had put a mile at least between us and the line of sentries.

'Now,' said I, as we paused for breath on the banks of a rivulet, 'who's for pushing on, and who's for lying hid?'

Harlowe and Smutchy were for pushing on, but I argued that it was better to lurk close to the camp. In the first place, the searchers would expect us to go off as far as possible; in the second, if unluckily we were apprehended, it would be better that this should happen before the twenty-four hours had elapsed that would make us deserters. If we pushed on and were caught at a distance we might be sent back too late to benefit by the grace.

Harlowe held that the farther we ran, the less likely were we to be caught and brought back; but against this I argued that the farther we ran the more people we were likely to meet who might inform upon us.

'How do you expect to get to New York then, you sot?' he asked.

I patiently explained that, though our prime intention was to get safe through, we must reckon with the danger of apprehension. In the latter event, our hope lay in being caught either soon or so much later that our guards would by then have given up the search – which they would shorten doubtless in order not to miss their sight of General Washington, whom they looked upon as a national hero – and would have crossed the river. I believed that the Dutchmen, if they caught us, would not trouble to row us across the river under guard; for desertions in general were encouraged. Our greatest peril would be in the last stage of our flight, when we attempted to rejoin the British Army.

Smutchy then came over to my opinion, so that we were in a majority against Harlowe. We crossed the rivulet and soon perceived a small hut on the verge of a wood. Smutchy went forward to reconnoitre, and after a while motioned to us that all was well. We came up, knocked, entered and there found a poor woman, with two young children, in the act of filling their maple-wood bowls with 'soupaun' or maize porridge, as they sat at table.

The woman proved to be a Mrs Eder, a New York woman, widow to a Dutchman who had been lately killed by a falling tree. The family was in very poor circumstances, as we could learn from the poverty of the kitchen furniture, and the pinched faces of the children. The little boy was sadly crying as we came in: 'No more 'lasses, Mama? No more 'lasses!' And she answered as sadly: 'No, my little one, no molasses and no milk neither, for the cow's gone dry!'

I apologized to Mrs Eder for our early visit and entreated her to hide us in her house for a few hours. I told her that our German guards would soon miss us and make search for us, adding: 'I do not know what your politics are, Madam, and shall not enquire; but I can see that your little ones would do well this winter on a little butter and milk and molasses, which this money will purchase for them.' Here I showed her three Spanish silver dollars, and could see at once that I had come to the right market with them. The widow, who was young but had lost all title to beauty through the hard life she had evidently led, living alone in this wilderness, eagerly agreed to all that I asked. She even undertook to observe the movements of the guards, and if necessary mislead them by giving them false information.

'Where will you hide us?' I asked. 'Is there perhaps a hollow tree that you know in the woods, or a cave?'

She shook her head. 'The best place for you,' she said, 'is right here in this house. I will go out and lock up, and you may be sure that if any guard comes he will not be at pains to break down the door, unless he has previous information that you are here.'

When Harlowe asked her, how did he know she was not a double-dealer, she replied that she would leave her youngest child in our care as a pledge of her sincerity.

I said: 'Madam, we do not doubt your sincerity, but we accept your offer gladly. The little lass is a sweet child and will be good company to us. Can you give us some provisions into the bargain, for we have not yet breakfasted?'

She gave us what little remained of the soupaun, a few sour apples and a pickled pig's tail, which was all that she had in the house to offer. Presently she went off with her little boy, after locking us all into a small, clean apartment, where the little girl amused us with her prattle, of which we could understand hardly a word, being lisping English of the back-woods, mixed with Dutch.

We spent our time compiling our geographical knowledge of Hudson's River and reckoning on our chances of successful evasion. There were some Dutch books in a case, but they treated of law and theology, with not an Atlas among them. We knew that we were now about a day's march above the fortress of West Point, but upon the opposite bank, and that General Washington's Continental army lay squarely between us and safety, posted on the Eastern Highlands. Smutchy was of opinion that we must, if possible (using this woman as a first link in the chain), obtain recommendations from stage to stage that would persuade persons well disposed to our cause to help us through to safety, and travel only by night. I believed him to be right and Harlowe did not disagree.

About ten o'clock in the morning we heard voices: a German talking in halting English to an American. The German said in a deep voice: 'We must make search inside this hut, brother.'

'No, Hans,' drawled the American, 'Cannot you see, the key hangs on the nail outside? You can save yourself the pains. If the prisoners were there, I calculate the door would be locked from the inside.'

'Dumbhead,' returned the German, 'the people of the hut, perhaps they have locked the Englanders in from outside, not so?'

The American retorted: 'You are a dumbhead yourself. If the people of the hut wished to shelter deserters against us, I reckon, they would not have left the key hanging up where we could kind it; unless perhaps they were dumbheads, too. It an't reasonable.'

The German insisted: 'Perhaps they have forgotten it in their haste. I go to see.'

'You're a mighty thorough man, damn you!' was the reply.

'At least I will look in at the window,' the obstinate Hans said.

We had been unaware that Mrs Eder had left the key hanging on the door, and quaked inwardly when we heard the German approaching the hut with a heavy tread. He went first to peer in at the kitchen window, where he reported that nobody was at home.

Then he came to our window. We shuffled and lay close against the wall under the sill, to put ourselves below the angle of his vision as he looked through the glass. The child was lying in her cradle, sucking a stick of coarse sugar that I had found in my pocket and given her as a means of pacification. The German must have made some ludicrous grimaces at the child, for she set up a howl.

He told her playfully that she was a naughty child and must not fear a poor honest German. Then we heard him depart.

He shouted back to the American: 'Excuse me, I was wrong. There is one pretty child in that apartment who eats candy. The mother, she go away and lock it in there, so that it shall not fall in the fire, and do it a mischief, yes? Pardon! Let us go, brother!'

We could then hear them searching in the barns and sheds contiguous, and the attic over our heads, reached by a ladder from without; but they never entered the house. However, the American, standing close to our window, reported to an officer who had come up that they had investigated the whole place and found nothing.

Then the voices died away in the distance. The danger having passed, I said to Smutchy Steel: 'Now, faith, only a woman could have contrived that trick of hanging the key so invitingly on the nail! And I swear no man but a German would have been industrious enough even to peep in at the windows.'

'Ay, just like a woman,' asserted Smutchy.

'She nearly ruined us by over-shrewdness,' said the contrary Harlowe. 'And that is just like a woman, too.'

There were no further disturbances, and at nightfall the woman returned and, finding us still where she had left us, evinced great relief. She picked up her little girl and hugged her close. 'O I declare,' she cried, between tears and laughter, 'you have mussed your nice dress with a candy stick! What a pickle you are in, you greedy little wretch.'

Then she turned to us: 'You see, my friends, that I have been faithful to you. Your comrades have by now all crossed the River with most of their guards. There were very few American soldiers to be seen when I came away.'

To the three promised dollars I added a fourth from our store, believing that the outlay would justify itself. Then we told her that we intended to make our escape into New York, which we had not yet disclosed to her.

'You have set yourselves a very hard task, my friends,' she said. 'Now, sweet Pieterkin, run off and play with your little sister, for I wish to think in peace.' She pressed her knuckles hard against her temples. We did not interrupt her cogitations, which presently bore fruit. She gave us very minute directions to the house of her husband's sister. This woman was married to a Rhode Islander who was very lukewarm in his loyalty to the revolutionary cause. We must pass through a pine forest, around a naked hill and over a considerable stream. She herself had not been that way since the heavy flood of a month before, and feared that we might find the bridge carried away. Thereafter our route lay through cornfields and cleared ground for another two miles; and on the northern skirts of the next forest we would find the house we required, which lay remote from any others and was to be recognized by a ring of clipped red cedars which enclosed a duck-pond. The husband's name was Captain Webber.

We took affectionate leave of our faithful hostess and her children. I gave the little boy the crystal prism I had obtained from Diamond Island on Lake George in the previous year; which greatly delighted him. I told him to set it in the window when the sun was up next morning, for it would throw 'jackies' (or rainbows) upon the ceiling.

We followed our directions with care and picked up each consequent landmark until we hit the stream, which had the same name, Fishkill Creek, as that which watered General Schuyler's domain at Saratoga. The current was rapid, and I could not plumb the depth with a long stick; nor was there any sign of a bridge where our track ended. Neither Harlowe nor Smutchy knew how to swim, but I proposed to go across myself, taking one of them at a time with me. I assured them that if they would faithfully and courageously do as I said, namely gently lay their hands on my loins, striking out with their feet at the same time, I would soon ferry them over. However, they both declined my offer, as too hazardous an attempt in the dark, and proposed to trace the creek upwards in order to discover a fording place.

We were in luck; for we had not gone more than two hundred yards upstream before we found a tall tree that had been felled to lie across the river at a narrow place; and so went over dry-shod, after all. Such conveniences for crossing rivers are very common in America.

We considered now that we were well on our way, and must henceforth get along in good earnest.

CHAPTER V

AT LENGTH we arrived at Captain Webber's substantial house, to which we had been directed, and recognized it by the ring of cedars. There was no light showing in any of the windows, which was not surprising, for it had passed midnight. We went up to the door and rapped loudly.

A man's voice called to us: 'Who's there?'

I replied: 'Three friends of your sister-in-law, the widow Eder.'

'What friends?' the same man enquired, in some alarm.

Smutchy was bold enough to reply: 'Three British soldiers.'

A woman's voice then cried: 'Begone, soldiers. We want no Britainers here, and my brother Yan's sister should be ashamed to foist any such upon us. She was ever a troublemaker in the family.'

The man here evidently remonstrated with his wife, for upon our continuing to plead for admittance he came downstairs in his shirt, carrying a lantern, and unbolted the door for us. He w as a tall, large man and wore a night-cap. 'Now, gentlemen,' he said, 'what is your business? My wife is greatly alarmed by your appearance at this hour and asks you to hasten your explanations. Besides, it is very cold.'

We went into the kitchen, which had a brick floor arid was tolerably well furnished with papered walls, pewter platters on the shelves, and furniture in the heavy Dutch style. A tremendous ducking gun was suspended above tile chimney shelf and a tall brass-faced clock ticked in a corner. I also observed a stuffed Bengalese parrot in a glass case.

'Put this about your legs, Sir,' said Richard Harlowe, taking from his haversack a new English blanket, one of those that had been issued to us just before we began our march, 'and you will feel warmer.'

'This is good wool,' he said, admiring it. 'We have but two thin blankets left to us: the rest were taken from us for the use of the militia, though I am a captain myself.'

'It is yours, and another as good besides, if you can conduct us safely to New York,' Smutchy assured him.

'It is mighty good wool,' he said again. 'But I should require a deal of money from you, if I were to consent. It is a dangerous piece of work, very dangerous, that you propose.'

'Take us to the British outposts,' I said, 'and you shall have all the hard money in our possession, which amounts in gold and silver to twenty dollars, besides the two blankets as advance payment. Moreover, the Commander-in-Chief, Sir Henry Clinton, will give you a further reward, a bounty of three guineas a man. That will cock you up for a whole winter, Captain Webber.'

But Mrs Webber, who was gaunt and grey-haired, was by now standing in the doorway of the parlour where we were discoursing, and overheard what I had said. 'William,' she cried fiercely, 'you shall not go. As your devoted wife and the mother of your three fine boys, I will not permit you to go – no, though I have to offer you violence to prevent it.'

'Why, wife,' he said, attempting to conciliate her, 'times are hard, you know, and I confess the fee they offer is very advantageous, if I could be sure of that bounty. It would buy you a new dress and stockings and shoes for all the boys, besides the sheep of which we spoke to-day.'

She burst into tears, whether real or feigned I cannot pretend to judge. 'What!' said she, dramatically: 'Do you mean to break my heart, by running into the jaws of death? Would you deprive me of a husband, like my poor sister-in-law Eder, and orphan our boys? You know well that there are several camps and garrisons on the East Highlands between this and New York. You would not be able to go ten miles before you would be taken, and then you would be hung up like a dog.'

Her rude reasonings operated with all the power of simple nature upon Captain Webber. He changed his mind in a moment.

'Gentlemen,' said he, 'as I told you before, this is a very dangerous piece of work. All that my wife has said is true. Our people have very strong outposts all along the river as far as King's Bridge; and if I were taken in the act of bringing you into the British lines, I could obtain no mercy. Yet, unless I went with you to your journey's end, I should miss the bounty.'

All our arguments after this could not prevail with him, though we promised to add twelve dollars to the English blankets as an advance payment. However, he at last, for a single silver dollar, agreed to conduct us to another friend, a poor man known simply as Old Joe, who lived two miles further on our journey and who might probably go with us. Captain Webber assured us that he only consented to help us thus far from his not wishing to disoblige Mrs Eder.

We set off at about one o'clock in the morning and arrived after an hour at the poor man's hut, which was situated on the top of a high mountain. A light was burning, and we found Old Joe and a young woman, a niece, attending his wife who was ill of a swamp-fever. The light was supplied by a green wax-candle, made from the berries of the tallow shrub, which burned with an agreeable odour. True tallow candles were seldom seen in the Northern States during the war, since all the fat cattle were taken for the supply of the armies. We explained our circumstances and I informed

Old Joe, who seemed in a condition of great anxiety on account of his wife, that I had some medical knowledge. I recommended for his wife a decoction of the bark of a sort of willow which the Indians used against the disorder, and he appeared greatly relieved to have a physician in the house. For a dollar he agreed to bring us six miles further on our journey to a German settler whom there was every probability we might obtain for a guide, for this German had lost nearly all his sheep in the late floods and was in great want of money. We set off immediately and after making our way for near six hours, through a trackless desert, full of swamps, we found ourselves at the fringe of a wood, and at fifty yards' distance, an American barracks. Soldiers in buff and blue were carrying buckets of water and bundles of forage across a parade ground under the direction of a sergeant, whose back was fortunately turned to us. We shrank into the trees and Old Joe, being much terrified, fled from us with the greatest precipitation.

Harlowe ran after and caught him by the collar, asking him what he meant by this desertion of us. He confessed that he had missed his path and only now knew our whereabouts. We were in the midst of our enemies. The place was called Red Mills, close to Lake Mahopac and about six miles from Goolden's Bridge over the Croton River. As a last act of attention, Old Joe told us of a footpath which led to this bridge beyond the American camp. He advised us to cast a compass about the camp through the woods until we hit it. This path would pass by the hut of friends, who lay under an obligation to him; he described the hut but omitted to name the inhabitants. We thanked him and took his advice. The track appeared before long and we continued cautiously in the woods that fringed it, until we came to the hut about noon.

These were good people, Loyalist by inclination and, I believe, tenants of the Colden family who were landed proprietors thereabouts. When I asked the woman her name, she replied after a little hesitation that she was Hannah Sniffen, wife to James Sniffen. The husband was not at home, but only the wife, a grown daughter, and two boys. They were astonished by our appearance but evidently pleased with our company, the names of Captain Webber and Old Joe carrying weight with them. They inquired after the health of these families. When I told of the sickness of Old Joe's wife and what I had prescribed for her cure, Mrs Sniffen, a bustling and red-checked woman, seemed interested and asked whether I were a tooth-drawer as well as surgeon and physician. She could, she said, not sleep of nights for a toothache, nor could she trust her husband with the pincers, lest he snap off the crown of the tooth, which was rotten, and thus make matters worse.

I replied that, in exchange for a good meal, I would cleanly draw every tooth in her head and welcome; for it happened to be in the range of my powers, given a small pair of steel pincers. So the bargain was concluded.

She gave us a cold roast of pork and boiled potatoes, together with a tart conserve of quince, and to each of us a great pewter tankard of spruce beer. Apart from the soupaun and apples at Mrs Eder's – for we had not gnawed at the pig's tail there offered us – we had eaten nothing since our dinner at Nine Partners two days previously; this repast therefore, I need not add, proved highly acceptable to us. When it was done I felt sleep stealing across my eyes, so that I could scarcely keep them open. But I was bound first to conclude my bargain, by drawing her tooth, and had the good fortune to fetch it out whole, though its roots were very crooked, without injuring the gum. This feat excited admiration in the family and cries of 'Well, I declare now!' and 'Wasn't that a dandy pull?' The two boys also offered to submit themselves to my professional skill. But I refused them, as being greatly fatigued by my journey, and said that I proposed, with Mrs Sniffen's permission, to lie down and take a nap on my blanket in the corner. My comrades were already preparing to do the same.

This intention, however, she warmly opposed, though her daughter sighed: 'They have earned a nap, the poor fellows, let 'em lie there, they won't be in the way of our feet, surely.'

'Don't be a fool, Mary,' cried the mother. 'Don't you know that our own soldiers often straggle here from White Plains? Some of them are as likely as not to come in upon us while these red-coats sleep. Then what will we not suffer for the crime of harbouring! I declare now I hear footsteps – run off, soldiers, run quick, I say, and hide in the garret!' She bustled us out.

It was only her husband, however, a little pale-faced, irresolute man. Looking at him, I could well understand his wife's hesitation in entrusting the pincers and her tooth to his care. He seemed glad to see us. We revealed to him our intention of escaping into New York; but he repeated the words of our other directors, as to the number of American posts, particularly on the River. He added: 'Boys, I swear now it will be an hundred chances to one, if you are not taken up.'

We promised to reward him liberally if he would conduct us. After a while he said: 'A young man lives several miles off from this spot, over to Pine's Bridge: van Wart is his name. He's a mighty smart boy and has friends both with the Cowboys and the Skinners. I reckon he will under-take the task. If he should, I have no objection to come too, for he knows the lie of the land. But I well know the dangers which we shall be exposed to, and will not go myself without a second guide.'

I asked, who were these Cowboys and Skinners. Mrs Sniffen told me that they were the plague of Westchester County, into the northern confines of which we had just entered. The principal landowners of the county, who had been very prosperous, favoured the British cause but were soon forced to take refuge in the City of New York. Their tenant farmers and other persons of substance had suffered enormous losses from the foragers of both armies; while such of the labourers and common people who remained had agreed to form robber bands as pretended auxiliaries of one army or the other. Those who belonged to the 'upper party', that is, to the Loyalists, called themselves 'Cowboys' from their habit of driving off the cattle of the revolutionaries; but cattle were not their only prey. Those who belonged to the 'lower party', the revolutionary, were known as 'Skinners', for they had harder hearts yet and would strip a victim of everything that he-or she had in the world, down to the merest trifle, not scrupling to remove even stockings and under-linen. These Cowboys and Skinners ranged about in the neuter ground between the two lines of outposts, and while pretending to pillage only from opposing partisans were in reality perfectly indifferent whose throat or purse they cut. There was a close understanding, Mrs Sniffen assured us, between these sworn foes who, after a mock-skirmish to satisfy the regular troops that they were in the way of their duty, would meet secretly as friends in some ruined farmhouse, there jocosely intermingling the strains of *Yankee Doodle* with the *Grenadiers' March* and *Hot Stuff.* The object of these encounters was the bartering of cattle and goods stolen on the one hand by the Cowboys from their fellow Loyalists, and on the other by the Skinners from their fellow-revolutionaries. These goods being dangerous to dispose of in home territory could be exchanged with the enemy, and what each side got was made to appear as rightful booty taken in a pretended fight. Each side always claimed to have inflicted crushing losses on its foes and to have left many of them lying dead. When the celebrated Aaron Burr commanded the American advanced lines in this neuter land, and became aware of the depredations and cruelties practised by the Skinners, he is said to have exclaimed in indignation: 'I could gibbet half a dozen *good Whigs* with all the venom of an inveterate Tory!' For a party of these wretches, seeking to screw from an aged Quaker more money than he possessed, had roasted him naked in hot ashes as one would a potato, until the skin rose in blisters on his flesh. Then they thrice hanged him up to a rafter for a spell, and as often cut him down; and in the end left him for dead upon the ground.

Isaac van Wart was summoned, and arrived a few hours later, by which time we were refreshed by sleeping in the woods, where we had concealed ourselves in a drift of fallen leaves. He was, he avowed, a Cowboy in politics; but we could see at once that his courage was not equal to his profession. He was a wild-looking rogue and could neither read nor write. He boasted a great deal of his successes and stratagems in neuter ground, and how often the 'balls had sung like bees about his head'; but we were convinced that Mr Sniffen entertained too high an opinion of his smartness. He agreed at first to undertake any desperate work, but on one pretext or another continually postponed the hour of our departure; nor would Mr Sniffen consent to go forward without him.

It was two days before van Wart 'allowed that he would come', being constantly taunted by Miss Mary Sniffen with cowardice; and then only when we had presented him with five Spanish silver dollars on account and one of the two English blankets. Mr Sniffen accepted the same fee and remarked on the unusual goodness of the dollars as coin; meaning that they had not been carved or clipped. An immense number of gold and silver pieces in Spanish, Portuguese and English currency had found its way into America since the war began; where they circulated in a variety of mutilated forms. The blame for the clipping of the coins was by the Americans uniformly fastened upon Lieutenant-General Archibald Robertson, a Scottish Engineer and Deputy-Quartermaster-General to our Army; so that the diminished coins were known as 'Robertsons'. However, each individual, on either side, would cut up any coin into halves, quarters, or eighth parts, for the sake of small change, and naturally many an eighth was in reality a ninth or a tenth. These frauds, known as 'sharp-skinned money', were nevertheless highly preferred to paper.

We set out at six o'clock in the evening on the fourth day of our adventure and travelled all night through deep swamp, thick woods and over difficult mountains, until three hours before dawn. Isaac van Wart then stopped suddenly and, said he: 'This is a dangerous, troublesome piece of work, I vow. I heartily wish I had never engaged myself in it; but your daughter, friend Sniffen, prevailed by her beauty over my prudent inclinations. Well, she is ten hours' journey away from us now, and the force of her fascination over me has spent itself. We are now perhaps four miles from Tarry Town and an equal distance from White Plains. There is an American encampment of a thousand men within a mile of us. I was there a few days ago and know where all the sentries are posted. There is one at the corner of that coppice yonder. If I should be taken, I would lose my life, for they already have cause to suspect me as a driver of Whig cows.'

He seemed to be under great terror and fear, which did not abate when Smutchy said roughly: 'We are not afraid of one or two sentries. Only conduct us the best way you can. If we unavoidably fall in with any of them, you may leave the matter to us and fly for your life.'

All that we could say had no effect upon him, and although we offered him on the spot twelve more dollars in hard money he would not advance one step further. To our surprise, Mr James Sniffen, who had made no claims to courage and had insisted that he would not proceed without this van Wart, now changed colour. He undertook, of his own impulse, to carry us forward to our destination if van Wart only advised him how to avoid these sentries. This van Wart did.

Mr Sniffen said, when van Wart had hurried off: 'It was but to reassure my wife that I showed such caution. I am greatly devoted to King George and if I prove the means of restoring three good soldiers to His Majesty's service, I shall count myself a good subject. Be damned to the rebels! Now, forward with good courage!'

It had been raining very hard during the whole night and was very dark, even when the moon rose, and therefore though we expected every moment to fall in with the line of sentries, we went through them unchallenged. Mr Sniffen even led us in safety past a block-house which was full of sleeping troops, and remarked very coolly as we struck off into the woods to avoid it: 'Gentlemen, these block-houses are of remarkable construction, being made for lack of nails with jointed timber throughout. I reckon that in your country it would be difficult to find a barrack composed wholly of wood without a pennyworth of iron in the whole building, barring only the pot-hook and chain that hangs in the chimney?'

We agreed that America was a very remarkable country and the inhabitants ingenious beyond the ordinary; which seemed to please him very much.

We then climbed up precipices and waded through swamps and not long before dawn arrived at the house of some friends of Mr Sniffen's, midway between Tarry Town and White Plains; and he rapped them up. We remained hidden outside until he gave us the signal that all was well and we might enter. We never learned the name of these people, who withheld it from us in case, being taken up, we might inform against them. They gave us refreshment of cold beef-steaks with lettuce, and cider, with hickory nuts as a side dish; but begged us not to remain in the house, which would be highly dangerous to us and them, as the American soldiery were scattered over almost the whole face of the country and were constant visitors.

We held a consultation: what was to be done? Mr Sniffen proposed that we should hide ourselves in the haystack which stood near the house, until he could explore the country and find out the safest way for our escape. He told us that we should be as snug there as fleas in a sheepskin. We agreed unanimously and, just as dawn was breaking through the heavy rain, we climbed up into the hay-stack, which was unthatched, and each buried himself up to the chin in the hay. The downpour continued all day. At about noon, during a lull, someone rode up on a horse which he hitched to a rail close by. Presently he brought out our host to view the stack. We heard him saying in the Connecticut accent: 'Yes, Mister, that's a right elegant bit of hay and it will come in handy for our beasts. They consume a terrible amount of fodder. I expect I'll send a party along in about two hours' time to fetch it off to the camp. You'll be allowing us the use of your wagon, no doubt.'

'I declare that you are very hard on us, Captain,' expostulated the poor farmer. 'I'm sure I don't know how I'm to keep my beasts alive this winter if you now seize what remains of my fodder. They be'nt in too good a case already.'

'Well, I expect what you can't feed you must kill, and we'll pay you a fair price for your beef, be sure. The men must eat, the same as the cattle, and a good sight of them have right busy guts.'

'And my hen-roost regularly robbed by the soldiery and all my fences broke down! It is a hard life indeed for a family in the neighbourhood of a military camp,' continued the farmer.

'Ay, the boys will have their fun and cut their pranks,' returned the other lightly. 'But war is war, and you know, you can count yourself lucky that you an't situated on the other side of King's Bridge. The Commissaries there are pretty considerable harder than officers like myself.'

'I an't just capable to say as to that, Captain,' replied our host, 'but I hear at least that they pay in money that jingles and rings.'

'Well, I reckon you may say that,' commiserated the commissary. 'But war is war, and I'll trouble you to leave that stack where it stands till we come to fetch it off this afternoon.'

We were greatly alarmed at the prospect of our hay-stack being removed from about us; but, the Commissary riding away, our host stayed to reassure us that more rain was due to fall, and no party would come for the fodder. If they did, he would descry them at some distance and would warn us in time to run off and hide elsewhere.

Smutchy remarked: 'A thousand blessings fall upon the prophet Daniel George and upon his seed for ever.'

'Amen to that,' I responded.

We remained all that day in the wet hay-stack, snatching a little sleep in turns, one of us always acting as watchman. At six o'clock in the evening our host provided us with very good ham, for the curing of which this county was noted, and a glass apiece of cherry-rum. We emerged from the hay-stack and stretched our legs, but were still not permitted to enter the house. The rain coming down hard again, we returned to the stack and stayed there all night. Richard Harlowe spoke as few words as possible to me, though a sort of truce existed between us because of our common interest and danger. He now sullenly acknowledged my leadership and, if a dispute arose as to the course to be adopted, was always forced to yield to my way of thinking; for Smutchy regarded me as infallible and Harlowe lacked the resolution to part company with us. At this place Smutchy, who was helping Harlowe to descend the hay-stack, muttered: 'Hello, what's here?' and then to me: 'Sergeant Gerry, come now, feel what I have discovered!' He pulled my fingers towards him and I felt a row of coins sewn in the seam of Harlowe's breeches.

This ran against the articles upon which we had agreed before we set out: which was to share, and share alike, all the money and other property in our possession, with Smutchy acting as our treasurer. Harlowe had only admitted to three dollars, and here was a further store which he had not declared. We took five guineas from him. He tried to save his character by saying carelessly that he had forgotten that they were there. However, Smutchy searched him more thoroughly and found another guinea, a

Portuguese half-joe, a coin worth thirty-five shillings in English currency, and three badly clipped Spanish moidores concealed under the arm of his jacket. Smutchy then said hotly: 'I remember, Sergeant Gerry, a stroll that we three once took in company, when we were recruits together. When I laughed at this Gentleman Harlowe for his airs, you resented it on his behalf, did you not? What have you to say for his gentleman-like behaviour now, eh?'

I reproved Smutchy. 'This is no time for recrimination, for God's sake. Harlowe says that he forgot to put the guineas into the common stock. We have them now, at all events, and so much the better for the whole party.'

No more was said on the subject. We began to grow uneasy as this night advanced, lest James Sniffen also had forsaken us and left us to shift for ourselves; however, our kind host, when he visited us a little before dawn, bringing us breakfast, assured us that James Sniffen was a thorough man and a man of his word. His long absence was a proof that he had been vigilant in picking up all the intelligence he could with regard to the disposition of the camps and posts through which we must pass. Richard Harlowe would not believe this, and was for continuing without a guide; but we dissuaded him. Fortunately for us, the storm continued all day, blowing from the South; and the hay-stack, with ourselves in it, was not fetched away. Smutchy again loudly blessed Daniel George of Newbury-Port on this second day, and swore he should be kidnapped and appointed Astronomer-General to our Forces. Time passed for us very slowly.

At last, James Sniffen returned. He told us in a low voice from below that all was well; we must be prepared to follow him when darkness fell. We had twenty miles still to travel, but we might with determination reach King's Bridge that same night.

That evening at dark, when we had passed near thirty-six hours in the hay-stack, we said good-bye to those who had harboured us (and who would accept no recompense for all their kindness) and set off in high spirits on this final stage of our attempt. I could not say exactly what route we followed, but we crossed and recrossed the Bronx stream by fords and passed over several steep heights; the storm meanwhile not abating its violence and the darkness shrouding us so completely that it was difficult to believe that our guide. knew his whereabouts. We had agreed not to ply him with any talk or questions, in order to give him no excuse for missing his direction. But never once did he seem at a loss. At last he told us with relief: 'We stand now on the forward slopes of the Heights of Fordham, and must proceed with the greatest caution, for there are American advanced troops hereabouts of whose stations I am ignorant. We are but three miles distant from King's Bridge. A mile further down this slope is Musholu Brook which leads directly to the bridge. I will come this last stage with you if you desire, but I think now that I can leave it to yourselves; for I am sure you would spare me the hazard of passing and repassing these outposts, being sensible of what risks I have already run in your service.'

Harlowe asked: 'But what of the Commander-in-Chief's bounty? Surely you will be coming to New York to draw the bounty?'

'No, Sir,' he replied. 'What I already have received, and what you have undertaken to pay in addition, will be sufficient to my needs, I expect.'

We soldiers consulted together and subsequently told him: 'If we come safe through, it will be due chiefly to your skill and vigilance. We believe that we have arrived where you say, and are prepared to proceed by ourselves. Here are the twenty dollars, which we promised to you and van Wart together, and here are three more guineas as a thank-offering. For if we get through, very well – our freedom is worth ten times that sum; but if we are caught and hanged it is better that you and your family should benefit than our captors. Go off now and all good luck go with you and yours, Friend Sniffen.'

Nevertheless he came a little further, from a sense of gratitude, and showed us the head of the Musholu Brook, where he clasped our hands in affectionate farewell and told us that we were now safe. This was no-man's-land and lay under the fire of the British batteries at Fort Charles, which commanded King's Bridge. We never saw our excellent guide again, but I trust that he got safe home.

We next came to a small hut beside a cabbage-patch, where a sudden doubt seized Harlowe but that our guide had betrayed us into the American lines. He was of opinion that we should instantly confirm the truth of Mr Sniffen's story by questioning the people of the house. I myself had the fullest confidence in Sniffen. Since therefore he had assured us that we were now in neuter ground, with nothing to fear, I did not oppose Harlowe's resolution. He went up and boldly rapped at the door. The inhabitants, an old negro and his wife, were much terrified by our approach. Their fears increased when we ordered them to light a candle and kindle the fire in order to dry our drenched clothing. The old negro, falling on his knees, implored us not to insist on this service, for if the least light were seen at that hour, the whole habitation would soon be tumbled about our ears by shells from Fort Charles.

Then we knew for sure that all was well; and were not irked to remain in the dark and cold for the few hours that remained of this seventh night of our journey: we knew that to approach the bridge in the dark would be highly dangerous.

The rain ceased, the skies cleared, and soon a slow red dawn began to spread across the hills to our leftward. A rosy light glinted upon the waters of Harlem Creek which separates Manhattan Island, upon which New York stands, from the township of Westchester. With joyful hearts we went forward to the bridge.

'Halt, who goes there?' came in ringing accents from the out-sentry.

Such a moment must be imagined, it cannot be described. 'A sergeant and two men of The Ninth. We have made good our escape,' I answered.

'Advance and be recognized,' was the order, and, to the scandal of the sergeant of the Guard who had been summoned, the out-sentry grounded his firelock, tossed his hat in the air and rushed forward to hug us in delight. It was Mad Johnny Maguire!

'Och Gerry and Smutchy, my darlings,' he yelled, 'is it really yourselves now? And Gentleman Harlowe too!' (Here he gave us an arch look.) 'Oh, on my soul, what sad company you are keeping these days, Gerry, my jewel!'

I was almost as much astonished as Mad Johnny Maguire himself by this encounter. 'Yes, indeed it is ourselves, Johnny – deserting backwards again, the three of us!'

Smutchy said: 'Give that Tower musket into my hand, dear Johnny. Let me feel its weight. I have been a sick man these thirteen months without my old musket, Johnny – a sick man and a slave.'

The Guard through whom we passed were Royal Welch Fusiliers, and showed a very soldier-like appearance, or all but poor Johnny himself. He was now, very properly I own, ordered to be confined, on account of his unsentry-like behaviour towards us. For private feelings should not relax discipline.

CHAPTER VI

I ASKED permission from the sergeant of the Guard to converse with Mad Johnny Maguire before he was confined; which was granted. Maguire then related how he came to be in New York. He had gone to join his brother Cornelius, who was farming near Norwalk, in the southern part of Connecticut, which lies across the Sound from Long Island. Reaching this place without adventure, he had been instructed by Cornelius in the care of the cattle, trees, crops and poultry. When Cornelius was satisfied that Mad Johnny could be trusted, with the help of the family, to manage the three hundred acres of his property, he eyed his ducking-gun where it hung on the nail and announced that he was about to rejoin General Washington on the East Highlands. Johnny thereupon refused to remain in the house if Corny went off soldiering, pointing out very rightly that this would amount to treason: freeing a soldier for service against the King was a crime equal to thus serving himself. So they came to loggerheads, in the literal sense of the phrase. Each seized up one of the heavy iron loggerheads, which they used red-hot in this part of the country for scorching their flip (a nasty mixture of ale, rum and molasses, but good against the cold), and began whacking at each other with intent to maim or kill. Johnny stretched his brother out the whole length of the kitchen with a blow on the crown, and then took to his heels and ran for New York; which was about two days' march away.

'Had you no guide, Johnny?' I asked.

'The Devil a one,' he said.

'Did you travel by night?' I asked.

'What would I be doing, travelling by night? The sun's good enough for me,' he said.

'Then how in the world did you come safe through?' I asked in bewilderment. 'Weren't you wearing scarlet?'

He winked at me and said very simply: 'Well, there was only one of me, you know, and I had the Irish way of speaking, so they thought me a deserter – why, faith, so I was – and naturally inclined to disaffection. It seems that there's a Doctor Ben Franklin, who has been addressing very persuasive letters of late to the Old Country, saying that rebellion is the whole duty and salvation of the Irishman. I walked towards New York along the Eastchester road, and whenever I saw a man approaching, I sat me down by the roadside and nursed my foot as if I were kibed, and let him come up. Then I would eagerly ask him, how far was it to the place I had just left; and I'd tell him that I was Johnny Maguire, a deserter from the army of New York, who was running off, with a sore heel, to join my brother Cornelius Maguire at Norwalk. I would limp a few paces with him, and then sit down again and nurse my foot. When he had passed out of sight, I would start up again and continue my journey.'

'That must have been an inconvenient method of travel when there were many people on the road,' I observed.

'Yes,' he agreed solemnly. 'On some days I gained two miles and lost three. But I got along better as the rain cleared the roads of travellers. Well, the nearer I came, the greater joy I feigned of having broken the chains of British slavery and run out into the free air of patriot America. Many a good meal that sentiment won me, and more drink than I could well hold, for with all their great cleverness they are very easily deceived. But I codded them with too much success, by Jesus God! One kind fellow invited me to ride in his fine yellow carriage and would not take "no". He fetched me half-way back to Norwalk and it was with difficulty that I gave him the slip. Well, in the end I came within three miles of this place, and now whenever I met anyone I made as if desperate of escape from my pursuers, and my heel troubled me more and more. At last a pretended friend betrayed me, in hope of a reward: he peached on me to a British sentinel who came and fetched me safely in! So now there's deserting backwards for you – cap that tale, Sergeant Gerry Lamb!'

We were now entertained at the guard-house to British victuals and British ale. The men were exceedingly hearty and the officers most obliging. When this repast was finished, though I would fain have slept all day, we were conducted forward to New York City, a distance of about fifteen miles, in order to report to General Headquarters. We were the first party to have escaped from the Convention Army since September.

The sergeant who accompanied us, by name Collins, a native of London, was to prove a good friend of mine. Unlike most of the other non-commissioned officers in this regiment he was very talkative; however, most of his discourse was both informative and amusing. He told me: 'You'll be up before Major André, the Deputy-Adjutant-General – now there's the best brain and the kindest heart in the whole British Army. General Clinton thinks the world of him. Naturally, some of the officers consider him a thought too Frenchified – he is romantical, they say, and over-interested in millinery and the theatrical stage. Indeed, he designed all the costumes to be worn at our stage-plays fat the Theatre in Philadelphia, took leading parts, wrote the prologues, painted the scenery, and all. The great Mischianza, General Howe's farewell celebration – now that was a prodigious fine show, and Major André, he invented and produced it all. Knights of the Burning Mountain, Knights of the Blended Rose, a regatta, a tournament, queens of beauty, maids of honour, ornamental fireworks – by God, there was a beautiful, sweet phantasy, a written romance come true before our awed gazer It made a mock of the desolations of war that spread about us – and breathed defiance at the French King, who had just declared against us.'

Our travel-worn appearance excited compassion among the soldiers whom we met on the road, and two or three times we were called aside into a tavern and persuaded to tell our adventures. We passed under the strong works of Fort Washington and through McGowans Pass, a place close to the village of Harlem, so strong that a few companies posted there might well keep an army at bay. About noon we arrived in New York itself, which lay at the extremity of this island, and was even then a considerable city of ten thousand native inhabitants, though by the half below its present magnitude and importance. It was greatly overcrowded by the influx of the military and of very large numbers of Loyalists from all parts of the country, who more than repaired the loss of so many families 'on the other side of the question'. This congestion was made worse by the loss of eleven hundred houses – more than one-fourth of the city – burned by the Americans when they evacuated the city. The ruins of these houses lay to the east of Broadway (the fine street, seventy feet in width, that passed along a ridge in the centre of the city) and to the south of Wall Street, the abode of the well-to-do. Hovels of planking and old sail-cloth had been put up around the chimneys and walls that still stood, and the poor, tattered wretches who inhabited these dens gave the city a very squalid air. They were in part the usual refuse of humanity that is littered about the gates of any garrison town the world over, but in part also the most pitiable victims of this fratricidal war – landed proprietors and their families, descended from the first settlers, whom mob-law and rapine had driven from their estates and reduced to beggary. Of the houses that remained, some were built with good effect in the English style, very strong and neat and several storeys high; but the most were sharp-roofed, sloping Dutch buildings, with the gable ends projecting towards the street. The Dutch spirit, I was to find, still governed the city: the custom of the Dutch, who practically engrossed the markets and shops, was to give little and ask much, to conceal gains and to live for themselves alone. Dutchmen could be recognized by their comical custom of smoking 'cigars', leaves of tobacco rolled in the form of a tube six inches long, the smoke of which was drunk without the aid of any instrument. They were now, Sergeant Collins informed me, making enormous gains by the renting of apartments and the sale of provisions. The prices that he mentioned were four or five times greater than those that had ruled in Dublin when I was stationed there. '

Other sights that surprised me on this first visit to the city were a long

procession of negro slaves carrying bales of merchandise on their heads –
near one-fourth of the inhabitants of New York were negroes or mulattoes
– and three mistresses of officers, each in an elegant conveyance and
wearing a coat of military cut with the regimental facings of her protector.
The main streets were paved and clean and lined with trees. There were
some very good shops in the streets about Broadway, a few of them as luxurious as any in Dame Street or Parliament Street in my native city, which
may be justly pronounced two of the first trading streets in Europe. The
contrast between these affluent surroundings and the frightful country
from which I had escaped that very morning struck me very forcibly.

Before one of these shops, where were sold enamelled snuff-boxes and
comfit cases, a handsome young fop in a sky-blue silk coat and flowered
waistcoat stood in a negligent attitude, sucking the top of his malacca cane;
which, when he pensively removed it from his mouth, proved to be of
clouded amber. He also wore a Spanish military cloak, of Canary yellow
silk with a pure white lining, and a sword with crystal pommel and Toledo
scabbard. He so closely resembled a wax-figure or the paragon of a fashion
plate that I had the fancy to make him talk, in order to see what language
would break out of those cupid's lips. I asked him the time.

He stared at me in a vacant way; but when I repeated my question in a
louder but still civil tone, he thought it wiser to answer me, as being
supported by three other soldiers. Leisurely taking a jewelled gold watch
from his right-hand fate-pocket, he regarded it for a few moments and then
pronounced: 'Honest red-coat, I will tell you: it wants but three minutes
of noon.' He so vividly recalled the motley fool in Shakespeare's Arden
that I dared to quote:

> 'Thus we may see, quoth he, how the world wags.'

At this sally, he was good enough to laugh. '*Touché*,' he lisped and
continued:

> 'And so, from hour to hour we ripe and ripe,
> And then from hour to hour we rot and rot,
> And thereby hangs a tale.'

I was for thanking him and proceeding on my way, having satisfied my
curiosity and wit; but he called me back. 'Not so fast, my sun-burned
Jaques,' he said. 'We have so far consulted only one chronological oracle.
Stand by me while we approach the other.' From the fob on the left-hand
side of his pearly white breeches he drew out another costly time-piece,
and then the first again, attempting evidently to strike a mean between
them in calculation. However, before he could arrive at any answer, the
noon gun was fired from the Battery commanding the entrance of the
North and East Rivers, and the noon chimes rang out from several sacred
edifices.

'It is now noon,' he then said confidently.

'I am greatly your debtor, Sir,' I replied with a slight bow, which he was gentleman enough to return, saying, very truly: 'No, Sir, I protest – it was nothing.'

So we continued towards the fine brick edifice at the very end of Broadway which, by the guard of honour posted at the gate and the Royal Standard surmounting it, we could see was the General Headquarters. But Richard Harlowe hung back and signalled to us to wait a short spell while he also addressed our friend the fop. We did not hear what was said, but the two spoke earnestly together for half a minute; whereupon Harlowe rejoined us.

Smutchy jested: 'Why, Gentleman Harlowe, was that pretty pet your young brother? And did he agree to buy your discharge?'

Harlowe shot a keen look at him and then replied in some confusion: 'No, he is only an Irish cousin.' We all laughed very heartily, though not yet sure where the joke lay.

At Headquarters we were instantly admitted by the Officer of the Guard who told us: 'The Deputy-Adjutant-General, Major André, has heard of your escape and is desirous of seeing you immediately.'

We were presented to Major André, who welcomed us all together, complimenting us upon our escape. He then asked me: 'Are you not Sergeant Lamb, who was in charge of this expedition?'

When I said that I was that person, the Major invited me into the parlour, first giving orders to his clerk to take my comrades and the escort to the buttery for entertainment. He then poured out a glass of Madeira for me with his own hand.

'Proceed, Sergeant Lamb!' he said simply.

I smiled: 'Where am I to begin, your Honour? You know it is a dangerous thing to ask an Irishman for his story.'

He broke into a very musical laughter. 'Well, you can tell me first, if you wish, how came you to join the Army.'

I replied: 'I think that it was because I was tired of being a clerk in the counting-house and longed for glory.'

He clapped me on the shoulder and cried: 'Why now, that was the very same reason that brought me into the service. But – I was lucky in a rich father who could purchase me a commission. What is your age?'

I told him: 'Twenty-three.'

'Well, it is more credit to be a sergeant at twenty-three than a colonel at twenty,' he observed very frankly. 'For, Heaven be blessed, it is rarely that purse or privilege have a say in the appointment of our non-commissioned officers – the mainstay of the Line.'

I have never before or since been spoken to by an officer in so easy and familiar a style, or by one to whom my heart immediately warmed with such spontaneous affection. His face, though of dark complexion, was mild, open and animated. He had a long and beautiful head of hair which, agreeably to the fashion of the day, was wound with a black ribband and hung down his back; the lace at his throat and cuffs was of Mechlin, exquisitely laundered; and the facings of his well-cut scarlet coat were of a rich green. In short, he was the handsomest man that ever I saw. Nor was there anything of the coxcomb in his manner, and when he came to business and asked me for particulars of my captivity and flight, I knew at once that Sergeant Collins had not erred in rating his intelligence so highly. It was characteristic of the Major, by the way, that he never referred to our American enemy by such terms as 'the Rebels' or 'the Yankees' or 'the Mohairs', but always very politely as 'the Colonists'.

First he enquired what I knew about the discipline, composition, arms and disposition of the Colonists' forces, the capacity and spirit of their officers, from experience or hearsay, and the present mood of the militia, the regular troops and the peasantry. He rapidly noted down my answers and, nodding, compared them with entries in a calf-bound ledger which he had by him.

'Did you ever see General Benedict Arnold?' he asked suddenly.

'Yes, your Honour,' I replied, 'I saw him galloping between the lines in the engagement at Freeman's Farm – a man without fear. It is a great pity that so judicious and gallant an officer should be major-general in the American service.'

'*Entre nous*, many Continental Congressmen seem to think the same,' he laughed. 'I regret that I am not personally acquainted with him. But I know the young lady to whom he has now given his heart; she is sentimental and good. I wish her joy of him. Her father was most agreeable to me when I was in Philadelphia. On this account I fear that, despite her having the Military Governor for a swain, poor Peggy Shippen will be suspected as a Tory by the jealous Whig ladies there, and pronounced "contraband" at social gatherings. As for the General himself, my intelligencers report him to be living highly beyond his income in that city – a very expensive place, you know. I fear that will get him into more trouble with his enemies. But come, to the matter of your flight. I'll fetch a map and we may trace out your wanderings together. Here we are now, at five miles south-west from Hopewell, was it not? Where shall we mark the Widow Eder's hut?'

We lightly traced out the route in lead pencil on the map, and I marked the block-houses and camps to the best of my ability; also the bridges over the creeks and other matters of military interest. When I told him the name of our guide and described his house, wife and person, he laughed: 'So he called himself James Sniffen, did he? That was not his name. He borrowed it from a Whig farmer of White Plains – no, I know your man, and could name him if I would. Well, I'll keep his secret from you since he withheld it himself; and I'll see that an adequate reward is paid him by my agents, as an encouragement to further works of mercy. He is a very bold man and has done a deal of work for our side.'

When I had given Major André all the information that I could, he expressed much satisfaction. 'Now, Sergeant Lamb,' he said, 'as a non-commissioned officer of The Ninth, you enjoy a privilege not accorded to private soldiers, which is to choose whether you will sail by the next packet to England, and there be posted to the Details of the Regiment; or whether you will continue to serve in America. I may say that I sincerely hope you will choose the latter course. We have need here of experienced soldiers.'

When I hesitated a moment before answering, he divined the reason. 'Let me assure you before you speak, that you will not be sent to any corps in which to serve would be distasteful to you – I know well how greatly regiments vary in quality. No, no, Sergeant Lamb, Sir Henry Clinton, the Commander-in-Chief, has authorized me to offer you your choice of entering in what regiment you please now serving in America.'

'That is easily answered then,' I said, 'I shall stay and serve. My choice is the Royal Welch Fusiliers. May I ask a favour, which is that Private Alexander Steel, who came with me, be posted to the same corps, but Private Richard Harlowe to another?'

'I will undertake that,' he said. 'And I will inform Colonel Balfour of the Royal Welch that you are a man of energy and education, and will desire him to retain you in your rank. Meanwhile, I thank you for your information and for your loyal decision. Good luck to you!' He warmly clasped my hand and then summoning his orderly sent me to Colonel Handfield (the present Commissary-General of Ireland) who was appointed to pay the men who escaped from captivity. I was given a bounty of three guineas in addition to the money that, according to the account I gave him, we were out of pocket by bribing our guides. I am inclined to think that much of this bounty that my comrades and I received was the result of Sir Henry's secret benevolence. Colonel Handfield used the term 'honourable desertion' for my quitting the Convention Army. This was the distinction that General Burgoyne himself made, when addressing the House of Parliament, between those soldiers who through every difficulty rejoined His Majesty's forces, and those who left their regiments for the purpose of settling among the Americans.

I caught a sight of Sir Henry before we left. He was a low man, stout and full-blooded with a lordly nose and an air of honesty and courage, though his reserve was not easily broken through nor was he so familiar with the troops as General Burgoyne had been.

We lay that night in the guard-room at Headquarters and the next morning, after viewing the sights of the Town, marched back to King's Bridge. Sergeant Collins complained much to me of the present expen-siveness of New York, but expressed the hope that before long we should be 'launched on a new campaign that will push the tottering forces of the rebels into the abyss'. He said that he had been engaged that summer against the French in a sea-battle, three companies of the Regiment having volunteered to act as marines under Admiral Richard Howe. He had been in the fifty-gun ship *Isis*, Captain Raynor, when she engaged with the French seventy-four Caesar, which was so mauled that she put before the wind and sailed for the shelter of Boston harbour. 'But,' said he, 'the chief war hereabouts is not against rebellion – it is against the Treasury of Great Britain. It makes me hot with indignation to witness the scandalous jobbery and peculation that persists here, under the shield of the military Government.'

I asked him for particulars to support this general indictment. 'Oh,' he replied, 'every sight you see has a moral. Observe those cattle being driven to the slaughter-house. Whence do they come, do you suppose?'

'Rebel cattle driven by the Cowboys from Westchester county, or bought by them from the Skinners? Or perhaps sequestered from Whigs on Long Island or Staten Island?'

'I see that you know a thing or two. Well, whatever their origin, at least they have since been taken over by the Commissaries of Cattle at perhaps two guineas a beast, and sold as beef to the Army at two shillings sterling the pound weight, the hides and tallow remaining as the Commissaries' perquisites. There's a profit, now! And what do you see yonder? That is King's College, which was the university of this place, with faculties of Arts and Physic. There are now troops quartered in it. The Barrack-Masters charge an extravagant rent to the Crown for the use of these buildings, as also for churches, Quaker meeting-houses, breweries and the like. Do you suppose that one copper halfpenny is returned to the owners by these jobbers? No, no. And observe the wood smoke issuing from that row of chimneys? That tells a tale too. The same Barrack-Masters fetch the wood from the forests of Long Island or Staten Island; they pay the Tory proprietors fifteen shillings a cord for it, and the Whigs nothing at all. Transport costs them less than nothing; the Treasurer is overcharged for that item. Yet at what price do they sell the fuel? At eighty shillings a cord!'

I doubted many of these tales as fabrications, but was later convinced of their truth. It was not only the lesser officials who benefited, either. In these years four successive Quartermasters-General of the Army in America retired to England, each reputedly worth not less than a quarter of a million pounds sterling. Two Deputy-Quartermasters-General, however, Archibald Robertson and Henry Bruen, being called upon at New York in 1782 to testify before a Board of General officers (where I happened to be employed as a clerk) to explain the prodigious expenses incurred by their department, insisted that the system of private contracts was preferable to that of direct purchase by the military government. They remarked in evidence: 'There is no man conversant in business, or that is capable of judging of human nature, who can suppose that a contract held by the public can or will be executed with that economy, care and attention as when the interests of individuals are immediately concerned. Nor could it, almost, be possible for the Head of any department, let his zeal and attention be ever so great, to see that strict justice was done in the purchasing of such a variety of articles as the land and water carriage of an army require, especially in this country.'

Sergeant Collins continued: 'Nevertheless New York is a pleasant and healthy station, compared with others in America. There are cooling breezes in summer, and a more temperate air in winter. I mean, rather, the part on the North River yonder where the well-to-do live; phoo, the trading part down by the East River stinks in the summer like the sick bay of a transport. September is very pleasant, with the apple-trees bearing fruit and blossom at the same time. But let me tell you: one of the most serious inconveniences is the want of good water, there being but few wells hereabouts. The city is supplied mostly from a spring almost a mile distant; the water is distributed to the people at the reservoir at the head of Queen Street which I will show you. That, and the high price of soap, accounts for prodigious charges for laundering. See here, my latest bill – seven shillings and sixpence for a mere dozen pieces!' Yes, there are many worse stations than New York in peace-time. We were here in 1773, two years before the troubles. Those were the days. Good beef was then at 3½d. a pound, very pretty mutton at the same; chickens at ninepence a couple, instead of the present four shillings for a single small bird. Those cursed Dutch shopkeepers, they are as trickish as Jews! Turtle-meat sevenpence a pound – we never see it now. Pineapples as large as a quart mug, for sixpence each – they are gone too. Still, there's one advantage in this prodigious rise of prices – the men can't get drunk so readily. In those days New English kill-devil sold at threepence the pint-measure; and a worse poison for the guts I never drank. In those days King George's fine statue still proudly rode his horse at Bowling Green; the damned rebels pulled him down and chopped him up and ran the pieces into bullet-moulds. Over forty thousand bullets he was made to yield, to be fired into the breasts of his loyal subjects – oh, the shame of the dogs!'

At King's Bridge I reported to Lieutenant-Colonel Balfour, to whose kind attention I must ever feel myself much indebted. The Colonel of the Regiment was General Howe; but naturally he did not command it in the field. Lieutenant-Colonel Balfour provided me with clothing and necessaries that same day and appointed me sergeant at the first vacancy.

The Twenty-Third, or Royal Welch Fusiliers, were then, as now, one of the proudest regiments in the Service and preserved a number of remarkable customs, most of them recording some glorious episode in history or preserving the titular connexion of the Regiment with Wales – a country, however, of which few of its men or officers were natives. We bore very fine devices on our colours and appointments. In the centre of the Colour the Prince of Wales' Feathers issuing out of a Coronet, and in three corners, the badges of Edward the Black Prince, namely: the Rising Sun, the Red Dragon and the Three Feathers with the motto *Ich Dien*. On our grenadier caps were the same Feathers and the White Horse of Hanover with the motto *Nec Aspera Terrent* – 'Difficulties daunt us not'. The Feathers and the motto *Ich Dien* were painted upon our drums and bells of arms. Our Colours and appointments also bore the honour 'MINDEN'. One privileged honour enjoyed by us was that of passing in review preceded by our fine regimental he-goat, with horns gilded and adorned with ringlets of flowers. We valued ourselves much on the ancientness of the custom.

Martial finery can be an encouragement to formal discipline and clean drill, and I must confess that it did my heart good to be included in a parade of this regiment: it took out of my mouth the taste of drills perfunctorily performed in captivity, with sticks instead of muskets, and the memory of the awkward squads who had been set as guards over us prisoners at Prospect Hill and Rutland.

In the next few months we had our camp in different parts of Manhattan Island, and once near the village of Harlem, contiguous to which was the remarkable Strait of Hell Gate, always attended with whirlpools and a roaring of the waters. The tremendous eddy was due to the narrowness and crookedness of the passage, where the waves were tossed on a bed of rock extending across it. On one side were sunken rocks named The Hog's Back, and on the other a point of similar danger, The Devil's Frying Pan, where the water hissed as if poured upon red-hot iron. In the midst, the whirl of the current caused a vast boiling motion, known as The Pot. This place had been famous for its enormous and excellent lobsters, which in peace-time had sold for only three halfpence a pound; but the tremendous cannonading in the battle of Long Island disturbed them from their retreat and they went away, not to return. More recently Sir James Wallace, pursued by the French fleet, had taken the *Experiment*, of fifty guns, safely into New York through this perilous passage; to the great astonishment of Admiral Howe. The principal credit, however, rightly went to the negro pilot. At the moment of the greatest danger Sir James gave some orders on the quarterdeck, which in the pilot's opinion interfered with the duties of his own office. Advancing therefore to Sir James and gently tapping him on the shoulder, this mungo said: 'Massa, you no speak here!' Sir James, feeling the full force of the brave fellow's remonstrance, was silent; and afterwards, in thankful recognition of his extraordinary feat of navigation, settled on him an annuity of £50 for life. The phrase 'Massa, you no speak here' became proverbial in the Regiment, and once I had the hardihood to employ it in addressing a young officer, who joined us about this time, when he attempted to interrupt some instruction I was giving my company in the practise of wood-fighting. He accepted the reproof in good part, as became a true gentleman. This second-lieutenant (as they are peculiarly called in the Regiment, rather than 'ensigns'), young Harry Calvert Esq. is now risen to be Lieutenant-General, and Adjutant-General of the British forces: it was he whose kind condescension lately won me my out-pension of a shilling a day from the Royal Hospital at Chelsea.

I was able on one or two occasions to visit the New Theatre, opened at John Street in the New Year, where the Surgeon-General to the Forces was manager and the chief parts were taken by officers of the Staff. I delighted especially in the acting of Major André, who spoke his words with great naturalness and feeling; and the performances I attended of *Macbeth* and *Richard III* made me ashamed of my self-satisfaction as a stage-player in the Rutland pen. The female parts were taken either by the mistresses of officers or, failing these, by boy-ensigns of the garrison.

The regimental celebrations of St David's Day, which fall on March 1st, were as usual the occasion of much good humour and drunkenness among the Royal Welch Fusiliers. The officers together, and the sergeants together, celebrated it in the customary banquet with set toasts. To every toast that is drunk in either mess, the name of St David is habitually added, which adds a ludicrous solemnity to proceedings. The first toast is always to 'His Royal Highness the Prince of Wales – and St David', the band playing the melody of *The Noble Race of Jenkin* while a handsome drum-boy, elegantly dressed and mounted upon the goat, which is richly caparisoned with the Regimental devices, is led thrice around the mess table by the drum-major. It had happened at Boston four years previously that the goat sprang suddenly from the floor, spilling the drum-boy upon the table among the glasses and flagons and, bounding over the heads of some officers, ran off to the barracks. Other toasts, to 'Toby Purcell's Spurs[1] – and St David', 'Jenkin ap Morgan, the first gentleman of Wales – and St David', 'The Ladies – and St David – God bless 'em!', 'The Glorious Roses of Minden – and St David', 'Old Comrades – and St David', keep the merriment in progress all night. All officers or sergeants who have not previously performed the service of 'eating the leek', in the manner immortalized by Shakespeare's Fluellen are now obliged to do so in St David's honour, standing upon a chair with one foot resting on the table while the drums play a continuous double-flam until the nauseous raw vegetable is wholly consumed – (after which they are consoled with a large bumper and acknowledged as honorary Welshmen. This duty I was

---

1   These spurs, worn by Major Toby Purcell, who was with the Regiment at the Victory of the Boyne, are kept in the possession of his successor, the senior major of the Regiment, and displayed every year at the Feast of St David. R. L. [They were destroyed in a fire at Montreal when the Regiment was stationed there in 1842; but the toast is still drunk at the St David's Day dinner. R.G.]

obliged by my fellow-sergeants to perform; and Colonel Balfour, who had
but recently joined the Regiment from he King's Own, did likewise in the
Officers' Mess. Thus I became a person of triple nationality: Irish by birth,
Mohawk Indian and Welsh by initiation and adoption. I hope that I never
disgraced any of these three nations in my quality as a warrior!

Though our service at New York was broken by four warlike expeditions and several forays, the Regiment conducted itself throughout just as
if all were 'peace, parade and St James's Park'; I mean, as to the formality
and regularity of our behaviour and the exquisite care that each soldier was
made to take of his personal appearance. Many hours every day were spent
upon the pipe-claying of crossbelts and breeches – which, however, dried
far more quickly here than in the humid air of Ireland – upon the shining
of shoes, the polishing of buttons and buckles, and, above all, upon the
correct adornment of the hair. I recalled how, upon the disembarkation of
The Ninth at Three Rivers in Canada, Major Bolton had informed
company-officers that the tallow provided for us would now be better
daubed upon our shoes, to preserve them from the damps, than upon our
hair, to hold the flour with which we powdered it – and that this flour likewise would be of more service to us in the edible form of loaves. Few even
of the officers had thereafter attempted to keep themselves spick and span.
But the Royal Welch Fusiliers were no rough and ready regiment: the
comb, flour-dredge and pomatum box were as prime necessaries with us
as cartouche box, powder-flask and ramrod, and no slightest deviation
from correct soldierly behaviour in barracks was ever allowed to pass, nor
any gross conduct or unsoldier-like lounging in the streets. We were often
sneered at for macaronis; but we let that pass as a compliment, for we also
took correspondingly greater care of our arms than other regiments. For
example, I was very pleased to find that the company-officers, being
persons of substance and with a pride in their profession, had at their own
charges provided their men with the fine black flints which gentlemen use
in their sporting guns. These remained sharp even after fifty discharges,
whereas the ordinary Army issue of dull brown pebble was never good for
more than fifteen, and often less. What was still more to the point, when
we were at Harlem and a part of the Regiment quartered upon a wharf,
figures of men as large as life made of thin boards were anchored at a
proper distance from the end of the wharf; at these the platoons fired as a
practice in marksmanship. Floating objects such as glass bottles, bobbing
up and down with the tide, were also pointed out to them as targets, and
premiums given to the best shots. No other regiment to my knowledge
practised this sort of musketry, the colonels being content merely with
simultaneity of the volleys, and letting aim go hang.

I have always had a great love of the regular, the orderly and the neat;
and as a sergeant in this corps I was able to indulge it to the full. My
sergeant's wig, which was paid for by the Colonel, and fitted for me by the

Regimental perruquier, was of the finest hair; and I kept it always in irreproachable trim. Smutchy Steel took kindly to this mode of life, but it can be imagined that Mad Johnny Maguire found it difficult to alter his old slovenly habits. He was always in trouble.

Richard Harlowe was drafted to The Thirty-Third. It then proved that, by one of these extraordinary accidents that occur frequently on extraordinary occasions, Smutchy Steel had hit upon the exact truth. The Shakespearean fop was indeed a close relative of Harlowe's and rather than again risk the indignity of being accosted in the street by a common soldier who could call him cousin – or it may well have been brother – had undertaken to purchase his discharge: on condition that a substitute were found, which among the destitute Loyalists was not a difficult task. So this bad soldier was lost to the Army.

CHAPTER VII

OF THE expeditions which we made from our base of New York in 1779 I need not write in detail. The first was undertaken on May 30th, when we were sent up Hudson's River in boats against Stoney Point and Verplanck's Neck, some forty miles beyond New York, where the Americans had forts. These forts were placed at King's Ferry, a narrowing of the river, which was the way that the revolutionary forces habitually took when crossing from the middle provinces into New England, or contrariwise. If this passage were seized they must make a circuit of sixty miles through the mountains. To me the chief interest of the expedition was that I beheld for the first time the beautiful scenery on the lower reaches of Hudson's River, here about two miles in breadth, which surpassed description. The western bank showed at first a continuous dark wall of rock which by its vertical fissures suggested Palisades, and bore that name. It was occasionally broken by a watercourse and everywhere fringed and chequered with the bright foliage of early summer. The eastern shore – which I regarded with interest as the country which I had traversed as a fugitive in the previous winter – gradually assumed a wild and heroic character, with woods, pastures, towering cliffs. All the noblest combinations of forest and water, light and shade, were now here seen in the greatest perfection, and by the pleasure in Nature which I discovered, I knew that I was myself again, emerged from the slough of disgust and disinterest into which captivity had for awhile sunken me. Yet the American houses, sheds, sawmills and forts, that I beheld, all of undressed wood and many in ruins on account of the war, had for me a dishevelled and melancholy appearance when I contrasted them in memory with the neat whitewashed houses and handsome churches with glittering tin spires that had lined the St Lawrence River in Canada. Considering the matter in my mind, I decided: 'No, no, a modest and decent prosperity will always outweigh for me the most romantic prospect of peak, chasm and tangled forest.'

The division that we were in landed a little before noon at a point seven miles below King's Ferry. Another continued up the river, and before night had, with the loss of one man wounded, seized Stoney Point. This was a place of great natural strength but the works being not yet completed by the enemy were abandoned by them in haste. We meanwhile, advancing over rugged and difficult country, invested the fort on our side of the river, named Fort Lafayette, and bivouacked within musket-shot of it. By five in the morning our people on the other bank had hauled cannon and mortars from the fleet up to Stoney Point and bombarded Fort Lafayette from across the water. This proved to be a small but complete work with palisades, a double ditch, trees felled with branches outward, *chevaux-de-frise*, and a bomb-proof block-house in the middle. The seventy Americans in it soon beat a *chamade*, or demand for a parley, and Major André was sent in under a flag of truce by General Clinton to receive their surrender. The sole condition made by the Americans was that we should promise them good usage. Having garrisoned these two forts, we soon dropped down the river again.

On July 4th, the Regiment was sent in an expedition against the coast of Connecticut, a province which abounded with men as well as provisions and was a principal support to the American armies. Since the Connecticut people had long boasted that we feared to attack them because of their martial prowess, Sir Henry Clinton decided to undeceive them. By doing as much destruction as possible to public arsenals, stores, barracks and the like, he hoped to tempt General Washington into quitting the Highlands. If he took the bait, well and good – for his troops, though then being exercised by Baron von Steuben, a Prussian drillmaster, were no match for ours; or if he stayed behind, better still – he would earn a reputation, among the people of Connecticut, either of not caring at all what losses they might suffer or of not daring to come to their aid. The reason that Connecticut had been so long spared was that most inhabitants of the coastal districts were of the Episcopalian faith, and loyal by inclination, though kept in awe by the dissenting and revolutionary minority; it had been thought unwise to destroy the wheat with the tares. However, since these Loyalists were so slow to come out in their true colours, Sir Henry now gave them the chance to declare themselves – let them treat us either as foes or liberators, however they wished.

To be brief: our small expedition, of regulars and American Provincials intermixed, disembarked on either side of the Connecticut fort of New Haven, which lay about eighty miles up the coast from New York, and seized the fort which protected it. The vessels in the harbour and all artillery, ammunition, public stores ashore were either taken or destroyed; yet the town, which was a pleasant and substantial place, was not burned. However, as was to be expected, the presence of Colonel Fanning's Provincials among our forces caused some irregularities. They could not at first be restrained from the plunder of private houses; and the inhabitants, being thus provoked, fired from windows at the sentinels placed as guards to prevent any further damage. The people of New Haven were, by the bye, universally known in New England as Pumpkin-heads, because of an ancient law in Connecticut which enjoined every male to have his hair cut round his cap every Saturday; the hard shell of a pumpkin being often used instead of a cap. The intention was, it seems, to prevent those who had lost their ears for heresy from concealing their misfortune under long tresses. After a proclamation had been made to persuade these Pumpkin-heads to renewed allegiance the fort was dismantled and we re-embarked.

The expedition next proceeded to Fairfield, a town about twenty miles nearer to New York, and a little inland. Fairfield, and Norwalk its neigh-bour, had been spared from destruction two years previously during an expedition made by Governor Tryon of New York, who was now again in command, against the arsenal of Danbury. The Americans, therefore, trusting that the same indulgence would once more be shown to the place, used private houses as ambuscades against our people, when we advanced to the seizure of the public stores. We lost a number of men killed or wounded. Governor Tryon, remarking that the Americans must be taught to use private houses only for private purposes, or else accept the conse-quences, ordered the little town to be burned to the ground. This would have been a very painful sight to all our eyes, had not the resentment that we felt for the loss of our comrades mitigated our mercy. Yet I for one was grieved to see the English church go up in flames, among the secular build-ings; and a poor woman with an infant in her arms who came running to my platoon, calling upon us wildly to stay our hands, was the wife of the incumbent, the Reverend John Sayre. He had been very badly treated by the Whigs for the four years foregoing, his wife babblingly told us, and reduced to reading on a Sunday, to his congregation, no more than the Bible and the Homilies; for the Liturgy was forbidden him. Yet how had his forbearance and saintliness been served, she cried, even by those for whose victory he offered his private prayers to God nightly! His fine church was in ashes and his snug parsonage too, the Communion plate destroyed, and she and he, with eight children, were now left destitute of provisions, home and raiment. Our company commander offered her safe conduct back to New York, but she refused it. She had been separated from her husband, in the bustle, and from two of her children, and would not budge unless the whole flock were assembled. So we left her there raving distractedly.

Norwalk and Greenfield, places taken immediately afterward, suffered a similar fate, since the opposition of the militia, called out in great numbers, was of a nature that no regular army could patiently endure. Governor Tryon's name was productive of such hatred among the popu-lation, who regarded him as the main influence for the continuance of the war on our side (as we regarded King Hancock and the Adamses as the chief agitators on theirs), that every shed or barn became a fortress against our advance and, before we had done, our loss in killed, wounded and missing amounted to one hundred and fifty.

In the neighbourhood of Norwalk, Mad Johnny Maguire asked permission from our officer to leave the column for ten minutes while we halted in a field. The officer enquiring the reason, Maguire replied that he owed a native of the place a debt of four shillings and threepence and wished to discharge it. The officer, acceding to this curious request, sent a sergeant and two men with Maguire to observe what he did. I was the sergeant selected.

We passed up a wagon-track to a group of farm buildings through an orchard of cherry-trees, bearing a fine crop of the common black cherries which they used hereabouts for their cherry rum, and little red honey cherries which were good for eating. Maguire, leading confidently, said to me: 'This is the farm of my brother Cornelius the rebel; and yonder is my nephew and namesake Johnny. Come here, halloo, come here, Johnny, my fine rogue and greet your uncle!' But the little fellow hung back, and ran screaming to his mother at the sight of armed red-coats. She was gathering cherries in a tree, standing on a ladder; and being a little deaf had not heard our approach. When we came up, she screamed too, though with the presence of mind not to overset her basket. Descending the ladder precipitately, she fell at my feet and begged us to spare her life and that of the family.

'I think I have the pleasure of addressing Mrs Cornelius Maguire,' I said politely. 'Your brother-in-law has just come to the house to pay your husband a small debt.'

'Oh, it is but that rascal and thief of a Johnny?' she cried, fear giving way to an impetuous indignation. 'He that near killed my poor innocent husband, who was so good to him, cracking his head open with a cruel stroke of a loggerhead? Oh, by the Angels, I'll be equal with him.' She caught little Johnny by the hand and rushed towards the farm, picking up a hatchet from the wood-pile as she went.

We hurried after her and were spectators of a curious scene – a family tussle between Maguire and a swarm of his half-grown nephews and nieces, who had been at work on various household tasks in the kitchen, for the possession of Cornelius' ponderous firelock. Cornelius himself directed the operations of his family from where he lay, his head bound with a cloth, on a straw pallet in the corner of the kitchen. He was feebly calling: 'Trip him up, boys, fly at his eyes, girls, the black rapparee! Were it not for these cursed mumps I would be up myself, and oh, then wouldn't I knock him edgewise into Glory?'

Upon Mrs Maguire entering the fray with her hatchet, we interposed and disarmed her, and I received the captured firelock from Maguire. 'Now,' said I, 'what do you say, Private John Maguire' – for in our new regiment sergeants were required to distance themselves from the men and it was never 'Johnny' and 'Gerry' between us now, unless we were alone together – 'what do you say, are we to make a prisoner of your brother?'

Mrs Maguire began to sob and weep and to speak of the ingratitude of her brother-in-law, who thus returned evil for good, and how she would 'never see her darling Corny again; and him so bad with the mumps and all, so that his poor vitals were swelled to punkin-size'.

I did not wish to cause more hardship than could be prevented; and it seemed unjust that Johnny, whose only thought in visiting his brother had been to pay a debt of honour, should deprive this hardworking family of its 'king-post', as Mrs Maguire described him. However, that Cornelius Maguire was suffering from an infectious disease which also prevented him from walking was sufficient excuse for not taking him with us, especially as he was neither armed nor in military uniform. Yet we knew perfectly well that, the moment he was recovered of his complaint, he would return to his militia regiment. Johnny Maguire, nearly in tears himself because of the predicament into which his generous impulse had thrown us all equally, was struck by a helpful thought. 'Sergeant Lamb,' he cried, 'I have a notion where our duty lies. The greatest lack of General Washington's army is clothing and arms, but especially clothing. Now, listen, suppose we sequestrate this rogue's coat, gaiters, shoes, breeches, musket, powder flask and all – the same being private property to be returned to him after the war is won – that will be a deal better than either killing him or taking him off. For we shall deprive the enemy of a soldier without depriving this poor, decent family of a father.'

To this I acceded, and in spite of the screamed remonstrances of Mrs Maguire, we rendered her sullenly groaning husband an 'invalid'; which was the usual term for those many soldiers of the revolutionary forces who were unable to parade owing to mere nakedness. However, she had her revenge. As Johnny said good-bye to her and offered to kiss little Johnny, into whose palm he pressed a shilling, she seized a great handful of the black cherries from the basket by the door and; calling to her children to do likewise, began crushing them against his uniform and accoutrements. 'Pipe-clay that off, you thief, you villain, you wretch! You would strip your poor sick brother naked, would you, O fie, you blood-thirsty ogre! Now, what will your officers say, eh, Johnny, tell me that – won't they put you among the Invalids, the same as my poor Corny, that you won't disgrace them?'

This remarkable family then burst into a great cackle of laughter, in which Johnny Maguire himself joined as heartily as anyone.

Mrs Maguire was right about the disgrace. When we returned to the company, our officer put Maguire under arrest and returned him to the transport, such a poor spotted figure he cut amongst us. What is more, he took the mumps – which were very prevalent in the American army – from the contagion of the children with whom he struggled, and was very sick as a result.

The seaport town of Greenfield was next fired by Governor Tryon's order – I do not know upon what provocation; and we were proceeding to New London, the chief centre of the privateering trade in Connecticut, when news that the Americans were gathering in great force led us to postpone the attack until reinforcements could be fetched. We did not number three thousand men. In nine days we had caused the people of Connecticut such prodigious losses that Sir Henry Clinton was informed by his secret agents in this province that there was a movement on foot to make a separate peace with us, the inhabitants despairing of help from General Washington. However, New London was not attempted, since General Washington moved suddenly against Stoney Point and Fort Lafayette and dispossessed us of both forts by a charge-bayonet executed at night. Our forces were therefore drawn off to recover these important points, which was done.

It should be fairly said that General Washington could have effected no more than he did against us. He was starved of troops by Congress, who now evidently expected the active work of expelling us from their country to be accomplished chiefly by the French: as in previous wars the expulsion of the French had been left chiefly to us. General Washington himself expressed the fear that virtue and patriotism were extinct in America, and that, instead, 'speculation, peculation and an insatiable thirst for money' had got the better of almost every order of his fellow countrymen. This was written in despair; but the anxiety of rich and poor alike at the increasing depreciation of the paper currency and the great want of coin, must have spurred everyone to provide himself with some form of wealth that would still have value when Congress declared a bankruptcy. And so they not long afterwards did, by repudiating their paper, to the tune of nineteen shillings and sixpence in the pound.

The simple and impartial narrative of this Connecticut expedition, which I have just given, may be profitably set against the accounts given by the American writers Ramsay and Belsham. These have endeavoured with all the artifice of wilful misrepresentation so to colour the facts as to make the British name odious to humanity. In expeditions of this sort scenes naturally occur at which the feeling heart revolts; but in war the humane soldier can do no more than alleviate its horrors – he cannot prevent them entirely, especially if those whose residence unfortunately becomes the seat of war do not govern themselves prudently. Mr Ramsay strangely asserts: 'At New Haven the inhabitants were stripped of their household furniture and other moveable property. The harbour and waterside were covered with feathers discharged from open beds.' It is true that New Englanders and, indeed, all Americans, so far southward as the Carolinas, have an over-fondness for large feather beds, which the British find stifling and uneasy couches, yet no revenge was taken upon them for this peculiarity. Strange indeed that soldiers weighed down with arms, ammunition and provisions, should carry feather beds so far, merely in order to destroy them! And as for the household furniture, what were we to do with it? There was no space in our tents for wardrobes and clock-cases and the like, even had we exerted ourselves to remove them from the houses of the enemy. Such slanderous improbabilities refute themselves. I never saw anything of the kind.

Further, Mr Ramsay has the hardihood to write: 'An aged citizen, who laboured under a natural inability of speech, had his tongue cut out by one of the Royal army.' And again: 'A sucking infant was plundered of part of its clothing, while a bayonet was presented to the breast of its mother.' It is impossible for one who has been in America during a great part of the war, and actually taken part in much of the fighting, to read such gross falsehoods without being balanced between indignation and laughter. Any such wanton action as the former, proved on a British soldier, would have been punished by his officers with the greatest severity; as for the latter, the little cotton shirt that suffices an American infant in the heats of summer would be a curious booty for any but a madman.

Mr Belsham, though somewhat more cautious than Mr Ramsay, is equally off the mark. His assertion that 'all the buildings and farmhouses for two miles in extent round the town were laid in ashes', I can take upon me to contradict as a most cruel slander; and grieve that such misrepresentations can be transmitted under the pompous name of history to generations yet unborn.

Let me add that our cause was ill-served by Members of Parliament who sought to justify the burning of the towns not by a plain statement of the provocation that made such sad acts necessary, but by reference to the tomes of Puffendorf and Grotius. These two learned legal authorities had, it seems, long before declared that the burning of unfortified towns, which were the nurseries of soldiers, was consonant with the accepted rules of war. Mr Burke, for the Opposition, however, protested that our acts had exceeded all that the rights of warfare could sanction, in annihilating humanity from the face of the earth! The Prime Minister and the Attorney-General successively rose to rebuke Mr Burke for this exaggeration and falsification of fact, but Mr George Johnstone, who had been a rapacious Governor of the Floridas in the year 1763, and, more lately, a Commissioner of Peace, in company with the Earl of Carlisle, impetuously agreed with Mr Burke that a war of destruction was indeed being waged against the American people. 'No quarter should be shown to the American Congress, and if the Infernals could be let loose upon them I, for one, Mr Speaker, would approve the measure.' Governor Johnstone's foolish warmth was due to his resentment against Congress for repudiating the Saratoga Convention, and for treating him and his fellow-Commissioners with studied coolness.

On September 23rd, we were embarked at Sandy Hook, close to New

York, four thousand of us, under the command of Lieutenant-General the Earl of Cornwallis, whom I have mentioned in my previous volume as the exemplary Colonel of The Thirty-third when I was at Dublin learning the new light-infantry movements. We were told that we were bound for the West Indies, for Jamaica was threatened by the French fleet. After succouring our garrison there we would seize all the French Sugar Islands, and the Spanish possessions too, for the Spaniards had by now entered the war against us. We were glad to learn of this expedition, as providing at least a change of climate. A new draft of recruits from England had brought the fever with them, which soon swept through the city and the island, so that within six weeks six thousand men of the garrison were unfit for duty. Our officers, who always took good care of our health, saw that we disinfected our tents frequently and also supplied us with Bark; nevertheless we had many men on the sick list and a few deaths. New York was extremely subject to such fevers, chiefly on account of the dirtiness and narrowness of the streets on the East Side of the town, where houses were set as closely as possible and the riverside crowded with confused heaps of wooden stores, built upon wharfs projecting one beyond the other in every direction. Companies of negro slaves employed by the City Council used to carry through the streets, balanced on their heads, stinking buckets of night soil from the privies of the well-to-do, and empty them upon the mud of the water-fronts, where noxious vapours were bred. The hovels of the poor destitute Tories in the burned-out part of the city were also centres of infection.

Our voyage to Jamaica was cancelled when we had been but two days at sea (in very foul weather), since it had been reported that the French fleet had left the West Indies and were making again for the mainland of America. We returned on September 29th, and had two months to wait before we were re-embarked for the South.

News came that greatly grieved me. The American General Sullivan had been ordered with four thousand men to attack those settlements of the Six Nations through which I had passed two winters before, in the company of my friend Thayendanegea; the Indians, supported by some Loyalist troops, had met the General in battle at Chemung by the Susquehanna River and been entirely defeated. He had thereupon burned all their villages and towns, some of which consisted of sixty, eighty and even one hundred houses, and visited upon them a far severer destruction than we upon the settlements of Connecticut. For his men destroyed the crops of the Indians with the greatest thoroughness, even pulling up the vegetables and currant-bushes in the gardens, and killed every orchard of cherry, apple and peach, by girdling the trees. In my later travels in the back country of America I fell in with a soldier who had served in this campaign and happened to be a man of finer feelings. Said he: 'When we burned down the Indian huts, that was well enough. It seemed a just vengeance for what had been done to our own houses in the Wyoming valley. We laughed at the crackling flames. But when we came, according to orders, to cut down the corn-patches, then, I swear, my soul revolted. Who could see without tears the stalks that stood so stately with broad green leaves and gaily tasselled shooks – filled with sweet milky fluid, and flour – who could see these sacred plants bowing under our knives, to wither and rot untasted in the fields?'

The Indians, who were commanded by Thayendanegea, got safely away, but were forced that winter to move up into Canada and there rely upon General Carleton's charity. The news, as it first reached us, described the massacre by the Americans of the whole population of the Six Nations, and it may be imagined what gloomy thoughts oppressed me. From the moment that I had bidden farewell to Thayendanegea in the woods near Saratoga before the capitulation I had never for a day ceased to think of Kate Harlowe and our child, and still played with the fancy that some accident of war or the eventual signature of peace would happily reunite us. In planning my escape from the Convention Army I had even first considered whether or no I should run, not downstream to New York, but upstream past Albany – with a view to making my way through the American frontier settlements, following up the Mohawk River, and attaching myself to the Rangers under Colonel Guy Johnson, who were operating in company with the Six Nations. For I believed that Kate would still be living in the Indian town of Genesee, where Thayendanegea had reported her to be. Kate was a magnet that I had found it exceedingly hard to pull against.

The grief that the false news of the massacre engendered did not have the expected effect upon me, of driving me to drink and debauch: I was now too old a soldier to take that foolish course. On the contrary, I bent all my energies upon improving my military knowledge by the reading of books borrowed from my officers and upon making myself worthy of the regiment in which I was now fortunately enrolled, by a strict attention to my duty. Though winter here did not usually set in until the New Year, snow fell in the middle of November, with premature frosts; and very hard weather was predicted by the behaviour of the birds and beasts. It proved to be the hardest winter of two centuries; when such common wild game as deer, turkeys, squirrels and partridges were almost exterminated throughout the Northern colonies, when every privet hedge in Pennsylvania was destroyed by the frost, and when Hudson's River froze over as far down as New York City, and afforded a solid causeway of salt-water ice from shore to shore, a distance of above a mile. However, we escaped it. On the day after Christmas, 1779, the Commander-in-Chief, having received orders from Lord George Germaine in London to carry the war into the Southern provinces, sailed with us and a great part of the army to recapture Charleston, the capital city of South Carolina, which was then in the hands of the American General Lincoln. There was already a great deal of ice in New York Harbour when we sailed.

We expected to arrive at our destination by Ladies' Christmas, as we call Twelfth Night in my country, but soon were made to understand that we could not expect a continuance of the fair weather with which we set out. On December 28th, it blew a very hard gale of wind dead on the shore, from which we were distant thirty miles; we had to lie to until the next morning. The troops in our transport were very sick and in the morning the seas were still high and the fleet was scattered: one transport in the night had lost two masts. On the next day, fine weather; on the New Year's Eve, an extraordinary fog on the surface of the water – the north wind blowing, and the sea boiling under a sort of steam which never rose more than a few feet from the surface. New Year's day fine, as an augury for the year, but then suddenly another storm which blew from the north-west for no less than a week, forcing us to take down all our sail and lie to the whole while.

Our sick men grew very weak from this continual buffeting and, the hatches being battened down because of the huge seas, we could not ventilate the part where we were quartered, so that the air grew very foul. Salt pork and biscuit were never the proper medicine for sea-sickness, yet no other food was procurable. The water was cured with alum, which prevented it from rotting but was very disagreeable to the palate.

Sergeant Collins was the most active of us. When asked by what means he avoided this perpetual retching and vomiting, he gave us the old naval remedy, in rather a shamefast way: which was, to swallow a lump of greasy pork and as often as the stomach refused it, to swallow it again. At the fourth attempt the stomach being dominated, he said, by this expression of the throat's firm will, the pork was no longer bandied about between them, but decently passed on to the guts. However, not one of us cared to try this receipt, though it were as old as Noah's ark itself. I had brought two pounds of Souchong tea with me, and this was a great comfort to the sufferers while it lasted, as I laced it with rum.

There was one day's abatement of the gale on the 9th, and then it blew continuously from the west for six days more, during which we again lay to. The green water poured continually over us and carried everything away that was on deck. Many men were hurt by being flung against oak or iron by the rolling and pitching of our craft. We shipped a deal of salt water, and our supply of fresh water began to get very low in the scuttle-butts. I believe that it was in this gale that the ship foundered which carried the heavy guns of the expedition, and three or four other ships. The *Russia Merchant*, a transport carrying artillerymen, their wives and children, settled down slowly within sight of us, having sprung her timbers beyond hope of caulking. She was an old, crank vessel and should never have been commissioned for so important a service. We were unable to render any help, being pooped ourselves by the heavy sea, and all our boats and the mizzen-mast carried away. However, in spite of the tremendous seas, the *Lady Dunmore*, a privateer sloop of ours, went alongside and took off the crew and passengers. We gave her three hearty cheers for this bold action. The last boat had hardly got away when the *Russian Merchant* turned on her side and went down in a great boiling of water.

Our scattered fleet was crossed a few days later by an American fleet of twenty-six sail, come from the Dutch island of Eustacia, the greatest depot for smugglers in the Indies – the Dutch not yet having openly joined the alliance against us. The sea was then calm. The Americans took a few of our ships which had become separated from our escorting fleet and plundered others. In return, a vessel of the Royal Navy captured a schooner of theirs which had lost its rudder. The transport that we were in, the name of which I disremember, being a difficult Dutch one, was hard put to it to escape from an American schooner; but we caught a wind which they missed and so drew out of range of her guns. This was most extraordinary, for she was gaining on us, and was within a mile and a half, when suddenly she lay becalmed. Our breeze then failed too, but a new one sprang up from another quarter which we caught while she continued to be 'held in irons'. We had rigged up a jury mizzen-mast.

These trials continued until the first week of February, when having overshot South Carolina, we arrived at Tybee in Georgia, a port at the mouth of the River Savannah which separates the two provinces. Our company behaved throughout with the greatest discipline and fortitude; so that it was easy for me too to laugh in the face of danger and to appear indifferent whether we sank or swam. Much pity was expressed for the horses which we had on board, that starved for lack of forage; we were obliged to shoot six of them and the remainder did not live out the voyage. Indeed, of all the two hundred horses that we had with us, for the cavalry and artillery, not one came safe ashore.

Ours was among the last of the transports to reach Tybee, with hardly time to get water and fresh fruit aboard, especially oranges and lemons of which we stood greatly in need for the cleansing of our blood, before we sailed again. We arrived back again in the summer season, and I saw for the first time palm-trees and aloes, with other trees and plants which I knew only from the Scriptures. A heavy and delicious perfume mingled strangely with the stench of the harbour; for Georgia lies some fourteen hundred miles to the southward of Quebec, nine hundred from New York, and in the same degree of latitude as Jerusalem and the Delta of the Nile. The prodigious extent of North America is hardly realized in Europe: it equals that of the whole North Atlantic Ocean.

I should greatly have enjoyed a visit to Savannah, the principal town in Georgia, which lay a few miles up the river of the same name, but it was not to be. The small garrison of Savannah, a few weeks before, had success-fully repulsed the first combined assault of a French fleet and an American army. Following the failure, there had been recriminations, as before, between these ill-assorted allies. The French fleet had then sailed away, part to Europe, part to the West Indies; and General Lincoln, the American commander, was now wintering his troops at the polite city of Charleston, a hundred miles up the coast. We meant to catch him there, and accordingly sailed from Tybec on February 10th, to a place called North Edisto, which lay thirty miles short of the city; arriving there without further misadventure. We took part of the garrison of Savannah with us, who had suffered greatly of late from the yellow fever.

CHAPTER VIII

CHARLESTON, our object, was situated near the Ocean on a tongue of land formed by the confluence of Cooper River on the north side and Ashley River on the south: their united stream met the ocean below Sullivan's Island, where the Americans had a fort provided with heavy batteries. Between the city and the island was a harbour commodious for ships. The swelling tides of these rivers, together with pleasant sea-breezes, made Charleston more healthy than the neighbouring low country, so that invalids from the West India islands frequently came there to recuperate from fevers. However, the drinking water was frequently putrid and the sultry climate had reduced all the white people thereabouts to a bilious suet-colour and so diminished their energies that any sustained physical effort seemed impossible to them. Every white man of consequence kept a number of slaves and none would think to demean himself by performing the least action that could be performed as well by dusky hands, whether it were loading his sporting gun, combing his hair, or cutting up the meat on his trencher preparatory to eating it. Even the schoolboy going to his lessons had a little slave to carry his satchel, and the young miss who let a fan fall from her relaxed fingers to the carpet would scream for a slave rather than stoop to recover it herself. Contempt or pity was expressed by these people for the 'poor whites' who, for lack of money to buy and support a slave or two, were obliged to do menial tasks themselves.

The institution of slavery being the most striking aspect of the Southern States, I shall be excused for enlarging upon it in the course of this account. Its familiarity prevented the inhabitants of Charleston from looking upon it as in any way shameful or odious, though they professed, as American citizens, to cherish civil liberty and to assert the freedom and honour of human nature. The Charlestonians were indeed known throughout America for their hospitality, urbanity and enlightened minds; and it should be mentioned in their praise that throughout the war they continued to import books and all the new improvements of the arts from England and other countries of the old world. Charleston was the centre, especially, of the musical art in America and almost every man could scrape on a fiddle, toot on a flute, or perform pleasantly on some other instrument; and every woman sang.

On the coast this side of Ashley River were a number of low-lying islands which we must successively occupy: Edisto Island, St John's Island, St James Island. On our arrival at the village of North Edisto, the day after leaving Tybee, we landed unopposed and took possession of St John's Island, the further shores of which were bounded by Stono Creek. From this creek a winding canal called Wappo Cut led into Ashley River, directly opposite Charleston, with St James Island lying on the right hand of it. I mention these particulars because on the day after our arrival at St John's Island I was selected to go with a detachment under Major Moncrieff, our Chief Engineer, to take soundings of Stono Creek. He wished to determine whether provision boats could be taken up to our camp from the sea. This was my first adventure in the Southern States and though little of military importance happened during it, I recall the whole itinerary with a vividness of first impressions that survive untarnished when many more notable later circumstances fade altogether away.

Major Moncrieff, a talented Scotsman, when we had almost finished our task, felt the heat in our boat highly oppressive and called for a halt and refreshment. We were passing a swampy field in which a number of negro slaves, both men and women, clad only in loin-cloths, were dabbling about. They were attending to the cultivation of the young rice. Rice was the staple of this province and required very much labour. We pulled to the bank and Lieutenant Sutherland of the Engineers, who was with us, beckoned to a young negro, who came towards us. To my surprise the unfortunate creature hardly knew three words of English but jargoned in an incomprehensible gibberish – no doubt the native language of the Congo jungle from which he was stolen to be a slave.

However, a woman wearing a ragged cotton shift came to his aid and addressed Lieutenant Sutherland: 'Good day, Massa Cunnel. You want him, darra driber? Him driber sleep ober dere, under darra tree.'

'Then go wake the Driver, my good woman,' said the Lieutenant, not ill-pleased to be addressed as Colonel – 'Tell him that the Chief Engineer to the British Forces wishes to speak to his master.'

'Hilloo now, darra's a mighty hard word, Massa Cunnel, my honey, darra ole Chief Ingy-what-you-say! I tell him "British Cunnel him come: wake up, or masse vexed."'

So off she bounded and soon a young mulatto overseer, or driver, came walking his horse slowly across the ricefield. He appeared annoyed at having his noon-time sleep interrupted, but durst not show it for fear of punishment.

'Take me to your master,' Major Moncrieff ordered.

The Driver objected: 'Massa mebbe sleep. Him good massa but mighty angry man, him bery fierce be waked up.'

'I'll take the consequences,' said the Major. 'I understand that the gentlemen in these parts are most civil to strangers.'

When the Driver saw that we were determined on our visit he changed his tone: 'No, me lie to you. Massa not sleep, him right glad to welcome you, nobody neber so glad, nothing can be like.' He spoke to the slaves, threatening them with dire punishments if they idled in his absence, and then showed us where to tie up the boat and disembark. He led the way to the planter's house, which stood behind a grove of palmetto-trees, with a large barn beside it and two or three stacks of rice-straw. Before we reached it, we passed a row of tumbledown huts, about thirty of them, thatched with palmetto leaves, from which a fetid animal smell issued. Two old naked hags of negresses, with white wool on their heads, and shrivelled bosoms, peered out as we passed. They uttered cries of astonishment and admiration at our weapons and clothes.

'Dem's de meat-houses,' said the Driver, pointing. 'Massa's a consid'able warm man. Own one hun'ed good working niggers. All de urras but ole grand-mammy and ole grand-daddy, dey work in de rice swamp.'

He rode ahead to warn his master of our approach. This gentleman was named Captain Gale – every person throughout the South held a military rank of some sort, even though he had never spent but a single day with the provincial militia – and was the complete Master Planter. He appeared to us in undress – cambric shirt, canvas breeches, and a night-cap, his feet stockingless, a riding-whip in his left hand (for the correction of his slaves) which was always at the waggle. He came forward with the right hand outstretched to welcome the officers. He was neither drunk nor sober, but in a state of confused exhilaration. 'Egad, gentlemen, I am right down glad to welcome you! Upon my soul, it does my eyes good to feast them upon British regimentals again. This is a prelude, damme, to a fine show. You Britons will soon settle the hash of the damned rebels across to Charleston. Why, since they nested there I have been quite cut off from society, but for the Bennets and Mottes and M'Cordes, my neighbours. Huzza, now! What do you say to twigging a tickler of old peach to His Majesty King George's health? Heigh, Cudjo, *Cudjo*, CUDJO, you plaguey black dog, must I ever split my throat bawling to you? Bring us the old peach and three peachers instantly!'

A startled voice came from a room behind: 'Hi, Massa! Sure Cudjo always answer when he hear Massa halloa!'

Cudjo, another young mulatto, then came running up with the guilty air of one who has been caught napping. He brought with him a bottle of peach-brandy and three glasses on a tray. Captain Gale playfully cracked his whip at the fellow and called him a cursed, lazy Jack.

His Majesty's health was then duly drunk on the verandah, while I posted sentinels about the grounds; having done so, I reported to Major

Moncrieff for orders. He was good enough to suggest to his host that I would be the better off for a tickler too, remarking that I was a non-commissioned officer who had already seen considerable service in the war and been rewarded with a bounty by Sir Henry Clinton for bringing a party of escaped prisoners safely through General Washington's lines.

Captain Gale was at once all affability towards me and sent Cudjo flying for another glass. 'Well, my fine hero,' he cried, 'so you outwitted that old Virginian Fabius, did you, like a Hannibal and breached his fence? That's right, that's right! And now you'd be revenged on those damned Yankee pedlars for what they did to you? O the rogues! That's right! There's a great sight of 'em within Charleston. Show them no quarter, but give it to them handsomely! Break their backs like dogs! Cut them over the face and eyes like cats! Bang them like asses! Huzza! Britons, lay on! Were it not for my cursed loins which trouble me, I'd be with you too, I swear, staving at full butt against the sons of bitches.'

I respectfully drank the King's health in the 'old peach', which was very good liquor but with a powerful effect upon an empty belly.

Major Moncrieff spoke a few words in praise of the plantation, which Captain Gale heard with complacence; and Lieutenant Sutherland remarked that a planter's life must be pleasant enough.

'God's mercy, I have nothing to rail against, but only this damned war. It has swept the country clear of yellow boys and shining silver Carols and landed us with bushel-loads of Continental prock which crackle insult and treachery at a man the instant he takes them into his fist. Thank God, that you gentlemen have come to our rescue at last, for things were getting mighty difficult for honest men.'

He boasted about his 'black cattle', by which it seems he intended the negroes. He had six house-boys and wenches, all of them mulattoes, as best for domestic work. 'I breed 'em myself,' he said jovially, 'for, egad, then I have nobody to blame but myself for their weak points. Cudjo's mother, she was a strapping fine Gold Coast lass, a virgin, and I got her for nothing: that is, I won her from an old dried-up Frenchman of Tradd Street in Charleston, after an all-night sitting of cards. A pretty long heat that was before I wore the old Frog down, point by point, and at last the prize was mine. Cudjo favours me a little, I think – see the big nose on him and my lumpish thighs – and I had another son by the same wench, who's my groom, and a pretty smart creature too, though I do boast of him. The Driver I had by another Coaster whom I used as cook wench: she was the devil and all, for she grew jealous of Cudjo's mother and poisoned her – well, I forgave her that, ha-ha, jealousy is no bad fault in a woman – but then, damme, she got lined by a big black buck who came over with a musical party from Bennet's. So I lost patience with the jolter-headed bitch and returned her to the hoeing team. What do you think of that now, Major?'

Major Moncrieff replied, for he was accustomed to this sort of gentry, that it was an ill trick the wench played him.

'Ah, but that's not the half of it,' Captain Gale proceeded. 'She cast her brat at three months, as if to spite me, and fearing she would play me some such wry trick again, I traded her for a Virginia mare in foal to old Bennet. However, she proved a good breeder after all, and my mare lost her foal, so old Bennet had the laugh on me. Oh, to be sure, they're difficult cattle, these female blackamoors.'

'They must indeed keep you busy, night and day,' said the Lieutenant very drily.

'We dine at two o'clock, gentlemen,' Captain Gale continued, 'and I insist you'll honour us with your company, and there's good feeding for your men too – a trencher of fat pork with sweet potatoes and hearth-cakes, if that's to their taste. How say you, Sergeant?'

I replied: 'That would be very welcome, your Honour, I'm sure.'

'As for ourselves, gentlemen,' he proceeded, 'I know what our fare will be.' Here he leered archly and poked both the officers in the belly with his forefinger. 'A green goose with currant jelly and a bottle of old Madeira to wash it down, do you see? Something nice for you, do you see, Major Moncrieff, my noble son of thunder!'

I remained listening with attention to the extraordinary talk of this planter, and soon was privileged to see his white wife and daughter appear to greet the British officers. Both wore very handsome French dresses in a new fashion, and enormous poke-bonnets of blue gauze of the sort that all the better class of women affected thereabouts; they were made with a caul fitting close on the back part of the head. The front, stiffened with small pieces of cane, projected two feet or more forward above the face and was adorned with cherry-coloured ribbands.

Major Moncrieff paid the lady, and Lieutenant Sutherland paid the daughter, a few compliments in the New York style, which they swallowed as avidly as sugar-candy, simpering and casting such looks at the officers as were perfectly surprising to me. I noted that Miss Arabella, who had been born in this mansion, had contracted a negroish kind of accent and dialect. For it was the custom in the Carolinas to deliver a white child, as soon as it was born, to a negro foster-mother, so that it never tasted a drop of its mother's milk; and by constant association with negro servants a planter's daughter would carry their accent and vitiated manners with her through life.

The company now disappeared into the house and I took my leave, in order to look after the men. As I went, I thought to myself: 'These are people whom I shall never understand.' Nor was my perplexity eased when, upon discreet enquiry from one of the Motte family, a week later, I found that Captain Gale, though reputedly a 'jack of both sides', that is to say a trimmer between the loyal and revolutionary causes, was a man very

well spoken of in St John's Island. He was a considerate master to his slaves
– as one might say that a drover was considerate of his cattle in not over-
driving them or over-whacking them or stinting them in drink or forage;
and they repaid him with a dog-like loyalty, which was very touching when
I caught a glint of it in Cudjo's eyes. To his wife he was affectionate, never
'taking the timber to her' even when egregiously drunk; his breeding of
mulatto bastards she accepted very calmly as a part of the rustic economy,
and did not think it a nasty act. To his daughter he was an indulgent father,
and winked at her amours while they did not bring him into disgrace. He
had a son whom he had sent to an English college.

The Captain's manner of life, like that of most of his fellow-planters,
seems to have been as follows. He would rise about eight o'clock, drink off
a morning sling of strong apple-brandy and water, sweetened with sugar,
and then mount his blood-horse and ride round his plantation to view his
stock of human and beef cattle, returning about ten to breakfast on ham,
fried maize cakes, toast and cider. He then sauntered about the house,
playing on a flute or throwing dice, left hand against right. About noon he
drank his midday draught of old peach and water to give him an appetite
for dinner and pleasantly teased his servants and the little dark children
sprawling about on the verandah. At two he dined and thereafter slept for
three hours. Lastly, after sipping a little tea with Mrs Gale and Miss
Arabella, he began his serious work of the day, that of tippling himself into
stupefaction with apple-brandy; which achieved, his mulatto house-boys
would convey him to bed for the night. This routine he interrupted about
once a week, to attend a horse-race, a cock-fight or an auction of slaves or
cattle; and on court-days to visit the neighbouring Court House in his
capacity as magistrate. On the first of every month he took his wife and
daughter into Charleston for a taste of society, where they stayed three
days, and from whence he returned in a state of insensibility laid out on
the bottom of his carriage.

Major André, as Adjutant-General, came to visit us on February 20th,
where we bivouacked at Stono Ferry. He remarked to our commanding
officer, Lieutenant-Colonel Balfour, in my hearing: 'We must be very
careful not to flush General Lincoln's army from cover by any hasty show
of force until we can cut off his retreat. The Commander-in-Chief is very
positive on this point. He is glad now of our delay in reaching this place,
since it has given General Lincoln courage to muster all his militia and set
them to work at improving his fortifications. I wish to Heaven we could be
sure that he will not make a bolt for it.' Colonel Balfour expressed as his
opinion that: 'General Lincoln would be most unwise if he did not retreat,
when informed that more than seven thousand trained troops are come
against his five thousand half-trained, and under officers skilled in siege
warfare. Five thousand are hardly sufficient, I believe, to man such extensive works. Yet he may perhaps be tempted to stand a siege, if what our

people did at Savannah last summer, against much greater odds, touches and challenges his pride as an American.'

'Pray Heaven that he has such a pride,' said Major André.

'Well,' said Colonel Balfour, 'Sir Henry's pride is touched too. For he failed against Charleston four years ago, though that was owing to no fault of his own.'

Colonel Balfour then excusing himself and going away, I had the hardihood to address Major André and ask permission to inform him of something. He was sitting, hand at hip, on a handsome grey charger which was cropping the grass under a flowering Judas – a strange crooked tree whose red flowers burst directly from the bark and suggested the blood which poured from the traitor Judas at his hanging. He appeared deep in anxious thought. He started at the sound of my voice, but was good enough to recognise me; and encouraged me to say whatever was on my mind. I then begged pardon for interfering in matters which did not concern me, but continued: 'Your Honour may rest assured that General Clinton will hold his ground. For I heard positively from my guards at Rutland that he had been very hot against Generals Schuyler and St Clair for their abandonment of Ticonderoga Fortress when we invested it – he swore that any American who would not defend to the last shot a city entrusted to his defence deserved to be hanged without mercy. General Arnold disputing the point with him, and applauding General St Clair's decision, I am told they nearly came to blows. I overlooked to mention this item to you when you were condescending enough to call me into your parlour last September.'

He struck his brow with his knuckles. 'Why now, Sergeant Lamb, call me a fool not to have thought of that before! Ay, it's true enough, I heard of it too at the time. I am indeed infinitely obliged to you, my friend, for recalling the matter to my recollection. Now I can set Sir Henry Clinton's mind at rest. Oh, we'll bag that bold fox, I warrant.'

St David's Day led in March with the usual regimental jollity: in which we Fusiliers invited all our neighbours to join. Major André sang in our officers' mess a comical parody he had written, *Yankee Doodle's Expedition to Rhode Island*, of which I can recollect only the verse:

> In dread array their tattered crew
> Advanced with colours spread, Sir;
> Their fifes played Yankee-doodle-doo,
> King Hancock at their head, Sir.

He was loudly applauded. On being called upon for a speech he made a remarkable statement: 'My Lords and gentlemen,' he said, 'this has been a long war, but *it will be won this year*. Do not, I pray, press me for an explanation when I tell you that an American sheep-dog will soon come secretly into our fold, bringing the whole flock with him.' This obscure promise was bandied from mouth to mouth, and by some held to mean that General Washington was privately treating with General Clinton for terms. Others thought that General Charles Lee was going to 'play General Monk', and head a loyal counter-revolution. But Major André spoke with such conviction that all believed him as to the approaching end of hostilities.

Then came Easter, a prime festival season in Virginia and the Carolinas; and notwithstanding the war the inhabitants of the country about Charleston abated little of their customary ceremonies of drinking, wrestling, quarter-racing and egg-rolling. This last practice being something of a novelty I shall take the liberty of describing it. They boiled hens' eggs in log-wood, which dyed the shell a fine crimson. This colour would not rub off, yet one might with a pin scratch on the shells any figure or amatory device that struck the fancy. The favourite devices were true lovers' knots, Cupids, flowers, and pierced hearts; and the adorned egg, marked with the name of the Valentine (for Easter here had much of the fourteenth of February about it) was a sentimental gift between young people in love. The little children, being also provided by their parents with these gaudy eggs, rolled them towards one another down into a grassy hollow, so that they struck together at the bottom; and the egg whose shell was dinted became the property of him whose egg remained whole. The ultimate winner of these childish lists was named 'King Easter'. However, this Easter jollity was turned to disgust by news that Congress had repudiated their paper-money. It was recalled that in the previous September Congress had proclaimed: 'A bankrupt faithless republic would be a novelty in the political world, and would appear among respectable nations like a common prostitute among chaste matrons.' Now the rouge-pot was unblushingly applied by this chaste matron to her own cheeks. There had been gross abuse of the exchange all over the Continent: instead of creditor pursuing debtor, the position was reversed. The debtor came running with a sack-load of paper, purchased for a very little hard money, to pay off a loan or a mortgage; and the creditor could not refuse it. Many orphans and minors were similarly cheated by their guardians and trustees.

Wappo Cut was bridged and a large division of our army, crossing over it from St James Island, marched twelve miles up Ashley River. They were then ferried over to the root of that tongue of land, the tip of which was the city of Charleston. By then it was already the end of March, for Sir Henry was proceeding with great caution and careful method, making sure of his communications and supplies, seizing and fortifying all places of military importance, and building bridges over rivers and causeways over swamps. General Lincoln meanwhile had not only held his ground but even sent north for reinforcements. News of this caused general satisfaction in our ranks. We never for a moment had any doubt as to the happy issue of a general engagement, or an attempt at storm.

None the less, General Lincoln might well hope to wear down our patience, if he could keep his twenty thousand mouths well fed: for the entrenchments that he had raised since our fleet was first sighted were strong enough. They extended in the rear of the city from Ashley River across the whole tongue of land to Cooper River, a distance of one mile and a half. The first obstruction presented to our people was a broad canal filled with water; this terminated at either end in a morass, commanded by a fort with a clear held of fire along the canal. Next came *abattis* – trees buried slant-wise in the earth, their sharply lopped branches pointed outward – then a dry ditch with two rows of palisades, and lastly a chain of redoubts connected by trenches. There was also a big horn-work made of masonry in the centre of the line, which formed a sort of advanced citadel. Such were their defences against our sole approach by land; and on the waterfronts numerous strong batteries forbade the approach of ships, while stakes and other obstructions discouraged a landing from boats. Our fleet lay outside the harbour, below Sullivan's Island, but came no nearer because of the fort there, which was provided with heavy guns to dispute the passage.

A part of the army was busy as bees in a tar-barrel on the night of All Fool's Day when Sir Henry, or rather Major Moncrieff who conducted the siege as Chief Engineer, set two thousand men digging siege-works within half a mile of the American lines. Our regiment now lay at a place named Linning's, on the further bank of Ashley River immediately opposite these works, and our task was to carry over tools, wooden frames and other engineers' stores in small boats. During the night the working parties threw up two strong redoubts, each enclosing about a quarter of an acre of ground, which were not discovered by the enemy until daybreak. On the next night, they added a third redoubt sited between the two others, and for a whole week every night continued digging like beavers in the wet soil and constructing emplacements for our artillery.

On April 9th, in the early afternoon, we heard very heavy gun-fire from beyond the town and presently learned that the fleet had courageously forced the river passage, with only trifling loss, and become masters of the harbour. However, General Lincoln had sunk a number of vessels across Cooper River from Charleston, which made an impassable boom against our fleet; he also held the opposing bank of the river with three regiments of cavalry. The Americans were thus able to convey a regular supply of provisions across Cooper River into the city; and on April 10th seven hundred good Virginian troops came down the stream in small craft and joined the garrison unopposed. 'So much the better,' we thought. 'The more fish in the seine, the greater will be our haul.' We were now ourselves reinforced by three thousand troops from New York.

That same day a white flag was sent to General Lincoln summoning him to surrender his army as prisoners of war, with a promise of protection to the inhabitants' persons and property; for Sir Henry had not yet bombarded the city and did not wish to do so without fair warning. General Lincoln replied shortly that he would have quitted the city two months before had he intended to avoid battle.

So the siege was on, and our ten-inch mortars soon began dropping carcasses, or incendiary metal, into the city; which fired five or six houses and greatly alarmed the inhabitants. Besides that, we had three eight-inch howitzers at work and seventeen twenty-four-pounders, with Coehorns, Royals and other guns. They made a deal of noise. Through a spy-glass I saw a shell break against the tower of St Michael's church where the enemy had an observation-post. The fleet also assisted in this bombardment.

Another week, and our people across Ashley River had sapped forward and completed another parallel of trenches a quarter of a mile nearer the enemy. Meanwhile our cavalry, having found horses to replace those lost, by a forced sale from the planters of Port Royal near Savannah, had crossed Cooper River thirty miles upstream and cut to pieces the whole American cavalry division posted there. Infantry followed them, securing all the posts on the further banks, so that now the net was closed. Charleston was invested from every side.

On April 21st, General Lincoln sent a white flag to our lines and called for a truce. He proposed to march out with his garrison, drums playing and colours flying, and to take all his arms and ammunition too. Sir Henry must undertake not to pursue this column for ten days, and the few American ships anchored under cover of the batteries must be allowed to put out to sea equally unmolested. This offer was of course refused, as based upon a comical misreading of the true situation.

On with the siege again! A third parallel was now advanced close to the enemy's moat, which was bled at the northern, or Cooper River end, by a ditch driven forward into it. The moat was dry in two days: and a company of German Jaegers, or sharpshooters, used it for cover to gall with close rifle-fire the American sentinels in the trenches. Our losses by enemy fire were now about seven or eight a day. On May 8th, some batteries of guns being advanced within a hundred yards of the garrison, Sir Henry, from motives of humanity, offered the same terms as before. But General Lincoln still played his hand as if it were richer in tricks than we knew it to be. He returned a haughty answer and there was a great deal of defiant huzzaing heard and a violent cannonade from every gun that they could fire, seemingly in a drunken frenzy, but without any loss to us. It was true that when the hot weather came our army might well lose many thousands of men from fever; and that the French might be expected soon to attempt to raise the siege. But Sir Henry was aware that no more than one week's supply of fresh provisions remained in the city, and that the daily ration of maize was reduced to six ounces for every person. He knew too, by spies in Congress, that no plans of combined operations between the French expedition and General Washington's armies were to be concerted until the former arrived in American waters. He therefore ordered the cannonade to continue.

The first shot sent was a shell filled not with explosive powder but with rice and molasses, as an indication that we were aware of their shortage of food. This shell was returned half an hour later with a message chalked upon it: 'Intended for the 71st Regiment and their brother Scots.' It then contained sulphur and hog's lard. This laborious joke referred no doubt to the famous Scottish itch, caused by the overheating of Caledonian blood with too simple a diet of oatmeal. The lard was for external use as an emollient and the sulphur as an internal purificant. The Scots were among the most loyal subjects of King George, and those settled in the Carolinas had not budged from their principles either. After this raillery the earnest shot and shell began to fly again.

Our people sapped closer still and preparations for a general assault were made. Yet, after all, it did not come to a storm, for citizens and militia very soon forced General Lincoln to surrender; the original terms being still generously held out to them. The capitulation took place on May 12th. The garrison were allowed some of the honours of war: for example, all officers were to keep their swords and pistols, and their baggage was to remain unsearched. The troops in general were to march out of the town, their arms clubbed, not at the shoulder, and abandon them by the canal. Their drums were not given the honour of beating a British or German march – though they might play *Yankee Doodle* if they pleased – nor might their colours be unfurled from the casings. The regular troops and seamen were then to become prisoners of war; the militia to disperse to their homes on parole and, while they kept the same, to continue safe in their lives and properties; other able-bodied citizens to be treated in the same manner.

Out they all came at two o'clock in the afternoon of the 12th, to be disarmed: five thousand, six hundred of them, with seven generals, two hundred other officers, and a thousand seamen. The Americans never pile up their arms, but lay them upon wooden racks, or, more generally, ground them; which was now done. We were also yielded four hundred guns, quantities of ammunition, five stout warships and a vast amount of public stores. The regular troops who took over the city (the Loyalists not being trusted to enter, lest they should rob and insult their fellow-countrymen) behaved very discreetly and without exultation. There was satisfaction among us all to know that, with this surrender of the whole American Southern army, at a cost to ourselves of only two hundred and fifty killed and wounded, about the same as theirs, an enormous extent of country had been restored to the Crown. It had been hoped among the rank and file that the order for storm would be given, which would have meant the wild intoxication of battle and, by ancient usage, liberty to plunder when the city was taken. But I, for one, was glad that it had not come to this. I had seen enough of blood and detested the notion of plunder, which evokes from the breast of man all that is most brutal and odious.

This, by the bye, was the first instance in which the Americans had ventured to defend a town against regular troops; and the result demonstrated General Washington's wisdom in advising against such an attempt. It is, however, just to remark that Charleston was the only considerable city in the Southern part of the Confederacy, and worth preserving by every possible exertion; and that near ten thousand Americans were fast marching to its relief. Some turned back upon hearing news of the capitulation; others were caught and routed by our cavalry. A large French fleet, convoying six thousand soldiers in transports, was also on the way; but, hearing the news at Bermuda, sailed instead against our Northern forces.

CHAPTER IX

SIR HENRY CLINTON returned to New York with most of the army, the French fleet being soon expected in Northern waters. He left behind four thousand men under the Earl of Cornwallis; among whom were the Royal Welch Fusiliers, then numbering about five hundred men. Before he sailed, he issued a proclamation, freeing from their parole all prisoners except regular soldiers; but declared at the same time that any person who refused allegiance to King George would be considered a rebel. He promised the Carolinians reinstatement in their ancient rights and immunities, and exemption from all taxes except those imposed by their own provincial government. Lord Cornwallis was instructed to keep his hold on the province at all events, and to encourage or oblige its able-bodied men to form a militia to assist him in this task.

South Carolina was inhabited by a great variety of peoples. Since its foundation a hundred years before by a small number of English settlers, it had successively received French, Swiss, Germans, Dutch, Scottish and Irish immigrants, all of the Protestant faith. To them had recently been added fortune-seekers from Pennsylvania and Virginia. These races did not readily mix, but formed separate settlements on the several broad rivers, or their numerous tributaries, which watered the country. Each race had its own political convictions. There were seven main classes of opinion: viz. staunch Whigs, timid Whigs, Whigs, jacks of both sides, Tories, moderate Tories, and furious Tories.

The hot climate of the South encouraged the passions, so that crimes of violence were extraordinarily frequent, by comparison with the settled parts of the Northern States. In the North, in time of peace at least, no man ever troubled to take a gun with him on any excursion except in hope of game, and did not even bar his door at night. In the South, robberies on the road, burglaries by night, and perpetual family feuds were the general rule. A man who went even to his place of worship without a loaded pistol in his belt would be considered a fool. Drunkenness was universal and the morning slings and midday draughts of strong grog were rightly admitted by the people themselves as the chief curse of their country; though the great sultry heat was advanced as sufficient excuse for the error. It can therefore readily be understood why the merciless, cruel deeds that the rival partisans of King and Congress did to one another were in this torrid zone often beyond description in print.

On the whole, the white people of the Carolinas, and of the South in general, formed two classes: the rich and the poor. The poor were not (as is usual in other climes) supported by the rich, since the rich owned slaves whose labour was cheaper and whose black and oily skins tatted them better to withstand the climate than did that of the poor whites. The rich engrossing all the land and all the trade, the poor whites grew still poorer and more low-spirited. Enough food to live upon was easily come by in the South, where sixpence would buy rice for a month, fruit abounded and every creek was populous with fish – why, that noblest fish of all, the sturgeon, who in England is accounted royal and whenever caught must be rendered to the King's household as a right, him the negroes and poor whites captured easily and often, for their own use, as he took his midday sleep in the muddy waters of the great rivers. This 'white trash', as the poor whites were called, seldom got money and what little they did get they laid out in apple or peach brandy. A more indolent, vicious and uncivilized race of men I never met, yet they would boast themselves as the Lords of Creation when speaking of the negroes. It was a great misfortune that so many of them attached themselves to our forces, in hopes of plunder, and with their cries of 'God Save the King' as they robbed, burned and ravished, disgraced our own good name.

The Royal Welch Fusiliers were ordered to Camden. This small township lay one hundred miles inland from Charleston, but not two hundred feet above the level of the ocean, and in a very hot, damp situation near the banks of the Catawba River which ran between swamps. These swamps abounded with juniper and cypress; live oaks, bearded with lichen; and a long rich grass which fattened the cattle driven into it. Parts of these swamps were absolutely impervious to travellers because of close tangled thickets, the chosen lurking-places of foxes and racoons. Other parts were quaking bog or mere morass filled with strange creatures, horny or slimy, and gave off a sickly, putrescent smell, which breathed of fever.

Our men were warned by the Surgeon to avoid water that was not cleansed with a small addition of spirits. Nor should they eat any fruit, such as the luscious pineapple, or the golden persimmon that puckered the mouth, if it were still warm with the sun; else these would surely give the eater colic. We were also warned against eating fresh pork in these hot months, and some who disobeyed died of poisoning. Moses was a wise lawgiver in forbidding pork to the Jews in sultry Palestine. We acquired a taste for the great green water-melon with its pink flesh and black seed. We used, overnight, to pour a gill of rum into a hole bored at one end, which became absorbed and deliciously incorporated in the fruit by breakfast time.

Life in tents was excessively hot and it was not until the summer was well advanced that materials were brought us for making huts. Our drills we performed in the early morning and we were often taken for route-marches at night; partly in order to accustom us to finding our way through difficult country in the dark, but partly to shake the heavy humours out of our blood. In spite of every such precaution against fever, and the constant taking of Bark, we lost a number of men, though not so many as the other regiments. If any continuous labour was required of us by day, we sweated so profusely that we became quite faint. For this we found a remedy in adding a little salt to our drink, which restored what had been lost by sweating. The cattle and hogs of the Dutch plantation near us used the same remedy. They would come out from the swamp and down to the quay where our barrels of salted provisions were landed; crowding around them to lick off the brine. By their greediness they made it very difficult for us to roll the barrels up to the encampment. Their need of salt was so great that I once saw a great old hog come up to a sweating mare, tied to a post by an officer's marquee, and rearing up on his hind legs greedily lick her neck, flanks and legs.

A good deal of maize was grown hereabouts. The slaves who tended the crops of this plantation went stark naked and seemed a most discontented cattle, compared with Captain Gale's property. I heard that in the West India Islands there was a descending gradation in the humanity severally shown by the different European races, and that the same rule generally applied on the American continent. The most indulgent were the Spaniards; the next most indulgent were the French; the English were not so kind; but the most severe and merciless of all were the Dutch. It was strange that this was the same order into which the political governments then fell, in descending gradation of absoluteness – from the sacred autocracy of Spain to the obstinate republicanism of the Dutch. But that 'Republicans are always the worst masters' is an old saying, and a good argument (if any were needed) in favour of Royalty.

The poor negroes here were over-worked and under-fed in a manner that would have been considered shameful had they been horned cattle. They were called up at daybreak, and herded out immediately into the corn field. There they laboured without any intermission until noon, when half an hour was allowed them for their meal, which invariably consisted of maize-flour made into coarse cakes and baked on their working hoes. To this was added a little brine washed from the salted herrings which the Dutch household ate. At dusk they returned, after labouring all the remaining hours of daylight, and to keep them out of mischief were given a large quantity of Indian corn to husk. If they did not complete their allotted task, they were tied up in the morning and ruthlessly lashed by their drivers. The hours for sleep were seven, nor was the least rest or refreshment allowed them on Sundays or holidays. They slept on the bare ground. If any negro tried to escape into the swamp he was flogged nearly to death when apprehended; and after, if it was his second attempt, he was hanged in sight of his fellows. A negro who dared to raise his hand against a white man, even in defence against barbarity and outrage, was sentenced by the Law to have the whole limb lopped off. However, this was seldom done, because it was more profitable merely to give the fellow as many lashes as his constitution would stand, and then sell him to another master. Our proximity to this barbarous plantation was very disagreeable to us, and a party of sergeants privately warned the driver that if he did not at once mitigate his severity towards 'the cattle', his own back would be scarred.

The situation of these poor wretches was very different from that of the swarm of slaves, the property of revolutionaries, who had joined themselves to us during our march from Charleston. On our approach they had thought themselves absolved from all respect to their masters, and quit of their servitude. The pity that we felt for them, and also the great use to which we could put them as labourers, prevented us from undeceiving them: they might live upon the scraps that fell from our tables, and welcome. They made very good servants and I employed one myself, by name Jonah, who had been 'raised' in Virginia and was very expert at fishing and at racoon-hunting in the swamps. These emancipated slaves at first lived a luxurious life with us in the matter of high feeding and short hours. Afterwards they were industriously employed, when orders came to build a magazine near our camp and to unload, from the boats that came up from Charleston, large stores of rum, ammunition, salt provisions, &c. They soon learned to swear – a luxury denied to negroes in servitude – to gamble with dice, and to sing Dr Watts' hymns in chorus, which they performed with surprising tunefulness and devotion, though knowing nothing of the Christian religion.

Our retention of these negroes, who became greatly attached to us, was characterized by the settlers of the Catawba as sheer robbery; they said that we also encouraged desertion and neglect of work among their own slaves. Many thousands of negroes, indeed, were now camp-followers of the various detachments of the Royal army. In order therefore to conciliate the inhabitants, all slaves whose owners were not in arms against us were, if claimed, sent back to their bonds. Thus I soon lost my Jonah, whose freedom unfortunately I could not afford to purchase at the eighty guineas which was his declared value. He was in a lamentable state of mind when informed that he must return to his master, who, he said, was a drunken old wretch and would flog him nearly to death. However, upon my interceding with some of my officers and describing Jonah's excellent qualities, they agreed to purchase him jointly as a servant for their Mess. When I informed Jonah that he was promoted, from a mere sergeant's orderly, to being the slave of two captains and three lieutenants, he first fell at my feet and nearly overset me with his embraces; and then capered about, shouting in an ecstasy all the oaths and hymns that he knew, like a poll-parrot before visitors.

Despite the continual oppressive heat, which seldom broke in a thunder-storm, I was greatly interested in the curiosities of the country. Early in the summer, enormous quantities of fireflies danced about the Camp and its environs, from dusk to dawn at a height of a few feet above the earth. I had seen them before in the North, but never to such entrancing effect. A dozen of them enclosed in a small phial would provide enough light to read even small print by; and a hundred thousand of them, all darting and dipping at once give out an illumination which was perfectly surprising and outshone any artificial fireworks that I have ever witnessed. The hissing rise and fall of the towering rocket was missing to this display, but the perfect silence of the interlacing glints was both beautiful and awesome. The light emitted by any single insect was continuous, but shut off at will from swoop to swoop. As with the glow-worm, the light of the firefly is used for purposes of courtship: it shines no more as the summer advances. Fireflies could be very annoying to sentries and travellers by night, dazzling and distracting their gaze.

I also saw the humming-bird, the smallest and most beautiful bird in all Creation. It appeared to be jewelled rather than feathered, and fed only on honey. This it extracted from flowers with its long beak, hovering over them like a humble-bee, which in size it did not exceed. The smallest gun-shot would blow the humming-bird to bits; so those who would satisfy their curiosity with a sight of his corpse must put a bladder of water into their musket, which knocked him dead without injury to the feathers. When the honey season was over he hibernated, but whether his lurking-place was earth, wood or water nobody could inform me. I recollect also a Southern thrush, of twice the size of our European bird, that sang at night very finely; and a carrion-bird called the turkey-buzzard whom the natives shot for the sake of his feet – these when dissolved into an oil were very salutary in the sciatica and for easing rheumatic aches and pains.

There were noble fish in the Catawba River, and excellent eels in the smaller creeks. In the swamp crept the terrapin, a small sort of turtle which makes the best-tasting soup in the world – unless that were the oyster soup which we enjoyed at Harlem near New York from the fine oyster-beds contiguous. But I must mention two very troublesome insects to set against these other beautiful and beneficial creatures: viz. the wood-tick and the seed-tick. The wood-tick was a sort of bug which infested the bushes of the swamp. He drank blood through his proboscis like a vampire and swelled to a huge size before dropping off. He fastened especially upon the cattle. The seed-tick, also called the chigger, was much worse; he lurked in the long grass and attacked the feet and ankles. He was small enough to creep into the pores of the skin, where he would throw up blisters constantly for days on end. To rub the affected part was very dangerous, because the inflammation sometimes mortified. I myself had three such blisters, very painful, on my right ankle, which I got from going out injudiciously in grass one early morning without my cloth gaiters. I was advised to avoid duty for a day or two and meanwhile to cure my foot in tobacco smoke, like a herring in a chimney, in order to fumigate the pores and kill the vermin. This had the desired effect.

The continuance of the war had become most tedious; and its unpopularity in the army in America, as well as among the merchants and manufacturers at home, was reflected in the price of officers' commissions which had descended to less than one quarter of their peace-time value. In the officers' mess the toast was no longer drunk: 'A glorious war and a long one.' It was now: 'A speedy accommodation of our present unnatural differences.' There was much talk of a truce – the Empress Catherine of Russia was offering to act in the capacity of mediatrix. It was considered evident that the whole of America could not be conquered while Britain had also to face, single-handed, the united navies and armies of France and Spain; and the Ministry was therefore willing to compound, if King George would consent, by granting the Northern States their independence while we retained our conquests in the South. The Americans feared that they would be forced to accept these terms if we continued to hold Charleston: for present possession in all legal disputes, private or public, is a title very difficult to shake. The Revolution was now languishing for lack of money, and of soldiers willing to engage themselves for long periods; and the news of Charleston had made a very sharp impression on the common people. It was therefore resolved by Congress to restore public confidence by a daring use of their fast-dwindling forces. A pretended invasion of Canada would be undertaken, in order to draw off our New York troops, and then an expedition would strike southward at our small army with as much speed as was commensurate with safety.

General Washington recommended Major-General Nathaniel Greene, the American Quartermaster-General, to command this expedition; but General Horatio Gates, whose laurels were still green from Saratoga, impressed upon Congress that only himself was fit for the command, and that his popularity with the troops was such that they would mutiny were any other leader appointed. General Washington's recommendation was overruled and in July of that year, 1780, General Gates came marching towards us with as many regular troops as General Washington could spare from his small army, and whatever militia he could pick up by the way.

It will be remembered that Captain Gale had sneered at General Washington as an 'old Fabius', Fabius being the name of a Roman general who by avoiding an engagement with the Carthaginian invaders had restored the broken fortunes of Rome. General Washington's Fabian policy was equally derided by General Gates who, as it was expressed, had lately 'been brought forward on the military turf by his backers in Congress and run for the generalissimoship'.

It is reported that, on his way from Philadelphia, General Gates passed through Frederick Town in Maryland, where he fell in with his fellow-General, Charles Lee.

'Where are you going?' asked Lee.

'Why, to take Cornwallis,' replied Gates.

'I am afraid,' said Lee, 'that you will find him a tough steak to chew.'

'Tough, sir!' cried Gates. 'Tough, is it? Then, by Heavens, I'll tender him. I'll make *piloo* of him, Sir, and eat him alive.'

General Lee bawled after Gates as he rode off: 'Take care, General Horatio Gates! Take care, lest your Northern laurels degenerate into Southern willows.'

The army that Gates now commanded had been assembled for some weeks at Hillsborough in North Carolina. The regulars were regiments from the States of Maryland and Delaware; the militia had been recruited in North Carolina, and the army by the later addition of a Virginian regiment was brought up to about four thousand. After issuing a proclamation inviting the patriots of Carolina to 'vindicate the rights of America', and holding out an amnesty to all those who had been forced 'by the ruffian hand of conquest' to give their paroles, he hastened against us.

This was our position. South Carolina, though apparently pacified, was in a state of extreme unrest. Besides the matter I have mentioned, of the negroes who had run off to follow the drum, there was great dissatisfaction caused by the pressing of the planters' horses, for the use of our cavalry and transport: they feared that they would not be paid sufficient compensation, if any. Moreover, enormous stocks of rice, indigo, tobacco and other riches of the province were seized from the houses of absentee Whigs and sold to Loyalists at below the market price. The submission made by the people was therefore only nominal, and when a levy was raised among the young unmarried men, who alone were required to serve, it soon appeared that they had no notion of taking up arms in support of their King; nor could they be persuaded by any means to become good soldiers. To hold the vast territories of South Carolina and Georgia we had no more than four thousand dependable troops, of whom near a thousand were now sick of fever.

Thus, because of the detachments that had to be left to garrison Charleston and other places of importance, and to guard our lines of communication, we could only bring against the Americans about seven hundred regular troops, and twelve hundred volunteers and militia. Lord Cornwallis, when he came up from Charleston to command us in person, found our striking forces concentrated in the neighbourhood of Camden. He might have retired behind the Charleston lines, but this course did not commend itself to him. We had sick at Camden in the hospital, and the magazine contained powder and provisions that we could not afford to abandon. A retreat also would encourage the South Carolina militia to renounce their new allegiance and to be revenged for their surrender at Charleston. Indeed, two regiments had already mutinied and carried some of our sick away into North Carolina.

Upon arriving at the borders of North Carolina, General Gates was advised that the longer of the two possible routes which he could take in his advance against us was the better: this was a westerly circuit by Charlotte and Salisbury through fertile country inhabited by revolution-aries. He chose instead to come direct at us through a country of sandy hills and what were called pine-barrens, interspersed with swamps.

A prisoner from his army later told me: 'It was a country poor enough to have starved a forlorn-hope of caterpillars. Hearts alive, what hope had we at this August season when the old corn-crop was gone and the new not yet in? Especially in a miserable piney-wood Tory desert, where even in peace-time many a family must starve, unless they can hit lucky – knock down a squirrel from the pines or pick up a terrapin from the swamp! We chewed the corn still green, stripped from the thin patches that we came across, and sinned against our bellies with unripe peaches. A few half-starved Tory cattle, met in the woods, we butchered; and one day my mess made a soup of an old bitch fox and the powder we kept for our queues. On the night before we came against you we were still very hungry; and, for want of rum, General Gates ladled us out molasses. That may be good enough fare for a Yankee, but it turns any honest Southern stomach inside out; by jing, many of us were mighty sick that night and fell out along the road by companies!'

On August 13th, the American army reached Rugeley's Mills, about fifteen miles to our north. This was a place that the Royal Welch Fusiliers knew very well; for we had been sent forward there a few days previously, but soon withdrawn to Camden lest we be overwhelmed. On August 15th, at ten o'clock at night the order was given us to march against General Gates and surprise him at dawn in his encampment, if he were still there – for Lord Cornwallis had information that at this very hour General Gates was to march against Camden and surprise us at dawn in our own encamp-ment. We set off in the most profound silence, with orders not to sing, whistle or raise our voices above a whisper. But the loud undisciplined noises of night birds and insects from the swamps would have made the most animated discourse inaudible at twenty paces. At midnight we came to a river called Saunders' Creek, and this occasioned some delay, the front of the column waiting for the rear to catch up. There was a scouting party ahead, of Tarleton's Greens, a volunteer force of mixed cavalry and infantry, very bold and bloodthirsty men. Their uniforms were light-green, they wore waistcoats without skirts, and black cuffs and capes, and were armed with one sabre and one pistol apiece. The spare pistol-holsters were receptacles for their bread and cheese. Behind them came a half-battalion of regular light infantry, then ourselves, then The Thirty-Third (Lord Cornwallis' own regiment) and then the rest of the army. About two in the morning, when we had made some nine miles, halting every now and then to await reports from our scouts, we heard a brisk sound of firing ahead of us. We were soon informed by a Green, who galloped back, that his scouting party had met enemy cavalry, and had instantly charged them. The enemy were in greater force, however, than the Greens had bargained for, and an officer being wounded they broke off the skirmish.

We were now ordered to shake out from our column and form a line across the road; which we did, though it was very dark, with no moon that I remember. Soon we perceived the dim forms of the enemy advancing, also in line, and opened platoon fire. For about a quarter of an hour there was a brisk exchange of volleys; but since neither side knew what was in opposition, or would venture to charge until the main body of its own army could form up in support, this fire soon ceased. General Cornwallis was delighted to find that the position in which we now found ourselves was most favourable, being narrowed by swamps on either hand, which prevented us from being outflanked by the superior numbers of the enemy. Had we started our march but an hour later, General Gates would have been able to seize a most advantageous position near Saunders' Creek; but we had forestalled him.

We rested on our arms all night. The ground was sandy, with scrub and a few very straggling trees. The nearest human dwelling was a wretched farm about a mile away.

I was the youngest sergeant in the Regiment and the proud honour therefore devolved upon me of carrying one standard of the Regimental Colours. The Goat did not come with us into action, for he had been bled so badly by the wood-ticks that he could hardly stand, much less march fifteen miles. My position was in the middle of the right wing, which consisted of ourselves, the Light Infantry, and The Thirty-Third. In the centre were our artillery – but only light pieces, two six-pounders and two three-pounders. The left wing, commanded by young Lord Rawdon (accounted as at once the ugliest man in Europe and the bravest), consisted of the infantry of the Greens; five hundred undependable American Loyalists; and The Volunteers of Ireland, a regiment which had been raised at Philadelphia during our occupation. These compatriots of mine were almost all deserters from the American army. Many of them, Dublin men, had been customers at my father's shop and knew me as a child. Colonel Ferguson, their commander, was troubled one day that a volunteer had been caught in the act of deserting back to the enemy; he did not wish to order a flogging and therefore left the man's fate to be adjudged by his comrades – they tucked him up at once from the nearest tree. In reserve stood the Seventy-First Highlanders and the cavalry of the Greens, with two more six-pounders.

Colonel Balfour, by the bye, was not with us, being now Governor of Charleston, and the Regiment was therefore commanded by Captain Forbes Champagné, our senior captain. Being the eldest regiment we held the right of the line, according to tradition.

As soon as daylight appeared we saw the enemy drawn up in two lines, very close to us. There was a dead calm, with a little haziness in the air. Opposite us were the Virginian militia who had joined the enemy only the day before; with the North Carolina militia posted next to them, facing The Thirty-Third who were on our left. We recognized these corps by their facings. Only a few random shots had been exchanged when General Gates, dissatisfied with the position of the militia, ordered them to re-form on a more extensive front. This movement was intended to prelude an assault, but Lord Cornwallis, observing what General Gates was about, decided 'to catch him on one foot', as a boxer would say, and desired Lieutenant-Colonel Webster of The Thirty-Third, who led the right wing, to advance forthwith. The order was sung out: 'Make ready, present, fire!' and the whole line crashed out in a volley which filled the air with acrid smoke. The enemy replied in a ragged manner; then came 'Charge bayonets!' and all around me, slap! every Fusilier's hand came smartly against the sling of his musket as if it were a parade for the King's birthday. The officers, pale and resolute, drew their hangers and with a huzza we went forward at a run in perfect alignment. There was not enough air to shake out the silken folds of the standard in display of Rising Sun, Red Dragon, White Horse and Three Feathers, but I wagged the staff as I ran. The heaviness of the air also prevented the smoke from rising; and, the action becoming general all along the line, so thick a darkness overspread the field that it was impossible to see the effect of the fire on either side. The Virginian militia, uncertain whether to continue the extending movement which had been ordered them, or whether to stand their ground, or whether to advance immediately against us, were thrown into total confusion. First some, and then all, ran back to the protection of their second line; but the North Carolina militiamen, who were posted there, caught contagion and ran too. Another North Carolina regiment, however, opposed to The Thirty-Third, behaved very well and fought to their last cartridge; for they had an excellent commanding officer, a General Gregory. Men of all races, I believe, are equally brave in battle if led by dependable and beloved officers.

The smoke became so dense that we could not see what we were about, but the British huzza and the 'Southern yell' of the Americans – which they had adopted, I think, from their neighbours, the Cherokee Indians – gave us an indication of who was friend and who foe. We did not pause to pursue the militia, but wheeled sharply to the left and with charge-bayonet

and volley engaged the flank of the Maryland regiment as it came up from
the rear.

The action continued for three-quarters of an hour, being very obstinate in the centre, where The Thirty-Third and The Volunteers of Ireland
lost heavily from artillery and small-arms fire. At last the cavalry of
Tarleton's Greens came around under cover of the smoke and charged
with their sabres. I had never before witnessed a cavalry charge and its
excitement intoxicated me, as I saw through the smoke the green uniforms
sweep down, with sabres slashing and hacking, on the buff and blue ranks
of the Continentals. Only remarkably well-trained and well-posted
infantry can accept a cavalry charge; these were resolute enough men, but
not cavalry-proof. They began to break.

Soon it was all over, though their right wing, unaware that the game
was already lost, were making a brave push against the Loyalist corps
opposed to them. The American commander here was Major-General
Baron de Kale, a German in the French service, whose ruddy youthful
looks made him seem twenty years younger than the sixty-three which
were his true age. He fell with eleven bayonet wounds in him, after having
killed one or two of our people with his sword; and Lord Cornwallis afterwards buried him, very properly, with all the honours of war.

About one hundred Americans escaped in a compact body by wading
through a swamp on our left, and got clear away. The remainder fled indiscriminately down the Rugeley road, and were pursued about twenty miles
by the cavalry of The Greens; the road was covered with abandoned arms
and baggage. Almost all the officers overtaken had lost their commands.
One thousand Americans surrendered, six hundred lay dead, three
hundred severely wounded were conveyed to our hospital at Camden.
They lost the whole of their artillery (eight brass held-pieces), all their
ammunition, all their baggage, all their two hundred wagons; and seventy
officers, killed, wounded or prisoners.

The Regiment's losses were not heavy, being only six killed and seventeen wounded, of the two hundred and ninety to which sickness and skirmishing had now reduced our five hundred. Captain Drury, a valuable
officer of ours, who was lying under a tree wounded in the leg, was hotly
reproached by a party of twenty prisoners, two of them sergeants, because
he ordered them back to the rear under the command of the slave Jonah.
They told him that it was a monstrous indignity for white men to be left
to the tender mercies of 'a rascal blackamoor', who threatened, if they
attempted to escape, to 'blow them through'. Said the Captain, pretty
testily, for his wound irked him: 'My good fellows, I cannot spare soldiers
for the service. And let me tell you: your Massachusetts allies boast in their
newspapers that my friend, Major Pitcairne of the Marines, was shot dead
at Bunker's Hill by a negro, Peter Salem. If negroes are qualified to shoot
British officers, God damn it, they are equally capable to act as escort to

American rank and file. If you prefer, however, to be shot out of hand, that can be arranged too, by Heaven!' However, on the whole, the prisoners behaved with politeness and gave no trouble.

Jonah was very scornful of the defeated Americans. He said: 'It am high time for dem damned rebels to turn deir bayonets into pitchforks, den dey go foddering de beeves.' For this sentiment I severely reproved him.

It was nearly three years since Mad Johnny Maguire and I had fought side by side against General Gates' men. Maguire came up to me after the fight, his face and regimental well grimed with gunpowder, as ours all were. With that relaxation of decorum allowed, among the Fusiliers, only after a conspicuous victory or on St David's Night, he cried: 'By my soul, Gerry my jewel, we are at last revenged for Saratoga. Now I wonder what in the holy name of God has become of that spectacled scoundrel Gates? I was looking for him in the smoke with my bayonet, like Diogenes with his lantern, whoever that same busy Diogenes may have been. But the Devil a sight of him did I get.'

Says I: 'Well, Johnny, you know I could never forgive General Gates for charging our officers and ourselves, after we were in his power, with depredations that never existed but in his own imagination. Ay, where is he? I haven't heard that he's been taken, or his body found among the slain.'

General Gates had attempted, as he afterwards explained to Congress, to rally the flying militiamen. Indeed, he was heard to vociferate: 'I will bring the rascals back into line.' He was then 'swept away by the torrent of fugitives'. However, he soon shook himself free of them. He was mounted on a race-horse of some reputation, which took him sixty miles before it foundered. It is said that he killed two more horses of lesser value before he reached Hillsborough in North Carolina, from whence he had started. An old letter, by the bye, was lately published, written from General Gates to General Lee, which he concluded with the following emphatic and patriotic lines:

> 'On this condition would I build my fame,
> And emulate the Greek and Roman name;
> Think Freedom's rights bought cheaply with my blood,
> And die with pleasure for my Country's good!'

Congress never trusted General Gates with an army again, and presently noticed him officially to resign his command. He was greatly chagrined that, for one little defeat, his victory at Saratoga trumpeted across the whole of America, and indeed the world, had been blotted from the page of glory and made as if it had never been. He turned away to his private affairs, in disgust with political and party distractions. But now his former admirers and well-wishers suddenly struck their heads in surprise, and 'Heigh!' they cried, 'why did we never think of it? – in that whole

Northern campaign he contrived never once to come under fire. And did
he not shirk taking part in the famous battle of Trenton when invited to do
so by General Washington?' General Benedict Arnold, now commanding
the chief fortress in America, West Point on Hudson's River, was at last
remembered by these feather-headed critics as the true victor of Saratoga.
Yet their praise came too late, and was soon stifled; as will appear.

I was kept very busy for some days after this battle, being appointed
temporary surgeon to the Regiment; a duty for the performance of which
I earned my officers' thanks.

CHAPTER X

OUR VICTORY at Camden opened the way for a British invasion of North Carolina; and in September 1780, so soon as sufficient provisions arrived, we were marched up the Catawba River to Charlotte, which lies in that province. Movement was the best cure, Lord Cornwallis thought, for the increasing sickness of the army, which had reduced its strength to an alarming extent. Charlotte, which yielded after a slight skirmish, was a place of importance to us on account of its many flour-mills and several large, well-cultivated farms, rich in cattle. The town itself consisted of but two streets, dominated at their intersection by a large brick building, Court House above and market-house below.

While we were there, we were well enough fed: at one mill alone, Colonel Polk's, twenty-five tons of flour were seized and a quantity of wheat. Fresh beef there was in plenty, for the woods abounded with grass both in summer and winter and black cattle ran wild in them; but the grass being coarse they were exceedingly lean. These cattle were in ordinary times sold to drovers from Pennsylvania at a low price; who took them back to fatten on the rich pastures of the Delaware. The oxen being in general mere hide and bones, unfit to kill, we found it our unpleasant necessity to kill milch-cows, and even cows in calf. We butchered upon an average one hundred head a day. This slaughter caused great indignation among the inhabitants, who were among the most revolutionary people in the whole Southern States. Several messengers with despatches for the Commander-in-Chief were murdered on the road, and our foraging parties were frequently fired upon by marksmen lurking behind trees.

The country about was covered with close, thick woods. The roads were narrow and crossed in every direction; and the outlying plantations small and ill-cultivated. There may have been a few Loyalists in this district, but the vigilance and animosity of the revolutionaries checked them, and we could not rely upon any information that came to us of the movements of the enemy. For though their field force had been destroyed, the war was by no means at an end. Three bold and intelligent partisan leaders, Sumpter, Marion and Horry, with a few score of active horsemen, armed with sabres hammered from mill-saws and well mounted, kept the flame of rebellion alight. These harried our communications, struck at our isolated posts; they had no base or garrison town against which we could strike, but seemed to be both nowhere and everywhere. They were brave men and lived very frugally upon hoe-cake and sweet-potatoes baked in the embers. Colonel Tarleton with his Greens was always on their track, but the country people in general, to whom these guerrillas seemed heroes, gave them the assistance that they denied our people. A party of them even dared to attack Polk's Mill, where my company happened to be on piques duty under Lieutenant Guyon. Our sentinels were vigilant. We drove them off with fire from a loopholed building near by.

In the baggage captured at Camden was found correspondence proving thirty substantial citizens of Charleston to have been our secret enemies, in correspondence with the revolutionaries; and several prisoners taken in the same battle were found to hold certificates of allegiance to King George in their pockets. The former persons, except some who escaped, from being warned in time, were arrested and confined to the hulks; the latter were executed. This strong action inflamed the feeling of the province against us to a still greater degree.

Towards the end of September I fell sick of a dangerous fever and my comrades despaired of my life. It was a month before I was fit for duty again, and I remained very listless and feeble for some time after. I owed my life to the faithfulness of poor Jonah, who played truant from the Mess on my account. He sat by me all night, where I lay in the Camden market-house which had been converted into a hospital. He prevented me by main force from flinging off my clothes in my delirium and rushing down to swim in the river, which I persisted in naming the Liffey; and he was always ready with hot or cold drinks as I needed them. The febrifuge he supplied was salts of wormwood, mixed with lemon-juice, sugar and water. When I could fancy no meat, or heavy diet, this poor mungo caught fish and made me broth, and treated me in short with a solicitous affection that I have never before or since enjoyed at the hand of any man, and seldom from a woman's.

Sergeant Collins often came to visit me in my sickness. When I was able to converse intelligently with him he said: 'How now, Gerry Lamb! You seemed to recognize me in the height of your delirium. Do you recollect what you told me?'

'I remember nothing,' I assured him. 'My mind is like a lake over which a storm has raged. It reflects only the blue sky and forgets the thunder and lightning.'

'Well,' he said laughing. 'You were in terrible concern about Major André, the Deputy-Adjutant-General, and declared that he was about to be hanged upon a Judas-tree at Linning's. You begged me to plead with General Washington for his life. Soon it was not a Judas-tree, it seems, but a gallows. You gave me a very pitiful account of how the Major comported himself during the execution, exactly as if you were a witness of it. "Oh, that villain of a hangman with his black face and his impudent leer," you shouted. "Is Major André to suffer at the hands of a slouch like him?" Then you muttered: "Look, look, who is the chaplain! Who else would it be but the Reverend John Martin? He was at Pretty Jimmy's wake, you know. He's the Devil himself, so he is. And look who stands beside him! It's Isaac van Wart, the Skinner, with thirty Robertson dollars jingling in his pockets. Thirty Robertson dollars and a Judas-tree – there's a charming concurrence!"'

I began sweating at Sergeant Collins' recital, and asked for a drink of grog, which he found for me. 'Tell me more,' said I.

'Why,' said Sergeant Collins, 'it was only the delirium. Would you really hear more?'

'Ay, tell me everything,' I said.

'It was really most singular,' he continued. 'You described how the Major stood rolling a pebble under the ball of his foot, and how his little dwarf servant burst out weeping and was reproved by him. Then how, with courage and disgust blended, the Major leapt into the cart under an immense gibbet, snatching the halter from the hangman and setting it with dignity about his own neck, with the knot under his right ear; and how he bound his eyes with his own handkerchief. Then, not in your own Irish brogue, but in a gentle English accent, you cried: "All that I request of you, gentlemen, is that you will bear witness to the world that I die like a brave man!" And again a whisper: "It will but be a momentary pang." You spoke no more after this, though the flesh crawled upon your face, and a few instants later, a violent shock seemed to pass through you and you fell back upon the pallet as if dead.'

'I remember nothing of that,' I said aghast. 'You are not codding me?'

He continued: 'Jonah set up a howl, thinking you had gone from us; and indeed you had every appearance of a dead man. I could not feel the least tremor in your pulse. But the faithful creature flung himself upon you, breathing into your lungs and slapping your cheeks and hands; and you at last gave a slight groan and returned to life. From that instant your fever abated and you were in a fair way to health.'

It was not for three or four weeks that we heard a report that struck us with stupefaction. The first article was that General Benedict Arnold had deserted to our army at New York, and the second that Major André had been captured by a party of Skinners in neuter ground on the eastern bank of Hudson's River and was now threatened with death as a spy! Sergeant Collins brought me the news, white to the lips, and 'I misdoubt,' said he, 'that he is already hanged. October 2nd was the day upon which you recounted the particulars of his execution.'

Alas, he was right! The bare report that reached us concealed a most extraordinary story; and before long we knew what the Major had meant when he hopefully assured our officers at the St David's Day banquet that an American sheep-dog was soon to lead his flock into our fold, and so end the war. The history is as follows. Major André had written in a private manner to his friend, Miss Margaret Shippen (whose name he had mentioned to me when I waited upon him in New York), now wife to General Arnold; offering her his services in procuring such slight millinery for her as cap-wire, needles and gauze, which were unobtainable in Philadelphia because of the war. This letter he intended her to show to her husband, whom he believed to be the secret correspondent 'Gustavus' who had lately been sending General Clinton most valuable information about the American army. It seems that when she innocently replied, General Arnold, unknown to her, added a note to hers, confirming his identity, and arranging for a safe channel of correspondence between André and himself.

General Arnold, by his own account, had originally taken arms against King George because a redress of American grievances could then only be obtained by force. This reason was, he said, later removed when decent redress was offered by the King's Commissioners; and when the French alliance was ratified by Congress all his ideas of the justice and policy of the war were changed – he became a secret Loyalist. This does not seem unlikely; and add to this that Congress had from the first goaded him into disaffection by slighting his merits and delaying his promotion. As Governor of Philadelphia, in 1779, he was treated in the same shabby style. The Executive Council of the city laid before Congress a packet of complaints from citizens against his 'imperious and crooked way of conducting public business'; and Congress was highly pleased to order a court-martial. Then, despite General Arnold's plea for a speedy trial, his accusers kept the matter suspended over his head for nine months, during which he fretted without cease. After a long investigation he was, indeed, fully acquitted of all charges that touched his honour; but was sentenced to be reprimanded for his 'imprudence' in having employed certain public wagons, then lying idle, for removing private property from the reach of our foragers, and for having once given a pass to a trading vessel on the Delaware River without mentioning the matter to General Washington!

This reprimand General Washington conveyed, as delicately as he could, to General Arnold; but later showed his disapproval of Congress by bestowing upon him the command of the fortress of West Point. West Point, which commanded Hudson's River a few miles above the fortress of Stoney Point, was the Gibraltar of America. Rocky ridges, ascending one behind the other, protected it against investment by any force less than twenty thousand strong. It was the magazine of immense quantities of stores, and also kept open for the Americans the passage between New England and the middle provinces. Half a million pounds sterling, and immense labour, had been spent in its construction and three thousand men formed its garrison. It was this place that General Arnold now proposed to hand over to King George – a blow that, Sir Henry Clinton thought, would end the war at a stroke. General Arnold asked in return for his gift not a million pounds or so – which would have fallen far short of the real value, since the war, directly or indirectly, was costing us millions every month: he desired only that he should be given a rank in the British Army equal to his rank in the American service, and compensation for the loss of his private property, which he modestly estimated at £6,000. Major André obtained permission from Sir Henry Clinton to attend a private meeting with General Arnold and arrange details for the admission of the British Army into the fortress.

To be brief, in September 1780, Major André secretly met General Arnold near Fort Lafayette, and there arranged and settled everything; but by some accident was prevented from returning to the ship that had brought him up the river under a flag of truce. He therefore returned on horseback by a roundabout way, with a safe conduct from General Arnold made out in the feigned name of 'John Anderson'. He had the plans of West Point, and a Detail of the state of the forces there, hid in his stockings. He passed safely over Pine's Bridge, the same that I had passed in my escape to New York two years before; but, near Tarrytown, came upon a party of eight men gambling under a tulip-tree by the road-side. One of them was dressed in stolen British uniform and Major André concluded that he was among friends; for he had passed over the Croton River, then considered the boundary between the British and American sides of the Debateable Ground. He acknowledged that he was a British officer on important business and asked them to assist him safely to King's Bridge. But they proved to be American Skinners, nominally members of the Westchester militia. They were here awaiting the return of some friends who had gone to sell stolen cattle to the Cowboys. When they declared themselves, he altered his tone and told them that he also was in the American service, but had pretended to be British as a ruse to get him through; he then produced General Arnold's pass. 'Damn Arnold's pass,' they said. The truth was that they wanted money and his first introduction of himself as British afforded them an excuse for 'skinning' him. They proceeded to rob him of his two watches (silver and gold), and a few guineas; and then stripped him of his riding boots, which were a very valuable commodity in the revolutionary lines. They thus accidentally came across the papers hid in the stockings, and pulled them out, believing them to be paper-currency. Their leader, the only one of them who could read, cried out: 'A spy, by God!' Major André then grew alarmed and offered them a thousand guineas between the party if they would bring him safe to King's Bridge. They debated whether to do so: but either they distrusted his ability to provide so great a sum at short notice, or feared that, once in safety, he would go back on the bargain. They therefore concluded to bring him back into their own lines, in the hope of being rewarded for the capture of a spy; but were equally unaware of the worth of their prize as innocent of any true patriotic spirit – being Skinners, not regular soldiers.

Major André, pretending indignation at his detention, desired the American officer before whom he was brought to inform General Arnold that John Anderson had been arrested with General Arnold's own pass; which was granted. General Arnold, on receipt of this report, abandoned everything. He leapt upon a horse and was soon at the river, where his own barge was waiting with its crew; in this he hurried downstream, with a white flag, to the British ship which was waiting for Major André, and so came safe away.

'Whom can we trust now?' cried General Washington in despair when the news reached him, and the shock was very great; for it seems that he himself was to have inspected West Point about the time of its proposed abandonment to our forces and would therefore have been seized. Moreover, he had shown such favour to General Arnold, notwithstanding all that had been whispered against that strange man by his enemies in Congress, that he now stood suspect of being himself concerned in the treason. ·

The unfortunate Major André had been persuaded by General Arnold to discard his regimentals for the purpose of his ride; and, being under an assumed name, was therefore in the character of a spy. A court-martial by American and French generals sentenced him to death. They hoped thereby to oblige Sir Henry Clinton to give up General Arnold to their country's vengeance, in exchange for Major André. But to do so was plainly not consistent with British honour. Sir Henry offered to barter the Major against six American colonels; but this was refused. General Arnold then himself proposed to Sir Henry that he might be permitted to ride out and surrender himself to General Washington in exchange for the man whom he had involuntarily betrayed to his death. Sir Henry replied: 'Your proposal, Sir, does you great honour; but were Major André my own brother, I could not consent to such a transaction.'

Every possible argument was tried upon General Washington to persuade him to save the Major's life – appeals to his humanity, to his honour, to justice; rich promises; threats of retaliation against the Charleston traitors then in our hands. But nothing availed. The American people demanded a victim and, since General Arnold had escaped, this must be Major André. General Washington could not save the Major, even had he wished, nor even substitute an honourable fusillade for the disgrace of the gibbet. Unless he displayed the same ruthless fury as the rest of his countrymen, his own position would be knocked from under him; and he knew that there was none capable of replacing him as Commander-in-

Chief. Moreover; General Greene, the Marquis de La Fayette and others, whether from private rancour against Arnold or a desire to appear as single-minded partisans of the cause of Liberty, were so insistent upon the disgraceful sentence being carried out that they seemed to be literally thirsting for Major André's blood. General Washington therefore signed the death-warrant; and, to the extraordinary grief and horror of the whole British Army, the execution was carried out. It took place in the same manner exactly that I had described in my delirious vision, and at the very hour. No doubt the profound affection with which the Major had inspired me contributed to my vision, nor was I the only one so favoured. His sister and several other persons were warned in dreams of his melancholy fate. The officers and sergeants of the Royal Welch Fusiliers went into mourning for him, and so did several other regiments.

As for the eight Skinners: they were rewarded by being each given a farm and a yearly pension of two hundred dollars for life. Three of them, one of whom was my faithless guide Isaac van Wart, were awarded silver Congressional medals inscribed *Fidelity* and (in Latin) *Patriotism Triumphs*. There is a popular stanza that runs something in this style:

> Treason doth never prosper: what's the reason?
> If treason prospers, 'tis no longer treason.

But for a succession of trivial accidents, Major André would have come safely back into the British lines; West Point would have been yielded up; and Benedict Arnold, playing the General Monk, might well have restored the Colonies, for a time at least, to their former allegiance and won the thanks of posterity. But it happened otherwise, and the cause of Liberty was revived by that excess of indignation which discovered treason excites in the breasts of lukewarm patriots. General Arnold was burned in effigy in towns and villages, often with obscene and disgusting circumstance; and every man who happened to bear the same surname as he, whether related to him or not, was obliged to change it, in order to quit himself of the odium that it now conveyed.

About this time, we in the Carolinas suffered a great setback. We were waiting at Charlotte for the order to advance further into North Carolina and strike at Hillsborough, when news came that an unsuccessful attack by the enemy had been made on a post in Georgia, far to the south. Major Ferguson, with eleven hundred Loyalist militia and volunteers, was detached to intercept the enemy on their return. But he was himself intercepted by enemy forces of whose existence Lord Cornwallis was unaware – an army of three thousand backwoodsmen from across the Blue Mountains. Their anger had been stirred by the news that the Cherokee Indians, their bitterest enemies, were now on the war-path as King George's allies. They had also been promised pay for their service in the unusual currency of human flesh – so many negroes, taken from the

Tories, for each man according to his rank! At King's Mountain a swarm of these rough, uncivilized men, armed with Deckard rifles, surrounded Major Ferguson's people and shot them to pieces from behind trees and boulders; the Major himself was mortally wounded, and nearly half his force were either wounded or killed before the remainder clubbed their firelocks in surrender. The mountainy men hanged up a score of prisoners, and then returned home.

This Major Ferguson was, after Major André, the most beloved officer in the Army and had the greatest power of any to enlist Loyalists in our service. He was also the most remarkable marksman then living.

A curious instance, by the bye, of the disparity of British and American ideas of honour and policy in warfare, is afforded by contrasting Colonel Daniel Morgan's order for the concerted attempt upon General Fraser's life, near Saratoga (which was carried out), with Major Ferguson's adventure at the time of the Brandywine fighting in 1777. According to his own account, he was out scouting when he observed an American officer, remarkable for Hussar dress, pass slowly within a hundred yards of him, followed by another dressed in dark green with a large cocked hat and mounted on a bay. Major Ferguson ordered three good shots to steal near and fire at the horsemen; but 'the idea disgusted me; I recalled the order'. Major Ferguson's account continues: 'In returning, the Hussar made a wide circuit, but the other passed within a hundred yards of us; upon which I advanced from the woods towards him. On my calling, he stopped, but after looking at me, he proceeded. I again drew his attention, but he slowly continued on his way and I was within that distance at which, in the quickest firing, I could have lodged half a dozen balls in or about him before he was out of my reach. I had only to determine; but it was not pleasant to fire at the back of an unoffending individual, who was acquitting himself very coolly at his duties; so I let him alone.'

It was afterwards proved that the gentleman in the cocked hat was General Washington himself, the Hussar being a French aide-de-camp!

Major Ferguson's defeat at King's Mountain obliged us to defer our hopes of conquest and retire back into South Carolina. It was as miserable a march as I remember, for retirement is never agreeable even in fine weather, and it now rained for several days without intermission. Lord Cornwallis was sick of a fever and the command devolved on Lord Rawdon. We had no tents with us, and at night, when we encamped, it was in the wet and stinking woods; nor for several days had we any rum but only water as thick as puddle. The roads were over our shoes in mud and water. Sometimes we had bread but no beef, sometimes beef but no bread; seldom both together. On two occasions we were without food for fully forty-eight hours. For another five days we lived upon unground Indian corn, two and a half heads being a man's daily ration. At first we merely parched it before a fire; but soon we discovered a better way of treating this hearty but difficult grain. Two men of every mess converted their canteens into rasps by punching holes in them with a bayonet. The ear was then scraped against the rasp and the flour that resulted was made into hoe-cakes, baked on our entrenching tools. We were in a very weak state, I can assure my readers. When we came to a river called Sugar Creek, swollen with a rapid flood, and the steep clay banks as slippery as ice, we could not get the wagons over except by using as draught-animals the Loyalist militia that remained to us. They were our chief reliance in this retreat, as knowing the country and not only protecting us from treachery and surprise but acting as foragers. They also had the difficult art of driving black cattle into the open from the recesses of swamps.

Up to our breasts in yellow water, we forded the Catawba River which at that spot was nearly half a mile over. Fortunately our crossing was not opposed by hidden riflemen. So, after a journey of a fortnight, in which I am proud to say that the men never even murmured against the hardships they underwent, we came to the small town of Wynnsborough, which lies between the Catawba and Congaree Rivers; and there remained for the rest of the year 1780.

CHAPTER XI

HOW DID the war go for our arms at the close of 1780? The French alliance
was so far of no assistance to the Americans, and the six thousand white-
uniformed Frenchmen who had failed to relieve Charleston were landed
at Newport, Rhode Island, and there blockaded by the British Atlantic
fleet. A second division of Frenchmen, who were to have followed, were
locked up in Brest by the British Channel fleet. General Washington's
troops found Congress a cruel stepmother in the matter of pay and
supplies; they were ragged and half-starved and lived from hand to mouth.
Lately their condition had become worse, for General Nathaniel Greene
was intrigued against by Samuel Adams and other Congressmen and
forced to resign his post as Quartermaster-General. General Greene wrote
to General Washington that he had 'lost all confidence in the justice and
rectitude of Congress. Honest intentions and faithful service are but a poor
shield against men without principles, honesty or modesty.' The troops
had not been paid for one whole year even in Continental currency, and
those whose time had expired were refused discharge. In the New Year
there was a serious mutiny at Morristown in Pennsylvania: thirteen
hundred Pennsylvania Ulstermen marching towards Philadelphia, under
the command of three sergeants, with the resolve to force Congress to pay
them. Before they set out, they had been ridden against by their officers
armed with swords, and had killed one of them, a captain. They were met
half-way with promises of redress and persuaded to return to duty.
Another mutiny, of New Jersey men, was put down by shooting, and
General Washington presently asked leave from Congress to raise the
amount of lashes that might be awarded for such ill-behaviour to five
hundred. Who were now the Bloody Backs?

On the other hand, the war was bearing very heavily upon the spirits
and pockets of the British people. Towards the end of August 1780 came
exceedingly grave news. Our outward-bound East India and West India
merchant fleets, sailing in company, had been convoyed by the Channel
Fleet as far south as the north-western promontory of Spain. There the
Admiral in command, obeying the explicit orders of the Earl of Sandwich,
from Admiralty House, turned homewards; leaving the protection of this

glittering prize to a single line-of-battle ship and two or three frigates. On the 9th of August, the convoy was intercepted by a combined Spanish and French fleet of great strength. The commodore of the escort being forbidden to engage an enemy that so greatly exceeded him in strength, abandoned the convoy to the enemy. Thus were lost forty-seven West India merchantmen and transports, with cargoes valued at £600,000; five large East Indiamen with coin, bullion and other valuables aboard to the amount of £1,000,000; also two thousand sailors, eight hundred passengers, twelve hundred soldiers, eighty thousand muskets; and an immense quantity of naval stores destined for Madras as a means of re-equipping our squadron in those waters that had been mauled in battle with the French. In the memory of the oldest man, the Royal Exchange at London had never presented so dull and melancholy an aspect as on the Tuesday afternoon when the notice of this double loss was issued by the Admiralty. No instance had ever been known in the mercantile annals of England where so many ships had been captured at once, nor where loss was recorded of above one-fourth the sum of this. In the same month news reached London that an unescorted Quebec fleet of fifteen ships had been met off the Banks of Newfoundland by an American frigate and two brigantine privateers. Only three of our ships escaped. This came as a very serious blow to the garrison and people of Quebec. I may here append that in the course of this war against the combined fleets of France, Spain, Holland and the United States we lost three thousand merchant ships captured or sunk, besides other naval damage.

The fault for these calamities did not lie with our sailors or their captains. The Earl of Sandwich, alias 'Jeremy Twitcher', it has already been noted, had wickedly thrown away our command of the seas. He had starved the dockyards, lied to the House of Lords about the number of warships in commission, bullied and betrayed his admirals; and condemned the few lonely frigates still afloat to choose, in their encounters with the magnificent fleets of our enemies, between fighting against dismal odds or running for safety. Often enough they chose the former alternative, and sometimes snatched an unhoped-for victory. The names of Howe, Rodney, Hyde Parker and Keppel need no recommendation from my humble pen! Yet I must not omit mention of Sir George Collier's feat at Penobscot Bay; for this glorious action (which by the spite of Lord Sandwich was acknowledged by no ringing of bells or other public acclamation – Sir George, indeed, being superseded in his American command and on his return left unemployed and unpromoted) struck directly against the Americans in their own waters.

Penobscot is a harbour on the wild northern coast of Massachusetts, lying in what is now known as the State of Maine. In the summer of 1779 a settlement of distressed Loyalists was there planted; and the erection of a fort begun by a few companies of the Eighty-Second and Seventy-

Fourth Regiments. No sooner did the people of Boston receive news of this work than they determined to mar it. Twenty-four transports, containing three thousand troops, and nineteen warships, manned by two thousand sailors and mounting 324 guns – the whole constructed at a cost of near £2,000,000 – were despatched to Penobscot. Yet our small garrison, posted behind slight works held off the Bostonians for near three weeks. Sir George Collier then sailed to the rescue with a squadron mounting no more than two hundred guns. The American ships formed a line of battle, but broke at the first attack and were driven up the Penobscot River. I have seen a copy of a letter written by the American military commander, General Solomon Lovell, to the following effect: 'To give a description of this terrible day is out of my power – to see four British ships pursuing seventeen sail of our armed vessels, nineteen of which were stout ships; transports on fire, men of war blowing up, and as much confusion as can possibly be conceived.' To be brief, none of all the American ships escaped capture or destruction, and those of the Bostonians who escaped to the shore found themselves a hundred miles from any base, and without a morsel of food. A grand argument then ensued between the sailors and soldiers, the latter accusing the former of cowardice, the former returning the insult, and, weapons being snatched up, sixty men fell in fratricidal battle. Hundreds more perished of famine or exhaustion on their march back through the wilderness to the settled parts of the province.

This disaster dulled the martial ardour of 'the Saints' for the remainder of the war; yet we were not greatly benefited by it. The British troops in America were insufficient for its conquest and more could not be spared from our Islands. The contesting nations resembled two boxers, badly battered, struggling in a clench, hardly able to stand, each unable to raise raw knuckles and deal a deciding blow to the other's jaw. General Arnold believed that he knew how victory could be achieved. 'Money will go farther than arms in America,' he wrote to Lord George Germaine. 'Offer the Continental troops all the arrears of pay owing to them, equal to about £400,000, half-pay for seven years, two hundred acres for every private soldier, and proportionately more for every officer, together with a bounty of twenty guineas hard money on their coming over. Thus you shall draw two or three thousand of the best soldiers in America to the King's Service.' He believed that this force would be sufficient to take West Point and cut off the Northern States from the rest. General Washington would then be obliged either to fight on our ground or disband his army; for his supplies of meat were on the East side, and his supplies of bread-stuffs on the West. If this operation were deemed too hazardous, another plan offered, which was to leave but a small garrison in New York and concentrate the whole army to seize Baltimore, at the head of the Chesapeak Bay which divides the State of Maryland; and, after overawing Maryland, Delaware and Virginia, which lie contiguous, proceed against Philadelphia from the south. Natural obstacles, such as mountains, swamps, forests, rivers were few in this quarter. However, General Arnold was not heeded; and is likely to have been in error at least about the expected desertion of so many American soldiers. When, in fact, the mutinous Ulstermen of Morristown were approached by British emissaries, with offers to receive them in the Royal camp, they turned these tempters over to the hangman.

It is, however, to be remarked that Joseph Galloway, the Congressman from Pennsylvania who came over to our side from disgust with the Adamses and with the French alliance, declared that not one soldier in four of General Washington's army was a native-born American, one half being Irishmen and the remainder British, with some German deserters and a sprinkling of Northern negroes; and, if his testimony is to be doubted, we have General Greene's word for it that he fought us towards the close of the war largely with British soldiers. The American has ever 'been impatient of discipline and long engagements to the degree that he loves independence, and General Washington's regular army was trained in the European style. Few native-born Americans were therefore inclined to enlist in it, but preferred the easy and insubordinate militia life, where the ranks ruled the officers, not the officers the men, and all fought in Indian fashion, shooting from ambush and avoiding the onset.

The Commander-in-Chief, Sir Henry Clinton, was for commencing no further military operations on a grand scale, but conserving his gains and 'breaking windows' until the Revolution collapsed from exhaustion. Perhaps his way was wisest, though it depended for its success upon British supremacy at sea, which by the Earl of Sandwich's criminal neglect of our fleet and dockyards we had now forfeited to the French, Spanish and Americans. Yet Sir Henry did not have the last word, for Lord George Germaine was still bent upon conducting the war from Downing Street in his own remarkable fashion.

In South Carolina, Major Ferguson's defeat had encouraged the revolutionary cause to a dangerous degree. Our rear and flanks were threatened, our provisions cut off, our posts attacked.

Colonel Tarleton, with his Greens, returned blow for blow, but the guerrilla bands could not be exterminated and now overran the whole province. General Washington appointed General Greene to replace General Gates in North Carolina, to oppose our expected invasion of North Carolina, and in December he arrived at Charlotte, where he collected two thousand men – insufficient to attack us, but enough to do us mischief if used in detachment. The Earl of Cornwallis immediately broke camp and marched us up the right bank of the Catawba against him. General Greene then divided his army into two columns, one of which, under General Daniel Morgan, was ordered to work around our front and harass our posts in Georgia. This column contained the famous Virginian riflemen, and some good regular troops, cavalry and infantry, of the

Continental Line. Lord Cornwallis made a similar division of his forces; sending Colonel Tarleton with a strong column in pursuit of General Morgan, who decisively defeated him at The Cowpens, fifty miles north of Wynnsborough and half that distance from the camp that we had reached on our advance up the river.

At The Cowpens, Colonel Tarleton lost eight hundred men, including the whole of our Light Infantry, two guns, the Colours of the Seventh Regiment, and the confidence of all the remaining Loyalists in the province. He had over-marched his men – an imprudence characteristic of cavalry-commanders – and besides, General Morgan's riflemen were the best light troops in the whole American Army. As usual, they concentrated their fire upon our officers, and disposed of a great number at the first onset. General Morgan also had a stroke of luck, for which he was honest enough not to claim credit: the left wing of his second line at a late stage of the fighting decided to retire two hundred paces, in order to conform with a manoeuvre of the right. This increased the distance of the charge that our people, already out of breath from hustling back the first line of militi-amen, were called upon to make; and coming on in a broken crowd were halted and confused by a very cool volley. They broke under the counter-attack. Colonel Tarleton escaped, with most of his cavalry; but the news of the disaster shook us greatly, especially as General Morgan's force had been rather the weaker in numbers and suffered almost no loss in the fighting.

Yet even so Lord Cornwallis could not bring himself to abandon once more his proposed invasion of North Carolina. Valuable reinforcements had arrived from New York, including the Brigade of Footguards; and these (until the disaster of The Cowpens) had brought our numbers up to the total of four thousand men. The reinforcements were intended by Sir Henry Clinton for defensive rather than offensive use, but Lord Cornwallis, who had obtained from Lord George Germaine the right to communicate directly with him rather than at second hand through Sir Henry Clinton, now felt himself at liberty to behave as though his army were an independent command. He should have been warned by the fate of General Burgoyne, who had similarly embarked upon an independent invasion, trusting to the same broken reed to concert the movements of the New York Army with his own. His Lordship had even so disobeyed General Clinton's instructions, about securing South Carolina at all costs, that he had dismantled the fortifications of Charleston – to prevent Loyalists from seizing and holding it, I suppose, while we were away. He had now assembled enough arms, guns and provisions for a regular campaign and it seemed a pity not to use them. At least, he must do his utmost to cut off General Morgan's retreat and prevent him from rejoining General Greene.

Since we had lost our light troops, Lord Cornwallis determined that the whole Army should, for the sake of speed, travel as light as possible. He therefore ordered the destruction of all our superfluous baggage; no wagons were kept except those that carried ammunition, salt, and hospital stores, and four empty ones for the conveyance of the sick and wounded. He set an example to his officers, whose coffers were crammed with a superfluity of hats, clothes and footwear, novels, plays, wine, condiments, perfumery, silver, glass and bed-linen, by first reducing the size and quantity of his own possessions. There was no objection raised by either officers or men to this sacrifice, even though it deprived us of all future prospect of spirituous liquors. It was a sorry sight to see so many hogsheads of good rum staved in; and a great novelty for the quarters of a British General, and an Earl at that, to be incapable of affording even a glass of wine to visitors, and for his table to be as destitute of comforts as a common soldier's.

Lord Rawdon remained behind with a small force at Camden, which had now been well fortified.

The first difficulty that faced us on our march was the re-crossing of the upper Catawba River, the opposing banks of which were strongly held by the enemy. This our main army was to accomplish at a point well across the North Carolina frontier, by a private ford, M'Gowan's, while a diversion was made six miles lower down by another of our columns. M'Gowan's Ford, which was about half a mile over, lay within a short distance of the Blue Mountains, now covered with snow; and the crossing was made just before dawn on February 1st, 1781, on a dark and rainy morning.

I will not trouble my readers with a close geographical account of our three-hundred-mile pursuit of General Greene's divisions, which succeeded in re-uniting in the second week of February. We were endeavouring to cut him off from Virginia, the next province to the north, whence he received his supplies. Suffice it to tell that we marched through North Carolina, at the average rate of nearly twenty miles a day, by way of Salibury and the pine-clad, clayey foot-hills of the Blue Mountains; gaining every day upon our adversaries and unmolested by their rear-guard. The air was invigorating and the sunshine on fine days delightful. But it rained very heavily, with intervals of snow and sleet, fully half the time, and we were greatly fatigued by our exertions. General Greene was making for the Dan River, across which lay Virginia and safety. We should have caught him and compelled to give battle, had Lord Cornwallis not been deceived by pretended Loyalists who told him that the lower fords of this river were impassable, which they were not, and persuaded him to use the upper ones. General Greene by forced marches reached the lower fords, and Ending a sufficiency of boats got his last stragglers across on February 15th, just as our vanguard arrived. But a great part of his militia had already deserted and dispersed to their homes. His line troops were in a very bad case, having but one blanket for every three men and very few boots; so that we might have followed them by the trail of blood the poor fellows left, like wounded animals. Like us, they had no tents.

Since General Greene had escaped us, we were marched slowly back to Hillsborough which, though the chief town of upper North Carolina, did not boast a hundred houses. There Lord Cornwallis erected the Royal Standard and issued a proclamation calling upon the province to return to its allegiance. We were greeted upon our arrival with the news that General Benedict Arnold, now fighting upon our side, had taken a force of American Loyalists up the James River into Lower Virginia, and for three weeks 'broken windows' to some purpose. He had captured several ships in cargo, blown up an iron-foundry where cannon were manufactured and burned a vast quantity of public and private stores. The fragrant smoke of tobacco rolled in clouds over the country, not diffused through day pipes, calumets or cigars, but issuing from the roofs of burning warehouses at Richmond and Norfolk. General Arnold returned without loss to his base at Portsmouth, at the mouth of the river.

I cannot omit to mention a most foul transaction that took place not far from Hillsborough on February 25th. The Loyalists to our immediate south having risen in numbers in answer to the Proclamation, Colonel Tarleton was sent forward to assist their organization; but Colonel Harry Lee of the American Light Horse was there beforehand and the three hundred Loyalists mistaking Lee's column, whom they met in a narrow lane, for Colonel Tarleton's, approached them with friendly shouts. They were at once surrounded; though they begged for quarter, the relentless Americans refused it, and they were all butchered in cold blood. Had twenty revolutionary Americans thus fallen to British arms, how would the pages of Ramsay, Belsham and the rest have foamed with the charges of murder, massacre, blood and malice! But very bloody deeds were done between partisans throughout the campaign; even some of Colonel Tarleton's Greens were guilty of rape, murder and indiscriminate hanging. A troop of British dragoons attached to the Greens were so disgusted with these proceedings that they refused to 'wear the Green', and remained in their scarlet.

The inhabitants of the hilly upper parts of North and South Carolina differed very greatly from those of the swampy lower parts, both in vigour and complexion. They were a fine, strong, ruddy people, combining hospitality with savagery to a remarkable degree and greatly addicted to drink. Hardly a man but was six foot tall and broad in proportion; hardly a two-roomed cabin but had its still for the brewing of peach-brandy. The women were erect and beautiful; not drunkards, but reputedly of relaxed morals. There was a custom here in vogue of 'swapping wives' which they took to a remarkable pitch of wantonness: one man who thought his daughter-in-law more handsome than his wife, proposed an exchange to his son, who consented on the condition that his father gave, with the mother, two cows and two horses. The women concerned, so far from being the victims, were said to have been the instigators of this unnatural transaction.

Most of our officers had brought dogs with them, and at Hillsborough enjoyed great sport in quail-shooting and rabbit-hunting. The American rabbits disdained to burrow in the ground, so that we had no use for ferrets; after a good chase they would go to earth (if I may so express myself) by running up a hollow tree. The slave Jonah, who acted as our huntsman, showed us the 'Virginia ferret'. He cut us a hickory pole, and split it at the top, which was to be poked up the tree and twisted in the animal's fur, to haul him down kicking. This proved very practical. On one occasion when I assisted at such a hunt an oppossum was caught, which is a sort of rat with a long, bushy, prehensile tail. It was seen suspended by this tail to the extremity of a branch and knocked down with the hickory pole. Where it fell it lay perfectly motionless, feigning death; and the officers' spaniels, though they barked at it and worried it so that I heard the bones crack, yet would not eat it up, from the natural horror that almost every animal, but the jackal and hyaena, feels of devouring what he has not himself slain. Lieutenant Guyon, my officer, out of humanity took up the poor creature, which lay limp in his hands, and brought it back to the house where he lodged. There he laid it upon the window-ledge in the sun, sitting still at the further end of the room and watching it attentively. After a while it furtively opened one eye, twisted its head slowly about to see whether it was observed, then suddenly sprang up and out of the window and disappeared. Jonah remarked very sagely: 'Him like rebel Whig in Ca'lina. Pertend him good dead rebel, den up he jump, do murrer mischief to dem poor Tories.'

No sooner were we halted at this place than we began to remedy our uncouth appearance, by washing our soiled linen and brushing our muddy regimental clothing. But the several yellow and reddish streams that we had forded made mock of our most industrious efforts. Pipe-clay we had none, and though we dressed our hair as we should, and polished buttons and buckles, our appearance suggested a debtors' prison where decayed gentlemen with more pride than luck barely subsist upon fourpence a day. Provisions were also exceedingly scarce, since the country was in any case but sparsely settled, and the American army stationed here before us had eaten up the surplus stocks of corn and beef. When we had gleaned after their reaping, the country was swept bare; and though Lord Cornwallis had promised that the draught-oxen, the only cattle that survived in the neighbourhood, should not be slaughtered except in case of necessity, that necessity arose, and even the Loyalists complained loudly of the hardships they incurred because of it. The Commissary of Supplies was obliged, as a most unpleasant duty, to go from house to house in the town with a file

of men, commanding the citizens to yield up their provisions: for in time
of war an army is never allowed to starve while the citizens whom it is
defending still have grain in their bins.

We retired southward about thirty miles to the upper tributaries of the
Cape Fear River. (This river meets the ocean at Wilmington, two hundred
miles to the south-east, where we had a detachment.) Here we were obliged
by General Greene with the offer of battle. His army had been augmented
to five thousand men and, crossing again into North Carolina, he took
position at Guildford Court House, where Lord Cornwallis hurried to
attack him.

We lay at this time twelve miles southward from Guildford Court
House, with our headquarters at a Quakers' meeting-house of New
Garden, in the forks of Deep River. I remember that being sent on detachment with the Commissary, Mr Stedman, to command provisions from
the plantations in the neighbourhood, a venerable Quaker from whom we
obtained a considerable quantity of corn made some very sensible remarks.

'How is the general spirit of the Province hereabouts?' asked Mr
Stedman.

'The greater part wish to be united to Britain, Friend,' he replied.

'Then why do they not join us?' Mr Stedman asked. 'Or if they join us,
why do they quit the Colours so soon?'

'Alas, Friend, canst thou ask this? Art thou ignorant of the resentment
of the revolutioners against those who wish thy cause well? And of the
many times that these well-wishers have been deceived in hopes of
support, or abandoned to their enemies when thy army has relinquished
its posts? And of the revenge that these bloody-minded men take upon the
families of those who serve King George?'

'Pray inform me upon this point, Sir,' said Mr Stedman.

'Friend, fear of injury works upon men's hearts more powerfully than
hope of reward for honest or loyal dealings. The Tories of North Carolina
live in terror of the Whigs. There are some who have dwelt like hunted
beasts in the wilderness for two and even three years, not daring to return
to their homes, and are secretly supported by their families, or faithful
slaves, with hoe-cakes and jerked meat hid now and then in the recesses of
the wood for them to find. Others, promised safety by their neighbours,
have been shot at from behind a tree as they worked in their corn-patch;
or tied to a tree and flogged until insensible. Not far from here a suspected
Loyalist was shot dead in the early morning as he lay in bed with his wife.'

'These circumstances are indeed abominable,' cried Mr Stedman. 'But
do these poor people expect to live so happily or so undisturbed under any
rule but that of the British King?'

'No, Friend,' the Quaker replied. 'Nor does that come in question. The
people have experienced such distress between the ebb and flow of revolution and royalism that they would submit to any government in the

world, Christian, Jew or Turk in order only to obtain peace. And so great are the odds against which thy nation is contending and so foolish are thy Ministers (forgive my boldness) that they despair of victory for you. They tend to the side of Congress. Yet be assured of this much – as soldiers in the rebel militia they are of small comfort to General Greene.'

CHAPTER XII

GENERAL GREENE was unlucky to have lost the services of General Daniel Morgan who after his resounding victory at The Cowpens had retired from the service, pleading the ague and rheumatic pains. These ailments, though painful, would not have been sufficient to keep so courageous and patriotic a soldier from battle had General Morgan felt that he was estimated by Congress at his just worth; but he had too often been disappointed by deferred promotion and given cold thanks for his extraordinary services, nor did he agree very well in policy with General Greene. He retired to his farm and never served against us again. General Greene was what they termed in the South a 'judgmatical' man, that is, a man of careful judgment. His military knowledge was wholly derived from reading, not from experience in the field, but his dispositions on this occasion were pretty well. The ground he chose was certainly most favourable for defence.

The whitewashed Court House stood on a gentle slope at the skirt of an irregular clearing of about one hundred and twenty acres. The only other buildings in this clearing were two small farmhouses and three barns. The Court House had been, I suppose, sited here as lying at a road-junction and at a point nearly equidistant from several scattered plantations which formed the township of Guildford. Our approach to it from the south was by a narrow defile with thick woods on either hand. On emerging from the defile, we would first come upon a smaller clearing of about fifty acres, with the road running between. General Greene's advanced line of defence, consisting of North Carolina militiamen, was posted behind a rail fence on the further edge of the smaller clearing, where the woods began again. Two guns were mounted ahead of this line to distress us as we debouched from the defile; also companies of picked riflemen were thrown forward on either flank, and two squadrons of cavalry were ready to charge if we showed panic. The North Carolina men were to be discouraged from breaking, by a few veteran troops posted immediately in their rear with orders to shoot any man who flinched. This wood extended for half a mile until our road reached the larger clearing at the back of which the Court House stood; in the middle of the wood, behind a stout breastwork,

General Greene had placed a second line, of better militia, including the famous riflemen trained by General Morgan. The last line, posted on the slopes about the Court House consisted of the regular and veteran troops. Three-quarters of a mile separated the leading militia from the veterans in reserve.

It may well be wondered why General Greene had placed his lines at so great a distance from one another. The fact was: he knew that General Morgan's victory at The Cowpens had been gained by defending his position with successive lines of infantry, each strongly posted, so that when one line was dislodged our charge would spend its force before it reached the second position; and he trusted that after we were staggered by the first skirmish the density of the woods would make us break our alignment and come against his best troops in exhaustion and disorder. Had General Morgan been present he would have approved General Greene's dispositions in principle, but criticized the detail. It is a good thing to separate one's lines in such a way that the defence is in depth, and the enemy is exhausted in attempting to pierce it; but a bad thing to separate these lines by too great a distance. The front companies will feel lonely, and suspect that they have been devoted to destruction for the benefit of those behind. Unless they are seasoned troops they will not hold their ground for long.

The full circumstances of the battle, which took place on March 15th, 1781, are so complicated and have been so ably presented by Mr Stedman in his History that it would be an impertinence on my part to attempt to improve upon him. I will therefore content myself with giving my own experiences in the battle, recommending my readers to study Mr Stedman for a more general account.

The Royal Welch Fusiliers went into action about two hundred and twenty officers and men strong; some eighty having been lost by sickness and skirmishing since the Camden battle. We were marched off at dawn from New Garden, without having eaten our breakfast – and not from our officers' negligence, but only because there was no breakfast to eat. We had been on very short rations for a week and now possessed no food at all. After a frosty night, the sun shone benignantly and warmed our stiff bodies; while the croaking of frogs and the twittering of birds pleasantly reminded us that the Spring was now well advanced. Life without a daily issue of grog was uncomfortable, I own, for the old soldiers especially. Even Saint David had been cheated of his customary bumpers: the amount of peach-brandy that Captain Champagné had contrived to collect for that pious purpose on March 1st did not amount to more than half a gill for each mess.

At about noon, our cavalry scouts brushed with theirs about four miles from Guildford Court House, and Lord Cornwallis, unable to get any information from prisoners or natives as to the enemy dispositions, was forced to fight blind. We Fusiliers were in the centre of the advancing army, and heard confused artillery and musket fire ahead of us. Presently a rider came down the column with orders to Lieutenant-Colonel Webster of The Thirty-Third, who commanded our division, to hurry forward and deploy to the left so soon as we reached the first clearing. At about half-past one o'clock in the afternoon, we found ourselves advancing across the wet, red clay of a ploughed field, with The Thirty-Third on our left and The Seventy-First on our right. Music of fife and drum was not lacking; but, the regimental drummers being now employed as musketmen, we used young American boys who had joined the Colours at Camden. Our chief fifer was the negro Jonah, who played the *Grenadiers' March* and *The Noble Race of Jenkin* with great spirit.

We were the leading troops, and first came under rifle-fire at about a hundred and fifty paces from the wood towards which we were hurrying. Since our Tower muskets were, as usual, greatly outranged by the American rifles, we were obliged to hold our volley and continue our advance, despite great losses. The marksmen on the flanks especially galled us. Here fell Mad Johnny Maguire with a bullet through the heart; but I did not know of my poor friend's fate until the next day when he was found by Smutchy Steel lying in a furrow upon his back, his rugged features bent in the pleasant smile which in life had seldom left them.

At sixty paces we halted to fire a volley; then Colonel Webster gave the word 'Charge!' But The Thirty-Third, who had suffered heavily, not yet being up in line with us on the left, we paused for a moment, at forty paces from the enemy, to allow them to come up. Colonel Webster, misunder-standing our hesitation, cried out in more than his usual commanding voice, which was well known to our Brigade: '*Come on, my brave Fusiliers!*' The North Carolina militia were massed with arms presented behind the rail-fence and taking aim with the nicest precision. We went forward at a smart run, and they would not meet our bayonets. Despite the guards set over them to prevent this very thing, five hundred fled away to the flanks and thence dispersed to their homes: 'to kiss their wives and sweethearts', as General Greene afterwards amiably expressed it.

Next we came against the Virginians in the middle of the wood, who fired very sharply at us from behind their breastworks of brushwood. We could not get at them because of the trees that they had felled in our path, and must change direction, working round to our left.

I happened to run ahead with a party of about ten men, Smutchy Steel among them. As we gained the end of the breastwork, which had cost us many valuable lives, and went in among the Virginians with the bayonet, I observed an American officer attempting to fly across our front. I imme-diately left my comrades, whom I put under Smutchy's orders, and darted after him. He saw my intention to capture him and fled with the utmost speed. I pursued – I do not know how far – to where the trees were less dense, but the underwood high and tangled. He fell once or twice, and was slow in rising, and I was gaining on him when suddenly he turned about and threw up his hands. Like a dream is a battle, when the spirit is so highly inflamed that the soldier hopes not, fears not, repines not, but proceeds without astonishment or reflexion from one remarkable or terrible circumstance to the next. It appeared natural enough to me that the American officer should be my former comrade Richard Harlowe – though how he came to be in the enemy's service I knew not and do not know to this day – and that I should deny him quarter, as I did, shooting him through the head with my fusil in summary conviction of his traitorous dealing. His sword I drew from the scabbard in detestation, and with an effort snapped it across my knee.

I was now aware of a confused noise upon my left, where I saw several bodies of riflemen drawn up behind brushwood, the cast of a crust from me. A vigorous contest had evidently been in progress here between the Second Battalion of Guards and these people: for several dead Guardsmen and Americans lay about me. I stopped by a dead Guardsman, and stooping down, replenished my pouch with the cartridges remaining in his. Then I reloaded my fusil in a very deliberate manner, as one who walks in his sleep, careless of danger; they shouted and fired several shots at me, but not one took effect. Glancing my eye the other way, I saw a company of Guards advancing to the attack, and was glad to observe that they had been belied by popular rumour: so far from being effeminated by the luxuries of the Metropolis or enervated by idleness, they fought with vigour and majesty. I would have joined them now, but to do so I should have had to run the gauntlet of the Americans who lay between. How to act I knew not. I wished to join in the fight, but could effect nothing. I fell back a few paces.

On the instant, however, another remarkable vision seemed to swim up before me: the Earl of Cornwallis himself, riding towards me across the clear part of the wood, unaccompanied by any *aide*. He was mounted on a common dragoon's horse, his own charger having been shot. The saddle-bags were under the creature's belly, which much retarded his progress, because of the underwood that caught against it. I immediately ran forward and snatched at the bridle, turning the horse's head. 'Your Lordship,' I cried, 'another few yards and you will be surrounded by the enemy. This way, I beg of you.'

He thanked me, mentioned that he was unconscious of the danger, and observing the White Horse on my cap, asked where the Royal Welch Fusiliers were. I told him that I had become detached from them by the pursuit of an officer, but believed, by the shouting and cheering of a few minutes before, that they had now broken the second line. Still keeping the bridle in my hand I ran alongside of the horse in the direction from which the shouts had proceeded, until we came upon the Royal Welch Fusiliers. They were re-formed in the skirt of the wood just short of the farm-land behind which the Court House stood. To their left ran a road and on their right was a small hill. His Lordship noted this hill at once as commanding the Court House, and the very place to post our batteries, which were now coming up the road.

'General Greene should not have overlooked this place,' he said in my hearing, as one who mildly reproaches an opponent in a game of chess for a neglected opportunity. The guns were hauled up the hill and unlimbered, and at once opened fire upon the American third line. There was heavy fighting already in that quarter, where Lieutenant-Colonel Webster, who had become separated from us, had led The Thirty-Third and other troops. Presently we heard distant huzzas, and then these drowned by a tremendous Southern yell; and we saw a sight which surprised and dismayed us. The Second Guards, caught in the rear by Colonel Lee's sabres and in the flank by the bayonets of the First Maryland Regiment, were fairly on the run across an open field. Lord Cornwallis did not hesitate: he ordered Lieutenant Macleod of the gunners to fire grapeshot point-blank into the mêlée! This in a moment broke the American pursuit, by making the horses unmanageable, but it was at great cost to our own people. 'A necessary evil,' said his Lordship, returning very pale to where we were formed. 'So a man would do right to shoot off his own finger where a rattlesnake bit him, lest the poison lose him his whole arm and life itself.' The Marylanders then returned to their original post in the neighbourhood of the Court House.

Ourselves and The Seventy-First formed a solid line to which five regiments now rallied, including the survivors of the Guards. It was now about three o'clock and the crisis of the battle. But Colonel Tarleton with a cavalry charge broke the enemy militia on our right, where fighting was in progress about a mile distant from us; our re-formed line then swept forward across the farm-land, which was deeply seamed with gullies, and the Americans went off in haste.

The Royal Welch Fusiliers had the luck to capture two of the four brass six-pounders close to the Court House, which General Greene abandoned with their ammunition. A few prisoners were taken. Ourselves and The Seventy-First as the troops least exhausted were ordered to pursue the enemy as they fell back to our left towards a river called Troublesome Creek: but we were near fainting from hunger and our long exertions and could do little against them.

In this desperate battle, we lost in killed and wounded above five hundred men, near one-third of our whole army. Among the mortally wounded was Lieutenant-Colonel Webster, whose death a few days later struck Lord Cornwallis with such pungent sorrow that he exclaimed: 'I have lost my scabbard.' The Royal Welch Fusiliers were reduced by sixty-eight officers and men to a total strength of but one hundred and fifty. The Americans left between two and three hundred dead on the battlefield; by which we could estimate their losses in killed and wounded at twice as many as ours. Well, it was a victory, but such a victory as my old commander General Phillips said, when he heard the news, as 'the sort of victory that ruins an army'. (General Phillips had lately been exchanged against an American prisoner of equal rank and was now with General Arnold at Portsmouth in Virginia. While in captivity he had caused great resentment among the Americans by his downright manner of speech and by telling his officers 'not to heed the Americans more than a flock of cackling geese'. Many of our veteran officers and men, I confess, made troublesome prisoners.)

We camped that night upon the field of battle. It was a very black night, and the battle had been scattered over so wild and difficult a country that darkness fell before we had brought in our own and the American wounded. The Court House, with the meagre farm-buildings and sheds, was insufficient to shelter even those whom we found. It rained in torrents all night and the cries of the wounded and dying, for whom no shelter could be found, exceeded all description for painfulness. We had no food, no drink, no shelter. So complicated a scene of horror and distress rarely occurs even in military life; yet I had experienced as bad or worse in the Saratoga fighting, where the gloomy necessity of constant retreat had weighed upon our hearts like lead. Today at least we had won a resounding victory against a courageous and well-fed enemy, advantageously posted, whose numbers exceeded us by nearly three to one. As for myself, I admit that my heart was strangely elated in spite of all. The death of so many good comrades, especially of Mad Johnny Maguire, should have stilled it to sobriety. But one consideration now dominated every other: Richard Harlowe (or Pearce) was killed, and I was now free to marry the woman whom I had widowed with my own fusil, and who was the mother of my child. For I was convinced by a strong intuition not only that she still lived, but that I would meet her once more, and before many months had passed. I should dearly have loved to seek out Richard Harlowe's corpse and search it to find his commission or some other proof of his death; but I could not be spared from duty.

Smutchy Steel was promoted to Corporal as a reward for his soldierlike services that day, and I was glad to be able once more to discourse with him on equal and familiar terms, we being now both of non-commissioned rank. Though originally of a low and vicious disposition, he had been insensibly improved by the exacting round of duty and discipline: so much so that he was entirely changed in mind and character into an honourable and moral person, whom I was proud to call my friend. Such cases in the Army are as frequent as they are surprising, and constitute a strong argument for the military life; if the officers be worthy of their trust.

The morning after the battle we buried the dead, from whom we took such shoes as were in better condition than our own, and marched back to the New Garden Meeting House. There we left seventy of our most severely wounded under the charge of the good Quakers, with a flag of truce and a petition to the Americans to relieve their distresses. That same afternoon we were fed for the first time for forty-eight hours, the ration being a quarter of a pound of maize flour and the same amount of very lean beef. The nearest place whence we could hope for regular provisions was Wilmington on the North Carolina coast, above two hundred miles away, following the bank of the Cape Fear River. So off we marched, by short stages. General Greene then turned to pursue us; but our rear-guard fought only slight skirmishes with his van, and he did not follow us above forty miles. We were very hungry and for bread we were one day served with liver, and another day with turnips, which roots have small nourishment in them.

A settlement of Highland Loyalists at Cross Creek lay on our route, but even there we could not find four days' forage within twenty miles, and could not therefore halt for refreshment. These Highlanders, notwithstanding the cruel persecution that they had constantly endured from the Revolutionaries, had shown great affection and zeal towards us, collecting and conveying to us all the flour and spirits in the neighbourhood. Their attention saved the lives of a number of our wounded, worn out by traversing this barren desert; none the less, we lost a great many on the road. The enemy militia did not appear in arms against us, but contented themselves with driving the cattle out of our reach, carrying off supplies of corn and breaking down bridges over the numerous creeks which we must pass.

The only commerce of which this remote country was capable was in horses. They multiplied very fast in the swamps and were sold in the Spring to drovers from Pennsylvania who grazed them upon the road on their return. Agriculture here was patriarchal, that is to say, only enough crops were raised for the consumption of the growers. Each plantation raised and dressed its own wool and leather, and the chief lack appeared to be nails and salt. Yet so skilful were the settlers with axe and hatchet that at a pinch they could construct and roof huts without a single nail—a most tedious business.

The day before we reached Cross Creek an incident occurred which went far to prove that the Quaker of New Garden had been telling the truth. An extraordinary-looking person came to join our Colours, who looked (so someone truly remarked) as if he had escaped from the collection of natural monstrosities exhibited at Surgeons' Hall in London. He was bent with rheumatic pains, and shaken with ague; his hair was white as snow, his body utterly emaciated. He was but thirty-eight years old, he said, but for three years had lived the life of a beast in the swamps, having scooped a den for himself in the bank of a river and provided it with a concealed entrance. Nobody of his kin or acquaintance remained to supply him with necessaries, except some cousins who lived at a great distance and once or twice in a year ventured to visit him. He had often been pursued and shot at by his rancorous enemies, but always escaped. His meat was terrapin, fish and small animals, generally eaten raw; and his bread was acorns, which from long use had become quite agreeable to him. His clothing was composed entirely of skins, jobbed together with sinews. On his head was a racoon-skin cap. But for having no umbrella, no musket and no Man Friday, he would have well served for a cut in illustration of Mr De Foe's *Robinson Crusoe*. He was now enlisted in the Provincial Forces. By living so much alone, this poor fellow had contracted the habit of talking to himself in a debate of two voices, and his wits were almost turned; but he proved a valuable scout and had not lost his skill with a rifle. When Mr Brice, who distributed the rations of the Provincial Forces, gave him his share, the new recruit let great tears fall into the pannikin of flour and exclaimed: 'At last, Sir, I know myself for a human being again, by the token of beef and flour.'

Of this very disagreeable march, there are two more incidents worthy of the reader's attention. The first happened at Ramsay's Crossing, about March 22nd. That evening I was called upon to mount guard upon the American officer-prisoners, which was a duty given to regular sergeants, though the guards themselves were American militia. The Provost-Marshal of the Army, instructing me in my duties, warned me that a certain cavalry officer was a very dangerous person and would do all in his power to escape: since conscious that he had not only violated his oath of allegiance but acted with great cruelty against the inhabitants of the Carolinas. He feared the gibbet were he sent to trial at Charleston, of which he was a native. I desired to have the officer pointed out to me, and the Provost-Marshal did so. 'I know the gentleman,' said I, 'I have even eaten and drunk at his expense. He is Captain Gale, is he not, of Wappo Creek? He was a Furious Tory when I last heard him declaim. Well, your Honour, I shall take all precautions to keep him with us.'

'Do so, Sergeant,' said the Provost-Marshal, 'for if he escapes, I fear he will prove unlucky to the river-people who have assisted us in our march.'

He went off, and not being able to lock the prisoners into any hut, none being available for that purpose, I bound Captain Gale's wrists and ankles with a cord, one end of which I fastened to my own wrist as I slept. Towards morning I awoke, at some slight noise, but jerking the cord found it still attached, as I thought, to the captive, and resumed my sleep. To my astonishment and alarm, when dawn came, I discovered that the Captain was gone, and the other end of the cord was tied to a little bush. I questioned the sentinel who had been on guard, but he professed to know nothing. I instantly confined him, raised the alarm and reported my loss to the Provost-Marshal, who sent out cavalry in pursuit; but to no purpose. We never caught Captain Gale.

Lord Cornwallis was highly displeased when the circumstance was made known to him, and commanded the Sergeant of the Guard to be brought before him; threatening to 'break him for so gross a dereliction of duty'. I was thereupon summoned to Headquarters and felt very bad as I approached his Lordship's presence; but to my great relief his stern frown changed into a smile when he recognized me. He said to his aide-de-camp: 'Why 'tis the sergeant of whom I told you – he who proved a good fairy to me in the wood during the battle. This case is over before it has begun. The sentinel was bribed, that's clear. Put him on trial for his life: the Sergeant may return to his regiment and will act as witness.'

I may add that Lord Cornwallis frequently addressed a 'good morning' or a few kind words to me afterwards when we met; and I was often employed by him to copy out the duplicates of his despatches. The latter circumstance accounts for the knowledge that I acquired, from casual talk and the confidence of his military family, of the direction of the war by Lord George Germaine and Sir Henry Clinton.

The second interesting circumstance of the march happened when we were at Grange's plantation, but two days' march from Wilmington, on April 5th. It was then that I first witnessed at close range one of the great wonders of nature for which the American Continent is famous. It was an unusually sultry day, provocative of petulant tempers, and bred no less than three duels (one fatal) among the Hessian officers of Bose's Regiment. Hot streams of air now were felt and sudden gusts from different points of the compass. One gust twitched off my cap and wig as I was passing across the yard of the plantation where we were about to be quartered. They were cleverly caught before they fell by two little negro boys, who laughed merrily at me as I restored the honours of my head. All at once a great cloud of darkness rose in the north, and from the distance I heard a great roaring, grinding noise gradually approaching, like the noise of crunched sugar prodigiously magnified. I knew it at once for a tornado. I was for taking shelter in the great red barn opposite; but thought better of it and remained where I was in the open yard.

Now with a resounding clap the tornado struck. It carried with it a great cloud of green leaves, torn branches, dust, hay and rotten wood, and cut a twisted path a hundred yards across in which barns, trees, houses were alike levelled with the ground. I turned, clutching at my cap with both hands and was thrown flat on my face as the whirlwind passed over me. All the breath was sucked out of my lungs and I nearly choked. Down went the great barn, collapsing inwards by some atmospheric trick, and the 'meat-houses', or negro cabins, beyond, were blown clean away. As I raised myself on my elbows, and looked up, I saw a most remarkable sight: a great empty butt (of the sort in which the stinking mash is kept when they make their peach-brandy) sailing through the air as if it had been fired from a mortar. It crashed squelch against a stable wall, which went down like a house of balanced playing-cards. Stones, planks and bricks were now flying about me, as hot as under a cannonade, and this continued for three minutes during the whole of which I found it very difficult to breathe. A slight lull followed and then came a storm of thunder and lightning and drenching cold rain which lasted for another hour. A tall tulip-tree that had escaped the whirlwind, from standing a little outside its track, was struck before my eyes and scathed the whole length of its smooth grey trunk. Two of the wounded and a number of negroes were killed. That storm proved very annoying to me, for it carried away, with my other poor baggage, the journal that I had kept posted every day throughout the campaign; my memory, being none of the best, has played many tricks with me in attempting, so many years since, to reconstruct the sequence of my adventures.

CHAPTER XIII

WE WERE fast approaching the end of the War, which had now been six years in progress, and Guildford Court House proved the last pitched battle in which I took part. I had fought in six. Yet I was by no means yet at the end of my fighting, still less of my wide wanderings, and I may affirm without boasting or fear of contradiction that, before I had done, the track of my feet upon the American Continent marked a longer and more distant route than that of any other soldier in the Royal armies.

Wilmington was a poor place and though we found stores awaiting us there which were very grateful, especially rum and a few hundred pairs of shoes, our necessities could not yet be wholly supplied. We had eighteen days' rest, which together with sea-baths restored most of the convalescents to duty.

It was here that Captain Champagné, who was an assiduous fox-hunter, called for volunteers among us to learn the equestrian art; for he said that this was cavalry country and horses' legs could save our own on innumerable occasions, especially in scouting and foraging. About half the regiment came forward, Smutchy Steel and myself among them, and Colonel Tarleton, who was an old friend of the Captain's, obliged him with a number of horses. So I became a recruit again, in a manner of speaking, though with this advantage over most of the other rank and file that as a boy in Ireland I had learned the rudiments of horsemanship from my patron, young Mr Howard. The other marching regiments flocked as spectators to our riding-school, in order to laugh at our ungainly seats and awkward tumbles. But we knew that they secretly envied us, and we persevered. A sergeant of the Seventeenth Dragoons acted as our instructor, and taught us the proper care of our horses, besides. He said to me one day in a condescending manner: 'Upon my word, Sergeant Lamb, I don't wonder that as men of honour you are bent on learning our profession. For my part, I cannot comprehend how any man can enlist, without mortification, in any other arm of the service but the cavalry! I believe I would as fief be a churchwarden as a sergeant in the Line.'

'Why,' said I, disguising my resentment with a smile, 'it is not all psalms and long faces in our poor foot-swinging congregation. I assure you that we have very lively meetings in the vestry on occasion.'

'Ay, no doubt,' he said magnificently. 'But the cavalry rules the battle.'

'At least it did not rule at Minden,' said I, growing more nettled, 'when six British regiments, mine among them, tumbled the whole French cavalry to ruin; and when the British cavalry never entered the action at all. And what is more, when shells and grape-shot are flying, I am thankful that I chose the Line. For I can answer for my own legs that they will not play the coward or prove unmanageable: as the boldest cavalryman cannot answer for the legs of his mount. You forget, Sergeant Haws, that an infantryman has his own proper pride.'

He was a stupid man, but presently concluded that he had come near to a positive insult; and soon he begged my pardon, which I was glad to give, and we had a long drink together. Yet we never became close friends. The cavalryman in general regards the infantryman no more than a Jew does a pig; being raised three feet above him, he absurdly seeks to translate this superiority of altitude into a moral superiority. But it is generally accepted that, as a rule, mounted infantry fall less short of their duty in action than do dismounted cavalry.

Sergeant Haws had a continuous complaint against the horses of Virginia, which he owned were fine animals, that they were marred for riding by the false gaits taught them by their lazy masters. For to a Southern planter a trot was odious, as unsettling to his liver; and a fair gallop he found most fatiguing. The horse was therefore taught those unnatural modes of progression, the pace and the wrack. In the first the animal moves his two legs on one side together alternatively with the other two, and, being therefore unable to spring from the ground as in a trot, proceeds with a sort of shuffling motion. The Virginian planter habitually sat with his toes just beneath his horse's nose, the stirrups being extremely long and the saddle put about three or four inches forward on the mane. English ladies, monks, priests and lawyers once favoured the pace, under the name of the amble, but it disappeared from the manège about the time of the first George. A passage in Chambers' *Cyclopedia*, I find, contradicts Sergeant Haws as to the unnaturalness of this gait, declaring that the pace or amble is usually the first natural step of young colts. In the wrack the horse gallops with his fore-feet and trots with those behind. This is a gait that looks very odd to the European, and greatly fatigues the horse; but the gentlemen of Virginia found it conducive to their ease, which was all that they considered. It was also judged to be a safer motion for a sleepy man, or a man far gone in liquor, than a trot or a gallop. The pace and the wrack were taught to the horses, when foals, by hoppling them – in the first case with two bands, one linking the two off legs, the other the near legs; in the second case with a single band for the hind legs.

General Greene's defeat had gained him as much as a victory. Our lack of stores and our great train of sick and wounded, had forced us to come so far away from our base in South Carolina, that he was now at liberty to enter that province himself with what remained of his army. I may note here that General Greene never won a battle in his whole career, yet always managed, as in this case, to obtain the fruits of victory. He wrote very frankly about himself that few generals had run faster and more lustily than he; but that he had taken care not to run too far and had commonly run as fast forward as backward. 'Our army,' he said, 'has frequently been beaten but, like the stockfish, grows the better for it.' Lord Cornwallis was indeed in a quandary when he had a clear and positive report that General Greene was pressing hard against Camden, where Lord Rawdon's garrison was pitifully small. We did not have sufficient stores for marching back across the five hundred miles of barren country which intervened, and several broad rivers must be crossed, from which the enemy would no doubt remove all boats as we approached. To return by sea to Charleston, his Lordship thought disgraceful. Besides, sea-voyages usually proved ruinous to cavalry horses; and some weeks would be wasted in waiting for transports, during which time our army, already reduced to a mere fourteen hundred men, would suffer severely from sickness in the heats of this unhealthy station. A third and bolder course, however, remained, which was to go forward into the rich province of Virginia. There we could join forces with General Phillips' army and perhaps do such widespread damage as to draw General Greene hurriedly away from South Carolina.

In the event, the courage and determination of Lord Rawdon checked General Greene for a time; yet South Carolina was lost, except only Charleston. Even this would have gone, and none of our frontier garrisons have been brought away safe but for an accident – the arrival of three British regiments from Ireland. These had been intended by Lord George Germaine to reinforce Lord Cornwallis in South Carolina for his campaign against General Gates; but when the news of our victory at Camden arrived, Lord George had assumed that the province was finally reduced and sent a packet in pursuit of the transports with orders for them to sail to New York instead. An American privateer fortunately intercepted this despatch, and the troops continued to Charleston, where they arrived in the nick of time. General Greene remained encamped on the Neck near the city. Do what he might, he could not prevent the Whigs of South Carolina from attempting to extirpate the Tories, nor the Tories from retaliating in kind upon the Whigs. Thousands of men were hanged by grapevines from trees, or by cords from the poles of fodder stacks, in the very sight of their children and women-folk. A civil war is always more cruel and vengeful than a foreign war; but here the angry climate was chiefly to blame.

Sir Henry Clinton was grieved when he heard that Lord Cornwallis had abandoned the Carolinas to their fate. He also trembled for his own safety at New York, were he the object of a combined attack of French and

Americans. It lies outside the scope of this work to attempt to disentangle the web of cross-purposes that was then woven between Sir Henry Clinton and Lord Cornwallis. Each had his own different plan of campaign and carried it out as best he could according to the limited knowledge that he had of the other's situation and his own; both were equally hampered by orders and counter-orders from Lord George Germaine (whose plan of campaign differed from that of either) and by their ignorance of what help they could count upon from Lord George in Downing Street, and from the Earl of Sandwich at Admiralty House. None of the despatches that each wrote the other cleared up the mist of misunderstanding but only increased it. The Earl of Cornwallis was in the worse case, as being expected to serve two masters, Sir Henry and Lord George, who contradicted each other and each continually countermanded his own successive plans as he became aware of altered circumstances; moreover, most of these despatches reached their destination either too late or not at all. Lord Cornwallis must therefore incur no blame for acting upon his own judgment, even if that proved at fault. He confessed himself greatly disappointed with the Loyalists of the Carolinas; the hope of their rising in large numbers, as expressed by Lord George Germaine, being totally disappointed. Many hundreds of them at different times had ridden into camp to shake hands with him and congratulate him upon his victory; but not two companies could be persuaded to remain with our Standard. His Lordship told an officer too, in my hearing that he was quite tired of marching about the great American Continent as it were in search of adventures.

There were no memorable occurrences in our forward march from Wilmington on April 25th, 1781. Since many rivers and creeks intervened between the Cape Fear River and the James River in Virginia, including the considerable floods of Nuse, Tar and Roanoke, two boats mounted on wagons were drawn along with the army. We had sufficient rum, salt and flour for a three-weeks' journey, and set off in good heart. The country was as barren as it had been described to us, but we were not molested in our march. Colonel Tarleton went ahead with his Greens and sixty mounted Royal Welch Fusiliers. Whenever he reached a settlement he was at pains greatly to magnify the size and power of our forces. I remained behind with the rest of the regiment, but was mounted and did some scouting and foraging.

It was not until we came to Tar River after a crooked journey of two hundred miles that, the country becoming more populous, we were able to supplement the stores carried upon the wagons; but at the same time met with some opposition at the river crossings. The militia of Halifax on the Roanoke River turned out in force. but our advanced troops bustled them away; and on May 20th, we joined forces on the borders of Virginia with General Phillips' army.

I was much grieved to hear that General Phillips himself was dead, only the week before, of a fever. He was a man equally beloved and respected for his virtues and his military talents. The Marquis de La Fayette, who had led down a small army with the prime object of capturing and hanging General Arnold, was not far off, but broke camp as soon as he was aware of our arrival. It seems that the young Marquis had lost his boasted French *politesse* since his arrival in America, for when a flag was sent to him across the river to inform him that General Phillips lay dying in a certain house, and request him to drop no more shells about it, he disregarded this embassy, and the cannonade continued. One ball passed through the room next to the death chamber. General Phillips' last words were: 'Now why in the world cannot that vainglorious boy let me die in peace? 'Tis very cruel.'

The junction of the armies was at Petersburgh, a town of about three hundred houses on a tributary of the James River, which runs into Chesapeak Bay. There were fine falls at the upper end of the town and some of the best flour-mills in the country. The houses were of wood roofed with shingles: the better sort were white-plastered, with brick chimneys and glazed windows; the poorer sort were left rough outside, with wooden chimneys clay-lined and only shutters to the windows. This was an important centre of the tobacco trade and also contained a number of general stores which used to supply the back country. Now trade was at a standstill, the merchants being unable to export their tobacco, for fear of British men-of-war and privateers, and thus to replenish their shelves.

The great warehouses and the mills of Petersburgh belonged to a Mrs Bowling, whose mansion General Phillips, and now Lord Cornwallis, used as their headquarters. This fine mansion was situated on a vast grassy platform on a considerable slope above the town. I was quartered in the stables there, at his Lordship's request, in order to be at hand for copying out his despatches. I remember how, early one Sunday morning, I paused entranced in the garden and thought to myself: 'Ah, what a sweet green oasis in the desert of War!' In my nostrils was the scent of clove pinks, of which a long border stretched down the garden path on either hand, and my eye feasted on the ripe apricots and nectarines hanging upon the well-pruned trees, the swelling green peas trained upon their sticks, and strawberries of enormous size netted against the depredations of birds. At the same time a mocking-bird was singing very finely from a plum-tree above my head, hopping incessantly from branch to branch; he was about the size of a thrush, but more slender. The mocking-bird would imitate the note of every other bird, but with increased strength and sweetness – to the discomfiture of the bird he mocked, who would fall silent and fly off. He imitated for me on this occasion the cardinal and the painted plover, and then (as if to raise a laugh) the wail and whimper of a black piccaninny! I clapped my hands and called out 'bravo!'; whereupon he flew off.

The interior of the mansion, one wing of which, by Virginian custom, was wholly dedicated to guests, appeared solidly but not exquisitely furnished, and rather for good cheer than for the cultivation of the polite arts; with much massive silver but no books or albums; several comfortable sofas but no cabinets of curios, and so forth.

The people of Virginia felt sentimentally about their great magnolia bushes with the broad leaves and heavily perfumed flowers; and about a very sweet white flower of smaller size called the 'bubby-flower' because it was presented by gallant young men to their sweethearts to place between their breasts. In New England, contrariwise, flowers and music were alike considered luxurious and 'a sign of slavery'. Virginia was the most mature and agreeable province in America that I had yet visited, and the nearest to my own country in manners. Fox-hunting with hounds, unknown in New England (where the chase was only for the sake of the pot), and cock-fighting (which the Yankees held un-Christian and barbarous), were with drinking and horse-racing the chief amusements of the Virginians. The fortune of the province, I must add, was founded upon tobacco, as firmly as that of the Northern provinces upon the cod-fish.

In our passage by the James River and other streams we observed to our surprise a great deal of derelict land in what seemed to us advantageous situations. The fact was that tobacco is a crop that soon exhausts the soil, and the settlers, when they had sucked all the richness out of a piece of land did not trouble to put it into good heart again but, with the money it had fetched, bought fresh land in the interior and settled there until that in turn was worn out. The exhausted land soon threw up a spontaneous growth of pine and cedar, but did not recover its fertility for about twenty years.

This was the season when the young plants of tobacco had just been removed from the seed-beds and transplanted into fields, where they were set out in hillocks at about a yard's interval, each from each; as hops are planted in Great Britain. Now the slaves, who were in general less brutish, since more humanely treated then those of the Carolinas or Georgia, were constantly tending the plants, picking off a large black fly of the beetle kind and all manner of other greedy insects, and removing weeds and worms with their hoes. When the plants attained about a foot in height the slaves would break off the tops, the suckers and the coarse lower leaves, in order to encourage the fine upper leaves. The plants would reach maturity in August and then be cut down for removal to the drying-houses, where they would be smoked, damped, sweated and smoked again. This work required the most delicate judgment, lest the leaves should crumble or rot. When sufficiently dry they were then stripped from the stems, sorted, and packed by means of strong presses into hogsheads of a thousand-pound capacity. The hogsheads were sent for inspection to a State warehouse – trundled along by a couple of strong pins at either end, by way of axles –

and certificates given in exchange for them; which certificates passed as currency in the province, and a man generally reckoned the value of a horse, a watch or a silver dish not in coin but in so many hogsheads of tobacco. However, much of this paper, the only American currency that had not hitherto depreciated in value, was now worthless from the raids made by General Arnold upon the tobacco warehouses.

When we arrived at Petersburgh we found a bitter dispute in progress between General Arnold and the Royal Navy, each side claiming the tobacco stored in Mrs Bowling's warehouse as its own prize. Lord Cornwallis settled the dispute, in Indian fashion, by burning the whole stock, amounting to four thousand hogsheads. However, from consideration for his hostess, Mrs Bowling, he first had it removed from the warehouses. It was a pleasure to us to learn that this tobacco, with what had been destroyed at Richmond and other places, was the property of the French Government and amounted to almost the whole of their annual remittance. We were surprised that with such discouragement the planters continued the manufacture of tobacco, but they must keep their slaves employed, and I suppose they hoped for better times. The Virginians, by the way, unlike the Carolinians, neither took snuff nor chewed tobacco, and few of them smoked – out of consideration for their women-folk, whose nostrils were easily offended.

The province now raised a deal of cotton, a shrub which flourished better on inferior land, or on land that had already had its first richness taken from it by tobacco; on virgin soil it produced more wood than cotton. This substance was contained in the swollen pistil of the flower, which burst open when ripe. The flocks intermixed with the seeds were then gathered by negroes; and the seeds later removed by means of a gin, a contrivance of two smooth rollers moving in contrary directions. The plant, which was set in regular walks, was kept down by cropping to a height of four feet. Though previously all cotton had been sent for manufacture to England, since the war the provincials had of necessity carded, spun and woven their own cotton-cloth, but little inferior to Manchester goods; the labour employed being that of female slaves. Much of this cloth here dyed blue with indigo, also of native growth.

Reinforcements now arrived from New York. They had been sent by Sir Henry before he knew of Lord Cornwallis' intention to come into this country, and they brought up the combined armies, of which his Lordship now took command, to above five thousand men. This made us greatly superior to the American forces in Virginia, and he determined to chase the Marquis out of the province. We crossed the James River without opposition at a place called Westover where the river was two miles broad. The Marquis decamped from his position at the tobacco town of Richmond and retreated north up the York River, ourselves in pursuit. However, he went too fast for us and Lord Cornwallis contented himself with ordering the destruction of tobacco and other public stores wherever they were found. General Arnold was not with us: he was recalled by Sir Henry to New York, whence he undertook a very successful raid against New London, in his own State of Connecticut, and did frightful damage. Congress would have done well to treat him with more decency and gratitude when his outstanding powers were exerted in the American cause.

We were near a place called Hanover in early June when orders came from Lord Cornwallis that greatly interested the Royal Welch Fusiliers. All the seventy horsemen among us were to be mounted upon blood-horses, numbers of which had been seized from the plantations of revolutionary officers, and sent upon a very enterprising jaunt under Colonel Tarleton, in company with one hundred and eighty Greens. The Virginia General Assembly were shortly to assemble at Charlotteville, in the foothills of the mountains seventy miles from us, where were the head-waters of the Rivanna, a tributary of the James River. They would meet under guard, for the purpose of voting taxes, drafting the militia and making an addition to the regular forces of the State. Their president was the famous Mr Thomas Jefferson, a citizen of Charlotteville, and the chief author (or rather compiler) of the Declaration of Independence. To break up this meeting was the object confided to us.

At dawn on June 4th, we set out, making our way between the North and South Anna Rivers. Our horses went unshod, as is customary in the South during the summer. It was an exceedingly hot day, but to have one's back unencumbered by the great luggage of a marching soldier, and even to be provided with pistols in place of a heavy musket, was delightful to us. The country was wooded and uncultivated and for several miles we did not pass a single human habitation or meet with a single person. We halted at midday to refresh ourselves, but pressed on again after two hours, and by eleven o'clock at night had reached Louisa after about forty miles' ride. Whenever we passed over a bridge we first blanketed it to prevent the drumming of our horses' hooves from giving the signal of our approach. At Louisa we were regaled with hearth-cake, bacon and peach-brandy by a Loyalist planter. At two o'clock we were in the saddle again and before the dawn of June 5th, struck the great road which ran along the skirt of the mountains and communicated between Maryland and the Southern States.

Here we were in luck. The rumble of wheels was heard in the distance, the crack of whips and the shouting of drivers to sleepy horses: it was twelve heavy wagons under a slight escort coming down the road from Alexandria. These we seized, taking the escort prisoner. They were found to be laden with clothing and French arms for General Greene's forces. We could not waste time or men in conveying these goods back to our army, and therefore burned them. This was a great disservice for the enemy, for long before this, according to General Greene's own account, more than two-thirds of his men were entirely naked but for a breech-cloth, and never came out of their tents; and the rest were as ragged as wolves, and shoeless. Soon after daybreak, at Dr Walker's plantation and in its neighbourhood, the Greens took from their beds a number of the principal gentlemen of Virginia, who had fled to this mountain border for safety. We had with us two Loyalist gentlemen who knew the records and characters of these persons, one of whom was a member of Congress. Some they recommended for mercy, some for capture, and a third sort for imme-diate slaughter. However, Colonel Tarleton was careful to do nothing violent: a month before, Lord Cornwallis had read the Greens a lecture on their brutal rapacity and, two of them, being picked out of a parade by country people as the authors of rape and murder, he had executed as an example to the rest. His Lordship had likewise forbidden all acts of terror and revenge. The more active enemies of King George were therefore secured and put under guard, the remainder paroled and allowed to remain with their families. We now halted for half an hour, having come seventy miles in twenty-four hours. We were very saddle-sore, those of us who were but horsemen for the occasion.

Precautions were taken to secure every person going in the direction of Charlotteville, which lay seven miles ahead of us, so that our arrival there might come as a surprise. Among those we seized was a great plump negro, driving a gaudy yellow cart, who acted as the Charlotteville post-rider. In his mail bags several important letters were discovered. Negroes in Virginia were forbidden by law to bear the consequential dignity of post-rider, but this one was, by a fiction, deputy to a four-year old white boy who rode in the cart with him. It was the child who wore the laced hat of office and had taken the oath before a magistrate, 'by the Almighty God', to carry the mail safely through. His childish lips were not, however, equal to a blast upon the post-horn, nor his fingers to the management of a pistol; and even the shrill cries of alarm raised by his black deputy failed to disturb his slumbers when we surrounded the cart and impounded the bags.

Various were the accounts given by this negro and other persons on the road as to the force assembled in Charlotteville: some trying to dissuade us from our adventure by magnifying the State Guard, others encouraging us by denying that any soldiers whatever were there. But we must strike at once or not at all. We were therefore ordered to urge our horses forward with all possible expedition. Captain Champagné begged as a favour from Colonel Tarleton that, should a charge be made into the town, our people might be given the honour of leading it. This was granted.

It was about breakfast time when, despite the warning of our scouts that the ford of the Rivanna was guarded by a company of Americans, we swept down the banks and across the water in a headlong gallop, losing but three men wounded, and pistolled the flying guards. The town was erected on the opposite bank: it was but a small place, consisting of about a dozen gentlemen's houses, with their negro-cabins and tobacco-houses, one 'ordinary' (or tavern), a Court House; and some barracks. We were immediately directed to charge up the street, which we did. So animated was my spirit that to the surprise of my comrades and the terror of my horse, who swerved, plunged and nearly threw me, I uttered a loud war-whoop in the Mohawk style. Some American officers now came running out from the houses, pistol in hand, to oppose us. They were shot down, and while one troop continued to the Court House, where the Assembly met, and another to the magazine, Captain Champagné led forty of us for some distance up a mountain in an attempt to catch Mr Jefferson.

A good carriage road of about three miles brought us to a large mansion in the Italian style, with columned porticoes, which was Mr Jefferson's residence, named Monticello. We were told by his servants, as soon as we arrived, that their master had heard the distant noise of shots and seen our red-coats coming up the hill. He had then provided for his personal liberty by a precipitate retreat: his horse was fresh and good and he was not to be overtaken by our exhausted ones. Captain Champagné entered the mansion, taking me with him, to make a close search; but Mr Jefferson was indeed gone.

Monticello, which occupied about an acre and a half on the extreme summit of the mountain, was a place which greatly differed from the other plantations of Virginia. Mr Jefferson was not a sportsman and no trophies of the chase adorned the house, of which he was himself the architect and to which he had given this Italian name. Instead, we found evidences of his philosophic studies, viz. terrestrial and celestial globes, a large telescope through which he had observed our approach, meteorological instruments and observations, and a sort of alchemist's den with phials, retorts and alembics. The centre of the mansion consisted of a large octagonal saloon, with glass folding doors opening upon a portico at either side. From one window there was an extensive prospect of the Blue Mountains rising for about three thousand feet, from the other, across a well-tended vineyard, we could see the wooded valley of the Rivanna. There was also a library upstairs with decorations in the antique Roman style, but not yet completed. The Captain apologized to the lady of the house (whom I suppose to have been Mrs Jefferson) for our intrusion and after a short examination of the premises, from which he removed some papers of an official kind found in a chest, led us down the hill again.

Meanwhile at Charlotteville seven members of the Assembly had been captured, with a few officers and men; one thousand new firelocks from the Fredericksburg manufactory had been broken; four hundred barrels of gunpowder, several hogsheads of tobacco and a store of Continental uniform clothing destroyed. We abstained from the plundering or destruction of private property, but spent all day in searching the district for what could be considered of public ownership or capable of hostile use against us.

We remained in the town for the night. Early the next day a party of twenty ragged men came into our piquets on the hill, huzzaing and singing. I was on duty not far away and strolled up with Smutchy Steel to see who they might be. The man who led them cried out at sight of me and came running to me with hand outstretched. I confess that I did not give a very cordial greeting to this savage, who had a great black beard, red moustachios and long matted hair, and was clad only in a pair of cotton trousers, with half one leg missing. But Smutchy had a sharper eye. 'Why, Terry Reeves,' he cried, 'is it not yourself?'

The meeting between the three of us was truly affecting – Corporal Reeves' companions were all members of the Army taken at Saratoga, chiefly men of the Twentieth and Fourteenth Regiments, but there were two others of The Ninth. They told of their long march from the pen at Rutland, during which they had suffered very great hardships. On their arrival they had been informed that they were not expected to arrive until the Spring, and thereupon led into a wood, where were a few log huts in the course of construction, but unroofed and filled with snow. The provisions were very bad, with only a little maize-flour and no meat or rum: to keep themselves warm the soldiers had drunk hot water in which red peppers had been steeped. They had lived a most miserable life for the last year and a half, the huts being made miserable by a plague of rats of enormous size. By sickness and desertion The Ninth, Terry said, was reduced to about sixty men; the inordinate drinking of cheap spirits had accounted for above a score. They had lately been ordered up to Little York in Pennsylvania. It was at the same time decided that their officers, in further violation of the Convention, were to be removed from them. When Terry Reeves heard this, he had asked permission of the American Colonel Cole, at whose plantation he had been working as a mechanic, to stay behind. A regiment without officers, Terry held, was no longer a regiment. Besides, the climate of Virginia was more agreeable to naked and hungry men than that of the Northern and Middle States; and Colonel Cole had behaved in a gentlemanly fashion. These other men had obtained the same permission from their masters. Terry told me that he was sorry now not to have joined Smutchy and myself in our escape from Hopewell; however, the war was not yet over and he hoped to strike another blow for his King and Country. He mentioned that the person who had done most for The Ninth in settling disputes, in organizing amusements and profitable labours, and in a thousand other ways, had been Jane Crumer, who still remained very faithful to her poor innocent husband and was called 'The Mother of the Regiment'.

Upon my warm recommendation of Terry Reeves to Captain Champagné, he was immediately taken upon the strength of the Regiment in his own rank. He had become a proficient horseman during his captivity and on our homeward journey that afternoon rode by my side, dressed in a captured Continental uniform and armed with two fine pistols taken from a dead officer. The other men were also incorporated in the Regiment, which with the sick and wounded now returned to duty, and a small draft, was brought up to the strength of about two hundred and fifty officers and men.

Our route was more southerly, down the valley of the Rivanna. Two of the captured Assembly-men rode close behind us, conversing with the Captain. They seemed relieved at the courteous treatment that they received and were very frank about the war. They said that the American cause was now at its last gasp, with the Congress armies unpaid, ill-fed and mutinous, the statesmen and officers of the North and South at odds, and the British raids upon the more prosperous parts of the country most crippling in their effect.

'It all turns now upon this,' said one of them, very earnestly, 'whether your people can prevent the intended co-operation between the French fleet and army and ours before the fall of the year. Hitherto the French have been a hindrance rather than a help, from raising hopes which they have always continually disappointed. They hold it against us that they have been disappointed in the shipments of tobacco, rice and indigo that they hoped from us in exchange for the muskets they sent. But that was no fault of ours. The vigilance of your fleet and the destructive raids of that traitor Arnold have prevented us from fulfilling our obligations. However, it is possible that they will respond to the pressing appeal now made to them, and then we shall see. But it is now crack and crack how matters turn; and let me tell you fairly, Sir, that if once more the French prove, like Egypt, a broken reed, then the jig is over. We Virginians at least will gladly dissolve our alliance with them and enter into honourable treaty with Great Britain. For, by God, we are now in a bad box.'

We came back safe, with no more adventure to myself than a rotten old pine suddenly crashing down in front of my horse, which, like myself, was sleepy from weariness and the hot sun. The woods hereabouts were full of such old rascals tottering with the slightest breeze.

CHAPTER XIV

NO OTHER event of remarkable interest took place during the whole of that summer. More public stores were taken and destroyed at various towns through which we passed, but Lord Cornwallis durst not lead us up into the Middle provinces without reinforcements. He hoped that Sir Henry Clinton would now evacuate New York and join him in Virginia, using Portsmouth or some other nearer seaport for a base. But Sir Henry was aware that the French had at last listened to the appeal of Congress – who were totally bankrupt and forced to obtain supplies by bills of impress, since nobody would accept their bills of credit – and were sending to their aid chests of coin, a fleet of overpowering size and a considerable army. General Washington called upon the country for one last effort to refill his depleted ranks, and now proposed with French help to drive Sir Henry out of New York, where were less than four thousand men. Sir Henry therefore ordered Lord Cornwallis to abandon his operations in Virginia and send every man he could spare to succour New York.

We had passed through the town of Richmond and were now encamped at Williamsburgh, an ancient place by American standards, lying in a plain between the James and York Rivers. It was a pretty place of three streets, with neat white houses surrounding a green, in the English style. Here was the University College of William and Mary, of which the Bishop of Virginia was president a heavy building like a brick-kiln; and the former Capitol of Virginia, a spacious brick edifice, in the hall of which stood the statue of a former Regal Governor, the head and one arm knocked off by Revolutionaries. There was also a hospital here for lunatics, but it appeared ill-regulated.

On receiving these new orders, Lord Cornwallis, though he would have preferred to return to South Carolina to assist Lord Rawdon, left Williamsburgh and marched us down towards Portsmouth. The Marquis de La Fayette who funding himself unpursued when we halted at Hanover, had returned to harass us, now tried to cut off our re02rguard during our crossing of the James River. Lord Cornwallis allowed our piquets to be driven in, to encourage the Marquis, and then with a counter-attack completely routed him and took two guns. This engagement, in which I had no part, took place near Jamestown, famous as the first settlement made by the English in Virginia. But no sooner had we crossed the river than another express arrived from Sir Henry, asking instead for three thousand troops to assist him in a raid through New Jersey on the enemy magazines at Philadelphia. We continued our march to Portsmouth. On our way we skirted the great Dismal Swamp, which extended southward into North Carolina and occupied about one hundred and fifty thousand acres. In the interior were large herds of wild cattle, the descendants of cattle lost on being turned into the swamp to feed, also indigenous bears, wolves, deer and, more remarkable, wild white men who were lost there as children and were perfect beasts. The swamp and its neighbourhood were remarkably healthy, and the water of a medicinal quality sovereign against fevers and bilious complaints: it was of the colour of brandy and tasted strongly of the juniper, a tree which abounded in it. Before the war, a very great quantity of barrel-staves had been cut and shaped on the swamp by negroes in the employment of The Dismal Swamp Company, but the work was carried on from Norfolk, close to Portsmouth, which was burned down in the second year of the war by order of the Regal Governor, and the enterprise abandoned. In that single burning £300,000 worth of damage was done; and even this was a very small part of the material loss incurred by the province because of the war. War was ever an expensive luxury to any nation but to such poor carnivores as the Huns and Vikings who had little to lose and much to gain.

When we arrived at Portsmouth, three thousand of us were duly embarked on transports for New York; but, just as we were putting out to sea, still another express arrived from Sir Henry to prevent our sailing. Lord Cornwallis was to keep the whole of his forces and return to Williamsburgh. There based, he was to fortify an adjacent harbour, where our larger ships could lie under cover of shore batteries, either at Old Point Comfort or Hampton Roads. Sir Henry's change of plan was due to a direct command from Lord George Germaine that not a single man was to be withdrawn from Virginia. Lord Cornwallis, disgusted with this continual chopping and changing, visited the two ports mentioned, taking his Engineer with him; but found that for geographical reasons they did not answer Sir Henry's purpose. We therefore were taken in the transports down the estuary of the James River and then by sea into the York River. Here, at a little distance from the mouth, where the stream suddenly narrowed to less than a mile across and ran five fathoms deep, were two ports, opposite to each other – Gloucester on the northern and York Town on the southern bank. These Lord Cornwallis believed, though they had faults, would correspond better with Sir Henry's requirements. He evacuated Portsmouth, an unhealthy and inconvenient station, at the end of August. A large number of Loyalists and their families, who had taken refuge in Portsmouth, could not be left behind there to the fury of the returning Revolutionaries; and were brought with us into Gloucester and York Town.

York Town, to which the Royal Welch Fusiliers went, contained about two hundred houses, a few taverns and stores, a jail and a church. The church was Episcopalian, the common religious persuasion in Virginia. Religion, however, had been totally interrupted by the war, the clergy being Loyalists, and the English bishops patriotically refusing to ordain Revolutionaries in their place. The churches, never well attended, had been allowed to fall into ruin. This did not greatly discommode the Virginians, I believe. Most of the gentry, including General Washington and Mr Jefferson, were little better than Deists, and the lower orders quite pagan. The fact was that General Washington, on first assuming his command, had forbidden the clergy to offer prayers for their Sovereign and Royal Family. He had asseverated that he was 'disposed to indulge the professors of Christianity with that road to Heaven which to them shall seem the most direct, plainest, easiest and least liable to exception'; but to sanction prayers for the Monarchy to which he was so inveterate did not suit his humour. Of near a hundred incumbents in Virginia, no more than twenty-eight, being Whiggishly inclined, or trimmers, remained in their parishes throughout the war. It was the same story in all other provinces of America. I heard tell of one parson, the Rev. Jonathan Boucher, at Annapolis in Maryland, who while the Revolution was first brewing preached always with a brace of loaded pistols on the cushion before him, chastening 'all silly clowns and illiterate mechanics who take upon them to censure their Prince'. One day the mob set a brawny blacksmith to waylay and beat him. In the event, the priest of God struck down the priest of Vulcan with a single punch below the ear, which earned him the admiration even of his foes. Yet he took no pride in this victory, and when the day came when he could continue no more in his cure, he told the people of Annapolis: 'You shall see my face no more among you, brethren. For so long as I live I shall cry with Zadok the priest, and with Nathan the prophet – GOD SAVE THE KING!'

At York Town, swamps drained by creeks lay on either side of the town, which was built along a slight cliff above the river; between them was half a mile of firm ground. These swamps were covered with red cedars and pine-trees, and an important industry hereabouts had been burning them for tar. The felled trees were simply heaped in a shallow pit, and the tar, running out, was later gathered up, cleared of the charcoal mixed with it, and put into barrels. Most of the tar-makers, however, had quitted the country, and no labour was anywhere to be had for fortifying York Town. We soldiers must rely upon our own exertions. The task was rendered very disagreeable because of the sultry weather, and the ground being baked exceedingly hard. We had but four hundred tools for the work, half of which were unserviceable. Sir Henry Clinton indeed ordered a great quantity of picks and shovels to be sent to us from New York, but these had not arrived. In the whole neighbourhood no more were procurable; for the agricultural work hereabouts was done with hoes.

At the very end of August, in a fatal moment which may be said to have turned the wavering scale of fortune in favour of the Americans, the French Admiral, Count de Grasse, arrived in the Chesapeak Bay with twenty-eight ships of the line. The sight was mortifying and astonishing to us, for five days before our Admiral Hood had been in those waters with fourteen ships, but, not finding the Frenchmen there, had sailed off to join Admiral Thomas Graves at New York. Admiral Hood had been positive that de Grasse would not bring with him more than ten ships – yet here was the best part of the French fleet!

Count de Grasse surprised two British frigates anchored in the mouth of York River, taking one and driving the other upstream beyond us. Then four of his frigates sailed past us, convoying a large force of French soldiers to join the Marquis de La Fayette at Williamsburgh; they went by night and we could not stop them with fire from our batteries. A week later we heard a cannonade from the sea. It was Admiral Graves who had sailed from New York with eighteen ships in order to intercept another French fleet of eight ships and a convoy of military stores and heavy artillery, that had slipped out of Newport, Rhode Island, and was thought to be coming our way. Instead of these eight ships of war, he found Count de Grasse with four-and-twenty, and immediately attempted to engage him; but, from the wind and other circumstances, he could not force the enemy to a battle which he preferred to decline. Our ships suffered some damage and Admiral Graves returned to New York to refit and fetch assistance. In his absence the eight ships from Newport arrived with their important convoy.

Lord Cornwallis would now dearly have loved to go out against the Marquis de La Fayette and his five thousand men. But he considered it wiser to employ us in improving our position, since his orders were to provide a secure base for the British fleet: true, our united squadrons would be inferior to the enemy, but the British had often before fought at a great numerical disadvantage and gained the victory. We therefore continued at our work of entrenchment, but because of the same scarcity of tools we made slow progress. We were unable to do more than raise an inner line of defences with parapet and stockade, which were to be protected at some distance forward by three redoubts. Other posts covered the passages through the swamps, including the road to Williamsburgh, which followed the bank of the river. The soil, when we broke through the hard outer crust, was very light and more suitable for the growth of cotton than for the construction of ramparts; we eyed it with mistrust. The defences at Gloucester across the river were completed in a shorter time, the earth lending itself more agreeably to military purposes.

News now came that General Washington, who had so long been immobile with his army on the Highlands of Hudson's River, had moved at last. He was coming down against us with a large army, paid in hard money from the French military chest, to which was joined the French army from Rhode Island: in all eighteen thousand men, to swell La Fayette's five thousand. But we remembered the successful defence of Savannah against a similar combination of arms, and consequently feared nothing. On September 28th, York Town was invested by the enemy, who camped at a distance of two miles away, General Washington's men facing the open half-mile between the swamps. Unfortunately our three advanced redoubts were not yet completed. We marched out to meet the enemy and formed in open ground, between these poor works, but he would not give battle. The next day we were pleased to hear that a message had come for Lord Cornwallis from Sir Henry Clinton, who, finding that Washington had slipped away from Hudson's River, undertook to sail to our relief on October 5th, with twenty-six ships of war and five thousand men.

Since the unfinished redoubts were untenable against heavy artillery, Lord Cornwallis withdrew us to the inner line, which we continued industriously to improve. The enemy occupied the positions that we had left. Half of the Regiment had been sent out along the Williamsburgh road on the extreme right, where assisted by a force of forty Marines they held the star-shaped advance redoubt on the cliff beyond the creek. Opposed to them was a French division under the Count de St Simon. These felt the defences of the redoubt but were driven off by a salvo of grape. Forty more of our mounted men skirmished across the York River under Colonel Tarleton against the French Hussars, or rather Lancers, of the Duke de Lanzun. The rest of us, myself included, were on fatigue duty in the town, which was excessively crowded. Over six thousand troops, and perhaps three thousand civilians, were cramped into a space about five hundred paces in breadth, by twelve hundred in length. Sickness soon broke out and raged through the camp, the sanitary conveniences of the town being very bad, and the weather continuing hot.

Orders came to my company on the morning of October 4th, to attend Lieutenant Sutherland, now the Chief Engineer, on the cliff above the river, where he set us to excavating a deep bomb-proof magazine. We worked at this task for a couple of days, and erected a wooden framework to support the roof. On the third afternoon the Earl of Cornwallis came himself to supervise the task, and criticized a few particulars. I overheard him instructing Lieutenant Sutherland, who came with him, how the window embrasure was to be cut overlooking the river, and how the stairway was to run. 'It is to be hung with green baize,' said his Lordship, 'which I will provide; and do you see that there is width on the stair for bringing down the bed, the *pondreuse* and the large *armoire*.' I cocked up my ears then; for this was clearly not to be a magazine for storing ammunition but a safe retreat for some lady. Two years before the Earl of Cornwallis had lost his beautiful wife, to whom he was greatly attached, and though at Charleston he had rejected the rather shameless advances of many Tory ladies, it was rumoured that at Portsmouth he had fallen in love with a beautiful Irishwoman, lately arrived from New York, and brought her here with him. However, his Lordship had been so discreet in this affair that nobody knew for certain who she might be.

Said Terry Reeves to me when I told him what I had heard: 'Good luck to his Lordship and the lass! It is unnatural for a man to live single, especially when he has so many cares upon his shoulders as has Lord Cornwallis.'

'He is a man whom I hold in great esteem,' I said.

'Ay, esteem,' said Terry, 'but for all that I wish another commanded us. A cross-eyed officer never brought an army good luck.'

This was October 6th, on the evening of which, in heavy rain, the enemy completed their first parallel of trenches at about six hundred yards from our parapet. Our cannon and mortars from the forward redoubts continually disturbed them at this work, which was done at night. They replied with occasional shots from their heavy artillery at a distance, which knocked up great clouds of dust, demolished houses and did much military damage.

Two days later I was sent for to Headquarters for my usual task of duplicating despatches – for which, by the bye, I was rewarded by his Lordship at the rate of one shilling a page – but by some error, when I arrived at Mr Secretary Neilson's house, where Lord Cornwallis lodged, I was conducted by the negro servant to his private apartment and desired to wait.

I heard a female voice in the corridor singing a song from Mr Gay's *Beggar's Opera*, which was very popular at the time, to the tune of 'Patie's Mill'.

> 'I, like the fox, shall grieve
> Whose mate hath left her side'

and, as the door opened, it continued:

> 'Whom hounds from morn to eve
> Chase o'er the country wide.
> Where can my lover hide,
> Where cheat the wary pack?
> If love be not his guide,
> He never will...'

Here it broke off suddenly, like a musical box demolished with a blow of a hammer; for seeing me, Kate Harlowe (who was dressed and coiffed in the finest French style) could only gasp and shudder. 'You, Gerry! O, it is not you, Gerry? I thought you dead – I heard it for certain. O, had I been so advised I should never have taken to this life!'

'You are his Lordship's mistress?' I asked in agitation.

She nodded in answer and began to weep. It was clear that she had altogether forgotten her resolve of coldness towards me.

'Where is our child? Does she live?' was my next question.

She wept still more and told me that she did not know. When General Sullivan's army had laid waste Genesee village, the child, who was being suckled by an Indian woman, had been among a small party of fugitives whom the Americans had cut off. Kate had done her utmost to obtain news of the child and even made a long solitary journey into American territory for that purpose; but could learn nothing. She had then made her way to New York, where an exchanged officer of The Ninth had informed her that I was killed. She had in despair become the mistress of an artillery captain, who brought her to Portsmouth; but there he grossly abused her, when in liquor, and Lord Cornwallis happening to pass the house and hear her cries, entered and gave the officer a severe beating. She then passed under his Lordship's protection, and he had since treated her with great affection and gentility.

'But, Gerry,' she cried. 'Even had I known you lived, how could we have continued together? I am married to Richard Harlowe; and be sure he is the sort of salamander who will never die of gunfire.'

'He is dead already,' said I. 'O, Kate, I killed him myself in battle in Carolina. He was fighting under General Greene.'

'You are telling the truth?' she demanded, her eyes now shining with joy.

'I never lied to you,' I replied. 'My dearest, I have dreamed of this meeting for so many years, and your image alone has sustained me in my long misery. Cannot you break your connexion with his Lordship and marry me?'

'When the siege is over, I will,' she said. 'But it would be most cruel to him at present, when he has such need of me and ungrateful too.'

'Will you not give me a kiss?' I asked, seizing her hand, which was stone cold. 'One single loving salutation in token of this promise?'

'Until I pass from his Lordship's protection, I cannot,' she said. 'I am his mistress. To kiss another man meanwhile would be to wrong him and make a common prostitute of me. Go now, dear Gerry. Be patient, and I will be true to you with my heart, since not with my body. Forgive me; but I cannot come to you now.'

I retired from the room, my breast tormented with mingled feelings of joy and mortification, pride and shame. Hearing his Lordship below giving some instruction to an officer, I slipped into a closet to avoid encountering him as he ascended the stairs. Soon he came up, two steps at a time, and I heard him greeting Kate in his merry, manly voice, as he entered the parlour. My great esteem for him at once prevailed over my jealousy and baser feelings. He was saying: 'Your bower is very prettily furnished, my lovely girl. You will be as safe there from the rebel shot as if you were in the Town of London itself. I will escort you there tonight, I promise you.'

I then went below and, his aide giving me the despatches which I was to copy, I concentrated my mind upon the task; but my hand shook, and though I made no blots or errors, my penmanship was not what it should have been. I excused myself to the officer, alleging that I was overtaken by a return of an old fever – as was, figuratively at least, true enough.

That evening our company was sent up to Fusilier Redoubt, as the right-hand post across the creek was named, to relieve another company. The French were constructing a counter-work at a short distance from us, and there was a hot exchange of fire. Captain Apthorpe commanded us, a very officer-like gentleman, who rejoiced that at last we stood confronted by our natural enemies the French, who fought moreover in a way that we understood.

'I believe,' he said, addressing Lieutenant Guyon, 'that the Regiment of Touraine is in the Count de St Simon's division. Our Regiment has already had the pleasure of engaging them more than once, when we fought under the Duke of Marlborough. And were they not also at Dettingen?'

Lieutenant Guyon replied: 'I believe you are right, Captain Apthorpe; and that we took them down handsomely.'

On October 9th, the enemy batteries opened upon the town from their first parallel, a distance of six hundred yards, making a very ominous noise. We sprang to arms, and soon the shells began flying about our own ears at Fusilier Redoubt, and in great numbers. This was by no means the first time that I had suffered a cannonade, but so well-nourished and violent a one did not lie in my experience. The whizz and roar was almost continuous, and the air was grey with the dust of our shattered parapet. Besides mortars and howitzers, they were pounding us with a battery of nine nine-pounders at only sixty paces distance. Our fraizing, that is to say the rows of palisades on the exterior of our parapet, was breached at several points and a number of men were killed and wounded. A shell broke directly over my head, so that I fell with my ears ringing and blood gushing from my nose and ears; and I imagined that I was mortally wounded. However, no metal had struck me and I staggered to my feet, prepared to continue with the fight.

Of what ensued I have no clear memory, on account of the dizziness of my head, but I was a veteran soldier by now, to whom battle was become second nature, and I gave my people their orders, I am told, in a very cool and sensible manner. At least, I remember tall French Grenadiers, in white

uniforms with sky-blue facings, issuing from their works and advancing at
a trot towards us; led on by officers who waved their swords and plumed
hats and cried *En avant, mes enfants!* or some such encouragement. Our
guns were trained point-blank on them, like infernal pointers at a dead set,
and blew their leading files to ruin with grape-shot as they struggled
through the obstacles of felled trees that intervened. On they came again
in a great crowd with *Vive le Roi!* and *Vive St Simon!* Our musketry halted
them on the glacis, and then down we swarmed at them with charged bayonets and drove them back.

They re-formed out of range and came on again; but I cannot distinguish between the first onset and the second. They numbered three thousand in all, and were volunteers, not impressed men, the best to be had in
France. This time, I am told, they gained the lip of the parapet and it was
very bloody work before we could dislodge them. Lieutenant Guyon
engaged their leader (who wore a brilliant order), sword against sword, and
took him with the *point d'arrête* in the throat. I have a confused recollection of seeing Lieutenant Guyon killed with a bayonet thrust and of seizing
his weapon from him as he fell, and reviving my old practice of small-
sword fencing in a combat with a French officer. But some person intervened, and then the smoke of battle cleared and the French were gone.

A bullet struck my head, furrowing through my scalp, and what then
occurred I can only relate *as it appeared to me,* for its actual occurrence can
only appear an absurdity to a judicious mind. From the tangle of trees a
man came strolling very calmly up the glacis, wearing the dress of a French
chaplain, with a little purple cap and lace at his neck. He had in his hand
what appeared to be a breviary, and stooping over the prostrate bodies of
the French soldiers he gave them each in turn the valedictory sacrament.
So far my account will pass muster, but then, as it appeared to me, he rose
and came towards me with pointed forefinger, revealing the wet black lock
and sallow features of the Reverend John Martin! He said to me in a cold,
sneering voice: 'How now, friend Lamb, have we met again? And will you
take the stick to me as you promised? But listen, for I have news for you: I
shall never have the pleasure of joining your hand with Mrs Kate's in holy
matrimony. For she was killed this morning at about nine o'clock by a
bomb-splinter at the entrance to her green-baized retreat.'

I ran at him with my sword. But my feet caught on a broken palisade
and I fell, and seemed to continue falling and falling, for a thousand years
into a bottomless pit, such as that which is said to be prepared for the
reception of the damned souls at the second coming of the Saviour.

I came to my senses some hours later. I was still in the redoubt. Smutchy
Steel was by me, and grinned with delight to see me recover. I asked him
in a weak voice, that seemed to proceed from a great distance away, what
had occurred.

'Oh,' he said, 'we beat 'em off, the third time, and that. was the end.
Your wits were a little turned, I think. You went rushing out with a sword
against a poor harmless French priest – now I had thought better of you,
Gerry – you always told me that you had no quarrel with the Papists. But
here's sorrowful news for you and me. When you fell in a faint and were
carried back, poor Terry Reeves was given your command. He is dead. A
nine-pounder ball struck him.'

I fell to sobbing from mere weakness, but soon as I had rallied my forces
I called the faithful Jonah to me. I told him that, when he went down that
evening with the party to draw the rations, he should enquire whether the
rumour was true that a lady had been killed at such and such a spot by the
cliff, that morning at nine. When he returned, it was to tell me that it was
true: a 'very beautiful young woman in a green sprigged dress', killed with
a bomb-splinter through the throat. But nobody seemed to know her
name.

For the next three days I rambled in my speech, so Smutchy told me
after, wept frequently and said many ridiculous things, telling of sights
that were mere mirage and invisible to other eyes. But I was kept at my
duty, for I had no fever.

The enemy meanwhile had battered our unfinished defences on the left
of the town, silenced the guns that we mounted on them and searched the
whole line of houses at the cliff top. Mr Secretary Nielson's house was
holed in a number of places, but Mr Nielson himself was so philosophical
as not to quit until his negro servant was blown to pieces at his side. On
October 11th, the enemy crept nearer, and established his second parallel
at but three hundred yards from our parapet. Our people defended themselves with howitzers and coehorns (or light mortars of four and a half
inches calibre), but the guns at our embrasures were dismounted as soon
as shown. For the enemy worked sixty powerful breaching-guns and a
number of heavy mortars. About this time a despatch from Sir Henry
Clinton came up the river for Lord Cornwallis, informing him that the
departure of the relieving fleet had been delayed by a complexity of
mischances, and expressing great anxiety for his situation.

A desperate project was pressed upon Lord Cornwallis by Colonel
Tarleton and others; which was to remove the greater part of the garrison
by night and take it across the river for an attack upon the forces of the
French General, Choisy, who was investing Gloucester. It was believed
that we might easily break our way through; and by travelling very light
and seizing all the horses of the Roanoke country, which was rich in provisions and fodder, we might force a passage through Maryland,
Pennsylvania and the Jerseys and attain New York. His Lordship seemed
confused in his mind and unable to agree to this project. His vacillation
surprised his officers, for he had hitherto shown himself very collected and
resolute. But I heard privately from his chief clerk, under whose direction

I had worked and with whom I was intimate, who had it from his Lordship's own valet, that his Lordship on the morning of October 9th, had been 'struck with great horror and grief by the news of pretty Miss Kate's death'. He had since been drinking more than was his habit, and soliloquizing to himself as he paced about his parlour alone. The valet added that Lord Cornwallis had not shown himself so unmanned since news had reached him two years before of the death of his lovely Countess. I must decline to enlarge upon my own feelings of grief, not wishing to present them as it were in rivalry to those of Lord Cornwallis.

It was not until October 14th that his Lordship could be persuaded to agree to the plan of escape; by which time our palisades were all down and but one single shell remained for the remaining eight-inch mortar, and a few boxes of coehorn shells. Undismayed by a sortie from our lines, in which eleven of their guns had been spiked, the combined armies of the enemy were preparing for the assault. The spiking of these guns, it may be observed, was a botched task, the soldiers who took part in the sortie not being provided with spiking irons. They merely broke off the points of their bayonets in the touch-holes, and these were readily removed afterwards. By now our effective forces were reduced to four thousand men, two thousand being unfit for duty from sickness or wounds; but continued of undaunted spirit; and since we were seasoned troops, who could march and starve with the best, we had no doubt at all but that we would pull the chestnuts out of the fire.

On the evening of October 15th, therefore, the Light Infantry, the greater part of the Brigade of Guards, and seventy Royal Welch Fusiliers (Smutchy and myself among them) were embarked upon boats and taken across the river to Gloucester Point. We were to effect a landing there and with our fire cover the passage of the rest of the army. But hardly had we reached the other side, which was about midnight, when the weather, from being calm and moderate, changed to a most violent storm of wind and rain. Our boats were blown down the river nearly to the Ocean. The passage of the rest of the troops, who counted upon these same boats, now became impracticable, and though the storm abated and we managed to make our way back to York Town before morning, we were greatly harassed by fire from the banks and lost a number of men.

Thus expired the last hope of the British army. Our defences were tumbled to ruin and it was the opinion of the principal officers at a Council of War that it would be madness to maintain them. In the morning, at Lord Cornwallis' orders, a drummer mounted upon our parapet and beat a parley. The Duke de Lanzun then came forward alone, waving a white silk handkerchief; and was informed that Lord Cornwallis proposed a cessation of hostilities in order to settle terms for a capitulation.

To be short: this was granted by General Washington and terms adjusted for our surrender as prisoners of war on the following day. The capitulation was signed on October 19th – the very day that Sir Henry Clinton, after long delays, sailed to our relief from New York with seven thousand men.

The honours of war granted to us were much the same as General Lincoln had obtained at Charleston, and he himself, being now exchanged, received the surrender of Lord Cornwallis' sword; but at General O'Hara's hands, his Lordship being sick. We marched between a long lane, with well-groomed French troops on one side, ragged Americans'on the other; and piled up our arms. We were forbidden, in revenge for the Savannah terms, to use either a French or an American march. Our musicians therefore very properly played *The World Turned Upside Down*. Our standards were cased, not flowing, and this enabled two of our officers – Captain Peter and, I believe, Lieutenant Julian – to remove the Colours from the staves and conceal them upon their persons. The field officers of the Count de St Simon's Brigade sought out Captain Apthorpe and highly praised him upon our defence of the star-shaped Redoubt. They could hardly credit it when they learned that we had fought that day against odds of nearly twenty to one. They observed at the same time what a pleasure to them it was to converse thus agreeably with Englishmen of distinction and sensibility – glancing rather severely at their American allies as almost totally ignorant of the 'language of culture', namely French. At the same time the young Duke de Lanzun sought out Captain Champagné to congratulate him upon the fine bearing of his mounted Fusiliers in the skirmish near Gloucester. These compliments to some degree comforted our people for the disgrace of the surrender, which was the first (as I trust the last) occasion that the Royal Welch Fusiliers were ever forced to yield since their first enrolment in the year 1689. Our losses, of thirty-one officers and men, had left us the weakest corps in the whole army.

The usual jealous quarrels broke out between the officers in the victorious army. An Ensign Denny, of the Marquis de La Fayette's division, was in the act of planting the American flag on our broken parapet in sight of the three armies, when up galloped Major-General Baron Steuben, General Washington's Prussian drill-master, seized it from him and planted it himself. This raised great laughter among our people and great scandal and argument among theirs. An American colonel challenged the Baron to a duel. But General Washington hushed the matter up, for the old Baron was better acquainted with the laws of war than the Marquis de La Fayette. The Baron had commanded in the enemy trenches when the drum first beat the parley, and the honour of planting the flag was therefore his.

I had by now somewhat recovered my health of mind, and was naturally curious to gaze upon the person of General George Washington, for whose patience, uprightness and courage the British army in general had conceived a great respect; though there were many who could not abide him for his part in condemning poor Major André to the rope. I espied him in the company of a group of high French officers, with whom, however, he was unable to converse in their own language. He was as plainly clothed as he was well mounted. His body was tall, but not stout, his face much pock-marked and with the largest eye-sockets I ever saw in a man. The expression was severe, as of one who has struggled successfully for many years against malice and disloyalty in his associates, and against the sins of pride and anger in himself.

CHAPTER XV

THIS SURRENDER was to prove fatal to our cause in America, though we still had a quantity of troops stationed on that Continent, and though King George, who received the ill news with perfect composure, was for a continuance of the struggle at all events. Lord George Germaine resigned at last, which was something gained by the country he had so ill served, and was rewarded for his extraordinary services with a viscountcy. The universally detested Earl of Sandwich, alias Jemmy Twitcher, continued in office a few months longer. (His latter years were lonely, for two years before this he had lost his arrogant, greedy but devoted helpmeet, Miss Ray, whom a former lover of hers, the Reverend James Hackman, shot dead with a pistol at the door of Covent Garden Theatre.) The Ministry now declared that none but defensive operations could be conducted against the Americans, and in effect no engagement upon a grand scale was thereafter fought. The fact was, we were waging several important wars at the same time: with the Spaniards at Gibraltar and Minorca – with the massed hordes of India, with the Dutch in almost every sea and ocean of the world – with the French in the West India Islands and India, besides here in America. The poet William Cowper wrote truly and feelingly at this time:

> Poor England! Thou art a devoted deer,
> Beset with every ill but that of fear.
> Thee nations hunt. All mark thee for a prey.
> They swarm around thee, and thou standst at bay,
> Undaunted still.

Moreover, the Armed Neutrality of Europe, a league consisting of Russia, Prussia, the Scandinavian and Baltic nations, Portugal, Turkey, and in fact nearly the whole of Europe, was opposed to us. These countries were banded together to resist by force the 'brigandage and cupidity' of our Navy, when we stopped and searched neutral vessels bringing munitions of war to our numerous foes.

The Opposition now howled for a complete withdrawal of all our forces from America, the better to preserve our own islands. Yes: and we might never have found ourselves in such a fix but for their leaders, who had put party interest before national honour. Careless of the lives of our poor fellows in America, they had secretly promoted the American cause by traitorous correspondence with Dr Franklin and Mr Silas Deane, as well as by false reports and libels printed in their scurrilous newspapers. Yet between politicians, who shall judge? Of the Tory leaders, most of those who were not merely idle and incompetent in their duties were downright evil. In Shakespeare's phrase one might cry: 'A plague on both your houses!'

It was truly grievous to perceive the style of exultation in which the party writers of the Opposition indulged on the capitulation of Lord Cornwallis. One of them, in direct terms, spoke of 'the pride of Lord Cornwallis'. What pride? The very reverse was his Lordship's true character. In this campaign (I declare these facts from my own knowledge) he fared like a common soldier. He assumed, he would admit of, no distinction, not even indulging himself in that of a tent. When a beloved officer is the object of viperous attack, it must rouse a resentment in the mind of every old soldier still living, *who knows the contrary to be fact*, which it is not very easy for military feeling to bear, or even for Christian forgiveness to pardon. Mr Ramsay, too, has a very prettily manufactured tale on this occasion: 'The door-keeper of Congress, an aged man, died suddenly, immediately after hearing of the capture of Lord Cornwallis' army. His death was universally ascribed to a violent emotion of political joy.' Mr Ramsay strongly reminds me of a celebrated Republican preacher, in England, who had the impiety to take for his text the words of good old Simeon, 'Lord now lettest thou thy servant depart in peace, for mine eyes have seen thy Salvation', when he preached a sermon to celebrate the French Revolution!

It is interesting to recall that the American Revolution was the means of introducing into France novel ideas of independency, which, gaining a hold among the common people, proved fatal to the established Government. The young French officers of the Newport army who travelled about America and were entertained by a vigorous, hospitable and self-sufficient peasantry, impatient of Government, returned to Europe and there, with great enthusiasm, propagated philanthropical notions. Indeed, they lighted a train of gunpowder that blew their own magazine sky-high. Europe would have been spared thirty years of bloodshed, had these red-heeled young philosophers stayed at Court. It is said that Queen Marie Antoinette's party had difficulty in forcing on the unfortunate King Louis XVI the treaty with America. Though not averse to depressing Britain, he regarded it as an unfair measure and, when asked to sanction it with his signature, threw away the pen. On repeated importunity, however, he relented and signed the instrument which was indirectly to prove the death-warrant for himself and his lovely young Queen. A large number of the high officers before whom we defiled (including the Duke de Lanzun) were before many years to die under the knife of Dr Guillotine's humane instrument or languish for years in prison; and among the rank and file were numerous men destined to be their judges, jailers and executioners.

The Spanish monarchy was likewise ruined by the same contagion and so served out for the part that it took against us.

Let me here append, as a curiosity, an extract from a speech delivered in Congress, when the news of our surrender arrived, by the famous Dr Witherspoon, President of Nassau College at Princeton, and the first Classical scholar of America. I must, let me make clear, take exception to his severe and ungrateful attack upon General Washington, as also to his censure upon Admiral Sir Thomas Graves (who afterwards fought very gallantly under Admiral Howe at the Glorious First of June). In the Chesapeak fighting Sir Thomas did all that could have been expected of him; but he was unlucky. However, Dr Witherspoon's praise of Lord Cornwallis at least is not amiss, and I trust that the speech will not prove uninteresting as showing the disunion and uncertainty of American opinion at this time.

It is incumbent on us to thank Heaven for the victory which we have just obtained, and though over a handful of troops, yet they were flushed with success, and led on by a General, whose valour is no less illustrious than his discretion; by a General not equalled in courage by the Macedonian madman, or, in wise and solemn deliberation, by the Roman Fabius; nor has his defeat tarnished his fame; for he was encompassed about with a mighty host of the picked troops of France and America, aided by a formidable navy; and, to sum up his difficulties, he was attacked by famine in his camp.

It would be criminal in me to be silent on this occasion, which has diffused such joy in every breast. To procure America freedom and happiness has ever been my study, ever since I arrived among you; for this I have encountered a variety of hardships, and suffered not a little in my private fortune and reputation.

Now, gentlemen, since victory irradiates our arms, let us snatch this opportunity of securing to ourselves advantageous terms of peace; so shall we reap a profitable benefit from the example of all the wise states so eminent in history.

Some may think it very censurable, and highly derogatory to the dignity of this mighty Commonwealth to crouch and offer terms of peace, when we have been gathering such blooming laurels; but when we duly weigh all the circumstances of our overrated victory, the reasonableness of my advice may more fully appear to every dispassionate man.

Lord Cornwallis's troops had boldly marched through the heart of our country, opposed not only by woods, rivers and swamps, but also by all the force we could send against him, which was greatly superior to him in numbers; his whole army, I would say his foraging party (for it does not deserve the name of army) did not exceed four thousand; and, small as it was, it had spread universal dismay; it had struck terror even into General Washington's camp, and wondrous to relate (!) brought that man of valour out of his lurking place (which it would seem he had taken a lease of) at the head of no less than thirteen thousand troops, whom he had been training to arms, and teaching to storm mock castles these three years, in a strong impregnable camp, where no enemy would ever think it worth while to disturb his slumbers, and so panic-struck was the American hero, that even with the great and formidable army under his command, would he not dare to attack an English foraging party; no, he must first be sure the French were before him with eight thousand of the gens d'armes, as a breastwork, to save his gallant troops, whose blood has ever been so precious to him. And to complete his safety, that thirty sail of the line-of-battle ships, manned with twenty-five thousand seamen (half of whom might act ashore) were within call of him. Heavens! Gentlemen, if every victory is to cost us so dear, if we must send into the field fifty thousand men before we can capture four thousand fatigued, half-starved English, we must view at a very remote distance, our so much wished for Independency: to bring this about if we go on as we have, for these long seven years, we ought to have more than all the wealth of all Mexico and Peru, and our women must bring forth four males at one birth. O dauntless spirit of immortal Cromwell behold how enervated are thy descendants!

Gentlemen, trivial and contemptible as our success is, we got it by mere accident; we got it not by the vigilance of our allies, or the powers of our arms; we got it by the neglect or cowardice of the British Admiral, who would not, when he had the golden opportunity, take possession of the Chesapeak; and to this gross blunder alone are we to ascribe our fortune. But, gentlemen, although one commander has abandoned his post, and betrayed the best interests of his country, can we suppose that his guilt will not meet that severe and exemplary punishment it deserves? Can we hope that British vengeance will never wake, that it will always sleep? When that culpable Admiral is put to death, do you foolishly imagine his successor will not be alarmed for himself, and profit by his fate? Yes; he will exert himself, he will be master of the Chesapeak, upon which you know our destiny hangs; for if that is once shut up, Virginia and Maryland, the springs of all our resources, the objects which enticed your good and great ally to aid you, are no morel Then a few British soldiers may harass our planters, lay waste their lands, set their tobacco in flames, destroy their docks, and block up such ships as they cannot burn or capture.

It is a painful task, gentlemen, for me to set before your eyes a true picture of your affairs, but it is the duty of a friend. He who flatters you at this awful period smiles in your face while he stabs you in the vitals; it is by exhibiting to you such a picture, that you will be convinced you ought to send Commissioners to treat with Britain for peace, without a moment's delay. Our enemies, I own, are surrounded with danger; a strong confederacy is in arms against them; yet although they possess but a speck of land, the fortitude of Britons, their exertions and supplies, have astonished the wondering world; they are by no means exhausted: they have hitherto asked for no alliance, they have singly and alone kept all their combined foes at bay. Britain has yet in store very tempting offers to hold out to any potentate whom she may court; she is mistress of our seaports; the large and fruitful colony of Canada is hers; her fleets have all arrived from Quebec, the Baltic, the West Indies and East Indies, without the loss of a ship; her arms in Asia have carried conquest before them; so long as they hold their dominions there, they will have a perennial source of riches. Such is the situation of our foe; but how much more terrible may she become, if she joins to her already resist-less marine the fleet of another power!

Suffer me to use the words of the prophet Jeremiah, and ask you, 'If thou hast run with footmen, and they have wearied thee, how then canst thou contend with horses?' When your enemy has once made such an addition to her strength, she will rise in her terms upon you, and in the paroxysm of her fury insist upon your submission, your unconditional submission! In order that I may not displease some of you, who hold a man a traitor for telling you wholesome truths, I will suppose all I have said to be exaggerated; I will suppose Britain to be in a galloping consumption; then let me interrogate you. Do you increase in power and wealth? The very reverse is your case. Your maladies, I am sorry to tell you, are incurable. Where are your numerous fleets of merchant ships, which were wont to cover old Ocean? Have you so much as one to convoy your cargoes, or save them from capture? Have you any goods to export? Where are your luxuriant glebes and smiling meads? Alas! they are now an unculti-vated waste. Your commerce is extinct; the premium of insurance on the very few ships which dare to peep out, never more to see their natal shore, so enormous, seamens' wages so high (for nothing but death or an English dungeon is before them!) that ruin and bank-ruptcy have overwhelmed all descriptions of men; hardly any possess the conveniences, none the luxuries of life but faithless secretaries avaricious commissaries, and griping contractors. These, indeed, loll in their coaches, live in princely palaces, have a numerous train of vermin to attend them, and fare sumptuously every day. 'Curse on the wretch who owes his greatness to his country's ruin!'

Would to God I could here draw a veil over our calamities! but the zeal I have to serve you will not allow it. I must thunder in your ears that your trade is annihilated; your fisheries, that fertile nursery of seamen, that fountain of all we could ever boast, are no more! Our ploughshares beat into bayonets, our soldiers mutinying for want of pay; our planters beggared, and our farmers ruined! You are oppressed with taxes; not to emancipate you from bondage – no, with taxes to support the lazy; to pamper the proud; to exalt mean, cunning knaves and dissipated gamblers to the first offices of the State, to pay armies who have the figures of men, but the hearts of hares; they are, God knows, numerous enough; but of what use? Why do we call in soup-meagre[1] soldiers? Are our own cowards? Are they not disciplined after so many years dancing a jig to the fife and drum? Will they not look an enemy in the face when their religion, their liberty, is at stake; when their wives and children are butchered before their eyes?

O America! America! Thou art now ruined and past redemption, consigned to destruction! Curse on this French connexion! I see thee prostrate on the ground, imploring mercy at the feet of the Gallic monarch. If France conquers Britain (which, for your sakes, I pray God to prevent!) I tremble when I think of the accumulated miseries with which you will be loaded. The French have already cheated you out of Rhode Island from whence, as from a flaming volcano, will stream fire to burn your ships, and lay your seaports in smoking ruins. Methinks I see already the Canadians rush in upon your possessions in the North, and the French and Spaniards overrun your southern colonies! Like an impetuous torrent they sweep all before them! And even those of your own flesh and blood, whose lands you have confiscated, whose fathers and brothers you have murdered, join to lay you desolate! I see you turned into a desert, exposed to the ruthless elements, calling upon some hospitable roof to hide you from the storm! May Heaven save you from calamities, and dispose you to sue for peace! 'Now is the appointed time; now is the day of salvation!'

---

1   That is to say French soldiers who subsist upon thin soup. – R.L.

CHAPTER XVI

MY OFFICERS, made aware from my attention to the wounded after the battles of Camden and Guildford Court House that I was a surgeon of sorts, sent me over the river from York Town to the General Hospital at Gloucester, a town of not more than twenty houses, to supervise our wounded; for the Regimental Surgeon was sick. Captains Champagné and Apthorpe, as well as the junior officers, were very obliging when they bade me farewell; and professed their deep regret that sergeants could not, equally with themselves, be permitted to return to Europe on parole. The most affecting good-bye was spoken to me by the negro Jonah, whose condition as a slave inscribed him among the officers' baggage which the terms allowed them to retain. He was to sail to England with them, as steward to their mess, by the next packet. When he learned that we were to be parted, he fell at my feet and blubbered. Said he: 'Sarnt Lamb, massa, you be de best friend poor old black Jonah ebber hab. You done rescue me from de meat-house and make me mighty consequential military nigger. Jonah, him nebber forget darra good Sarnt Lamb, nebber kind murrer like to him.'

Only Captain de Saumerez continued with the men of the Regiment, in order to protect them from abuses while in the quality of captives. They were now marched off with the rest of the troops to Winchester, in the back-country of Virginia.

I remained behind in the hospital at Gloucester for five weeks, by which time my wounded comrades had either succumbed to their wounds or were in a fair way to recover. Being sent back across the river one day I went to muse at the grave of poor Kate. It lay close to the entrance of the bomb-proof boudoir, which still remained handsomely furnished for her pleasure and that of Lord Cornwallis, and attracted numerous sightseers. I wished that the Quaker Jonah were there to pray with me: my heart was still stunned and mute.

The only cure for melancholy being action, I resolved upon another escapade from the hands of my enemies. Rather than rot again in a prisoners' pen as I would be bound to do as soon as the hospital was removed from this place – I would willingly face any conceivable hardship and danger, in the wilds of America, as a free man. With this object in view, I waited the next day, November 28th, upon the Surgeon-General, and resigned my situation in the General Hospital; acquainting him that I intended to follow the troops to Winchester. Having then received the balance of pay due to me for the hospital service, which was forty shillings, I relinquished my wig and epaulettes and put on the clothes of a private soldier who had that day died of a wound. I packed my knapsack with shirts, stockings and other necessaries; and also took about half a pound of flour, some dried beef and a small bottle of rum – but these were to be a reserve and only drawn upon in an extremity. My next consideration was how to elude the French and American sentinels who guarded the barriers on the road to the North. This was likely to prove a difficult task, but I was aware that both the French guard and the American were relieved at ten o'clock in the forenoon and I judged that the best time to elude them was when the relief was in progress and their attention therefore distracted.

I was right in this conclusion. I found the French guard, who were Soissonais and wore fine rose-coloured facings, more concerned with the ceremony and show of the guard-changing than with the chief object in hand, which was to prevent prisoners from escaping. I wrapped a blanket around my regimentals and appeared as an innocent sightseer, seating myself on the barrier. While the old guard were inspected by their officer before dismissal, and the new guard were being addressed by theirs – the sentinel of the old guard being already withdrawn, and that of the new guard not yet posted – I climbed down on the other side of the barrier and strolled along the Rappahannock road.

The American method of guard-changing was equally characteristic of the newer nation. At ten o'clock the old guard was due to be relieved and therefore merely walked off, trusting that a few minutes later the new guard would arrive. I found the post deserted and, passing the barrier, immediately struck right-handed into the tangled pine-woods that fringed the road.

I made a circuit of about a mile in order to avoid the piquet guard, which was thrown out at a convenient distance to protect the camp from possible attack, and then made for the road at a point a few miles beyond. Unfortunately, not knowing that the road took a sharp turn to the left after a few miles, I did not strike it again so soon as I had expected. I grew confused and alarmed and thus became aware how weak my health still was. To extricate myself from this wood seemed like a task set a dreamer in a nightmare. There were many ponds, which to a romantic eye would have seemed delightful but grossly offended mine. I climbed upon a slight hill above one of them just as the sun was setting, but could make out nothing save continued forest, nor keep my teeth from chattering in the sudden chill that ascended from the pond.

Before it was completely dark I came upon a rough track that led from a clearing where some trees had lately been burned for tar, and this fetched me to a collection of poor houses standing close to the road of my search.

I went to the nearest house and knocked. A rough man came to the door, swaying on his legs. He had but one eye and, as I descried in the blaze of a huge pine-wood fire that burned in the grate, very long nails.

'What do you want?' he asked in a ruffianly voice, his whole person reeking very strongly of apple-brandy.

'A lodging for the night, if you please,' I replied.

'Do you see these talons of mine?' he asked, displaying them in uncination. 'Now ain't they a pretty set? I suppose you wouldn't like to fight me, would you – nothing barred? Bite, bollock and gouge is my trade – in which I lost one eye, over to Hob's Hole, last quarter-races. Yet I would be happy to risk another peeper in a good cause. I warrant you're a redcoat son of a bitch, run off from Gloucester, heigh? Now I'm surprised you dare show your cursed face at my door: phoo, you lousy fellow! You redcoats ain't fighters: all that you are equal to is swaggering about at the grogshops and nanny-houses. Who turned you out of the Carolinas, tell me that? Little dried-up General Marion did, he and his patriot crew on their poor starved tackles, with grape-vine bridles and sheep-skin saddles: ay, they made you run all right, I'll warrant 'em. Well, say now, will you fight? Or shall I swing you back by the collar to Gloucester Point?'

A woman's voice came from the room within. 'Dear me now, Joe my honey, why will you ever be picking quarrels? Perhaps this traveller has a little hard money to pay his score. Hearts alive, in these times, we surely can't quarrel with hard money?'

I naturally did not own to the possession of coin, lest it be all stripped from me on some pretext or other. Instead I begged them to take me in as a charity.

'Charity, eh, a pretty story! I swear you're in the wrong furrow,' cried the woman warmly, coming forward; and I observed that she was very fat and had only one eye, like her husband, and that the flesh about it was bruised red, blue and yellow. Her face was blowsy, and scratched from cheek to chin. 'Charity indeed, you ugly jack? Those that have no money have no business to travel. Get you gone!'

Here her husband interposed, thrusting her aside: 'No, stay, you poor bastard,' he said. 'I'll fight you for the price of a night's lodging.'

I told him I could not oblige him, being unskilled in the manner of fighting in use thereabouts (compared with which an Irish boxing match is mere kiss-in-the-ring) and but lately recovered from a severe illness. He called me a white-livered gallow's fruit and rushed out from the door to kick at me with his hob-nailed shoes; but tripped over his spaniel in the half-light and measured his length in the mud.

The sight of this couple disgusted me. I had never witnessed a rough

Virginia fight, but the mode had been described to me as resembling that of wild beasts. The practitioners, who were of course all men of the lower orders, prided themselves upon the dexterity with which they could gouge or scoop out an eye. To perform this horrid operation the combatant would twist his forefingers in his adversary's long side-locks and then apply his thumbs to the base of the orb. What was worse than all, these wretches would endeavour to the utmost to castrate each other.

I went away into the woods, my stomach sick, my heart low, and my head ringing again as when the shell had broken above me; so that I was scarcely able to determine what course to take. The weather turning very cold with a violent wind from the north, I made a desperate effort and brought myself to the door of a house a few hundred yards away. Through the chink of a window-shutter I saw a severe-looking woman of about thirty years old seated at a table surrounded by a number of children. She was ladling them out a meal of rice and boiled bacon, with a bowl of milk for each poured from a pitcher.

I knocked, and she bade me enter.

'What do you want?' she demanded.

'Please, madam, only the favour of a corner of your house to sleep in. I have lately been ill and have lost my way upon the road.'

She looked at me very sternly and asked: 'How can you expect such a favour from me, or any woman of Virginia, seeing you came from England with an intent to destroy our country?'

I replied very humbly: 'Indeed, madam, you are wrong. I was never in England in my life. I was first sent from Ireland to protect the homesteads of Canada from an unprovoked invasion by Americans.'

She startled at this. I continued: 'But you know how wars go, madam: one campaign leads to another. I have at least always refrained from plunder and private injury, and obeyed my officers, as a soldier is bound to do.'

A little girl slipped down from her stool and came up to me: 'I have a little red bird in a cage,' she said. 'It is very clever, you know. It eats the crumbs I give it. Come and see it, poor man.'

'Child, go back to your food, instantly,' the mother said scoldingly but not unpleased.

'Then I will show the poor man my bird afterwards,' said the child gravely.

'Your little maid has a sweet nature,' I remarked. 'She knows that I am unfortunate and wishes to do what she can to cheer me.'

The woman almost angrily ladled me out some of the rice, together with a small piece of the bacon, and drew up a chair for me. 'Eat,' she commanded. I ate.

She then drew me a pewter pot of cider. 'Drink,' she commanded. I drank.

The little girl said: 'My name is Henrietta. My brothers provoke me by calling me Etta. What is your name?'

I told her that it was Roger Lamb and she simply laughed. The other children were abashed and said nothing. The woman began asking me questions about Ireland, which I was at pains to answer as fully as I could. While we were talking, her husband came in, with a large bundle of faggots on his shoulder, which he threw on the floor. He was a large, heavy man with a humane countenance.

'Whom have we here?' he asked.

'A straggler from Lord Cornwallis' army,' I replied. 'A Cyclops and his wife refused me lodging further down the road, though I could hardly stand from faintness. But your good wife has been very kind to me.'

He considered for a moment. 'I served with Dan Morgan in Canada. But twenty-five men of our whole regiment saw home again. The sufferings that I experienced in that year are burned in my soul. Well, upon my word, it would be very hard indeed to turn you out of my door on such a severe evening as this. You may bide here this night. Wife, fetch a little straw from the barn, and shake it down here by the fire.'

She did so, and the husband and I talked amicably, as fellow-soldiers, upon the hardships and cruelties of war, and the wife interposed now and again, speaking very sharp against the French connexion. She said that at Alexandria on their way to these parts, the French officers had danced minuets with several handsome young American ladies, in the middle of the camp; and this was very well, though she did not hold with dancing herself. But the nasty French soldiers who watched the dance in a great circle had from the heat of the weather disengaged themselves from their clothes, and stood around dressed only in their shirts, which were neither long nor in good repair. 'Moreover,' she said, 'the officers themselves were very sly and lecherous. Each had brought a fashionable assortment of coloured ribbands from Paris, such as our ladies of Virginia tie in their poke-bonnets, with which they counted upon buying the honour of the best-bred girls in the dominion.'

The husband judiciously remarked: 'Indeed, wife, I hope that they found they had reckoned amiss. But, as you know, when such girls are confronted with officers of rank and title, there is "no wisdom below the girdle".'

'La, husband,' she cried indignantly. 'How coarse you talk, and before a stranger too!'

The good man, before I retired to rest, showed me two Cherokee Indian scalps, properly dressed and mounted on frames, that he had taken in revenge for the murder of his wife's brother. I slept soundly, and awoke greatly refreshed. I gave the children some trifling presents: to one a lump of chalk, to another a Fusilier's button, to little Henrietta a Virginia bill for (I believe) eighteenpence or some such small amount. It was printed upon the silver paper used by English hatters – a consignment of this paper having been seized by an American privateer, and made into money by the Virginian Assembly, as difficult to counterfeit. Tobacco money, Congress money and the earlier Assembly money were all now highly suspect, because of the reams of counterfeit circulated by loyal Americans. The children and their parents seemed much gratified by my gifts, and after a breakfast of milk and stirabout I left them with the warmest emotions of thankfulness.

Henrietta kissed me, before I went; and I reflected fondly as I marched along the high road that my lost daughter must, by now, be about the same age as this dear child namely four years and a piece.

During this day, November 29th, I marched very hard on the main road, which was sandy, without meeting any interruption: for a party of convalescents had marched this way, two days before, from the hospital and it was supposed that I had not been able to keep up with them, and was trying to overtake them. I came to the Rancatank River at a place called Turk's Ferry, where a negro, who was conveying several fine hogs over the stream, allowed me a free passage in his scowl, or fat-bottomed boat, upon my agreeing to help him manage his unruly drove. Like the Prodigal Son of the Parable this worn-out mungo envied his swine. He told me: 'Him Bockarorra Gentleman' – meaning the white planter – 'make de poor black man workee, make the hoss workee, make the ox workee, make ebberyting all workee togarrer, only de hog. Him, de hog, no workee: him eat, him drink, him saunter, him sleep at pleasure, him old hog libb like murrer gentleman.' By evening I reached the town of Urbanna on the Rappahannock River, above forty miles from Gloucester Point.

I entered the town boldly, keeping to the account of myself as a conva-lescent straggler, which the travellers I met had fastened upon me by their inquisitive guesses as to my condition and intention. I came to a large building which proved to be an 'ordinary', and a stout, florid gentleman in a gay waistcoat accosted me from his chair on the portico. 'Heigh, Soldier, there is plenty of room inside for such as you, and plenty of drink.'

I enquired: 'How for such as me?'

He laughed. 'Well, you look mighty innocent, but you can't deceive me. You are looking for a master, I'll be bound.'

'I do not understand you,' said I.

'Then I'll be plain,' he said. 'There are a great many of your men in my house, who are determined to remain in the country. They have hired themselves to different gentlemen. You had better join with them. You shall be well used and in a short time you may become a citizen of America.'

I thanked him, and thought it wise to go in, for I did not wish to offend him, lest my true character might appear.

On the porch hung a placard which read:

Four pence a night for a bed.
Six pence with supper.
No more than five to sleep in one bed.
No boots to be worn in bed.
No dogs allowed upstairs.
No drinking tolerated in the kitchen.
New England travellers to pay on the nail.

Inside I found about forty British soldiers, none of them of my own regiment, but one of The Thirty-Third, who had hired themselves to different gentlemen about the country as mechanics, grooms, overseers and such. Each plantation in Virginia resembled a small village and now carried on various novel industries, by slave labour, to supply the manufactured goods that had formerly been imported from England. Experienced tailors, potters, weavers, whitesmiths and the like who would initiate or superintend such labours were therefore highly useful to the planters. I was strongly importuned by these soldiers to follow their example, rather than be conveyed to a prison pen in a barren country; but my mind revolted at the thought.

Towards midnight in came a shift-eyed person with a wide hat and a silver-headed cane. He represented himself as a lawyer and a close comrade of the famous Mr Daniel Boone, of Bridnorth in Somersetshire, who had passed westward over the Alleghany Mountains in the year 1759, and become an enthusiastic admirer of the territory he found on the further side of the range, called Kentucke. This eloquent person, drawing me into a corner, enlarged upon the diversity and glories of nature met with in that delightful clime of Kentucke: her fruits and flowers so beautifully coloured, elegantly shaped and charmingly flavoured, the great quantity of game, the fertile soil, the enormous and dignified Ohio rolling through the plains in inconceivable grandeur, the distant mountains penetrating the clouds with their venerable brows. Just before the war he informed me, Mr Boone had made his first settlement in this same favourite though forlorn district; and there engaged the Indians in a conflict of great savagery, losing two of his own sons and two brothers at their hands. Now, however, 'peace crowned the sylvan shade', for Mr Boone had been reinforced by a great number of settlers, who had removed across the mountains with their families in order to avoid the exactions of Congress and the raids of King George's soldiers.

I observed that his account was interesting, and believed that much of reality and fact must belong to his description – which to some would appear greatly exaggerated. He appeared somewhat offended at my saying this and warmed up to a peroration recalling that of a recruiting sergeant in search of 'prime young fellows to exercise the profession of arms'. At the close he offered me, free and without charges, a debenture of three hundred acres, with a fine deep bottom, in a fertile location upon the Ohio – and now wasn't that a handsome offer, he asked.

I enquired, to what sort of a trap was this cheese set as the bait?

He solemnly assured me that there was no trap at all. Mr Boone wanted brave and hardy men to strengthen the infant settlement, which would soon be a new State sending its own delegates to Congress, and therefore offered land free to likely settlers in order to increase the common wealth.

Here I had to affect the clown, and asked this recruiting sergeant whether it were not true that Indians carried off and roasted white men at a slow fire, then hacked them gradually in pieces, as one might snip slices oft a prime Virginia ham?

He asked, was I then a coward?

For reply I chanted, in a close parody of a song from Mr Bickerstaffe's comedy, *The Recruiting Sergeant:*

> Ay, ay, master Lawyer, I wish you good day,
> You have *no need* at present, I thank you, to stay:
> My stomach for Kentucke's gone from me, I bow.
> When it comes back again, I'll take care you shall know.

My companions set up a shout of laughter at this declamation; and the gentleman from Kentucke flew in a rage and rushed out of the room. I wished the soldiers good-night and soon fell fast asleep.

Early on the next morning their masters came with horses and took them all away. I retired out of the way to the privy, lest I be accosted with an offer of odious service.

When all had ridden off, I prepared to discharge my debt. But the land-lord, who was a militia colonel, refused my coin with a wave of his hand. He said to me: 'Why, now, I swear I thought you had given me leg-bail! You are Sergeant Lamb of The Twenty-Third, are you not? An acquaintance of yours in The Thirty-Third gives you a high character. He says that you write a very good hand and understand accounts.'

'Yes,' I replied, 'I may own to those accomplishments. If there is some task in that way that you wish to put upon me, I shall be pleased to undertake it immediately. You have been very hospitable to me.'

'Well, now,' he said, 'I have a proposition to make. You are an Irishman, I am told. Then I will build a school house for you and make you as comfortable as I can, and you shall stay here with us and instruct the children of Urbanna, who have run wild these three years and forgotten even their alphabet. You shall eat and drink at this house and earn ten dollars a month besides.'

I felt my whole frame agitated at the proposal: the more so because, though the proposal was dishonourable to a soldier, the man who made it, unlike the shifty Kentucke lawyer, was evidently of a liberal and philanthropic mind. Smothering my indignation, I stammered out as graceful excuses as I could find; then, though the weather was stormy and I felt very unwell, I immediately left his house. As we parted, I tried to insist upon payment, but he would not go back on his word, and shook his head at me for 'a most perverse, proud fellow who did not know what was good for him'.

The country beyond Urbanna wore but a poor aspect. The road, which was level and very sandy, ran through woods of black oak, pine and cedar for miles together: there were several bridges across creeks and causeways across swamps which abounded with snipe. After a few miles on the road I overtook a Sergeant Macleod of The Seventy-First, who was an acquaintance of mine, and a drummer of my own company, named Darby Kelly. They were in fact what I was by a fiction, namely stragglers from the convalescent party. Drummer Kelly suffered from a leg wound and Sergeant Macleod, a man of great hardiness and enterprise, had nearly died of the yellow fever. When the Sergeant asked me how I came to be on the road, I replied: 'I am escaping to New York. I did so once before after the Saratoga capitulation, together with two companions; and, please God, I shall do it again. Will you join me?'

Sergeant Macleod replied solemnly in his slow, thick Scottish way: 'You ken well, Sergeant Lamb, how entwined about the very heart of man is the love of liberty. But though 'tis easy enough to brag about pushing through a tract of land, of five or six hundred miles covered with enemies, I misdoubt how it can be realized in practice.'

'By a stout heart, and a trust in the humanity of the better sort of Americans,' I replied, '– especially of the women.'

When I recounted my former experiences, Sergeant Macleod was convinced that I was not 'just havering', as he expressed it; and both he and Kelly decided to throw in their lot with me. We lay that night in a fodder-stack near Hob's Hole, or Tappahannock, twenty-five miles beyond Urbanna. It was a sad-looking town of about a hundred houses. As dawn came and we resumed our march we came upon a mulatto fish-pedlar. He was calling tunefully as we met him:

> Fishee, fishee!
> Flounder and Blackfish!
> Shark-steaks – for dem darra likes 'em;
> Swordfish – for dem darra fights 'em.
> Fishee, fishee!

We bought shark-steaks from him, which was all the wares he had for sale. He informed us that the Rappahannock River, which ran three-quarters of a mile broad at this point, was full of sharks, which the negroes caught on strong hooks baited with shark-flesh and then despatched with spears. We roasted the steaks on sticks held over a fire of pine-branches, and they ate very well.

We addressed ourselves to our journey with confidence the next morning, but Drummer Kelly presently complained that we marched too hard for him. He said in great despondency, when we halted for awhile: 'It is impossible, you know well, ever to make good our escape. For my part, I will go no further with you towards the cold North. I will stay where I am and solace myself after all my hardships. Hob's Hole was no bad place. I shall find employment there, I do not doubt.'

We could not alter his determination by any arguments and therefore left him sitting by the roadside. Sergeant Macleod remarked, morosely, as we resumed our march: 'Ay, no trained drummer should ever lack employment in this sultry airs, where no son born to woman will willingly labour unless he be oft and scientifically flogged.'

I replied: 'Drummer Kelly could flog to a hair's breadth, and to watch him slowly slide the lash through his left hand before he laid on was the terror of all our criminals whose wounds still smarted. But, faith, it is strange that a man so lacking in compassion towards others should be so tender on his own behalf.'

The river now gradually narrowed. The same evening we reached a place called Port Royal, unremarkable except for the very noisome stench of its river front, and were now a day's march short of Fredericksburg, the tobacco town. Our night was passed in the drying-house of a derelict plantation. We had found in the mud on the road a heap of rice fallen from a wagon: we washed this and made a meal of it, with the crimson berries of the pokeplant and some shark-steak that we had saved.

On the following day, as we were coming out of Port Royal we overtook a fine wagon of the sort named Conestoga from a town in Pennsylvania where they were manufactured by the Dutch. The under-body was painted blue and the top part a bright red: there was a trooped tilt over it of tarred cotton cloth. The wagon was filled with sacks.

The wagoner rode one of the horses of his team – an old man with a smooth, very red face. We learned later that he was nicknamed Sops-in-Wine after an apple (called in Canada *pomme caille*) the flesh of which is red to the very core and of a remarkable sweetness. He hailed us with: 'Huzza, my hearties, how where might you be bound?'

We told him: 'To Winchester.'

He asked: 'You be'nt of that sort who sell themselves to the gentlemen hereabouts, I guess?'

'No,' said I, smiling. 'We are not for sale. Were you about to make a bid for us?'

For answer he pointed with his whip across the river and asked: 'Do you know how yonder land is named, hey?'

We said that we did not know.

'Well,' said he, ''Tis King George County, lying a matter of seven miles from here. *God bless King George*, I say; and those as hear me may believe, if they will, that I bless the township only.'

We understood by this speech that he was a Loyalist and therefore asked whether we might ride concealed in his wagon. He told us that we were welcome to come as far with him as we wished in the direction of Philadelphia, where his master Mr Benezet the Quaker lived. He had come southward three months before in the wake of the French army, with a load of tinware, cutlery, cloth and other manufactured articles from New England. He was now returning with rice, indigo, lemons and tobacco, by way of Frederick Town in Maryland and Little York in Pennsylvania. Four other wagons of the same train were a mile ahead. His offer of protection was gladly received on our part, and we promised him two shillings a day in hard money for the conveyance, he undertaking to keep us in corn-bread and cold bacon.

After an hour or two we passed the party of British convalescents resting by the roadside, but thought it prudent not to hail them.

We travelled undetected for five days, hidden among the sacks in the rear of the wagon and without any view of the country through which we were passing. We kept our own company while Mr Sops-in-Wine dined with the others of the train.

The wagon was a comfortable conveyance. I was surprised to learn that instead of axle-grease our protector used powdered soapstone – the same pale, greasy stone that was used by the Red Indians for their carved calumets and other ornamental instruments. We passed over the Rappahannock at Fredericksburg, being ferried across in a flat which our protector cursed as very dangerous and leaky.

We now passed through Colchester and crossed the Potomack River at Alexandria. where was a large glass manufactory and where the women dressed more luxuriously than in any city of America, especially in the matter of plumed bonnets. We were now in the Romish state of Maryland. On the fifth day the wagon was unfortunately hailed by an American Continental soldier who had been wounded in the foot at York Town and was hobbling along with the aid of a stick; his destination, he said, was Frederick Town. Ours happened to be the leading wagon of the train that day and the driver dared not refuse to take the man in. He was a talkative, knowing fellow and when we heard the manner in which he addressed Mr Sops-in-Wine, we thought fit to come out from our concealment before he entered. I will not attempt to recall his precise manner of addressing us, but it was most opprobrious, and he told us that his people had given us a good whacking at York Town and who were the cowards now, hey, ourselves, or they? We told him that we had never accused the Americans of cowardice; but he wagged his finger at us and cried: 'So I dare say! So I dare say!'

Sergeant Macleod thought it best to inform this soldier that we had fallen sick and stayed behind on the road, being members of a party that left York Town for Frederick Town – whom we were now rejoining. But he replied only with a knowing leer: 'Ay, so I dare say, lobsters, so I dare say!'

This disconcerted our plan for the present. We were fast approaching Frederick Town, through which we could not pass concealed in the wagon on account of the American soldier. When therefore we were at about six miles' distance from the town we considered it both more prudent for our own sakes, and more honest dealing with Mr Sops-in-Wine, to quit the wagon entirely and boldly go through the town on foot, trusting to the inspiration of the moment to satisfy any awkward questionings. This happened on December 10th, 1781. The good wagoner, before he left us, promised to wait a few miles on the other side of the town. But in the event he must have waited in vain. We crossed the Little Monocaccy Creek, by a ford where the stones were very loose, the current rapid, and the water rising to our breasts. Four miles more and we came to Frederick Town, which was a substantial town built chiefly of brick and stone, with several churches, and inhabited by near two thousand Germans. Soon as we entered, the American soldier gave the alarm from behind us. He had obliged the wagoner to whip up his team to keep up with us, for we were marching fast; and now he helloed to two guards posted at the entrance of the principal street: 'Heigh, brothers, there go two more birds for the cage! They thought to give me the slip, but I was too smart for the sons of bitches.'

We were seized and led through the town in triumph, two guards walking a little behind each of us, with one hand gripping a wrist and the other a shoulder. The Seventy-First, who had numbered 248 rank and file at the surrender, but were reduced by desertions and sickness to two hundred, were here imprisoned in barracks with some other regiments. We were put among them and found ourselves in a most deplorable situation: nearly fifty British soldiers huddled together in a room that had been built for the accommodation of eight Americans. It is true that we had an extensive parade to walk about during the day, but as the weather was already remarkably cold, very few men availed themselves of that privilege and the room, though warm, grew fetid to a nauseating degree.

Sergeant Macleod exclaimed to me: 'Faugh, Sergeant Lamb, you do not think to bide here many more days, I dare say?'

'No,' said I, 'I value the health of my lungs more than the society of my fellow-unfortunates.'

CHAPTER XVII

THE BARRACKS and parade at Frederick Town were surrounded by numerous sentinels, but before Sergeant Macleod and I attempted to find a weak link in this chain we would try another plan. We learned that small parties of prisoners, under a strong guard, were often ordered out to get wood for firing. We soon prevailed on the quartermaster-sergeant of The Seventy-First, who was in charge of the hut, to enrol us in the next wood-cutting party, which was set for December 12th. We then strove to persuade as many of the party as possible to venture an escapade with us. But only one other man, a private soldier also named Macleod, would consent.

When the day came, I waited with anxious suspense for the call which would summon us out to our task. First I emptied my knapsack, and distributed my superfluous necessaries among my comrades, but I put on three shirts, took my spare pair of shoes in my pocket, wrapped my blanket about my shoulders and carried my hatchet in my hand.

We arrived at the wood about half a mile from the place of confinement, at ten o'clock, and immediately set to the work of cutting. The two Macleods kept close to me, and we felled a pine together and chopped it up into logs. I then observed to one of our guards: 'Pine-wood burns bright, but is all consumed in a short space of time. Pray, will you let me and my companions fell that fine large maple that stands just beyond you?'

He consented, but with that rudeness which ever characterizes the low mind when in office, he grinningly detailed to us several disagreeable uses to which, for aught he cared, we might put the timber when we had reduced it to small pieces. We strolled together in a leisurely manner to the maple and, the better to colour our pretence, began loudly disputing as to the best manner of felling it; and then set about the work, keeping our eyes constantly fixed on the guard. At last, he turned himself about to watch the other prisoners.

We seized the opportunity and darted into the thickest part of the wood. Anxiety and hope, being pretty nearly balanced in our minds, were the twin wings which urged our flight. Our guards must have possessed the feet of deer before they could have overtaken us. We ran on through the woods, as near as I could conjecture for two hours, scarcely stopping to take breath. We steered due north. At last we considered it safe to walk, and continued for another three hours or more, alternately walking and running until we struck the Great Monocaccy just below Bennet's Creek. Here we paid our fare to a negligent old boatman and crossed without being examined – for the blankets wrapped about us disguised our regimentals and gave us rather the appearance of Indians than British soldiers.

Luck went against us once more. We were proceeding through a wood when we suddenly ran into an armed party of Americans who instantly surrounded us, and marched us back prisoners to Frederick Town, which happened to be their destination. They bantered us in a not unfriendly way upon our folly in 'not knowing our places'. But worse was to follow. Soon as we entered the town, very footsore, about evening, a man lounging on the *stoep*, or elevated porch, of a tavern, called out: 'Now, I'll be damned if it an't that indefatigable Sergeant Gerry Lamb again. He's the very devil and all for escaping. Why, he ran off from the Convention Army near Fishkill Creek, when I served in the Engineers, and won safe to New York. Last week I saw him brought prisoner into this town after escaping from the Gloucester Hospital. Take good care of him, soldiers, or he'll give you the slip again. He has quicksilver at his heels, has Gerry Lamb.'

This deserter was intoxicated, and perhaps intended me no injury, but my captors paid attention to what he said and passed me on with a bad character to the prison guard. Sergeant Macleod and the private soldier, his namesake, were then separated from me. They were turned in along with their regiment again, but I was sent a prisoner to the American guard-house.

The weather was extremely cold, and the guard-house was an open block-house, through which the snow and frost made their way unopposed. With much trouble I prevailed on a guard, for sixpence, to bring me a little straw to lie upon, in one corner. But I soon found that my lodging would be a very hard one; for whenever the guard discovered that I had fallen asleep, they applied a firebrand to the straw, and as it blazed, they set up a yell like the Indians, rejoicing in my distress, and deriding my endeavours to extinguish the flames. When the relief used to be turned out, I sometimes took the liberty of drawing near the fire, to warm my half-frozen limbs; but this indulgence was of short duration, for when the sentinels were relieved they came pouring into the guard-house, and, if found near the fire, I was usually buffeted about from one to the other, and perhaps a dozen fixed bayonets at once placed at my breast. When I found that I could obtain no mercy from these savages, and that every day I was worse used than on the preceding, I wrote a letter to the American commanding officer. In this letter, which I handed to the Lieutenant who inspected the guard, I informed the commanding officer of the treatment that I daily received, and entreated him to have me rather confined to the Town Jail.

This request was granted three days before Christmas Day, but my condition was not bettered by it. My remaining money and possessions were taken from me and I was placed in the upper part of the prison, to which I had to climb by a long board, furnished with slats, which was almost perpendicular. In this dreary place, without any fire-place, I found twelve criminals chained to the walls. Some were deserters from the militia; some horse-thieves; two were pedlars confined for pursuing their trade without a licence; one had insulted a Congressman; one had tried to pass counterfeit money. Soon I was secured beside them, and gave them a civil greeting. After asking me a great variety of questions, which I answered carefully, they resumed their single and perpetual business, which was to argue on politics together. Not one man of them, by the bye, had a good word to say for Congress. For Generals Washington and Greene they professed considerable esteem, and were pleased that I judged this esteem as on the whole well founded. The poor fellows received a very small allowance of provisions, which was hoe-cake and a little rusty bacon, with water to wash it down; however, not a morsel was allotted me, as not being on the charge of the prison, but a military prisoner confined by my own request. However, these 'jail birds', though some of them may have lived very vicious lives – I know not – took compassion on me. The man who had insulted the Member of Congress and ruled the roast here, declared that it was 'kind of hard' that I should starve to death. At his suggestion they agreed each to set aside for my subsistence a twelfth portion of their pittance. Had it not been for their humanity this work would never have been written: I should have starved to death.

I must here fairly account for the bad usage that I received: the regiment of horse that was cut to pieces in August 1776, at Long Island, was composed very largely of young men from the Western confines of Maryland. This was a source of general inveteracy to all British prisoners, it being represented that the regiment was refused quarter and massacred; how true this may have been, I cannot say. I had also become an object of particular severity because it was believed that I still meditated my escape – as was indeed the case.

In this jail I remained for twelve days, until past the New Year of 1782, suffering the bitings of hunger by day, and shivering all night with the cold. The only remission from our fetters was when once a day we were fetched down to the necessary-house under guard of two men with muskets. Though it can hardly be imagined that aught was wanting to our sufferings, yet the case was indeed worse. We were continually annoyed with the yellings of an emancipated black woman, confined at the bottom of the jail for the murder of her child. She used to yell the whole night long, weeping and wailing for her 'poor honey lamb', her 'lill' peach blossom', who had 'done gone to be an Angel', as she hoped, 'in Hebben'.

I cudgelled my brains to devise some means of escape and in the end bargained with the negro who brought the victuals and water-jug that I would give him one of my three shirts (which I still had on) if he provided me with pen, ink and a sheet of paper and conveyed a letter for me to an officer whom I knew to be in the town. This was Major Gordon of The Eighth, for whom I had undertaken the service of cleansing a small offensive wound that he suffered at York Town and of attending to the eleven wounded men his regiment left behind at Gloucester Point. He was a most generous gentleman: indeed he had voluntarily offered to take the place of Lieutenant-Colonel Lake, the field-officer appointed by Lord Cornwallis to command the captive army – and this only because he was a bachelor, whereas Colonel Lake had a wife and children at home.

The negro brought me the instruments I required and I wrote to the Major, acquainting him with my distressed condition and begging him to intercede with the American commander on my behalf. All I asked was to be liberated from jail and placed with other British soldiers.

The negro soon came back to tell me that he had delivered the letter, and therefore claimed the shirt. I did not know whether or no to believe him, but fulfilled my part of the bargain and waited anxiously for the event. On the morrow a soldier arrived at the foot of the board and bawled out: 'Is there a prisoner here named Robert Land?'

No one replying, the soldier was going away, when I had the inspiration to call out: 'Ay, pardon, here I am!' for I guessed that my name had been miswritten on a warrant of release, and I would in any case rather be enlarged for awhile as Robert Land than remain fast in my fetters as Roger Lamb.

He said to me, 'Come now, Land, look sharp and put your best foot forward. Do you love jail so much that you are thus slow to quit it?'

'You must first unfetter me,' said I.

'Now, isn't that a plaguey thing!' he cried. 'Heigh, turnkey, where are your cursed keys, you wretch? Now, quick, nip up that board and unfetter Mr Land, the British soldier, or I'll blow you through with my blazing iron. I'm in a pretty considerable tearing hurry this forenoon.'

In a twinkling I was unconfined and, trembling for weakness, descended the awkward board. The soldier took compassion on me when he saw my pale and hollow cheeks, and permitted me, despite his haste, to recover my money from the prison officer; though this greedy personage would not return me my spare shoes, which I saw that he was wearing himself. I then entrusted five shillings to the negro, with an extra shilling for himself, to lay out on victuals for my companions in misery. I believe him to have been a humane and honest fellow and hope that he discharged this duty.

The soldier now told me: 'I have orders to take you to Captain Coote.' I feared that after all I might have been mistaken in answering to the appellation 'Land', but was comforted when, on being conducted through the town to the quarters of Captain Eyre Coote of the Thirty-Third Regiment, that gentleman greeted me in my right name. 'Why, Sergeant Lamb,' he cried, when we were alone, 'what have these rascals done to you? You look like a spectre!'

I related him my experiences in a few simple words and confessed my determination and hope still to effect my escape into New York.

The tears of sympathy filled his eyes. Said he: 'Ay, Sergeant, we are all unfortunate, but must keep up our courage still. Major Gordon wishes to convey his regards to you: he has laboured under a complication of disorders since he first came here. He is not unmindful of your case but has referred it to me. You will be glad when I tell you, I have obtained from the American commander an order for your release. You are now to come under my command.'

I hastily thanked Captain Coote (later to become Lieutenant-General Sir Eyre Coote) for his kindness, and took the liberty of congratulating him upon the news, that had but lately arrived in the country, of the victory of his uncle and namesake over an enormous horde of Indians under Hyder Ali at the battle of Porto Novo. 'Ay, Sergeant,' he said, heaving a sigh, 'but my poor uncle has yet a long course to run. The sick old man, with his handful of half-starved men, and the dice loaded against him by the treachery of the Madras Government, marching and countermarching in that pestilential climate – it grieves me to turn my thoughts thither, and towards those other brave commanders of ours distressed with terrible odds in distant parts of our Empire. In India, Goddard, Popham and Camac; and my friend Flint at Wandewash reduced, I hear, to constructing wooden mortars and grenades of fuller's earth! General Elliott besieged and bombarded these long months at Gibraltar, and poor Murray whose flag still flies – as I hope – at Port Mahon. Our comrades pent up in Charleston, and several other garrisons languishing in Pensacola and the West India Islands under constant threat of destruction by fever or the French and Spanish fleets. The Americans have but one war to fight, and a host of allies; we are fighting now alone and for our lives, like a bull set upon by three mastiffs in front, while a couple more sneak round to lay hold on his vitals. Would to Heaven I were free of my parole: I would attempt to escape in your company.'

While the faculties of my nature remain entire I shall never forget the affecting manner in which Captain Coote addressed me. Said I, 'Your Honour, my reasons for deserting were love of liberty and loyalty to my Sovereign. You have confirmed me in them and I will never rest until I find a chink in my prison door and break out again.'

Captain Coote then said: 'Hark 'ee now, Sergeant Lamb: I have already directed my sergeants to build you a hut in the pen and to take you into their mess. This they are glad to do, for they all esteem you. Here, will you accept this guinea from me as a tribute to your steadfastness? And when you have rested yourself somewhat and resumed your purpose, my hope and prayer is that you come safe through.'

I went off in triumph to join The Thirty-Third in their pen, and there found my hut nearly constructed; but hardly was I settled in some degree of ease and comfort with these excellent people, when an order came that, for regularity, all men who were quartered with regiments not their own should be returned where they belonged. I was to be sent under guard to the Royal Welch Fusiliers who were confined at Winchester, about eighty miles away to the westward.

This journey of five days, by way of the South Mountains and Harper's Ferry, was unremarkable. My two guards were silent and surly both with each other and with me. They guarded me very close by day and secured me by night with heavy fetters, which I must carry during the march. All the way along the Potomack River, the soil was rich and chiefly, it seemed, given up to wheat-growing Beyond the gorge through the South Mountains lay a broad limestone valley, the water of which at first caused me severe gripings. In the middle of this valley, with the snow-covered Devil's Backbone behind it, lay Winchester, which I found to be an irregularly built town of about two hundred houses. The Royal Welch Fusiliers occupied a pen in a fort near by, which had been constructed during the previous war by General (then Colonel) Washington as a protection against the Red Indians.

Here I was welcomed by Captain de Saumarez, who commanded the Regiment in captivity and had heard of my hardships. He said: 'Sergeant Lamb, will you take a hint from me? I understand from the guards who brought you here that you are a marked man. The sergeant says that his comrades have been constantly employed in apprehending you and escorting you from one place to another. It is my notion that when in three days' time we march up to Little York in Pennsylvania, they will arrest you, as soon as you fall into the ranks, and confine you here in Winchester Jail; from whence you will not obtain release, except by death, until the war ends.'

I thanked the Captain for his warning; and on the morning of January 16th, when the Regiment, with all the others, marched up to Little York, I reported sick and remained behind at the hospital. The Surgeon, to whom I was known, very obligingly sent me to lie on a pallet in the death-hut, appropriated to the men whose lives were despaired of.

The two days that I spent here proved of some refreshment to me. When they had passed and the American guards had all moved away from the town in order to escort the army to Little York, it was not difficult to escape from the hut. It was left unguarded, because of the fatal purpose to which it was devoted. I must here say that I had confided to Smutchy Steel that I intended to follow behind the Regiment; and had asked him to do a service for me if he could. This was, to inform our old comrades of The

Ninth, who were now quartered in the neighbourhood of Little York and there enjoyed a considerable degree of liberty, that I was on the way. I told him that I would represent myself as never having escaped from The Ninth at all, since their first surrender at Saratoga. My tale would be that I had stayed behind at Charlotteville working (like poor Terry Reeves) on Colonel Cole's plantation, when The Ninth removed from thence in the previous April; but now was rejoining them.

The road, I found, ran very straight for about a hundred miles, with seven rivers or large creeks to pass, and a ridge of hills. I set off early on the morning of January 18th. The weather was extremely cold, but I had Captain Coote's guinea, or rather its change in quarters, picayunes and coppers; as also my blanket and a few necessaries which I had obtained in the death-hut, from the effects of a Fusilier who died while I was there. In my knapsack were four pounds of flour, a gill bottle of rum and some dressed meat.

The severe treatment which I had received from the Americans seemed, in my mind, to excuse me from revealing the truth about myself. I was resolved only that I would not attempt to win the favour of any person whom I met by speaking with pretended disloyalty of my King and Country. This was one of my hardest marches, since it was made in the depth of winter and I was sick, alone and always in fear of being haled back to the jail. The wind was from the north-west and bitter beyond description. However, the very severity of the weather aided my purpose, since I met nobody upon the road who troubled to ask me questions, except one foolish old man who smelled like a pig-drover, though he had no hogs with him. He stopped me a few miles short of Spurgent, where I must recross the Potomack.

'Stop, Mister!' he cried. 'Why, I guess now you be coming from Charlotteville by way of Wood Gap.'

'Nein,' said I, pretending to be German, for I could not abide the fellow. It was almost the one word in the German tongue which I knew at this time but 'ja', which is its opposite.

'Why, then, I guess as how you be coming from Kentucke?' he offered again.

'Nein,' said I again, dully.

'O, why then, pray now where might you be coming from?' he persisted.

To shake him off I reeled off some such unintelligible nonsense as: 'Twankydillo, lilliput, finicky blitzen, niminy-piminy buzz-buzz potsdam finicky-fanicky, ulallo hot-pot *Fredericksburg.*'

He caught at the last word and said, as if he understood every word that I had spoken: 'Why, then, you must have heard all the news. Pray now, Mister, what might the ruling price of bacon be in those parts?'

I pretended to grow angry: 'Keen kein Englisch,' cried I, providentially recalling the words with which our German guards at Rutland pen had always put us off, did we ask them any slight favour.

This he understood. 'Ay, ay, Mister, I see now you be'nt one of us. Well, I must be going on my way. I have a long tack before me.'

'Ja, ja,' said I, leaving him and continuing my march to the Potomack, which I crossed without question, proffering my fare to the ferryman without a word and pretending to suffer very violently from the toothache. During this time I lived on my rations, sleeping by night in sheds or fodder stacks. Often the snow was up to my knees, and the rivers that I had to ford were full of floating ice. I nearly lost two toes from frostbite, in my passage of the South Mountains, but rubbed them well with snow before it was too late. I made about fifteen miles a day. I passed on my way four freshly made graves of the army that had gone ahead of me.

I was now in the Commonwealth of Pennsylvania and from the language which I heard spoken knew that I was in a German part. These Germans were industrious, quiet, sober people and alone of all Americans abstained from asking impertinent questions of travellers. They always made for the richest lands, where they settled down in orderly communities and both built and farmed as for a lifetime there was none of that hasty, restless pioneering manner with which English-speaking Americans staked out a plot in the wilderness, felled trees, ran up a slight hut, ploughed between the stumps, took their toll of the soil, and after a few years sold their plot cheap and passed on again to new ground. These Germans, and the Dutch intermixed with them, built fine solid houses and great red barns, tilled the land lovingly, keeping it always in good heart by a rotation of crops, and employed themselves and their households in all manner of artistic industries.

About January 25th, as I was stumbling along the road, very sick now, about five miles from Little York, a woman called out merrily from behind a stone wall:

'How now, Spirit, whither wander you?'

My heart lifted with joy and I declaimed in reply:

'Over hill, over dale,
  Thorough bush, thorough brier,
Over park, over pale,
  Thorough flood, thorough fire
I do wander everywhere ——

Why, dear Mrs Jane, do you recall at Rutland what trouble we took with the Fairy, the little drum-boy who would not learn those very lines?'

'I have expected you to pass here these two days. Was the road so bad?' asked Mrs Jane Crumer. 'You look very sick, Gerry Lamb. Come, my poor husband is down the road. He will give you a drink of peach-whiskey.'

Crumer's wits were still turned, I found. He said to me: 'Why, Sergeant Lamb, are you back so soon? Yesterday my Jane wept, when she told me that you had run away. See how she smiles now!' He had lost all sense of the passage of time, and thought himself still in the year 1779, when I had escaped to New York from Hopewell. That Jane Crumer had wept then, touched my heart – and that she smiled now.

The peach-whiskey warmed me and I went along the road with them very cheerfully. But the happiest surprise was to come: Smutchy had contrived to convey my message to the sergeants of The Ninth and they had already obtained, from the unsuspecting American officer set over them, a pass in my own name in which I was described as belonging to their regiment. This precious piece of paper was handed to me as I entered the town, for several of my old comrades besides Jane Crumer and her husband had kindly and attentively watched for my arrival.

I thus avoided being put into the pen which had been constructed for the Royal Welch Fusiliers, and was adopted as an inhabitant of Convention Village, that had been built about two hundred yards away from the pen by the small remains of General Burgoyne's army. The villagers were allowed very great liberties and regarded as almost citizens of America. I found that the pass gave me the privilege of ten miles of the neighbouring country, while I behaved well and orderly. I was conducted into the hut which my poor loving comrades had built for me here as soon as they heard of my approach. They had furnished it very comfortably with bed and blankets, chair and table, candles, liquor and even an iron stove.

CHAPTER XVIII

I REMAINED for six weeks at Convention Village, visiting my former companions from hut to hut. I was astonished by the spirit of industry which prevailed among them. Men and women were employed in a variety of mechanical trades which they had either driven before they followed the drum or had learned during their captivity. Even the children were impressed into usefulness. One of my former comrades had married a 'She-Kener' or gipsy, a tribe that had been brought to the country from Germany by Dutch slave-traders as 'redemptioners', but had soon bought their freedom and were now settled down in this part. This gipsy taught the women lace-making and basket-weaving. Some soldiers whittled wooden spoons and likewise learned the trade of cutting bowls, plates, skimmers, cups and saucers from dish-timber: that is to say, from the large knots that occurred in old sugar-maples, soft-maples, beech and ash. From a single such lump of dish-timber a whole nest of bowls could be scooped. A man who had been a brass-worker sent his fellows around the country-side with money from the common stock to buy up old candlesticks, lamps, kettles and other brass and copper, paying by weight, then hammered the metal out and re-worked it into buttons, knee-buckles and shoe-buckles. Some of the soldiers he took on as apprentices; others became pedlars and sold the articles about the country, adding lace, brooms, wooden ware (inclusive of carved butter-stamps) and baskets to their stock.

I was called upon by my comrades, almost as soon as arrived in the village, to take the part of Richard Plantagenet in a public performance of the *History of Henry the Sixth*; Jane Crumer playing that of Queen Margaret. A chief reason for the esteem and seven affection in which the Villagers were held by the people of Little York was these regular dramatic entertainments. The Americans had hitherto been almost unacquainted with stage plays and the impression made upon them by their first hearing poetry spoken with feeling and intelligence was very remarkable; I believe that they have never since lost their taste for the works of Shakespeare. When later I mentioned the matter to Major Mackenzie of my regiment, he remarked: 'Why, now, what a lazy jade the Muse of History is – how she repeats herself! Two thousand years ago an expeditionary force sailed

westward from the ancient maritime state of Athens against the vigorous
Greek colonists of the New World of Sicily. The affair miscarried and a
great number of Athenians were taken prisoners; but these mitigated the
severity of their lot by performing the Comedies of the playwright
Euripides, which greatly delighted their Syracusan captors.'

Jane Crumer was indeed the Mother of the Regiment: she even formed
the workers into a guild or brotherhood and with the monthly contribu-
tions that they paid compiled a respectable sum of money which could be
drawn upon by persons in ill-health or those desirous of borrowing money
for the purchase of tools or materials. She administered this fund very
wisely, but not knowing how to cast accounts in due form now took lessons
from me in that art. She begged me to remain with them and act as schoolmaster to the children of the Village, of whom there were a great number,
since the married men had in general not deserted their regiments; but
when I informed her that I could not relinquish my intention of escaping,
she desisted, with a sigh for my obstinacy.

So well had she tamed the 'rough and ready Ninth' by the gentle bonds
of female discipline that when I strove by every argument to arouse that
animation that ought to possess the breast of the soldier, I made no impression at all upon them. I offered to head any number of them and make a
noble effort to escape into New York, but none of them would listen to me.
They were very well off here, they said, and here they would continue at
least until Peace were signed, and perhaps for the rest of their lives. The
climate suited them, they liked the people of Pennsylvania, and they had
had enough of war. Twenty or thirty of them had taken wives, German
women for the most part.

Jane Crumer smiled at me when I told her of my ill-success, assuring
me that peace had its victories no less than war. She pointed across the
parade at Long Winifried (the woman who had stolen the Town Bull at
Boston and vanquished the Select-man) seated outside her hut, the
familiar clay-pipe still between her teeth. She was transformed from a
harpy of the camp into a very respectable basket-maker and the best of
housewives, though her tongue was still tart. 'Gerry Lamb,' said Jane
Crumer, 'you are but young. When you have overpassed the Fourth Age
of Man, and ceased in Shakespeare's words to "seek the bubble,
Reputation, even in the cannon's mouth" you will, I believe, enter upon
the Fifth Age very decently. You will become a most judicious Justice –
and I hope then to know you better.'

Said I: 'Now, Mrs Jane, you must cease funning, I beg. You know that
it is not glory that I seek, but we British are plunged up to our ears in war,
and for my part, like poor Terry Reeves, I intend to "stand up for my King
and Country till I die!"'

She begged my pardon and cried: 'No, no, Gerry Lamb, I did not mean
to thwart your ways. I admire your steadfastness and I wish you every

success. It is only that these poor remains of the Regiment are those who always lacked the resolution to escape, men of peace, not natural soldiers like yourself, and it is better that they remain here. The rest have all run off long ago and many came safe through, as you know. But the most part were apprehended and some shot, some hanged, some cast into prison. The news of their fate has discouraged the remainder.'

Accordingly, I sent a message to my comrades of the Royal Welch Fusiliers in the pen, wrapping a paper around a stone and tossing it over the palisade when the sentinel's back was turned. It was addressed to Sergeant Collins, and in it I wrote that I intended to head a party for escape to New York, upon St David's Day. I considered that in all the British Army the seven men named in my letter could not be excelled for courage and intrepidity. They were three sergeants, viz.: Collins, Smutchy Steel and Robert Prout the transport-sergeant; and four private soldiers, Tyce, Penny, Evans and Owen. I mentioned that if they decided to come they were to meet me in my hut at midnight on the last day of February. At the same time I sought out Captain de Saumarez at his quarters in the town and told him of my intention, mentioning the names of the men. As my money was almost expended, I begged him to advance me as much as was convenient. He applauded both my intention and my choice of a day; and the same evening sent me no less than eight guineas, one for every man of the party.

Although my old comrades of The Ninth would none of them venture with us, they did all that lay in their power to further our escapade. Two of them even consented to hold the sentinel in play at the hour for which the evasion from the pen was planned, by pretending to be drunk and cutting capers in the vicinity of his box. The night fortunately was very dark, and at midnight the seven men duly entered my hut, having scaled the palisade unobserved. There they remained for the rest of the night. I took the precaution to bind them to certain Articles of War. The expedition that we were now undertaking must be conducted under military discipline, and being unanimously chosen their leader I demanded perfect obedience. Smutchy, who had been with me during my previous successful escapade, and now bought a cavalry pistol from one of the villagers, volunteered to execute the sentence of death upon any man who disobeyed my orders. In return, I undertook to hold a Council of War whenever I was myself in doubt as to the course to follow; but my own decisions must be obeyed as if they were those of Lord Cornwallis himself.

On March 1st, therefore, after drinking a few parting glasses in my hut to the success of our venture, 'and St David', we set out westward in two parties towards the frozen Susquehannah River, which lay ten miles off. With the leading party went Jane Crumer, who was by now so well known in the country that it would be supposed that the men with her were members of the Convention army. The rear party I myself conducted, and my pass, which was good as far as the river, would no doubt cover the other four men, who would say that they had left theirs behind. We passed through the country without challenge and said our thanks and farewell to Jane as we came in sight of the river. Looking back, I observed that she walked away very disconsolately as if she would readily have come with us, but for the responsibilities that she had undertaken at the Village, and her poor disabled husband. She then turned herself about, and observed my backward looks. We both returned to the place where we had parted, moved by a common sympathy; our eyes filled with tears, I kissed her hand, but neither of us found words for this second good-bye.

The ice when we came to the river was rotten with thaw; for the weather had been mild during the day, and it was evident that we could not attempt to cross. However, a severe north wind now blew up and I judged that it was now freezing again. The Susquehannah at this point was about a mile over. We resolved to remain on its banks all night in the hope that by morning the ice would bear our weight. In a thicket some of us felled a few saplings and made a hut of hurdles to protect us against the wind, while others collected brushwood. I went along the bank to where I had noticed a man setting fishing-lines at a hole in the ice. I believed that he might have observed us, and wished to assure myself that he was of no danger to us. His face appeared familiar and I had no difficulty when I approached to put a name to him. 'Why, now, Happy Billy Broadribb,' I cried, 'how goes the fishing?'

This Broadribb was a Royal Welch Fusilier. He had received his nick-name because of the gloom which was permanently settled upon his countenance; he had deserted us during our expedition against Fort Lafayette two years before. He had been very negligent of his hair and accoutrements on that occasion and had impertinently answered the Sergeant who reproved the fault, protesting that 'pipe-clay and pomatum will lose us the war' and that 'the Americans at least have a great deal more sense than to waste their time in such fribbling ways'. The Sergeant ordered him a lashing of twenty strokes, to be carried out the next morning; but he deserted rather than submit. 'Happy' Broadribb seemed very shy of me at first, as a sergeant in the regiment from which he had 'deserted in the face of the enemy'; but it occurred to me that he might be of assistance to us, and I therefore showed him every possible friendliness.

'Why, Happy Billy,' said I. 'Sergeant Farr who ordered you that lashing is dead, poor fellow, these eighteen months. He was a very severe officer. I believe that nobody blamed you in his heart for answering him back as you did. But were you not a friend of Harry Tyce? He is yonder in the bushes with a few others of the Regiment, and would, I am sure, be glad to shake your hand again.'

'Nay, I must be going,' said Broadribb, looking very ill at ease. 'I am sure I cannot look any Welch Fusilier in the face. Besides, it is very cold.'

'We have a gallon of peach-whiskey between us,' I said, 'and you shall warm yourself with a dram.'

He then consented to accompany me into the thicket. But first, I asked him: 'Well, pray, old Happy, how have you spent the last two years? Have the people of America fulfilled your expectations of them?'

He sighed and replied lugubriously: 'To tell you the truth, Sergeant Lamb, I have passed a most miserable existence since I left the Service. The Americans universally profess scorn for me as having deserted my King yet being averse from an engagement to fight for Congress. It is very hard. I have roved about Pennsylvania and New York and the Jerseys ever since, working most industriously for my livelihood; but have ever met with more kicks than halfpence.'

'What sort of work have you done?' I asked.

'Why, now, any and every sort of work – "whipping the stump", with an axe over my shoulder, peddling Notions, helping in a saw-mill, rowing at a ferry, hoeing turnips for a Dutch farmer, even "goose-herding", though I am a sad hand with the needle. I believe I know every inch of the country between here and the British lines. The Loyalists have been better friends to me than the Rebels, for I have made no bones about regretting my desertion.'

We went together into the thicket, and in a tone that I hoped my comrades would understand I cried out: 'Here comes a friend in need, Fusilier William Broadribb who once deserted the Regiment in a huff but has lived to regret it. I believe that he will now make amends for his single error by acting as our guide back to New York. He knows the whole lie of the land as well as General Washington himself. Come, comrades, where is that peach? A deep swig of benbooze for old Happy Billy Broadribb.'

Private Tyce, who was a Yorkshireman, took the cue well and slapped his old mess-mate on the back. 'I'm right glad to see you, Billy Broadribb. It will all be plain sailing. You will guide us by the paths you know, and when we win safe through to New York we will as one man intercede for your pardon with Sir Henry Clinton – how say you, Sergeant Lamb?'

'He will grant it,' I replied with assurance. 'There is no doubt whatever on that score. And what is more, when I ran over the same course three years ago, Sir Henry was most liberal in his reward of our guide, as Sergeant Steel here will testify.'

Here Sergeant Probert interposed in his excitable Welsh way: 'I care not what Sir Henry gives, but I do know this, by damn, that I my own self will reward Billy with a great deals of money, and with a great many drops of drink too.'

We made Broadribb happy indeed with repeated drams of peach-whiskey and encouragement of him as a misunderstood and ill-used person; and he finally consented to guide us throughout the journey. But, drunk though he was, I was pleased to observe that he did not on that account lose his judgment, but on the contrary gave us very valuable advice. He said that he knew the temper of the country very well, and that whereas two or three men might pass through it unmolested, nine in number were too many altogether. We must divide up, as soon as we had passed the river, for so great a body of British soldiers would soon spread an alarm through the country and cause immediate pursuit. He also strongly advised us to change our regimental clothes for 'coloured' ones at the first opportunity.

We told him that we would sleep on the proposal. We had a merry supper party upon the fish he had caught, which we roasted at the fire, also some slices of sour German bread and the peach-whiskey.

We took turns to keep watch and at dawn I went down to the river to test the condition of the ice. It cracked under my feet, yet bore me. I brought the good news back to the party, and we resolved to make the crossing without delay. Though the ice was exceedingly weak and broken up in many places, we ventured with the firmest resolution. It shivered and complained beneath us at every step we took. We proceeded in Indian file at a few paces' distance and had armed ourselves with long saplings so that if any man were engulphed the others might haul him to safety; but in the event we crossed without accident. Having gained the further bank, Sergeant Collins said to me: 'Well, now, Lamb, I believe that Broadribb is right. We must divide our forces if we are to succeed. How do you say?'

'I am very reluctant to do that,' I replied, 'but I can see no alternative. The Loyalists, who might be willing to assist two men or three, would most probably be fearful of entertaining so great a party as ours is now. I propose therefore that we break up into four and four. Broadribb can choose which party he would care to guide. Do you and I, Collins, each choose a man in turn; for since you are the senior sergeant you must command the other party.'

We made our choices. My first was Smutchy Steel, my second Sergeant Probert, my third was Private Jack Tyce. Sergeant Collins chose the other three private soldiers as being men of his own company. Happy Broadribb elected to accompany me, because of his friendship for Tyce and because he believed that I would have more influence than Sergeant Collins, should we succeed in our attempt, in the matter of obtaining his pardon from Sir Henry Clinton. Then I said: 'Very well, that is decided. Collins, my advice is to travel by night and hide by day, and to use a chain of friends, making certain of each next link as you go.'

'Why, for sure, that is what I shall do. But what of the first link? Happy, can you not direct me to a place from which to make a start?'

He undertook to do that and gave Sergeant Collins the name of a Loyalist widow living seven miles off, who would doubtless be friendly to them if they approached her discreetly. We then took leave of one another with aching hearts, while expressing full expectation of meeting all together at New York: we even considered what dishes and wines would grace our banquet of celebration. After some argument we compounded for beef-steaks, a fricassee of chicken, a prime leg of mutton, a boiled goose well stuffed, a sweet sauce of cranberries, copious Madeira, eggs and bacon, and a pineapple apiece – if such a fruit could be procured. Smutchy protested that for him no board was well spread without a steaming dish of 'Irish Roots' boiled in their jackets. We engaged to provide him with half a peck on his trencher, with salt and fresh butter to eat them with.

Sergeant Collins and his men continued towards the house proposed to them, but we hid all day among the trees on the snowy hill-side that formed the further bank of the river. In the morning our guide brought us to the house of one of the King's Friends, as Loyalists were here termed. He proved more useful to us than agreeable. His business was the collection and sorting of silk, linen and cotton rags for paper-making, and he was able to provide us from his stock with four suits of very bad coloured clothes, taking our regimentals in exchange. He was a grim, unsmiling man and would not permit us to enter his house, warning us that though we might use his shed, we must expect him to disown all knowledge of us if we were apprehended on his grounds. We asked him for a few cold potatoes or a little bread, but he had nothing to spare, he said. We did not see him again, nor did he wish us 'God speed'.

I put on my suit with disgust, for it had the rank musky smell of negro in it. Private Tyce, smiling a little to see the usually correct and formal Sergeant Lamb dressed in such a rig, I struck an attitude and declaimed in theatrical style, from my favourite character of Edgar in *King* Lear:

> No port is free; no place
> That guard and most unusual vigilance
> Does not attend my taking. Whiles I may scape
> I will preserve myself: and am bethought
> To take the basest and most poorest shape
> That ever penury, in contempt of man,
> Brought near to beast; my face I'll grime with filth,
> Blanket my loins, elf all my hair in knots,
> &c., &c., &c.

At eleven o'clock that night we began our march, making towards Lancaster, an industrious German town of eleven hundred houses; but we decided to avoid its streets and brought up our right shoulders a little, keeping always to the woods. To have passed to the south of the town would have been dangerous: it would have taken us into territory inhabited by the inveterate Presbyterians of Ulster, whose town of Londonderry was a chief focus of revolution as well as the seat of the young American linen industry. As Irishmen, Smutchy and I could expect no mercy did we fall into their hands. But the Germans were not, so Broadribb assured us, either inquisitive to travellers or cruel to the unfortunate.

At dawn we arrived at a village named Litiz. There was a house a little distant from the others with an ill-written sign to the effect that refreshment for man and horse was to be had there. Broadribb informed us that the warmth of the whiskey had died down in him and that he needed more of the same, and a good breakfast to settle it. We judged it necessary to humour him, and since we had no spirit to spare, it was natural to allow him a little money for a drink. Unfortunately, we had no smaller coin with us than a silver dollar, and I could not trust Broadribb in a tavern alone with such a sum. He would soon become intoxicated and might forget us altogether while we waited outside in the woods. So we must go in with him. We therefore rapped at the door, and I suppose that the landlord must have taken a peep at us from the window and thought us ill-looking customers; for he scrambled out of the backdoor, bare-footed and half-dressed, buttoning himself as he went. We were apprehensive that he had run out to alarm the neighbours and therefore ourselves ran in the opposite direction and took shelter in a small wood.

Here we remained, almost perishing with hunger and cold until night, not daring either to light a fire or to resume our march until nightfall. Broadribb grew very gloomy and we were forced to give him our remaining peach-whiskey. He told us that we were heading towards the township of Caernarvon, where was a barn in which he had, not long before, rested himself all night. On that occasion, the farmer when he had passed through the barn in the morning had not discovered the presence of his visitor, even when a loud sneeze escaped him: he must have been either sunken in a brown study or, more likely, stone deaf. Broadribb led us without a fault across the Conestoga Creek by a footbridge and along a woodland trail until at dawn he halted us and 'there is the place', he said. It was a stone dwelling-house with a great red barn contiguous, as also a boarded maize-shed of the sort that broadens upward like a wheat-rick and has half an inch of interval between the boards to allow ventilation for the maize-heads stored in it. We deliberated whether or not to steal a few heads of maize where a broken board permitted, but we had no rasp to grate them into flour; so with one consent we went to repose our hungry and weary selves in the red barn. The door was open, we soon entered and, climbing up a long ladder, concealed ourselves under some sheaves of wheat which were in the loft. We rubbed a few ears in our hands in Galilean fashion and chewed the grain; but fell asleep still chewing. I kept a spy-hole open between the sheaves in case we were surprised.

We were cheated of our rest, for just as sleep was deliciously stealing over my senses, with many coloured images and confused dancing lights, a shrill whistling of *Yankee Doodle* spoilt all, and I awoke with a start to see a tousle-headed, lanky boy with a pitchfork coming up the ladder. It was clear that he was about to remove the wheat for thrashing.

I aroused the others and instantly disclosed myself. Says I: 'We arrived to see your master pretty late last night and took the liberty of spending the night in his barn.'

He stared at us and, evidently misliking our looks, backed down the ladder again, carrying his pitchfork at the charge, and then ran out of the barn. In my haste to forestall him with his master I jumped from the loft upon a heap of hay and ran after, entering the house almost as soon as he. The boy was shouting about us to the farmer, a big, blinking, grey-bearded German, who made a trumpet of one hand placed to his ear, and replied, 'Yes, yes, my child,' very indulgently.

We saluted him with politesse and he desired us to sit down. Though it appeared that he was a widower and childless, the place was spotlessly clean. There was a collection of curiosities ranged in well-made glass cabinets: such as Indian arrowheads of red, grey and black flint, tropical nuts, lumps of ore, fossils, a carved whale's-tooth and a wampum-belt. I happened to admire a gaily decorated fire-board (used to fill the fire-place in summer time) which was suspended from a nail on the wall. The intricate design of birds, trees and flowers had evidently been scratched into the soft wood, then filled in with colour and varnished over.

He smiled complacently. 'Mine own work,' he said in a thick German accent. He then pointed to a painted chest, decorated in the same style, with houses and people portrayed among birds and flowers. 'Mine own work,' he said again. We all expressed great admiration for the chest, and indeed it was most pleasingly painted, though the figures were crude and the flowers ill-sorted with them as to size. Then he showed us a work upon which he had been engaged as we came in: a sheet of illuminated handwriting, nearly complete, under a painting of the Whale spewing up the prophet Jonah. The writing was German verse and appeared to be a hymn. He had on the table beside him a colour-box containing quill pens, brushes (which he told us were of cat's hair), a small bottle of cherry-gum varnish, and others of coloured inks – red, green, blue, yellow and cuttle-fish brown.

I smote him upon the back, and uttered some resounding compliment. It was clear that, hungry and sleepless though we were, we could not hurry matters, but must cultivate the friendship of this artist by the easiest and most natural means – a regard for his work. After a while he said to me, in the mixed whispering and shouting characteristic of deaf people: 'Ha, can you do Fractur, ha? ha? It is not easy, ha?' He thrust a quill into my hand and rummaged in a box for a sheet of paper, then grinned at me as he laid it down before me. Thus challenged, I limned a neat little picture of four starving children with platters in their hands, standing meekly at the door of a house, where a benignant gentleman, the very spit and image of our present host, blinked down at them. Underneath, I wrote in my best penmanship with delicate flourishes and seraphs and an intricate rubric below, the first verse of the Souling Song as it is sung in my country by children from door to door at the vigil of All Souls'.

> A Soul, a Soul, a Soul cake!
> Pray, good master, a Soul cake!
> An apple? a pear, a plum, a cherry,
> A loaf or a cake to rest us merry:
> One for Peter, two for Paul,
> Three for HIM who made us all.
> A Soul cake!

Then it was he who slapped me upon the back, roaring with laughter that I had hit him off so luckily, and immediately shouted to his little cook-wench to bring us breakfast.

This consisted only of maize-flour stirabout, but since we had eaten nothing since our meal beyond the Susquehannah, fifty hours previously, we made a hearty breakfast. He eyed us with a quizzical expression, for we ate most voraciously, but abstained from asking us a single question as to our condition and destination. However, when we had finished, and he had given each of us a bowl of fresh milk he said solemnly: 'Gentlemen, I spy who and how you be. I spy your intention well. But I shall have nothings to do with you. For the sake of your good leader, who is mine brother in Fractur, I say as follows: "Depart now in peace"!'

I offered him money, but he would not accept of it, saying very obligingly that my little picture (which after breakfast I completed by giving the beggar children little scarlet coats) had paid our score. We thanked him warmly and withdrew to our usual hiding-place, the woods, where we remained for several hours.

'Well, Happy,' said Smutchy Steel, 'what is our next port of call?'

Broadribb told us that there was a gentleman, one of the King's Friends, who lived ten miles further on the great road leading to Pennsylvania. We should certainly receive entertainment from him. He was a native of Manchester in England and had grown very rich from the export of flour. Flour shipped on board at Philadelphia cost five dollars the barrel of 196 lb.; and, if it eluded the vigilance of the King's ships and privateers at the mouth of the Delaware River and won safe through to the Havannah, produced at least thirty dollars the barrel in hard money. Very many vessels were captured, but new ones were always in the stocks to take their places, and this gentleman had been more than usually fortunate of late. There was, I believe, scarcely a captain or even a common seaman who had not been taken six or seven times during the war – nor, for the matter of that, any merchant who had not been more than once rich, ruined and rich again.

When we arrived at this gentleman's fine mansion at dusk, we remained concealed in the orchard while Broadribb went ahead into the house. He soon returned and told us to follow him in by the side-door. We found ourselves in a most luxurious apartment, furnished in the English style. Tyce, Probert and Smutchy seemed ashamed to trespass into this elegance, clad as they were in sad rags, with cracked wet shoes on their feet and beards of five days' growth. But I determined not to be put out of countenance, and saluted the old yellow-wigged gentleman who rose from his wide elbow-chair to welcome us, as if I were in all the glory of full regimentals.

He bade us sit down at a fine wide fire until refreshment could be got ready for us. Then, in a most feeling manner he observed: 'You know the great hazard I run in receiving you as friends. It is now eight o'clock. I will let you remain under my roof till midnight. You must then depart. I will not ask your names, and if you know mine, I must ask you to forget it.'

'That we undertake, Sir,' I said.

A most excellent supper was then set before us by the old gentlemen's widowed daughter, who acted as his housekeeper. There was boiled ham, cranberry jelly, venison pastry, hot coffee with plenty of brown sugar as a sweetening; also apples, hickory nuts, wheaten bread and butter and plentiful cider out of silver goblets. The mahogany table glistened under the light of several white wax candles, and our instruments were ivory-handled Sheffield knives, and heavy silver spoons and forks. Our host asked us a number of questions relative to our experiences in the Carolinas and Virginia, which I answered at some length, for I could see that his mind was working upon problems of commerce and considering what new markets might lie open to him in that quarter, now that the Royal armies had removed. I was left to do all the talking, for my comrades had none of them sat at such a table before, and kept their mouths shut all the while except for an occasional 'Yes, your Honour' and 'No, your Honour' and 'That I cannot tell you, your Honour'.

The night proved very stormy, and the rain poured down like a deluge: we could hear it beating a continuous ruffle upon the roof of the portico outside. The hands of the tall clock drew nearer to midnight, and we eyed them wistfully, like the lady in the old wives' tale, who must leave the ballroom at that same hour lest the spell break and her fine ball dress be transmogrified into its original rags. But gratitude to our host forbade us to overstay our welcome. I asked a great favour of him, that he would write down for us a list of the King's Friends who lived in our line of march. This he did on condition that we learned the names by rote without taking the paper from him; and that we never, so long as we lived, revealed them to any questioner. 'Remember,' he said, 'that if by some great mischance the worst should happen, and by a treaty of peace the United States be granted their independence, these good people, unlike yourselves, must remain in America, where their fortunes lie. To be known as disaffected would prove as fatal then as now.'

We promised to abide by this condition, and I have ever since kept my word. Just before we braved the dark and boisterous weather, the old gentleman told us: 'Wait a minute, and we will drink a toast together.'

He brought out a very large bottle of rum from an armoury, filled up six Waterford rummers, and then, stepping up to a picture of General Washington which hung over the chimney, turned its face to the wall; so revealing to our admiring eyes another painting executed on the reverse of the canvas.

'To His Gracious Majesty, King George, gentlemen,' he said, and drank the glassful down at one blow. We followed his example and gazed for a full minute in silence at the Royal features in the portrait. Then we saluted and trooped out.

CHAPTER XIX

THE NIGHT was so dark that we ventured to march on the main road to Philadelphia. The nearest of the King's Friends mentioned in the list lived near Hilltown, about seventeen miles away. We marched on hopefully, despite the increasing inclemency of the weather. We had not gone a mile before we were well drenched to the skin, and what made our journey yet more distressing was that the road was all puddle from the great fall of water. Broadribb began to murmur at the hardships which he endured, saying that his shoes were almost worn out and that the stones cut his feet. Indeed, all our shoes were in a wretched condition: we could scarcely keep them on our feet. Both my soles had come away from the toes, and to prevent them catching as I walked I had secured them with twists of wire.

We told Broadribb to be of good courage, enlarging upon the better aspects of the situation. Rain, we said, was at least better than snow, since it portended fine Spring weather. Besides, we had a good meal in our bellies and a recommended friend at the end of our march. We swore that we were proud of his company and would sing his praises very loudly upon our arrival at New York. Yet he stopped in his course, like a recalcitrant ass, and fetching a deep groan cried: 'No, comrades, no, I can go no further with you. You know that I am a deserter and a drunkard and a poor lost wretch, and you despise me in your hearts. Come, come, you can't deny your true opinion of me.'

Private Tyce put an arm about the wretched fellow and, 'Billy Broadribb,' said he, 'you take a delight in belittling yourself. You were a fine soldier once, and will be so again when you have shaken yourself free of your despondency. You, Sergeant Probert, weren't you present aboard the *Isis* three and a half years since, when we engaged the *Caesar* seventy-four, and didn't Captain Raynor, our Commander, pick upon Happy Billy Broadribb, out of our whole Fusilier company, and call him a "damned cool soldier"?'

Probert clearly could not recollect any such occasion, but came out with an 'O yes indeed, I swear by damn those were the Captain's very words.'

This encouragement helped the unhappy fellow for another mile or two upon his journey, but then he stopped again, to observe with another groan: 'No, no, I have been thinking that perhaps all my hardships will be of no avail: when I get into New York I shall be denied my pardon and sentenced to the halberts. In my present weak state two strokes only with the lash would kill me.'

It still wanted an hour or so of dawn, but the rain now ceased and in the grey light we saw a small hovel on the road-side, and a solid house a little further on. I suggested that we should take shelter in it, and Tyce very nobly said: 'Yes, indeed, Billy Broadribb, I see now that your shoes are very bad. Suppose that you and I exchange, for as our guide it is only justice that you should be the best shod.' But it proved that the only man besides myself with a shoe of the right size was Smutchy Steel, so Smutchy devoted his to the common cause. I would have yielded mine, but they were in worse repair even than Broadribb's.

We pushed open the crazy door of the hovel, where to our great mortification we were saluted with the roaring and loud grunting of the pigs which were inside. We marched off at once, lest by their outcries they might alarm the people of the house, and Broadribb, who now understood how greatly we depended upon him, found a fresh complaint, namely that the coloured clothes he had received from the Scot were much thinner and more wretched than any of ours. Rather than that he should make an outcry as we passed the house, we undertook to give him, presently, the best clothes we had in exchange for his bad ones. At last we came in sight of a large barn. We had been cheated of rest on the previous morning and resolved to take shelter here; but were again disappointed, for as we drew nearer we saw that someone was inside with a lighted lantern. We heard some sheep coughing from the barn and guessed that here was one of those careful shepherds who sit up with their ewes in the lambing season.

Broadribb now began to whimper and sob and vowed that not another step would he march without rest and sleep. Behind the barn was a large dung-hill and, as the last resource to humour him, we agreed to lie upon it, covering ourselves with the loose litter. Here we remained about half an hour, but could not continue longer because of the extreme cold, and the shooting pains in our bones caused by the damp of the dung.

Smutchy Steel suddenly leaped up with a curse. 'Now, you wretch of a Broadribb, we have been subject to your megrims and fancies for too long. Why, you might be a breeding woman, not a Fusilier! For sixpence in old Continental paper, I'd break your lolling neck for you. Up now, you tapeworm, you poltroon, and lead forward or, by God, I will shoot you dead and bury you here in this charming muck-heap.'

This sharp speech had the looked-for effect. Broadribb started to his feet and declared himself ready to continue. The house recommended to us would not be far off, and morning was breaking fast on us. We reached the place after about a mile. It was a tavern, and as we approached we heard a neighing from the stable. I went forward to reconnoitre, but found to my unspeakable disgust that six army chargers were tied up in the stalls, with furniture which showed pretty clearly that the house was filled with American officers of rank.

I put a good face upon it, and returning to my comrades, remarked: 'The whole of General Washington's family appears to be sleeping in our beds. Do you proceed half a mile down the road while I get some liquor for us all, and if I am not back among you within five minutes, continue under Sergeant Steel's command, for I will be a lost man.' They moved off and I returned to the tavern.

As I approached, I was aware of two men talking behind a shuttered window – the one in thick drawling tones, and the other in the brisker accents of New York. I paused to listen. As nearly as I can recall the dialogue, it ran after this style:

'Captain Cuyler, I say you are a damned son of a bitch, yet I swear I love you.'

'Fie now, my dear Major M'Corde, I must take exception to that sentiment. Yet I forgive you with all my heart. For it is as plain as a cat's nose that you are altogether Addled and Awash.'

'How say you, damme? I want none of your plaguey Dutch forgiveness. I addled, sirree? Egad now, it is you who are addled. I am Sobriety's sweet self. You are, moreover, Boozy, Buzzy and Bepunched.'

'I deny that with blasphemous oaths, Major M'Corde, and will cap you, Tappahanock toper, throughout the English alphabet, if you dare. I say: you are customarily Cocked, Cock-eyed and Crocus, as my name is Cuyler.'

'I take you up, you dog! You are damnably Dagged and Drunk – yet I love you, I swear.'

'Dagged, am I? You are Ebrious.'

'And you, Fettered.'

'You, Glazed.'

'Hammerish, Sirree.'

'Intoxicate.'

'Juicy.'

'Knapt and Kill-Devilled.'

'Lappy, my trickish friend.'

'Mimbo'd, Mumbo'd and Momentous, my mighty Major.'

'Nimtoposical as old Noah.'

'Oiled, Sir.'

'Pungey with peach.'

'Raddled, Roaring and Rumfustianate, rascal.'

'Stingo'd, Stewed and Soaked, stinkard.'

'Tagged and tarnation Trammelled.'

'Unhinged and unusual Unsteady.'

'Vinous and Virginia-valiant.'

'Wine-logged and Whiskey-wet.'

'– Have at you, Major! To crown all, you are altogether X-Y-Zee'd. And there's my hand on it.'

'I kiss it, you most lovable rogue of a Captain. God's mercy, now, let us toss down another glass of I care not what – whether peach julep, or brandy-sling, or rank Boston kill-devil, or sweet sangree mantled over with nutmeg – to seal fast our enduring friendship, and drink damnation to Congress!'

A silence then falling, I passed on from below the window and pushed open the side door. Spying a man who proved to be the landlord, I said: 'Mr —, over by Hilltown, recommended your peach-whiskey to me. May I pray you to fill my can?'

He filled it without a word, refused the money I tendered, slapped me on the shoulder, wrapped a cold beef-steak in a newspaper, which he then thrust into my hand, and with an expressive command to silence, by squeezing his own lips between forefinger and thumb, pushed me gently out again into the yard.

With the meat and the peach-whiskey we managed to coax another few miles of travel from Happy Billy Broadribb. He led us off the great road and down the track which led to Valley Forge, where General Washington's men had shivered and starved during the winter that Smutchy and I had starved and shivered in the open huts at Prospect Hill. Near the cross-roads was a sign directing us to a shoemaker's dwelling, and there we had all our shoes repaired by a German workman and his apprentice while we sat by the fire in a corner. They were Hessian deserters, I believe, and showed more anxiety lest we be displeased than curiosity as to our history or intentions. For ten shillings we were all now tolerably well-shod but only Broadribb, and for another five we bought a new pair of shoes for him. We then returned into the woods and exchanged our good clothes for his bad, as we had promised. After another deep draught of the peach-whiskey he seemed determined for the present to continue with us to New York. That evening we made no mistake, but were nobly entertained in a mansion on the banks of the Schuykill by a lady who was a near relation of General Lee. She provided us with straw pallets in the attic of her house and then, after a lavish supper brought us by a negro, we slept like pigs for near twenty hours.

Her husband, a nervous and loquacious gentleman, dressed in a very dandiacal fashion, came up to discourse with us as soon as he learned that we had awakened; and enlarged upon his firm attachment to the Royal Cause. His observations, however, always came round to the same point, namely what a monstrously dull city Philadelphia had become since the British had marched out. He said that the subscription dances which had succeeded the fashionable balls of those golden days were a mere mockery, that even the best-bred ladies must now spend all their days in sewing shirts for Washington's rabble, that the odious French strutted and leered about the fine brick walks of the City as if they were conquerors. 'Ichabod, Ichabod,' was the burden of his song, 'the Glory has departed.' We let him run on, listening sympathetically, though we could not feel that in times like these a curtailment of his frivolous enjoyments warranted so loud a howl. At least he had a good and handsome wife, a fine house, attentive servants, money in both breeches pockets, which he jingled all the while as he spoke, and, by his own boast, 'a hale constitution, thank God'.

On the evening of March 8th, after we had eaten a very good supper of turkey and cold meats, this poor, forlorn lover of pleasure came to tell us that his canoe was at our disposal at midnight, and that his servant would put us across the river. He gave us the name and place of abode of a friend, a young Quaker, who lived a few miles this side of Germantown and would assuredly take us in. This Quaker, whose house we reached without misadventure, lodged us in a loft above his stable. He happened to have been acquainted with Major André, when that amiable and unfortunate gentleman was imprisoned at Lancaster in 1776, and his children had taken drawing lessons from him. He was as strict in his persuasion as my former friend Josiah, and confirmed me in my good opinion of the sect. He told us among other things that the Friends of Philadelphia had a year or two previously passed a law to excommunicate from their society any member who should pay a debt in depreciated Continental money; even though at this time it was treason to doubt the goodness of the paper, and though they themselves must accept it from their own debtors at its face value. They had also concurred not to take part in any privateering or contraband trade; and our host mentioned without self-glorification that he had been obliged by this law to restore to the English owner his part of a prize captured by a merchant ship in which he was interested. But he regretted that a number of his fellows had taken an active part in the war, forgetting their principles: so that he had been often accosted with 'Wilt thou take a gun?' and 'Can we expect thee on the parade tomorrow?' He told us that: 'Our poor *halting* brother, Nathaniel Greene' – the glancing reference was to the General's limp – 'is of that company of backsliders.'

Upon leaving his house at midnight, we came about dawn to a creek, the name of which escapes me, that lay between Germantown and Bristol. It was swollen with the late rains. We chose to cross at a place where it was very broad, but only about four feet deep. Half-way over was a small island. No bridge or ferry or other means of passage offering, 'Come,' I said, 'there's nothing else for it but to wade over.'

'Ay,' said Smutchy, 'now to strip off our clothes and make bundles of them to tie about our necks! Heigh, you, Billy Broadribb, you have sleep still in your eyes. The cold dip will freshen you.'

Broadribb slowly removed one shoe and stocking and felt the water

with his bare toes. He drew them out again with a cry. 'Now, in the name
of Almighty God,' he complained, 'you cannot surely expect me to pass
through this liquid ice before I have breakfasted?' He began to blubber. He
had been so pampered by the gentleman of pleasure and by the honest
Quaker, that he could not return to his former hardships. 'O, Sergeant
Lamb,' he cried, 'my heart is almost broken, you know, with hardships. I
am sure I will never survive if I wade into this river. And you can't deceive
me about my pardon – the Commander-in-Chief will never grant it, that
I swear.'

We proposed to carry him over on our backs, to give him half the money
we had with us, which would have amounted to near two guineas, and of
course renewed our assurances as to interceding for his pardon; but all in
vain. He drew on his stocking and shoe again.

'Very well, then,' cried Smutchy, 'with Sergeant Lamb's permission, I
will now carry out in earnest what I threatened before. I will beat the bad
manners and cowardice out of you with the butt of this horse-pistol and
then I'll shoot you out of hand.'

'You have my permission, Sergeant Steel,' said I, for this seemed the
only means left of persuasion – the Quaker not having supplied us with any
intoxicants, and our can being now empty.

Happy Billy Broadribb turned about in great terror and was off like a
mountainy hare. We ran after him, but we were all bare-footed in readiness for the crossing, and could not pursue him far because of thorns and
stones. He abandoned us there, taking with him his new shoes, our better
rags, and the money we had advanced to him. We never saw him again, but
agreed that it was good riddance: his cowardice had depressed our spirits.

We were already shaking with cold but, not wishing to postpone our
trial further, waded in. That half-mile of water was indescribably cold.
When we reached the island, we found that we had almost lost the power
of our limbs. We rubbed and slapped one another to restore the flow of
blood and danced about like Indians. Robert Probert, whose skin was
bluish white in colour and his body shaken with a sort of palsy, cried in his
sing-song Welsh voice: 'By Devil's damnation, no indeed, I cannot blame
that poor fellow Happy. It is awful cold, I am. Indeed, I cannot blame poor
old Happy.' Yet he was the first to wade into the second branch of the creek
and the first to emerge. Smutchy gashed his foot very badly in the course
of his passage, an injury which he did not discover until some time after
leaving the water, all feeling being departed from his legs. We had to
support him, for the next two miles of our journey, as he could not put his
injured foot to the ground. Fortunately the house to which the Quaker
recommended us proved hospitable. We were there concealed in the barn,
and I was given salve and bandage for dressing Smutchy's foot. Our victuals, though plentiful, consisted wholly of corn-bread, honey and cider.
Pennsylvania produces a remarkable quantity of honey, near every house

boasting seven or eight bee-hives. It is said that bees were altogether unknown in America before the coming of the white men, as is proved by the name for the bee in most Indian languages being 'the Englishman's fly'.

Thus far we had been most successful. We were close to the great Delaware River, about twenty miles above Philadelphia. Somehow we must find a way across it into the State of New Jersey. Unfortunately our hostess, who was the widow of a former British officer, could give us neither assistance nor recommendation in this matter. She told us that it was as much as her life was worth to make fresh enquiries on our behalf: she was already highly suspect to her neighbours. We must act on our own initiative.

We set off at nine o'clock the same evening and passing a small house, observed a poor old woman chopping kindling wood in a shed. 'Depend on it,' said Tyce in an undertone, 'either the woman is a widow or else her husband is away. It is the men hereabouts who chop the kindling, and in the early morning.'

My experience having been that widows and other lonely women are seldom vindictive, and that they welcome company, I ventured to follow this one into the house. I asked her, could she direct me to the nearest ferry-house. She eyed me attentively from crown to foot and seeming to approve of her examination, replied in very genteel accents: 'Come in, with your companions. You will be safe. I can see that you are a British soldier by your walk and carriage. If you would pass for American you must relax the muscles of your neck and not pout out your breast so proudly; and in putting down your feet you must not crack down the heel first as if to wound the ground, but must use the ball of your foot.'

She had a bed-ridden husband upstairs, who had been in the service of the regal governor of Georgia, and her only son was at New York with Fanning's Provincials, in the King's Service. We were entertained very kindly and insisted upon paying her for her bacon and stirabout, when we left her in the morning and went to the ferry-house two miles away.

We had hardly entered the building before we found that we had run into a nest of hornets. Eight boatmen had just come in from the river to refresh themselves with apple-jack. They were from the neighbourhood of Trenton, forty miles up the river, and were bringing a raft of seasoned timber down on the flood-water to Philadelphia for use in the shipyards. Two of them carried rifle-guns. One, who had already, as we watched, drunk off two gills of apple-jack in succession, and now called for more, sang out: 'These four scarecrows keep very mum. Why don't they speak? Why don't they declare themselves? I'll be blamed if I don't believe that they are on the other side of the question. How say you, neighbour Melchizedek?'

The landlord spoke up: 'Now, now, boatmen, don't seek trouble for yourselves or this house. They are poor, honest Germans, I warrant, who haven't the gift of English. *Kommen Sie, mein Freund,*' he added, addressing me. '*Trinken Sie etwas?*'

I thought it best to appear cheerful and undismayed, and adopting a North of Ireland accent, which came easy, I called for four gills of apple-jack and told him that 'we Londonderry people aye keep our own company'. Then I added fiercely: 'Drink up, Phil, drink up, Corny and Sandy and you too, you big lump of a Robbie, before any good liquor be spilt. If these impudent tarry-faced rogues mislike our company, they must mind themselves.'

At this they rose with one accord and went into an inner room, the land-lord running after them, I suppose to deter them from violence. Smutchy said: 'I have my pistol, but that will only be good for a single shot.'

'Let us sell our lives very dear,' cried Probert with all the ardour of a Fluellen.

'I believe that no buying or selling is necessary,' said the imperturbable Tyce, 'if we now seize the ferry-boat and make across the river. How say you, Sergeant Lamb?'

He was right. I bade them go ahead to the ferry, since Smutchy was delayed by his bandaged foot, while I called the landlord out and discharged the reckoning. I protested very angrily to this Melchizedek at the uncivility of the boatmen, and vowed to be revenged on them, soon as the remainder of my party of ten men came along the road. This speech covered our retreat in good order. I then sallied out and hurrying down to the river found my companions already in the boat, and Smutchy sitting behind the terrified negro-boatman with the pistol pressed against his black nape. I leaped in, we cast loose, Tyce seized the spare pair of oars and we were half-way over the river before the alarm was given. We were within range of their rifle-guns but Smutchy helloed at them as a bullet whizzed by us: 'Another shot, and by God, we kill your old mungo.' They then desisted.

Soon as the boat touched the opposite shore, we ran into the woods and were before long secure from our pursuers, as we had above a mile and a half start of them.

It would be tedious to continue detailing our travels in the same particular style: it is enough to say that in all the different places in America through which I have marched as a soldier, been carried as a captive or travelled in regaining my freedom, I never found people more strongly attached to the British Government than the inhabitants of New Jersey. I aver this with the most awful appeal for the verity of my words, despite the malignant assertions of the historian Belsham that 'such havoc spoil and ruin' had been made in this very part of the country by our licentious soldiery, particularly the Germans, under General Howe's personal inspection and command as 'to excite the utmost resentment and detestation of the inhabitants'. A historian ought to record the truth, and the truth only, whether of friend or foe. It must be admitted that the Hessians were addicted to plundering in the European style, so that their officers found difficulty in curbing their petty thieving of poultry, forage and the like; and that even so fine a corps as The Thirty-Third, when short of fuel in wintry weather, had here distrained upon the fences of the Whig farmers. I will also grant that there are rogues in every army, whose occasional crimes discredit their comrades. But had the British troops in America coolly and deliberately murdered Mr Belsham's father, mother and all his relatives before his very eyes, he could hardly have been more rancorous or uncandid in attributing to British officers the direction or encouragement of atrocities. The officers who served in these campaigns were gentlemen, or noblemen, of the first families in the Empire for wealth as well as honour: men without any earthly temptation to the acts charged against them, and whose high spirits would have revolted at the bare mention of petty plunder and rapine.

But to return to my narrative. For the next week these good people of New Jersey ventured their own lives and property to secure ours, and smuggled us on from house to house in short stages, as the slipper is passed from haunch to haunch in the children's game of 'Cobbler, Mend my Shoe'. This country was full of troops, and the nearer we came to New York, the more numerous they grew. We went by way of Moonstown, Mountholly and Princeton, at which last place we were actually hid overnight by one of the masters in Nassau College. It was a fine, plain stone building of four storeys and a wide extension, but seemed to us rather a grammar-school, than an University College. We were concealed in the College Library. It surprised me that the books consisted almost wholly of old theological works, some placed in the shelves upside down, and all without any regularity, and having no scientific, historical or geographical treatises among them that I could see. At one end of the Library stood the famous Mr Rittenhouse's orrery, but a year or two previously it had been hurriedly taken in pieces and removed from this place by the Americans – for fear, I suppose, that our officers would wish to add it to their plunder! Nor had anyone been found to restore it to working order. At the other end of the room were two small cupboards, named 'the Museum'. They contained merely a couple of small stuffed alligators and some curious fishes: which presented a very dilapidated appearance from having been the constant playthings of students at the commencement festival each year. No studious youth with a taste for the sermons of Attenborough, South or Bishop Berkeley came to disturb us during the hours we were here.

Since writing the above passage I have heard it asseverated by an American gentleman of some credit, a graduate of Nassau College, that the smallness of the library as I found it was due to the depredations of the rude Hessian soldiers quartered there, before General Washington's victory, at the close of the year 1777, dispossessed them of the place. He added with indignation that scores of the choicest volumes were used for fuel by them in the Franklin stoves. I sympathized with him that by perfect exactness of stupidity these boors had rejected all the dead and dry tomes as unsuitable for burning, while choosing only the greenest and least combustible timber of the tree of knowledge.

The last stage of our journey was to the town of Amboy, which lay opposite Staten Island, divided only by a river from the British outposts. We arrived within two days' march of it on March 19th. We had a guide with us, whom we believed to be worthy of trust. He took us to Elizabethtown at eleven o'clock that night, and pausing outside the place told us that we might safely march through, as the inhabitants were in bed and no Americans were stationed in it. However, the news had that day reached us, published in a Philadelphia newspaper to the following effect: 'William Broadribb, an acknowledged English deserter, was on March 9th taken up at Germantown by an Officer. He was tried the next day by a Military Court at Philadelphia on the charge of conducting four men, supposed to be British soldiers, towards New York; and the fact being proved he was summarily condemned to be hanged. The sentence will be publicly carried out in *terrorem similium*, in the usual place of execution, punctually at noon to-morrow, unless it rains.' This warning struck terror in our guide's heart. He now said to us: 'Lest I should happen to be seen with you, and they serve me as they served this Broadribb, I will make a circuit. Let us meet on the great road at the top of the next hill beyond the town.'

The people of Elizabethtown slept soundly and we were not challenged; but our guide was not to be found at the place appointed. We waited two hours for him and then gave up all hopes. We saw clearly that he had given us the slip. There was a piercing north wind which whirled heavy snow with it. We could not support the notion of waiting longer, our clothes being in tatters and our shoes having broken open again in our recent marching for the leather was too rotten to hold the stitches of the German cobblers. We at last resolved to proceed by ourselves, though we had no notion upon what point of the compass South Amboy lay. The snowstorm abated and we saw the North Star shining rather bright; we knew we could not be materially wrong if we steered due north. We marched on, very hard, over broken, uneven ground, sometimes on the road, and sometimes through the woods.

At four o'clock in the morning, Smutchy Steel suddenly stumbled and fell prone on the rutted ground. He exclaimed in a very weak voice: 'Gerry Lamb, I have endeavoured to keep my troubles to myself and not let out a cry. But I have long overpassed the limit of my possible exertions. The pains of Hell are in my wounded foot, which is greatly inflamed, and not another step can I go.'

I knew that Smutchy was no 'malingerer' or skulker: if he said that he could not march another step, that was the mere truth. I therefore said to the other two: 'Come now, comrades, I know your feet are all very bad, but we must not abandon our friend so close to our goal. Come, hoist him up on my back, will you? We can carry him by turns until daylight. Then we will rest.'

'No, Gerry,' said he, 'leave me here! You are yourselves at the very end of your tether. Better that one should die than all be lost. If I live till morning, I will strive to creep to the next house; and if I have luck, I will follow you in a day or two.'

We tried to take him with us, none the less, but he was a heavy man and we could not support his weight: we fell down under it. We saw that we must after all leave him, and this was peculiarly distressing to me as his comrade in so many hazards. But for Tyce and Sergeant Probert being dependent upon my leadership, I should have elected to remain with Smutchy. He gave us his pistol, we wrung his hand, and marched on.

The whole of the next day we spent marching through the snowy woods. We were quite without provisions, nor did we break our fast before two o'clock of the following morning, which was March 22nd. Then we stopped at a house on the side of a narrow road, which was unconnected with any other building. We heard voices downstairs and rapped at the door. An old man quickly opened and, said he: 'I don't know who you may be, but step inside if you are a good man, and stop outside if you are not. My old woman and I are lonely old folk, but select in company.'

I said: 'Pray, Sir, I believe you are a Dubliner by your manner of speech. It is long since I heard the true Dublin speech from other than soldiers. May I ask from what part of the City do you come?'

This bold questioning drew a hearty laugh from the old man and a cackle from his old wife. 'Glory be to God,' he cried. 'Do you mean, after all, that thirty years in this land of sharp speech have not cured me of my soft voice? Now, tell me, you night-prowler, whom in the name of Nick do you resemble? I have seen those eyes before now, and that manner of widening them as you speak. Well, I'll not think – it will come the easier to me, the harder I thrust the thought away. But I'll tell you, my fine, large man, that my abode was by Bloody Bridge, and that I worked about St Patrick's Cathedral, for the old Dean, the dear man.'

I told him: 'The Cathedral was having that grand spire added to the steeple about the time you came away, was it not?'

He looked very grave: 'Truth, and I came away on account of that same spire. I had the misfortune to drop a hammer on the skull of a drunken, lying mason who was walking beneath me, and they all misdoubted it an accident: for I had the good fortune a few days later to marry my Molly here, whom I widowed. They gave me black looks in the Cathedral, did my fellow masons, and I came away here. Tell me now, isn't it true that there have been many fine churches and other edifices built or rebuilt in Dublin of late years? Answer me now, quickly, for I'm dying to hear.'

I here begged permission first to bring in my comrades; though I did not yet declare who we were. This he granted, and with a brisk nod at them immediately began plying me with numerous questions relative to these new churches – their style, materials, decoration and capacity. His wife chid him for his lack of hospitality to a fellow-countryman and began hastily to peel about twelve pounds of fine potatoes and made her husband mend the fire with the bellows, which she thrust into his hand.

It is very hard for a man caught in a hostile wilderness and near fainting with cold, hunger and sleeplessness to be obliged to read a lecture upon the ecclesiastical architecture of Dublin! Yet I was equal to the task, for I knew how much depended upon it. He was a choleric old man and would not be crossed. I told him of the elegant symmetry of St Werburgh spire – a fine octagon supported by pillars and terminating in a gilt ball, and of the re-edification of St Catherine's in Thomas Street, and of the new St Thomas' church, the latest foundation of that kind in the City; and of the handsome front of hewn stone with columns and pediment which was added to St John's in Fishamble Street about the time I left the City.

From churches I was obliged to proceed to the new Royal Exchange, which was a fairy-tale to my host, and to the rebuilding of Arran Bridge (now Queen's Bridge) which was destroyed by the floods in my eleventh year and soon after rebuilt in hewn stone. He suddenly smote his knee and cried: 'Now, isn't this an agreeable packet of news? Come, Molly, my duck, the whiskey! Here are two Irishmen who would be sociable together.' The potatoes were now bubbling in the pot and demanded eating, and had it not been for thoughts of poor Smutchy Steel, as another Dubliner, it would have been a truly merry evening.

My host informed us, as if accidentally, where were the American posts on the banks of the river, which flowed only two miles away. But he made no clear profession of politics, and neither did his old wife. She kissed me very affectionately when we presently left their abode.

Off we went, avoiding the American posts, and as soon as daylight dawned, we saw the woods of Staten Island in the distance, but a deep and broad river rolling between. We wandered up and down the shore in search of a canoe or boat, but found nothing. The broad appearance of day much alarmed us, and after a hurried consultation we agreed to return to my fellow-countryman's house, discover who we were and throw ourselves upon his protection.

He came running out of the house to meet me, snapping his fingers and crying: 'I have it, I have it!'

I tried to address him, but he would have his say first: 'Tell me this, my poor, ragged friend: who was the fine man with the pale blue eyes like yours who kept a marine store convenient to Arran Bridge?'

I replied, laughing: 'Now, why wouldn't his name be Lamb, the same as his son's?'

'That's the name, by Jesus God! It was from him I bought my seaman's clothes when I took ship for this country. He widened his pale blue eyes at me in the same way as yourself. Now, Mr Lamb, I am yours entirely. You are British soldiers, are you not? Be guided by me. I love King George as much as any man.'

It was late that evening that we entered a small row-boat, owned by two friends of our Dubliner, and put off from the shore. We had agreed to pay them for the passage all the money in our possession. The river here was more than three miles broad.

The men had not rowed a quarter of a mile when the wind, which had hitherto blown fair for us, changed around and blew very fresh. The boat made a great deal of water, which alarmed the boatmen: they immediately brought the helm over and made for the shore whence we came. There was an English sloop of war that constantly cruised at night in these waters to intercept American privateers and other craft, but we had not yet caught a sight of her. We ordered the boatmen to turn the boat again and either attempt to gain this sloop or, failing that, row us at all events across to the Island. They declared that a boat could not live in such a wind and that we should all be drowned if we persisted. At this I pulled Smutchy's pistol from my shirt and peremptorily ordered them to do as I said.

After beating against the wind and waves for near two hours, and being almost perished with wet and cold, we espied a square-rigged vessel at half a mile from us. The boatmen declared her to be an American privateer, but as our boat was within a few minutes of sinking, despite vigorous bailing, we resolved to make towards her. Tyce could not swim at all, and Probert very ill. We must take the risk, I said. As we approached, we were hailed and ordered to come alongside. To our unspeakable joy, when a lantern was shown, we saw British soldiers standing on the deck.

They hauled us aboard and, as the leader of the party, I was ordered down to the cabin to give an account to Captain Skinner, her commander, who we were. Arrived before him, I could only gape, having lost for awhile the power of articulation. However, he humanely ordered a large glass of rum to be given me. This soon brought me to my speech. 'Thank God,' I cried, 'we are back among our own people!'

CHAPTER XX

THE AUTHOR has conducted his readers over varied herds of adventure and trouble, marching and sailing them some four thousand miles from his first enlistment at Dublin to his half-way house at Boston; and perhaps another four thousand miles on his complicated journeys, by way of New York, through the Southern and Middle States and back to New York again. However trying these scenes have proved, he hopes that the faithful local description contained in them will convey a certain degree of amusement and interest, as being the work of an eye-witness. Now, having almost reached the close of his career as a soldier, the author will make a quick exit from the literary stage, aware that the awful blaze of war alone could foot-light so obscure a character as himself into public notice.

Captain Skinner set us ashore on the next morning with a letter to his father, the Colonel of a regiment of Loyal Americans. We waited on Colonel Skinner, who immediately ordered a boat to convey us to New York. Our appearance astonished the soldiers of the Garrison as with cheerful steps we marched up to Headquarters. Never had sergeants of the Royal Welch Fusiliers appeared in such scarecrow wretchedness. Sir Guy Carleton, whom we found to have superseded Sir Henry Clinton as Commander-in-Chief, received us with great kindness, and we communicated to him all the information we possessed that could tend to the good of the service. But it was with a pang, as I stood in the parlour, that I thought how I had stood here last in much the same pickle and how familiarly and sweetly poor Major André had talked with me. There were some framed sketches and silhouettes by his hand still hanging upon the walls. His appointment as Deputy-Adjutant-General was now held by Major Frederick Mackenzie, who had been adjutant of the Royal Welch Fusiliers during the siege of Boston, and therefore took great interest in us. He desired me to write out a narrative of our escape, and then sent us to the officer who should pay us the usual bounty. This officer, after he had entered my name in the book, turned his eye to the top of the first page. 'Why,' said he, 'the Lambs are famous for this sort of work. Here is another Roger Lamb, a sergeant of The Ninth, one of the first who made good his escape from General Burgoyne's army, in the winter of 1778.'

I answered: 'I am the same man. I afterwards entered the Royal Welch Fusiliers.'

'Indeed, then,' he said, 'if you can prove that you are identical with the other, I have good news for you. Colonel John Hill who was exchanged and went to England has left here all your arrears of pay.' The proof was not difficult, there being officers of both regiments in New York at this time; and the money was paid me, amounting to forty pounds.

Major Mackenzie then recommended me to General Birch, the Commandant of New York, who appointed me his first clerk, at a good salary. Nor did the Major's kindness stop there: through his interest I was later made adjutant to the Merchants' Corps of Volunteers who were on permanent duty in the town. With them for two months I enjoyed the only repose, I may truly say, which I had during the eight years I was in America! Sir Guy Carleton, it may be remarked, had been appointed to his command by Lord Rockingham (whose Ministry had displaced that of Lord North) largely as being an honest and vigorous administrator who would root out from their seat at New York the parasites and plunderers who, under the negligent eyes of Generals Sir William Howe and Sir Henry Clinton, had sucked such immense private fortunes from the war. Sir Guy at once instituted a General Court of Inquiry and soon sent packing a number of officers, commissaries and contractors.

Later in the year when the preliminaries of peace were signed between Spain, France, America and Great Britain, I was at King's Bridge in charge of the recruits of the Royal Welch Fusiliers who were doing duty there. I heard the news with a sort of apathy, but high indignation was expressed by very many Loyalists and British. They were aware that General Washington's army were as naked and destitute as ever, and incapable of making a march of one day, even often plotting mutiny and held down only by the shooting of their ringleaders. General Washington himself afterwards confessed that his people were in a sort of stupor, that had we been permitted to march we could certainly have taken the Highlands above Hudson's River. The terms of the peace conceded the United States total independence; the great back-country territories from the middle Mississippi northward to the Great Lakes, formerly a part of Canada; the enjoyment of the cod-fisheries on the banks of Newfoundland; and the retention of the confiscated estates of the Loyalists. The Loyalists, twenty-five regiments of whom had served in our armies, now tore the British facings from their coats and stamped them under foot. They had lost all.

Thus ended a contest which had dismembered England of much more than half her territory. How far her commerce and her true interest as a nation were affected by it, was a point upon which it was then useless to speculate, and upon which innumerable and contradictory opinions have since been given. This at least can be written without fear of contradiction:

that for the sake of enforcing duties upon tea and other commodities, which would only have brought in a few thousand pounds sterling – even had the expense of collection not greatly outweighed the receipts! – a war was precipitated which added no less than £120,000,000 to the National Debt, already very heavy, and doubled the burden of interest upon it. (The French, by the bye, were also £50,000,000 out of pocket as a result of this same war.) However, money is dross, and much money is much dross, and in the long run I believe it to have been for the best that the two nations were thus at last separate, in fact as well as by a fiction. It may even come about some day that, remembering the ancient ties of affection and language that, despite all, yet bind the two nations, the Americans will join in armed alliance with us against the French or other relentless foes who threaten our common liberties. However, from the loss of their Tories, they have been unhappily slow in settling down as a nation upon an even keel; and in this very year in which I write[1] we have fallen foul of them again, and been forced to land troops who have burned down their new capital city of Washington.

I have hoarded up two happy surprises for the reader; and may now disclose them. Sergeant Collins and his party came safe into New York about the end of April. They had endured the same great hardships as ourselves, and had been unfortunately taken prisoners in Jericho Valley as they prepared to cross the Delaware River a few miles below Trenton. They were confined in the famous Reformatory Prison of Philadelphia. There the treatment of prisoners was wisely designed to eradicate vice and make them look forward to their re-establishment as honest members of society: by allowing them to continue at their trades during their servitude, or teaching them trades if they were ignorant of any. Sergeant Collins and his party did not own to the knowledge of any trade and were therefore all together instructed in nail-making; just as ignorant females were commonly set to beat hemp. Had my comrades, who preferred liberty to reformation, been made into hemp-beaters they would have stolen strands to twist into light rope for their escape; but as nail-makers they stole iron bars instead and escaped by undermining the foundation of their cell. They smuggled themselves aboard a trading vessel at the docks and were rescued, as she sailed out of the river, by a British privateer.

We celebrated our banquet of reunion, as agreed upon, with the same choice viands that we had named as we crouched in the snow by the Susquehannah River, though we had to forgo our pineapples as unobtainable. The expense, I can assure my readers, was no paltry one, for in New York market at this time a leg of mutton sold for a guinea, a fowl for six shillings, a good egg for threepence, and the other articles proportionately.

1 1814.

Liquor also stood extravagantly high. I proposed a silent toast to 'An absent face', meaning of course Smutchy Steel, and as we raised our glasses to our lips, then pat, as if by a theatrical cue, someone knocked at the door. 'Enter,' we cried. A well-known head craned in and a well-known voice enquired: 'Is the table set for eight or only for seven? And where is my great trencherful of potatoes that you promised me?'

'Why, Smutchy!' we cried, and ran to him, pressing him to our breasts. 'How came you here?'

He said: 'By the same way as you did, Gerry. I had the luck after you left me by Elizabethtown. The guide had not deserted us, but by an error waited at another hill closer to the village. When he found his mistake he went after us, and came upon me lying insensible by the roadside. He revived me with some warm rum and carried me to a friend's house, where I remained for three weeks until my foot had been healed with poultices. My next stage was the house of an old Irishman by the river who wished to be kindly recommended to you; and so across to Staten Island by boat with a fair wind and a starry sky.'

You may well imagine what a night was that!

In May, 1783, Captain de Saumarez, who was one of the twelve captains who had drawn lots for their lives at General Washington's order, led the Royal Welch Fusiliers, unbroken in spirit, back to the army in Staten Island. Colonel Balfour was already at New York, Charleston having been evacuated by the British some months before; I added my recruit company to the Regiment and on December 5th we sailed all together from Sandy Hook. As I watched the coasts recede, I remarked to Sergeant Collins who stood by me: 'Pray, Collins, how do you feel on this solemn occasion?' He replied: 'Well pleased at having seen so many interesting sights and scenes, but without the slightest desire ever to revisit that shore. I have had my belly-full of fighting too. Dr Franklin was not far out when he declared that there was never a good war, nor a bad peace. Let the Americans keep America, I say: it will be both their reward and their punishment. They are a lively, sensible and not ill-natured folk: but if the Archangel Gabriel himself descended from Heaven to govern them, they would the next day indict him as a bloody tyrant, a profligate and a thief – so jealous are they of their liberties.'

When Sergeant Collins had gone below, the words of Richard Plantagenet in Shakespeare's *Henry the Sixth*, in which he mourns the loss of British possessions in France, came involuntarily to my lips. I declaimed in a melancholy voice to the gulls that sailed in our wake:

> Is all our travail turned to this effect?
> After the slaughter of so many peers,
> So many captains, gentlemen and soldiers

That in this quarrel have been overthrown,
And sold their bodies for their country's benefit?
&c., &c.

After a short and prosperous voyage we landed at Portsmouth in England. From Portsmouth we marched to Winchester, where I requested my discharge, though I had very great privileges allowed me in the Army and was making money fast. Colonel Balfour kindly and humanely reasoned with me, in order to prevail on me to remain in the Service; but I had a notion to return to my own land.

He regretfully signed my discharge and with a number of my companions marched up to London in order to pass the board. Here I was considered too young to receive the pension, and likewise, it was judged, had not been long enough in the Service. I left the Metropolis, which I visited for the first and last time, on March 15th and four days later landed in Dublin, to the inexpressible joy of my aged mother and two surviving sisters.

The Ninth Regiment had also returned from captivity in the Spring of 1783, but sadly shrunken in numbers. They were soon brought up to strength and given the title of the East Norfolk Regiment, but they are now more generally known in jest as 'The Holy Boys'. They are still rough and ready; for the characters of regiments do not change. How heroically and steadfastly both they and the Royal Welch Fusiliers have conducted themselves in the wars against Napoleon Buonaparte is common knowledge.

Jane Crumer and her husband remained at Little York together with a number of married villagers. However, as it proved, I was later to renew my acquaintance with this very admirable woman.

On my arrival at Dublin I had determined, after long cogitation, that my duty to my Country had by no means terminated upon the battlefield, and that the frequent solicitations made me by Americans to remain in their townships in the quality of schoolmaster were clear signs of the destiny that Providence had marked out for me. Returned to Ireland, I would devote the rest of my life to educating the poor children of my fellow-countrymen in moral virtues and the simpler requirements of the useful citizens: viz. to read, write a fair hand, and cast accounts.

My affectionate recollections of Sergeant Fitzpatrick, to whose children I had first served as a teacher, suggested that I should undertake the charge of a new free school at the Methodist Chapel in White Friar Lane; where I soon had forty boys confined to me. We met daily in the Chapel lobby until, after some years, a school house was by subscription erected for me at the back of the sacred edifice. In the autumn of 1785, Mrs Jane Crumer returned to Dublin. I met her again at the house of Sergeant Fitzpatrick's widow, her aunt. Poor Crumer, her imbecile husband, had been killed in Little York by the fall of a rotten pine. Since she and I agreed very well together, we were married by banns on January 15th, in the following year, in the Parish Church of St Anne's, Dublin. We have had together a numerous progeny, many hard trials and much to be thankful for. I may add that my wandering feet have long ceased to travel. I have now taught in the same crowded school, with, I believe, an equal fidelity to that I gave my Regiment, for more than thirty years.

Before my marriage, I revealed to my dear wife the story of Kate Harlowe and the lost child; and was glad in the event that I had done so. For, ten years later, a handsome young female sought me out, having obtained my address from a soldier of The Ninth, and declared herself my child! She had with her my silver groat, wrapped in a paper on which was written:

> The gift of Roger Lamb, Sergeant of the Ninth Regiment, to his daughter: Eliza Lamb.

K. H.

This charming young creature whose face and form recalled that of Kate at her most enchanting, had, I learned, been taken from the Indians by an American officer who wished to adopt her as his child. But the *bardash* Sweet Yellow Head, of whom I have written in my previous volume, sought her out and carried her back to his Chief, Thayendanegea, or Captain Brant, who brought her at five years old to the house of the Quaker Josiah, that she might be among people of her own race. Upon the Quaker's moving to Montreal she had been brought up in that city until the good man died, bequeathing her a modest competence. Shortly after her arrival in Ireland she married, with my consent, a man in the band of a militia regiment and soon made me a grandfather.

From my daughter I had news of Thayendanegea. She told me that he had visited London again in the year after I came to Dublin, and was presented to the King – but from some scruple of honour declined kissing his hand; observing, however, that he would gladly kiss that of the Queen. The Prince of Wales took a delight in his company and my daughter had heard Thayendanegea remark that the Prince sometimes took him 'to places very queer for a prince to attend'. While in London he had attended a masquerade in the Prince's company, at which were many of the nobility and gentry, appearing in war paint with one side of his face adorned with a black hand and his nose incarnadined. A member of the Turkish Embassy was so much struck with Thayendanegea's appearance that he ventured to touch his nose, to satisfy curiosity. No sooner did he do this when Thayendanegea, much amused but simulating a rage, uttered a tremendous war-whoop and flourished his tomahawk about the ears of the terrified Ottoman. Men shouted and drew their swords, ladies screamed and fainted dead away; and His Royal Highness could scarce contain himself for laughing. This was the same year that Thayendanegea published the Gospel of St Mark in the Mohican tongue. After a war against the American General St Clair, whom he defeated and killed in the year 1791, at the battle of Miami, Thayendanegea settled down to farm his rich estate at Niagara, on the Canadian side, having thirty negroes under him, whom he treated with the utmost rigour. He died in the year 1807.

POSTSCRIPT, 1823

I was hob-nobbing with Smutchy Steel, a few days since, at his respectable tavern in Parliament Street. He asked me: 'Now, Gerry, why do you look so pensive, and neglect your good porter?'

I replied that I was meditating on the fates of the few American generals opposed to us who had come out of the war with honour. General Nathaniel Greene had died of a sun-stroke, on the fine estate presented him in Georgia, but before he could enjoy it; and General George Washington, by his surgeons over-bleeding him. This was after two difficult terms as President of the United States; during which popular rancour had forced him to relieve his character from the charge of peculation, and he was accused of 'polluting the Presidential ermine to an extent almost irremediable'.

'Now what happened to that whipper-snapper of a Frenchman, that Marquis de La Fayette?' Smutchy asked.

I informed him: 'When the Revolution that he had fostered in America spread to his own country, the National Assembly declared him a traitor. He was immured in a fortress. Efforts were made to procure the intercession of England on his behalf, and the King himself was approached; but his Majesty cut the speaker short with but the two words: "Remember André!"'

'Ay,' said Smutchy. 'But, as you have shown, those that condemned the poor Major to hanging, never had much luck after. I wonder they had the heart to tuck up so handsome, so sentimental, so officer-like a gentleman. Our people would never have done so, had he been a dog of Rebel. We were ever too soft-hearted in such matters.'

'Yet even Major André's melancholy fate,' said I, 'was preferable to that of the man who occasioned it: General Benedict Arnold. He sought to end the war at a stroke and without bloodshed, for the betterment of his country. Had he succeeded, he would have won imperishable glory and the thanks of posterity. He failed, and was constrained to carry fire and sword against his own people. The war ended, America was lost. He came to England, and though he was brought into the Royal presence leaning upon the arm of Sir Guy Carleton, was avoided by the best society, and publicly hissed when he entered the playhouse. He died twenty years later, bitter, broken and debt-ridden.'

Then said Smutchy: 'Yet I would rather a thousand times have been in General Arnold's shoes than in another's – a hearty, well-intentioned, bustling man whose standing upon a point of honour plunged two worlds into death and disaster – who becoming aware of the incestuous alliance of his favourite daughter with his natural son went mad; and was put away for many years; and was daily whipped by his keepers; and went blind, and lingered on and on among the wreck of his hopes, and could not die – '

'His gracious Majesty the late King George, ay, truth,' I said, fetching a deep sigh, 'in whose service we suffered terrible things. I believe that even the Americans who wrote with such detestation of him in their Declaration of Independence must have forgiven the poor Royal creature before he died.'

THE END